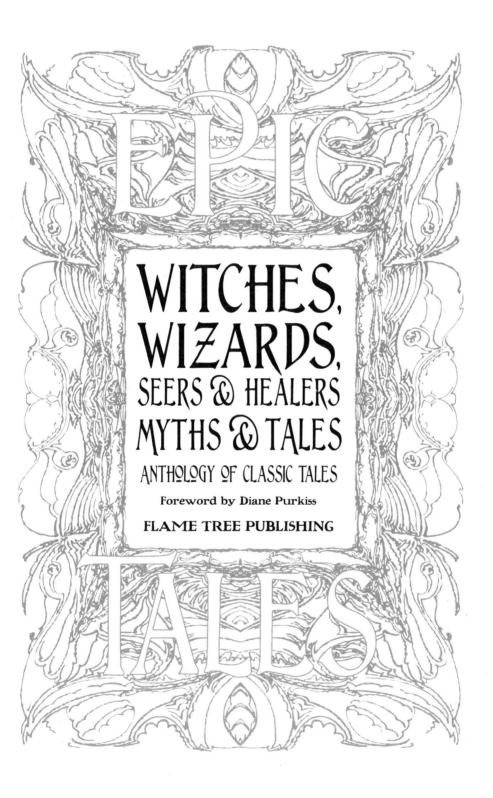

EPIC

WITCHES, WIZARDS, SEERS & HEALERS MYTHS & TALES

ANTHOLOGY OF CLASSIC TALES

Foreword by Diane Purkiss

FLAME TREE PUBLISHING

TALES

This is a FLAME TREE Book

Publisher & Creative Director: Nick Wells
Editorial Director: Catherine Taylor
Special thanks to Federica Ciaravella and Tim Leng

FLAME TREE PUBLISHING
6 Melbray Mews, Fulham,
London SW6 3NS, United Kingdom
www.flametreepublishing.com

First published 2020
Copyright © 2020 Flame Tree Publishing Ltd

22 24 23
3 5 7 9 10 8 6 4 2

ISBN: 978-1-83964-236-4

The cover image is created by Flame Tree Studio
based on artwork courtesy of Shutterstock.com.

Incidental motif images courtesy of Shutterstock.com:
EssentiallyNomadic, Gorbash Varvara, Svet_Lana, Karlionau, Jef Thompson

A copy of the CIP data for this book is available from the British Library.

Printed and bound in China

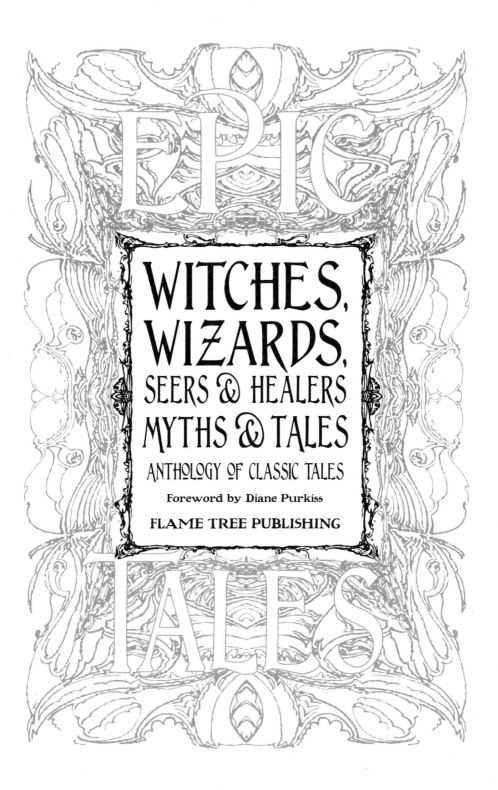

EPIC

WITCHES, WIZARDS, SEERS & HEALERS MYTHS & TALES

ANTHOLOGY OF CLASSIC TALES

Foreword by Diane Purkiss

FLAME TREE PUBLISHING

TALES

Contents

CONTENTS

WITCHES, SORCERESSES, HAGS & CRONES

Magic, Spells, Enchantments & Curses

HEALERS, SEERS & SOOTHSAYERS

Foreword

WE NEED THESE STORIES because of the darkness in ourselves. It is a darkness generated by fear. We know we will all go into the dark. We know quick bright things die everyday. We fear an end that catches up with us before we have even begun. We fear one another. We fear impingement. Why does one person die while another lives? Why do some lack for nothing while others have more than enough? Stories are one way to talk about these feelings and to manage them.

Human beings do not much like the inconvenient truth that the individual is not in control. The mother of all stories, including conspiracy theory stories, is the wish to be sure of causes. When rape victim Susan J. Brison blames herself for the attack she suffered, she observes that this is preferable to believing that the attack was random, and could therefore take place again at any moment in the future. In stories, unlike in life, everything has a meaning. If a gun falls off the wall in act one, we can be sure that somebody will fire it by the end of act three. Stories of magic and witchcraft also explain the randomness of life in causal terms. If sickness comes from one evil person, it can be controlled.

If we want to go back into a past closed to us, then stories are the slender clue that will let us trace a way through the thick dark of the labyrinth. We will have to be brave to make the journey. We will have to confront our fear. There is no single centre to the maze, and there is no single idea of the witch. In all cultures, the witch is at home in the dark that terrifies others. Wizards, male magic users, know how to manage the dark with words and numbers. Medieval writers thought of both Plato and Virgil as magicians, while we hear of mathmagicians as late as the gunpowder plot. For those who approached the dark with heads full of books, and sought to drive that seething unknown back, the stories may end happily or sadly, but the storytellers themselves are wiser. They know that the story needs the darkness to be powerful. That's why so many cultures represent the witch as an old crone. She is close to death, too close; she is old age, the withering of skin and flesh. Yet still she hungers. She reminds us of our fate.

However, in these stories, that connection to the darkness and the dead allow the witch to act as a bridge, perhaps most touchingly in the tale of the Korean magistrate who learns from a witch to speak with his deceased friend. Initially, the magistrate is a vicious witch hunter, and the story cleverly suggests that such old bigots are grieving inside. They tried to hold back the dark they crave. As Maria Tatar writes, magic only happens at the margins of the forbidden. Even the tale of Hansel and Gretel speaks to deep psychic caverns we hide within ourselves. Here, mothers want to eat children, and in other tales, children devour mothers. One reason all these stories still resonate and are still told and retold is that storytelling itself is often the only way to talk about deep trauma and dark desires – the insane longing for a child, the longing to be without a lovechild for half-an-hour, the prison of the female body, whether you are the fairest of them all or the ugliest, the body as object of unimaginable desire. Tatar again: why do we ritually repeat stories, all over the world, time and again? Because only then can we feel we know the dark well enough to manage it. Any nonsense words – 'abracadabra', 'shazam', 'hocus-pocus' – carry a darkness of meaninglessness within them. You have that darkness in your hands here, and the slender story-threads to lead you through it.

Diane Purkiss
Professor of English Literature and Fellow in English, Keble College Oxford

Publisher's Note

AS TALES FROM MYTHOLOGY AND FOLKLORE are principally derived from an oral storytelling tradition, their written representation depends on the transcription, translation and interpretation by those who heard them and first put them to paper, and also on whether they are recently re-told versions or more directly sourced from original first-hand accounts. The stories in this book are a mixture, and you can learn more about the sources and authors at the back of the book. This collection presents a thoughtfully selected cross-section of stories from all over the world, though some countries may seem more heavily represented than others since their cultures more readily define characters with a magical or mystical status. For the purposes of simplicity and consistency, most diacritical marks have been removed, since their usage in the original sources was sometimes inconsistent or would represent different pronunciation, depending on the original language of the story, not to mention that quite a sophisticated understanding of phonetic conventions would be required to understand how to pronounce them anyway.

We also ask the reader to remember that while the myths and tales are timeless, much of the factual information, opinions regarding the nature of countries and their peoples, as well as the style of writing in this anthology, are of the era during which they were written.

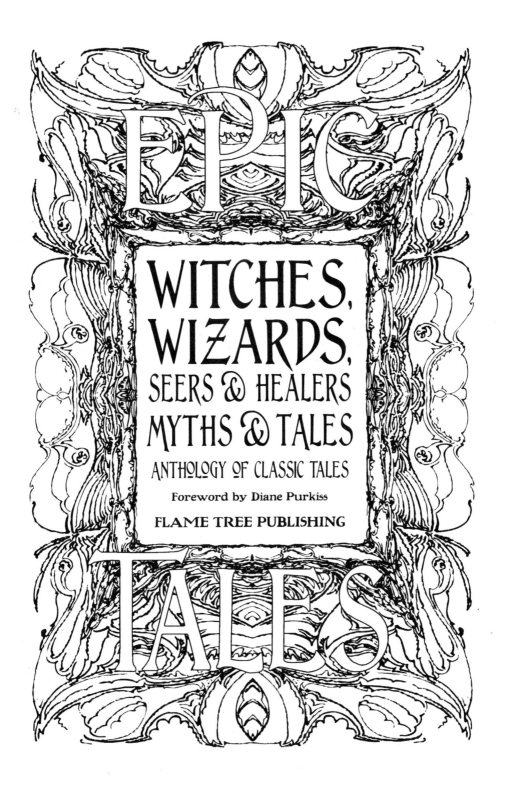

EPIC

WITCHES,
WIZARDS,
SEERS & HEALERS
MYTHS & TALES
ANTHOLOGY OF CLASSIC TALES

Foreword by Diane Purkiss

FLAME TREE PUBLISHING

TALES

Witches, Wizards & Magic in Folklore

Introduction

'THE SAIDE AGNIS TOMPSON was after brought againe before the Kings Maiestie and his Counsell,' the record shows,

and being examined of the meetings and detestable dealings of those witches, she confessed that upon the night of Allhallow's Euen last, she was accompanied as well with the persons aforesaide, as also with a great many other witches, to the number of two hundreth: and that all they together went by Sea each one in a Riddle or Sieve, and went in the same very substantially with Flaggons of wine making merrie and drinking by the waye in the same Riddles or Sieves, to the Kerke of North Barrick in Lowthian, and that after they had landed, tooke handes on the land and daunced this reill or short daunce, singing all with one voice:

> *Commer goe ye before, commer goe ye,*
> *If ye will not goe before, commer let me.*

Such a simple, straightforward narrative, and yet so strange. Should we be more unsettled or amused? The former, obviously, in that scores of men and women were to be tortured and executed on the strength of Thompson's testimony at the North Berwick Witch Trials of 1590. Yet it's undeniably utterly ludicrous as well...

Fearefull Aboundinges

How are we to begin to understand the mindset that set down this stuff so seriously? Or empathize with the anxiety it clearly represents? Why does this testimony trouble us so much? Is it the gravity of the overall tone in which such an outlandish story is reported? The matter-of-factness with which Agnes admits to having literally sailed on the North Sea in a 'sieve'? The news that, not only did she herself do this, but that she did it in the company of a couple of hundred fellow witches? Or that the 'Kings Majestie' was actually present in person in the court to hear her speak? King James VI of Scotland, later to be James I of England, was a ruler renowned for his intelligence and learning – and author of a treatise, the *Daemonologie* (1597) in which he set out to study *'the fearefull aboundinge at this time in this countrie, of these detestable slaues of the Deuill, the Witches or enchaunters.'* And to warn his people:

> both that such assaultes of Sathan are most certainly practised, & that the instrumentes thereof, merits most severly to be punished.

Subversive Spirits

Then there are the other little oddities – not quite questions, maybe, but irksome inklings of curiosity or doubt. To what extent were the King and court officials really affronted, in what were coming to be dour, drab, puritanical times, by the fact that the 'witches' and 'wizards' had drunk and danced and sung – in short had fun? And had fun together – 200 people singing 'all in one voice' – how far was this just the suspicion any state with repressive leanings has for large gatherings and mass movements of any kind? How far were the authorities reacting to the fact that – though men were to be caught up in these prosecutions and to lose their lives – these supposed festivities had been strongly female-led? Did the fact that the whole thing had happened on All Souls' Eve – a traditionally Catholic feast – have any significance? The spirits supposedly unloosed that night had to come from Purgatory – a sort of half-way house to heavenly salvation; a place where the good but less-than-perfect were purged of the sins that stained them; and one which had no place in a Protestant scheme that acknowledged only the damned or saved. In a Scotland whose Reformation was a very recent (and violent) memory, the slightest suggestion of 'Popery' was provocative. Such interpretative subtleties should not of course blind us to the anything-but-nuanced nature of the witch-hunts that resulted: 4,000 men and women were to die.

No single explanation can hope to cover all the different questions that we've raised; no single definition of 'witchcraft' addresses all these doubts. Which is why a book like this one has to extend its scope so widely, from the islands of Polynesia to the deserts and forests of America's West; from Scandinavia to China and Japan. And, chronologically, through the entire sweep of human history, all the way back to Babylonia and Ancient Egypt. In seventeenth-century Scotland, we've seen, the fear of witchcraft articulated the unacknowledged preoccupations of a complex culture in a time of transition. The same might be said for any other time or place.

Community Concerns

One common theme we can see is the extent to which witchcraft is in the eye of the beholder. One civilization's wizardry is another's wisdom. For a 'primitive' people at home with the idea that it lives attended by its ancestors, what we see as 'magic' may be no more than common sense. Not only can the spirits be contacted through 'spells' in such a culture but they surely should be: it is only fitting for them to be consulted on the community's concerns, problems or plans. Vulnerable as they were to what must have seemed completely arbitrary fluctuations of fortune – to drought and flood; crop-failure and cattle disease; not to mention epidemics afflicting humans – they naturally saw these as reflecting either displeasure on the part of their gods or ancestral spirits or foul play on the part of envious neighbours. What held at societal level went for the individual as well: for the sadly-smitten youth pining away for a beloved who wouldn't even look at him, or the woman desolate because she couldn't have a child. Whether these tribulations were the result of angry ancestors or the 'evil eye', they had to be offset by 'medicine' or magic.

Witchcraft and wickedness do not necessarily go together in this kind of scheme. Spells certainly may be malevolent in their intent; curses can be cast and lives badly afflicted. But the cures to these ills are to be found by magic too. Many of the stories in this collection reflect this: in African myth, the medicine man is as likely to be benevolent – a healer – as to be evil. Sometimes the so-called sorceror is really more a seer: India's Sumedha (actually an earlier incarnation of the great Gautama Buddha himself) might be better characterized as a 'sage'. China's Chang Tao-Ling, who discovered a magic elixir of immortality, is also the 'Heavenly Teacher' of the religious Taoist tradition. Mishosha, the Magician of Lake Superior, in Native American legend, starts out as a sort of subcontracted creator: he darts about the lake in his magic canoe, conjuring up bays and beaches, woods and streams. Only later does he grow in pride and acquire a less appealing personality and have to be overthrown by a mortal hero.

A Woman's Place

There has always been male magic. As the stories in this book make clear, wizards, sorcerors and 'medicine men' have abounded in world myth. Men have been pursued in 'witch-hunts' too. The widespread view that the Scottish persecutions were essentially a spree of misogynistic violence oversimplifies things, as we have seen. At the same time, it is difficult to dispute that this kind of enchantment has at some level been felt to represent some sort of feminine principle. The archetypal witch is a woman, that's for sure. To some extent, this is easy enough to account for: hatred of women has arguably been a by-product of the way we have ordered things through much of human history. The extreme misogynism displayed by the online 'incels' of the twenty-first century is no more than a distillation of the fury felt by many males, tantalized by the erotic promise apparently held out to them – but ultimately withheld – in what is supposed to be (and in so many obvious ways has been) 'a man's world'. Where women are responsible for providing men with both sexual reward and social affirmation (the 'trophy wife'), the potential for resentment is always there.

Heaven and Earth

But the prejudice is at once more ancient and much deeper. We can trace it back through many millennia of myth. Those great heavenly patriarchs who had command of the thunder, the lightning and the rain (Greece's Zeus; Thor in Scandinavia; the Anu of the Hittites…) generally represent a second generation in an older line. What we might call an 'Earth Mother' generally preceded them. In the Minoan civilization of Crete (third millennium BCE), for instance, the great goddess Potnia far outranked the male deity who was at once her consort and her son. Indeed, he seems to have existed primarily so that his annual death and rebirth from his mother/lover's loins could be carefully recorded to mark the successive passing of each agricultural year.

The superimposition upon a matriarchal culture of stone-age subsistence farming of a patriarchal civilization that raised its eyes to the heavens can be seen represented symbolically in the story of the war between the Titans and Olympians in classical Greek tradition. As recorded by Hesiod's *Theogony*, c. 700 BCE, the world was once ruled by the Titans, the children of Gaia, the Earth, and Uranus (Heaven), her son and husband. Thus far, the antique order corresponds with the sort of matriarchy imagined by the Minoans, with their goddess Potnia, but events would take a decidedly different turn in the developing Greek tradition. The story goes that Kronos, Gaia's youngest son, castrated his father and usurped his throne, marrying his sister Rhea, but swallowing all their children as they were born to secure his own position. One alone escaped: the infant Zeus was smuggled to safety in Crete, where he grew to manhood plotting revenge against his unnatural sire. The god of open sky and mountaintop, he was armed with flashing thunderbolts, and established his seat on the heights of Greece's highest peak, Mount Olympus, from where he led his own family in war against the Titans (now regurgitated so as to be able to help in their father's defence). The final victory of Zeus and his Olympians marked not only the end of the region's pre-Greek period but the inauguration of a new, and more recognizably 'modern' male-supremacist theology.

Ancient Archetypes

It went without saying that the sort of powers wielded by wise women in the older, 'earth mother' mythologies would have to be downgraded in a patriarchal order of this new kind. Hence the 'hag' by which the witch has usually been represented in the West in recent times. Old and wizened as she is, she embodies the antiquity of the 'Earth Mother' figure – but emblematizes too the extent to which that figure has been devalued. She has neither the physical attractiveness that might make the younger woman alluring; nor, in her crabbed misanthropy, the nurturing nature, the empathy. (The sexual promise that might once have redeemed her endures only in a sort of fossilized form in the black 'pussy' cat that is her inseparable companion.)

Even here, there are dangers in generalizing, though: Celtic legend abounds in hags who, though tough and exacting, are yet benign. The type endured into modern mythology in the figure of the Sean-Bhean bhocht (Shan Van Vocht) or Kathleen Ni Houlihan. This 'Poor Old Woman' became emblematic of a weakened and impoverished Ireland. Pitiably put-upon as she was, she had a profoundly passive-aggressive streak: her loyal sons were expected to sacrifice themselves for her sake.

Fatal Attraction

Not that the hag's younger, more outwardly appealing, sister is necessarily to be preferred. We see this very clearly in the cases of Calypso and Circe, from Greek myth. They are most famously described in Homer's epic poem, *The Odyssey* (c. 800 BCE). Young, enticing and bewitchingly (literally) beautiful, they represent the power of a malevolent femininity to beguile and to betray. Calypso, a beautiful, alluring goddess-myth, lives on her own island in the Aegean. She casts a spell over the hero Odysseus with her lovely, ensnaring singing voice, diverting him from his homeward voyage to rejoin his wife Penelope in Ithaca. Circe holds him prisoner for seven years, only releasing him when Zeus himself intervenes. Circe is a sorceress: she lives on another island on to which she invites Odysseus with all his crew. She casts a spell over the hero's men and turns them into swine, while she keeps Odysseus captive for a year. Both these enchantresses may be seen as standing symbolically for what the psychoanalyst Sigmund Freud (1856–1939) would define as the 'vagina dentata' – literally, the fanged vagina, which men believed castrated them even as it offered to fulfil them sexually.

Even when women seem sympathetic, their sexual and emotional incontinence in some stories can make them dangerous. As with Medea, who comes to the rescue of Jason and the Argonauts. In an earlier tradition, her special powers might have made her admirable – and the help she offers the hero is accepted with alacrity in the classical Greek myth. But her love for Jason is frighteningly fierce. Not only does she murder and dismember her own brother, Absyrtus, when he seems to bar her way to having Jason: she erupts into insane fury when the hero leaves her. In some versions of her myth, indeed, she murders her own children in her lust to exact revenge for her abandonment. As alarming in her way is Kiyo, the tea-house maiden in the Japanese story 'A Bell and the Power of Karma'. In her rage at being rejected by her young lover, a Buddhist priest, she studies sorcery and ultimately transforms herself into an avenging dragon-serpent. Does the shocking reaction of the ancient Egyptian Ubaaner to his young wife's infidelity just make clear that hell hath no fury like a male magician scorned? Or does it suggest more deeply that, whatever the sex of the sorceror, witchcraft represents a destructive principle that is always ultimately feminine underneath?

Changing Times

As for why witches and wizards have been intrinsically wicked in some traditions; benign healers and teachers in others: that's a difficult question, with different answers in different places. In England, for the most part, the steady advance of industrialism and the expansion of education that went along with this finished rather more gently the job so brutally begun in the Scottish witch-hunts of the seventeenth century. Colonial North America to a considerable extent followed Britain – even to the extent, notoriously, of having witch-trials of its own in Salem, Massachusetts (1692–93).

By contrast, in Ireland (and in the UK's Celtic fringes), cultural nationalism dictated that people should hold on to an earlier view, in which enchantment represented ancestral wisdom. The same went for the Native American peoples of the United States. In many countries in eastern and southern Asia, Africa and elsewhere, colonialism abruptly imposed a version of modernity atop a traditional culture (rather as the ancient sky-religions had imposed themselves atop older, female-founded faiths). Sometimes this was further overlayered by capitalism (as in Japan or South Korea) or Communism as in China and Vietnam. Often, in such rapidly (and consequently imperfectly) modernized societies, ancestral attitudes continued to some extent to influence life, feeling and belief at a more intimate, everyday level. This led to a situation in many communities around the world in which modern ways and 'folk traditions' coexist.

Not that this coexistence has always been harmonious by any means. In much of Africa, witch-hunts still continue. The kind of stresses and strains that radical transformation to new ways of living bring are always liable to find expression in angry scapegoating. In post-colonial Africa, as in Reformation Scotland, the witch-hunt is a 'thing'. The reality is, Selina H. Stenberg has observed, that belief in witchcraft has proven 'resilient to change'. And brought a backlash, in which innocent men, women and children are caught up. 'Despite the fact that most African societies have undergone major structural changes generating convergence toward the liberal model,' Stenberg says; 'the fear of witchcraft in Africa is actually increasing in the contemporary period.'

Development and Its Discontents

In the advanced industrial societies, meanwhile, belief in witchcraft has also been 'resilient'. It has, however, changed more or less completely. Partly, of course, because we feel less threatened, less completely in thrall to the sort of natural disasters which left poor communities so reliant on village healers and on magic spells. (Granted, global warming has increased the incidence of catastrophic floods and crop disease; pandemic has revived folk-memories of plague. For the moment, though, we feel – albeit with a certain trepidation – in control of our living circumstances in a way of which our remoter ancestors could scarcely even have dreamed.)

Also, though, because we've had to learn to be a little less rigid in our thinking. We've been forced to open up our minds to some extent. Not only has Newtonian physics been found, if not exactly wanting, then at least incomplete in its cosmic vision. What little most of us know of its Einsteinian replacement has allowed us to assume that science is 'softer' than it was, with all that 'relativity'; that 'bendy' space and time. Other answers we thought we'd found have proven just as inadequate. Our ancestors may for centuries have yearned for the liberty and democracy so many of us have today, but do we really feel we're free or represented?

There has, accordingly, been an insatiable hunger for new perspectives. Mainly, cynics sneer, because modern science and economics have abolished actual hunger, in the 'First World', at least. Be that as it may: widespread affluence has left many unfulfilled. It is true, though, that it has allowed a great many of us the luxury of thinking more broadly, and in some ways maybe more adventurously, now. The ecologically conscious look for an alternative frame through which to examine the limitations of a western scientific, technological and industrial history they see as having damaged their world – perhaps irreparably. Witchcraft represents an approach to life that for centuries stood outside that modernizing mainstream: doesn't it make sense to explore the possibilities it might open up? From feminists fighting to rehabilitate their 'herstorical' heritage through students of 'traditional medicine' to anarchistic followers of Wicca: the witches of the past have had enthusiastic champions.

A World of Wonder

That diversity is key. The mainstream culture that for so long sought to sideline witchcraft made a virtue not only of religious monotheism but of the maintenance of a single, universalizing view. Paganism, in its plurality, its local particularity, was deemed 'primitive' by comparison with an 'objectivity' underwritten by one coherent and all-encompassing spiritual and scientific system. Increasingly, though, we're becoming conscious of what was lost. This is one reason why the present collection casts its net so widely to bring in tales from so many different, far-flung folk traditions, representing such a range of perspectives on witchcraft and wizardry. The other reason is, of course, the abundance of entertainment to be had from so big and colourful a collection of stories, by turns disturbing and delightful, harrowing and heartening, unsettling and inspiring.

WIZARDS, MAGICIANS & MEN OF MAGIC

Introduction

FOR BETTER OR FOR WORSE, the male sorcerer represents patriarchal power. Whether he uses that power to protect or destroy makes all the difference. He may be benign, like Merlin, the magical mentor to King Arthur; or like Hsu Sun, the dragon-slayer of Chinese myth. Or, like the 'Ngaka or witch-doctor in the Lesotho story of 'How Ra-Molo Became a Snake', he may be wicked: an accomplice to all the evil in the world.

Frequently, we find, the sorcerer has some of the qualities of a creator – like Tangled-Hair, son of the West Wind, and the 'Great Wizard' of the Native American myth. He accidentally drops some seeds into water and they fly off as birds; the oil he squeezes from a fish he's caught drips into a hollow and becomes a mighty lake. But no one knew better than the Native Americans that Nature was red in tooth and claw and that a world-maker wasn't necessarily to be trusted. 'He was able to heal wounds and sicknesses and to conquer all his enemies,' the story says admiringly: 'but for all this he was a bad spirit nearly all his life.'

How Ra-Molo Became a Snake

LONG, LONG AGO, before the time of the great chief Mosheshue, there lived, behind the mountains, a wicked chief called Ra-Molo (the father of fire), who ruled his people with the hand of hardness. His village lay at the foot of a high hill, and down below flowed the Sinkou, deep and dark and cold.

Every year, when the harvest feasts began, would Ra-Molo cause to die the black death all those upon whom his displeasure had fallen during the past year; and when the moon was big in the heavens, he would come out from his dwelling to gaze upon his victims, and to listen to their screams of agony. Many, many times have the cries of the poor unfortunates echoed from rock to rock, while the people hid their heads in their blankets and trembled with fear and horror.

When the last feeble moans died away, the chief would return to his dwelling, and a great silence would descend upon the village. Then softly, by ones and by twos, the frightened people would creep away to some quiet spot out of sight of the village, and there offer up their prayers to the spirits of their fathers to rescue them from Ra-Molo; but for many many moons no help came.

Despair seized upon their hearts and hung in darkness over their homes. What hope was there for them when even the spirits were silent?

Now Ra-Molo had a brother who bore the name of Tau (the lion). This brother Ra-Molo hated with a great and bitter hatred, and gladly would he have put him to death, but he feared the vengeance of the spirits, for Tau was as brave and good as Ra-Molo was wicked and cruel. Then also he knew that all the people loved Tau, and would flee from the one who murdered him, as from the Evil Eye itself.

At length the evil counsels of the Ngaka (witch doctor) and the desire of Ra-Molo's heart overcame all fears, and one night, when the silence of sleep had come down upon the village, Ra-Molo called his Ngaka to bring his followers, and to enter the dwelling of Tau and put him to death.

The Ngaka needed no urging to begin his vile work. His heart glowed with delight as he thought of what a big strong man Tau was, and how long it would take him to die. Soon the whole village was aroused by the shrieks which the torturers extracted from the helpless victim. "Help, oh, help me, my brothers!" cried Tau, "lest I die, and my blood stain the hands of my father's son." They strove to rescue him, but the hut was well guarded, and their chief stood in the doorway, and forbade them to enter, using many threats to frighten them.

When the grey shadow in mercy came down to end his sufferings, Tau raised his eyes to the stars, and cried, "Oh, spirits of my fathers, receive me, and bring down upon Ra-Molo the heavy hand of vengeance, that his power may be destroyed, and no more innocent blood be spilled upon the earth to cry to the spirits. Oh, let my cry be heard, because of my great suffering!" So saying, he passed to the land of shadows, and a great darkness descended upon the village. All the people crept together and waited in tears for the dawn. At length the sun came forth, the darkness was lifted up; but what awful horror now held the people? What was that towards which all eyes were turned? Behold! at the door of the chief's dwelling lay a gigantic snake, so great that his like had never before been seen. Slowly he uncoiled himself and raised his head, when a wild cry went up from all the people. The body was the body of a snake, but the head was the head of a sheep, with a snake's tongue, which darted in and out from its wide-open mouth, while from the eyes the lightning flew. With a long loud hiss-s-s the thing began to crawl towards the river bank, then, raising its head to cast one long backward glance upon the village, it plunged into the waters of the Sinkou, there to remain a prisoner for all time. The spirits had, indeed, heard the dying cry of Tau, and had turned Ra-Molo into the awful thing the people had just beheld.

Once in each year, as the day comes round, does Ra-Molo rise to the surface of the giant pool, where he lies hid, and woe, woe to the one who sees the silver flash of his great body as he rises, for surely will that poor one be drawn by the power of those evil eyes down, down to the water's edge. Then will the serpent seize him and carry him away from the sight of men to the bottom of the pool, there to sleep cold and still till all men shall be gathered to the land of the spirits of their fathers on the day when the Great Spirit shall call from the stars.

The Magician and the Sultan's Son

THERE WAS ONCE a sultan who had three little sons, and no one seemed to be able to teach them anything; which greatly grieved both the sultan and his wife.

One day a magician came to the sultan and said, "If I take your three boys and teach them to read and write, and make great scholars of them, what will you give me?"

And the sultan said, "I will give you half of my property."

"No," said the magician; "that won't do."

"I'll give you half of the towns I own."

"No; that will not satisfy me."

"What do you want, then?"

"When I have made them scholars and bring them back to you, choose two of them for yourself and give me the third; for I want to have a companion of my own."

"Agreed," said the sultan.

So the magician took them away, and in a remarkably short time taught them to read, and to make letters, and made them quite good scholars. Then he took them back to the sultan and said: "Here are the children. They are all equally good scholars. Choose."

So the sultan took the two he preferred, and the magician went away with the third, whose name was Keejaanaa, to his own house, which was a very large one.

When they arrived, Mchaawee, the magician, gave the youth all the keys, saying, "Open whatever you wish to." Then he told him that he was his father, and that he was going away for a month.

When he was gone, Keejaanaa took the keys and went to examine the house. He opened one door, and saw a room full of liquid gold. He put his finger in, and the gold stuck to it, and, wipe and rub as he would, the gold would not come off; so he wrapped a piece of rag around it, and when his supposed father came home and saw the rag, and asked him what he had been doing to his finger, he was afraid to tell him the truth, so he said that he had cut it.

Not very long after, Mchaawee went away again, and the youth took the keys and continued his investigations.

The first room he opened was filled with the bones of goats, the next with sheep's bones, the next with the bones of oxen, the fourth with the bones of donkeys, the fifth with those of horses, the sixth contained men's skulls, and in the seventh was a live horse.

"Hullo!" said the horse; "where do you come from, you son of Adam?"

"This is my father's house," said Keejaanaa.

"Oh, indeed!" was the reply. "Well, you've got a pretty nice parent! Do you know that he occupies himself with eating people, and donkeys, and horses, and oxen and goats and everything he can lay his hands on? You and I are the only living things left."

This scared the youth pretty badly, and he faltered, "What are we to do?"

"What's your name?" said the horse.

"Keejaanaa."

"Well, I'm Faaraasee. Now, Keejaanaa, first of all, come and unfasten me."

The youth did so at once.

"Now, then, open the door of the room with the gold in it, and I will swallow it all; then I'll go and wait for you under the big tree down the road a little way. When the magician comes home, he will say to you, 'Let us go for firewood;' then you answer, 'I don't understand that work;' and he will go by himself. When he comes back, he will put a great big pot on the hook and will tell you to make a fire under it. Tell him you don't know how to make a fire, and he will make it himself.

"Then he will bring a large quantity of butter, and while it is getting hot he will put up a swing and say to you, 'Get up there, and I'll swing you.' But you tell him you never played at that game, and ask him to swing first, that you may see how it is done. Then he will get up to show you; and you must push him into the big pot, and then come to me as quickly as you can."

Then the horse went away.

Now, Mchaawee had invited some of his friends to a feast at his house that evening; so, returning home early, he said to Keejaanaa, "Let us go for firewood;" but the youth answered, "I don't understand that work." So he went by himself and brought the wood.

Then he hung up the big pot and said, "Light the fire;" but the youth said, "I don't know how to do it." So the magician laid the wood under the pot and lighted it himself.

Then he said, "Put all that butter in the pot;" but the youth answered, "I can't lift it; I'm not strong enough." So he put in the butter himself.

Next Mchaawee said, "Have you seen our country game?" And Keejaanaa answered, "I think not."

"Well," said the magician, "let's play at it while the butter is getting hot."

So he tied up the swing and said to Keejaanaa, "Get up here, and learn the game." But the youth said: "You get up first and show me. I'll learn quicker that way."

The magician got into the swing, and just as he got started Keejaanaa gave him a push right into the big pot; and as the butter was by this time boiling, it not only killed him, but cooked him also.

As soon as the youth had pushed the magician into the big pot, he ran as fast as he could to the big tree, where the horse was waiting for him.

"Come on," said Faaraasee; "jump on my back and let's be going."

So he mounted and they started off.

When the magician's guests arrived they looked everywhere for him, but, of course, could not find him. Then, after waiting a while, they began to be very hungry; so, looking around for something to eat, they saw that the stew in the big pot was done, and, saying to each other, "Let's begin, anyway," they started in and ate the entire contents of the pot. After they had finished, they searched for Mchaawee again, and finding lots of provisions in the house, they thought they would stay there until he came; but after they had waited a couple of days and eaten all the food in the place, they gave him up and returned to their homes.

Meanwhile Keejaanaa and the horse continued on their way until they had gone a great distance, and at last they stopped near a large town.

"Let us stay here," said the youth, "and build a house."

As Faaraasee was agreeable, they did so. The horse coughed up all the gold he had swallowed, with which they purchased slaves, and cattle, and everything they needed.

When the people of the town saw the beautiful new house and all the slaves, and cattle, and riches it contained, they went and told their sultan, who at once made up his mind that the owner of such a place must be of sufficient importance to be visited and taken notice of, as an acquisition to the neighbourhood.

So he called on Keejaanaa, and inquired who he was.

"Oh, I'm just an ordinary being, like other people."

"Are you a traveller?"

"Well, I have been; but I like this place, and think I'll settle down here."

"Why don't you come and walk in our town?"

"I should like to very much, but I need someone to show me around."

"Oh, I'll show you around," said the sultan, eagerly, for he was quite taken with the young man.

After this Keejaanaa and the sultan became great friends; and in the course of time the young man married the sultan's daughter, and they had one son.

They lived very happily together, and Keejaanaa loved Faaraasee as his own soul.

The Three Magicians

A CERTAIN KING had engaged in a series of wars, during which he employed three magicians or medicine-men to make charms for him, so that he might destroy his enemies.

At the end of the war these three magicians came to the King and humbly asked to be allowed to return home. The King foolishly refused, and at this the magicians said:

"We asked your permission out of courtesy, O King, but we can very easily depart without it."

Thereupon the first magician fell down on the ground and disappeared. The second threw a ball of twine into the air, climbed up the thread and disappeared likewise. The third magician, Elenre, remained standing.

"It is your turn to disappear," said the King, trembling with anger, "or I will slay you."

"You cannot harm me," replied the magician.

At this the King ordered him to be beheaded, but the sword broke in two, and the executioner's arm withered away. The King then ordered him to be speared, but the spear crumpled up and was useless. An attempt was made to crush the magician with a rock, but it rolled over his body as lightly as a child's ball.

The King then sent for the magician's wife and asked her to reveal his secret charm. At last the woman confessed that if they took one blade of grass from the thatched roof of a house, they could easily cut off his head with it.

This was done, and the magician's head rolled off and stuck to the King's hand. It could not by any means be removed. When food and drink was brought to the King, the head consumed it all, so that the King seemed likely to die.

Magicians were hastily summoned from all over the kingdom, but the head laughed at all their charms and remained fast.

Finally came one who prostrated himself before the head and cried out:

"Who am I to oppose you, great Elenre? I come only because the King commands me."

To this Elenre replied:

"You are wiser than all the rest!" and the head fell at once to the ground, where it became a flowing river, which to this day is called Odo Elenre, or Elenre's river.

The magician's wife was likewise changed into a river, but because she had betrayed him, Elenre commanded the river not to flow, and it became instead a stagnant pool.

Hsu Sun, the Dragon Slayer

AT FORTY-ONE YEARS OF AGE, when Hsu Sun was Magistrate of Ching-yang, near the modern Chih-chiang Hsien, in Hupei, during times of drought he had only to touch a piece of tile to turn it into gold in order to relieve the people of their distress. He also saved many lives by curing sickness through the use of talismans and magic formulae.

During the period of the dynastic troubles, he resigned and joined the famous magician Kuo P'o. Together they went to the minister Wang Tun, who had risen against the Eastern Chin dynasty. Kuo P'o's remonstrance only irritated the minister, who cut off his head.

Hsu Sun then threw his chalice on the ridgepole of the room, causing it to be whirled into the air. As Wang Tun watched this unfold, Hsu disappeared and escaped. When he reached Lu-chiang K'ou, in Anhui, he boarded a boat, which two dragons towed into the offing and then raised into the air. In an instant they had borne it to the Lu Shan Mountains, to the south of Kiukiang, in Kiangsi. The perplexed boatman opened the window of his boat and looked out. The dragons, finding themselves discovered by an infidel, set the boat down on the top of the mountain and fled.

In this country was a dragon, or spiritual alligator, which transformed itself into a young man named Shen Lang. He married Chia Yu, daughter of the Chief Judge of T'an Chou. The young people lived in rooms below the official apartments. During spring and summer Shen Lang roamed in the rivers and lakes. One day Hsu met him, recognized him as a dragon and knew that he was the cause of the numerous floods that were devastating Kiangsi Province. He determined to find a means of getting rid of him.

Shen Lang, aware of the steps being taken against him, changed himself into a yellow ox and fled. Hsu at once transformed himself into a black ox and started in pursuit. The yellow ox jumped down a well to hide, but the black ox followed suit. The yellow ox then jumped out again and escaped to Ch'ang-sha, where he reassumed a human form.

Hsu Sun, returning to the town, hastened to the yamen and called to Shen Lang to come out and show himself, addressing him in a severe tone of voice: "Dragon, how dare you hide yourself there under a borrowed form?" Shen Lang then reassumed the form of a spiritual alligator and Hsu Sun ordered the spiritual soldiers to kill him. He then commanded his two sons to come out of their abode. By merely spurting a mouthful of water on them he transformed them into young dragons. Chia Yu was told to vacate the rooms at once and in the twinkling of an eye the whole yamen sank beneath the earth. Nothing but a lake remained where it had been.

After his victory over the dragon, Hsu Sun assembled the members of his family on Hsi Shan, outside the city of Nan-ch'ang Fu and all ascended to Heaven in full daylight, taking with them even the dogs and chickens. He was then 133 years old. Subsequently a temple was erected to him and he was canonized as Just Prince, Admirable and Beneficent.

Lo Hsuan and the Ministry of Fire

IT IS BELIEVED that Lo Hsuan was originally a Taoist priest known as Yen-chung Hsien, of the island Huo-lung, meaning 'Fire-dragon'. His face was the colour of ripe fruit of the jujube-tree, his hair and beard red, the former done up in the shape of a fish-tail. He is also said to have had three eyes. He wore a red cloak ornamented with the pa kua; his horse snorted flames from its nostrils and fire darted from its hoofs.

While fighting in the service of the son of the tyrant emperor, Lo Hsuan suddenly changed himself into a giant with three heads and six arms. In each of his hands he held a magic weapon. These were a seal which reflected the heavens and the earth, a wheel of the five fire-dragons, a gourd containing ten thousand fire-crows, and, in the other hands, two swords which floated like smoke and a tall column of smoke enclosing swords of fire.

Having arrived at the city of Hsi Ch'i, Lo Hsuan sent forth his smoke-column and the air was filled with swords of fire. The ten thousand fire-crows, emerging from the gourd, spread themselves over the town and a terrible fire broke out, the whole place being ablaze in just a few minutes.

It was then that Princess Lung Chi, daughter of Wang-mu Niang-niang appeared in the sky. She spread her shroud of mist and dew over the city and the fire was extinguished by a heavy downpour of rain. All the mysterious mechanisms of Lo Hsuan lost their power and the magician took to his heels down the side of the mountain. There he was met by Li, the Pagoda-bearer, who threw his golden pagoda into the air. The pagoda fell on Lo Hsuan's head and broke his skull.

Hui Lu, God of Fire

THE MOST POPULAR God of Fire is Hui Lu, a celebrated magician who lived some time before the reign of Ti K'u, the father of Yao the Great, and had a mysterious bird named Pi Fang and a hundred other fire birds shut up in a gourd. He had only to let them out to set up an extensive fire that would extend over the whole country.

Huang Ti ordered Chu Jung to fight Hui Lu and also to subdue the rebel Chih Yu. Chu Jung had a large bracelet of pure gold – a most wonderful and effective weapon. He hurled it into the air and it fell on Hui Lu's neck, throwing him to the ground and rendering him incapable of moving. Finding resistance impossible, he asked for mercy from his victor and promised to be his follower in the spiritual contests. Subsequently he always called himself Huo-shih Chih T'u, 'the Disciple of the Master of Fire'.

Chang Tao-Ling, the Heavenly Teacher

CHANG TAO-LING, the first Taoist pope, was born in AD 35, in the reign of the Emperor Kuang Wu Ti of the Han dynasty. His birthplace is variously given as the T'ien-mu Shan, 'Eye of Heaven Mountain', in Lin-an Hsien, in Chekiang, and Feng-yang Fu, in Anhui. He devoted himself wholly to study and meditation, declining all offers to enter the service of the State. He preferred to live in the mountains of Western China, where he persevered in the study of alchemy and in cultivating the virtues of purity and mental abstraction. From the hands of Lao Tzu he received a mystic treatise. Any by following the instructions in it he was successful in his search for the elixir of life.

One day when he was engaged in experimenting with the 'Dragon-tiger elixir' a spiritual being appeared to him and said: "On Po-sung Mountain is a stone house in which are concealed the writings of the Three Emperors of antiquity and a canonical work. By obtaining these you may ascend to Heaven, if you undergo the course of discipline they prescribe."

Chang Tao-ling found these works and by means of them he obtained the power of flying, of hearing distant sounds and of leaving his body. After going through a thousand days of discipline and after receiving instruction from a goddess, who taught him to walk about among the stars, he began to fight with the king of the demons, to divide mountains and seas and to command the wind and thunder. All the demons fled before him. On account of the immense slaughter of demons by this hero, the wind and thunder were reduced to subjection, and various divinities hurried to acknowledge their faults. In nine years he gained the power to ascend to Heaven.

Chang Tao-ling may rightly be considered as the true founder of modern Taoism. The recipes for the pills of immortality contained in the mysterious books, and the invention of talismans for the cure of all sorts of diseases, not only elevated him to the high position he has since occupied in the minds of his numerous disciples, but enabled them in turn to successfully exploit this new source of power and wealth. From that time the Taoist sect began to specialize in the art of healing. Protecting or curing talismans bearing the Master's seal were purchased for enormous sums. It is therefore seen that he was after all a deceiver of the people, and unbelievers or rival partisans of other sects have dubbed him a 'rice thief'.

He is generally represented as dressed in richly decorated garments, brandishing his magic sword with his right hand, holding a cup containing the draught of immortality in his left, and riding a tiger which in one paw grasps his magic seal and with the others tramples down the five venomous creatures: lizard, snake, spider, toad and centipede. Pictures of him with these accessories are pasted up in houses on the fifth day of the fifth moon to protect from calamity and sickness.

Another legend relating to Chang Tao-ling is that, not wishing to ascend to Heaven too soon, he took of only half of the pill of immortality, dividing the other half among several of his admirers. Also that he had at least two selves or personalities, one of which used to amuse itself in a boat on a small lake in front of his house. The other self would receive his visitors, entertaining them with food, drink and conversation.

On one occasion this self said to them: "You are unable to quit the world altogether as I can, but by imitating my example in the matter of family relations you could obtain a medicine which would prolong your lives by several centuries. I have given the crucible in which Huang Ti prepared the draught of immortality to my disciple Wang Ch'ang. Later on, a man will come from the East, who will also make use of it. He will arrive on the seventh day of the first moon."

Exactly on that day a man named Chao Sheng arrived from the East. Chang then led all three hundred of his disciples to the highest peak of the Yun-t'ai. Below them they saw a peach tree growing near a pointed rock, stretching out its branches like arms above a fathomless abyss. It was a large tree, covered with ripe fruit.

Chang said to his disciples: "I will communicate a spiritual formula to the one among you who will dare to gather the fruit of that tree." They all leaned over to look, but each declared the feat to be impossible. Chao Sheng alone had the courage to rush out to the point of the rock and up the tree stretching out into space. He stood and gathered the peaches, placing them in the folds of his cloak, as many as it would hold, but when he wished to climb back up the precipitous slope, his hands slipped on the smooth rock and all his attempts were in vain. So he threw the peaches, three hundred and two in all, one by one up to Chang Tao-ling, who distributed them. Each disciple ate one, as did Chang, who reserved the remaining one for Chao Sheng, whom he helped to climb up again. To do this Chang extended his arm to a length of thirty feet, everyone present marvelling at the miracle.

After Chao had eaten his peach Chang stood on the edge of the precipice and said with a laugh, "Chao Sheng was brave enough to climb out to that tree and his foot never tripped. I too will make the attempt. If I succeed I will have a big peach as a reward."

Having said this, he leapt into space and jumped into the branches of the peach tree. Wang Ch'ang and Chao Sheng also jumped into the tree and stood one on each side of him. There Chang communicated to them the mysterious formula. Three days later they returned to their homes; then, having made final arrangements, they returned once more to the mountain peak. From here, in the presence of the other disciples, who followed them with their eyes until they had completely disappeared from view, all three ascended to Heaven in broad daylight.

The name of Chang Tao-ling, the Heavenly Teacher, is a household name in China. He is the earthly representative of the Pearly Emperor in Heaven and the Commander-in-Chief of the hosts of Taoism. He, the chief of the wizards, the 'true man', as he is known, wields an immense spiritual power throughout the land. The present pope boasts of an unbroken line for many generations. His family obtained possession of the Dragon-tiger Mountain in Kiangsi around AD 1000.

The Two Jugglers

ONE BEAUTIFUL spring day two men strolled into the public square of a well-known Chinese city. They were plainly dressed and looked like ordinary countrymen who had come in to see the sights. Judging by their faces, they were father and son. The elder, a wrinkled man of perhaps fifty, wore a scant grey beard. The younger had a small box on his shoulder.

At the hour when these strangers entered the public square, a large crowd had gathered, for it was a feast day, and everyone was bent on having a good time. All the people seemed very happy. Some, seated in little open-air booths, were eating, drinking, and smoking. Others were buying odds and ends from the street-vendors, tossing coins, and playing various games of chance.

The two men walked about aimlessly. They seemed to have no friends among the pleasure-seekers. At last, however, as they stood reading a public notice posted at the entrance of the town-hall or yamen, a bystander asked them who they were.

"Oh, we are jugglers from a distant province," said the elder, smiling and pointing towards the box. "We can do many tricks for the amusement of the people."

Soon it was spread about among the crowd that two famous jugglers had just arrived from the capital, and that they were able to perform many wonderful deeds. Now it happened that the mandarin or mayor of the city, at that very moment was entertaining a number of guests in the yamen. They had just finished eating, and the host was wondering what he should do to amuse his friends, when a servant told him of the jugglers.

"Ask them what they can do," said the mandarin eagerly. "I will pay them well if they can really amuse us, but I want something more than the old tricks of knife-throwing and balancing. They must show us something new."

The servant went outside and spoke to the jugglers: "The great man bids you tell him what you can do. If you can amuse his visitors he will bring them out to the private grand stand, and let you perform before them and the people who are gathered together."

"Tell your honourable master," said the elder, whom we shall call Chang, "that, try us as he will, he will not be disappointed. Tell him that we come from the unknown land of dreams and visions, that we can turn rocks into mountains, rivers into oceans, mice into elephants, in short, that there is nothing in magic too difficult for us to do."

The official was delighted when he heard the report of his servant. "Now we may have a little fun," he said to his guests, "for there are jugglers outside who will perform their wonderful tricks before us."

The guests filed out on to the grand stand at one side of the public square. The mandarin commanded that a rope should be stretched across so as to leave an open space in full view of the crowd, where the two Changs might give their exhibition.

For a time the two strangers entertained the people with some of the simpler tricks, such as spinning plates in the air, tossing bowls up and catching them on chopsticks, making flowers grow from empty pots, and transforming one object into another. At last, however, the mandarin cried out: "These tricks are very good of their kind, but how about those idle boasts of changing rivers into oceans and mice into elephants? Did you not say that you came from the land of dreams? These tricks you have done are stale and shopworn. Have you nothing new with which to regale my guests on this holiday?"

"Most certainly, your excellency. But surely you would not have a labourer do more than his employer requires? Would that not be quite contrary to the teachings of our fathers? Be assured, sir, anything that you demand I can do for you. Only say the word."

The mandarin laughed outright at this boasting language. "Take care, my man! Do not go too far with your promises. There are too many impostors around for me to believe every stranger. Hark you! no lying, for if you lie in the presence of my guests, I shall take great pleasure in having you beaten."

"My words are quite true, your excellency," repeated Chang earnestly. "What have we to gain by deceit, we who have performed our miracles before the countless hosts of yonder Western Heaven?"

"Ha, ha! hear the braggarts!" shouted the guests. "What shall we command them to do?"

For a moment they consulted together, whispering and laughing.

"I have it," cried the host finally. "Our feast was short of fruit, since this is the off season. Suppose we let this fellow supply us. Here, fellow, produce us a peach, and be quick about it. We have no time for fooling."

"What, masters, a peach?" exclaimed the elder Chang in mock dismay. "Surely at this season you do not expect a peach."

"Caught at his own game," laughed the guests, and the people began to hoot derisively.

"But, father, you promised to do anything he required," urged the son. "If he asks even a peach, how can you refuse and at the same time save your face?"

"Hear the boy talk," mumbled the father, "and yet, perhaps he's right. Very well, masters," turning to the crowd, "if it's a peach you want, why, a peach you shall have, even though I must send into the garden of the Western Heaven for the fruit."

The people became silent and the mandarin's guests forgot to laugh. The old man, still muttering, opened the box from which he had been taking the magic bowls, plates, and other articles. "To think of people wanting peaches at this season! What is the world coming to?"

After fumbling in the box for some moments he drew out a skein of golden thread, fine spun and as light as gossamer. No sooner had he unwound a portion of this thread than a sudden gust of wind carried it up into the air above the heads of the onlookers. Faster and faster the old man paid out the magic coil, higher and higher the free end rose into the heavens, until, strain his eyes as he would, no one present could see into what far-region it had vanished.

"Wonderful, wonderful!" shouted the people with one voice, "the old man is a fairy."

For a moment they forgot all about the mandarin, the jugglers, and the peach, so amazed were they at beholding the flight of the magic thread.

At last the old man seemed satisfied with the distance to which his cord had sailed, and, with a bow to the spectators, he tied the end to a large wooden pillar which helped to support the roof of the grand stand. For a moment the structure trembled and swayed as if it too would be carried off into the blue ether, the guests turned pale and clutched their chairs for support, but not even the mandarin dared to speak, so sure were they now that they were in the presence of fairies.

"Everything is ready for the journey," said old Chang calmly.

"What! shall you leave us?" asked the mayor, finding his voice again.

"I? Oh, no, my old bones are not spry enough for quick climbing. My son here will bring us the magic peach. He is handsome and active enough to enter that heavenly garden. Graceful, oh graceful is that peach tree – of course, you remember the line from the poem – and a graceful man must pluck the fruit."

The mandarin was still more surprised at the juggler's knowledge of a famous poem from the classics. It made him and his friends all the more certain that the newcomers were indeed fairies.

The young man at a sign from his father tightened his belt and the bands about his ankles, and then, with a graceful gesture to the astonished people, sprang upon the magic string, balanced himself for a moment on the steep incline, and then ran as nimbly up as a sailor would have mounted a rope ladder. Higher and higher he climbed till he seemed no bigger than a lark ascending into the blue sky, and then, like some tiny speck, far, far away, on the western horizon.

The people gazed in open-mouthed wonder. They were struck dumb and filled with some nameless fear; they hardly dared to look at the enchanter who stood calmly in their midst, smoking his long-stemmed pipe.

The mandarin, ashamed of having laughed at and threatened this man who was clearly a fairy, did not know what to say. He snapped his long finger nails and looked at his guests in mute astonishment. The visitors silently drank their tea, and the crowd of sightseers craned their necks in a vain effort to catch sight of the vanished fairy. Only one in all that assembly, a bright-eyed little boy of eight, dared to break the silence, and he caused a hearty burst of merriment by crying out, "Oh, daddy, will the bad young man fly off into the sky and leave his poor father all alone?"

The greybeard laughed loudly with the others, and tossed the lad a copper. "Ah, the good boy," he said smiling, "he has been well trained to love his father; no fear of foreign ways spoiling his filial piety."

After a few moments of waiting, old Chang laid aside his pipe and fixed his eyes once more on the western sky. "It is coming," he said quietly. "The peach will soon be here."

Suddenly he held out his hand as if to catch some falling object, but, look as they would, the people could see nothing. Swish! thud! it came like a streak of light, and, lo, there in the magician's fingers was a peach, the most beautiful specimen the people had ever seen, large and rosy. "Straight from the garden of the gods," said Chang, handing the fruit to the mandarin, "a peach in the Second Moon, and the snow hardly off the ground."

Trembling with excitement, the official took the peach and cut it open. It was large enough for all his guests to have a taste, and such a taste it was! They smacked their lips and wished for more, secretly thinking that never again would ordinary fruit be worth the eating.

But all this time the old juggler, magician, fairy or whatever you choose to call him, was looking anxiously into the sky. The result of this trick was more than he had bargained for. True, he had been able to produce the magic peach which the mandarin had called for, but his son, where was his son? He shaded his eyes and looked far up into the blue heavens, and so did the people, but no one could catch a glimpse of the departed youth.

"Oh, my son, my son," cried the old man in despair, "how cruel is the fate that has robbed me of you, the only prop of my declining years! Oh, my boy, my boy, would that I had not sent you on so perilous a journey! Who now will look after my grave when I am gone?"

Suddenly the silken cord on which the young man had sped so daringly into the sky, gave a quick jerk which almost toppled over the post to which it was tied, and there, before the very eyes of the people, it fell from the lofty height, a silken pile on the ground in front of them.

The greybeard uttered a loud cry and covered his face with his hands. "Alas! the whole story is plain enough," he sobbed. "My boy was caught in the act of plucking the magic peach from the garden of the gods, and they have thrown him into prison. Woe is me! Ah! woe is me!"

The mandarin and his friends were deeply touched by the old man's grief, and tried in vain to comfort him. "Perhaps he will return," they said. "Have courage!"

"Yes, but in what a shape?" replied the magician. "See! even now they are restoring him to his father."

The people looked, and they saw twirling and twisting through the air the young man's arm. It fell upon the ground in front of them at the fairy's feet. Next came the head, a leg, the body. One by one before the gasping, shuddering people, the parts of the unfortunate young man were restored to his father.

After the first outburst of wild, frantic grief the old man by a great effort gained control of his feelings, and began to gather up these parts, putting them tenderly into the wooden box.

By this time many of the spectators were weeping at the sight of the father's affliction. "Come," said the mandarin at last, deeply moved, "let us present the old man with sufficient money to give his boy a decent burial."

All present agreed willingly, for there is no sight in China that causes greater pity than that of an aged parent robbed by death of an only son. The copper cash fell in a shower at the juggler's feet, and soon tears of gratitude were mingled with those of sorrow. He gathered up the money and tied it in a large black cloth. Then a wonderful change came over his face. He seemed all of a sudden to forget his grief. Turning to the box, he raised the lid. The people heard him say: "Come, my son; the crowd is waiting for you to thank them. Hurry up! They have been very kind to us."

In an instant the box was thrown open with a bang, and before the mandarin and his friends, before the eyes of all the sightseers the young man, strong and whole once more, stepped forth and bowed, clasping his hands and giving the national salute.

For a moment all were silent. Then, as the wonder of the whole thing dawned upon them, the people broke forth into a tumult of shouts, laughter, and compliments. "The fairies have surely come to visit us!" they shouted. "The city will be blessed with good fortune! Perhaps it is Fairy Old Boy himself who is among us!"

The mandarin rose and addressed the jugglers, thanking them in the name of the city for their visit and for the taste they had given to him and his guests of the peach from the heavenly orchard.

Even as he spoke, the magic box opened again; the two fairies disappeared inside, the lid closed, and the chest rose from the ground above the heads of the people. For a moment it floated round in a circle like some homing pigeon trying to find its bearings before starting on a return journey. Then, with a sudden burst of speed, it shot off into the heavens and vanished from the sight of those below, and not a thing remained as proof of the strange visitors except the magic peach seed that lay beside the teacups on the mandarin's table.

According to the most ancient writings there is now nothing left to tell of this story. It has been declared, however, by later scholars that the official and his friends who had eaten the magic peach, at once began to feel a change in their lives. While, before the coming of the fairies, they had lived unfairly, accepting bribes and taking part in many shameful practices, now, after tasting of the heavenly fruit, they began to grow better. The people soon began to honour and love them, saying, "Surely these great men are not like others of their kind, for these men are just and honest in their dealings with us. They seem not to be ruling for their own reward!"

However this may be, we do know that before many years their city became the centre of the greatest peach-growing section of China, and even yet when strangers walk in the orchards and look up admiringly at the beautiful sweet-smelling fruit, the natives sometimes ask proudly, "And have you never heard about the wonderful peach which was the beginning of all our orchards, the magic peach the fairies brought us from the Western Heaven?"

King Mu of Dschou

IN THE DAYS of King Mu of Dschou a magician came out of the uttermost West, who could walk through water and fire, and pass through metal and stone. He could make mountains and rivers change place, shift about cities and castles, rise into emptiness without falling, strike against solid matter without finding it an obstruction; and he knew a thousand transformations in all their inexhaustible variety. And he could not only change the shape of things but he could change men's thoughts. The King honored him like a god, and served him as he would a master. He resigned his own apartments that the magician might be lodged in them, had beasts of sacrifice brought to offer him, and selected sweet singers to give him pleasure. But the rooms in the King's palace were too humble – the magician could not dwell in them; and the King's singers were not musical enough to be allowed to be near him. So King Mu had a new palace built for him. The work of bricklayers and carpenters, of painters and stainers left nothing to be desired with regard to skill. The King's treasury was empty when the tower had reached its full height. It was a thousand fathoms high, and rose above the top of the mountain before the capital. The King selected maidens, the loveliest and most dainty, gave them fragrant essences, had their eyebrows curved in lines of beauty, and adorned their hair and ears with jewels. He garbed them in fine cloth, and with white silks fluttering about them, and had their faces painted white and their eyebrows stained black. He had them put on armlets of precious stones and mix sweet-smelling herbs. They filled the palace and sang the songs of the ancient kings in order to please the magician. Every month the most costly garments were brought him, and every morning the most delicate food. The magician allowed them to do so, and since he had no choice, made the best of it.

Not long afterward the magician invited the King to go traveling with him. The King grasped the magician's sleeve, and thus they flew up through the air to the middle of the skies. When they stopped they found they had reached the palace of the magician. It was built of gold and silver, and adorned with pearls and precious stones. It towered high over the clouds and rain; and none could say whereon it rested. To the eye it had the appearance of heaped-up clouds. All that it offered the senses was different from the things of the world of men. It seemed to the King as though he were bodily present in the midst of the purple depths of the city of the air, of the divine harmony of the spheres, where the Great God dwells. The King looked down, and his castles and pleasure-houses appeared to him like hills of earth and heaps of straw. And there the King remained for some decades and thought no more of his kingdom.

Then the magician again invited the King to go traveling with him once more. And in the place to which they came there was to be seen neither sun nor moon above, nor rivers or sea below. The King's dazzled eyes could not see the radiant shapes which showed themselves; the King's dulled ears could not hear the sounds which played about them. It seemed as though his body were dissolving in confusion; his thoughts began to stray, and consciousness threatened to leave him. So he begged the magician to return. The magician put his spell upon him, and it seemed to the King as though he were falling into empty space.

When he regained consciousness, he was sitting at the same place where he had been sitting when the magician had asked him to travel with him for the first time. The servants waiting on him were the same, and when he looked down, his goblet was not yet empty, and his food had not yet grown cold.

The King asked what had happened. And the servants answered, "The King sat for a space in silence." Whereupon the King was quite bereft of reason, and it was three months before he regained his right mind. Then he questioned the magician. The magician said: "I was traveling with you in the spirit, O King! What need was there for the body to go along? And the place in which we stayed at that time was no less real than your own castle and your own gardens. But you are used only to permanent conditions, therefore visions which dissolve so suddenly appear strange to you."

The King was content with the explanation. He gave no further thought to the business of government and took no more interest in his servants, but resolved to travel afar. So he had the eight famous steeds harnessed, and accompanied by a few faithful retainers, drove a thousand miles away. There he came to the country of the great hunters. The great hunters brought the King the blood of the white brant to drink, and washed his feet in the milk of mares and cows. When the King and his followers had quenched their thirst, they drove on and camped for the night on the slope of the Kunlun Mountain, south of the Red River. The next day they climbed to the peak of Kunlun Mountain and gazed at the castle of the Lord of the Yellow Earth. Then they traveled on to the Queen-Mother of the West. Before they got there they had to pass the Weak River. This is a river whose waters will bear neither floats nor ships. All that attempts to float over it sinks into its depths. When the King reached the shore, fish and turtles, crabs and salamanders came swimming up and formed a bridge, so that he could drive across with the wagon.

It is said of the Queen-Mother of the West that she goes about with hair unkempt, with a bird's beak and tiger's teeth, and that she is skilled in playing the flute. Yet this is not her true figure, but that of a spirit who serves her, and rules over the Western sky. The Queen-Mother entertained King Mu in her castle by the Springs of Jade. And she gave him rock-marrow to drink and fed him with the fruit of the jade-trees. Then she sang him a song and taught him a magic formula by means of which one could obtain long life. The Queen-Mother of the West gathers the immortals around her, and gives them to eat of the peaches of long life; and then they come to her with wagons with purple canopies, drawn by flying dragons. Ordinary mortals sink in the Weak River when they try to cross. But she was kindly disposed to King Mu.

When he took leave of her, he also went on to the spot where the sun turns in after running three thousand miles a day. Then he returned again to his kingdom.

When King Mu was a hundred years old, the Queen-Mother of the West drew near his palace and led him away with her into the clouds.

And from that day on he was seen no more.

The Kindly Magician

ONCE UPON A TIME there was a man named Du Dsi Tschun. In his youth he was a spendthrift and paid no heed to his property. He was given to drink and idling. When he had run through all his money, his relatives cast him out. One winter day he was walking barefoot about the city, with an empty stomach and torn clothes. Evening came on and still he had not found any food. Without end or aim he wandered about the market place. He was hungry, and the cold seemed well nigh unendurable. So he turned his eyes upward and began to lament aloud.

Suddenly an ancient man stood before him, leaning on a staff, who said: "What do you lack since you complain so?"

"I am dying of hunger," replied Du Dsi Tschun, "and not a soul will take pity on me!"

The ancient man said: "How much money would you need in order to live in all comfort?"

"If I had fifty thousand pieces of copper it would answer my purpose," replied Du Dsi Tschun.

The ancient said: "That would not answer."

"Well, then, a million!"

"That is still too little!"

"Well, then, three million!"

The ancient man said: "That is well spoken!" He fetched a thousand pieces of copper out of his sleeve and said: "That is for this evening. Expect me tomorrow by noon, at the Persian Bazaar!"

At the time set Du Dsi Tschun went there, and, sure enough, there was the ancient, who gave him three million pieces of copper. Then he disappeared, without giving his name.

When Du Dsi Tschun held the money in his hand, his love for prodigality once more awoke. He rode pampered steeds, clothed himself in the finest furs, went back to his wine, and led such an extravagant life that the money gradually came to an end. Instead of wearing brocade he had to wear cotton, and instead of riding horseback he went to the dogs. Finally he was again running about barefoot and in rags as before, and did not know how to satisfy his hunger. Once more he stood in the market-place and sighed. But the ancient was already there, took him by the hand and said: "Are you back already to where you were? That is strange! However, I will aid you once more!"

But Du Dsi Tschun was ashamed and did not want to accept his help. Yet the ancient insisted, and led him along to the Persian Bazaar. This time he gave him ten million pieces of copper, and Du Dsi Tschun thanked him with shame in his heart.

With money in hand, he tried to give time to adding to it, and saving in order to gain great wealth. But, as is always the case, it is hard to overcome ingrown faults. Gradually he began to fling his money away again, and gave free rein to all his desires. And once more his purse grew empty. In a couple of years he was as poor as ever he had been.

Then he met the ancient the third time, but was so ashamed of himself that he hid his face when he passed him.

The ancient seized his arm and said: "Where are you going? I will help you once more. I will give you thirty million. But if then you do not improve you are past all aid!"

Full of gratitude, Du Dsi Tschun bowed before him and said: "In the days of my poverty my wealthy relatives did not seek me out. You alone have thrice aided me. The money you give me to-day shall not be squandered, that I swear; but I will devote it to good works in order to repay your great kindness. And when I have done this I will follow you, if needs be through fire and through water."

The ancient replied: "That is right! When you have ordered these things ask for me in the temple of Laotsze beneath the two mulberry trees!"

Du Dsi Tschun took the money and went to Yangdschou. There he bought a hundred acres of the best land, and built a lofty house with many hundreds of rooms on the highway. And there he allowed widows and orphans to live. Then he bought a burial-place for his ancestors, and supported his needy relations. Countless people were indebted to him for their livelihood.

When all was finished, he went to inquire after the ancient in the temple of Laotsze. The ancient was sitting in the shade of the mulberry trees blowing the flute. He took Du Dsi Tschun along with him to the cloudy peaks of the holy mountains of the West. When they had gone some forty miles into the mountains, he saw a dwelling, fair and clean. It was surrounded by many-colored clouds, and peacocks and cranes were flying about it. Within the house was a herb-oven nine feet high. The fire burned with a purple flame, and its glow leaped along the walls. Nine fairies stood at the oven, and a green dragon and a white tiger crouched beside it. Evening came. The ancient was no longer clad like an ordinary man; but wore a yellow cap and wide, flowing garments. He took three pellets of the White Stone, put them into a flagon of wine, and gave them to Du Dsi Tschun to drink. He spread out a tiger-skin against the western wall of the inner chamber, and bade Du Dsi Tschun sit down on it, with his face turned toward the East. Then he said to him: "Now beware of speaking a single word – no matter what happens to you, whether you encounter powerful gods or terrible demons, wild beasts or ogres, or all the tortures of the nether world, or even if you see your own relatives suffer – for all these things are only deceitful images! They cannot harm you. Think only of what I have said, and let your soul be at rest!" And when he had said this the ancient disappeared.

Then Du Dsi Tschun saw only a large stone jug full of clear water standing before him. Fairies, dragon and tiger had all vanished. Suddenly he heard a tremendous crash, which made heaven and earth tremble. A man towering more than ten feet in height appeared. He called himself the great captain, and he and his horse were covered with golden armor. He was surrounded by more than a hundred soldiers, who drew their bows and swung their swords, and halted in the courtyard.

The giant called out harshly: "Who are you? Get out of my way!"

Du Dsi Tschun did not move. And he returned no answer to his questions.

Then the giant flew into a passion and cried with a thundering voice: "Chop off his head!"

But Du Dsi Tschun remained unmoved, so the giant went off raging.

Then a furious tiger and a poisonous serpent came up roaring and hissing. They made as though to bite him and leaped over him. But Du Dsi Tschun remained unperturbed in spirit, and after a time they dissolved and vanished.

Suddenly a great rain began to fall in streams. It thundered and lightninged incessantly, so that his ears rang and his eyes were blinded. It seemed as though the house would fall. The water rose to a flood in a few moments' time, and streamed up to the place where he was sitting. But Du Dsi Tschun remained motionless and paid no attention to it. And after a time the water receded.

Then came a great demon with the head of an ox. He set up a kettle in the middle of the courtyard, in which bubbled boiling oil. He caught Du Dsi Tschun by the neck with an iron fork and said: "If you will tell me who you are I will let you go!"

Du Dsi Tschun shut his eyes and kept silent. Then the demon picked him up with the fork and flung him into the kettle. He withstood the pain, and the boiling oil did not harm him. Finally the demon dragged him out again, and drew him down the steps of the house before a man with red hair and a blue face, who looked like the prince of the nether world. The latter cried: "Drag in his wife!"

After a time Du Dsi Tschun's wife was brought on in chains. Her hair was torn and she wept bitterly.

The demon pointed to Du Dsi Tschun and said: "If you will speak your name we will let her go!" But he answered not a word.

Then the prince of evil had the woman tormented in all sorts of ways. And she pleaded with Du Dsi Tschun: "I have been your wife now for ten years. Will you not speak one little word to save me? I can endure no more!" And the tears ran in streams from her eyes. She screamed and scolded. Yet he spoke not a word.

Thereupon the prince of evil shouted: "Chop her into bits!" And there, before his eyes, it seemed as though she were really being chopped to pieces. But Du Dsi Tschun did not move.

"The scoundrel's measure is full!" cried the prince of evil. "He shall dwell no longer among the living! Off with his head!" And so they killed him, and it seemed to him that his soul fled his body. The ox-headed demon dragged him down into the nether regions, where he tasted all the tortures in turn. But Du Dsi Tschun remembered the words of the ancient. And the tortures, too, seemed bearable. So he did not scream and said not a word.

Now he was once more dragged before the prince of evil. The latter said: "As punishment for his obstinacy this man shall come to earth again in the shape of a woman!"

The demon dragged him to the wheel of life and he returned to earth in the shape of a girl. He was often ill, had to take medicine continually, and was pricked and burned with hot needles. Yet he never uttered a sound. Gradually he grew into a beautiful maiden. But since he never spoke, he was known as the dumb maid. A scholar finally took him for his bride, and they lived in peace and good fellowship. And a son came to them who, in the course of two years was already beyond measure wise and intelligent. One day the father was carrying the son on his arm. He spoke jestingly to his wife and said: "When I look at you it seems to me that you are not really dumb. Won't you say one little word to me? How delightful it would be if you were to become my speaking rose!"

The woman remained silent. No matter how he might coax and try to make her smile, she would return no answer.

Then his features changed: "If you will not speak to me, it is a sign that you scorn me; and in that case your son is nothing to me, either!" And with that he seized the boy and flung him against the wall.

But since Du Dsi Tschun loved this little boy so dearly, he forgot the ancient's warning, and cried out: "Oh, oh!"

And before the cry had died away Du Dsi Tschun awoke as though from a dream and found himself seated in his former place. The ancient was there as well. It must have been about the fifth hour of the night. Purple flames rose wildly from the oven, and flared up to the sky. The whole house caught fire and burned like a torch.

"You have deceived me!" cried the ancient. Then he seized him by the hair and thrust him into the jug of water. And in a minute the fire went out. The ancient spoke: "You overcame joy and rage, grief and fear, hate and desire, it is true; but love you had not driven from your soul. Had you not cried out when the child was flung against the wall, then my elixir would have taken shape and you would have attained immortality. But in the last moment you failed me. Now it is too late. Now I can begin brewing my elixir of life once more from the beginning and you will remain a mere mortal man!"

Du Dsi Tschun saw that the oven had burst, and that instead of the philosopher's stone it held only a lump of iron. The ancient man cast aside his garments and chopped it up with a magic knife. Du Dsi Tschun took leave of him and returned to Yangdschou, where he lived in great affluence. In his old age he regretted that he had not completed his task. He once more went to the mountain to look for the ancient. But the ancient had vanished without leaving a trace.

Tales of Ancient Egyptian Magicians

THE FOLLOWING THREE SHORT STORIES tell of the wonderful deeds of ancient Egyptian magicians and are based on those found in the Westcar Papyrus, which was discovered in 1823 by British adventurer Henry Westcar and is currently preserved in the Egyptian Museum of Berlin.

The surviving material of the Westcar Papyrus consists of 12 columns of hieratic script written in classical Middle Egyptian. It was written probably at some period between the twelfth and eighteenth dynasties (c. 18th–16th century BC). The first attempt at a complete translation was made by German Egyptologist Adolf Erman in 1890, but as the hieretic signs were still insufficiently understood, the papyrus was first displayed as a curiosity. Since then the text has been translated many times, resulting in numerous different outcomes.

Each of the stories are told at the royal court by the sons of King Khufu (Cheops) of the fourth dynasty.

Ubaaner and the Wax Crocodile

THE FIRST STORY describes an event that happened during the reign of Nebka, a king of the third dynasty. It was told by Prince Khafra to King Khufu (Cheops). The tale tells of a magician named Ubaaner (meaning 'splitter of stones'), who was the chief Kher-heb in the temple of Ptah of Memphis, and a very learned man. He was a married man, but unfortunately his wife had fallen in love with a young man who worked in the fields.

One day, the wife sent one of her maids to deliver a box containing a supply of very fine clothes to the young man. Soon after receiving this gift, the young man suggested to the magician's wife that they should meet and talk in a certain lodge in her garden. So she instructed the steward to have the lodge made ready for her to receive her friend. When this was done, she went to the lodge and she sat there with the young man and drank beer with him until the evening, when he went on his way.

The steward, knowing what had happened, made up his mind to report the matter to his master, and as soon as morning came, he went to Ubaaner and informed him that his wife had spent the previous day drinking beer with the young man. Ubaaner then told the steward to bring him his casket made of ebony, silver and gold, which contained materials and instruments used for working magic. When it was brought him, Ubaaner took out some wax and fashioned a figure of a crocodile seven spans long. He then recited certain magical words over the crocodile and said to it, "When the young man comes to bathe in my lake you shall seize him." Then giving the wax crocodile to the steward, Ubaaner said to him, "When the young man goes down to the lake to bathe according to his daily habit, you shall throw the crocodile into the water after him." Having taken the crocodile from his master, the steward departed.

A little later the wife of Ubaaner told the steward to set the little lodge in the garden in order, because she was going to spend some time there. When the steward had furnished the lodge, she went there and the young man paid her a visit. After leaving the lodge he went and bathed in the lake. So the steward followed him and threw the wax crocodile into the water; it immediately turned into a large crocodile 7 cubits (about 3.5 metres/11 feet) long. It seized the young man and swallowed him up.

As this was unfolding, Ubaaner was visiting the king and he remained with him for seven days, during which time the young man was in the lake with no air to breathe. When the seven days were almost up, King Nebka suggested taking a walk with the magician. Whilst they were walking Ubaaner asked the king if he would like to see a wonderful thing that had happened to a young peasant. The king said he would and the pair immediately set off walking towards the lake. When they arrived Ubaaner uttered a spell over the crocodile and commanded it to come up out of the water bringing the young man with him; and the crocodile did so. When the king saw the beast he exclaimed at its hideousness and seemed to be afraid of it, but the magician stooped down fearlessly and took the crocodile up in his hand. Amazingly the living crocodile had disappeared and only a wax crocodile remained in its place.

Then Ubaaner told King Nebka the story of how this young man had spent days in the lodge of his garden talking and drinking beer with his wife. His Majesty said to the wax crocodile, "Be gone and take what is yours with you." The wax crocodile leaped out of the magician's hand into the lake and once more became a large, living crocodile. It swam away with the young man and no one ever knew what became of it afterwards. Then the king commanded his servants to seize Ubaaner's wife. They carried her off to the grounds on the north side of the royal palace, where they burned her and scattered her ashes in the river.

Once King Khufu had heard the story of Ubaaner and the wax crocodile he ordered many offerings to be made in the tomb of his predecessor Nebka and gifts to be presented to the magician.

Tchatchamankh and the Gold Ornament

PRINCE BAIUFRA STOOD UP and offered to tell King Khufu a story of a magician called Tchatchamankh, who flourished in the reign of Seneferu, the king's father. The offer having been accepted, Baiufra proceeded to relate the following tale.

One day King Seneferu was in a perplexed and gloomy state of mind. He wandered distractedly about the rooms and courts of his palace looking to find something to amuse himself with, but he failed to do so. Then he thought of the court magician Tchatchamankh and ordered his servants to summon him. When the great Kher-heb and scribe arrived, the king addressed him as "my brother" and told him that he had been wandering around his palace seeking some amusement, but had failed to find any. The magician promptly suggested to the king that he should have a boat got ready, decorated with pretty things that would give pleasure, and should go for a row on the lake. The motions of the rowers as they rowed the boat would interest him, and the sight of the depths of the waters and the pretty fields and gardens round about the lake would give him great pleasure. "Let me arrange the matter," said the magician. "Give me twenty ebony paddles inlaid with gold and silver, twenty pretty maidens with flowing hair and twenty beautiful garments to dress them in."

The king gave orders for all these things to be provided, and when the boat was ready and the maidens who were to row had taken their places, he entered the boat and sat in his little pavilion and was rowed about on the lake. The magician's views proved to be correct. The king enjoyed himself and was greatly amused by watching the maidens row. Before long one of the maidens caught the handle of her paddle in her long hair. In trying to free it a gold ornament that she had been wearing in her hair fell into the water and disappeared.

The maiden was distressed over her loss, so she stopped rowing, as did the other maidens. After the king had asked why the rowing had ceased, one of the maidens told him what had happened. Immediately, the king promised the maiden that the precious ornament would be recovered, to which the maiden responded, "I have no doubt that it will be returned to me."

Straightaway King Seneferu summoned Tchatchamankh to be brought to his presence. When the magician arrived, the king told him all that had happened. Then the magician began to recite certain spells, the effect of which was to cause the water of the lake first to divide into two parts, and then the water on one side to rise up and place itself on the water on the other side. The boat sank down gently onto the ground of the lake near where the gold ornament was seen lying. The magician fetched it and returned it to its owner. As soon as the ornament was restored to the maiden, the magician recited further spells and the water lowered itself and spread over the ground of the lake. The lake soon regained its normal level.

After returning to the royal palace His Majesty, King Seneferu made a handsome gift to his clever magician. When King Khufu had heard the story he ordered a large supply of funerary offerings to be sent to the tomb of Seneferu, and bread, beer, meat and incense to be sent to the tomb of Tchatchamankh.

The Magician Teta

ONCE PRINCE BAIUFRA had finished telling the story of Tchatchamankh and the gold ornament, Prince Herutataf, the son of King Khufu and a very wise man, stood up before his father and said to him, "Up until now you have only heard tales about the wisdom of magicians who are dead and gone. It is quite impossible to know whether they are true or not. Now, I want Your Majesty to see a certain sage who is actually alive and whom you do not know."

His Majesty Khufu said, "Who is it, Herutataf?" The Prince replied, "He is a certain peasant named Teta who lives in Tet-Seneferu. He is 110 years old, and up to this very day he eats 500 bread-cakes and a leg of beef, and drinks 100 pots of beer. He knows how to reunite to its body a head which has been cut off, he knows how to make a lion follow him whilst the rope with which he is tied drags behind him on the ground, and he knows the number of the Apet chambers of the shrine of Thoth." Now for a long time His Majesty had been searching for the number of the Apet chambers of Thoth, because he had wished to make something like it for his own 'horizon' (thought to be the books and instruments which the ancient Egyptian magicians used in working magic). So King Khufu said to Herutataf, "My son, you yourself shall go and bring the sage to me."

A boat was made ready for Prince Herutataf, who set out on his journey to Tet-Seneferu, the home of the sage. When the prince came to the spot on the river bank that was nearest to the sage's village, he had the boat tied up and continued his journey overland seated in a sort of sedan chair made of ebony, which was carried on bearing poles made of wood inlaid with gold. When Herutataf arrived at the village, the chair was set down on the ground and he stood up ready to greet the old man, whom he found lying on a bed, with the door of his house lying on the ground. One servant stood by the bed holding the sage's head and fanning him, and another was engaged in rubbing his feet.

Herutataf addressed a highly poetical speech to Teta, the gist of which was that the old man seemed to be able to defy the usual effects of old age, and to be like one who had obtained the secret of everlasting youth, and then expressed the hope that he was well. Having paid these compliments, which were couched in dignified and archaic language, Herutataf went on to say that he had come with a message from his father Khufu, who hereby summoned Teta to his presence. "I have come," he said, "a long way to invite you, so that you may eat the food, and enjoy the good things which the king bestows on those who follow him, and so that he may lead you after a happy life to your fathers who rest in the grave." The sage replied, "Welcome, Prince Herutataf, welcome, Oh son who loves his father. Your father shall reward you with gifts, and he shall promote you to the rank of the senior officials of his court. Your vital force shall fight successfully against your enemy. Your soul knows the ways of the Other World ... I salute you, Prince Herutataf."

Herutataf then held out his hands to the sage and helped him to rise from the bed, and he went with him to the river bank, Teta leaning on his arm. When they arrived there Teta asked for a boat for his children and his books, and the prince put at his disposal two boats, with crews complete. Teta himself, however, was ushered to the prince's boat and sailed with him. When they came to the palace, Prince Herutataf went to the king to announce their arrival, and said to him, "Oh king my lord, I have brought Teta." His Majesty replied, "Bring him in quickly." Then the king went out into the large hall of his palace, and Teta was led into his presence. His Majesty said, "How is it, Teta, that I have never seen you?" To this Teta answered, "Only the man who is summoned to the presence comes; so as soon as the king summoned me, I came."

Then His Majesty asked him, "Is it indeed true, as is asserted, that you know how to rejoin to its body the head which has been cut off?" Teta answered, "Most assuredly do I know how to do this, Oh king my lord." His Majesty said, "Let them bring in from the prison a prisoner, so that his death sentence may be carried out." But Teta rejoined, "Let them not bring a man, Oh king my lord. Perhaps it may be ordered that the head shall be cut off some other living creature." So a goose was brought to him and he cut off its head. He laid the body of the goose on the west side of the hall and its head on the east side. Then Teta recited certain magical spells and the goose stood up and waddled towards its head and its head moved towards its body. When the body and the head came close together, the head leaped onto the body and the goose stood up on its legs and cackled.

Then a goose of another kind called khetâa was brought to Teta, and he did with it as he had done with the first goose. Next His Majesty caused an ox to be taken to Teta, and when he had cut off its head, and recited magical spells over the head and the body, the head rejoined itself to the body, and the ox stood up on its feet. A lion was next brought to Teta, and when he had recited spells over it, the lion went behind him, and followed him (like a dog), and the rope with which he had been tied up trailed on the ground behind the animal.

King Khufu then said to Teta, "Is it true what they say that you know the number of the Apet chambers of the shrine of Thoth?" Teta replied, "No. I do not know their number, Oh king my lord, but I do know the place where they can be found." His Majesty asked, "Where is that?" To this Teta replied, "There is a box made of flint in a house called Sapti in Heliopolis." The king asked, "Who will bring me this box?" Teta replied, "Oh king my lord, I cannot bring the box to you." His Majesty asked, "Who then can bring it to me?" Teta answered, "The oldest of the three children of Rut-tetet can bring it to you." His Majesty said, "It is my wish that you tell me who this Rut-tetet is." Teta answered, "Rut-tetet is the wife of a priest of Ra of Sakhabu, who is about to give birth to three children of Ra. He told her that these children should attain to the highest dignities in the whole country, and that the oldest of them should become high priest of Heliopolis."

On hearing these words the heart of the king became sad; and Teta said, "Why are you so sad, Oh king my lord? Is it because of the three children?" His Majesty asked, "When will these three children be born?" Teta explained that the children would be born on the fifteenth day of the first month of Pert (which in today's calendar would have been around 1 December).

The king then expressed his determination to go and visit the temple of Ra of Sakhabu, which was situated near the great canal of the Letopolite district of Lower Egypt. In reply Teta declared that he would ensure that the water in the canal should be deep enough for the royal barge to sail on the canal without difficulty. The king then returned to his palace and gave orders that Teta should have lodgings provided to him in the house of Prince Herutataf, that he should live with him, and that he should be given 1,000 bread-cakes, 100 pots of beer, one ox, and 100 bundles of vegetables. And all that the king commanded concerning Teta was done.

The Death Stone

*"The Death-Stone stands on Nasu's moor
Through winter snows and summer heat;
The moss grows grey upon its sides,
But the foul-demon haunts it yet.*

*"Chill blows the blast: the owl's sad choir
Hoots hoarsely through the moaning pines;
Among the low chrysanthemums
The skulking fox, the jackal whines,
As o'er the moor the autumn light declines."*

THE BUDDHIST PRIEST GENNO, after much weary travel, came to the moor of Nasu, and was about to rest under the shadow of a great stone, when a spirit suddenly appeared, and said: "Rest not under this stone. This is the Death-Stone. Men, birds, and beasts have perished by merely touching it!"

These mysterious and warning remarks naturally awakened Genno's curiosity, and he begged that the spirit would favour him with the story of the Death-Stone.

Thus the spirit began: "Long ago there was a fair girl living at the Japanese Court. She was so charming that she was called the Jewel Maiden. Her wisdom equalled her beauty, for she understood Buddhist lore and the Confucian classics, science, and the poetry of China."

"One night," went on the spirit, "the Mikado gave a great feast in the Summer Palace, and there he assembled the wit, wisdom, and beauty of the land. It was a brilliant gathering; but while the company ate and drank, accompanied by the strains of sweet music, darkness crept over the great apartment. Black clouds raced across the sky, and there was not a star to be seen. While the guests sat rigid with fear a mysterious wind arose. It howled through the Summer Palace and blew out all the lanterns. The complete darkness produced a state of panic, and during the uproar someone cried out, 'A light! A light!'"

> *"And lo! from out the Jewel Maiden's frame*
> *There's seen to dart a weirdly lustrous flame!*
> *It grows, it spreads, it fills th' imperial halls;*
> *The painted screens, the costly panell'd walls,*
> *Erst the pale viewless damask of the night*
> *Sparkling stand forth as in the moon's full light."*

"From that very hour the Mikado sickened," continued the spirit. "He grew so ill that the Court Magician was sent for, and this worthy soul speedily ascertained the cause of his Majesty's decline. He stated, with much warmth of language, that the Jewel Maiden was a harlot and a fiend, 'who, with insidious art, the State to ravage, captivates thy heart!'

"The Magician's words turned the Mikado's heart against the Jewel Maiden. When this sorceress was spurned she resumed her original shape, that of a fox, and ran away to this very stone on Nasu moor."

The priest looked at the spirit critically. "Who are you?" he said at length.

"I am the demon that once dwelt in the breast of the Jewel Maiden! Now I inhabit the Death-Stone for evermore!"

The good Genno was much horrified by this dreadful confession, but, remembering his duty as a priest, he said: "Though you have sunk low in wickedness, you shall rise to virtue again. Take this priestly robe and begging-bowl, and reveal to me your fox form."

Then this wicked spirit cried pitifully:

> *"In the garish light of day*
> *I hide myself away,*
> *Like pale Asama's fires:*
> *With the night I'll come again,*
> *Confess my guilt with pain*
> *And new-born pure desires."*

With these words the spirit suddenly vanished.

Genno did not relinquish his good intentions. He strove more ardently than ever for this erring soul's salvation. In order that she might attain Nirvana, he offered flowers, burnt incense, and recited the sacred Scriptures in front of the stone.

When Genno had performed these religious duties, he said: "Spirit of the Death-Stone, I conjure thee! what was it in a former world that did cause thee to assume in this so foul a shape?"

Suddenly the Death-Stone was rent and the spirit once more appeared, crying:

> *"In stones there are spirits,*
> *In the waters is a voice heard:*
> *The winds sweep across the firmament!"*

Genno saw a lurid glare about him and, in the shining light, a fox that suddenly turned into a beautiful maiden.

Thus spoke the spirit of the Death-Stone: "I am she who first, in Ind, was the demon to whom Prince Hazoku paid homage.... In Great Cathay I took the form of Hoji, consort of the Emperor Iuwao; and at the Court of the Rising Sun I became the Flawless Jewel Maiden, concubine to the Emperor Toba."

The spirit confessed to Genno that in the form of the Jewel Maiden she had desired to bring destruction to the Imperial line. "Already," said the spirit, "I was making my plans, already I was gloating over the thought of the Mikado's death, and had it not been for the power of the Court Magician I should have succeeded in my scheme. As I have told you, I was driven from the Court. I was pursued by dogs and arrows, and finally sank exhausted into the Death-Stone. From time to time I haunted the moor. Now the Lord Buddha has had compassion upon me, and he has sent his priest to point out the way of true religion and to bring peace."

The legend concludes with the following pious utterances poured forth by the now contrite spirit:

> *"'I swear, O man of God! I swear,' she cries,*
> *'To thee whose blessing wafts me to the skies,*
> *I swear a solemn oath, that shall endure*
> *Firm as the Death-Stone standing on the moor,*
> *That from this hour I'm virtue's child alone!'*
> *Thus spake the ghoul, and vanished 'neath the Stone."*

The Wizard and His Pupil

THERE WAS ONCE a woman who had a son. To whatever school she sent him, he always ran away. Perplexed, the mother asked the boy "Where shall I send you?" To which he answered: "Do not send me, but go with me; if I like the place I will not run away." So she took him with her to market, and there they watched a number of men working at various handicrafts, and among them was a wizard.

The boy was very much attracted by this last, and requested his mother to apprentice him to the wizard. She went to the man and told him her son's desire. The matter was soon arranged to their mutual satisfaction, and the boy was left with his master, as the wizard was henceforth to be.

In the course of time the youth had learnt all that the wizard was able to teach him, and one day his master said: "I will transform myself into a ram; take me to market and sell me, but be sure to keep the rope." The youth agreed, and the wizard accordingly changed himself into a ram. The youth took the animal to the auctioneer, who sold it in the marketplace. It was bought by a man for five hundred piastres, but the youth kept the rope as he was instructed. In the evening the master, having resumed his human form, escaped from the buyer of the ram and came home.

Next day the wizard said to his pupil: "I am now going to transform myself into a horse; take me and sell me, but guard the rope." "I understand," answered the youth, and led the horse to market, where it was sold by auction for a thousand piastres. The pupil kept the rope, however, and came home. An idea struck him: "Now let me see," said he to himself, "whether I cannot help myself," and he went to his mother. "Mother," said he when they met, "I have learnt all that was to be learnt. Many thanks for apprenticing me to that wizard; I shall now be able to make a great deal of money." The poor woman did not understand what he meant, and said: "My son, what will you do? I hope you are not going to run away again and give me further trouble." "No," he answered. "Tomorrow I shall change myself into a bathing establishment, which you will sell; but take care not to sell the key of the door with it, or I am lost."

While the youth was thus discoursing with his mother, the wizard escaped from the man who had bought him as a horse, and came home. Finding his apprentice not there, he became angry. "You good-for-nothing; you have sold me completely this time, it seems; but wait until you fall into my hands again!" That night he remained at home, and next morning went out in search of his truant pupil.

The youth transformed himself into a beautiful bathing establishment, which his mother put up for sale by auction. All the people of the town were astonished at its magnificence, and multitudes collected round the auctioneer. The wizard was among the crowd, and guessed at once that this stately building was in reality his rascally pupil. He said nothing of that, however, but when all the pashas, beys, and other people had bid their highest he bid higher still, and the building was knocked down to him. The woman was called, and when the wizard was about to hand her the money she explained that she could not give up the key. Then the wizard said he would not pay unless he received it. He showed her that he had plenty of money, and observed to the woman that that particular key was of no importance to her; she could easily buy another if she must have one. Many of the bystanders expressed their agreement with the purchaser, and as the woman knew not the true significance of keeping the key, she parted with it to the wizard in return for the price of the bathing establishment. When she gave up the key the youth felt that his time had come, so he changed himself into a bird and flew away. His master, however, changed himself into a falcon and pursued him. They both flew a long distance until they reached another town, where the Padishah was entertaining himself with his court in the palace garden.

As a last resource, the youth now changed himself into a beautiful rose and fell at the feet of the Padishah. The King expressed his surprise at seeing the rose, as that flower was not then in season. "It is a gift from Allah," he concluded. "It smells so sweetly that not even in the rose-flowering season could its equal be found."

The wizard now resumed his human form and entered the garden, lute in hand, as a minnesinger. As he was striking his instrument he was observed by the Padishah, who, calling him, ordered him to play and sing his songs. In one of his impromptu ballads the singer requested the Padishah to give him the rose. Hearing this the King was angry, and said: "What say you, fellow? This rose was given me by Allah! How dare you, a mere wanderer, demand it?" "O Shah," answered the singer, "my occupation is obvious; I have fallen in love with the rose you possess. I have been seeking it for many years, but till now have been unable to find it. If you give it not to me I shall kill myself. Would not that be a pity? I have followed it over hill and fell, to find it now in the hands of the mild and gracious Padishah. Have you no pity for a poor man like me, who has lost love and light and happiness? Is it seemly to afflict me thus? I will not move from this spot until you give me the rose."

The Padishah was moved, and said to himself: "After all, of what consequence is the rose to me? Let the unfortunate man attain his object." Saying these words he stepped forward and handed the flower to the singer. But before the latter could grasp it, it fell to the ground and was changed into millet pulp. Quickly the wizard transformed himself into a cock and ate it up. One grain, however, fell under the Padishah's foot and so escaped the cock's attention. This grain suddenly changed into the youth, who picked up the cock and wrung its neck – in other words, he disposed of his master.

The Padishah was astonished at these strange proceedings, and commanded the young man to explain the riddle. He told the King every thing from beginning to end, and the monarch was so delighted with his skill in magic that he appointed him Grand Vezir and gave him his daughter in marriage. The young man was now able to provide for his mother, and thus everybody lived happily ever after.

The Wizard

THERE WAS HERE once in our village a certain Avstriyat, who was such a wizard that he could cause rain or hail to pass away when he chose. It happened that we were cutting corn in the country; a cloud came up. We began to hurry off the sheaves, but he took no notice, cut and cut away by himself, smoked his pipe, and said: "Don't be frightened – there'll be no rain." Lo and behold, there was no rain. Once – all this I saw with my own eyes – we were cutting rye, when the sky became black, the wind rose: it began to whistle at first afar off, then over our very heads. There was thunder, lightning, whirlwind – such a tempest, that – O God! Thy will be done! We went after our sheaves, but he – "Don't be frightened, there'll be no rain." "Where won't it be?" We didn't hearken to him. But he smoked his pipe out, and cut away quietly by himself. Up came a man on a black horse, and all black himself: he darted straight up to Avstriyat: "Hey! give permission!" said he. Avstriyat replied: "No, I won't!" "Give permission; be merciful!" "I won't. It would be impossible to get such a quantity in." The black horseman bowed to the man, and hastened off over the country.

Then the black cloud became gray and whitened. Our elders feared that there would be hail. But Avstriyat took no notice. He cut the corn by himself and smoked his pipe. But again a horseman came up; he hastened over the country still quicker than the first. But this one was all in white, and on a white horse. "Give permission," he shouted to Avstriyat. "I won't!" "Give permission, for God's sake!" "I won't. It wouldn't be possible to get such a quantity in." "Hey! give permission; I can't hold out!" Then, and not till then, did Avstriyat relent. "Well, then, go now, but only into the glen, which is beyond the plain." Scarcely had he spoken, when the horseman disappeared, and hail poured down as out of a basket. In the course of a short hour it filled the glen brimful, level with the banks.

The Magician and the Merchant

ONE DAY A MERCHANT, going for a stroll, came across a date tree; reaching up his hand, he plucked a date and threw the stone away.

Now, near the spot where it fell there lived a wicked magician, who suddenly appeared before the frightened merchant, and told him he was going to kill him.

"You have put out my son's eye," said he, "by throwing the stone into it, and now you shall pay for the deed with your life."

The poor merchant begged and implored for mercy, but the magician refused. At last the merchant asked that he might be allowed to go home and settle his affairs. and distribute his goods amongst his family, after which he promised to return.

To this the magician consented, so the merchant departed, and spent a last happy year with his wife and children. Then, after dividing his goods amongst them, bade them farewell, and with many tears, left them, that he might return to the magician and fulfil his promise.

Arrived at the spot, he saw an old man, who asked him why he came to such a place. "A wicked magician lives here," said he, "who kills people, or else changes them into animals or birds."

"Alas!" cried the unfortunate merchant, "that is just what my fate will be, for I have come in fulfilment of a promise to return after a year and be killed."

Just then two other old men came, and, while the four were conversing together, the magician, sword in hand, suddenly appeared and rushed at the merchant to kill him.

On this the old man interceded, and said: "O Magician, if what I have suffered be more than you have suffered in the loss of your son's eye, then indeed give this man double punishment: let me, I beg you, tell my story."

"Say on," said the magician.

"Do you see this deer?" said the old man; "it is my wife. I was once married to a wife, but after a time I wearied of her, and married another wife, who presented me with a son. I took both the woman and her child to my first wife, and asked her to feed and take care of them; but she, being jealous, changed my wife into a cow, and my son into a calf. After a year I returned and enquired after my wife and child. My first wife said: 'Your wife is dead, and for the last two days your child has been missing.'

"Now it happened at that time that I wanted to offer a sacrifice, and, asking for a suitable offering, my second wife was brought to me. She fell at my feet, and looked so unhappy that I could not kill her, and sent her away. Then my wife grew very angry, and insisted upon the sacrifice. At last I consented, and the poor cow was killed.

"Then I asked for another offering, and the calf was brought. It too looked at me with tearful eyes, and I had not the heart to kill it, but gave it to a cowherd, and told him to bring it back to me after a year. He kept it with his other cattle, and one day a young girl who saw it began to laugh and cry. On this the cowherd asked her reason for such conduct, and she replied: 'That calf is not really what it appears to be, but is a young man, and his mother was the cow who was sacrificed some time ago.'

"Then the cowherd ran to me and told me the girl's story, and I went at once to her to ask whether it was really true, and if she could not restore my son to his original shape again. 'Yes,' she replied, 'on two conditions. One, that I may be allowed to marry your son, and the other, that I may do as I please with your first wife.'

"To this I consented, so she took some water and sprinkled it upon the calf, which at once turned into my son again. With some of the same water she sprinkled my wife, who there and then turned into a deer.

"Now, I might easily kill her if I liked; but, knowing that she is my wife, I take her with me wherever I go."

Then the second old man said: "Hear my story. I was one of three brothers. My father died, and we divided his clothes and money amongst us. My eldest brother and I became merchants, but my third brother ran away, wasted and squandered his money, and became a beggar. He returned home, and begged us to forgive him, which we did, and gave him one thousand rupees to buy merchandise.

"We three then went across the seas to buy goods. On the seashore I saw a very beautiful woman, and asked her if she would come across the sea with me. She consented; but when my brothers saw her they grew jealous, and, as soon as the ship sailed, they took her and threw her into the sea, and me after her. But she, being an Enchanted Being, rose to the surface of the water unhurt, and, taking me up, carried me to a place of safety on the seashore.

"Then she said she was very angry with my brothers and meant to kill them both. I begged in vain that she would spare them, so at last she consented to punish them in some other way instead of killing them.

"When next I visited at the house of my brothers, two dogs fell at my feet and cowered before me. Then the woman told me that they were my brothers, and would remain dogs for twelve years, after which time they would resume their natural shapes."

The third old man began to tell his story. "I had the misfortune to marry a witch, who, soon after my marriage, turned me into a dog. I fled from the house, and ate such scraps of food as were thrown away by the store-keepers in the market place.

"One day one of the men there took me home, but his daughter turned away her head each time she looked at me. At last her father enquired her reason for doing this, and she replied: 'Father, that is not a dog, but a man whose wife is a witch, and it is she who has changed him into a dog. I will restore him again to his former shape.' So she sprinkled water upon me, and I forthwith regained the shape of a man. I then asked her if I might not punish my wife, and she gave me some water and told me to go and sprinkle it upon the wicked witch.

"I did this, and she became a donkey! Yet I keep her, and take care of her, and pray you, even as we had mercy, to so have mercy upon this man."

So the magician forgave the man, and let him go.

Yun Se-Pyong, the Wizard

YUN SE-PYONG was a military man who rose to the rank of minister in the days of King Choong-jong. It seems that Yun learned the doctrine of magic from a passing stranger, whom he met on his way to Peking in company with the envoy. When at home he lived in a separate house, quite apart from the other members of his family. He was a man so greatly feared that even his wife and children dared not approach him. What he did in secret no one seemed to know. In winter he was seen to put iron cleats under each arm and to change them frequently, and when they were put off they seemed to be red-hot.

At the same time there was a magician in Korea called Chon U-chi, who used to go about Seoul plying his craft. So skilful was he that he could even simulate the form of the master of a house and go freely into the women's quarters. On this account he was greatly feared and detested. Yun heard of him on more than one occasion, and determined to rid the earth of him. Chon heard also of Yun and gave him a wide berth, never appearing in his presence. He used frequently to say, "I am a magician only; Yun is a God."

On a certain day Chon informed his wife that Yun would come that afternoon and try to kill him, "and so," said he, "I shall change my shape in order to escape his clutches. If any one comes asking for me just say that I am not at home." He then metamorphosed himself into a beetle, and crawled under a crock that stood overturned in the courtyard.

When evening began to fall a young woman came to Chon's house, a very beautiful woman too, and asked, "Is the master Chon at home?"

The wife replied, "He has just gone out."

The woman laughingly said, "Master Chon and I have been special friend's for a long time, and I have an appointment with him to-day. Please say to him that I have come."

Chon's wife, seeing a pretty woman come thus, and ask in such a familiar way for her husband, flew into a rage and said, "The rascal has evidently a second wife that he has never told me of. What he said just now is all false," so she went out in a fury, and with a club smashed the crock. When the crock was broken there was the beetle underneath it. Then the woman who had called suddenly changed into a bee, and flew at and stung the beetle. Chon, metamorphosed into his accustomed form, fell over and died, and the bee flew away.

Yun lived at his own house as usual, when suddenly he broke down one day in a fit of tears. The members of his family in alarm asked the reason.

He replied, "My sister living in Chulla Province has just at this moment died." He then called his servants, and had them prepare funeral supplies, saying, "They are poor where she lives, and so I must help them."

He wrote a letter, and after sealing it, said to one of his attendants, "If you go just outside the gate you will meet a man wearing a horsehair cap and a soldier's uniform. Call him in. He is standing there ready to be summoned."

He was called in, and sure enough he was a Kon-yun-no (servant of the gods). He came in and at once prostrated himself before Yun. Yun said, "My sister has just now died in such a place in Chulla Province. Take this letter and go at once. I shall expect you back to-night with the answer. The matter is of such great importance that if you do not bring it as I order, and within the time appointed, I shall have you punished."

He replied, "I shall be in time, be not anxious."

Yun then gave him the letter and the bundle, and he went outside the main gateway and disappeared.

Before dark he returned with the answer. The letter read: "She died at such an hour to-day and we were in straits as to what to do, when your letter came with the supplies, just as though we had seen each other. Wonderful it is!" The man who brought the answer immediately went out and disappeared. The house of mourning is situated over ten days' journey from Seoul, but he returned ere sunset, in the space of two or three hours.

The Two Sorcerers

KIKI WAS A CELEBRATED SORCERER, and skilled in magical arts; he lived upon the river Waikato. The inhabitants of that river still have this proverb: 'The offspring of Kiki wither shrubs.' This proverb had its origin in the circumstance of Kiki being such a magician, that he could not go abroad in the sunshine; for if his shadow fell upon any place not protected from his magic, it at once became tapu, and all the plants there withered.

This Kiki was thoroughly skilled in the practice of sorcery. If any parties coming up the river called at his village in their canoes as they paddled by, he still remained quietly at home, and never troubled himself to come out, but just drew back the sliding door of his house, so that it might stand open, and the strangers stiffened and died; or even as canoes came paddling down from the upper parts of the river, he drew back the sliding wooden shutter to the window of his house, and the crews on board of them were sure to die.

At length, the fame of this sorcerer spread exceedingly, and resounded through every tribe, until Tamure, a chief who dwelt at Kawhia, heard with others, reports of the magical powers of Kiki, for his fame extended over the whole country. At length Tamure thought he would go and contend in the arts of sorcery with Kiki, that it might be seen which of them was most skilled in magic; and he arranged in his own mind a fortunate season for his visit.

When this time came, he selected two of his people as his companions, and he took his young daughter with him also; and they all crossed over the mountain range from Kawhia, and came down upon the river Waipa, which runs into the Waikato, and embarking there in a canoe, paddled down the river towards the village of Kiki; and they managed so well, that before they were seen by anybody, they had arrived at the landing-place. Tamure was not only skilled in magic, but he was also a very cautious man; so whilst they were still afloat upon the river, he repeated an incantation of the kind called 'Mata-tawhito,' to preserve him safe from all arts of sorcery; and he repeated other incantations, to ward off spells, to protect him from magic, to collect good genii round him, to keep off evil spirits, and to shield him from demons; when these preparations were all finished, they landed, and drew up their canoe on the beach, at the landing-place of Kiki.

As soon as they had landed, the old sorcerer called out to them that they were welcome to his village, and invited them to come up to it: so they went up to the village: and when they reached the square in the centre, they seated themselves upon the ground; and some of Kiki's people kindled fire in an enchanted oven, and began to cook food in it for the strangers. Kiki sat in this house, and Tamure on the ground just outside the entrance to it, and he there availed himself of this opportunity to repeat incantations over the threshold of the house, so that Kiki might be enchanted as he stepped over it to come out. When the food in the enchanted oven was cooked, they pulled off the coverings, and spread it out upon clean mats. The old sorcerer now made his appearance out of his house and he invited Tamure to come and eat food with him; but the food was all enchanted, and his object in asking Tamure to eat with him was, that the enchanted food might kill him; therefore Tamure said that his young daughter was very hungry, and would eat of the food offered to them; he in the meantime kept on repeating incantations of the kind called Mata-tawhito, Whakangungu, and Parepare, protections against enchanted food, and as she ate she also continued to repeat them; even when she stretched out her hand to take a sweet potato, or any other food, she dropped the greater part of it at her feet, and hid it under her clothes, and then only ate a little bit. After she had done, the old sorcerer, Kiki, kept waiting for Tamure to begin to eat also of the enchanted food, that he might soon die. Kiki having gone into his house again, Tamure still sat on the ground outside the door, and as he had enchanted the threshold of the house, he now repeated incantations which might render the door enchanted also, so that Kiki might be certain not to escape when he passed out of it. By this time Tamure's daughter had quite finished her meal, but neither her father nor either of his people had partaken of the enchanted food.

Tamure now ordered his people to launch his canoe, and they paddled away, and a little time after they had left the village, Kiki became unwell; in the meanwhile, Tamure and his people were paddling homewards in all haste, and as they passed a village where there were a good many people on the river's bank, Tamure stopped, and said to them: "If you should see any canoe pulling after us, and the people in the canoe ask you, have you seen a canoe pass up the river, would you be good enough to say: 'Yes, a canoe has passed by here?' – and then, if they ask you: 'How far has it got?' would you be good enough to say: 'Oh, by this time it has got very far up the river?'" – and having thus said to the people of that village, Tamure paddled away again in his canoe with all haste.

Some time after Tamure's party had left the village of Kiki, the old sorcerer became very ill indeed, and his people then knew that this had been brought about by the magical arts of Tamure, and they sprang into a canoe to follow after him, and puffed up the river as hard as they could; and when they reached the village where the people were on the river's bank, they called out and asked them: "How far has the canoe reached, which passed up the river?" – and the villagers answered: "Oh, that canoe must got very far up the river by this time." The people in the canoe that was pursuing Tamure, upon hearing this, returned again to their own village, and Kiki died from the incantations of Tamure.

Some of Kiki's descendants are still living – one of them, named Mokahi, recently died at Tauranga-a-Ruru, but Te Maioha is still living on the river Waipa. Yes, some of the descendants of Kiki, whose shadow withered trees, are still living. He was indeed a great sorcerer: he overcame every other sorcerer until he met Tamure, but be was vanquished by him, and had to bend the knee before him.

Tamure has also some descendants living, amongst whom are Mahu and Kiake of the Ngati-Mariu tribe; these men are also skilled in magic: if a father skilled in magic died, he left his incantation to his children; so that if a man was skilled in sorcery, it was known that his children would have a good knowledge of the same arts, as they were certain to have derived it from their parent.

The Prince and the Wizard

THERE WAS A KING, and he had an only son. Now, that lad was heroic, nought-heeding. And he set out in quest of heroic achievements. And he went a long time nought-heeding. And he came to a forest, and lay down to sleep in the shadow of a tree, and slept. Then he saw a dream, that he arises and goes to the hill where the dragon's horses are, and that if you keep straight on you will come to the man with no kidneys, screaming and roaring. So he arose and departed, and came to the man with no kidneys. And when he came there, he asked him, "Mercy! what are you screaming for?"

He said, "Why, a wizard has taken my kidneys, and has left me here in the road as you see me."

Then the lad said to him, "Wait a bit longer till I return from somewhere."

And he left him, and journeyed three more days and three nights. And he came to that hill, and sat down, and ate, and rested. And he arose and went to the hill. And the horses, when they saw him, ran to eat him. And the lad said, "Do not eat me, for I will give you pearly hay and fresh water."

Then the horses said, "Be our master. But see you do as you've promised."

The lad said, "Horses, if I don't, why, eat me and slay me."

So he took them and departed with them home. And he put them in the stable, and gave them fresh water and pearly hay. And he mounted the smallest horse, and set out for the man with no kidneys, and found him there. And he asked him what was the name of the wizard who had taken his kidneys.

"What his name is I know not, but I do know where he is gone to. He is gone to the other world."

Then the lad took and went a long time nought-heeding, and came to the edge of the earth, and let himself down, and came to the other world. And he went to the wizard's there, and said, "Come forth, O wizard, that I may see the sort of man you are."

So when the wizard heard, he came forth to eat him and slay him. Then the lad took his heroic club and his sabre; and the instant he hurled his club, the wizard's hands were bound behind his back. And the lad said to him, "Here, you wizard, tell quick, my brother's kidneys, or I slay thee this very hour."

And the wizard said, "They are there in a jar. Go and get them."

And the lad said, "And when I've got them, what am I to do with them?"

The wizard said, "Why, when you've got them, put them in water and give him them to drink."

Then the lad went and took them, and departed to him. And he put the kidneys in water, and gave him to drink, and he drank. And when he had drunk he was whole. And he took the lad, and kissed him, and said, "Be my brother till my death or thine, and so too in the world to come."

So they became brothers. And having done so, they took and journeyed in quest of heroic achievements. So they set out and slew every man that they found in their road. Then the man who had had no kidneys said he was going after the wizard, and would pass to the other world. Then they took and went there to the edge of the earth, and let themselves in. And they came there, and went to the wizard. And when they got there, how they set themselves to fight, and fought with him two whole days. Then when the lad, his brother, took and hurled his club, the wizard's hands were bound behind his back. And he cut his throat, and took his houses, made them two apples.

And they went further, and came on a certain house, and there were three maidens. And the lad hurled his club, and carried away half their house. And when the maidens saw that, they came out, and saw them coming. And they flung a comb on their path, and it became a forest – no needle could thread it. So when the lad saw that, he flung his club and his sabre. And the sabre cut and the club battered. And it cut all the forest till nothing was left.

And when the maidens saw that they had felled the forest, they flung a whetstone, and it became a fortress of stone, so that there was no getting further. And he flung the club, and demolished the stone, and made dust of it. And when the maidens saw that they had demolished the stone, they flung a mirror before them, and it became a lake, and there was no getting over. And the lad flung his sabre, and it cleft the water, and they passed through, and went there to the maidens. When they came there they said, "And what were you playing your cantrips on us for, maidens?"

Then the maidens said, "Why, lad, we thought that you were coming to kill us."

Then the lad shook hands with them, the three sisters, and said to them, "There, maidens, and will you have us?"

And they took them to wife – one for himself, and one for him who had lost his kidneys, and one they gave to another lad. And he went with them home. And they made a marriage.

And I came away, and I have told the story.

The Great Wizard

TANGLED-HAIR, SON OF THE WEST-WIND, was a giant in size and his face was as black as the feathers of the crow. His hair was of twisted snakes, gray, black and spotted, with an adder raising its copper-colored head for his crown, while a rattlesnake spread itself across his shoulders. He was the greatest of all wizards, and could change himself into any bird or beast at will, could disguise his voice, and did both good and evil as he felt inclined.

He lived with his grandmother, who had been thrown from the moon by a jealous rival. Their lodge was on the edge of the prairie not far from the Big Sea Water.

He himself did not know his power until one day while playing with a beautiful snake, whose colors were brighter than any of those upon his head, he found that by means of it he could do magic. He had caught the snake and kept it in a bowl of water, feeding it every day on birds and insects. By chance he let fall some seeds, which were turned into birds as they touched the water, and the snake greedily devoured them. Then he discovered that everything he put into the water became alive.

He went to the swamp where he had caught the snake, for others, which he put into the bowl. Happening to rub his eyes while his fingers were still wet he was surprised to find how much clearer things at a distance appeared.

He gathered some roots, powdered them, and put them into the water. Then he took a little of the water into his mouth and blew it out in spray which made a bright light. When he put the water on his eyes he could see in the dark. By bathing his body with it he could pass through narrow or slippery places. A feather dipped into it would shoot any bird at which it was aimed, and would enter its body like an arrow.

He was able to heal wounds and sicknesses and to conquer all his enemies, but for all this he was a bad spirit nearly all his life.

His father, the West-wind, had intrusted Tangled Hair's brothers with the care of three-fourths of the earth, the north, the south, and the east; but gave nothing to him, the youngest. When he was old enough to know how he had been slighted, he was very angry and sought to fight his father.

He took his bearskin mittens and dipped them into the snake-water, thereby making them strong with magic, so that he could break off great boulders by merely striking them. He chased his father across the mountains, hurling boulder after boulder at him until he drove him to the very edge of the earth. He would have killed the West-wind if he had dared, but he was afraid of his brothers, who were friendly to one another, and he knew that he could not stand against the three. So he compelled his father to give him power over serpents, beasts and monsters of all kinds, and to promise him a place in his own kingdom after he should have rid the earth of them.

Having thus secured his share, he returned to his lodge, where he was sick for a long time from the wounds that he had received.

One of his first adventures after he had recovered was capturing a great fish, from which he took so much oil, that when he poured it into a hollow in the woods, it formed a small lake, to which he invited all the animals for a feast.

As fast as they arrived he told them to jump in and drink. The bear went in first, followed by the deer and the oppossum. The moose and the buffalo were late and did not get as much as the others. The partridge looked on until nearly all the oil was gone, while the hare and the marten were so long in coming, that they did not get any. That is why animals differ so much in fatness.

When they had done feasting, Tangled Hair took up his drum, beat upon it, and invited his guests to dance. He told them to pass round him in a circle, keeping their eyes shut all the time.

When he saw a fat fowl pass by him he wrung its neck, beating loudly on his drum to drown its cries, and the noise of its fluttering. After killing each one, he would call out, "That's the way, my brothers, that's the way!"

At last a small duck, being suspicious of him, opened one eye, and seeing what he was doing, called as loudly as she could, "Tangled Hair is killing us," and jumped and flew towards the water.

Tangled Hair followed her, and just as she was getting into the water, gave her a kick which flattened her back, and straightened her legs out backward, so that she can no longer walk on land, and her tail-feathers are few to this day.

The other birds took advantage of the confusion to fly away, and the animals ran off in all directions.

After this Tangled Hair set out to travel, to see if there were any wizards greater than himself. He saw all the nations of red men, and was returning quite satisfied, when he met a great magician in the form of an old wolf, who was journeying with six young ones.

As soon as the wolf saw him, he told the whelps to keep out of the way, for Tangled Hair's fame for cruelty and wickedness had been carried everywhere by the animals and birds he had tried to kill.

As the young wolves were running off, Tangled Hair said to them, "My grandchildren, where are you going? Stop and I will go with you."

The old wolf was watching him and came up in time to answer, "We are going to a place where we can find most game, where we may pass the winter."

Tangled Hair said he would like to go with them and asked the old wolf to change him into a wolf. Now this was very foolish, for he thereby lost his power, whereas if he had changed himself into one he might still have kept it, but even the greatest wizard did not know everything.

The old wolf was only too glad to grant his wish, and changed him into a wolf like himself. Tangled Hair was not satisfied and asked to be made a little larger. The wolf made him larger; and as he was still dissatisfied, he made him twice as large as the others.

Tangled Hair was better pleased, but he still thought he might be improved, so he said to the old wolf, "Do, please make my tail a little larger and more bushy."

The wolf did this, and Tangled Hair found a large tail very heavy to drag about with him.

Presently they came to the bottom of a ravine up which they rushed into the thick woods where they discovered the track of a moose. The young wolves followed it, while the old wolf and Tangled Hair walked on after them, taking their time.

"Which do you think is the swiftest runner among my whelps?" said the wolf.

"Why the foremost one, that takes such long leaps," said Tangled Hair.

The old wolf laughed sneeringly.

"You are mistaken," he said, "he will soon tire out. The one who seems to be slowest will capture the game."

Shortly afterward they reached a place where one of the young wolves had dropped a small bundle.

"Pick it up," said the wolf to Tangled Hair.

"No," replied he, "what do I want with a dirty dog-skin?"

The wolf took it up and it was turned into a beautiful robe.

"I will carry it now," said Tangled Hair.

"Oh, no," said the wolf, "I cannot trust you with a robe of pearls," and immediately the robe shone, for nothing could be seen but pearls.

They had gone about six arrow-flights farther when they saw a broken tooth that one of the young wolves had dropped in biting at the moose as it passed.

"Tangled Hair," said the wolf, "one of the children has shot at the game, pick up his arrow."

"No," he replied, "what do I want with a dirty dog's tooth?"

The old wolf took it up, and it became a beautiful silver arrow.

They found that the young wolves had killed a very fat moose. Tangled Hair was hungry, but the wolf charmed him so that he saw nothing but the bones picked bare. After a time the wolf gave him a heap of fresh ruddy meat cut, so it seemed to Tangled Hair, from the skeleton.

"How firm it is!" he exclaimed.

"Yes," answered the wolf, "our game always is. It is not a long tail that makes the best hunter."

Tangled Hair was a good hunter when he was not too lazy to undertake the chase. One day he went out and killed a large fat moose, but having lived well in the wolf's lodge he was not very hungry, and so turned the carcass from side to side, uncertain where to begin. He had learned to dread the ridicule of the wolves, who were always showing him how little he knew as a wolf, yet he could not change himself into a man again.

"If I begin at the head," he said, "they will say I ate it backwards. If I cut the side first, they will say I ate it sideways." He turned it round so that the hindquarter was in front of him. "If I begin here, they will say I ate it forwards." But he began to be hungry, so he said, "I will begin here, let them say what they will."

He cut a piece off the flank and was just about to put it into his mouth when he heard the branches of a large tree creaking. "Stop, stop," he said to the tree, for the sound annoyed him. The tree paid no attention to him, so he threw down his meat, exclaiming, "I cannot eat with such a noise about!"

He climbed the tree and was pulling at the branch which by rubbing against another had caused the creaking, when it was suddenly blown towards him and his paw was caught so that he could not get it out. Pretty soon a pack of wolves came along and he called out to them,

"Go away, go away!"

The chief of the wolves knew Tangled Hair's voice and said to the others, "Let us go on, for I am sure he has something there he does not want us to see."

They found the moose and began eating it. Tangled Hair could not get to them, so they finished the animal, leaving nothing but the bones. After they had gone a storm arose which blew the branches of the trees apart, and Tangled Hair was able to get out, but he had to go home hungry.

The next day the old wolf said to him, "My brother, I am going to leave you, for we cannot live together always."

"Let me have one of your children for my grandson," said Tangled Hair.

The old wolf left the one who was the best hunter, and also the lodge.

Tangled Hair was disenchanted after the wolves had gone, and when he assumed his natural shape, his power as a wizard came back. He was very fond of his grandson and took good care of him, giving much thought night and day to his welfare. One day he said to him, "My grandson, I dreamed of you last night, and I feel that trouble will come to you unless you will heed what I say. You must not cross the lake that lies in the thick woods. No matter what may the need or how tired you may be, go around it, even though the ice looks strong and safe."

In the early spring when the ice was breaking up on the lakes and rivers, the little wolf came to the edge of the water late in the evening. He was tired and it was such a long way round. He stood and thought to himself, "My grandfather is too cautious about this lake," and he tried the ice with his foot, pressing his weight upon it. It seemed strong to him, so he ventured to cross. He had not gone half way, however, when it broke and he fell in, and was seized by the serpents whose lodge was under the water.

Tangled Hair guessed what had happened to him when night came and again the day and he did not return. He mourned many days first in his lodge, and then by a small brook that ran into the lake.

A bird that had been watching him said, "What are you doing here?"

"Nothing," said Tangled Hair, "but can you tell me who lives in this lake?"

"Yes," said the bird, "the Prince of Serpents lives here, and I am set by him to watch for the body of Tangled Hair's grandson, whom they killed three moons since. You are Tangled Hair, are you not?"

"No," was the answer, "Why do you think he would wish to come here? Tell me about these serpents."

The bird pointed to a beautiful beach of white sand where he said the serpents came just after mid-day to bask in the sun. "You may know when they are coming," said he, "because all the ripples will disappear and the water will be smooth and still before they rise."

"Thank you," said Tangled Hair, "I am the wizard Tangled Hair. Do not fear me. Come and I will give you a reward."

The bird went to him and Tangled Hair placed a white medal round his neck, which the Kingfisher wears to this day. While putting it on he tried to wring the bird's neck. He did this for fear it might go to the serpents and tell them he was watching for them. It escaped him, however, with only the crown feathers ruffled.

He went to the beach of white sand and changing himself into an oak stump waited for the serpents. Before long the water became smooth as the lake of oil he himself had once made. Soon hundreds of serpents came crawling up on the beach. The Prince was beautifully white, the others were red and yellow.

The Prince spoke to the others and said, "I never saw that black stump there before; it may be the wizard, Tangled Hair."

Then one of the largest serpents went to the stump and coiled itself round the top, pressing it very hard. The greatest pressure was on Tangled Hair's throat, and he was just ready to cry out when the serpent let go. Eight of the others did the same to him, but each let go just in time. They then coiled themselves up on the beach near their Prince, and after a long time fell asleep.

Tangled Hair was watching them closely, and when he saw the last one breathing heavily in sleep, he took his bow and arrows and stepped cautiously about until he was near the Prince, whom he shot and wounded.

The serpents were roused by his cry, and plunging into the water, they lashed the waves so that a great flood was raised and Tangled Hair was nearly drowned. He climbed into a tall tree, and when the water was up to his chin he looked about for some means of escape. He saw a loon and said to him, "Dive down, my brother, and bring up some earth so that I can make a new world."

The bird obeyed him, but came up lifeless. He next asked the muskrat to do him the service, and promised him if he succeeded, a chain of beautiful little lakes surrounded by rushes for his lodge in future. The muskrat dived down, but floated up senseless. Tangled Hair took the body and breathed into the nostrils, which restored the animal to life. It tried again and came up the second time senseless, but it had some earth in its paws.

Tangled Hair charmed the earth till it spread out into an island, and then into a new world. As he was walking upon it, he met an old woman, the mother of the Prince of Serpents, looking for herbs to cure her son. She had a pack of cedar cords on her back. In answer to his questions she said she intended it for a snare for Tangled Hair.

Having found out all he wished, Tangled Hair killed her, took off her skin, wrapped it about him, and placing the cedar cord on his back, went to her lodge.

There he saw the skin of his beloved grandson hanging in the doorway. This made him so angry that he could hardly keep up the disguise. He sat down outside the door and began weaving a snare of the cedar cord, rocking himself to and fro and sobbing like an old woman. Some one called to him to make less noise and to come and attend to the Prince.

He put down the snare, and wiping his eyes, went in, singing the songs the old woman had told him would cure her son.

No one suspected him, and he pretended to make ready to pull out the arrow which he found was not deeply embedded in the Prince's side. Instead of pulling it out he gave it a sudden thrust and killed the Prince; but he had used so much force that he burst the old woman's skin. The serpents hissed and he fled quickly from the place.

He took refuge with the badger, and with its help he threw a wall of earth against the opening of their lodge so that no one could get at him. They had another opening behind the rock, through which they could bring in food so that they could not be starved out by the serpents.

Tangled Hair soon grew tired of living under ground, so he started to go out, and, as the badger stood in his way, and did not move quickly enough to please him, he kicked the poor animal and killed him.

He then ran back towards the serpent's lodge, and finding the dead body of the Prince, which the serpents in their haste to follow him had left unburied, he put the skin around him and went boldly up to the serpent tribe. They were so frightened that they fell into the lake and never again ventured forth.

After many years of wickedness, Tangled Hair repented, and traveled to the end of the earth, where he built himself a lodge, and tried, by good deeds, to rid himself of remembrances. But even there he was a terror to men and beasts.

Having shown, however, that he was really sorry for his misdeeds, his father, the West-wind gave him a part of his kingdom. He went to live beyond the Rocky mountains, and took the name of the North-west wind.

White Cloud's Visit to the Sun-Prince

ONCE UPON A TIME, when there were no large cities in the western world, all the land being forest or prairie, five young men set out to hunt. They took with them a boy named White Cloud. He was only ten years old, but he was a swift runner and his sight was keen, so there were many ways in which he was useful to them.

They started before daylight, and had traveled a long way when, on reaching the top of a high hill, the sun suddenly burst forth. The air was free from mist, and there being but few trees or tall bushes near, the brightness dazzled then as it had never done before, and they exclaimed, "How near it is!"

Then one of them said, "Let us go to it," and they all agreed. They did not wish to take White Cloud with them, but he insisted upon going. When they continued to refuse he threatened to tell their parents and the Chief, who would surely prevent them from undertaking such a journey. Finally they consented, and each went home to make preparations. They shot some birds and a red deer on the way so as not to arouse the suspicions of their friends.

Before they parted they agreed to get all the moccasins they could and a new suit of leather apiece, in case they should be gone a long time and might not be able to procure clothes.

White Cloud had most difficulty in getting these things, but after coaxing to no purpose, he burst out crying and said, "Don't you see I am not dressed like my s companions, they all have new leggings?" This plea was successful, and he was provided with a new outfit.

As the party went forth the next day they whispered mysteriously to one another, taking care that such phrases should be overheard as "a grand hunt," and "we'll see who brings home most game." They did this to deceive their friends.

Upon reaching the spot from which they had seen the sun so near on the previous day, they were surprised to find that it looked as far away as it did from their own village. They traveled day after day, but seemed to come no nearer. At last they encamped for a season and consulted with one another as to the direction in which they should go. White Cloud settled it by saying, "There is the place of light (pointing towards the east), if we keep on we must reach it some time."

So they journeyed toward the east. They crossed the prairie and entered a deep forest, where it was dark in the middle of the day. There the Prince of the rattlesnakes had his warriors gathered round him, but the eldest of the party wore a "medicine" of snake-skin, so he and his companions were allowed to go through the woods unharmed.

They went on day after day and night after night through forests that seemed to have no end. When the Morning Star painted her face, and when the beautiful red glowed in the west, when the Storm-fool gathered his harvest, when the south wind blew silver from the dandelion, they kept on, but came no nearer to their object.

Once they rested a long time to make snowshoes and more arrows. They built a lodge and hunted daily until they had a good store of dried meat, as much as they could carry, and again they went on their way.

After many moons they reached a river that was running swiftly towards the east. They kept close to it until it flowed between high hills. One of these they climbed and caught sight of something white between the trees. They hurried on and rested but little that night, for they thought surely the white line must be the path that leads to the splendid lodge of the sun.

Next morning they came suddenly in view of a large lake. No land was on any side of it except where they stood. Some of them being thirsty, stooped to drink. As soon as they had tasted, they spat out the liquid, exclaiming, "Salt water!"

When the sun arose he seemed to lead forth out of the farthest waves. They looked with wonder, then they grew sad, for they were as far away as ever.

After smoking together in council, they resolved not to go back, but to walk around the great lake. They started towards the north, but had only gone a short distance when they came to a broad river flowing between mountains. Here they stayed the night. While seated round their fire, some one thought to ask whether any of them had dreamed of water.

After a long silence the eldest said, "I dreamt last night that we had come wrong, that we should have gone towards the south. But a little way beyond the place where we encamped yesterday is a river. There we shall see an island not far out in the lake. It will come to us and we are to go upon it, for it will carry us to the lodge of the sun."

The travelers were well pleased with the dream and went back towards the south. A few hours' journey from their old camp brought them to a river. At first they saw no island, but as they walked they came to a rise of ground and the island appeared to them in the distance. As they looked, it seemed to approach.

Some were frightened and wanted to go away, but the courage of White Cloud shamed them, and they waited to see what would happen. They saw three bare trees on the island, such as pine trees that have been robbed of their leaves by fire. As they looked, lo! a canoe with wings that flapped like those of a loon when it flies low down to the lake, left the island.

It came swiftly over the water, and when it touched the land, a man with a white face and a hat on, stepped upon the shore and spoke to them, but they could not understand what he said. He motioned to them to mount the bird canoe, which they did, and were carried to the island.

There was a horrible noise and rattle like that made by the magician when he conjures the evil spirit from a sick man, then white wings sprang from the bare tree trunks, and they felt themselves moving over the water, as the deer bounds across the trail in the forest.

The night came and they saw the familiar stars above them, so they lay down to sleep, fearing nothing.

When the day dawned, they could see no shore anywhere, only the water of the lake. The Pale-faces were kind, and gave them food and drink, and taught them words, such as they said to one another.

One moon had passed and another had come and nearly gone, when the Pale-face Chief said they would soon find the shore, and he would take them to his Prince, who would direct them to their journey's end.

The Prince lived in a beautiful lodge of white stone. The walls were of silver, hung with silver shields and arrows. His throne was of white horn carved with many figures. His robe was ermine, and he had many sparkling stones in his headdress.

He talked to White Cloud and listened to the story of their wanderings, their dreams and their disappointments, and spoke gently, trying to persuade them to' give up their purpose. "See," said he, "here are hunting-grounds, and fat deer, and game and fish enough for you, and none shall make war or trouble you, why go farther?"

But they would not stay. Whereupon, the Prince proved himself a magician, for he told them in what direction they should go, and what would befall them. At the last they would come to the wigwam of the great wizard, Tangled Hair. They would hear his dreadful rattle three days before they reached his lodge, and the wizard would do his best to destroy them.

The Prince tried again to keep them, but as they would not stay, he gave them presents of food and clothing, and his warriors led them to the end of his country.

They went through many forests, but the trees were strange to them. They saw flowers springing in their path and vines upon the rocks and about the trees, but none were those they knew. Even the birds were strange, and talked in voices which they could not understand. But all this made them believe they wire getting nearer to the Sun-Prince.

After many moons the clothing which the Prince of the Pale-faces had given was worn out, so they put on their leather dresses again. Hardly had they done this, when they heard a fierce rattle and knew that they were near the wigwam of the wizard. The noise was dreadful and seemed to come from the centre of the earth.

They had traveled far that day. The ground had been rough and stony and in many places covered with water through which they had been obliged to wade. They lighted a fire and sat down to dry their clothes and to rest. The noise of the rattle continued and increased so much that they broke up their camp and went toward the place which they knew must be Tangled Hair's lodge.

It was not a wigwam, but a lodge with many fireplaces, and it had eyes which glared like their camp fire. Two of the travelers wished to go back or to try to get around the lodge, but White Cloud said, "Let the wizard see we are no cowards." So they went up to the door.

There they were met by Tangled Hair himself, who said, "Welcome, my grandsons!"

When they were seated in his lodge, he gave each some smoking mixture, and as they sat and smoked he said that he knew their history, and had seen them when they left their village. He took the trouble to do this so that they might believe what he was about to say.

"I do not know that all of you will reach your journey's end, though you have gone three-fourth's of the way and are very near the edge of the earth. When you reach that place you will see a chasm below you and will be deafened by the noise of the sky descending upon the world. It keeps moving up and down. You must watch, and when it lifts you will see a little space. You must leap through this, fearing nothing, and you will find yourselves on a beautiful plain."

The wizard then told them who he was and that they had no need to fear him if they were brave men. He was not permitted to help weak men and cowards.

When the first arrow of daylight came into the lodge, the young men started up and refused to rest longer, so Tangled Hair showed them the direction they were to take in going to the edge of the world. Before they left he pointed out a lodge in the shape of an egg standing upon its larger end and said, "Ask for what you want and he who lives in that lodge will give it to you."

The first two asked that they might live forever and never be in want. The third and fourth asked to live longer than many others and always to be successful in war. White Cloud spoke for his favorite companion and for himself. Their wish was to live as long as other braves and to have success in hunting that they might provide for their parents and relatives.

The wizard smiled upon them and a voice from the pointed lodge said, "Your wishes shall be granted."

They were anxious to be gone, more especially when they found that they had been in Tangled Hair's lodge not a day, as they had supposed, but a year.

"Stop," cried Tangled Hair, as they prepared to depart, "you who wished to live forever shall have that wish granted now." Thereupon he turned one of them into a cedar tree and the other into a gray rock.

"Now," said he to the others, "you may go."

They went on their way trembling, and said to one another, "We were fortunate to get away at all, for the Prince told us he was an evil spirit."

They had not gone far when they heard the beating of the sky. As they went nearer and nearer to the edge it grew deafening, and strong gusts of wind blew them off their feet. When they reached the very edge everything was dark, for the sky had settled down, but it soon lifted and the sun passed but a short distance above their heads.

It was some time before they could get courage enough to jump through the space. White Cloud and his friend at last gave a great leap and landed on the plain of which they had been told.

"Leap, leap quickly," called White Cloud to the others, "the sky is on its way down."

They reached out timidly with their hands, but just then the sky came down with terrific force and hurled them into the chasm. There they found themselves changed into monstrous serpents which no man could kill, so their wish was granted.

Meanwhile, White Cloud and his companion found themselves in a beautiful country lighted by the moon. As they walked on all weariness left them and they felt as if they had wings. They saw a hill not far off and started to climb it, that they might look abroad over the country.

When they reached it, a little old woman met them. She had a white face and white hair, but her eyes were soft and dark and bright in spite of her great age.

She spoke kindly and told them that she was the Princess of the Moon, that they were now half way to the lodge of her brother, the Sun-prince. She led them up a steep hill which sloped on the other side directly to the lodge of the Sun.

The Moon-princess introduced them to her brother, who wore a robe of a rich, golden color, and shining as if it had points of silver all over it. He took down from the wall a splendid pipe and a pouch of smoking mixture, which he handed to them.

He put many questions to them about their country and their people, and asked them why they had undertaken this journey. They told him all he wished to know, and in return asked him to favor their nation, to shine upon their corn and make it grow and to light their way in the forest.

The Prince promised to do all these things, and was much pleased because they had asked for favors for their friends rather than for themselves.

"Come with me," he said, "and I will show you much that you could not see elsewhere."

Before starting he took down from his walls arrows tipped with silver and with gold, and placed them in a golden quiver. Then they set out on their journey through the sky.

Their path lay across a broad plain covered with many brilliant flowers. These were half hidden many times by the long grass, the scent of which was as fragrant as the flowers it hid. They passed tall trees with wide spreading branches and thick foliage. The most luxuriant were on the banks of a river as clear as crystal stone, or on the edge of little lakes which in their stony trails looked like bowls of water set there for the use of a mighty giant. Tribes of water-fowl flew about, and birds of bright plumage darted through the forest like a shower of arrows. They saw some long, low lodges with cages filled with singing birds hanging on the walls, but the people were away.

When they had traveled half across the sky, they came to a place where there were fine, soft mats, which the young men discovered were white clouds. There they sat down, and the Sun-prince began making preparations for dinner.

At this place there was a hole in the sky, and they could look down upon the earth. They could see all its hills, plains, rivers, lakes and trees, and the big salt lake they had crossed.

While they were looking at a tribe of Indians dancing, something bright flew past them, downwards through the hole in the sky and struck the merriest dancer of them all, a young boy, son of a great chief.

The warriors of his tribe ran to him and raised him with great cries and sounds of sorrow. A wizard spoke and told them to offer a white dog to the Sun-prince.

The animal was brought, and the master of the feast held the choicest portion above his head, saying: "We send this to thee, Great Spirit," and immediately the roasted animal was drawn upwards and passed through the sky. Then the boy recovered and went on dancing.

After White Cloud and his companion had feasted with the Sun-prince, they walked on till they saw before them a long slope that was like a river of gold, flowing across silver sands.

"Keep close to me," said the Sun-prince, "and have no fear. You will reach your home in safety."

So they took hold of his belt, one on either side of him, and felt themselves lowered as if by ropes. Then they fell asleep.

When they awoke they found themselves in their own country, and their friends and relatives were standing near them, rejoicing over their return. They related all their adventures, and lived many years in honor and in plenty, the Sun-prince smiling upon them in all their undertakings.

Mishosha, or The Magician of Lake Superior

IN AN EARLY AGE OF THE WORLD, when there were fewer inhabitants than there now are, there lived an Indian, in a remote place, who had a wife and two children. They seldom saw any one out of the circle of their own lodge. Animals were abundant in so secluded a situation, and the man found no difficulty in supplying his family with food.

In this way they lived in peace and happiness, which might have continued if the hunter had not found cause to suspect his wife. She secretly cherished an attachment for a young man whom she accidentally met one day in the woods. She even planned the death of her husband for his sake, for she knew if she did not kill her husband, her husband, the moment he detected her crime, would kill her.

The husband, however, eluded her project by his readiness and decision. He narrowly watched her movements. One day he secretly followed her footsteps into the forest, and having concealed himself behind a tree, he soon beheld a tall young man approach and lead away his wife. His arrows were in his hands, but he did not use them. He thought he would kill her the moment she returned.

Meantime, he went home and sat down to think. At last he came to the determination of quitting her forever, thinking that her own conscience would punish her sufficiently, and relying on her maternal feelings to take care of the two children, who were boys, he immediately took up his arms and departed.

When the wife returned she was disappointed in not finding her husband, for she had now concerted her plan, and intended to have dispatched him. She waited several days, thinking he might have been led away by the chase, but finding he did not return, she suspected the true cause. Leaving her two children in the lodge, she told them she was going a short distance and would return. She then fled to her paramour and came back no more.

The children, thus abandoned, soon made way with the food left in the lodge, and were compelled to quit it in search of more. The eldest boy, who was of an intrepid temper, was strongly attached to his brother, frequently carrying him when he became weary, and gathering all the wild fruit he saw. They wandered deeper and deeper into the forest, losing all traces of their former habitation, until they were completely lost in its mazes.

The eldest boy had a knife, with which he made a bow and arrows, and was thus enabled to kill a few birds for himself and brother. In this manner they continued to pass on, from one piece of forest to another, not knowing whither they were going. At length they saw an opening through the woods, and were shortly afterward delighted to find themselves on the borders of a large lake. Here the elder brother busied himself in picking the seed pods of the wild rose, which he reserved as food. In the mean time, the younger brother amused himself by shooting arrows in the sand, one of which happened to fall into the lake. Panigwun, the elder brother, not willing to lose the arrow, waded in the water to reach it. Just as he was about to grasp the arrow, a canoe passed up to him with great rapidity. An old man, sitting in the centre, seized the affrighted youth and placed him in the canoe. In vain the boy addressed him – "My grandfather (a term of respect for old people), pray take my little brother also. Alone, I cannot go with you; he will starve if I leave him." Mishosha (the old man) only laughed at him. Then uttering the charm, Chemaun Poll, and giving his canoe a slap, it glided through the water with inconceivable swiftness. In a few moments they reached the habitation of the magician, standing on an island in the centre of the lake. Here he lived with his two daughters, who managed the affairs of his household. Leading the young man up to the lodge, he addressed his eldest daughter. "Here," said he, "my daughter, I have brought a young man to be your husband." Husband! thought the young woman; rather another victim of your bad arts, and your insatiate enmity to the human race. But she made no reply, seeming thereby to acquiesce in her father's will.

The young man thought he saw surprise depicted in the eyes of the daughter, during the scene of this introduction, and determined to watch events narrowly. In the evening he overheard the two daughters in conversation. "There," said the eldest daughter, "I told you he would not be satisfied with his last sacrifice. He has brought another victim, under the pretence of providing me a husband. Husband, indeed! the poor youth will be in some horrible predicament before another sun has set. When shall we be spared the scenes of vice and wickedness which are daily taking place before our eyes?"

Panigwun took the first opportunity of acquainting the daughters how he had been carried off, and been compelled to leave his little brother on the shore. They told him to wait until their father was asleep, then to get up and take his canoe, and using the charm he had obtained, it would carry him quickly to his brother. That he could carry him food, prepare a lodge for him, and be back before daybreak. He did, in every respect, as he had been directed – the canoe obeyed the charm, and carried him safely over, and after providing for the subsistence of his brother, he told him that in a short time he should come for him. Then returning to the enchanted island, he resumed his place in the lodge, before the magician awoke. Once, during the night, Mishosha awoke, and not seeing his destined son-in-law, asked his daughter what had become of him. She replied that he had merely stepped out, and would be back soon. This satisfied him. In the morning, finding the young man in the lodge, his suspicions were completely lulled. "I see, my daughter," said he, "you have told the truth."

As soon as the sun arose, Mishosha thus addressed the young man. "Come, my son, I have a mind to gather gulls' eggs. I know an island where there are great quantities, and I wish your aid in getting them." The young man saw no reasonable excuse; and getting into the canoe, the magician gave it a slap, and uttering a command, they were in an instant at the island. They found the shores strown with gulls' eggs, and the island full of birds of this species. "Go, my son," said the old man, "and gather the eggs, while I remain in the canoe."

But Panigwun had no sooner got ashore, than Mishosha pushed his canoe a little from the land, and exclaimed – "Listen, ye gulls! you have long expected an offering from me. I now give you a victim. Fly down and devour him." Then striking his canoe, he left the young man to his fate

The birds immediately came in clouds around their victim, darkening the air with their numbers. But the youth seizing the first that came near him, and drawing his knife, cut off its head. He immediately skinned the bird and hung the feathers as a trophy on his breast. "Thus," he exclaimed, "will I treat every one of you who approaches me. Forbear, therefore, and listen to my words. It is not for you to eat human flesh. You have been given by the Great Spirit as food for man. Neither is it in the power of that old magician to do you any good. Take me on your backs and carry me to his lodge, and you shall see that I am not ungrateful." The gulls obeyed; collecting in a cloud for him to rest upon, and quickly flew to the lodge, where they arrived before the magician. The daughters were surprised at his return, but Mishosha, on entering the lodge, conducted himself as if nothing extraordinary had taken place.

The next day he again addressed the youth: "Come, my son," said he, "I will take you to an island covered with the most beautiful stones and pebbles, looking like silver. I wish you to assist me in gathering some of them. They will make handsome ornaments, and possess great medicinal virtues." Entering the canoe, the magician made use of his charm, and they were carried in a few moments to a solitary bay in an island, where there was a smooth sandy beach. The young man went ashore as usual, and began to search. "A little further, a little further," cried the old man. "Upon that rock you will get some fine ones." Then pushing his canoe from land – "Come, thou great king of fishes," cried the old man; "you have long expected an offering from me. Come, and eat the stranger whom I have just put ashore on your island." So saying, he commanded his canoe to return, and it was soon out of sight.

Immediately a monstrous fish thrust his long snout from the water, crawling partially on the beach, and opening wide his jaws to receive his victim. "When!" exclaimed the young man, drawing his knife and putting himself in a threatening attitude, "when did you ever taste human flesh? Have a care of yourself. You were given by the Great Spirit to man, and if you, or any of your tribe eat human flesh you will fall sick and die. Listen not to the words of that wicked man, but carry me back to his island, in return for which I will present you a piece of red cloth." The fish complied, raising his back out of the water, to allow the young man to get on. Then taking his way through the lake, he landed his charge safely on the island before the return of the magician. The daughters were still more surprised to see that he had escaped the arts of their father the second time. But the old man on his return maintained his taciturnity and self-composure. He could not, however, help saying to himself – "What manner of boy is this, who is ever escaping from my power? But his spirit shall not save him. I will entrap him to-morrow. Ha, ha, ha!"

Next day the magician addressed the young man as follows: "Come, my son," said he, "you must go with me to procure some young eagles. I wish to tame them. I have discovered an island where they are in great abundance." When they had reached the island, Mishosha led him inland until they came to the foot of a tall pine, upon which the nests were. "Now, my son," said he, "climb up this tree and bring down the birds." The young man obeyed. When he had with great difficulty got near the nest, "Now," exclaimed the magician, addressing the tree, "stretch yourself up and be very tall." The tree rose up at the command. "Listen, ye eagles," continued the old man, "you have long expected a gift from me. I now present you this boy, who has had the presumption to molest your young. Stretch forth your claws and seize him." So saying, he left the young man to his fate, and returned.

But the intrepid youth, drawing his knife, and cutting off the head of the first eagle that menaced him, raised his voice and exclaimed, "Thus will I deal with all who come near me. What right have you, ye ravenous birds, who were made to feed on beasts, to eat human flesh? Is it because that cowardly old canoe-man has bid you do so? He is an old woman. He can neither do you good nor harm. See, I have already slain one of your number. Respect my bravery, and carry me back that I may show you how I shall treat you."

The eagles, pleased with his spirit, assented, and clustering thick around him formed a seat with their backs, and flew toward the enchanted island. As they crossed the water they passed over the magician, lying half asleep in his canoe.

The return of the young man was hailed with joy by the daughters, who now plainly saw that he was under the guidance of a strong spirit. But the ire of the old man was excited, although he kept his temper under subjection. He taxed his wits for some new mode of ridding himself of the youth, who had so successfully baffled his skill. He next invited him to go a hunting.

Taking his canoe, they proceeded to an island and built a lodge to shelter themselves during the night. In the mean while the magician caused a deep fall of snow, with a storm of wind and severe cold. According to custom, the young man pulled off his moccasins and leggings, and hung them before the fire to dry. After he had gone to sleep, the magician, watching his opportunity, got up, and taking one moccasin and one legging, threw them into the fire. He then went to sleep. In the morning, stretching himself as he arose and uttering an exclamation of surprise, "My son," said he, "what has become of your moccasin and legging? I believe this is the moon in which fire attracts, and I fear they have been drawn in." The young man suspected the true cause of his loss, and rightly attributed it to a design of the magician to freeze him to death on the march. But he maintained the strictest silence, and drawing his conaus over his head, thus communed with himself: "I have full faith in the Manito who has preserved me thus far, I do not fear that he will forsake me in this cruel emergency. Great is his power, and I invoke it now that he may enable me to prevail over this wicked enemy of mankind."

He then drew on the remaining moccasin and legging, and taking a dead coal from the fireplace, invoked his spirit to give it efficacy, and blackened his foot and leg as far as the lost garment usually reached. He then got up and announced himself ready for the march. In vain Mishosha led him through snows and over morasses, hoping to see the lad sink at every moment. But in this he was disappointed, and for the first time they returned home together.

Taking courage from this success, the young man now determined to try his own power, having previously consulted with the daughters. They all agreed that the life the old man led was detestable, and that whoever would rid the world of him, would entitle himself to the thanks of the human race.

On the following day the young man thus addressed his hoary captor: "My grandfather, I have often gone with you on perilous excursions, and never murmured. I must now request that you will accompany me. I wish to visit my little brother, and to bring him home with me." They accordingly went on a visit to the main land, and found the little lad in the spot where he had been left. After taking him into the canoe, the young man again addressed the magician: "My grandfather, will you go and cut me a few of those red willows on the bank, I wish to prepare some smoking mixture." "Certainly, my son," replied the old man; "what you wish is not very hard. Ha, ha, ha! do you think me too old to get up there?" No sooner was Mishosha ashore, than the young man, placing himself in the proper position struck the canoe with his hand, and pronouncing the charm, N'chimaun Poll, the canoe immediately flew through the water on its return to the island. It was evening when the two brothers arrived, and carried the canoe ashore. But the elder daughter informed the young man that unless he sat up and watched the canoe, and kept his hand upon it, such was the power of their father, it would slip off and return to him. Panigwun watched faithfully till near the dawn of day, when he could no longer resist the drowsiness which oppressed him, and he fell into a short doze. In the mean time, the canoe slipped off and sought its master, who soon returned in high glee. "Ha, ha, ha! my son," said he; "you thought to play me a trick. It was very clever. But you see I am too old for you."

A short time after, the youth again addressed the magician. "My grandfather, I wish to try my skill in hunting. It is said there is plenty of game on an island not far off, and I have to request that you will take me there in your canoe." They accordingly went to the island and spent the day in hunting. Night coming on they put up a temporary lodge.

When the magician had sunk into a profound sleep, the young man got up, and taking one of Mishosha's leggings and moccasins from the place where they hung, threw them into the fire, thus retaliating the artifice before played upon himself. He had discovered that the foot and leg were the only vulnerable parts of the magician's body. Having committed these articles to the fire, he besought his Manito that he would raise a great storm of snow, wind, and hail, and then laid himself down beside the old man. Consternation was depicted on the countenance of the latter, when he awoke in the morning and found his moccasin and legging missing. "I believe, my grandfather," said the young man, "that this is the moon in which fire attracts, and I fear your foot and leg garments have been drawn in." Then rising and bidding the old man follow him, he began the morning's hunt, frequently turning to see how Mishosha kept up. He saw him faltering at every step, and almost benumbed with cold, but encouraged him to follow, saying, we shall soon get through and reach the shore; although he took pains, at the same time, to lead him in roundabout ways, so as to let the frost take complete effect. At length the old man reached the brink of the island where the woods are succeeded by a border of smooth sand. But he could go no farther; his legs became stiff and refused motion, and he found himself fixed to the spot. But he still kept stretching out his arms and swinging his body to and fro. Every moment he found the numbness creeping higher. He felt his legs growing downward like roots, the feathers of his head turned to leaves, and in a few seconds he stood a tall and stiff sycamore, leaning toward the water.

Panigwun leaped into the canoe, and pronouncing the charm, was soon transported to the island, where he related his victory to the daughters. They applauded the deed, agreed to put on mortal shapes, become wives to the two young men, and forever quit the enchanted island. And passing immediately over to the main land, they lived lives of happiness and peace.

Bokwewa, or
The Humpback Magician

BOKWEWA AND HIS BROTHER LIVED in a secluded part of the country. They were considered as Manitoes, who had assumed mortal shapes. Bokwewa was the most gifted in supernatural endowments, although he was deformed in person. His brother partook more of the nature of the present race of beings. They lived retired from the world, and undisturbed by its cares, and passed their time in contentment and happiness.

Bokwewa, owing to his deformity, was very domestic in his habits, and gave his attention to household affairs. He instructed his brother in the manner of pursuing game, and made him acquainted with all the accomplishments of a sagacious and expert hunter. His brother possessed a fine form, and an active and robust constitution; and felt a disposition to show himself off among men. He was restive in his seclusion, and showed a fondness for visiting remote places.

One day he told his brother that he was going to leave him; that he wished to visit the habitations of men and procure a wife. Bokwewa objected to his going; but his brother overruled all that he said, and he finally departed on his travels. He travelled a long time. At length he fell in with the footsteps of men. They were moving by encampments, for he saw several places where they had encamped. It was in the winter. He came to a place where one of their number had died. They had placed the corpse on a scaffold. He went to it and took it down. He saw that it was the corpse of a beautiful young woman. "She shall be my wife!" he exclaimed.

He took her up, and placing her on his back, returned to his brother. "Brother," he said, "cannot you restore her to life? Oh, do me that favor!" Bokwewa said he would try. He performed numerous ceremonies, and at last succeeded in restoring her to life. They lived very happily for some time. Bokwewa was extremely kind to his brother, and did everything to render his life happy. Being deformed and crippled, he always remained at home, while his brother went out to hunt. And it was by following his directions, which were those of a skilful hunter, that he always succeeded in returning with a good store of meat.

One day he had gone out as usual, and Bokwewa was sitting in his lodge, on the opposite side of his brother's wife, when a tall, fine young man entered, and immediately took the woman by the hand and drew her to the door. She resisted and called on Bokwewa, who jumped up to her assistance. But their joint resistance was unavailing; the man succeeded in carrying her away. In the scuffle, Bokwewa had his hump back much bruised on the stones near the door. He crawled into the lodge and wept very sorely, for he knew that it was a powerful Manito who had taken the woman.

When his brother returned, he related all to him exactly as it happened. He would not taste food for several days. Sometimes he would fall to weeping for a long time, and appeared almost beside himself. At last he said he would go in search of her. Bokwewa tried to dissuade him from it, but he insisted.

"Well!" said he, "since you are bent on going, listen to my advice. You will have to go south. It is a long distance to the residence of your captive wife, and there are so many charms and temptations in the way, I am afraid you will be led astray by them, and forget your errand. For the people whom you will see in that country do nothing but amuse themselves. They are very idle, gay, and effeminate, and I am fearful they will lead you astray. Your journey is beset with difficulties. I will mention one or two things, which you must be on your guard against. In the course of your journey, you will come to a large grape-vine lying across your way. You must not even taste its fruit, for it is poisonous. Step over it. It is a snake. You will next come to something that looks like bear's fat, transparent and tremulous. Don't taste it, or you will be overcome by the pleasures of those people. It is frog's eggs. These are snares laid by the way for you."

He said he would follow the advice, and bid farewell to his brother. After travelling a long time, he came to the enchanted grape-vine. It looked so tempting, he forgot his brother's advice and tasted the fruit. He went on till he came to the frog's eggs. The substance so much resembled bear's fat that he tasted it. He still went on. At length he came to a very extensive plain. As he emerged from the forest the sun was setting, and cast its scarlet and golden shades over all the plain. The air was perfectly calm, and the whole prospect had the air of an enchanted land. The most inviting fruits and flowers spread out before the eye. At a distance he beheld a large village, filled with people without number, and as he drew near he saw women beating corn in silver mortars. When they saw him approaching, they cried out, "Bokwewa's brother has come to see us." Throngs of men and women, gayly dressed, came out to meet him. He was soon overcome by their flatteries and pleasures, and he was not long afterward seen beating corn with their women (the strongest proof of effeminacy), although his wife, for whom he had mourned so much, was in that Indian metropolis.

Meantime, Bokwewa waited patiently for the return of his brother. At length, after the lapse of several years, he set out in search of him, and arrived in safety among the luxuriant people of the South. He met with the same allurements on the road, and the same flattering reception that his brother did. But he was above all temptations. The pleasures he saw had no other effect upon him than to make him regret the weakness of mind of those who were led away by them. He shed tears of pity to see that his brother had laid aside the arms of a hunter, and was seen beating corn with the women.

He ascertained where his brother's wife remained. After deliberating some time, he went to the river where she usually came to draw water. He there changed himself into one of those hair-snakes which are sometimes seen in running water.

When she came down, he spoke to her, saying, "Take me up; I am Bokwewa." She then scooped him out and went home. In a short time the Manito who had taken her away asked her for water to drink. The lodge in which they lived was partitioned. He occupied a secret place, and was never seen by any one but the woman. She handed him the water containing the hair-snake, which he drank, with the snake, and soon after was a dead Manito.

Bokwewa then resumed his former shape. He went to his brother, and used every means to reclaim him. But he would not listen. He was so much taken up with the pleasures and dissipations into which he had fallen, that he refused to give them up, although Bokwewa, with tears, tried to convince him of his foolishness, and to show him that those pleasures could not endure for a long time. Finding that he was past reclaiming, Bokwewa left him, and disappeared forever.

The Adventures of Living Statue

LIVING STATUE WAS A GREAT MAGICIAN of the Ottawas, who lived on the shores of Lake Huron. His wigwam was of skin that had been scrubbed and bleached until it shone like snow when the sun falls upon it; and it could be seen at a great distance. From the lodge pole downwards it was covered with paintings, some done by the magician and others by his friends, each telling a wonderful tale of his magic.

His couch was of white buffalo skins, which are very rare and precious. His pipes were the admiration of all who saw them, for they were ornamented with red feathers from the breast of the robin, blue from the jay, purple from the neck of the pigeon, and green from the throat of the drake. His moccasins of rabbit skin, dyed scarlet, were the softest that could be made. They were worked with beads brought by a messenger from a far-distant tribe, who had received them from the Pale-faces that came across the Big Salt Lake. But the most wonderful thing about these moccasins was that they were magic shoes; for every stride he took in them carried him over a mile of ground.

His flute was a reed cut in the swamp forest. When he blew a loud note upon it the distant rocks answered him, and the little vanishing men who danced in the moonlight, took up the music and laughed it back to him. When he breathed softly upon it no Indian heard him; for the sound went straight into the heart of the flowers. The fairies hearing it crept forth and balanced themselves on the petals of the flowers that they might hear the better.

The magician's sister, Sweet Strawberry, whose fawn-skin robe may be seen in the moon on bright nights, sometimes rested on the topmost branches of the tall trees to listen. She had once lived with him, but the Moon Prince had taken her to be his bride, and all the tribe mourned for her as for one dead.

Living Statue talked with the birds and the squirrels, who laid down and died and rolled out of their skins when he asked for them. He was the friend of all the rabbits, who were proud to have him eat them. When he had finished the meal, he read the story of the animal's life in its bones, and if it had been good in its time he stroked its skin and it came to life again, and could nevermore be caught.

One day, as Living Statue was walking across the plain near the edge of the forest, he met a little man no higher than his knee. The dwarf was dressed all in green, and wore a green cap with a red plume in it.

"Fight me, fight me," said the dwarf, placing himself directly in front of the magician.

Living Statue tried to kick him out of his path. Thereupon his foot began to swell so that he could hardly move.

"Fight me, fight me," said the dwarf, who again danced in front of him.

Living Statue stooped and took hold of him, intending to throw him to one side, but he found the dwarf too strong for him. He strove in vain to lift him, so he wrestled with him till his arms were tired; but the dwarf was not overcome. At last, by a great effort he pushed him from him, then rushed at him with all his might and succeeded in throwing him to the ground. He sprang quickly upon him, and taking out his knife prepared to scalp him.

"Hold, hold," said the dwarf; "I see the Ottawa magician is a brave warrior, as well as a great wizard. He has fought and conquered me, though not by magic. I will show him greater magic than any he has ever known."

When he had done speaking he threw himself backwards and was changed into a crooked ear of corn, which rolled over and lay at the magician's feet.

"Take me," said the ear; "tear off the wrapper that is drawn so tightly about me and leave nothing to hide my body from your eyes. Then pull my body to pieces, taking all the flesh from the bones and throw the flesh upon different parts of the plain. Cover me with earth that the ravens may not feast upon me. My spine you shall break in pieces no larger than your thumb and shall scatter them near the edge of the forest. Go back to your village when you have done this and return to this place after one moon."

Living Statue did exactly what the dwarf had told him to do, but he said nothing to the Ottawas about his adventure. It was not for them to understand magic; they might try to do what he alone understood and the spirits would be offended.

When the hot moon had come Living Statue went back to the plain where he had wrestled with the dwarf, and there he saw a field of long, green plumes waving in the sunlight. They were smooth and glossy and dropped almost to the ground. In color they were like the robe of the dwarf, only bright and shining.

While he was looking and wondering, the dwarf suddenly sprang out of the broadest stalk and said, "You have done well. Let one moon pass and another appear before you come again. Then you will find a new food for the Ottawas, better than the wild rice, sweet as the blood of the maple, and strength-giving as the flesh of the deer."

At the time appointed, Living Statue went again to the spot and there he found the gift of the corn. He brought his tribe to witness, and to gather it. Then he and three other magicians painted their bodies with white clay and danced round the kettle in which it was being prepared, which done, they took out the ears and burnt them as a sacrifice. They then put out the fire and lighted a fresh one, with which they cooked "the spirits' berry" for themselves.

One night when Living Statue lay asleep, he heard the curtain of his tent flap, and presently two dwarfs entered and crept up to his couch. One climbed upon his legs and sat astride them; the other mounted to his breast and began feeling his throat.

"Choke him! choke him!" said the dwarf at his feet.

"I can't; my hands are too small and weak," said the other.

"Pull his heart out! Pull his heart out!" said the first.

The second dwarf began pounding and tugging at the breast of the sleeper. At this the one astride his legs gave his companion a vicious kick, and said in a hoarse whisper, "You stupid! pull it out through his mouth."

So the dwarf forced open the teeth of Living Statue and thrust his fingers far down his throat. Now, this was just what the magician thought he would do; so when the fingers were inside his mouth, he shut his teeth together quickly and bit them off. Then, slowly raising himself, he threw the dwarf who was on his legs, clear to the door of the wigwam.

"Oh! oh!" cried the one whose hand was bitten, and he howled like a dog.

"Oh! oh!" cried the other, and he howled like a wolf as the two disappeared in the darkness.

The magician kept very still, then crept to the door, raised the curtain and put his head outside to listen, so that he might know in what direction they went. He heard them hurrying through the forest towards the lake. There was a soft splash, as of water when a canoe bends to it beneath the weight of a man, and all was still.

In the morning Living Statue found that the fingers he had bitten off were long wampum beads, greatly prized by the Indians, and so valuable that they made him very rich. He had no trouble in following the trail of the dwarfs, for it was marked by drops of blood that were changed into wampum beads. He had enough to make a coat, a cap and leggings, so that ever after he was known to all nations as the Prince of Wampum.

When he reached the lake he saw a stone canoe which was four times the length of his prow and white as the waves when the strong wind races with them to the shore. Two men were seated in it, one at the bow and the other in the stern. They were bolt upright, with their hands upon their knees, and did not look towards him. On going closer he saw that they were the dwarfs turned into stone. The boat was filled with sacks of bear skin, in which was treasure such as the magician had never before seen or imagined.

As he was about to take some of it away, the dwarf whose fingers he had bitten off, spoke to him and said: "In this manner the canoes of your people shall be loaded as they go past these shores, and no enemy shall be able to rob them."

The magician took the statues to his wigwam and afterwards they were set up in the sacred lodge of the tribe, the white canoe being placed between them.

Many chiefs wished to give the Prince of Wampum their daughters in marriage, but he chose a star maiden, and they went to live in the fields of the sky, near the white, misty road of the dead.

The Red Swan

THREE BROTHERS WERE LEFT DESTITUTE, by the death of their parents, at an early age. The eldest was not yet able to provide fully for their support, but did all he could in hunting, and with his aid, and the stock of provisions left by their father, they were preserved and kept alive, rather, it seems, by miraculous interposition, than the adequacy of their own exertions. For the father had been a hermit, having removed far away from the body of the tribe, so that when he and his wife died they left their children without neighbors and friends, and the lads had no idea that there was a human being near them. They did not even know who their parents had been, for the eldest was too young, at the time of their death, to remember it. Forlorn as they were, they did not, however, give up to despondency, but made use of every exertion they could, and in process of time, learned the art of hunting and killing animals. The eldest soon became an expert hunter, and was very successful in procuring food. He was noted for his skill in killing buffalo, elk, and moose, and he instructed his brothers in the arts of the forest as soon as they became old enough to follow him. After they had become able to hunt and take care of themselves, the elder proposed to leave them, and go in search of habitations, promising to return as soon as he could procure them wives. In this project he was overruled by his brothers, who said they could not part with him. Maujeekewis, the second eldest, was loud in his disapproval, saying, "What will you do with those you propose to get – we have lived so long without them, and we can still do without them." His words prevailed, and the three brothers continued together for a time.

One day they agreed to kill each, a male of those kind of animals each was most expert in hunting, for the purpose of making quivers from their skins. They did so, and immediately commenced making arrows to fill their quivers, that they might be prepared for any emergency. Soon after, they hunted on a wager, to see who should come in first with game, and prepare it so as to regale the others. They were to shoot no other animal, but such as each was in the habit of killing. They set out different ways; Odjibwa, the youngest, had not gone far before he saw a bear, an animal he was not to kill, by the agreement. He followed him close, and drove an arrow through him, which brought him to the ground. Although contrary to the bet, he immediately commenced skinning him, when suddenly something red tinged all the air around him. He rubbed his eyes, thinking he was perhaps deceived, but without effect, for the red hue continued. At length he heard a strange noise at a distance. It first appeared like a human voice, but after following the sound for some distance, he reached the shores of a lake, and soon saw the object he was looking for. At a distance out in the lake, sat a most beautiful Red Swan, whose plumage glittered in the sun, and who would now and then make the same noise he had heard.

He was within long bow shot, and pulling the arrow from the bow-string up to his ear, took deliberate aim and shot. The arrow took no effect; and he shot and shot again till his quiver was empty. Still the swan remained, moving around and around, stretching its long neck and dipping its bill into the water, as if heedless of the arrows shot at it. Odjibwa ran home, and got all his own and his brothers' arrows, and shot them all away. He then stood and gazed at the beautiful bird. While standing, he remembered his brothers' saying that in their deceased father's medicine sack were three magic arrows. Off he started, his anxiety to kill the swan overcoming all scruples. At any other time, he would have deemed it sacrilege to open his father's medicine sack, but now he hastily seized the three arrows and ran back, leaving the other contents of the sack scattered over the lodge. The swan was still there. He shot the first arrow with great precision, and came very near to it. The second came still closer; as he took the last arrow, he felt his arm firmer, and drawing it up with vigor, saw it pass through the neck of the swan a little above the breast. Still it did not prevent the bird from flying off, which it did, however, at first slowly, flapping its wings and rising gradually into the air, and then flying off toward the sinking of the sun. Odjibwa was disappointed; he knew that his brothers would be displeased with him; he rushed into the water and rescued the two magic arrows, the third was carried off by the swan; but he thought that it could not fly very far with it, and let the consequences be what they might, he was bent on following it.

Off he started on the run; he was noted for speed, for he would shoot an arrow, and then run so fast that the arrow always fell behind him. I can run fast, he thought, and I can get up with the swan some time or other. He thus ran over hills and prairies, toward the west, till near night, and was only going to take one more run, and then seek a place to sleep for the night, when suddenly he heard noises at a distance, which he knew were from people; for some were cutting trees, and the strokes of their axes echoed through the woods. When he emerged from the forest, the sun was just falling below the horizon, and he felt pleased to find a place to sleep in, and get something to eat, as he had left home without a mouthful. All these circumstances could not damp his ardor for the accomplishment of his object, and he felt that if he only persevered, he would succeed. At a distance, on a rising piece of ground, he could see an extensive town. He went toward it, but soon heard the watchman, Mudjee-Kokokoho, who was placed on some height to overlook the place, and give notice of the approach of friends or foes – crying out, "We are visited;" and a loud holla indicated that they all heard it. The young man advanced, and was pointed by the watchman to the lodge of the chief, "It is there you must go in," he said, and left him. "Come in, come in," said the chief, "take a seat there," pointing to the side where his daughter sat. "It is there you must sit." Soon they gave him something to eat, and very few questions were asked him, being a stranger. It was only when he spoke, that the others answered him. "Daughter," said the chief, after dark, "take our son-in-law's moccasins, and see if they be torn; if so, mend them for him, and bring in his bundle." The young man thought it strange that he should be so warmly received, and married instantly, without his wishing it, although the young girl was pretty. It was some time before she would take his moccasins, which he had taken off. It displeased him to see her so reluctant to do so, and when she did reach them, he snatched them out of her hand and hung them up himself. He laid down and thought of the swan, and made up his mind to be off by dawn. He awoke early, and spoke to the young woman, but she gave no answer. He slightly touched her. "What do you want?" she said, and turned her back toward him. "Tell me," he said, "what time the swan passed. I am following it, and come out and point the direction." "Do you think you can catch up to it?" she said. "Yes," he answered. "Naubesah" (foolishness), she said. She, however, went out and pointed in the direction he should go. The young man went slowly till the sun arose, when he commenced travelling at his accustomed speed.

He passed the day in running, and when night came, he was unexpectedly pleased to find himself near another town; and when at a distance, he heard the watchman crying out, "We are visited;" and soon the men of the village stood out to see the stranger. He was again told to enter the lodge of the chief, and his reception was, in every respect, the same as he met the previous night; only that the young woman was more beautiful, and received him very kindly, but although urged to stay, his mind was fixed on the object of his journey. Before daylight he asked the young woman what time the Red Swan passed, and to point out the way. She did so, and said it passed yesterday when the sun was between midday and pungishemoo – its falling place. He again set out rather slowly, but when the sun had arisen he tried his speed by shooting an arrow ahead, and running after it; but it fell behind him.

Nothing remarkable happened in the course of the day, and he went on leisurely. Toward night, he came to the lodge of an old man. Some time after dark he saw a light emitted from a small low lodge. He went up to it very slyly, and peeping through the door, saw an old man alone, warming his back before the fire, with his head down on his breast. He thought the old man did not know that he was standing near the door, but in this he was disappointed; for so soon as he looked in, "Walk in, Nosis,"he said, "take a seat opposite to me, and take off your things and dry them, for you must be fatigued; and I will prepare you something to eat." Odjibwa did as he was requested. The old man, whom he perceived to be a magician, then said: "My kettle with water stands near the fire;" and immediately a small earthen or a kind of metallic pot with legs appeared by the fire. He then took one grain of corn, also one whortleberry, and put them in the pot. As the young man was very hungry, he thought that his chance for a supper was but small. Not a word or a look, however, revealed his feelings. The pot soon boiled, when the old man spoke, commanding it to stand some distance from the fire; "Nosis," said he, "feed yourself," and he handed him a dish and ladle made out of the same metal as the pot. The young man helped himself to all that was in the pot; he felt ashamed to think of his having done so, but before he could speak, the old man said, "Nosis, eat, eat;" and soon after he again said, "Help yourself from the pot." Odjibwa was surprised on looking into it to see it full; he kept on taking all out, and as soon as it was done, it was again filled, till he had amply satisfied his hunger. The magician then spoke, and the pot occupied its accustomed place in one part of the lodge. The young man then leisurely reclined back, and listened to the predictions of his entertainer, who told him to keep on, and he would obtain his object. "To tell you more," said he, "I am not permitted; but go on as you have commenced, and you will not be disappointed; to-morrow you will again reach one of my fellow old men; but the one you will see after him will tell you all, and the manner in which you will proceed to accomplish your journey. Often has this Red Swan passed, and those who have followed it have never returned: but you must be firm in your resolution, and be prepared for all events." "So will it be," answered Odjibwa, and they both laid down to sleep. Early in the morning, the old man had his magic kettle prepared, so that his guest should eat before leaving. When leaving, the old man gave him his parting advice.

Odjibwa set out in better spirits than he had done since leaving home. Night again found him in company with an old man, who received him kindly, and directed him on his way in the morning. He travelled with a light heart, expecting to meet the one who was to give him directions how to proceed to get the Red Swan. Toward nightfall, he reached the third old man's lodge. Before coming to the door, he heard him saying, "Nosis, come in," and going in immediately, he felt quite at home. The old man prepared him something to eat, acting as the other magicians had done, and his kettle was of the same dimensions and material. The old man waited till he had done eating, when he commenced addressing him. "Young man, the errand you are on is very difficult. Numbers of young men have passed with the same purpose, but never returned. Be careful, and if your guardian spirits are powerful, you may succeed. This Red Swan you are following, is the daughter of a magician, who has plenty of everything, but he values his daughter but little less than wampum. He wore a cap of wampum, which was attached to his scalp; but powerful Indians – warriors of a distant chief, came and told him, that their chief's daughter was on the brink of the grave, and she herself requested his scalp of wampum to effect a cure. 'If I can only see it, I will recover,' she said, and it was for this reason they came, and after long urging the magician, he at last consented to part with it, only from the idea of restoring the young woman to health; although when he took it off, it left his head bare and bloody. Several years have passed since, and it has not healed. The warriors' coming for it, was only a cheat, and they now are constantly making sport of it, dancing it about from village to village; and on every insult it receives, the old man groans from pain. Those Indians are too powerful for the magician, and numbers have sacrificed themselves to recover it for him, but without success. The Red Swan has enticed many a young man, as she has done you, in order to get them to procure it, and whoever is the fortunate one that succeeds, will receive the Red Swan as his reward. In the morning you will proceed on your way, and toward evening you will come to the magician's lodge, but before you enter you will hear his groans; he will immediately ask you in, and you will see no one but himself; he will make inquiries of you, as regards your dreams, and the powers of your guardian spirits; he will then ask you to attempt the recovery of his scalp; he will show you the direction, and if you feel inclined, as I dare say you do, go forward, my son, with a strong heart, persevere, and I have a presentiment you will succeed."

The young man answered, "I will try." Early next morning, after having eaten from the magic kettle, he started off on his journey. Toward evening he came to the lodge as he was told, and soon heard the groans of the magician. "Come in," he said, even before the young man reached the door. On entering he saw his head all bloody, and he was groaning most terribly. "Sit down, sit down," he said, "while I prepare you something to eat," at the same time doing as the other magicians had done, in preparing food – "You see," he said, "how poor I am; I have to attend to all my wants." He said this to conceal the fact that the Red Swan was there, but Odjibwa perceived that the lodge was partitioned, and he heard a rustling noise, now and then, in that quarter, which satisfied him that it was occupied. After having taken his leggings and moccasins off, and eaten, the old magician commenced telling him how he had lost his scalp – the insults it was receiving – the pain he was suffering in consequence – his wishes to regain it – the unsuccessful attempts that had already been made, and the numbers and power of those who detained it; stated the best and most probable way of getting it; touching the young man on his pride and ambition, by the proposed adventure, and last, he spoke of such things as would make an Indian rich. He would interrupt his discourse by now and then groaning, and saying, "Oh, how shamefully they are treating it." Odjibwa listened with solemn attention. The old man then asked him about his dreams – his dreams (or as he saw when asleep) at the particular time he had fasted and blackened his face to procure guardian spirits.

The young man then told him one dream; the magician groaned; "No, that is not it," he said. The young man told him another. He groaned again; "That is not it," he said. The young man told him of two or three others. The magician groaned at each recital, and said, rather peevishly, "No, those are not them." The young man then thought to himself, Who are you? you may groan as much as you please; I am inclined not to tell you any more dreams. The magician then spoke in rather a supplicating tone. "Have you no more dreams of another kind?" "Yes," said the young man, and told him one. "That is it, that is it," he cried; "you will cause me to live. That was what I was wishing you to say;" and he rejoiced greatly. "Will you then go and see if you cannot procure my scalp?" "Yes," said the young man, "I will go; and the day after to-morrow, when you hear the cries of the Kakak, you will know, by this sign, that I am successful, and you must prepare your head, and lean it out through the door, so that the moment I arrive, I may place your scalp on." "Yes, yes," said the magician; "as you say, it will be done." Early next morning, he set out on his perilous adventure, and about the time that the sun hangs toward home, (afternoon) he heard the shouts of a great many people. He was in a wood at the time, and saw, as he thought, only a few men; but the further he went, the more numerous they appeared. On emerging into a plain, their heads appeared like the hanging leaves for number. In the centre he perceived a post, and something waving on it, which was the scalp. Now and then the air was rent with the Sau-sau-quan, for they were dancing the war dance around it. Before he could be perceived, he turned himself into a No-noskau-see (hummingbird), and flew toward the scalp.

As he passed some of those who were standing by, he flew close to their ears, making the humming noise which this bird does when it flies. They jumped on one side, and asked each other what it could be. By this time he had nearly reached the scalp, but fearing he should be perceived while untying it, he changed himself into a Me-sau-be-wau-aun (the down of anything that floats lightly on the air), and then floated slowly and lightly on to the scalp. He untied it, and moved off slowly, as the weight was almost too great. It was as much as he could do to keep it up, and prevent the Indians from snatching it away. The moment they saw it was moving, they filled the air with their cries of "It is taken from us; it is taken from us." He continued moving a few feet above them; the rush and hum of the people was like the dead beating surges after a storm. He soon gained on them, and they gave up the pursuit. After going a little further he changed himself into a Kakak, and flew off with his prize, making that peculiar noise which this bird makes.

In the mean time, the magician had followed his instructions, placing his head outside of the lodge, as soon as he heard the cry of the Kakak, and soon after he heard the rustling of its wings. In a moment Odjibwa stood before him. He immediately gave the magician a severe blow on the head with the wampum scalp: his limbs extended and quivered in agony from the effects of the blow: the scalp adhered, and the young man walked in and sat down, feeling perfectly at home. The magician was so long in recovering from the stunning blow, that the young man feared he had killed him. He was however pleased to see him show signs of life; he first commenced moving, and soon sat up. But how surprised was Odjibwa to see, not an aged man, far in years and decrepitude, but one of the handsomest young men he ever saw stand up before him.

"Thank you, my friend," he said; "you see that your kindness and bravery have restored me to my former shape. It was so ordained, and you have now accomplished the victory."

The young magician urged the stay of his deliverer for a few days; and they soon formed a warm attachment for each other. The magician never alluded to the Red Swan in their conversations.

At last, the day arrived when Odjibwa made preparations to return. The young magician amply repaid him for his kindness and bravery, by various kinds of wampum, robes, and all such things as he had need of to make him an influential man. But though the young man's curiosity was at its height about the Red Swan, he controlled his feelings, and never so much as even hinted of her; feeling that he would surrender a point of propriety in so doing; while the one he had rendered such service to, whose hospitality he was now enjoying, and who had richly rewarded him, had never so much as even mentioned anything about her, but studiously concealed her.

Odjibwa's pack for travelling was ready, and he was taking his farewell smoke, when the young magician thus addressed him: "Friend, you know for what cause you came thus far. You have accomplished your object, and conferred a lasting obligation on me. Your perseverance shall not go unrewarded; and if you undertake other things with the same spirit you have this, you will never fail to accomplish them. My duty renders it necessary for me to remain where I am, although I should feel happy to go with you. I have given you all you will need as long as you live; but I see you feel backward to speak about the Red Swan. I vowed that whoever procured me my scalp, should be rewarded by possessing the Red Swan." He then spoke, and knocked on the partition. The door immediately opened, and the Red Swan met his eager gaze. She was a most beautiful female, and as she stood majestically before him, it would be impossible to describe her charms, for she looked as if she did not belong to earth. "Take her," the young magician said; "she is my sister, treat her well; she is worthy of you, and what you have done for me merits more. She is ready to go with you to your kindred and friends, and has been so ever since your arrival, and my good wishes go with you both." She then looked very kindly on her husband, who now bid farewell to his friend indeed, and accompanied by the object of his wishes, he commenced retracing his footsteps.

They travelled slowly, and after two or three days reached the lodge of the third old man, who had fed him from his small magic pot. He was very kind, and said, "You see what your perseverance has procured you; do so always and you will succeed in all things you undertake."

On the following morning when they were going to start, he pulled from the side of the lodge a bag, which he presented to the young man, saying, "Nosis, I give you this; it contains a present for you; and I hope you will live happily till old age." They then bid farewell to him and proceeded on.

They soon reached the second old man's lodge. Their reception there was the same as at the first; he also gave them a present, with the old man's wishes that they would be happy. They went on and reached the first town, which the young man had passed in his pursuit. The watchman gave notice, and he was shown into the chief's lodge. "Sit down there, son-in-law," said the chief, pointing to a place near his daughter. "And you also," he said to the Red Swan.

The young woman of the lodge was busy in making something, but she tried to show her indifference about what was taking place, for she did not even raise her head to see who was come. Soon the chief said, "Let some one bring in the bundle of our son-in-law." When it was brought in, the young man opened one of the bags, which he had received from one of the old men; it contained wampum, robes, and various other articles; he presented them to his father-in-law, and all expressed their surprise at the value and richness of the gift. The chief's daughter then only stole a glance at the present, then at Odjibwa and his beautiful wife; she stopped working, and remained silent and thoughtful all the evening. They conversed about his adventures; after this the chief told him that he should take his daughter along with him in the morning; the young man said "Yes." The chief then spoke out, saying, "Daughter, be ready to go with him in the morning."

There was a Maujeekewis in the lodge, who thought to have got the young woman to wife; he jumped up, saying, "Who is he (meaning the young man), that he should take her for a few presents. I will kill him," and he raised a knife which he had in his hand. But he only waited till some one held him back, and then sat down, for he was too great a coward to do as he had threatened. Early they took their departure, amid the greetings of their new friends, and toward evening reached the other town. The watchman gave the signal, and numbers of men, women, and children stood out to see them. They were again shown into the chief's lodge, who welcomed them by saying, "Son-in-law, you are welcome," and requested him to take a seat by his daughter; and the two women did the same.

After the usual formalities of smoking and eating, the chief requested the young man to relate his travels in the hearing of all the inmates of the lodge, and those who came to see. They looked with admiration and astonishment at the Red Swan, for she was so beautiful. Odjibwa gave them his whole history. The chief then told him that his brothers had been to their town in search of him, but had returned, and given up all hopes of ever seeing him again. He concluded by saying that since he had been so fortunate and so manly, he should take his daughter with him; "for although your brothers," said he, "were here, they were too timid to enter any of our lodges, and merely inquired for you and returned. You will take my daughter, treat her well, and that will bind us more closely together."

It is always the case in towns, that some one in it is foolish or clownish. It happened to be so here; for a Maujeekewis was in the lodge; and after the young man had given his father-in-law presents, as he did to the first, this Maujeekewis jumped up in a passion, saying, "Who is this stranger, that he should have her? I want her myself." The chief told him to be quiet, and not to disturb or quarrel with one who was enjoying their hospitality. "No, no," he boisterously cried, and made an attempt to strike the stranger. Odjibwa was above fearing his threats, and paid no attention to him. He cried the louder, "I will have her; I will have her." In an instant he was laid flat on the ground from a blow of a war club given by the chief. After he came to himself, the chief upbraided him for his foolishness, and told him to go out and tell stories to the old women.

Their arrangements were then made, and the stranger invited a number of families to go and visit their hunting grounds, as there was plenty of game. They consented, and in the morning a large party were assembled to accompany the young man; and the chief with a large party of warriors escorted them a long distance. When ready to return the chief made a speech, and invoked the blessing of the great good Spirit on his son-in-law and party.

After a number of days' travel, Odjibwa and his party came in sight of his home. The party rested while he went alone in advance to see his brothers. When he entered the lodge he found it all dirty and covered with ashes: on one side was his eldest brother, with his face blackened, and sitting amid ashes, crying aloud. On the other side was Maujeekewis, his other brother; his face was also blackened, but his head was covered with feathers and swan's down; he looked so odd, that the young man could not keep from laughing, for he appeared and pretended to be so absorbed with grief that he did not notice his brother's arrival. The eldest jumped up and shook hands with him, and kissed him, and felt very happy to see him again.

Odjibwa, after seeing all things put to rights, told them that he had brought each of them a wife. When Maujeekewis heard about the wife, he jumped up and said, "Why is it just now that you have come?" and made for the door and peeped out to see the woman. He then commenced jumping and laughing, saying, "Women! women!" That was the only reception he gave his brother. Odjibwa then told them to wash themselves and prepare, for he would go and fetch them in. Maujeekewis jumped and washed himself, but would every now and then go and peep out to see the women. When they came near, he said, "I will have this one, and that one;" he did not exactly know which – he would go and sit down for an instant, and then go and peep and laugh; he acted like a madman.

As soon as order was restored, and all seated, Odjibwa presented one of the women to his eldest brother, saying, "These women were given to me; I now give one to each; I intended so from the first." Maujeekewis spoke, and said, "I think three wives would have been enough for you." The young man led one to Maujeekewis, saying, "My brother, here is one for you, and live happily." Maujeekewis hung down his head as if he was ashamed, but would every now and then steal a glance at his wife, and also at the other women. By and by he turned toward his wife, and acted as if he had been married for years. "Wife," he said, "I will go and hunt," and off he started.

All lived peaceably for some time, and their town prospered, the inhabitants increased, and everything was abundant among them. One day dissatisfaction was manifested in the conduct of the two elder brothers, on account of Odjibwa's having taken their deceased father's magic arrows: they upbraided and urged him to procure others if he could. Their object was to get him away, so that one of them might afterward get his wife. One day, after listening to them, he told them he would go. Maujeekewis and himself went together into a sweating lodge to purify themselves. Even there, although it was held sacred, Maujeekewis upbraided him for the arrows. He told him again he would go; and next day, true to his word, he left them. After travelling a long way he came to an opening in the earth, and descending, it led him to the abode of departed spirits. The country appeared beautiful, the extent of it was lost in the distance: he saw animals of various kinds in abundance. The first he came near to were buffalo; his surprise was great when these animals addressed him as human beings. They asked him what he came for, how he descended, why he was so bold as to visit the abode of the dead. He told them he was in search of magic arrows to appease his brothers. "Very well," said the leader of the buffaloes, whose whole form was nothing but bone. "Yes, we know it," and he and his followers moved off a little space as if they were afraid of him. "You have come," resumed the Buffalo Spirit, "to a place where a living man has never before been. You will return immediately to your tribe, for your brothers are trying to dishonor your wife; and you will live to a very old age, and live and die happily; you can go no further in these abodes of ours." Odjibwa looked, as he thought to the west, and saw a bright light, as if the sun was shining in its splendor, but he saw no sun. "What light is that I see yonder?" he asked. The all-boned buffalo answered, "It is the place where those who were good dwell." "And that dark cloud?" Odjibwa again asked. "Mud-jee-izzhi-wabezewin," (wickedness) answered the buffalo. He asked no more questions, and, with the aid of his guardian spirits, again stood on this earth and saw the sun giving light as usual, and breathed the pure air. All else he saw in the abodes of the dead, and his travels and actions previous to his return, are unknown. After wandering a long time in quest of information to make his people happy, he one evening drew near to his village or town; passing all the other lodges and coming to his own, he heard his brothers at high words with each other; they were quarrelling for the possession of his wife. She had, however, remained constant, and mourned the absence and probable loss of her husband; but she had mourned him with the dignity of virtue. The noble youth listened till he was satisfied of the base principles of his brothers. He then entered the lodge, with the stern air and conscious dignity of a brave and honest man. He spoke not a word, but placing the magic arrows to his bow, drew them to their length and laid the brothers dead at his feet. Thus ended the contest between the hermit's sons, and a firm and happy union was consummated between Odjibwa, or him of the primitive or intonated voice, and the Red Swan.

The Giant Magicians

THERE WAS ONCE a man and his wife who lived by the sea, far away from other people. They had many children, and they were very poor. One day this couple were in their canoe, far from land. There came up a dense fog; they were quite lost.

They heard a noise as of paddles and voices. It drew nearer. They saw dimly a monstrous canoe filled with giants, who greeted the little folk like friends. "Uch keen, tahmee wejeaok?" "My little brother," said the leader, "where are you going?" "I am lost in the fog," said the poor Indian, very sadly. "Ah, come with us to our camp," said the giant, who seemed to be a good fellow, if there ever was one. "Truly, ye will be well treated, my small friends, for my father is the chief; so be of good cheer!" And they, being much amazed at this gentleness, sat still in awe, while two of the giants, each putting a tip of his paddle under their bark, lifted it up and put it into their own, as if it had been a chip. And truly the giants seemed to be as much pleased with the little folk as a boy would be who had found a flying squirrel.

And as they drew near the beach, lo! they beheld three wigwams, high as mountains, in size according to that of the giants. And coming to meet them was the chief, who was taller than the rest.

"Ha!" he cried. "Son, what have you there? Where did you pick up that little brother? Noo, my father, I found him lost in the fog." "Well, bring him home to the lodge, my son!" So the giant took the small canoe in the palm of his hand, the man and his wife sitting therein, and carried them home. Then they were taken into the wigwam, and the canoe was laid carefully in the eaves, but within easy reach, about a hundred and fifty yards from the ground.

Then an abundant meal was set before them, but the benevolent host, mindful of their small size, did not give them more to eat than they would have needed for about ten years to come, and informed them in a subdued whisper, which could hardly have been heard a hundred miles off, that his name was Oscoon.

Now it came to pass, a few days after, that a company of these well-grown people went hunting, and when they returned the guests must needs pity them that they had no game in their land which answered to their size; for they came in with strings of such small affairs as two or three dozen caribou hanging in their belts, as a Micmac would carry a string of squirrels, and swinging one or two moose in their hands like rabbits. Yet, what with these and many deer, bears, and beavers, they made up in the weight of their game what it lacked in size, and of what they had they were generous.

Now the giants became very fond of the small folk, and would not for the world that they should in any way come to harm. And it came to pass that one morning the chief told them that they were to have a grand battle, since they expected in three days to be attacked by a Chenoo. Therefore the Micmac saw that in all things it was even with the giants as with his own people at home, they having their troubles with the wicked, and the chiefs their share in being obliged to keep up their magic and know all that was going on in the world. Yea, for he would be a poor powwow and a necromancer worth nothing who could not foretell such a trifle as the day and hour when an enemy would be on them!

But this time the Sakumow, or sagamore, was forewarned, and bade his little guests stop their ears and bind up their heads, and roll themselves in many folds of dressed skins, lest they should hear the deadly war-scream of the Chenoo. And with all their care they hardly survived it; but the second scream hurt them less; and after the third the chief came to them with a cheerful countenance, and bade them arise and unpack themselves, for the monster was slain, and though his four sons, with two other giants, had been sorely tried, yet they had conquered.

But the sorrows of the good are never at an end, and so it was with these honest giants, who were always being pestered with some kind of scurvy knaves or others; who would not leave them in peace. For anon the chief announced that this time a Kookwes – a burly, beastly villain, not two points better than his cousin the Chenoo – was coming to play at rough murder with them. And, verily, by this time the Micmac began to believe, without bating an ace on it, that all of these tall people were like the wolves, who, meeting with nobody else, bite one another. So they were bound and bundled up as before, and put to bed like dolls. And again they heard the horrible shout, the moderate shout, and the smaller shout, until sooel moonoodooahdigool, which, being interpreted, meaneth that they hardly heard him at all.

Then the warriors, returning, gave proof that they had indeed done something more than kick the wind, for they were covered with blood, and their legs were stuck full of large pines, with here and there an oak or hemlock, for the fight had been in a forest; so that they had been as much troubled as men would be with thistles, nettles, and pine splinters, which is truly often a great trouble. But this was their least trial, for, as they told their chief, the enemy had well-nigh made Jack Drum's entertainment for them, and led them the devil's dance, had not one of them, by good luck, opened his eye for him with a rock which drove it into his brain. And as it was, the chief's youngest son had been so mauled that, coming home, he fell dead just before his father's door. Truly this might have been deemed almost an accident in some families; but lo! what a good thing it is to have an enchanter in the house, especially one who knows his business, as did the old chief, who, going out, asked the young man why he was lying there. To which he replying that it was because he was dead, his father bade him rise and walk, which he did straight to the supper table, and ate none the less for it.

Now the old chief, thinking that perhaps his dear little people found life dull and devoid of incident with him, asked them if they were aweary of him. They, with golden truth indeed, answered that they had never been so merry, but that they were anxious as to their children at home. He answered that they were indeed right, and that the next morning they might depart. So their canoe was reached down for them, and packed full of the finest furs and best meat, when they were told to tebah'-dikw', or get in. Then a small dog was put in, and this dog was solemnly charged that he should take the people home, while the people were told to paddle in the direction in which the dog should point. And to the Micmac he said, "Seven years hence you will be reminded of me." And then tokooboosijik (off they went).

The man sat in the stern, his wife in the prow, and the dog in the middle of the canoe. The dog pointed, the Indian paddled, the water was smooth. They soon reached home; the children with joy ran to meet them; the dog as joyfully ran to see the children, wagging his tail with great glee, just as if he had been like any other dog, and not a fairy. For, having made acquaintance, he without delay turned tail and trotted off for home again, running over the ocean surface as if it had been hard ice; which might, indeed, have once astonished the good man and his wife, but they had of late days seen so many wonders that they were past marvelling.

Now this Indian, who had in the past been always poor, seemed to have quite recovered from that complaint. When he let down his lines the biggest fish bit; all his sprats were salmon; he prayed for goslings, and got geese; moose were as mice to him now; yea, he had the best in the land, with all the fatness thereof. So seven years passed away, and then, as he slept, there came unto him divers dreams, and in them he went back to the Land of the Giants, and saw all those who had been so kind to him. And yet again he dreamed one night that he was standing by his wigwam near the sea, and that a great whale swam up to him and began to sing, and that the singing was the sweetest he had ever heard.

Then he remembered that the giant had told him he would think of him in seven years; and it came clearly before him what it all meant, and that he was erelong to have magical power given to him, and that he should become a Megumoowessoo. This he told his wife, who, not being learned in darksome lore, would fain know more nearly what kind of a being he expected to be, and whether a spirit or a man, good or bad; which was, indeed, not easy to explain, nor is it clearly set down in the chronicles beyond this, that, whatever it might be, it was all for the best, and that there was a great deal of magic in it.

That day they saw a great shark cruising about in their bay, chasing fish, and this they held for an evil omen. But, soon after, there came trotting towards them over the sea the same small dog who had been their pilot from the Land of the Giants. So he, full of joy, as before, at seeing them and the children, wagged his tail and danced for glee, and then looked earnestly at the man as if for some message. And to him the man said, "It is well. In three years' time I will make you a visit. I will look to the southwest." Then the dog licked the hands and the ears and the eyes of the man, and went home as before over the sea, running on the water.

And when the three years had passed the Indian entered his canoe, and, paddling without fear, found his way to the Land of the Giants. He saw the wigwams standing on the beach; the immense canoes were drawn up on the water's edge; from afar he beheld the old giant coming down to welcome him. But he was alone. And when he had been welcomed, and was in the wigwam, he learned that all the sons were dead. They had died three years before, when the shark, the great sorcerer, had been seen.

They had gone, and the old man had but lingered a little longer. They had made the magic change, they had departed, and he would soon join them in his own kingdom. But ere he went he would leave their great inheritance, their magic, to the man.

Therewith the giant brought out his son's clothes, and bade the Indian put them on. Truly this was as if he had been asked to clothe himself with a great house, since the smallest fold in them would have been to him as a cavern. But he stepped in, and as he did this he rose to great size; he filled out the garments till they fitted; he was a giant, of Giant-Land. With the clothes came the wisdom, the m'téoulin, the manitou power of the greatest and wisest of the olden time. He was indeed Megumoowessoo, and had attained to the Mystery.

The Wizard and His Wife

LONG AGO, THERE WAS AN OLD WOMAN and her little grandson who were so ragged and filthy that the people drove them from the camp and they lived alone, far away from anyone. She was a wise woman and taught the boy strange things so that when he was a young man, though he was still ragged and filthy, he knew how to talk with birds and beasts and to do magical things.

The chief had a beautiful daughter who was so beloved by all, that they would spread their robes on the ground for her to walk upon. This young man wanted the chief's daughter for his wife, but she scorned him because he was so filthy. He told his grandmother what he wanted and asked her to go to the camp and get a bladder for him. She was afraid to go to the camp or to ask anyone for anything, for she knew the people despised her and her grandson and that they would treat her with contempt and might abuse her.

The young man persuaded her to go. When she was near the camp she called to the people and asked if someone would give her a bladder. They made sport of her and told her to keep away from the camp. She was about to go to her tipi when a good woman gave her a bladder. She took it to her grandson and he made a rattle of it and conjured it so that it was magical. He then sat beside the creek where the chief's daughter came for water and when she came and stooped to fill her vessel, she saw his reflection in the water.

When she looked up at him, he told her he wanted her to be his wife. She answered him by scolding and bemeaning him and calling him vile names and ordered him to keep away from her so that she could not see him. He then shook his magic rattle at her and she became like a rattle and rattled at every step she made. She ran, but this only made her rattle the louder, so she began to weep. Her friends put a robe on her and carried her to her father's tipi and she told him of the filthy young man who had asked her to be his wife, and had brought this evil thing on her when she had refused.

The chief knew that the old woman had taught her grandson many wise things and that he was a wizard so he told his daughter that this young man and no other could relieve her of the evil upon her. He advised her to go to the young man and say that she would be his wife if he would relieve her of the spell that was upon her and then she could run away from him.

She went to the old woman's tipi and told the young man that she had always intended to be his wife, that what she had said to him at the creek was just to tease him, that if he would relieve her from the evil he had put upon her, she would be his wife. He relieved her of the evil and told her to go back to her father's tipi and he would come there and get her with her father's consent and take her in an honorable way, before all the people. This pleased her, for she thought that her father would never give his consent to such an arrangement. When she was relieved of the evil she hurried away.

The people were gathered at her father's tipi, waiting to learn the result of her visit to the young man and when they saw her coming, restored to her natural condition, they shouted their joy and congratulated her on her escape from the filthy young man. The young man perceived that he had been tricked into restoring her and that she did not intend to become his wife and would try to keep out of his power. He went to the creek and hid himself near where she came for water. Soon she came, looking cautiously about to see if he were there. At first she did not see him, but when she stooped to fill her vessel she saw his shadow in the water. She started to run but he shook the rattle at her and she became dry and hard and rattled as she moved.

The people again carried her to her father's tipi and she told him what had happened to her. He then understood that this young man was truly a wizard and told his daughter that she could not escape him and must be his wife. He then directed the people to go to the young man, to treat him well and invite him to come to his tipi, and tell him that he would give him his daughter to be his wife. They did so.

The young man came to the chief's tipi. The chief ordered three old women to take him and cleanse him, bathe him and clothe him in good clothing and put a new robe on him. They did so. When the young man was cleansed and clothed in good clothing all saw that he was a strong and handsome man and good to look upon, so they followed him to the chief's tipi, singing and laughing joyfully.

When the chief's daughter saw him, she smiled upon him and came and put her hand in his. He restored her to her natural condition and wrapped his robe about her and himself, and stood facing all the people, proud and commanding, so that they knew that he would be a chief. The chief then said to him, "You are a wizard, and you shall be known by that name forever."

He then gave his daughter to the wizard to be his wife and made a great feast and the people danced and sang and played games. The young people made love and the old people told stories and all were happy. The old women made a big tipi at the head of the camp, next to the chief's tipi and the wizard and his wife lived in it, happily for many moons.

One morning, the wizard awoke and found his wife gone. He inquired for her in her father's tipi and in all the camp, but could not find her, so the chief called all the people together and asked them about her, but no one could tell where she had gone or what had become of her.

The wizard was disconsolate and wandered aimlessly about until one day he came to his grandmother's tipi. He did not know her, but she said, "Come into my tipi, my grandson. I have been waiting for you. Your wife is gone and I will tell you how to find her." He went into the tipi and his grandmother gave him food. After he had eaten and rested, she gave him a gray bonnet and a big knife and told him that when he put the bonnet on, no one could see him, and when he struck anything with the big knife, it would be cut to pieces.

She showed him a trail and told him to follow it until he came to a lake and then put on the gray bonnet and dive into the lake where he would find a trail at the bottom and to go on this trail until he came to a river. When he came to the river, she told him to put on the gray bonnet and he could walk across the river. On the other side of the river was a great camp and his wife was in that camp.

The wizard did as his grandmother told him and traveled on the trail until he came to the lake where he put on the bonnet, dived into the lake, and found the trail at the bottom. He went on this trail until he came to a river and he put on the gray bonnet again and walked on the water across the river. On the other side of the river he saw a great camp and in the center of the camp he saw a large tipi. He put the gray bonnet on, so that no one could see him and walked into the camp and went into the big tipi in the center of the camp. Here, he found his wife, sitting in the tipi, making moccasins. He sat down near her and took off the gray bonnet.

She was surprised and pleased to see him and begged him to take her back to his tipi. She begged him to go quickly for she was afraid of the one who had stolen her and brought her there, because he was a strong and savage beast who would try to kill both the wizard and his wife if he found them together. The wizard told her to have no fear, for he wanted to see this evil one who had stolen her, but she begged him so hard to go before the beast came that he took her by the hand and led her out of the door. As they came out of the tipi, his wife cried, "Here it comes. It will kill both of us."

The wizard saw a great beast rushing at them and knew that it was the Magical Buffalo (Ganask inyan). He put on the gray bonnet and the Magical Buffalo could see neither him nor his wife. As it rushed by him, he struck it with the big knife and it was cut into pieces. He and his wife then went to the river and he put on the gray bonnet and followed the trail to his grandmother's tipi. They came to her tipi and found her waiting for them, and she said, "Come into my tipi, grandson. I knew that you would bring your wife with you." When they were in the tipi she said to him, "Hang the gray bonnet and the big knife on the side of the tipi, and when you are in trouble come to me." She then gave them food and when they had rested, they went on their way to their own tipi. When the people saw them, they rejoiced; the chief gave a great feast and all were happy.

The wizard and his wife lived happily in their tipi for many moons. One morning, the wizard awoke and found his wife gone again. He searched for her in her father's tipi and in all the camp but could not find her. The chief called the people together but no one could tell where she was or what had become of her. The wizard remembered his grandmother and went to her tipi and found her waiting for him. She said to him, "My grandson, you have lost your wife again. I will help you to find her."

She then gave him food. When he had rested she told him to take the gray bonnet and the big knife and follow her. She went into a wood on the bank of a large river where there was a log with a branch at one end. She twisted this branch round and round and the log rolled over and over towards the river and as it rolled became more and more like a boat, so that when it reached the water it was a boat with a head, two great eyes, and a tail. She told the wizard that this boat would carry him where he wanted to go and that when he got out of it, it would sink below the surface of the water until only its tail could be seen. She told him that when he wished to use the boat again he should shake the tail and the boat would rise and start away. She warned him that he must get into it quickly or it would go and leave him.

He sat in the boat and it carried him all day. At night he lay down and slept and it carried him all night. The next morning he saw something dark far away, and when the boat brought him near he saw that it was a summer cloud sitting on the bank of the river. The boat carried him to the bank. He got out of it and it sank in the water until only the tail could be seen. He found a trail under the cloud and followed it to the top of a high hill and in the valley beyond he saw a large yellow tipi. He put the gray bonnet on and went to the tipi and walked around it, examining it closely. Then he went into it and found his wife making moccasins and sat down near her.

He took off the gray bonnet. When his wife saw him, she was like one dead with fear. When she revived she begged him to take her away from that place, for the one who had stolen her and brought her there was a malicious and terrible bird with three brothers who were as evil as it, and that when they glared their glance would kill. The wizard told her to have no fear for him, as he wished to see the bird that had stolen her.

While they talked, there was a crash of thunder. The woman grew pale with fear and said that the thunder was one of the birds coming. The wizard told her to sit still as if she were making moccasins and if the bird came in to go out and hurry to the bank of the river and wait for him there.

In a short time, the bird came in and the wizard saw that it was the Thunderbird from the north. Its voice was loud and rough as it said, "Who has been here? There are tracks around the tipi." The woman said, "No one has been here and gone. Look about the tipi for yourself." It looked about the tipi but could see no one, so it said, "I will wait for my brothers."

Soon there was another crash of thunder and another bird came in. The wizard saw that it was the Thunderbird from the west. It said in a loud coarse voice, "Who has been here? There are tracks about the tipi and in the door?" The woman said, "No one has been here and gone. Look about the tipi for yourself." It looked about the tipi but could see no one, so it said, "We will wait for our brothers."

Then there was another crash of thunder and another bird came in. The wizard saw it was the Thunderbird from the south. It said in a loud coarse voice, "Who has been here? There are tracks around the tipi and in the door and near the fireplace." The woman said: "No one has been here and gone. Look about the tipi for yourself." It looked about the tipi but could see no one, so it said, "We will wait for our brother."

Then there was a crash of thunder louder than the others, which shook the tipi and the earth, and soon another bird came. It was larger and more terrible than either of the others. The wizard saw that it was the Thunderbird from the east. It said in a voice that sounded like the growling of an angry bear, "Who has been here? There are tracks around the tipi, and in the door, and near the fireplace and by the woman." The woman said, "No one has been here and gone. Look about the tipi for yourself." It looked about the tipi but could see no one and it said, "Woman, the tracks are tracks of a human. The tracks are of one of your kind. You must be hiding him. You may be sitting on him. Get up and go out of the tipi."

She went out of the tipi and hurried to the bank of the river as the wizard had told her. When she had gone, the Thunderbirds looked all about the tipi but could see no one, so they gathered up the robes and bags and everything that was in it, and threw them all out, but could find no one. Then the Thunderbird from the north searched all the north side of the tipi, and said, "There is no one in the north side of the tipi." The Thunderbird from the west, searched the west side and said, "There is no one in the west side of the tipi." The Thunderbird from the south searched the south side and said, "There is no one in the south side of the tipi." The Thunderbird from the east searched on one side of the door in the east, and said, "There is no one on this side of the door." As it crossed the doorway, the wizard struck it on the head and knocked it down. It jumped up and knocked down the Thunderbird from the north and it said, "Why did you do that?" and the Thunderbird from the east said, "Why did you knock me down?" The Thunderbird from the north said, "I did not knock you down."

Then the Thunderbird from the east knocked down the Thunderbird from the west, and it said, "Why did you do that?" and the Thunderbird from the east said, "Why did you knock me down?" and the Thunderbird from the west said, "I did not knock you down." Then the Thunderbird from the east knocked down the Thunderbird from the south, and it said, "Why did you do that?" The Thunderbird from the east said, "Why did you knock me down?" and the Thunderbird from the south said, "I did not knock you down." Then the Thunderbird from the east said, "One of you has lied to me, for one of you knocked me down." So they began to quarrel, and soon were fighting. They fought until three of the birds were killed and the other was weak and bloody.

The wizard saw that it was the Thunderbird from the west that was not killed and he took off the gray bonnet and said to the bird, "You are an evil thing. You delight in destroying and killing. You have even killed your own brothers. Now I will kill you." The Thunderbird saw that he was a wizard because he had appeared from nowhere. It was wounded and weak from the loss of blood, so it cried like a woman and begged the wizard to spare its life, but he said, "You have had no mercy on anything or anyone, and I will have no mercy on you."

He threw the gray bonnet down and took the big knife in his hand and stepped towards the bird to strike it, but the gray bonnet fell on the body of one of the dead birds and he could not see it and he stumbled over it and fell down. When he fell, the Thunderbird from the west snatched the gray bonnet and put it on, and the wizard could not see it. He searched long and carefully but could see neither the bird nor the bonnet. Then the Thunderbird mocked him and said, "My brothers are now dead. I am the Thunderbird. I shall keep the gray bonnet and no one shall ever see me again. I am weak now and cannot harm you, but I shall ever be your enemy. I will destroy and kill forever."

The wizard hurried to his wife on the bank of the river, but it was night when he got there and the summer cloud sitting on the bank made it very dark, so they waited for morning. During the night, they saw the glare of the Thunderbird's eye, weak and faint like the northern light, but towards morning it grew stronger and glanced towards them. As soon as it was light enough for them to see, the wizard shook the tail of the boat and it rose to the top of the water. They got into it quickly and it carried them away very fast. It carried them all day. At night, they slept in it and it carried them all night. The next morning, they saw something far away. When the boat brought them near it they saw that it was the wood on the bank of the river where the trail that led to his grandmother's tipi started.

The grandmother stood on the bank waiting for them. When they got out of the boat, she twisted its tail and it rolled over and over, up the bank and into the wood. Each time it rolled over, it grew smaller and rounder until it was a log again. They then went to the grandmother's tipi and she said to him, "Grandson, I knew you would bring your woman back with you. Now hang the gray bonnet and the big knife on the side of the tipi, and if you are ever in trouble come to me."

Then the wizard told her how he had lost the gray bonnet. She went to the top of a hill and wailed a song as if for the dead for she knew that it was gone forever and no man would again wear it. She returned to the tipi and said to the wizard, "My heart is heavy, for the gray bonnet is gone forever. The Thunder is your enemy and it will wear it always. Waziya and Iktomi are its friends and Heyoka and Iya will do its bidding. It will plague you with these evil ones. There is but one bonnet that will help you. That is the brown bonnet. It is far away, but you must get it. When you are in trouble come to me."

She then gave the wizard and his wife food. When they had rested they went on their way to their own tipi. When the people saw them they rejoiced and the chief made a great feast for all. The wizard and his wife lived happily until the winter moon had come when, one night his wife woke him and said, "Waziya is blowing his breath on me." He knew there would be trouble, so he went to his grandmother's tipi, and found her waiting for him. She said, "Grandson, Waziya is troubling your wife. You must get the brown bonnet. A stone wrapped the little brown bonnet in a little red ball and swallowed it. You must find this stone and take the brown bonnet from it. I will prepare you for this quest. Bring me three things. A wolf, a turtle and a meadowlark." She then gave him food and when he had rested, he went to find the wolf, turtle, and meadow lark.

He traveled far on the plains, and met a huge wolf and said to him, "My friend, come and eat with me." The wolf was hungry and sat beside the wizard and they feasted all that day and far into the night. The next morning the wizard told the wolf that he must go in quest of the brown bonnet, and what his grandmother must have to prepare him for the quest. The wolf said, "I have little hair. Waziya's breath pinches me. I will help you that I may be revenged on Waziya."

So the wolf and the wizard traveled on together and they came to a great muddy lake and met a huge turtle.

The wizard, whose name was Piya, said to the turtle, "My friend, come eat with us." The turtle sat and ate with Piya and the wolf. In the morning, Piya told the turtle as he had the wolf. The turtle said, "My skin is thin and insects bite me, but I will help you so that I maybe revenged on those who suck my blood." The wizard, the wolf, and the turtle traveled far into the night.

In the morning, Piya spoke to the lark as he had the wolf and turtle. The lark said, "My voice is harsh and I can sing but one note and the magpie laughs at me; but I will help you so that I can make the magpie ashamed." So Piya, the wolf, the turtle, and the lark went together to the tipi of the wizard's grandmother.

She stood outside and said, "Grandson, I knew you would come and bring that which I want." She then bade them go inside. She prepared a feast for them and they feasted far into the night. In the morning Piya told his grandmother what the wolf, the turtle, and the lark had said. She told them that if they would give her what she wished she would give each of them what he most wished. The wolf, the turtle, and the lark agreed to this. She said she wished the wolf to give her grandson the cunning by which he could follow a hidden trail and find hidden things; the turtle to give him the sense by which he could locate water; and the lark to give him the power to hide himself without a covering.

The wolf said he wished for fur clothing for himself and his people so that they could laugh at the Old Man, Wazi. The turtle said he wished for hard and tough clothing so that he could laugh at all insects that bite and suck blood. The lark said he wished for a pleasing voice so that he could sing and make the magpie ashamed.

The Old Woman then said that if they would first help her grandson as she wished, she would give them and all their people what they wished. She then told them how to go to a far region where there were neither trees, nor grass, nor open trail, and but little water in hidden springs. She gave Piya the big knife and a magic rattle and told him to go upon the barren region and find his wife.

The wizard, the wolf, the turtle and the lark traveled together as the Old Woman had instructed them. Piya was sad, for he thought of his wife, but the others were happy, for they thought of that which the Old Woman would give them. In the evening the wolf taught Piya how to lie hidden with no covering. Thus they traveled many days and came to the barren region. Piya took food and went alone upon this region, but he could see no trail and wandered about until he remembered the cunning the wolf had taught him. Then he found a hidden trail and traveled on it until evening, when he located a spring hidden under a stone, with little water in it. He camped there that night. In the morning a bear came and Piya hid himself as the lark had taught him. The bear saw the stone was taken from the spring, and he raged and sniffed about to find who had drunk from his spring. Piya showed himself and the bear reared and rushed to attack him. Piya shook the magic rattle toward the bear and he could not move. Piya showed the big knife and the bear whimpered and begged for pity and promised to help Piya in any manner. Then Piya told of his wife and why he was there. The bear said that the Crazy Buffalo had stolen his wife and kept her in his tipi which was four days' journey distant; that the hidden trail was to this tipi which was like a huge cactus; that no man could enter this cactus without wearing the brown bonnet; and that the brown bonnet was hidden in a red stone that was like a fruit on the cactus.

Piya traveled on the hidden trail for four days and then saw a huge cactus. He bid himself and watched it. The Crazy Buffalo came from the cactus. He hid himself and watched it. The Crazy Buffalo came from the cactus and bellowed that he smelled a man. He sniffed this way and that way and then rushed along the hidden trail, grunting and snorting.

When Piya could no longer see him he went to the cactus and saw what appeared to be a large fruit on it. He struck the fruit with the big knife. When it fell to the ground, he saw that it was a stone. He struck the stone with the big knife and cut it through. The brown bonnet was inside the stone and Piya put it on his head. A door opened in the cactus and he went inside and when his wife saw him she was much afraid.

She said that the Crazy Buffalo was a ferocious demon and would kill Piya when he came back. Piya, told her not to fear and do as he bade her. When the Crazy Buffalo came and saw the broken red stone he bellowed with rage. Piya hid. The demon came into the cactus and said, "I smell a man. Where is he?" The woman said, "No man has been here and gone." The Crazy Buffalo said, "You hid a man and I will gore you." Piya. said to the woman, "Runaway from here." The Crazy

Buffalo turned to see who spoke and the woman ran from the cactus and far away. When Piya showed himself and the Crazy Buffalo rushed to gore him, he shook the magic rattle. When the Crazy Buffalo heard the rattle he could not move. He said to Piya, "You are a wizard and have much power. We should be friends, for I also have much power. We can work together and we can do anything that we may wish." Piya said nothing. The Crazy Buffalo said, "If you will be my friend I will give you my power. You will be a chief and a brave and the women will sing your songs." Piya said nothing. The Crazy Buffalo said, "I will give you power so that you will have plenty of meat and robes and can take the wives of other men and ravish the young women and no one will harm you." Piya gazed far away, but said nothing. The Crazy Buffalo grew bold and said, "Let me take the brown bonnet and I will show you how to wear it so that you can do as you wish in anything." Then Piya said, "You tell me lies to escape from me, but you shall not escape." He drew the big knife and when the Crazy Buffalo saw it he begged for mercy.

Piya said, "You are a demon who has had no pity for anyone, and I will have no pity for you." He then struck the Crazy Buffalo with the big knife and cut him into four pieces. Piya then went and found his wife. Together they traveled on the hidden trail until they came to where the wolf, the turtle, and the lark waited for them. All rejoiced and they went to the Old Woman's tipi. She stood outside and said, "Grandson, I knew that you would get the brown bonnet and find your wife."

She then made a feast and all feasted until far into the night. In the morning she gave the wolf, the turtle, and the lark what each had wished for, and together they went on the trail. She told her grandson to hang the brown bonnet and big knife in the tipi, and keep the magic rattle, and as long as it was in his tipi no harm would come to him or his wife.

The wizard and his wife returned to her people and they rejoiced, singing songs, dancing, and playing games. The chief made a great feast and gave away all he possessed. The women put up a new tipi beside that of the chief and the wizard's wife led him through its door and seated him on the man's place.

The Beginning of Foot Racing

LONG AGO a chief left his camp to visit a camp far away. On the way, he came to a man running over hills and valleys and round and round. He asked the man why he did this and he said he was a magician and running was part of the mysteries he performed. As they talked together, the chief told the magician that he was going to visit a camp far away and invited him to go along. He agreed to do so. As they traveled together, the chief asked the magician what his name was. He told him it was Runner.

After a time, they saw a man lying on the ground, laughing. He continued to laugh and roll about on the ground as if he heard something funny. They asked him why he did this and he told them that he was listening to a very funny story about an old woman who lived in a camp far away and the people in that camp were talking about the strange things she did. They asked how he could hear people in a camp far away. He told them that he was a magician and could hear things far away by putting his ear to the ground. While they talked together, the Chief and Runner told the other man that they were going on a visit and asked him if he would go with them and he agreed to do so. They then asked what his name was and he said he was called Hears.

So the three traveled together. Soon they came to a man who was throwing dust and sand into the air and blowing on it so that it whirled about. They asked him why he did this and he told them that he was a magician who could control the winds and he did this to cool the earth. While they talked with him, they told him that they were going on a visit and asked if he would go with them and he agreed to do so. They asked what his name was and he told them he was called West Wind.

As these four men traveled together they agreed to go to the camp where the old woman lived who could run so fast and do such strange things, for they knew that she was a witch. When they got there, they found the people outside the camp watching the witch performing her antics. She would run very swiftly and then jump high in the air and prance about in a ludicrous manner and she twitted the men and dared them to run against her.

The Chief told the Runner that as he was a magician who could run fast he should run with the witch. He agreed to do so the next day. That night, Hears lay with his ear to the ground and heard the witch plotting with her friends to play witch tricks on Runner to frighten him, so he told Runner of this.

The next morning four men came to the Chief and his friends and told them that the old woman was a witch and advised them not to contest against her for she might do some harm to them. But the Runner said he would run and risk her harming him.

About the middle of the day all went from the camp to the place where the race was to be run. The witch said they would run once around a deep gully, then on level ground to the hills, and once around the bills and back through a gap in the hills to the place where they started. The Runner agreed to this. Then the witch cavorted around the Runner and jumped high in the air and over his head to frighten him, but he only smiled at her and walked leisurely about.

Then she said that when they came to the place to start the one that was ready first should go first and he agreed to that. He knew that she intended to play some trick on him so he watched her closely. When they were to start, the witch ran quickly to the starting place and ran on without stopping to see if he had started or not, but West Wind blew Runner ahead of the witch.

Runner ran beside the witch and she ran faster but could not outdistance him. When they came to the hills, the witch changed herself into a jackrabbit and as she ran up the hill ahead of Runner she kicked dust and sand into his face and mocked him and said, "Ho, you did not know that I am a witch." Then Runner changed himself into a hawk and as he flew over the hills ahead of her he said, "Ho, you did not know that I am a magician." The witch was angry and called the hawk "old crooked nose" and reviled him, but he only laughed at her.

When the witch had gone over the hill, she changed herself into a beautiful young woman and called to the hawk to come to her. The hawk came. When he saw the young woman he changed himself into a young man and sat beside the young woman. She took his head in her lap and soothed him so that he was soon asleep. Then she laid his head on a soft bundle of grass and ran to the gap in the hills, intending to get back to the people before he should awake. She said, "Ho. I have fooled you. You will sleep till I win the race."

But Hears had his ear to the ground and told West Wind that the witch was talking to Runner and what she said. Then West Wind blew sand and gravel in the face of Runner and awoke him. He saw that he had been fooled, so he changed himself into a hawk and flew swiftly after witch and overtook her and beat her back to the place where they started.

The people had bet everything on the witch, and they felt badly, so they persuaded the Chief and his friends to stay with them. They sent the witch to find someone to run and win back what they had lost. The witch went to the north and found one who said he could run swiftly and she brought him back with her, but Runner would not run with him. So the people called them cowards and bemeaned them until West Wind said he would run.

Then all the people went out to see the race. When they came there, the four friends saw that it was Waziya who was to ran and they feared some trick. Waziya was fat and wheezed when he breathed and he was clothed in a thick robe made of down of birds. They agreed to go to the hills and run from there to the people. They started from the hills and ran side by side. Soon the witch saw that Waziya was too fat to run so she pulled off his robe of down and threw it in front of West Wind intending to trip him, but he stepped on it and it disappeared. They ran on till they came near the people so that Waziya's breath was cold on them, but he got out of breath before he came to them. West Wind ran up to them and then ran on and back to them and said, "I have beaten the North Wind and I will always do so."

Hereafter men will run foot races and when they do so this shall be the rule, "He that cheats shall lose the race."

Why the Cat Always Falls Upon Her Feet

SOME MAGICIANS ARE CRUEL, but others are gentle and good to all the creatures of the earth. One of these good magicians was one day traveling in a great forest. The sun rose high in the heavens, and he lay down at the foot of a tree. Soft, green moss grew all about him. The sun shining through the leaves made flecks of light and shadow upon the earth. He heard the song of the bird and the lazy buzz of the wasp. The wind rustled the leafy boughs above him. All the music of the forest lulled him to slumber, and he closed his eyes.

As the magician lay asleep, a great serpent came softly from the thicket. It lifted high its shining crest and saw the man at the foot of the tree. "I will kill him!" it hissed. "I could have eaten that cat last night if he had not called, 'Watch, little cat, watch!' I will kill him, I will kill him!"

Closer and closer the deadly serpent moved. The magician stirred in his sleep. "Watch, little cat, watch!" he said softly. The serpent drew back, but the magician's eyes were shut, and it went closer. It hissed its war-cry. The sleeping magician did not move. The serpent was upon him – no, far up in the high branches of the tree above his head the little cat lay hidden. She had seen the serpent when it came from the thicket. She watched it as it went closer and closer to the sleeping man, and she heard it hiss its war-cry. The little cat's body quivered with anger and with fear, for she was so little and the serpent was so big. "The magician was very good to me," she thought, and she leaped down upon the serpent.

Oh, how angry the serpent was! It hissed, and the flames shot from its eyes. It struck wildly at the brave little cat, but now the cat had no fear. Again and again she leaped upon the serpent's head, and at last the creature lay dead beside the sleeping man whom it had wished to kill.

When the magician awoke, the little cat lay on the earth, and not far away was the dead serpent. He knew at once what the cat had done, and he said, "Little cat, what can I do to show you honor for your brave fight? Your eyes are quick to see, and your ears are quick to hear. You can run very swiftly. I know what I can do for you. You shall be known over the earth as the friend of man, and you shall always have a home in the home of man. And one thing more, little cat: you leaped from the high tree to kill the deadly serpent, and now as long as you live, you shall leap where you will, and you shall always fall upon your feet."

The Strange Banana Skin

KUKALI, ACCORDING TO THE FOLK-LORE OF HAWAII, was born at Kalapana, the most southerly point of the largest island of the Hawaiian group. Kukali lived hundreds of years ago in the days of the migrations of Polynesians from one group of islands to another throughout the length and breadth of the great Pacific Ocean. He visited strange lands, now known under the general name, Kahiki, or Tahiti. Here he killed the great bird Halulu, found the deep bottomless pit in which was a pool of the fabled water of life, married the sister of Halulu, and returned to his old home. All this he accomplished through the wonderful power of a banana skin.

Kukali's father was a priest, or kahuna, of great wisdom and ability, who taught his children how to exercise strange and magical powers. To Kukali he gave a banana with the impressive charge to preserve the skin whenever he ate the fruit, and be careful that it was always under his control. He taught Kukali the wisdom of the makers of canoes and also how to select the fine-grained lava for stone knives and hatchets, and fashion the blade to the best shape. He instructed the young man in the prayers and incantations of greatest efficacy and showed him charms which would be more powerful than any charms his enemies might use in attempting to destroy him, and taught him those omens which were too powerful to be overcome. Thus Kukali became a wizard, having great confidence in his ability to meet the craft of the wise men of distant islands.

Kukali went inland through the forests and up the mountains, carrying no food save the banana which his father had given him. Hunger came, and he carefully stripped back the skin and ate the banana, folding the skin once more together. In a little while the skin was filled with fruit. Again and again he ate, and as his hunger was satisfied the fruit always again filled the skin, which he was careful never to throw away or lose.

The fever of sea-roving was in the blood of the Hawaiian people in those days, and Kukali's heart burned within him with the desire to visit the far-away lands about which other men told marvelous tales and from which came strangers like to the Hawaiians in many ways.

After a while he went to the forests and selected trees approved by the omens, and with many prayers fashioned a great canoe in which to embark upon his journey. The story is not told of the days passed on the great stretches of water as he sailed on and on, guided by the sun in the day and the stars in the night, until he came to the strange lands about which he had dreamed for years.

His canoe was drawn up on the shore and he lay down for rest. Before falling asleep he secreted his magic banana in his malo, or loincloth, and then gave himself to deep slumber. His rest was troubled with strange dreams, but his weariness was great and his eyes heavy, and he could not arouse himself to meet the dangers which were swiftly surrounding him.

A great bird which lived on human flesh was the god of the land to which he had come. The name of the bird was Halulu. Each feather of its wings was provided with talons and seemed to be endowed with human powers. Nothing like this bird was ever known or seen in the beautiful Hawaiian Islands. But here in the mysterious foreign land it had its deep valley, walled in like the valley of the Arabian Nights, over which the great bird hovered looking into the depths for food. A strong wind always attended the coming of Halulu when he sought the valley for his victims.

Kukali was lifted on the wings of the bird-god and carried to this hole and quietly laid on the ground to finish his hour of deep sleep.

When Kukali awoke he found himself in the shut-in valley with many companions who had been captured by the great bird and placed in this prison hole. They had been without food and were very weak. Now and then one of the number would lie down to die. Halulu, the bird-god, would perch on a tree which grew on the edge of the precipice and let down its wing to sweep across the floor of the valley and pick up the victims lying on the ground. Those who were strong could escape the feathers as they brushed over the bottom and hide in the crevices in the walls, but day by day the weakest of the prisoners were lifted out and prepared for Halulu's feast.

Kukali pitied the helpless state of his fellow-prisoners and prepared his best incantations and prayers to help him overcome the great bird. He took his wonderful banana and fed all the people until they were very strong. He taught them how to seek stones best fitted for the manufacture of knives and hatchets. Then for days they worked until they were all well armed with sharp stone weapons.

While Kukali and his fellow-prisoners were making preparation for the final struggle, the bird-god had often come to his perch and put his wing down into the valley, brushing the feathers back and forth to catch his prey. Frequently the search was fruitless. At last he became very impatient, and sent his strongest feathers along the precipitous walls, seeking for victims.

Kukali and his companions then ran out from their hiding-places and fought the strong feathers, cutting them off and chopping them into small pieces.

Halulu cried out with pain and anger, and sent feather after feather into the prison. Soon one wing was entirely destroyed. Then the other wing was broken to pieces and the bird-god in his insane wrath put down a strong leg armed with great talons. Kukali uttered mighty invocations and prepared sacred charms for the protection of his friends.

After a fierce battle they cut off the leg and destroyed the talons. Then came the struggle with the remaining leg and claws, but Kukali's friends had become very bold. They fearlessly gathered around this enemy, hacking and pulling until the bird-god, screaming with pain, fell into the pit among the prisoners, who quickly cut the body into fragments.

The prisoners made steps in the walls, and by the aid of vines climbed out of their prison. When they had fully escaped, they gathered great piles of branches and trunks of trees and threw them into the prison until the body of the bird-god was covered. Fire was thrown down and Halulu was burned to ashes. Thus Kukali taught by his charms that Halulu could be completely destroyed.

But two of the breast feathers of the burning Halulu flew away to his sister, who lived in a great hole which had no bottom. The name of this sister was Namakaeha. She belonged to the family of Pele, the goddess of volcanic fires, who had journeyed to Hawaii and taken up her home in the crater of the volcano Kilauea.

Namakaeha smelled smoke on the feathers which came to her, and knew that her brother was dead. She also knew that he could have been conquered, only by one possessing great magical powers. So she called to his people: "Who is the great kupua [wizard] who has killed my brother? Oh, my people, keep careful watch."

Kukali was exploring all parts of the strange land in which he had already found marvelous adventures. By and by he came to the great pit in which Namakaeha lived. He could not see the bottom, so he told his companions he was going down to see what mysteries were concealed in this hole without a bottom. They made a rope of the hau tree bark. Fastening one end around his body he ordered his friends to let him down. Uttering prayers and incantations he went down and down until, owing to counter incantations of Namakaeha's priests, who had been watching, the rope broke and he fell.

Down he went swiftly, but, remembering the prayer which a falling man must use to keep him from injury, he cried, "O Ku! guard my life!"

In the ancient Hawaiian mythology there was frequent mention of 'the water of life.' Sometimes the sick bathed in it and were healed. Sometimes it was sprinkled upon the unconscious, bringing them back to life. Kukali's incantation was of great power, for it threw him into a pool of the water of life and he was saved.

One of the kahunas [priests] caring for Namakaeha was a very great wizard. He saw the wonderful preservation of Kukali and became his friend. He warned Kukali against eating anything that was ripe, because it would be poison, and even the most powerful charms could not save him.

Kukali thanked him and went out among the people. He had carefully preserved his wonderful banana skin, and was able to eat apparently ripe fruit and yet be perfectly safe.

The kahunas of Namakaeha tried to overcome him and destroy him, but he conquered them, killed those who were bad, and entered into friendship with those who were good.

At last he came to the place where the great chiefess dwelt. Here he was tested in many ways. He accepted the fruits offered him, but always ate the food in his magic banana. Thus he preserved his strength and conquered even the chiefess and married her. After living with her for a time he began to long for his old home in Hawaii. Then he persuaded her to do as her relative Pele had already done, and the family, taking their large canoe, sailed away to Hawaii, their future home.

The Story-Teller At Fault

AT THE TIME WHEN the Tuatha Dé Danann held the sovereignty of Ireland, there reigned in Leinster a king, who was remarkably fond of hearing stories. Like the other princes and chieftains of the island, he had a favourite story-teller, who held a large estate from his Majesty, on condition of telling him a new story every night of his life, before he went to sleep. Many indeed were the stories he knew, so that he had already reached a good old age without failing even for a single night in his task; and such was the skill he displayed that whatever cares of state or other annoyances might prey upon the monarch's mind, his story-teller was sure to send him to sleep.

One morning the story-teller arose early, and as his custom was, strolled out into his garden, turning over in his mind incidents which he might weave into a story for the king at night. But this morning he found himself quite at fault; after pacing his whole demesne, he returned to his house without being able to think of anything new or strange. He found no difficulty in 'there was once a king who had three sons' or 'one day the king of all Ireland,' but further than that he could not get. At length he went in to breakfast, and found his wife much perplexed at his delay.

"Why don't you come to breakfast, my dear?" said she.

"I have no mind to eat anything," replied the story-teller; "long as I have been in the service of the king of Leinster, I never sat down to breakfast without having a new story ready for the evening, bu this morning my mind is quite shut up, and I don't know what to do. I might as well lie down and die at once. I'll be disgraced for ever this evening, when the king calls for his story-teller."

Just at this moment the lady looked out of the window.

"Do you see that black thing at the end of the field?" said she.

"I do," replied her husband.

They drew nigh, and saw a miserable looking old man lying on the ground with a wooden leg placed beside him.

"Who are you, my good man?" asked the story-teller.

"Oh, then, 'tis little matter who I am. I'm a poor, old, lame, decrepit, miserable creature, sitting down here to rest awhile."

"An' what are you doing with that box and dice I see in your hand?"

"I am waiting here to see if any one will play a game with me," replied the beggar man.

"Play with you! Why what has a poor old man like you to play for?"

"I have one hundred pieces of gold in this leathern purse," replied the old man.

"You may as well play with him," said the story-teller's wife; "and perhaps you'll have something to tell the king in the evening."

A smooth stone was placed between them, and upon it they cast their throws.

It was but a little while and the story-teller lost every penny of his money.

"Much good may it do you, friend," said he. "What better hap could I look for, fool that I am!"

"Will you play again?" asked the old man.

"Don't be talking, man: you have all my money."

"Haven't you chariot and horses and hounds?"

"Well, what of them!"

"I'll stake all the money I have against thine."

"Nonsense, man! Do you think for all the money in Ireland, I'd run the risk of seeing my lady tramp home on foot?"

"Maybe you'd win," said the bocough.

"Maybe I wouldn't," said the story-teller.

"Play with him, husband," said his wife. "I don't mind walking, if you do, love."

"I never refused you before," said the story-teller, "and I won't do so now."

Down he sat again, and in one throw lost houses, hounds, and chariot.

"Will you play again?" asked the beggar.

"Are you making game of me, man; what else have I to stake?"

"I'll stake all my winnings against your wife," said the old man.

The story-teller turned away in silence, but his wife stopped him.

"Accept his offer," said she. "This is the third time, and who knows what luck you may have? You'll surely win now."

They played again, and the story-teller lost. No sooner had he done so, than to his sorrow and surprise, his wife went and sat down near the ugly old beggar.

"Is that the way you're leaving me?" said the story-teller.

"Sure I was won," said she. "You would not cheat the poor man, would you?"

"Have you any more to stake?" asked the old man.

"You know very well I have not," replied the story-teller.

"I'll stake the whole now, wife and all, against your own self," said the old man.

Again they played, and again the story-teller lost.

"Well! here I am, and what do you want with me?"

"I'll soon let you know," said the old man, and he took from his pocket a long cord and a wand.

"Now," said he to the story-teller, "what kind of animal would you rather be, a deer, a fox, or a hare? You have your choice now, but you may not have it later."

To make a long story short, the story-teller made his choice of a hare; the old man threw the cord round him, struck him with the wand, and lo! a long-eared, frisking hare was skipping and jumping on the green.

But it wasn't for long; who but his wife called the hounds, and set them on him. The hare fled, the dogs followed. Round the field ran a high wall, so that run as he might, he couldn't get out, and mightily diverted were beggar and lady to see him twist and double.

In vain did he take refuge with his wife, she kicked him back again to the hounds, until at length the beggar stopped the hounds, and with a stroke of the wand, panting and breathless, the story-teller stood before them again.

"And how did you like the sport?" said the beggar.

"It might be sport to others," replied the story-teller looking at his wife, "for my part I could well put up with the loss of it."

"Would it be asking too much," he went on to the beggar, "to know who you are at all, or where you come from, or why you take a pleasure in plaguing a poor old man like me?"

"Oh!" replied the stranger, "I'm an odd kind of good-for-little fellow, one day poor, another day rich, but if you wish to know more about me or my habits, come with me and perhaps I may show you more than you would make out if you went alone."

"I'm not my own master to go or stay," said the story-teller, with a sigh.

The stranger put one hand into his wallet and drew out of it before their eyes a well-looking middle-aged man, to whom he spoke as follows:

"By all you heard and saw since I put you into my wallet, take charge of this lady and of the carriage and horses, and have them ready for me whenever I want them."

Scarcely had he said these words when all vanished, and the story-teller found himself at the Foxes' Ford, near the castle of Red Hugh O'Donnell. He could see all but none could see him.

O'Donnell was in his hall, and heaviness of flesh and weariness of spirit were upon him.

"Go out," said he to his doorkeeper, "and see who or what may be coming."

The doorkeeper went, and what he saw was a lank, grey beggarman; half his sword bared behind his haunch, his two shoes full of cold road-a-wayish water sousing about him, the tips of his two ears out through his old hat, his two shoulders out through his scant tattered cloak, and in his hand a green wand of holly.

"Save you, O'Donnell," said the lank grey beggarman.

"And you likewise," said O'Donnell. "Whence come you, and what is your craft?"

"I come from the outmost stream of earth,
From the glens where the white swans glide,
A night in Islay, a night in Man,
A night on the cold hillside."

"It's the great traveller you are," said O'Donnell.

"Maybe you've learnt something on the road."

"I am a juggler," said the lank grey beggarman, "and for five pieces of silver you shall see a trick of mine."

"You shall have them," said O'Donnell; and the lank grey beggarman took three small straws and placed them in his hand.

"The middle one," said he, "I'll blow away; the other two I'll leave."

"Thou canst not do it," said one and all.

But the lank grey beggarman put a finger on either outside straw and, whiff, away he blew the middle one.

"'Tis a good trick," said O'Donnell; and he paid him his five pieces of silver.

"For half the money," said one of the chief's lads, "I'll do the same trick."

"Take him at his word, O'Donnell."

The lad put the three straws on his hand, and a finger on either outside straw and he blew; and what happened but that the fist was blown away with the straw.

"Thou art sore, and thou wilt be sorer," said O'Donnell.

"Six more pieces, O'Donnell, and I'll do another trick for thee," said the lank grey beggarman.

"Six shalt thou have."

"Seest thou my two ears! One I'll move but not t'other."

"'Tis easy to see them, they're big enough, but thou canst never move one ear and not the two together."

The lank grey beggarman put his hand to his ear, and he gave it a pull.

O'Donnell laughed and paid him the six pieces.

"Call that a trick," said the fistless lad, "any one can do that," and so saying, he put up his hand, pulled his ear, and what happened was that he pulled away ear and head.

"Sore thou art; and sorer thou'lt be," said O'Donnell.

"Well, O'Donnell," said the lank grey beggarman, "strange are the tricks I've shown thee, but I'll show thee a stranger one yet for the same money."

"Thou hast my word for it," said O'Donnell.

With that the lank grey beggarman took a bag from under his armpit, and from out the bag a ball of silk, and he unwound the ball and he flung it slantwise up into the clear blue heavens, and it became a ladder; then he took a hare and placed it upon the thread, and up it ran; again he took out a red-eared hound, and it swiftly ran up after the hare.

"Now," said the lank grey beggarman; "has any one a mind to run after the dog and on the course?"

"I will," said a lad of O'Donnell's.

"Up with you then," said the juggler; "but I warn you if you let my hare be killed I'll cut off your head when you come down."

The lad ran up the thread and all three soon disappeared. After looking up for a long time, the lank grey beggarman said: "I'm afraid the hound is eating the hare, and that our friend has fallen asleep."

Saying this he began to wind the thread, and down came the lad fast asleep; and down came the red-eared hound and in his mouth the last morsel of the hare.

He struck the lad a stroke with the edge of his sword, and so cast his head off. As for the hound, if he used it no worse, he used it no better.

"It's little I'm pleased, and sore I'm angered," said O'Donnell, "that a hound and a lad should be killed at my court."

"Five pieces of silver twice over for each of them," said the juggler, "and their heads shall be on them as before."

"Thou shalt get that," said O'Donnell.

Five pieces, and again five were paid him, and lo! the lad had his head and the hound his. And though they lived to the uttermost end of time, the hound would never touch a hare again, and the lad took good care to keep his eyes open.

Scarcely had the lank grey beggarman done this when he vanished from out their sight, and no one present could say if he had flown through the air or if the earth had swallowed him up.

> He moved as wave tumbling o'er wave
> As whirlwind following whirlwind,

As a furious wintry blast,
So swiftly, sprucely, cheerily,
Right proudly,
And no stop made
Until he came
To the court of Leinster's King,
He gave a cheery light leap
O'er top of turret,
Of court and city
Of Leinster's King.

Heavy was the flesh and weary the spirit of Leinster's king. 'Twas the hour he was wont to hear a story, but send he might right and left, not a jot of tidings about the story-teller could he get.

"Go to the door," said he to his doorkeeper, "and see if a soul is in sight who may tell me something about my story-teller."

The doorkeeper went, and what he saw was a lank grey beggarman, half his sword bared behind his haunch, his two old shoes full of cold road-a-wayish water sousing about him, the tips of his two ears out through his old hat, his two shoulders out through his scant tattered cloak, and in his hand a three-stringed harp.

"What canst thou do?" said the doorkeeper.

"I can play," said the lank grey beggarman.

"Never fear," added he to the story-teller, "thou shalt see all, and not a man shall see thee."

When the king heard a harper was outside, he bade him in.

"It is I that have the best harpers in the five-fifths of Ireland," said he, and he signed them to play. They did so, and if they played, the lank grey beggarman listened.

"Heardst thou ever the like?" said the king.

"Did you ever, O king, hear a cat purring over a bowl of broth, or the buzzing of beetles in the twilight, or a shrill tongued old woman scolding your head off?"

"That I have often," said the king.

"More melodious to me," said the lank grey beggarman, "were the worst of these sounds than the sweetest harping of thy harpers."

When the harpers heard this, they drew their swords and rushed at him, but instead of striking him, their blows fell on each other, and soon not a man but was cracking his neighbour's skull and getting his own cracked in turn.

When the king saw this, he thought it hard the harpers weren't content with murdering their music, but must needs murder each other.

"Hang the fellow who began it all," said he; "and if I can't have a story, let me have peace."

Up came the guards, seized the lank grey beggarman, marched him to the gallows and hanged him high and dry. Back they marched to the hall, and who should they see but the lank grey beggarman seated on a bench with his mouth to a flagon of ale.

"Never welcome you in," cried the captain of the guard, "didn't we hang you this minute, and what brings you here?"

"Is it me myself, you mean?"

"Who else?" said the captain.

"May your hand turn into a pig's foot with you when you think of tying the rope; why should you speak of hanging me?"

Back they scurried to the gallows, and there hung the king's favourite brother.

Back they hurried to the king who had fallen fast asleep.

"Please your Majesty," said the captain, "we hanged that strolling vagabond, but here he is back again as well as ever."

"Hang him again," said the king, and off he went to sleep once more.

They did as they were told, but what happened was that they found the king's chief harper hanging where the lank grey beggarman should have been.

The captain of the guard was sorely puzzled.

"Are you wishful to hang me a third time?" said the lank grey beggarman.

"Go where you will," said the captain, "and as fast as you please if you'll only go far enough. It's trouble enough you've given us already."

"Now you're reasonable," said the beggarman; "and since you've given up trying to hang a stranger because he finds fault with your music, I don't mind telling you that if you go back to the gallows you'll find your friends sitting on the sward none the worse for what has happened."

As he said these words he vanished; and the story-teller found himself on the spot where they first met, and where his wife still was with the carriage and horses.

"Now," said the lank grey beggarman, "I'll torment you no longer. There's your carriage and your horses, and your money and your wife; do what you please with them."

"For my carriage and my houses and my hounds," said the story-teller,

"I thank you; but my wife and my money you may keep."

"No," said the other. "I want neither, and as for your wife, don't think ill of her for what she did, she couldn't help it."

"Not help it! Not help kicking me into the mouth of my own hounds! Not help casting me off for the sake of a beggarly old –"

"I'm not as beggarly or as old as ye think. I am Angus of the Bruff; many a good turn you've done me with the King of Leinster. This morning my magic told me the difficulty you were in, and I made up my mind to get you out of it. As for your wife there, the power that changed your body changed her mind. Forget and forgive as man and wife should do, and now you have a story for the King of Leinster when he calls for one;" and with that he disappeared.

It's true enough he now had a story fit for a king. From first to last he told all that had befallen him; so long and loud laughed the king that he couldn't go to sleep at all. And he told the story-teller never to trouble for fresh stories, but every night as long as he lived he listened again and he laughed afresh at the tale of the lank grey beggarman.

The Wizard's Palace

LONG HUNDREDS OF YEARS AGO there was a fine palace on a mountain sloping up from the sea. It was like a palace in a dream, built of shining marble of all colours and having great doors covered with gold.

In it there lived the mighty Wizard who had made it for himself by his spells. But his hatred of other people was as great as his power, and he would not allow any person to come near him except his own servants, and they were evil spirits. If any man dared to go to see the palace, to ask for work or to beg for charity, he would never be heard of again. His friends might search for him, but they would never find him. Soon people began to whisper that some of the blocks of granite near the palace were like the men who had gone up the mountain and never came back. They began to believe that the Wizard had caught them and frozen them into grey stone. At length the Wizard became the terror of the whole island, so that no person would pass within several miles of his palace. The people of that side of the island fled from their homes, and the place was lonely and desolate.

So things went on for three years, until one day a poor man going on the houses happened to travel on that side of the island, not knowing anything of this Wizard. His road took him over the mountain, where the Wizard lived, and as he came near it, he was astonished to see the place so silent and desolate. He had been looking forward to the usual food and shelter, with the friendly welcome, but he found the houses empty ruins and the kindly country people gone. And where was the straw and hay which made such a snug bed in the barn? Weeds and stones were lying thick in the fields. Night came on him, and he walked and walked; but never a bit of shelter could he find, and he did not know where to go to get a bed. "It's a middlin' dark night," he thought; "but it's better to go on than back – a road a body is used on is no throuble to them, let it be night or not." He was travelling on the old road over the mountain, going ahead singing 'Colcheragh Raby' for company to himself, and after a long while he saw a light in the distance. The light got brighter and brighter until he came to a grand palace with every window lit up. The singing was all knocked out of him.

"In the name of Fortune where am I at all? This is a dreadful big house," he said to himself; "where did it come from, for all? Nobody never seen the like of it on this bare breas' before – else where am I at all, at all?"

He was hard set to get to the door with the blocks of stone lying about like frozen men.

"I'd swear," he said to himself as he stumbled over one, "that this was lil' Neddy Hom, the dwarf man tha's missin', only it's stone."

When he came to the big door it was locked. Through one of the windows he saw a table, and supper ready on it, but he saw no person. He was very tired and hungry, but he was afraid to knock at the door of such a fine place.

"Aw, that place is too gran' for the likes of me!" said he.

He sat down on one of the marble seats outside, saying:

"I'll stretch meself here till mornin', it's a middlin' sort of a night."

That day meat and bread had been given to him at the last town he had passed through. He was hungry and he thought he would eat, so he opened his wallet and took out a piece of bread and meat, then he put his hand into his pocket and drew out a pinch of salt in a screw of paper. As he opened the paper some grains of salt fell out, on to the ground. No sooner had this happened than up from the ground beneath came the sound of most terrible groans, high winds blew from every airt out of the heavens, lightnings flashed in the air, dreadful thunder crashed overhead, and the ground heaved beneath his feet; and he knew that there was plenty of company round him, though no man was to be seen. In less than a moment the grand palace burst into a hundred thousand bits, and vanished into the air. He found himself on a wide, lonely mountain, and in the grey light of dawn no trace of the palace was to be seen.

He went down on his knees and put up a prayer of thanksgiving for his escape, and then ran on to the next village, where he told the people all that he had seen, and glad they were to hear of the disappearance of the Wizard.

The Brazen Brogues,
or Too Many to Marry

THERE WAS A STRANGE PARTY ASSEMBLED at the young farmer Gille Macdonald's that late spring evening, the night of the tryst at Inveraray, from attending which all and sundry were making their way home to the southwards.

Though a fine dry evening, it was a bit chilly; there was still a touch of winter in the season, and so no one was too proud or too robust to join the circle round the ingle, and warm themselves by the cheerful blaze.

There was a fisherman from Strathlachlan, a drover from Kilmun, two farmers from away south about Bute, a merchant from Rothesay, and a pedlar from anywhere you please, for he was always on the road from there to somewhere else.

Each had much to say for himself about his luck or otherwise at the tryst, and they were good company; but far and away the best of them all for conversation and news was the little pedlar, who sat on the three-legged stool in the centre, and had an answer ready for each and advice for all.

The conversation turned, as likely it would (for you see they had all been bargaining and selling), on how fortunes were made or lost, and one said this, and the other said that, each one seeming to have his own view of the matter, and deeming his own way the best; but what the little pedlar remarked just before they broke up for the evening was the only thing that Gille Macdonald remembered or thought worth listening to.

For the pedlar had said in answer to how would he set to work to make his fortune, that, if he was a bit bigger, and was a younger and stronger man, he knew a place where a fortune could be got for the digging, only it needed a stouter heart and a more adventurous spirit than he possessed to attempt the search. So he for one would still stick to his pack.

After the cup had passed round for the last time, and all were moving off to the beds provided for them, Gille Macdonald gently touched the sleeve of the pedlar, and asked him if he would kindly wait a moment after the others had gone, as he wanted to ask him privately a certain question.

The pedlar was delighted to oblige so kind a host as Gille Macdonald, and said he certainly would.

So when the kitchen was clear of company, Gille Macdonald drew the little pedlar towards the ingle, and filling his glass once more, begged him to be seated, and if it so pleased him, to say what he meant by the place where a fortune was to be had for the digging, if only a brave heart and a stout spirit were there to attempt the deed.

"Oh!" replied the little pedlar, "that is it, is it? Well, the place I mean is over on the west side of Kintyre, a day's journey from here on horseback. Across the loch and by the road over the ridge from Tarbert, there is the castle of Taychronan, inhabited by an evil old gentleman who is reputed to be eminently rich; and that that is not a mere rumour I myself know, for he has a treasure buried in the well in the garden. With these two eyes I saw him shovelling in ducats and gold pieces just as if they were potatoes, only a month ago. I would have liked much to have secured some of them, but you know what a fragile little fellow I am, and I was too much afraid of the old gentleman to do anything of the kind.

"Now, don't let me induce you to go after the treasure; you are comfortably off, and can want nothing more than what you have got already. I should be sorry if you fell into the old gentleman's clutches, for evil things are spoken of him, and he is said to be not only a selfish old miser, but a powerful magician, and a cruel as well. Now, good night," and the pedlar walked off to his couch.

In the morning the whole party of the night before left the farm, thanking their host, and going their several ways. As to the pedlar, he had started at cock-crow, to be early on the road, so Gille Macdonald had no further chance to question him about the castle and the treasure, of which he had dreamed all night, waking up in the morning quite determined to investigate, and, if possible, secure it.

So he occupied himself that day in putting his farm in order, and gave instructions to his head servant that this and that should be done in his absence, and this and that should be done if he never came back at all; and this preparation finished, the very next morning he saddled his grey mare and took the road that led to the nearest ferry on Loch Fyne side.

The crossing was accomplished successfully, for it was fine weather for the time of the year, while a light breeze and sunny sky put him in good spirits for his adventure.

A fair was being held at Tarbert when he arrived there; booths were erected up and down the streets, and music and dancing were going on by the shore. There also many people were gathered together from the surrounding country, with mountebanks and singers and such like turning an honest penny among the crowd.

One little chap in especial Gille Macdonald could not help observing with interest, for he would throw three or four somersaults on the hard pavement without stopping – yes, and could throw them backwards and forwards at pleasure for what trifle the spectators might fling him in his upturned hat after each performance.

Amongst others the mannikin approached Gille as well.

"Well, then, a copper you must be satisfied with, small friend," said Gille Macdonald; "I can't give you more, for we are both seeking a fortune, I see, in our different ways."

"How so, friend?" said the mannikin. "Where and how do you seek a fortune?"

"With a strong arm and a stout heart," said Gille Macdonald. "I hope to get a fortune by digging;" and he passed up the street.

"Stay," said the mannikin, running after him; "where did you say a fortune was to be got for the digging?"

Well, Gille Macdonald did not like to be interrogated further, and in fact he was angry with himself for having been led to speak of his adventure at all; but he did not wish to seem rude to a poor little mite, so he said, "Oh, not far away; over the hills to the west. Good night."

"Good night," said the dwarf; and Gille Macdonald thought there was a queer tone in the way it was muttered, and somehow he did not like it at all; but everything was soon forgotten in the enjoyment of good company at the inn, where, the host being an old friend of his, he put up for the night.

Early next morning he was astir, and saddled his mare, giving her a good feed, for she had a long journey before her, and he wished to reach Castle Taychronan before nightfall, so that he might be able to have a look round unknown to the old man, and to find out where the well was situated.

As he journeyed on his thoughts naturally turned to the adventure before him, and in a brown study he let the mare jog along as she chose, taking no heed of anything till, with a start, he was aroused by a squeaky little voice beside him, which struck him as strangely familiar. Looking down, he was aware of a little man walking by his side, with a face exactly like the mannikin's he had seen at the fair the day before.

Yet it could not be the same, for that one was so very small and humpbacked, while this, though a wee bit creature, was not anything out of the run of little men. Yet he had the same hunch on his back, the same long pointed red nose and queer squint as had his acquaintance of the fair – yes, and his very voice too, only louder and stronger.

"Well met," quoth the little man.

"Well met," said Gille Macdonald.

"We are fellow-travellers, I see," said the wee man.

"For the present, yes," said Gille Macdonald, and he urged his mare on along the road.

"We'll meet again, maybe, before long," cried the wee man after him.

Now it made Gille Macdonald laugh to think such a crippled creature would ever catch him up again; but something about the dwarf he did not like, and he was not comfortable till he had galloped on a mile, and had lost sight of him.

It was about noon, and Gille Macdonald was giving his mare a quiet walk down that part of the highroad which, having kept to the upper moorland for some miles, here makes a rapid descent towards the sea again at Ronachan Bay. What was his astonishment to hear again the now familiar voice calling to him from the other side of the dyke, and before he regained his composure he saw the old, ugly face peering at him from behind a stunted willow, whose twisted roots crept in and out like snakes among the stonework.

"Well met," quoth the creature; and this time that which accosted him was a full-grown man just about his own size, and Gille Macdonald was not a small man by any means.

Gille Macdonald could not believe his eyes. There was the long red nose, and the squinting eyes, and the round bumpy back, but six foot the creature was if an inch. It could not be the same; but that it had some uncanny connections with the mannikin he met at Tarbert, and again already that morning, he felt certain.

You may be sure he liked the meeting less than ever; even his docile old mare shied on one side as the thing now stepped into the middle of the road. But Gille Macdonald thought civility could do no harm, so he gave him good-day as before.

"We are fellow-travellers, I see," said the thing, and he squinted horribly with his ugly eyes.

"For the present, yes," said Gille Macdonald; "but I must be jogging on," and he struck spurs into the mare.

"We'll meet again, maybe, before long," said the man.

It did not need much to make the mare go along the road at a good rate, and not for a while did Gille Macdonald feel the eerie thrill leave him; but young spirits are not easily upset for long, so before an hour had passed he was singing as blithely as before.

It's a long, straight bit of road from Ballochroy to Tayinloan, as every one knows who has made the journey, and at evening, just as Gille Macdonald chanced to be entering upon it, the sun was at his back, and he could see a long way down before him, with everything standing out very clearly.

"What a funny thing," said he, "for people to have planted a tree there right in the middle of the road!" for a little bit ahead there was what seemed to him a young fir-tree sticking up straight before him. "They do odd things in this part of the country, surely." But you may imagine what his astonishment was when he saw the thing move along in the direction in which he was going. He rubbed his eyes, and thought it must be some trick of light and shade. It couldn't be a human being! – yes, it was! and then the strange things he had seen that day flashed upon his mind, and he felt sure this was again another of the same nasty crew he had so wished to avoid.

"I shall most decidedly turn back," said he, and he was giving the rein a pull to one side when the gaunt figure in front turned round, and, stepping to one side, took off its hat with a low bow, and with the same voice as he had heard before said –

"Well met."

"Well met," said Gille Macdonald, shivering all over.

"Pray pass on," said the tall man; "we are fellow-travellers, I see;" and he rolled his squint eyes and shook his long red nose in a fearsome manner.

"For the present, yes," faltered Gille Macdonald. "But, excuse me; I must be pressing on," and he urged his steed past the creature, for now it was just as bad to go backward as forward.

"We'll meet again, maybe," cried the tall man after him, as Gille Macdonald sped along the straight road; for both man and beast were thoroughly frightened by this time, and they wanted to put as much country between themselves and that ugsome thing as they could.

Gille Macdonald did not forget the apparition this time, or his saying they would maybe meet again. At every turn he expected something terrible to appear; under every rock he thought he saw some horrid shape lurking, and ready to pounce. The evening also became dark and lowering, which added to his fears. The sun had set, and a fitful moonlight, now bright, now dark, made everything look larger and grimmer than it would appear by day. The trees by the roadside took fantastic shapes, and seemed to stretch out their arms fiercely over the path, with eager claws ready to seize him; in every sigh of the wind he heard again the croaky, familiar voice; in every echo of his mare's hoofs a weird footfall rang behind him.

Suddenly he came to a spot where the road seemingly had no outlet – rocks on this side, rocks on that, "Yet there must be some way through," thought he, "or the road would not lead this way," and he urged his horse forward into the darkness. A plunge! His faithful steed reared high in air, and, throwing his master, coursed back down the road, screaming with fear.

"Well met," said from somewhere above him the voice Gille Macdonald knew too well; and as he lay bruised on the road, he saw in the moonlight a gigantic figure blocking up the whole pass between the two steep rocks through which the road stretched beyond.

"Well met," again said the voice. "But you don't seem to have a civil answer for me as before;" for Gille Macdonald was so terrified his tongue stuck in his jaws, and he could not reply. "I said maybe we would meet again, and, by my troth, the pleasure seems to be all on my side."

"With your permission," said Gille Macdonald, gasping for breath, "I will now go and see if I can find my horse."

"With my permission you shall do nothing of the sort," replied the figure. "You have come a long way to see my castle, and within it you shall rest this night. Ay, and for many a night to come, for the matter of that."

"Your castle?" said Gille Macdonald. "What do you mean by that?"

"Where gold can be got for the digging: is it not so?" said the voice. "Come, you thief, you hypocrite, you wretched slave! know I am the magician, and Castle Taychronan is my home. There you shall have the digging you looked for, as my slave during your lifetime, with the digging of your own grave at the end of it."

Poor Gille Macdonald had not a word to say, so the giant – for he was a giant indeed of twenty feet by this time – took him up from the road and carried him by his waistbelt to the castle, which was a couple of miles off. Yet the journey only occupied but little time, for the giant's strides were long, and he was in a hurry to get home.

When they arrived at the castle gate he set Gille Macdonald down on the ground, and, putting his head down, he said a queer word below the lintel, and immediately, from being a giant over twenty feet high, he dwindled to the size of a man of seven feet or thereabouts, after which transformation he turned round and drove Gille Macdonald into the castle before him with a cudgel.

They entered now a large and lofty hall, roofed with black oak, dark and grim with smoke and age. There was spread some supper on an oaken board, huge and vast, fit for a giant; while on an open hearth blazed a great fire of pine logs, which lit the hall with a fitful gleam. In its ruddy light Gille Macdonald observed that the only furniture, besides the table and a huge couch in the corner, was five oaken presses set along the wall, all with panels carved in quaint devices, and hinges and locks of burnished brass.

"Serve my dinner," said the giant; "and be quick about it."

Gille Macdonald did so without any demur. He was getting his wits together as best he could, so he did his best to please in the meantime, meditating the while on his unfortunate fate, and wondering whether there was any chance of escape. An idea soon came into his head, and while handing a beaker of wine to the giant, he got up in a chair behind him, and held it for some moments right over his head.

"What are you doing? what are you up to?" said the giant. "What the mischief makes you hold it up there in that way?"

"Oh, I beg your pardon, I'm sure," explained Gille Macdonald; "you see I'm so accustomed –"

"Accustomed to what?" asked the giant sharply.

"To hand the cup to my master at home in this way; he likes me to hold it as near his mouth as he can."

"But that's ridiculously high," said the giant.

"Not a bit of it," explained Gille Macdonald; you are not the only giant in the kingdom." "Oh, ah!" said the giant, a bit taken by surprise.

Then, recovering himself, he said, "He must be a queer creature; but see you, I won't have any of your silly tricks here; so behave."

"You won't be troubled with them very long," said Gille.

"What d'ye mean by that?" said the giant.

"Only that my master will soon be here to take me away."

"Take you away when you are in my house! I'd like to see any one do that," remarked the giant with a snort.

"So should I," said Gille Macdonald; "and he will, too."

The giant got up with a bounce and went to the fire, where for a space he stood buried in thought. Meanwhile Gille Macdonald did not see any reason why he should not have a bit of the pasty and a sup of the wine; but he did not get long to do it, for the giant, turning round, said, as if to relieve his mind, "Well, he can't find you here, for he don't know where to look for you."

"Your attention, Sir, for a moment," said Gille Macdonald. "Do you see these brogues of mine? well, look at the heels; they are shod with brass. All my master's servants, men, women, and cattle, are shod with shoes of this description, so wherever they go, there he can trace them to the world's end."

"What sort of person do you say your master is?" said the giant, feigning composure.

"Oh! I can't be bothered to explain," said Gille Macdonald, plucking up his spirits as he saw the giant was losing his. "You'll see for yourself presently; he'll be here before to-morrow evening, most likely, and not in the best humour, either."

At this the giant got still more subdued, and said, "Oh! it does not matter, of course, to me whether your master comes or not; but just tell me, is he as big a man as I was when we met in the pass? I'm not curious, but I only want to know."

"Is that the very biggest you can make yourself?" said Gille Macdonald, not to be taken off his guard.

"Yes," said the giant, "it is, and bigger than what you've been accustomed to."

At this Gille Macdonald burst out laughing.

"You'll excuse me," said he, "but you'll be like a baby beside him, if that's all you can do."

At this the giant, in a great state of trepidation, again strode to the fireplace, and kicked the blazing logs about from one side of the hearth to the other in a most vicious manner, just to hide the fright he was now in.

"I think you had better be off at once," said he.

"I wish I had never seen your ugly face."

"That's not very civil," said Gille Macdonald, "especially as you were so very anxious for my acquaintance on the road here."

"Get out of the place this minute!" roared the giant. "Here's a piece to drink my health with, if you will only be quiet, and go."

Gille Macdonald took the piece and made for the door; but he was only pretending, for he saw now the giant was completely cowed, and he had no intention of leaving the castle without some treasure after all his troubles; so he turned round, just as he was leaving the hall, and said, "It is really very good of you to give me this piece, and to send me home; it is more than I would have expected, so I think it is only civil to tell you that whether I go or stay my master will come here after me, as once on the trail of the brazen brogues he never leaves it, so you had better be prepared. Hush! there, don't you hear that?" as a gust of wind swept round the tower; "there he is blowing his nose! Oh! don't alarm yourself; he is miles and miles off still."

"Come in and sit down," said the giant, "and I will make it worth your while to tell me how I can escape the notice of your master; for he seems to be an irascible kind of fellow, and I should not like a quarrel to take place with any friend of yours in my own house."

"Well," said Gille Macdonald, "just you hide till he has come and gone. But stay, I don't see how you are to do that; you're so very big."

"I'll get into that corner by the door," said the giant.

"Get into that corner?" cried Gille Macdonald.

"How can you with your size, indeed?"

"How can I?" roared the giant. "I'd have you to know there is no can or cannot in this house for me;" and he went behind the door and said a very queer word, and there the giant was about five feet high instantly, just the right size for the hiding-place.

"Oh," said Gille Macdonald, "that won't do at all; my master will be poking about all over the place. That's the worst of him, he is so curious, and will be certain to find you out."

"Rot his curiosity!" said the giant. "Then under the table will do," and he put his head under the table and said a very, very queer word, and in an instant there he was, just small enough to stand under the table.

"That's better," said Gille Macdonald, and he walked to the end of the hall. "But no; I can see you easily from here, and my master has such plaguy sharp eyes."

"Plaguy sharp eyes! Plague take them and you too! I wont diminish another inch to please anybody."

"Hush, hush!" said Gille Macdonald, as a louder gust of wind whirled round the castle; "there he is, still a good mile off; but coming fast, and oh! what a cold he's got in his nose! Just make the best of it. But don't blame me if he wrings your neck."

Then the giant rushed out from under the table and said a very, very, very queer word under the footstool, and there he was, sure enough, six inches high, a tiny mannikin squinting at Gille Macdonald from between its two legs.

"I really think be cannot see you there," said Gille Macdonald, "though he is most inquisitive, and does kick things about; so let's see, to make quite sure," and saying this, he gave the footstool a kick with his foot. "No, it won't do; I saw you then quite clearly when the stool moved. Can't you get under something smaller?"

"No, not for you or for your vile master," squeaked the mannikin. "I won't, I won't, I won't!"

"Then take the consequences! There he is at the door," as a fierce gust of wind roared down the chimney. "His nose will be as red as yours if he goes on blowing it at that rate."

Without a word the mannikin crawled out from under the footstool, and scrambling to the hearth, he said a very, very, very, very queer word under the hearthstone, and there he was in a moment, as small as a black beetle.

"Where have you got to?" said Gille Macdonald.

"Under the hearthstone," chirruped the mannikin.

"Nonsense; I can see you still under the footstool," replied Gille Macdonald.

"You can't," said the mannikin. "I'm under the hearthstone."

"Don't tell me lies!" said Gille Macdonald, "or I'll tell my master."

"Then will this satisfy you?" squeaked the mannikin, and a little, ugly black beetle crawled out from under the hearthstone. "Do you see me now? Are you satisfied now?" said he.

"I'm perfectly satisfied," said Gille Macdonald, and he put his foot on the beetle, and squish, sqrunch! there was nothing but a black patch seen on the floor.

"Well, that's over," and Gille Macdonald sank with a sigh of relief into the giant's chair.

But with a bang all the five doors of the five presses opened, and before he could say with your leave or by your leave, Gille Macdonald found himself surrounded by five maidens in seagreen-coloured attire, who clasped him round the neck and arms, kissing, tickling, and nearly throttling him, all the time laughing and giggling like wild lunatics.

"Have done! be off! Away with you, saucy wenches! Get off, I say!" choked Gille Macdonald, struggling to be free; but the more he pushed and kicked the closer they hung round about him and embraced him. What would have been the end of it I don't know, if he had not, with a violent effort, got clear, and, flying to the corner of the hall, he stood at bay with the giant's footstool held out before him in defence,

"Keep your distance," cried he. "I'll give the first one who comes within a foot of me a nasty smack, I vow I will!" and he whirled the footstool round and round in a circle in front of him.

And there were the five maidens dancing, laughing, kissing their hands to him, and kicking up their legs in a manner he had never seen before.

"Come out of the corner, you coward you!" cried they. "You call yourself a man, and go on in that way? Bah! ugh!" And oh! what faces they made when they said "Ugh!"

"I'll not come out or put the stool down," said Gille Macdonald, "till you promise to behave – that's flat. What is your business? tell me, go about it, and let me go about mine."

"That's just where it is; your business is ours," said they, "and whatever you have to go about, we must go about too. You've got to marry us all, so it is no use fretting about what must be."

"What can't be, you mean," said he. "All of you, did you say? What's the meaning of that? and don't all speak at once," for they began screeching and screaming together in return.

"Well," said the eldest, "look here. Now can we or you help it? We are the King of Loch Lin's daughters, and we have been locked up in those cupboards for three mortal years, because we vowed we would not marry that giant; and we must marry you, because we also vowed that whoever let us out should be our husband. You would not have us forswear ourselves, would you?"

"Well, if that's the case," said Gille Macdonald, "sit down quietly at that table, and we'll talk over the matter seriously; but mind, any misbehaviour, and I will bang each of you over the head."

So they promised to sit quietly at the table if he came out and sat at the end.

So they did, and so he did; but he kept the stool at easy reach of his hand, all the same.

After a great deal of arguing he explained that it was quite impossible for him to marry them all, but that they must choose which of the five should represent the others, and then he would see if anything could be done.

Then it was decided that the green maidens should play for a husband, and whoever won should be his wife. So they took the giant's dambrod from the top of the chimney-piece, and for two hours did they play; but such was the cheating and contriving that none won and none lost. So they said it was evident that he must marry them all.

"No," said Gille Macdonald; "this is ridiculous, and, what is more, it's getting late, and will be next morning very soon. Try each of you a cast of the dice, and we will see if it can be managed that way, perhaps."

So they took the bones and boxes from above the chimney, and threw for a husband; but they all cheated so and contrived so, that none won and none lost. So they said now he must marry them all, whatever he said or thought.

"No," said he, "I won't; but do get me some supper, I'm so famished, and then I'll tell you how we will settle it."

So they got his supper, and sat down, waiting, round the giant's table.

"This is the trial," said Gille Macdonald, when he had finished and collected his thoughts a bit. "Tomorrow I will ask you what colour I would my future bride should be dressed in, and whoever names the colour to my taste she shall be my wife. You can't cheat or contrive about that, I fancy."

"Very well," said the green maidens; but the youngest put a draught in Gille Macdonald's cup, when he was not looking, a potion that would make him dream – yes, and speak in his dream too. "Surely now he will tell us the secrets of his mind," said she.

After draining the cup, Gille Macdonald went and lay down before the fire on the giant's couch, and the green maidens made as if they were going upstairs, after giving him good-night; but as soon as he was fast asleep, they crept back into the room, and hid themselves about the room, waiting for what would come to pass.

Sure enough, very soon the draught began to take effect, and he dreamed of his farm and the hillsides of Strachur, speaking out aloud in his dreaming –

"Yellow is the corn in the glen of Ardkinglas;
And yellow is the bracken on the sides of Ben Ima;
Yellow is the hair of my loved one,
And yellow shall be the dye for her kirtle."

Then the green maidens arose, and with a low laugh they left the hall.

The next morning the sun shone through the window and woke Gille Macdonald, but not before the green maidens had come. down and prepared the breakfast; for they were so pleased at their liberty, their cheats, and contrivances, that whether the sun intended to get up or not, they did, and indeed, I don't think they closed an eye all night.

"Put your question," said the green maidens, when they perceived he was awake.

And Gille Macdonald put the question concerning the colour of his bride's robes to each in turn, and they all answered, "Yellow."

At this Gille Macdonald was so taken aback it was no use his saying they had not guessed right, for his looks said so.

"There now," said they; "you see there is no help for it; you must marry us all."

"Now, really," said Gille Macdonald, "in such a serious business you must give me another chance. But once more I will try you, and if that does not succeed, well, we'll see about it."

So the green maidens said they would have one more trial, and that in all conscience must be the very last; and they laughed together, for they felt quite confident of the result, and as they looked upon Gille Macdonald as a sort of fool to be easily taken in.

"Well, listen," said he; "whoever can tell me what favour it was the cod-fish of Ardminish asked of the widow woman of Gigha, that one I shall marry."

Then they said, "We must go out into the garden and think about the answer for a moment,"

"Do so," said Gille Macdonald, "and I will give you five hours for consideration."

So off they went; but, bless you, he knew perfectly well they had gone off to the Loch to see if the cod-fish would tell them for a consideration what favour he asked of the widow woman.

"Now is my chance," quoth Gille Macdonald, and he went without loss of time to the well in the garden, where he found, sure enough, the treasure the old pedlar had told him about. Having filled his wallet, without good-day or with your leave or by your leave to anything or anybody, he went straight out of the door and took the road home.

"Oh, if I could only find my dear old grey mare," he sighed, "how pleased I should be! Ah, then I should feel safe from these bold wenches."

Scarcely were the words out of his mouth, when, turning a corner, he saw his old grey mare grazing by the roadside, and at his call she came whinnying up to him; and I can't say which of the two was the gladder to meet with the other.

On her back he vaulted, and away towards Tarbert they galloped. His heart was as light as his wallet was full; and the mare's head being turned homewards, both were in a hurry, so there was no need for whip or spur. Nor did he wait at Tarbert that evening, but for a large sum (what was money to him now?) begot the ferryman to take him across there and then; and by midnight he was at his own hearthside, with his mare in her cosy stable.

Next morning he was out and about with his servants, so eager was he to begin improving his farm with his new wealth, and he worked, and kept his gillies working, till the evening star came and winked at the sun setting over Ben Dearg.

Then it was that, as he rested, leaning over the gate at the end of the field, he thought he heard voices up the road, and looking along there, what should he see about a mile off but five figures in green coming towards him, dancing, gesticulating, and chattering in a most unusual manner! No need, too, for him to ponder what visitors these might be, or what their errand was; so calling to his oldest and ugliest hind, he bade him cover himself with his plaid, and sit down by the hearth with a porridge bowl in his hands, just as if he were supping brose. Then running to the stable, he cut off a foot of his grey mare's tail, which he plaited over the forehead of the hind, letting it fall in grizzly ringlets over his nose.

"Now mind," said he, "to any visitors who chance to come, say you are the goodwife of the house, and ask them their business. As for myself, I will hide behind the peat-stack yonder, and bide the issue." In less time than I write this, there was a rare tapping at the door, and as the hind bid them enter the five green maidens hurried into the house.

"Is the goodman at home?" said the five green maidens, all at once.

"No; but I'm the goodwife, and may I ask you what is your business?"

At this answer the five green maidens stood for a moment transfixed with rage and wonder, then, shrieking aloud, they gathered up their coats and fled helter-skelter from the house down the road to the loch, and were seen no more.

So Gille Macdonald lived ever afterwards a life of wealth and comfort; and if he is not married yet, he can't say it is for the want of offers, can he?

Tales of Merlin

MERLIN IS A KEY FIGURE in the tales of King Arthur and the knights of the Round Table. Shown in different interpretations of the mythology as everything from a madman to a bard, prophet and seer, the most familiar version of Merlin to contemporary audiences is that of a wizard.

The following select chapters from Thomas Malory's *Le Morte d'Arthur* give an insight into this famed magician's character and his place in the greater Arthurian mythology.

The first three chapters reveal Merlin's role in the birth of the child who will later be his King…

Book I, Chapter I
How Uther Pendragon Sent for the Duke of Cornwall and Igraine his Wife, and of their Departing Suddenly Again

IT BEFELL IN THE DAYS OF UTHER PENDRAGON, when he was king of all England, and so reigned, that there was a mighty duke in Cornwall that held war against him long time. And the duke was called the Duke of Tintagil. And so by means King Uther sent for this duke, charging him to bring his wife with him, for she was called a fair lady, and a passing wise, and her name was called Igraine.

So when the duke and his wife were come unto the king, by the means of great lords they were accorded both. The king liked and loved this lady well, and he made them great cheer out of measure, and desired to have lain by her. But she was a passing good woman, and would not assent unto the king. And then she told the duke her husband, and said, "I suppose that we were sent for that I should be dishonoured; wherefore, husband, I counsel you, that we depart from hence suddenly, that we may ride all night unto our own castle."

And in like wise as she said so they departed, that neither the king nor none of his council were ware of their departing. All so soon as King Uther knew of their departing so suddenly, he was wonderly wroth. Then he called to him his privy council, and told them of the sudden departing of the duke and his wife.

Then they advised the king to send for the duke and his wife by a great charge; and if he will not come at your summons, then may ye do your best, then have ye cause to make mighty war upon him. So that was done, and the messengers had their answers; and that was this shortly, that neither he nor his wife would not come at him.

Then was the king wonderly wroth. And then the king sent him plain word again, and bade him be ready and stuff him and garnish him, for within forty days he would fetch him out of the biggest castle that he hath.

When the duke had this warning, anon he went and furnished and garnished two strong castles of his, of the which the one hight Tintagil, and the other castle hight Terrabil. So his wife Dame Igraine he put in the castle of Tintagil, and himself he put in the castle of Terrabil, the which had many issues and posterns out. Then in all haste came Uther with a great host, and laid a siege about the castle of Terrabil. And there he pight many pavilions, and there was great war made on both parties, and much people slain. Then for pure anger and for great love of fair Igraine the king Uther fell sick. So came to the king Uther Sir Ulfius, a noble knight, and asked the king why he was sick.

"I shall tell thee," said the king, "I am sick for anger and for love of fair Igraine, that I may not be whole."

"Well, my lord," said Sir Ulfius, "I shall seek Merlin, and he shall do you remedy, that your heart shall be pleased."

So Ulfius departed, and by adventure he met Merlin in a beggar's array, and there Merlin asked Ulfius whom he sought. And he said he had little ado to tell him.

"Well," said Merlin, "I know whom thou seekest, for thou seekest Merlin; therefore seek no farther, for I am he; and if King Uther will well reward me, and be sworn unto me to fulfil my desire, that shall be his honour and profit more than mine; for I shall cause him to have all his desire."

"All this will I undertake," said Ulfius, "that there shall be nothing reasonable but thou shalt have thy desire."

"Well," said Merlin, "he shall have his intent and desire. And therefore," said Merlin, "ride on your way, for I will not be long behind."

Book I, Chapter II
How Uther Pendragon Made War on the Duke of Cornwall, and How by the Mean of Merlin He Lay by the Duchess and Gat Arthur

THEN ULFIUS WAS GLAD, and rode on more than a pace till that he came to King Uther Pendragon, and told him he had met with Merlin.

"Where is he?" said the king.

"Sir," said Ulfius, "he will not dwell long."

Therewithal Ulfius was ware where Merlin stood at the porch of the pavilion's door. And then Merlin was bound to come to the king. When King Uther saw him, he said he was welcome.

"Sir," said Merlin, "I know all your heart every deal; so ye will be sworn unto me as ye be a true king anointed, to fulfil my desire, ye shall have your desire."

Then the king was sworn upon the Four Evangelists.

"Sir," said Merlin, "this is my desire: the first night that ye shall lie by Igraine ye shall get a child on her, and when that is born, that it shall be delivered to me for to nourish there as I will have it; for it shall be your worship, and the child's avail, as mickle as the child is worth."

"I will well," said the king, "as thou wilt have it."

"Now make you ready," said Merlin, "this night ye shall lie with Igraine in the castle of Tintagil; and ye shall be like the duke her husband, Ulfius shall be like Sir Brastias, a knight of the duke's, and I will be like a knight that hight Sir Jordanus, a knight of the duke's. But wait ye make not many questions with her nor her men, but say ye are diseased, and so hie you to bed, and rise not on the morn till I come to you, for the castle of Tintagil is but ten miles hence."

So this was done as they devised. But the duke of Tintagil espied how the king rode from the siege of Terrabil, and therefore that night he issued out of the castle at a postern for to have distressed the king's host. And so, through his own issue, the duke himself was slain or ever the king came at the castle of Tintagil.

So after the death of the duke, King Uther lay with Igraine more than three hours after his death, and begat on her that night Arthur, and on day came Merlin to the king, and bade him make him ready, and so he kissed the lady Igraine and departed in all haste. But when the lady heard tell of the duke her husband, and by all record he was dead or ever King Uther came to her, then she marvelled who that might be that lay with her in likeness of her lord; so she mourned privily and held her peace. Then all the barons by one assent prayed the king of accord betwixt the lady

Igraine and him; the king gave them leave, for fain would he have been accorded with her. So the king put all the trust in Ulfius to entreat between them, so by the entreaty at the last the king and she met together.

"Now will we do well," said Ulfius, "our king is a lusty knight and wifeless, and my lady Igraine is a passing fair lady; it were great joy unto us all, an it might please the king to make her his queen."

Unto that they all well accorded and moved it to the king. And anon, like a lusty knight, he assented thereto with good will, and so in all haste they were married in a morning with great mirth and joy.

And King Lot of Lothian and of Orkney then wedded Margawse that was Gawaine's mother, and King Nentres of the land of Garlot wedded Elaine. All this was done at the request of King Uther. And the third sister Morgan le Fay was put to school in a nunnery, and there she learned so much that she was a great clerk of necromancy. And after she was wedded to King Uriens of the land of Gore, that was Sir Ewain's le Blanchemain's father.

Book I, Chapter III
Of the Birth of King Arthur and of His Nurture

THEN QUEEN IGRAINE waxed daily greater and greater, so it befell after within half a year, as King Uther lay by his queen, he asked her, by the faith she owed to him, whose was the body; then she sore abashed to give answer.

"Dismay you not," said the king, "but tell me the truth, and I shall love you the better, by the faith of my body."

"Sir," said she, "I shall tell you the truth. The same night that my lord was dead, the hour of his death, as his knights record, there came into my castle of Tintagil a man like my lord in speech and in countenance, and two knights with him in likeness of his two knights Brastias and Jordanus, and so I went unto bed with him as I ought to do with my lord, and the same night, as I shall answer unto God, this child was begotten upon me."

"That is truth," said the king, "as ye say; for it was I myself that came in the likeness, and therefore dismay you not, for I am father of the child"; and there he told her all the cause, how it was by Merlin's counsel. Then the queen made great joy when she knew who was the father of her child.

Soon came Merlin unto the king, and said, "Sir, ye must purvey you for the nourishing of your child."

"As thou wilt," said the king, "be it."

"Well," said Merlin, "I know a lord of yours in this land, that is a passing true man and a faithful, and he shall have the nourishing of your child, and his name is Sir Ector, and he is a lord of fair livelihood in many parts in England and Wales; and this lord, Sir Ector, let him be sent for, for to come and speak with you, and desire him yourself, as he loveth you, that he will put his own child to nourishing to another woman, and that his wife nourish yours. And when the child is born let it be delivered to me at yonder privy postern unchristened."

So like as Merlin devised it was done. And when Sir Ector was come he made fiaunce to the king for to nourish the child like as the king desired; and there the king granted Sir Ector great rewards. Then when the lady was delivered, the king commanded two knights and two ladies to take the child, bound in a cloth of gold, and that ye deliver him to what poor man ye meet at the postern gate of the castle. So the child was delivered unto Merlin, and so he bare it forth unto Sir Ector, and made an holy man to christen him, and named him Arthur; and so Sir Ector's wife nourished him with her own pap.

LATER, WE SEE AN UNUSUAL ENCOUNTER between Arthur and Merlin, and a glimpse of the wizard's remarkable abilities.

Book I, Chapter XX
How King Pellinore Took Arthur's Horse and Followed the Questing Beast, and How Merlin Met with Arthur

"SIR KNIGHT," SAID THE KING, "leave that quest, and suffer me to have it, and I will follow it another twelvemonth."

"Ah, fool," said the knight unto Arthur, "it is in vain thy desire, for it shall never be achieved but by me, or my next kin."

Therewith he started unto the king's horse and mounted into the saddle, and said, "Gramercy, this horse is my own."

"Well," said the king, "thou mayst take my horse by force, but an I might prove thee whether thou were better on horseback or I."

"– Well," said the knight, "seek me here when thou wilt, and here nigh this well thou shalt find me, and so passed on his way."

Then the king sat in a study, and bade his men fetch his horse as fast as ever they might. Right so came by him Merlin like a child of fourteen year of age, and saluted the king, and asked him why he was so pensive.

"I may well be pensive," said the king, "for I have seen the marvellest sight that ever I saw."

"That know I well," said Merlin, "as well as thyself, and of all thy thoughts, but thou art but a fool to take thought, for it will not amend thee. Also I know what thou art, and who was thy father, and of whom thou wert begotten; King Uther Pendragon was thy father, and begat thee on Igraine."

"That is false," said King Arthur, "how shouldest thou know it, for thou art not so old of years to know my father?"

"Yes," said Merlin, "I know it better than ye or any man living."

"I will not believe thee," said Arthur, and was wroth with the child.

So departed Merlin, and came again in the likeness of an old man of fourscore year of age, whereof the king was right glad, for he seemed to be right wise.

Then said the old man, "Why are ye so sad?"

"I may well be heavy," said Arthur, "for many things. Also here was a child, and told me many things that meseemeth he should not know, for he was not of age to know my father."

"Yes," said the old man, "the child told you truth, and more would he have told you an ye would have suffered him. But ye have done a thing late that God is displeased with you, for ye have lain by your sister, and on her ye have gotten a child that shall destroy you and all the knights of your realm."

"What are ye," said Arthur, "that tell me these tidings?"

"I am Merlin, and I was he in the child's likeness."

"Ah," said King Arthur, "ye are a marvellous man, but I marvel much of thy words that I must die in battle."

"Marvel not," said Merlin, "for it is God's will your body to be punished for your foul deeds; but I may well be sorry," said Merlin, "for I shall die a shameful death, to be put in the earth quick, and ye shall die a worshipful death."

And as they talked this, came one with the king's horse, and so the king mounted on his horse, and Merlin on another, and so rode unto Carlion. And anon the king asked Ector and Ulfius how he was begotten, and they told him Uther Pendragon was his father and Queen Igraine his mother.

Then he said to Merlin, "I will that my mother be sent for that I may speak with her; and if she say so herself then will I believe it."

In all haste, the queen was sent for, and she came and brought with her Morgan le Fay, her daughter, that was as fair a lady as any might be, and the king welcomed Igraine in the best manner.

MERLIN'S POWERS AS A HEALER come to the fore in the following chapter, when he uses his powers of enchantment to heal King Arthur, who has been gravely injured in battle.

Book I, Chapter XXIV
How Merlin Saved Arthur's Life, and Threw an Enchantment on King Pellinore and Made Him to Sleep

THEREWITHAL CAME MERLIN and said, "Knight, hold thy hand, for an thou slay that knight thou puttest this realm in the greatest damage that ever was realm: for this knight is a man of more worship than thou wotest of."

"Why, who is he?" said the knight.

"It is King Arthur."

Then would he have slain him for dread of his wrath, and heaved up his sword, and therewith Merlin cast an enchantment to the knight, that he fell to the earth in a great sleep. Then Merlin took up King Arthur, and rode forth on the knight's horse.

"Alas!" said Arthur, "What hast thou done, Merlin? Hast thou slain this good knight by thy crafts? There liveth not so worshipful a knight as he was; I had liefer than the stint of my land a year that he were alive."

"Care ye not," said Merlin, "for he is wholer than ye; for he is but asleep, and will awake within three hours. I told you," said Merlin, "what a knight he was; here had ye been slain had I not been. Also there liveth not a bigger knight than he is one, and he shall hereafter do you right good service; and his name is Pellinore, and he shall have two sons that shall be passing good men; save one they shall have no fellow of prowess and of good living, and their names shall be Percivale of Wales and Lamerake of Wales, and he shall tell you the name of your own son, begotten of your sister, that shall be the destruction of all this realm."

MERLIN WAS NOT ONLY a man of great mystical power, but also a seer – as shown in the following excerpt where he foretells of a great battle to come.

Book II, Chapter VIII
How Merlin Prophesied that Two the Best Knights of the World Should Fight There, Which Were Sir Lancelot and Sir Tristram

THE MEANWHILE as this was a-doing, in came Merlin to King Mark, and seeing all his doing, said, "Here shall be in this same place the greatest battle betwixt two knights that was or ever shall be, and the truest lovers, and yet none of them shall slay other."

And there Merlin wrote their names upon the tomb with letters of gold that should fight in that place, whose names were Launcelot de Lake, and Tristram.

"Thou art a marvellous man," said King Mark unto Merlin, "that speakest of such marvels, thou art a boistous man and an unlikely to tell of such deeds. What is thy name?" said King Mark.

"At this time," said Merlin, "I will not tell, but at that time when Sir Tristram is taken with his sovereign lady, then ye shall hear and know my name, and at that time ye shall hear tidings that shall not please you." Then said Merlin to Balin, "Thou hast done thyself great hurt, because that thou savest not this lady that slew herself, that might have saved her an thou wouldest."

"By the faith of my body," said Balin, "I might not save her, for she slew herself suddenly."

"Me repenteth," said Merlin; "because of the death of that lady thou shalt strike a stroke most dolorous that ever man struck, except the stroke of our Lord, for thou shalt hurt the truest knight and the man of most worship that now liveth, and through that stroke three kingdoms shall be in great poverty, misery and wretchedness twelve years, and the knight shall not be whole of that wound for many years." Then Merlin took his leave of Balin.

And Balin said, "If I wist it were sooth that ye say I should do such a perilous deed as that, I would slay myself to make thee a liar."

Therewith Merlin vanished away suddenly. And then Balan and his brother took their leave of King Mark.

"First," said the king, "tell me your name."

"Sir," said Balan, "ye may see he beareth two swords, thereby ye may call him the Knight with the Two Swords."

And so departed King Mark unto Camelot to King Arthur, and Balin took the way toward King Rience; and as they rode together they met with Merlin disguised, but they knew him not.

"Whither ride you?" said Merlin.

"We have little to do," said the two knights, "to tell thee."

"But what is thy name?" said Balin.

"At this time," said Merlin, "I will not tell it thee. It is evil seen, said the knights, that thou art a true man that thou wilt not tell thy name. As for that," said Merlin, "be it as it be may, I can tell you wherefore ye ride this way, for to meet King Rience; but it will not avail you without ye have my counsel."

"Ah!" said Balin, "Ye are Merlin; we will be ruled by your counsel."

"Come on," said Merlin, "ye shall have great worship, and look that ye do knightly, for ye shall have great need."

"As for that," said Balin, "dread you not, we will do what we may."

FOLLOWING THE DEATH OF KING LOT in a great battle, Merlin once again shares knowledge of events still to come, this time with King Arthur.

Book II, Chapter XI
Of the Interment of Twelve Kings, and of the Prophecy of Merlin, and How Balin Should Give the Dolorous Stroke

SO AT THE INTERMENT came King Lot's wife Margawse with her four sons, Gawaine, Agravaine, Gaheris, and Gareth. Also there came thither King Uriens, Sir Ewaine's father, and Morgan le Fay his wife that was King Arthur's sister. All these came to the interment. But of all these twelve kings King Arthur let make the tomb of King Lot passing richly, and made his tomb by his own; and then Arthur let make twelve images of latten and copper, and over-gilt it with gold, in the sign of twelve kings, and each one of them held a taper of wax that burnt day and night; and King Arthur was made in sign of a figure standing above them with a sword drawn in his hand, and all the twelve figures had countenance like unto men that were overcome.

All this made Merlin by his subtle craft, and there he told the king, "When I am dead these tapers shall burn no longer, and soon after the adventures of the Sangreal shall come among you and be achieved." Also he told Arthur how Balin the worshipful knight shall give the dolorous stroke, whereof shall fall great vengeance.

"Oh, where is Balin and Balan and Pellinore?" said King Arthur.

"As for Pellinore," said Merlin, "he will meet with you soon; and as for Balin he will not be long from you; but the other brother will depart, ye shall see him no more."

"By my faith," said Arthur, "they are two marvellous knights, and namely Balin passeth of prowess of any knight that ever I found, for much beholden am I unto him; would God he would abide with me."

"Sir," said Merlin, "look ye keep well the scabbard of Excalibur, for ye shall lose no blood while ye have the scabbard upon you, though ye have as many wounds upon you as ye may have."

So after, for great trust, Arthur betook the scabbard to Morgan le Fay his sister, and she loved another knight better than her husband King Uriens or King Arthur, and she would have had Arthur her brother slain, and therefore she let make another scabbard like it by enchantment, and gave the scabbard Excalibur to her love; and the knight's name was called Accolon, that after had near slain King Arthur. After this Merlin told unto King Arthur of the prophecy that there should be a great battle beside Salisbury, and Mordred his own son should be against him. Also he told him that Bagdemegus was his cousin, and germain unto King Uriens.

THE GREAT FIGHT between brothers Balin and Balan culminates in the death of both men, and it is Merlin who subsequently lays them to rest together in a single tomb and sets Balin's sword in a marble stone knowing that one day it shall find itself in the hands of Sir Galahad.

Book II, Chapter XIX
How Merlin Buried Them Both in One Tomb, and of Balin's Sword

IN THE MORN came Merlin and let write Balin's name on the tomb with letters of gold, that:

Here lieth Balin le Savage that was the Knight with the Two Swords, and he that smote the Dolorous Stroke.

Also Merlin let make there a bed, that there should never man lie therein but he went out of his wit, yet Launcelot de Lake fordid that bed through his noblesse. And anon after Balin was dead, Merlin took his sword, and took off the pommel and set on another pommel. So Merlin bade a knight that stood afore him handle that sword, and he assayed, and he might not handle it. Then Merlin laughed.

"Why laugh ye?" said the knight.

"This is the cause," said Merlin: "there shall never man handle this sword but the best knight of the world, and that shall be Sir Launcelot or else Galahad his son, and Launcelot with this sword shall slay the man that in the world he loved best, that shall be Sir Gawaine."

All this he let write in the pommel of the sword. Then Merlin let make a bridge of iron and of steel into that island, and it was but half a foot broad, and there shall never man pass that bridge, nor have hardiness to go over, but if he were a passing good man and a good knight without treachery or villainy. Also the scabbard of Balin's sword Merlin left it on this side the island, that Galahad should find it. Also Merlin let make by his subtilty that Balin's sword was put in a marble stone standing upright as great as a mill stone, and the stone hoved always above the water and did many years, and so by adventure it swam down the stream to the City of Camelot, that is in English Winchester. And that same day Galahad the haut prince came with King Arthur, and so Galahad brought with him the scabbard and achieved the sword that was there in the marble stone hoving upon the water. And on Whitsunday he achieved the sword as it is rehearsed in the book of Sangreal.

Soon after this was done Merlin came to King Arthur and told him of the dolorous stroke that Balin gave to King Pellam, and how Balin and Balan fought together the marvellest battle that ever was heard of, and how they were buried both in one tomb.

"Alas," said King Arthur, this is the greatest pity that ever I heard tell of two knights, for in the world I know not such two knights. Thus endeth the tale of Balin and of Balan, two brethren born in Northumberland, good knights.

DESPITE HIS GREAT POWERS, Merlin is not infallible and has his own weaknesses – most notably his affections for the fairer sex. Enchanted by the beautiful Nimue, who does not reciprocate his love and instead fears him, the great wizard meets his end by her hand, as described in the following chapter.

Book IV, Chapter I
How Merlin Was Assotted and Doted on One of the Ladies of the Lake, and How He Was Shut in a Rock Under a Stone and There Died

SO AFTER THESE QUESTS of Sir Gawaine, Sir Tor, and King Pellinore, it fell so that Merlin fell in a dotage on the damosel that King Pellinore brought to court, and she was one of the damosels of the lake, that hight Nimue. But Merlin would let her have no rest, but always he would be with her. And ever she made Merlin good cheer till she had learned of him all manner thing that she desired; and he was assotted upon her, that he might not be from her. So on a time he told King Arthur that he should not dure long, but for all his crafts he should be put in the earth quick. And so he told the king many things that should befall, but always he warned the king to keep well his sword and the scabbard, for he told him how the sword and the scabbard should be stolen by a woman from him that he most trusted.

Also he told King Arthur that he should miss him – "Yet had ye liefer than all your lands to have me again."

"Ah," said the king, "since ye know of your adventure, purvey for it, and put away by your crafts that misadventure."

"Nay," said Merlin, "it will not be;" so he departed from the king.

And within a while the Damosel of the Lake departed, and Merlin went with her evermore wheresomever she went. And ofttimes Merlin would have had her privily away by his subtle crafts; then she made him to swear that he should never do none enchantment upon her if he would have his will. And so he sware; so she and Merlin went over the sea unto the land of Benwick, whereas King Ban was king that had great war against King Claudas, and there Merlin spake with King Ban's wife, a fair lady and a good, and her name was Elaine, and there he saw young Launcelot. There the queen made great sorrow for the mortal war that King Claudas made on her lord and on her lands.

"Take none heaviness," said Merlin, "for this same child within this twenty year shall revenge you on King Claudas, that all Christendom shall speak of it; and this same child shall be the most man of worship of the world, and his first name is Galahad, that know I well," said Merlin, "and since ye have confirmed him Launcelot."

"That is truth," said the queen, "his first name was Galahad. O Merlin," said the queen, "shall I live to see my son such a man of prowess?"

"Yea, lady, on my peril ye shall see it, and live many winters after."

And so, soon after, the lady and Merlin departed, and by the way Merlin showed her many wonders, and came into Cornwall. And always Merlin lay about the lady to have her maidenhood, and she was ever passing weary of him, and fain would have been delivered of him, for she was afeard of him because he was a devil's son, and she could not beskift him by no mean. And so on a time it happed that Merlin showed to her in a rock whereas was a great wonder, and wrought by enchantment, that went under a great stone. So by her subtle working she made Merlin to go under that stone to let her wit of the marvels there; but she wrought so there for him that he came never out for all the craft he could do. And so she departed and left Merlin.

Arthur in the Cave

ONCE UPON A TIME a Welshman was walking on London Bridge, staring at the traffic, and wondering why there were so many kites hovering about. He had come to London after many adventures with thieves and highwaymen, which need not be related here, in charge of a herd of black Welsh cattle. He had sold them with much profit, and with jingling gold in his pocket he was going about to see the sights of the city.

He was carrying a hazel staff in his hand, for you must know that a good staff is as necessary to a drover as teeth are to his dog. He stood still to gaze at some wares in a shop (for at that time London Bridge was shops from beginning to end), when he noticed that a man was looking at his stick with a long fixed look. The man after a while came to him and asked him where he came from. "I come from my own country," said the Welshman, rather surlily, for he could not see what business the man had to ask him such a question.

"Do not take it amiss," said the stranger: "if you will only answer my questions and take my advice, it will be of greater benefit to you than you imagine. Do you remember where you cut that stick."

The Welshman was still suspicious and said. "What does it matter where I cut it?"

"It matters," said his questioner, "because there is treasure hidden near the spot where you cut that stick. If you remember the place and can conduct me to it, I will put you in possession of great riches."

The Welshman now understood that he had to deal with a sorcerer, and he was greatly perplexed as to what to do. On the one hand, he was tempted by the prospect of wealth; on the other hand, he knew that the sorcerer must have derived his knowledge from devils, and he feared to have anything to do with the powers of darkness. The cunning man strove hard to persuade him, and at length made him promise to show the place where he had cut his hazel staff.

The Welshman and the magician journeyed together to Wales. They went to Craig y Dinas, the Rock of the Fortress, at the head of the Neath Valley, near Pont Nedd Fechan, and the Welshman, pointing to the stock or root of an old hazel, said, "This is where I cut my stick."

"Let us dig," said the sorcerer. They digged until they came to a broad, flat stone. Prising this up, they found some steps leading downwards. They went down the steps and along a narrow passage until they came to a door. "Are you brave," asked the sorcerer, "will you come in with me?"

"I will," said the Welshman, his curiosity getting the better of his fear.

They opened the door, and a great cave opened out before them. There was a faint red light in the cave, and they could see everything. The first thing they came to was a bell. "Do not touch that bell," said the sorcerer, "or it will be all over with us both."

As they went further in, the Welshman saw that the place was not empty. There were soldiers lying down asleep, thousands of them, as far as ever the eye could see. Each one was clad in bright armour, the steel helmet of each was on his head, the shining shield of each was on his arm, the sword of each was near his hand, each had his spear stuck in the ground near him, and each and all were asleep. In the middle of the cave was a great round table at which sat warriors, whose noble features and richly-dight armour proclaimed that they were not in the roll of common men.

Each of those, too, had his head bent down in sleep. On a golden throne on the further side of the round table was a King of gigantic stature and august presence. In his hand, held below the hilt, was a mighty sword with scabbard and haft of gold studded with gleaming gems; on his head was a crown set with precious stones which flashed and glinted like so many points of fire. Sleep had set its seal on his eyelids also.

"Are they asleep?" asked the Welshman, hardly believing his own eyes.

"Yes, each and all of them," answered the sorcerer, "but if you touch yonder bell, they will all awake."

"How long have they been asleep?"

"For over a thousand years!"

"Who are they?"

"Arthur's warriors, waiting for the time to come when they shall destroy all the enemies of the Cymry and repossess the Island of Britain, establishing their own King once more at Caer Lleon."

"Who are those sitting at the round table?"

"Those are Arthur's Knights, Owain, the son of Urien; Cai, the son of Cynyr; Gwalchmai, the son of Gwyar; Peredur, the son of Efrawc; Geraint, the son of Erbin; Trystan, the son of March; Bedwyr, the son of Bedrawd; Cilhwch, the son of Celyddon; Edeyrn, the son of Nudd; Cynon, the son of Clydno" – "And on the golden throne?" broke in the Welshman – "is Arthur himself, with his sword Excalibur in his hand," replied the sorcerer.

Impatient by this time at the Welshman's questions, the sorcerer hastened to a great heap of yellow gold on the floor of the cave. He took up as much as he could carry, and bade his companion do the same. "It is time for us to go," he then said, and he led the way towards the door by which they had entered.

But the Welshman was fascinated by the sight of the countless soldiers in their glittering arms, all asleep. "How I should like to see them all awaking!" he said to himself. "I will touch the bell – I must see them all arising from their sleep."

When they came to the bell, he struck it until it rang through the whole place. As soon as it rang, lo! the thousands of warriors leapt to their feet and the ground beneath them shook with the sound of the steel arms. And a, great voice came from their midst, "Who rang the bell? Has the day come?"

The sorcerer was so frightened that he shook like an aspen leaf. He shouted in answer," No, the day has not come. Sleep on."

The mighty host was all in motion, and the Welsh-man's eyes were dazzled as he looked at the bright steel arms which illumined the cave as with the light of myriad flames of fire.

"Arthur," said the voice again, "awake; the bell has rung, the day is breaking. Awake, Arthur the Great."

"No," shouted the sorcerer, "it is still night; sleep on, Arthur the Great."

A sound came from the throne. Arthur was standing, and the jewels in his crown shone like bright stars above the countless throng. His voice was strong and sweet like the sound of many waters, and he said, "My warriors, the day has not come when the Black Eagle and the Golden Eagle shall go to war. It is only a seeker after gold who has rung the bell. Sleep on, my warriors, the morn of Wales has not yet dawned."

A peaceful sound like the distant sigh of the sea came over the cave, and in a trice the soldiers were all asleep again. The sorcerer hurried the Welshman out of the cave, moved the stone back to its place, and vanished.

Many a time did the Welshman try to find the way into the cave again, but though he dug over every inch of the hill, he never found the entrance.

The Farmer Who Consulted the Conjuror; Or, The Familiar Spirits and the Lost Cows

A FARMER WHO LIVED in the Southern part of Carmarthenshire, lost three cows. Having searched in vain for them everywhere, he at last went to Cwrt-y-Cadno, though he had a very long journey to go. When he arrived there and consulted Dr. Harries, the worthy wizard told him that he could not give him any information concerning his lost cows till next day, as he wanted time to consult his magic books. The farmer was a little disappointed, as he wanted to go home that evening; but under the circumstances there was nothing to be done but try and get a bed for the night at some farm in the neighbourhood. So he left the wizard for the night with the intention of returning to him again in the morning, when he hoped to hear something of his lost cows. But after going out of the house, he noticed a barn close by, which he entered, and found in a corner a heap of straw where he thought he could lie down and sleep comfortably till next morning. This he did unknown to the wizard, who took for granted that the farmer had gone to stay for the night at some house in the neighbourhood. He slept comfortably in the barn for a while, but about one o'clock in the morning, he was awakened by the sound of the wizard's footsteps entering the place at that untimely hour, with a lantern in his hand. The disturbed farmer could not imagine what he wanted in the barn at this time of the night, and he was afraid of being discovered. Presently, however, he noticed the conjurer drawing a circle around himself in the middle of the room; that is the well-known Wizard's Circle. Then he stood right in the middle of this circle, and having opened a book, he summoned seven demons or familiar spirits to appear, and in an instant they came one after another and stood outside the circle. Then he addressed or called out to the first spirit something as follows: "Tell me where are the farmer's lost cows?" But the demon answered not. He repeated the question two or three times, but the Familiar was quite dumb. At last, however, it shouted out, "A pig in the straw" but this was no reply to the wizard's question.

Having failed with the first spirit, the wizard addressed the second one, and then the third, and so on till he had given the question to each one of the familiars except one, without any result; the spirits seemed very stupid on this occasion, and would not give the information required. Fortunately, however, when the question was given to the seventh and last of the demons, it shouted out, "The farmer's cows will be on Carmarthen Bridge at 12 o'clock to-morrow." Then the wizard left the barn and went to bed well pleased.

The farmer who was hiding in the straw heard everything, and made up his mind to travel to Carmarthen at once, so as to be there in time to find his cows on the bridge. So off he went to Carmarthen, and reached the bridge just at 12 o'clock, and to his great joy the cows were there. Then he drove them home, but when he had gone about half-a-mile from the bridge, the cows fell down as if half dead on the roadside, and in vain did he try to get them to move forward any further. So he had to go all the way to Cwrt-y-Cadno again, so as to consult what to do. When he arrived there, "Serve thee right," said the wizard to him, "I have cast a spell on thy cattle for running away secretly last night from the barn without paying me for the information obtained from the spirits."

Then the farmer gave the wizard a certain sum of money and returned to his three cows which he had left on the road half-a-mile from Carmarthen Bridge; and to his great joy the cows went home without any further trouble.

The Magic Apples

IT IS NOT VERY AMUSING to be a king. Father Odin often grew tired of sitting all day long upon his golden throne in Valhalla above the heavens. He wearied of welcoming the new heroes whom the Valkyrs brought him from wars upon the earth, and of watching the old heroes fight their daily deathless battles. He wearied of his wise ravens, and the constant gossip which they brought him from the four corners of the world; and he longed to escape from every one who knew him to some place where he could pass for a mere stranger, instead of the great king of the Aesir, the mightiest being in the whole universe, of whom every one was afraid.

Sometimes he longed so much that he could not bear it. Then – he would run away. He disguised himself as a tall old man, with white hair and a long gray beard. Around his shoulders he threw a huge blue cloak, that covered him from top to toe, and over his face he pulled a big slouch hat, to hide his eyes. For his eyes Odin could not change – no magician has ever learned how to do that. One was empty; he had given the eye to the giant Mimir in exchange for wisdom.

Usually Odin loved to go upon these wanderings alone; for an adventure is a double adventure when one meets it single-handed. It was a fine game for Odin to see how near he could come to danger without feeling the grip of its teeth. But sometimes, when he wanted company, he would whisper to his two brothers, Hoenir and red Loki. They three would creep out of the palace by the back way; and, with a finger on the lip to Heimdall, the watchman, would silently steal over the rainbow bridge which led from Asgard into the places of men and dwarfs and giants.

Wonderful adventures they had, these three, with Loki to help make things happen. Loki was a sly, mischievous fellow, full of his pranks and his capers, not always kindly ones. But he was clever, as well as malicious; and when he had pushed folk into trouble, he could often help them out again, as safe as ever. He could be the jolliest of companions when he chose, and Odin liked his merriment and his witty talk.

One day Loki did something which was no mere jest nor easily forgiven, for it brought all Asgard into danger. And after that Father Odin and his children thought twice before inviting Loki to join them in any journey or undertaking. This which I am about to tell was the first really wicked deed of which Loki was found guilty, though I am sure his red beard had dabbled in secret wrongs before.

One night the three high gods, Odin, Hoenir, and Loki, stole away from Asgard in search of adventure. Over mountains and deserts, great rivers and stony places, they wandered until they grew very hungry. But there was no food to be found – not even a berry or a nut.

Oh, how footsore and tired they were! And oh, how faint! The worst of it ever is that – as you must often have noticed – the heavier one's feet grow, the lighter and more hollow becomes one's stomach; which seems a strange thing, when you think of it. If only one's feet became as light as the rest of one feels, folk could fairly fly with hunger. Alas! This is not so.

The three Aesir drooped and drooped, and seemed on the point of starving, when they came to the edge of a valley. Here, looking down, they saw a herd of oxen feeding on the grass.

"Hola!" shouted Loki. "Behold our supper!" Going down into the valley, they caught and killed one of the oxen, and, building a great bonfire, hung up the meat to roast. Then the three sat around the fire and smacked their lips, waiting for the meat to cook. They waited for a long time.

"Surely, it is done now," said Loki, at last; and he took the meat from the fire. Strange to say, however, it was raw as ere the fire was lighted. What could it mean? Never before had meat required so long a time to roast. They made the fire brighter and re-hung the beef for a thorough basting, cooking it even longer than they had done at first. When again they came to carve the meat, they found it still uneatable. Then, indeed, they looked at one another in surprise.

"What can this mean?" cried Loki, with round eyes.

"There is some trick!" whispered Hoenir, looking around as if he expected to see a fairy or a witch meddling with the food.

"We must find out what this mystery betokens," said Odin thoughtfully. Just then there was a strange sound in the oak-tree under which they had built their fire.

"What is that?" Loki shouted, springing to his feet. They looked up into the tree, and far above in the branches, near the top, they spied an enormous eagle, who was staring down at them, and making a queer sound, as if he were laughing.

"Ho-ho!" croaked the eagle. "I know why your meat will not cook. It is all my doing, masters."

The three Aesir stared in surprise. Then Odin said sternly: "Who are you, Master Eagle? And what do you mean by those rude words?"

"Give me my share of the ox, and you shall see," rasped the eagle, in his harsh voice. "Give me my share, and you will find that your meat will cook as fast as you please."

Now the three on the ground were nearly famished. So, although it seemed very strange to be arguing with an eagle, they cried, as if in one voice: "Come down, then, and take your share." They thought that, being a mere bird, he would want but a small piece.

The eagle flapped down from the top of the tree. Dear me! What a mighty bird he was! Eight feet across the wings was the smallest measure, and his claws were as long and strong as ice-hooks. He fanned the air like a whirlwind as he flew down to perch beside the bonfire. Then in his beak and claws he seized a leg and both shoulders of the ox, and started to fly away.

"Hold, thief!" roared Loki angrily, when he saw how much the eagle was taking. "That is not your share; you are no lion, but you are taking the lion's share of our feast. Begone, Scarecrow, and leave the meat as you found it!" Thereat, seizing a pole, he struck at the eagle with all his might.

Then a strange thing happened. As the great bird flapped upward with his prey, giving a scream of malicious laughter, the pole which Loki still held stuck fast to the eagle's back, and Loki was unable to let go of the other end.

"Help, help!" he shouted to Odin and to Hoenir, as he felt himself lifted off his feet. But they could not help him. "Help, help!" he screamed, as the eagle flew with him, now high, now low, through brush and bog and briar, over treetops and the peaks of mountains. On and on they went, until Loki thought his arm would be pulled out, like a weed torn up by the roots. The eagle would not listen to his cries nor pause in his flight, until Loki was almost dead with pain and fatigue.

"Hark you, Loki," screamed the eagle, going a little more slowly; "no one can help you except me. You are bewitched, and you cannot pull away from this pole, nor loose the pole from me, until I choose. But if you will promise what I ask, you shall go free."

Then Loki groaned: "O eagle, only let me go, and tell me who you really are, and I will promise whatever you wish."

The eagle answered: "I am the giant Thiasse, the enemy of the Aesir. But you ought to love me, Loki, for you yourself married a giantess."

Loki moaned: "Oh, yes! I dearly love all my wife's family, great Thiasse. Tell me what you want of me?"

"I want this," quoth Thiasse gruffly. "I am growing old, and I want the apples which Idunn keeps in her golden casket, to make me young again. You must get them for me."

Now these apples were the fruit of a magic tree, and were more beautiful to look at and more delicious to taste than any fruit that ever grew. The best thing about them was that whoever tasted one, be he ever so old, grew young and strong again. The apples belonged to a beautiful lady named Idunn, who kept them in a golden casket. Every morning the Aesir came to her to be refreshed and made over by a bite of her precious fruit. That is why in Asgard no one ever waxed old or ugly. Even Father Odin, Hoenir, and Loki, the three travelers who had seen the very beginning of everything, when the world was made, were still sturdy and young. And so long as Idunn kept her apples safe, the faces of the family who sat about the table of Valhalla would be rosy and fair like the faces of children.

"O friend giant!" cried Loki. "You know not what you ask! The apples are the most precious treasure of Asgard, and Idunn keeps watch over them as if they were dearer to her than life itself. I never could steal them from her, Thiasse; for at her call all Asgard would rush to the rescue, and trouble would buzz about my ears like a hive of bees let loose."

"Then you must steal Idunn herself, apples and all. For the apples I must have, and you have promised, Loki, to do my bidding."

Loki sniffed and thought, thought and sniffed again. Already his mischievous heart was planning how he might steal Idunn away. He could hardly help laughing to think how angry the Aesir would be when they found their beauty-medicine gone forever. But he hoped that, when he had done this trick for Thiasse, now and then the giant would let him have a nibble of the magic apples; so that Loki himself would remain young long after the other Aesir were grown old and feeble. This thought suited Loki's malicious nature well.

"I think I can manage it for you, Thiasse," he said craftily. "In a week I promise to bring Idunn and her apples to you. But you must not forget the great risk which I am running, nor that I am your relative by marriage. I may have a favor to ask in return, Thiasse."

Then the eagle gently dropped Loki from his claws. Falling on a soft bed of moss, Loki jumped up and ran back to his traveling companions, who were glad and surprised to see him again. They had feared that the eagle was carrying him away to feed his young eaglets in some far-off nest. Ah, you may be sure that Loki did not tell them who the eagle really was, nor confess the wicked promise which he had made about Idunn and her apples.

After that the three went back to Asgard, for they had had adventure enough for one day.

The days flew by, and the time came when Loki must fulfill his promise to Thiasse. So one morning he strolled out into the meadow where Idunn loved to roam among the flowers. There he found her, sitting by a tiny spring, and holding her precious casket of apples on her lap. She was combing her long golden hair, which fell from under a wreath of spring flowers, and she was very beautiful. Her green robe was embroidered with buds and blossoms of silk in many colors, and she wore a golden girdle about her waist. She smiled as Loki came, and tossed him a posy, saying: "Good-morrow, red Loki. Have you come for a bite of my apples? I see a wrinkle over each of your eyes which I can smooth away."

"Nay, fair lady," answered Loki politely, "I have just nibbled of another apple, which I found this morning. Verily, I think it is sweeter and more magical than yours."

Idunn was hurt and surprised.

"That cannot be, Loki," she cried. "There are no apples anywhere like mine. Where found you this fine fruit?" and she wrinkled up her little nose scornfully.

"Oho! I will not tell any one the place," chuckled Loki, "except that it is not far, in a little wood. There is a gnarled old apple-tree, and on its branches grow the most beautiful red-cheeked apples you ever saw. But you could never find it."

"I should like to see these apples, Loki, if only to prove how far less good they are than mine. Will you bring me some?"

"That I will not," said Loki teasingly. "Oh, no! I have my own magic apples now, and folk will be coming to me for help instead of to you."

Idunn began to coax him, as he had guessed that she would: "Please, please, Loki, show me the place!"

At first he would not, for he was a sly fellow, and knew how to lead her on. At last, he pretended to yield.

"Well, then, because I love you, Idun, better than all the rest, I will show you the place, if you will come with me. But it must be a secret – no one must ever know."

All girls like secrets.

"Yes – yes!" cried Idunn eagerly. "Let us steal away now, while no one is looking."

This was just what Loki hoped for.

"Bring your own apples," he said, "that we may compare them with mine. But I know mine are better."

"I know mine are the best in all the world," returned Idun, pouting. "I will bring them, to show you the difference."

Off they started together, she with the golden casket under her arm; and Loki chuckled wickedly as they went. He led her for some distance, further than she had ever strayed before, and at last she grew frightened.

"Where are you taking me, Loki?" she cried. "You said it was not far. I see no little wood, no old apple-tree."

"It is just beyond, just a little step beyond," he answered. So on they went. But that little step took them beyond the boundary of Asgard – just a little step beyond, into the space where the giants lurked and waited for mischief.

Then there was a rustling of wings, and *whirr-rr-rr*! Down came Thiasse in his eagle dress. Before Idunn suspected what was happening, he fastened his claws into her girdle and flapped away with her, magic apples and all, to his palace in Jotunheim, the Land of Giants.

Loki stole back to Asgard, thinking that he was quite safe, and that no one would discover his villainy. At first Idunn was not missed. But after a little the gods began to feel signs of age, and went for their usual bite of her apples. Then they found that she had disappeared, and a great terror fell upon them. Where had she gone? Suppose she should not come back!

The hours and days went by, and still she did not return. Their fright became almost a panic. Their hair began to turn gray, and their limbs grew stiff and gouty so that they hobbled down Asgard streets. Even Freyia, the loveliest, was afraid to look in her mirror, and Balder the beautiful grew pale and haggard. The happy land of Asgard was like a garden over which a burning wind had blown, – all the flower-faces were faded and withered, and springtime was turned into yellow fall.

If Idunn and her apples were not quickly found, the gods seemed likely to shrivel and blow away like autumn leaves. They held a council to inquire into the matter, endeavoring to learn who had seen Idunn last, and whither she had gone. It turned out that one morning Heimdall had seen her strolling out of Asgard with Loki, and no one had seen her since. Then the gods understood; Loki was the last person who had been with her – this must be one of Loki's tricks. They were filled with anger. They seized and bound Loki and brought him before the council. They threatened him with torture and with death unless he should tell the truth. And Loki was so frightened that finally he confessed what he had done.

Then indeed there was horror in Asgard. Idunn stolen away by a wicked giant! Idunn and her apples lost, and Asgard growing older every minute! What was to be done? Big Thor seized Loki and threw him up in the air again and again, so that his heels touched first the moon and then the sea; you can still see the marks upon the moon's white face. "If you do not bring Idunn back from the land of your wicked wife, you shall have worse than this!" he roared. "Go and bring her *now*."

"How can I do that?" asked Loki, trembling.

"That is for you to find," growled Thor. "Bring her you must. Go!"

Loki thought for a moment. Then he said:

"I will bring her back if Freyia will loan me her falcon dress. The giant dresses as an eagle. I, too, must guise me as a bird, or we cannot outwit him."

Then Freyia hemmed and hawed. She did not wish to loan her feather dress, for it was very precious. But all the Aesir begged; and finally she consented.

It was a beautiful great dress of brown feathers and gray, and in it Freyia loved to skim like a falcon among the clouds and stars. Loki put it on, and when he had done so he looked exactly like a great brown hawk. Only his bright black eyes remained the same, glancing here and there, so that they lost sight of nothing.

With a whirr of his wings Loki flew off to the north, across mountains and valleys and the great river Ifing, which lay between Asgard and Giant Land. And at last he came to the palace of Thiasse the giant.

It happened, fortunately, that Thiasse had gone fishing in the sea, and Idunn was left alone, weeping and broken-hearted. Presently she heard a little tap on her window, and, looking up, she saw a great brown bird perching on the ledge. He was so big that Idunn was frightened and gave a scream. But the bird nodded pleasantly and croaked: "Don't be afraid, Idun. I am a friend. I am Loki, come to set you free."

"Loki! Loki is no friend of mine. He brought me here," she sobbed. "I don't believe you came to save me."

"That is indeed why I am here," he replied, "and a dangerous business it is, if Thiasse should come back before we start for home."

"How will you get me out?" asked Idunn doubtfully. "The door is locked, and the window is barred."

"I will change you into a nut," said he, "and carry you in my claws."

"What of the casket of apples?" queried Idun. "Can you carry that also?"

Then Loki laughed long and loudly.

"What welcome to Asgard do you think I should receive without the apples?" he cried. "Yes, we must take them, indeed."

Idunn came to the window, and Loki, who was a skillful magician, turned her into a nut and took her in one claw, while in the other he seized the casket of apples. Then off he whirred out of the palace grounds and away toward Asgard's safety.

In a little while Thiasse returned home, and when he found Idunn and her apples gone, there was a hubbub, you may be sure! However, he lost little time by smashing mountains and breaking trees in his giant rage; that fit was soon over. He put on his eagle plumage and started in pursuit of the falcon.

Now an eagle is bigger and stronger than any other bird, and usually in a long race he can beat even the swift hawk who has an hour's start. Presently Loki heard behind him the shrill scream of a giant eagle, and his heart turned sick. But he had crossed the great river, and already was in sight of Asgard. The aged Aesir were gathered on the rainbow bridge watching eagerly for Loki's return; and when they spied the falcon with the nut and the casket in his talons, they knew who it was. A great cheer went up, but it was hushed in a moment, for they saw the eagle close after the falcon; and they guessed that this must be the giant Thiasse, the stealer of Idun.

Then there was a great shouting of commands, and a rushing to and fro. All the gods, even Father Odin and his two wise ravens, were busy gathering chips into great heaps on the walls of Asgard. As soon as Loki, with his precious burden, had fluttered weakly over the wall, dropping to the ground beyond, the gods lighted the heaps of chips which they had piled, and soon there was a wall of fire, over which the eagle must fly. He was going too fast to stop. The flames roared and crackled, but Thiasse flew straight into them, with a scream of fear and rage. His feathers caught fire and burned, so that he could no longer fly, but fell headlong to the ground inside the walls. Then Thor, the thunder-lord, and Tyr, the mighty war-king, fell upon him and slew him, so that he could never trouble the Aesir any more.

There was great rejoicing in Asgard that night, for Loki changed Idunn again to a fair lady; whereupon she gave each of the eager gods a bite of her life-giving fruit, so that they grew young and happy once more, as if all these horrors had never happened.

Not one of them, however, forgot the evil part which Loki had played in these doings. They hid the memory, like a buried seed, deep in their hearts. Thenceforward the word of Loki and the honor of his name were poor coin in Asgard; which is no wonder.

Hermod

ANOTHER OF ODIN'S SONS was Hermod, his special attendant, a bright and beautiful young god, who was gifted with great rapidity of motion and was therefore designated as the swift or nimble god.

On account of this important attribute Hermod was usually employed by the gods as messenger, and at a mere sign from Odin he was always ready to speed to any par of creation. As a special mark of favour, Allfather gave him a magnificent corselet and helmet, which he often donned when he prepared to take part in war, and sometimes Odin entrusted to his care the precious spear Gungnir, bidding him cast it over the heads of combatants about to engage in battle, that their ardour might be kindled into murderous fury.

Hermod delighted in battle, and was often called 'the valiant in battle,' and confounded with the god of the universe, Irmin. It is said that he sometimes accompanied the Valkyrs on their ride to earth, and frequently escorted the warriors to Valhalla, wherefore he was considered the leader of the heroic dead.

Hermod's distinctive attribute, besides his corselet and helm, was a wand or staff called Gambantein, the emblem of his office, which he carried with him wherever he went.

Once, oppressed by shadowy fears for the future, and unable to obtain from the Norns satisfactory answers to his questions, Odin bade Hermod don his armour and saddle Sleipnir, which he alone, besides Odin, was allowed to ride, and hasten off to the land of the Finns. This people, who lived in the frozen regions of the pole, besides being able to call up the cold storms which swept down from the North, bringing much ice and snow in their train, were supposed to have great occult powers.

The most noted of these Finnish magicians was Rossthiof (the horse thief) who was wont to entice travellers into his realm by magic arts, that he might rob and slay them; and he had power to predict the future, although he was always very reluctant to do so.

Hermod, 'the swift,' rode rapidly northward, with directions to seek this Finn, and instead of his own wand, he carried Odin's runic staff, which Allfather had given him for the purpose of dispelling any obstacles that Rossthiof might conjure up to hinder his advance. In spite, therefore, of phantom-like monsters and of invisible snares and pitfalls, Hermod was enabled safely to reach the magician's abode, and upon the giant attacking him, he was able to master him with ease, and he bound him hand and foot, declaring that he would not set him free until he promised to reveal all that he wished to know.

Rossthiof, seeing that there was no hope of escape, pledged himself to do as his captor wished, and upon being set at liberty, he began forthwith to mutter incantations, at the mere sound of which the sun hid behind the clouds, the earth trembled and quivered, and the storm winds howled like a pack of hungry wolves.

Pointing to the horizon, the magician bade Hermod look, and the swift god saw in the distance a great stream of blood reddening the ground. While he gazed wonderingly at this stream, a beautiful woman suddenly appeared, and a moment later a little boy stood beside her. To the god's amazement, this child grew with such marvellous rapidity that he soon attained his full growth, and Hermod further noticed that he fiercely brandished a bow and arrows.

Rossthiof now began to explain the omens which his art had conjured up, and he declared that the stream of blood portended the murder of one of Odin's sons, but that if the father of the gods should woo and win Rinda, in the land of the Ruthenes (Russia), she would bear him a son who would attain his full growth in a few hours and would avenge his brother's death.

Hermod listened attentively to the words of Rossthiof and upon his return to Asgard he reported all he had seen and heard to Odin, whose fears were confirmed and who thus definitely ascertained that he was doomed to lose a son by violent death. He consoled himself, however, with the thought that another of his descendants would avenge the crime and thereby obtain the satisfaction which a true Northman ever required.

The Gifts of the Magician

ONCE UPON A TIME there was an old man who lived in a little hut in the middle of a forest. His wife was dead, and he had only one son, whom he loved dearly. Near their hut was a group of birch trees, in which some black-game had made their nests, and the youth had often begged his father's permission to shoot the birds, but the old man always strictly forbade him to do anything of the kind.

One day, however, when the father had gone to a little distance to collect some sticks for the fire, the boy fetched his bow, and shot at a bird that was just flying towards its nest. But he had not taken proper aim, and the bird was only wounded, and fluttered along the ground. The boy ran to catch it, but though he ran very fast, and the bird seemed to flutter along very slowly, he never could quite come up with it; it was always just a little in advance. But so absorbed was he in the chase that he did not notice for some time that he was now deep in the forest, in a place where he had never been before. Then he felt it would be foolish to go any further, and he turned to find his way home.

He thought it would be easy enough to follow the path along which he had come, but somehow it was always branching off in unexpected directions. He looked about for a house where he might stop and ask his way, but there was not a sign of one anywhere, and he was afraid to stand still, for it was cold, and there were many stories of wolves being seen in that part of the forest. Night fell, and he was beginning to start at every sound, when suddenly a magician came running towards him, with a pack of wolves snapping at his heels. Then all the boy's courage returned to him. He took his bow, and aiming an arrow at the largest wolf, shot him through the heart, and a few more arrows soon put the rest to flight. The magician was full of gratitude to his deliverer, and promised him a reward for his help if the youth would go back with him to his house.

"Indeed there is nothing that would be more welcome to me than a night's lodging," answered the boy; "I have been wandering all day in the forest, and did not know how to get home again."

"Come with me, you must be hungry as well as tired," said the magician, and led the way to his house, where the guest flung himself on a bed, and went fast asleep. But his host returned to the forest to get some food, for the larder was empty.

While he was absent the housekeeper went to the boy's room and tried to wake him. She stamped on the floor, and shook him and called to him, telling him that he was in great danger, and must take flight at once. But nothing would rouse him, and if he did ever open his eyes he shut them again directly.

Soon after, the magician came back from the forest, and told the housekeeper to bring them something to eat. The meal was quickly ready, and the magician called to the boy to come down and eat it, but he could not be wakened, and they had to sit down to supper without him. By-and-by the magician went out into the wood again for some more hunting, and on his return he tried afresh to waken the youth. But finding it quite impossible, he went back for the third time to the forest.

While he was absent the boy woke up and dressed himself. Then he came downstairs and began to talk to the housekeeper. The girl had heard how he had saved her master's life, so she said nothing more about his running away, but instead told him that if the magician offered him the choice of a reward, he was to ask for the horse which stood in the third stall of the stable.

By-and-by the old man came back and they all sat down to dinner. When they had finished the magician said: "Now, my son, tell me what you will have as the reward of your courage?"

"Give me the horse that stands in the third stall of your stable," answered the youth. "For I have a long way to go before I get home, and my feet will not carry me so far."

"Ah! my son," replied the magician, "it is the best horse in my stable that you want! Will not anything else please you as well?"

But the youth declared that it was the horse, and the horse only, that he desired, and in the end the old man gave way. And besides the horse, the magician gave him a zither, a fiddle, and a flute, saying: "If you are in danger, touch the zither; and if no one comes to your aid, then play on the fiddle; but if that brings no help, blow on the flute."

The youth thanked the magician, and fastening his treasures about him mounted the horse and rode off. He had already gone some miles when, to his great surprise, the horse spoke, and said: "It is no use your returning home just now, your father will only beat you. Let us visit a few towns first, and something lucky will be sure to happen to us."

This advice pleased the boy, for he felt himself almost a man by this time, and thought it was high time he saw the world. When they entered the capital of the country everyone stopped to admire the beauty of the horse. Even the king heard of it, and came to see the splendid creature with his own eyes. Indeed, he wanted directly to buy it, and told the youth he would give any price he liked. The young man hesitated for a moment, but before he could speak, the horse contrived to whisper to him:

"Do not sell me, but ask the king to take me to his stable, and feed me there; then his other horses will become just as beautiful as I."

The king was delighted when he was told what the horse had said, and took the animal at once to the stables, and placed it in his own particular stall. Sure enough, the horse had scarcely eaten a mouthful of corn out of the manger, when the rest of the horses seemed to have undergone a transformation. Some of them were old favourites which the king had ridden in many wars, and they bore the signs of age and of service. But now they arched their heads, and pawed the ground with their slender legs as they had been wont to do in days long gone by. The king's heart beat with delight, but the old groom who had had the care of them stood crossly by, and eyed the owner of this wonderful creature with hate and envy. Not a day passed without his bringing some story against the youth to his master, but the king understood all about the matter and paid no attention. At last the groom declared that the young man had boasted that he could find the king's war horse which had strayed into the forest several years ago, and had not been heard of since. Now the king had never ceased to mourn for his horse, so this time he listened to the tale which the groom had invented, and sent for the youth. "Find me my horse in three days," said he, "or it will be the worse for you."

The youth was thunderstruck at this command, but he only bowed, and went off at once to the stable.

"Do not worry yourself," answered his own horse. "Ask the king to give you a hundred oxen, and to let them be killed and cut into small pieces. Then we will start on our journey, and ride till we reach a certain river. There a horse will come up to you, but take no notice of him. Soon another will appear, and this also you must leave alone, but when the third horse shows itself, throw my bridle over it."

Everything happened just as the horse had said, and the third horse was safely bridled. Then the other horse spoke again: "The magician's raven will try to eat us as we ride away, but throw it some of the oxen's flesh, and then I will gallop like the wind, and carry you safe out of the dragon's clutches."

So the young man did as he was told, and brought the horse back to the king.

The old stableman was very jealous, when he heard of it, and wondered what he could do to injure the youth in the eyes of his royal master. At last he hit upon a plan, and told the king that the young man had boasted that he could bring home the king's wife, who had vanished many months before, without leaving a trace behind her. Then the king bade the young man come into his presence, and desired him to fetch the queen home again, as he had boasted he could do. And if he failed, his head would pay the penalty.

The poor youth's heart stood still as he listened. Find the queen? But how was he to do that, when nobody in the palace had been able to do so! Slowly he walked to the stable, and laying his head on his horse's shoulder, he said: "The king has ordered me to bring his wife home again, and how can I do that when she disappeared so long ago, and no one can tell me anything about her?" "Cheer up!" answered the horse, "we will manage to find her. You have only got to ride me back to the same river that we went to yesterday, and I will plunge into it and take my proper shape again. For I am the king's wife, who was turned into a horse by the magician from whom you saved me." Joyfully the young man sprang into the saddle and rode away to the banks of the river. Then he threw himself off, and waited while the horse plunged in. The moment it dipped its head into the water its black skin vanished, and the most beautiful woman in the world was floating on the water. She came smiling towards the youth, and held out her hand, and he took it and led her back to the palace. Great was the king's surprise and happiness when he beheld his lost wife stand before him, and in gratitude to her rescuer he loaded him with gifts.

You would have thought that after this the poor youth would have been left in peace; but no, his enemy the stableman hated him as much as ever, and laid a new plot for his undoing. This time he presented himself before the king and told him that the youth was so puffed up with what he had done that he had declared he would seize the king's throne for himself.

At this news the king waxed so furious that he ordered a gallows to be erected at once, and the young man to be hanged without a trial. He was not even allowed to speak in his own defence, but on the very steps of the gallows he sent a message to the king and begged, as a last favour, that he might play a tune on his zither. Leave was given him, and taking the instrument from under his cloak he touched the strings. Scarcely had the first notes sounded than the hangman and his helper began to dance, and the louder grew the music the higher they capered, till at last they cried for mercy. But the youth paid no heed, and the tunes rang out more merrily than before, and by the time the sun set they both sank on the ground exhausted, and declared that the hanging must be put off till to-morrow.

The story of the zither soon spread through the town, and on the following morning the king and his whole court and a large crowd of people were gathered at the foot of the gallows to see the youth hanged. Once more he asked a favour – permission to play on his fiddle, and this the king was graciously pleased to grant. But with the first notes, the leg of every man in the crowd was lifted high, and they danced to the sound of the music the whole day till darkness fell, and there was no light to hang the musician by.

The third day came, and the youth asked leave to play on his flute. "No, no," said the king, "you made me dance all day yesterday, and if I do it again it will certainly be my death. You shall play no more tunes. Quick! the rope round his neck."

At these words the young man looked so sorrowful that the courtiers said to the king: "He is very young to die. Let him play a tune if it will make him happy." So, very unwillingly, the king gave him leave; but first he had himself bound to a big fir tree, for fear that he should be made to dance.

When he was made fast, the young man began to blow softly on his flute, and bound though he was, the king's body moved to the sound, up and down the fir tree till his clothes were in tatters, and the skin nearly rubbed off his back. But the youth had no pity, and went on blowing, till suddenly the old magician appeared and asked: "What danger are you in, my son, that you have sent for me?"

"They want to hang me," answered the young man; "the gallows are all ready and the hangman is only waiting for me to stop playing."

"Oh, I will put that right," said the magician; and taking the gallows, he tore it up and flung it into the air, and no one knows where it came down. "Who has ordered you to be hanged?" asked he.

The young man pointed to the king, who was still bound to the fir; and without wasting words the magician took hold of the tree also, and with a mighty heave both fir and man went spinning through the air, and vanished in the clouds after the gallows.

Then the youth was declared to be free, and the people elected him for their king; and the stable helper drowned himself from envy, for, after all, if it had not been for him the young man would have remained poor all the days of his life.

The Young Man Who Would Have His Eyes Opened

ONCE UPON A TIME there lived a youth who was never happy unless he was prying into something that other people knew nothing about. After he had learned to understand the language of birds and beasts, he discovered accidentally that a great deal took place under cover of night which mortal eyes never saw. From that moment he felt he could not rest till these hidden secrets were laid bare to him, and he spent his whole time wandering from one wizard to another, begging them to open his eyes, but found none to help him. At length he reached an old magician called Mana, whose learning was greater than that of the rest, and who could tell him all he wanted to know. But when the old man had listened attentively to him, he said, warningly:

"My son, do not follow after empty knowledge, which will not bring you happiness, but rather evil. Much is hidden from the eyes of men, because did they know everything their hearts would no longer be at peace. Knowledge kills joy, therefore think well what you are doing, or some day you will repent. But if you will not take my advice, then truly I can show you the secrets of the night. Only you will need more than a man's courage to bear the sight."

He stopped and looked at the young man, who nodded his head, and then the wizard continued, "To-morrow night you must go to the place where, once in seven years, the serpent-king gives a great feast to his whole court. In front of him stands a golden bowl filled with goats' milk, and if you can manage to dip a piece of bread in this milk, and eat it before you are obliged to fly, you will understand all the secrets of the night that are hidden from other men. It is lucky for you that the serpent-king's feast happens to fall this year, otherwise you would have had long to wait for it. But take care to be quick and bold, or it will be the worse for you."

The young man thanked the wizard for his counsel, and went his way firmly resolved to carry out his purpose, even if he paid for it with his life; and when night came he set out for a wide, lonely moor, where the serpent-king held his feast. With sharpened eyes, he looked eagerly all round him, but could see nothing but a multitude of small hillocks, that lay motionless under the moonlight. He crouched behind a bush for some time, till he felt that midnight could not be far off, when suddenly there arose in the middle of the moor a brilliant glow, as if a star was shining over one of the hillocks. At the same moment all the hillocks began to writhe and to crawl, and from each one came hundreds of serpents and made straight for the glow, where they knew they should find their king. When they reached the hillock where he dwelt, which was higher and broader than the rest, and had a bright light hanging over the top, they coiled themselves up and waited. The whirr and confusion from all the serpent-houses were so great that the youth did not dare to advance one step, but remained where he was, watching intently all that went on; but at last he began to take courage, and moved on softly step by step.

What he saw was creepier than creepy, and surpassed all he had ever dreamt of. Thousands of snakes, big and little and of every colour, were gathered together in one great cluster round a huge serpent, whose body was as thick as a beam, and which had on its head a golden crown, from which the light sprang. Their hissings and darting tongues so terrified the young man that his heart sank, and he felt he should never have courage to push on to certain death, when suddenly he caught sight of the golden bowl in front of the serpent-king, and knew that if he lost this chance it would never come back. So, with his hair standing on end and his blood frozen in his veins, he crept forwards. Oh! what a noise and a whirr rose afresh among the serpents. Thousands of heads were reared, and tongues were stretched out to sting the intruder to death, but happily for him their bodies were so closely entwined one in the other that they could not disentangle themselves quickly. Like lightning he seized a bit of bread, dipped it in the bowl, and put it in his mouth, then dashed away as if fire was pursuing him. On he flew as if a whole army of foes were at his heels, and he seemed to hear the noise of their approach growing nearer and nearer. At length his breath failed him, and he threw himself almost senseless on the turf. While he lay there dreadful dreams haunted him. He thought that the serpent-king with the fiery crown had twined himself round him, and was crushing out his life. With a loud shriek he sprang up to do battle with his enemy, when he saw that it was rays of the sun which had wakened him. He rubbed his eyes and looked all round, but nothing could he see of the foes of the past night, and the moor where he had run into such danger must be at least a mile away. But it was no dream that he had run hard and far, or that he had drunk of the magic goats' milk. And when he felt his limbs, and found them whole, his joy was great that he had come through such perils with a sound skin.

After the fatigues and terrors of the night, he lay still till mid-day, but he made up his mind he would go that very evening into the forest to try what the goats' milk could really do for him, and if he would now be able to understand all that had been a mystery to him. And once in the forest his doubts were set at rest, for he saw what no mortal eyes had ever seen before. Beneath the trees were golden pavilions, with flags of silver all brightly lighted up. He was still wondering why the pavilions were there, when a noise was heard among the trees, as if the wind had suddenly got up, and on all sides beautiful maidens stepped from the trees into the bright light of the moon. These were the wood-nymphs, daughters of the earth-mother, who came every night to hold their dances, in the forest. The young man, watching from his hiding place, wished he had a hundred eyes in his head, for two were not nearly enough for the sight before him, the dances lasting till the first streaks of dawn. Then a silvery veil seemed to be drawn over the ladies, and they vanished from sight. But the young man remained where he was till the sun was high in the heavens, and then went home.

He felt that day to be endless, and counted the minutes till night should come, and he might return to the forest. But when at last he got there he found neither pavilions nor nymphs, and though he went back many nights after he never saw them again. Still, he thought about them night and day, and ceased to care about anything else in the world, and was sick to the end of his life with longing for that beautiful vision. And that was the way he learned that the wizard had spoken truly when he said, "Blindness is man's highest good."

The Wizard King

IN VERY ANCIENT TIMES there lived a King, whose power lay not only in the vast extent of his dominions, but also in the magic secrets of which he was master. After spending the greater part of his early youth in pleasure, he met a Princess of such remarkable beauty that he at once asked her hand in marriage, and, having obtained it, considered himself the happiest of men.

After a year's time a son was born, worthy in every way of such distinguished parents, and much admired by the whole Court. As soon as the Queen thought him strong enough for a journey she set out with him secretly to visit her Fairy godmother. I said secretly, because the Fairy had warned the Queen that the King was a magician; and as from time immemorial there had been a standing feud between the Fairies and the Wizards, he might not have approved of his wife's visit.

The Fairy godmother, who took the deepest interest in all the Queen's concerns, and who was much pleased with the little Prince, endowed him with the power of pleasing everybody from his cradle, as well as with a wonderful ease in learning everything which could help to make him a perfectly accomplished Prince. Accordingly, to the delight of his teachers, he made the most rapid progress in his education, constantly surpassing everyone's expectations. Before he was many years old, however, he had the great sorrow of losing his mother, whose last words were to advise him never to undertake anything of importance without consulting the Fairy under whose protection she had placed him.

The Prince's grief at the death of his mother was great, but it was nothing compared to that of the King, his father, who was quite inconsolable for the loss of his dear wife. Neither time nor reason seemed to lighten his sorrow, and the sight of all the familiar faces and things about him only served to remind him of his loss.

He therefore resolved to travel for change, and by means of his magic art was able to visit every country he came to see under different shapes, returning every few weeks to the place where he had left a few followers.

Having travelled from land to land in this fashion without finding anything to rivet his attention, it occurred to him to take the form of an eagle, and in this shape he flew across many countries and arrived at length in a new and lovely spot, where the air seemed filled with the scent of jessamine and orange flowers with which the ground was thickly planted. Attracted by the sweet perfume he flew lower, and perceived some large and beautiful gardens filled with the rarest flowers, and with fountains throwing up their clear waters into the air in a hundred different shapes. A wide stream flowed through the garden, and on it floated richly ornamented barges and gondolas filled with people dressed in the most elegant manner and covered with jewels.

In one of these barges sat the Queen of that country with her only daughter, a maiden more beautiful than the Day Star, and attended by the ladies of the Court. No more exquisitely lovely mortal was ever seen than this Princess, and it needed all an eagle's strength of sight to prevent the King being hopelessly dazzled. He perched on the top of a large orange tree, whence he was able to survey the scene and to gaze at pleasure on the Princess's charms.

Now, an eagle with a King's heart in his breast is apt to be bold, and accordingly he instantly made up his mind to carry off the lovely damsel, feeling sure that having once seen her he could not live without her.

He waited till he saw her in the act of stepping ashore, when, suddenly swooping down, he carried her off before her equerry in attendance had advanced to offer her his hand. The Princess, on finding herself in an eagle's talons, uttered the most heart-breaking shrieks and cries; but her captor, though touched by her distress, would not abandon his lovely prey, and continued to fly through the air too fast to allow of his saying anything to comfort her.

At length, when he thought they had reached a safe distance, he began to lower his flight, and gradually descending to earth, deposited his burden in a flowery meadow. He then entreated her pardon for his violence, and told her that he was about to carry her to a great kingdom over which he ruled, and where he desired she should rule with him, adding many tender and consoling expressions.

For some time the Princess remained speechless; but recovering herself a little, she burst into a flood of tears. The King, much moved, said, "Adorable Princess, dry your tears. I implore you. My only wish is to make you the happiest person in the world."

"If you speak truth, my lord," replied the Princess, "restore to me the liberty you have deprived me of. Otherwise I can only look on you as my worst enemy."

The King retorted that her opposition filled him with despair, but that he hoped to carry her to a place where all around would respect her, and where every pleasure would surround her. So saying, he seized her once more, and in spite of all her cries he rapidly bore her off to the neighbourhood of his capital. Here he gently placed her on a lawn, and as he did so she saw a magnificent palace spring up at her feet. The architecture was imposing and in the interior the rooms were handsome and furnished in the best possible taste.

The Princess, who expected to be quite alone, was pleased at finding herself surrounded by a number of pretty girls, all anxious to wait on her, whilst a brilliantly-coloured parrot said the most agreeable things in the world.

On arriving at this palace the King had resumed his own form, and though no longer young, he might well have pleased any other than this Princess, who had been so prejudiced against him by his violence that she could only regard him with feelings of hatred, which she was at no pains to conceal. The King hoped, however, that time might not only soften her anger, but accustom her to his sight. He took the precaution of surrounding the palace with a dense cloud, and then hastened to his Court, where his prolonged absence was causing much anxiety.

The Prince and all the courtiers were delighted to see their beloved King again, but they had to submit themselves to more frequent absences than ever on his part. He made business a pretext for shutting himself up in his study, but it was really in order to spend the time with the Princess, who remained inflexible.

Not being able to imagine what could be the cause of so much obstinacy the King began to fear, lest, in spite of all his precautions, she might have heard of the charms of the Prince his son, whose goodness, youth and beauty, made him adored at Court. This idea made him horribly uneasy, and he resolved to remove the cause of his fears by sending the Prince on his travels escorted by a magnificent retinue.

The Prince, after visiting several Courts, arrived at the one where the lost Princess was still deeply mourned. The King and Queen received him most graciously, and some festivities were revived to do him honour.

One day when the Prince was visiting the Queen in her own apartments he was much struck by a most beautiful portrait. He eagerly inquired whose it was, and the Queen, with many tears, told him it was all that was left her of her beloved daughter, who had suddenly been carried off, she knew neither where nor how.

The Prince was deeply moved, and vowed that he would search the world for the Princess, and take no rest till he had found and restored her to her mother's arms. The Queen assured him of her eternal gratitude, and promised, should he succeed, to give him her daughter in marriage, together with all the estates she herself owned.

The Prince, far more attracted by the thoughts of possessing the Princess than her promised dower, set forth in his quest after taking leave of the King and Queen, the latter giving him a miniature of her daughter which she was in the habit of wearing. His first act was to seek the Fairy under whose protection he had been placed, and he implored her to give him all the assistance of her art and counsel in this important matter.

After listening attentively to the whole adventure, the Fairy asked for time to consult her books. After due consideration she informed the Prince that the object of his search was not far distant, but that it was too difficult for him to attempt to enter the enchanted palace where she was, as the King his father had surrounded it with a thick cloud, and that the only expedient she could think of would be to gain possession of the Princess's parrot. This, she added, did not appear impossible, as it often flew about to some distance in the neighbourhood.

Having told the Prince all this, the Fairy went out in hopes of seeing the parrot, and soon returned with the bird in her hand. She promptly shut it up in a cage, and, touching the Prince with her wand, transformed him into an exactly similar parrot; after which, she instructed him how to reach the Princess.

The Prince reached the palace in safety, but was so dazzled at first by the Princess's beauty, which far surpassed his expectations, that he was quite dumb for a time. The

Princess was surprised and anxious, and fearing the parrot, who was her greatest comfort, had fallen ill, she took him in her hand and caressed him. This soon reassured the Prince, and encouraged him to play his part well, and he began to say a thousand agreeable things which charmed the Princess.

Presently the King appeared, and the parrot noticed with joy how much he was disliked. As soon as the King left, the Princess retired to her dressing-room, the parrot flew after her and overheard her lamentations at the continued persecutions of the King, who had pressed her to consent to their marriage. The parrot said so many clever and tender things to comfort her that she began to doubt whether this could indeed be her own parrot.

When he saw her well-disposed towards him, he exclaimed: "Madam, I have a most important secret to confide to you, and I beg you not to be alarmed by what I am about to say. I am here on behalf of the Queen your mother, with the object of delivering your Highness; to prove which, behold this portrait which she gave me herself." So saying he drew forth the miniature from under his wing. The Princess's surprise was great, but after what she had seen and heard it was impossible not to indulge in hope, for she had recognised the likeness of herself which her mother always wore.

The parrot, finding she was not much alarmed, told her who he was, all that her mother had promised him and the help he had already received from a Fairy who had assured him that she would give him means to transport the Princess to her mother's arms. When he found her listening attentively to him, he implored the Princess to allow him to resume his natural shape. She did not speak, so he drew a feather from his wing, and she beheld before her a Prince of such surpassing beauty that it was impossible not to hope that she might owe her liberty to so charming a person.

Meantime the Fairy had prepared a chariot, to which she harnessed two powerful eagles; then placing the cage, with the parrot in it, she charged the bird to conduct it to the window of the Princess's dressing-room. This was done in a few minutes, and the Princess, stepping into the chariot with the Prince, was delighted to find her parrot again.

As they rose through the air the Princess remarked a figure mounted on an eagle's back flying in front of the chariot. She was rather alarmed, but the Prince reassured her, telling her it was the good Fairy to whom she owed so much, and who was now conducting her in safety to her mother.

That same morning the King woke suddenly from a troubled sleep. He had dreamt that the Princess was being carried off from him, and, transforming himself into an eagle, he flew to the palace. When he failed to find her he flew into a terrible rage, and hastened home to consult his books, by which means he discovered that it was his son who had deprived him of this precious treasure. Immediately he took the shape of a harpy, and, filled with rage, was determined to devour his son, and even the Princess too, if only he could overtake them.

He set out at full speed; but he started too late, and was further delayed by a strong wind which the Fairy raised behind the young couple so as to baffle any pursuit.

You may imagine the rapture with which the Queen received the daughter she had given up for lost, as well as the amiable Prince who had rescued her. The Fairy entered with them, and warned the Queen that the Wizard King would shortly arrive, infuriated by his loss, and that nothing could preserve the Prince and Princess from his rage and magic unless they were actually married.

The Queen hastened to inform the King her husband, and the wedding took place on the spot.

As the ceremony was completed the Wizard King arrived. His despair at being so late bewildered him so entirely that he appeared in his natural form and attempted to sprinkle some black liquid over the bride and bridegroom, which was intended to kill them, but the Fairy stretched out her wand and the liquid dropped on the Magician himself. He fell down senseless, and the Princess's father, deeply offended at the cruel revenge which had been attempted, ordered him to be removed and locked up in prison.

Now as magicians lose all their power as soon as they are in prison, the King felt himself much embarrassed at being thus at the mercy of those he had so greatly offended. The Prince implored and obtained his father's pardon, and the prison doors were opened.

No sooner was this done than the Wizard King was seen in the air under the form of some unknown bird, exclaiming as he flew off that he would never forgive either his son or the Fairy the cruel wrong they had done him.

Everyone entreated the Fairy to settle in the kingdom where she now was, to which she consented. She built herself a magnificent palace, to which she transported her books and fairy secrets, and where she enjoyed the sight of the perfect happiness she had helped to bestow on the entire royal family.

Virgilius the Sorcerer

LONG, LONG AGO there was born to a Roman knight and his wife Maja a little boy called Virgilius. While he was still quite little, his father died, and the kinsmen, instead of being a help and protection to the child and his mother, robbed them of their lands and money, and the widow, fearing that they might take the boy's life also, sent him away to Spain, that he might study in the great University of Toledo.

Virgilius was fond of books, and pored over them all day long. But one afternoon, when the boys were given a holiday, he took a long walk, and found himself in a place where he had never been before. In front of him was a cave, and, as no boy ever sees a cave without entering it, he went in. The cave was so deep that it seemed to Virgilius as if it must run far into the heart of the mountain, and he thought he would like to see if it came out anywhere on the other side. For some time he walked on in pitch darkness, but he went steadily on, and by-and-by a glimmer of light shot across the floor, and he heard a voice calling, "Virgilius! Virgilius!"

"Who calls?" he asked, stopping and looking round.

"Virgilius!" answered the voice, "do you mark upon the ground where you are standing a slide or bolt?"

"I do," replied Virgilius.

"Then," said the voice, "draw back that bolt, and set me free."

"But who are you?" asked Virgilius, who never did anything in a hurry.

"I am an evil spirit," said the voice, "shut up here till Doomsday, unless a man sets me free. If you will let me out I will give you some magic books, which will make you wiser than any other man."

Now Virgilius loved wisdom, and was tempted by these promises, but again his prudence came to his aid, and he demanded that the books should be handed over to him first, and that he should be told how to use them. The evil spirit, unable to help itself, did as Virgilius bade him, and then the bolt was drawn back. Underneath was a small hole, and out of this the evil spirit gradually wriggled himself; but it took some time, for when at last he stood upon the ground he proved to be about three times as large as Virgilius himself, and coal black besides.

"Why, you can't have been as big as that when you were in the hole!" cried Virgilius.

"But I was!" replied the spirit.

"I don't believe it!" answered Virgilius.

"Well, I'll just get in and show you," said the spirit, and after turning and twisting, and curling himself up, then he lay neatly packed into the hole. Then Virgilius drew the bolt, and, picking the books up under his arm, he left the cave.

For the next few weeks Virgilius hardly ate or slept, so busy was he in learning the magic the books contained. But at the end of that time a messenger from his mother arrived in Toledo, begging him to come at once to Rome, as she had been ill, and could look after their affairs no longer.

Though sorry to leave Toledo, where he was much thought of as showing promise of great learning, Virgilius would willingly have set out at once, but there were many things he had first to see to. So he entrusted to the messenger four pack-horses laden with precious things, and a white palfrey on which she was to ride out every day. Then he set about his own preparations, and, followed by a large train of scholars, he at length started for Rome, from which he had been absent twelve years.

His mother welcomed him back with tears in her eyes, and his poor kinsmen pressed round him, but the rich ones kept away, for they feared that they would no longer be able to rob their kinsman as they had done for many years past. Of course, Virgilius paid no attention to this behaviour, though he noticed they looked with envy on the rich presents he bestowed on the poorer relations and on anyone who had been kind to his mother.

Soon after this had happened the season of tax-gathering came round, and everyone who owned land was bound to present himself before the emperor. Like the rest, Virgilius went to court, and demanded justice from the emperor against the men who had robbed him. But as these were kinsmen to the emperor he gained nothing, as the emperor told him he would think over the matter for the next four years, and then give judgment. This reply naturally did not satisfy Virgilius, and, turning on his heel, he went back to his own home, and, gathering in his harvest, he stored it up in his various houses.

When the enemies of Virgilius heard of this, they assembled together and laid siege to his castle. But Virgilius was a match for them. Coming forth from the castle so as to meet them face to face, he cast a spell over them of such power that they could not move, and then bade them defiance. After which he lifted the spell, and the invading army slunk back to Rome, and reported what Virgilius had said to the emperor.

Now the emperor was accustomed to have his lightest word obeyed, almost before it was uttered, and he hardly knew how to believe his ears. But he got together another army, and marched straight off to the castle. But directly they took up their position Virgilius girded them about with a great river, so that they could neither move hand nor foot, then, hailing the emperor, he offered him peace, and asked for his friendship. The emperor, however, was too angry to listen to anything, so Virgilius, whose patience was exhausted, feasted his own followers in the presence of the starving host, who could not stir hand or foot.

Things seemed getting desperate, when a magician arrived in the camp and offered to sell his services to the emperor. His proposals were gladly accepted, and in a moment the whole of the garrison sank down as if they were dead, and Virgilius himself had much ado to keep awake. He did not know how to fight the magician, but with a great effort struggled to open his Black Book, which told him what spells to use. In an instant all his foes seemed turned to stone, and where each man was there he stayed. Some were half way up the ladders, some had one foot over the wall, but wherever they might chance to be there every man remained, even the emperor and his sorcerer. All day they stayed there like flies upon the wall, but during the night Virgilius stole softly to the emperor, and offered him his freedom, as long as he would do him justice. The emperor, who by this time was thoroughly frightened, said he would agree to anything Virgilius desired. So Virgilius took off his spells, and, after feasting the army and bestowing on every man a gift, bade them return to Rome. And more than that, he built a square tower for the emperor, and in each corner all that was said in that quarter of the city might be heard, while if you stood in the centre every whisper throughout Rome would reach your ears.

Having settled his affairs with the emperor and his enemies, Virgilius had time to think of other things, and his first act was to fall in love! The lady's name was Febilla, and her family was noble, and her face fairer than any in Rome, but she only mocked Virgilius, and was always playing tricks upon him. To this end, she bade him one day come to visit her in the tower where she lived, promising to let down a basket to draw him up as far as the roof. Virgilius was enchanted at this quite unexpected favour, and stepped with glee into the basket. It was drawn up very slowly, and by-and-by came altogether to a standstill, while from above rang the voice of Febilla crying, "Rogue of a sorcerer, there shalt thou hang!" And there he hung over the market-place, which was soon thronged with people, who made fun of him till he was mad with rage. At last the emperor, hearing of his plight, commanded Febilla to release him, and Virgilius went home vowing vengeance.

The next morning every fire in Rome went out, and as there were no matches in those days this was a very serious matter. The emperor, guessing that this was the work of Virgilius, besought him to break the spell. Then Virgilius ordered a scaffold to be erected in the market-place, and Febilla to be brought clothed in a single white garment. And further, he bade every one to snatch fire from the maiden, and to suffer no neighbour to kindle it. And when the maiden appeared, clad in her white smock, flames of fire curled about her, and the Romans brought some torches, and some straw, and some shavings, and fires were kindled in Rome again.

For three days she stood there, till every hearth in Rome was alight, and then she was suffered to go where she would.

But the emperor was wroth at the vengeance of Virgilius, and threw him into prison, vowing that he should be put to death. And when everything was ready he was led out to the Viminal Hill, where he was to die.

He went quietly with his guards, but the day was hot, and on reaching his place of execution he begged for some water. A pail was brought, and he, crying "Emperor, all hail! seek for me in Sicily," jumped headlong into the pail, and vanished from their sight.

For some time we hear no more of Virgilius, or how he made his peace with the emperor, but the next event in his history was his being sent for to the palace to give the emperor advice how to guard Rome from foes within as well as foes without. Virgilius spent many days in deep thought, and at length invented a plan which was known to all as the 'Preservation of Rome.'

On the roof of the Capitol, which was the most famous public building in the city, he set up statues representing the gods worshipped by every nation subject to Rome, and in the middle stood the god of Rome herself. Each of the conquered gods held in its hand a bell, and if there was even a thought of treason in any of the countries its god turned its back upon the god of Rome and rang its bell furiously, and the senators came hurrying to see who was rebelling against the majesty of the empire. Then they made ready their armies, and marched against the foe.

Now there was a country which had long felt bitter jealousy of Rome, and was anxious for some way of bringing about its destruction. So the people chose three men who could be trusted, and, loading them with money, sent them to Rome, bidding them to pretend that they were diviners of dreams. No sooner had the messengers reached the city than they stole out at night and buried a pot of gold far down in the earth, and let down another into the bed of the Tiber, just where a bridge spans the river.

Next day they went to the senate house, where the laws were made, and, bowing low, they said, "Oh, noble lords, last night we dreamed that beneath the foot of a hill there lies buried a pot of gold. Have we your leave to dig for it?" And leave having been given, the messengers took workmen and dug up the gold and made merry with it.

A few days later the diviners again appeared before the senate, and said, "Oh, noble lords, grant us leave to seek out another treasure, which has been revealed to us in a dream as lying under the bridge over the river."

And the senators gave leave, and the messengers hired boats and men, and let down ropes with hooks, and at length drew up the pot of gold, some of which they gave as presents to the senators.

A week or two passed by, and once more they appeared in the senate house.

"O, noble lords!" said they, "last night in a vision we beheld twelve casks of gold lying under the foundation stone of the Capitol, on which stands the statue of the Preservation of Rome. Now, seeing that by your goodness we have been greatly enriched by our former dreams, we wish, in gratitude, to bestow this third treasure on you for your own profit; so give us workers, and we will begin to dig without delay."

And receiving permission they began to dig, and when the messengers had almost undermined the Capitol they stole away as secretly as they had come.

And next morning the stone gave way, and the sacred statue fell on its face and was broken. And the senators knew that their greed had been their ruin.

From that day things went from bad to worse, and every morning crowds presented themselves before the emperor, complaining of the robberies, murders, and other crimes that were committed nightly in the streets.

The emperor, desiring nothing so much as the safety of his subjects, took counsel with Virgilius how this violence could be put down.

Virgilius thought hard for a long time, and then he spoke:

"Great prince," said he, "cause a copper horse and rider to be made, and stationed in front of the Capitol. Then make a proclamation that at ten o'clock a bell will toll, and every man is to enter his house, and not leave it again."

The emperor did as Virgilius advised, but thieves and murderers laughed at the horse, and went about their misdeeds as usual.

But at the last stroke of the bell the horse set off at full gallop through the streets of Rome, and by daylight men counted over two hundred corpses that it had trodden down. The rest of the thieves – and there were still many remaining – instead of being frightened into honesty, as Virgilius had hoped, prepared rope ladders with hooks to them, and when they heard the sound of the horse's hoofs they stuck their ladders into the walls, and climbed up above the reach of the horse and its rider.

Then the emperor commanded two copper dogs to be made that would run after the horse, and when the thieves, hanging from the walls, mocked and jeered at Virgilius and the emperor, the dogs leaped high after them and pulled them to the ground, and bit them to death.

Thus did Virgilius restore peace and order to the city.

Now about this time there came to be noised abroad the fame of the daughter of the sultan who ruled over the province of Babylon, and indeed she was said to be the most beautiful princess in the world.

Virgilius, like the rest, listened to the stories that were told of her, and fell so violently in love with all he heard that he built a bridge in the air, which stretched all the way between Rome and Babylon. He then passed over it to visit the princess, who, though somewhat surprised to see him, gave him welcome, and after some conversation became in her turn anxious to see the distant country where this stranger lived, and he promised that he would carry her there himself, without wetting the soles of his feet.

The princess spent some days in the palace of Virgilius, looking at wonders of which she had never dreamed, though she declined to accept the presents he longed to heap on her. The hours passed as if they were minutes, till the princess said that she could be no longer absent from her father. Then Virgilius conducted her himself over the airy bridge, and laid her gently down on her own bed, where she was found next morning by her father.

She told him all that had happened to her, and he pretended to be very much interested, and begged that the next time Virgilius came he might be introduced to him.

Soon after, the sultan received a message from his daughter that the stranger was there, and he commanded that a feast should be made ready, and, sending for the princess delivered into her hands a cup, which he said she was to present to Virgilius herself, in order to do him honour.

When they were all seated at the feast the princess rose and presented the cup to Virgilius, who directly he had drunk fell into a deep sleep.

Then the sultan ordered his guards to bind him, and left him there till the following day.

Directly the sultan was up he summoned his lords and nobles into his great hall, and commanded that the cords which bound Virgilius should be taken off, and the prisoner brought before him. The moment he appeared the sultan's passion broke forth, and he accused his captive of the crime of conveying the princess into distant lands without his leave.

Virgilius replied that if he had taken her away he had also brought her back, when he might have kept her, and that if they would set him free to return to his own land he would come hither no more.

"Not so!" cried the sultan, "but a shameful death you shall die!" And the princess fell on her knees, and begged she might die with him.

"You are out in your reckoning, Sir Sultan!" said Virgilius, whose patience was at an end, and he cast a spell over the sultan and his lords, so that they believed that the great river of Babylon was flowing through the hall, and that they must swim for their lives. So, leaving them to plunge and leap like frogs and fishes, Virgilius took the princess in his arms, and carried her over the airy bridge back to Rome.

Now Virgilius did not think that either his palace, or even Rome itself, was good enough to contain such a pearl as the princess, so he built her a city whose foundations stood upon eggs, buried far away down in the depths of the sea. And in the city was a square tower, and on the roof of the tower was a rod of iron, and across the rod he laid a bottle, and on the bottle he placed an egg, and from the egg there hung chained an apple, which hangs there to this day. And when the egg shakes the city quakes, and when the egg shall be broken the city shall be destroyed. And the city Virgilius filled full of wonders, such as never were seen before, and he called its name Naples.

WITCHES, SORCERESSES, HAGS & CRONES

Introduction

THE WITCH IS MYTHOLOGICALLY INVESTED with all the world's experience and wisdom. And with all the wickedness of womankind. Hence her age, her hideousness – and (with honourable exceptions, like the old 'dame' who saves the Village Maidens in Basotho legend) her malice.

She's as ugly in action as in countenance, committing monstrous crimes on petty grounds – like the Manx witch of Slieu Whallian who sends a storm to sink a fishing fleet. If, like classical Circe, she's young and alluring, she is anything but beautiful inside. Her caress may promise love but it delivers death.

In the Turkish tale, 'The Horse-Dew and the Witch', she's the ultimate impossible mother-in-law. Today's sexist humour reflects an ancient anxiety that, far from promoting the perpetuation of the human race, older mothers may in their jealousy work to thwart it. This idea of the old woman as destructive 'anti-mother' reaches its logical conclusion in the children-devouring witches of eastern and central European fairy tale. (It's striking too how closely the trope of the rejecting stepmother relates to that of the wicked old enchantress, as in the Russian story, simply entitled 'The Witch', or the Armenian tale, 'The Wicked Stepmother'.)

How a Girl Reached the Land of the Ghosts and Came Back

MARWE AND HER BROTHER were ordered by their parents to watch the bean-field and drive away the monkeys. They kept at their post for the greater part of the day, but as their mother had not given them any food to take with them they grew very hungry.

They dug up the burrows of the field-rats, caught some, made a fire, roasted their game, and ate it. Then, being thirsty, they went to a pool and drank. It was some distance off, and when they came back they found that the monkeys had descended on the bean-patch and stripped it bare. They were terribly frightened, and Marwe said, "Let's go and jump into the pool." But her brother thought it would be better to go home without being seen and listen to what their parents were saying. So they stole up to the hut and listened through a gap in the banana leaves of the thatch. Father and mother were both very angry. "What are we to do with such good-for-nothing creatures? Shall we beat them? Or shall we strangle them?" The children did not wait to hear any more, but rushed off to the pool. Marwe threw herself in, but her brother's courage failed him, and he ran back home and told the parents: "Marwe has gone into the pool." They went down at once, quite forgetting the hasty words provoked by the sudden discovery of their loss, and called again and again, "Marwe, come home! Never mind about the beans; we can plant the patch again!" But there was no answer. Day after day the father went down to the pool and called her – always in vain. Marwe had gone into the country of the ghosts.

You entered it at the bottom of the pool. Before she had gone very far she came to a hut, where an old woman lived, with a number of children. This old woman called her in and told her she might stay with her. Next day she sent her out with the others to gather firewood, but said, "You need not do anything. Let the others do the work." Marwe, however, did her part with the rest, and the same when they were sent out to cut grass or perform any other tasks. She was offered food from time to time, but always made some excuse for refusing it. (The living who reach the land of the dead can never leave it again if they eat while there.) So time went on, till one day she began to weary, and said to the other girls, "I should like to go home." The girls advised her to go and tell the old woman, which she did, and the old body had no objection, but asked her, "Shall I hit you with the cold or with the hot?" and Marwe asked to be hit with the cold. The woman told her to dip her arms into a pot she had standing beside her. She did so, and drew them out covered with shining bangles. She was then told to dip her feet, and found her ankles adorned with fine brass and copper chains. Then the woman gave her a skin petticoat worked with beads, and said, "Your future husband is called Sawoye. It is he who will carry you home."

She went with her to the pool, rose to the surface and left her sitting on the bank. It happened that there was a famine in the land just then. Someone saw Marwe and ran to the village saying that there was a girl seated by the pool richly dressed and wearing the most beautiful ornaments, which no one else in the countryside could afford, the people having parted with all their valuables to the coast-traders in the time of scarcity. So the whole population turned out, with the chief at their head. They were filled with admiration of her beauty. They all greeted her most respectfully, and the chief wanted to carry her home; but she refused. Others offered, but she would listen to none till a certain man came along, who was known as Sawoye. Now Sawoye was disfigured by a disease from which he had suffered called woye, whence his name. As soon as she saw him Marwe said, "That is my husband." So he picked her up and carried her home and married her.

Sawoye soon lost his disfiguring skin disease and appeared as the handsomest man in the clan. With the old lady's bangles they bought a fine herd of cattle and built themselves the best house in the village. And they would have lived happy ever after if some of his neighbours had not envied him and plotted to kill him. They succeeded, but his faithful wife found means to revive him, and hid him in the inner compartment of the hut. Then, when the enemies came to divide the spoil and carry Marwe off to be given to the chief as his wife, Sawoye came out, fully armed, and killed them all. After which he and Marwe were left in peace.

The Village Maiden and the Cannibal

THE VILLAGE WAS STARVING, there was no running away from the fact; the men's eyes were big and hungry-looking, and even the plumpest girl was thin. What was to be done? The maidens must go out to find roots. Perhaps the spirits would take pity on their starved looks and guide them to where the roots grew; so early in the morning all the maidens, led by the chiefs two daughters, left the village to seek for food; they walked two by two, a maid and a little girl, side by side. Long they journeyed, and weary were their feet, yet they found nothing, and darkness was creeping over the land. So they laid themselves down to rest under the Great Above, with no shelter or covering over them, to wait for the coming dawn. Next day as they journeyed, behold one of the children espied a root, another, and yet another, until all were busy digging up the precious food. Now a strange thing happened, for, while the maidens only found long thin roots, the children gathered only thick large ones. At length enough had been found to last the village for a time, so the girls set off to return home. As they came near the river they saw it was terribly flooded, and an old, old woman sat crooning upon the bank.

As they approached they began to distinguish the words she was chanting: –

> "The Water Spirit loves not the thin roots,
> They are the food of swine –
> There is no safety for them.
> But the large root, how good it is –
> It is the food of spirits, even of the
> Great Water Spirit.
> Safety and strength are in it;
> The water flows on, flows on."

"Mother," said the elder of the chief's daughters, approaching the old woman, "tell us of your wisdom how we shall cross this swollen river, for we are in haste to reach our home."

Without lifting her eyes from the water, the dame replied, "To the swollen river a swollen root; in each maid's right hand a root that is large, then cross and fear not."

Accordingly the girls chose their largest root, which they threw upon the water, and then each child of her store of fat roots chose two; one she gave to one of the elder maidens, the other she held in her own right hand, then two by two they stepped into the river and in safety gained the opposite bank. But when it came to the turn of the chiefs two daughters, the child refused to give her sister one of her large roots, nor were threats or entreaties of any avail. The night was fast approaching, their companions were almost out of sight, and the river rolled at their feet, dark, swift, and deep.

At length the child relented, and soon the two girls were speeding after their friends; but it was too dark to see, and they missed their road and wandered far in the darkness. When midnight was fast approaching they saw a light shining near, and upon going up to it, found themselves at the door of a hut, over which a mat hung. "Let us ask for shelter for the night," said the elder girl, and shook the mat.

"Get up! get up! son of mine, and see if people are at the door; for I am hungry and would eat meat." The voice was that of a man, who was seated in front of some red-hot cinders in the middle of the hut.

The little boy ran to the door, and, upon seeing the two girls standing there, implored them to run away at once, as his father was a cannibal and would eat them up; but before they had time to do so, the old man appeared and dragged them into the hut.

Early the next morning the old cannibal left the hut to call two of his friends to share his feast. Before he left he securely fastened the two girls together, and told his son to watch them carefully.

Now, as soon as he was out of sight, there appeared at the door the old woman who yesterday had been sitting on the river bank. She at once set the girls free, but told them she must cut off all their hair. When this was done, she took a little and buried it under the floor of the hut, another bunch she buried under the refuse heap outside, another near the spring, and yet another halfway up the hill. She then returned to the hut and burnt the remaining hair.

"Now, my children," said she, "you must fly to your home. I shall follow you under the ground, but your guide shall be a bee. Follow where it leads, and you will be safe." So saying, she led them to the door and drew down the mat.

"Run!" said the boy; "make haste! There is the bee grandmother told you of. Follow quickly, lest my father find you and kill you."

Seeing a bee hovering near, the girls followed where it led. Presently they met two men, who stopped them, and asked, "Who are you? Are you not the two girls our friend has told us of? Did you not stay last night in a hut with an old man and a boy?"

"We know not of whom you speak," replied the girls. "We have seen no old man, nor little boy."

"Ho, ho! is that true? But yes, we see it is true. He told us his victims had plenty of hair, but you have none. No, no; these are not they; these are only people." So saying, they allowed the girls to continue their journey.

Now when the old man and his friends found the girls had escaped, they were very angry; but the little boy said he did not think they could be very far away. The old man went out and began calling, but, as he called, there answered him a voice from the hair under the hut, another voice from the hair by the spring, another from the mountain, and so on from each spot where the old woman had buried the hair, until he became mad with rage and disappointment; then, guessing that witchcraft had been used, and that the two girls his friends had spoken to were indeed his intended victims, he set off in pursuit; but when he caught sight of them, they were almost at their father's village, and a large swarm of bees was between him and them, which, when he tried to overtake the girls, stung him so terribly that he howled with agony, and dared not approach any nearer. Thus the girls escaped, and returned to bring the light of day to their parents' eyes.

Morena-Y-A-Letsatsi, or the Sun Chief

IN THE TIME OF THE GREAT FAMINE, when our fathers' fathers were young, there lived across the mountains, many days' journey, a great chief, who bore upon his breast the signs of the sun, the moon, and eleven stars. Greatly was he beloved, and marvellous was his power. When all around were starving, his people had plenty, and many journeyed to his village to implore his protection. Amongst others came two young girls, the daughters of one mother. Tall and lovely as a deep still river was the elder, gentle and timid as the wild deer, and her they called Siloane (the tear-drop.)

Of a different mould was her sister Mokete. Plump and round were her limbs, bright as the stars her eyes, like running water was the music of her voice, and she feared not man nor spirit. When the chief asked what they could do to repay him for helping them in their need, Mokete replied, "Lord, I can cook, I can grind corn, I can make 'leting', I can do all a woman's work."

Gravely the chief turned to Siloane – "And you," he asked, "what can you do?"

"Alas, lord!" Siloane replied, "what can I say, seeing that my sister has taken all words out of my mouth."

"It is enough," said the chief, "you shall be my wife. As for Mokete, since she is so clever, let her be your servant."

Now the heart of Mokete burned with black hate against her sister, and she vowed to humble her to the dust; but no one must see into her heart, so with a smiling face she embraced Siloane.

The next day the marriage feast took place, amidst great rejoicing, and continued for many days, as befitted the great Sun Chief. Many braves came from far to dance at the feast, and to delight the people with tales of the great deeds they had done in battle. Beautiful maidens were there, but none so beautiful as Siloane. How happy she was, how beloved! In the gladness of her heart she sang a song of praise to her lord – "Great is the sun in the heavens, and great are the moon and stars, but greater and more beautiful in the eyes of his handmaiden is my lord. Upon his breast are the signs of his greatness, and by their power I swear to love him with a love so strong, so true, that his son shall be in his image, and shall bear upon his breast the same tokens of the favour of the heavens."

Many moons came and went, and all was peace and joy in the hearts of the Sun Chief and his bride; but Mokete smiled darkly in her heart, for the time of her revenge approached. At length came the day, when Siloane should fulfil her vow, when the son should be born. The chief ordered that the child should be brought to him at once, that he might rejoice in the fulfilment of Siloane's vow. In the dark hut the young mother lay with great content, for had not Mokete assured her the child was his father's image, and upon his breast were the signs of the sun, the moon, and eleven stars?

Why then this angry frown on the chief's face, this look of triumph in the eyes of Mokete? What is this which she is holding covered with a skin? She turns back the covering, and, with a wicked laugh of triumph, shows the chief, not the beautiful son he had looked for, but an ugly, deformed child with the face of a baboon. "Here, my lord," she said, "is the long-desired son. See how well Siloane loves you, see how well she has kept her vow! Shall I tell her of your heart's content?"

"Woman," roared the disappointed chief, "speak not thus to me. Take from my sight both mother and child, and tell my headman it is my will that they be destroyed ere the sun hide his head in yonder mountains."

Sore at heart, angry and unhappy, the chief strode away into the lands, while Mokete hastened to the headman to bid him carry out his master's orders; but ere they could be obeyed, a messenger came from the chief to say the child alone was to be destroyed, but Siloane should become a servant, and on the morrow should witness his marriage to Mokete.

Bitter tears rolled down Siloane's cheeks. What evil thing had befallen her, that the babe she had borne, and whom she had felt in her arms, strong and straight, should have been so changed ere the eyes of his father had rested upon him? Not once did she doubt Mokete. Was she not her own sister? What reason would she have for casting the "Evil Eye" upon the child? It was hard to lose her child, hard indeed to lose the love of her lord; but he had not banished her altogether from his sight, and perhaps some day the spirits might be willing that she should once again find favour in his sight, and should bear him a child in his own image.

Meanwhile Mokete had taken the real baby to the pigs, hoping they would devour him, for each time she tried to kill him some unseen power held her hand; but the pigs took the babe and nourished him, and many weeks went by – weeks of triumph for Mokete, but of bitter sorrow for Siloane.

At length Mokete bethought her of the child, and wondered if the pigs had left any trace of him. When she reached the kraal, she started back in terror, for there, fat, healthy, and happy, lay the babe, while the young pigs played around him. What should she do? Had Siloane seen him? No, she hardly thought so, for the child was in every way the image of the chief. Siloane would at once have known who he was.

Hurriedly returning to her husband, Mokete begged him to get rid of all the pigs, and have their kraal burnt, as they were all ill of a terrible disease. So the chief gave orders to do as Mokete desired; but the spirits took the child to the elephant which lived in the great bush, and told it to guard him.

After this Mokete was at peace for many months, but no child came to gladden the heart of her lord, and to take away her reproach. In her anger and bitterness she longed to kill Siloane, but she was afraid.

One day she wandered far into the bush, and there she beheld the child, grown more beautiful than ever, playing with the elephant. Mad with rage, she returned home, and gave her lord no rest until he consented to burn the bush, which she told him was full of terrible wild beasts, which would one day devour the whole village if they were not destroyed. But the spirits took the child and gave him to the fishes in the great river, bidding them guard him safely.

Many moons passed, many crops were reaped and Mokete had almost forgotten about the child, when one day, as she walked by the river bank, she saw him, a beautiful youth, playing with the fishes. This was terrible. Would nothing kill him? In her rage she tore great rocks from their beds and rolled them into the water; but the spirits carried the youth to a mountain, where they gave him a wand. "This wand," said they, "will keep you safe. If danger threatens you from above, strike once with the wand upon the ground, and a path will be opened to you to the country beneath. If you wish to return to this upper world, strike twice with the wand, and the path will reopen."

So again they left him, and the youth, fearing the vengeance of his stepmother, struck once upon the ground with his wand. The earth opened, showing a long narrow passage. Down this the youth went, and, upon reaching the other end, found himself at the entrance to a large and very beautiful village. As he walked along, the people stood to gaze at him, and all, when they saw the signs upon his breast, fell down and worshipped him, saying, "Greetings, lord!" At length, he was informed that for many years these people had had no chief, but the spirits had told them that at the proper time a chief would appear who should bear strange signs upon his breast; him the people were to receive and to obey, for he would be the chosen one, and his name should be Tsepitso, or the promise.

From that day the youth bore the name of Tsepitso, and ruled over that land; but he never forgot his mother, and often wandered to the world above, to find how she fared and to watch over her. On these journeys he always clothed himself in old skins, and covered up his breast that none might behold the signs. One day, as he wandered, he found himself in a strange village, and as he passed the well, a maiden greeted him, saying, "Stranger, you look weary. Will you not rest and drink of this fountain?"

Tsepitso gazed into her eyes, and knew what love meant. Here, he felt, was the wife the spirits intended him to wed. He must not let her depart, so he sat down by the well and drank of the cool, delicious water, while he questioned the maid. She told him her name was Ma Thabo (mother of joy), and that her father was chief of that part of the country. Tsepitso told her he was a poor youth looking for work, whereupon she took him to her father, who consented to employ him.

One stipulation Tsepitso made, which was that for one hour every day before sunset he should be free from his duties. This was agreed to, and for several moons he worked for the old chief, and grew more and more in favour, both with him and with his daughter. The hour before sunset each day he spent amongst his own people, attending to their wants and giving judgment. At length he told Ma Thabo of his love, and read her answering love in her beautiful eyes. Together they sought the old chief, to whom Tsepitso told his story, and revealed his true self. The marriage was soon after celebrated, with much rejoicing, and Tsepitso bore his bride in triumph to his beautiful home in the world beneath, where she was received with every joy.

But amidst all his happiness Tsepitso did not forget his mother, and after the feasting and rejoicing were ended, he took Ma Thabo with him, for the time had at length come when he might free his mother forever from the power of Mokete.

When they approached his father's house, Mokete saw them, and, recognising Tsepitso, knew that her time had come. With a scream she fled to the hut, but Tsepitso followed her, and sternly demanded his mother. Mokete only moaned as she knelt at her lord's feet. The old chief arose, and said, "Young man, I know not who you are, nor who your mother is; but this woman is my wife, and I pray you speak to her not thus rudely."

Tsepitso replied, "Lord, I am thy son."

"Nay now, thou art a liar," said the old man sadly, "I have no son."

"Indeed, my father, I am thy son, and Siloane is my mother. Dost need proof of the truth of my words? Then look," and turning to the light, Tsepitso revealed to his father the signs upon his breast, and the old chief, with a great cry, threw himself upon his son's neck and wept. Siloane was soon called, and knew that indeed she had fulfilled her vow, that here before her stood in very truth the son she had borne, and a great content filled her heart. Tsepitso and Ma Thabo soon persuaded her to return with them, knowing full well that her life would no longer be safe were she to remain near Mokete; so, when the old chief was absent, in the dusk of the evening they departed to their own home.

When the Sun Chief discovered their flight, he determined to follow, and restore his beloved Siloane to her rightful place; but Mokete followed him, though many times he ordered her to return to the village, for that never again would she be wife of his, and that if she continued to follow him, he would kill her. At length he thought, "If I cut off her feet she will not be able to walk," so, turning round suddenly, he seized Mokete, and cut off her feet. "Now, wilt thou leave me in peace, woman? Take care nothing worse befall thee." So saying, he left her, and continued his journey.

But Mokete continued to follow him, till the sun was high in the heavens. Each time he saw her close behind him, he stopped and cut off more of her legs, till only her body was left; even then she was not conquered, but continued to roll after him. Thoroughly enraged, the Sun Chief seized her, and called down fire from the heavens to consume her, and a wind from the edge of the world to scatter her ashes.

When this was done, he went on his way rejoicing, for surely now she would trouble him no more. Then as he journeyed, a voice rose in the evening air, "I follow, I follow, to the edge of the world, yea, even beyond, shall I follow thee."

Placing his hands over his ears to shut out the voice, the Sun Chief ran with the fleetness of a young brave, until, at the hour when the spirits visit the abodes of men, he overtook Tsepitso and the two women, and with them entered the kingdom of his son.

How he won pardon from Siloane, and gained his son's love, and how it was arranged that he and Siloane should again be married, are old tales now in the country of Tsepitso. When the marriage feast was begun, a cloud of ashes dashed against the Sun Chief, and an angry voice was heard from the midst of the cloud, saying, "Nay, thou shalt not wed Siloane, for I have found thee, and I shall claim thee forever." Hastily the witch doctor was called to free the Sun Chief from the power of Mokete. As the old man approached the cloud, chanting a hymn to the gods, everyone gazed in silence. Raising his wand, the wizard made some mystic signs, the cloud vanished, and only a handful of ashes lay upon the ground.

Thus was the Evil Eye of Mokete stilled for evermore, and peace reigned in the hearts of the Sun Chief and his wife Siloane.

The Woman with Two Skins

EYAMBA I OF CALABAR was a very powerful king. He fought and conquered all the surrounding countries, killing all the old men and women, but the able-bodied men and girls he caught and brought back as slaves, and they worked on the farms until they died.

This king had two hundred wives, but none of them had borne a son to him. His subjects, seeing that he was becoming an old man, begged him to marry one of the spider's daughters, as they always had plenty of children. But when the king saw the spider's daughter he did not like her, as she was ugly, and the people said it was because her mother had had so many children at the same time. However, in order to please his people he married the ugly girl, and placed her among his other wives, but they all complained because she was so ugly, and said she could not live with them. The king, therefore, built her a separate house for herself, where she was given food and drink the same as the other wives. Everyone jeered at her on account of her ugliness; but she was not really ugly, but beautiful, as she was born with two skins, and at her birth her mother was made to promise that she should never remove the ugly skin until a certain time arrived save only during the night, and that she must put it on again before dawn. Now the king's head wife knew this, and was very fearful lest the king should find it out and fall in love with the spider's daughter; so she went to a Ju Ju man and offered him two hundred rods to make a potion that would make the king forget altogether that the spider's daughter was his wife. This the Ju Ju man finally consented to do, after much haggling over the price, for three hundred and fifty rods; and he made up some 'medicine', which the head wife mixed with the king's food.

For some months this had the effect of making the king forget the spider's daughter, and he used to pass quite close to her without recognising her in any way. When four months had elapsed and the king had not once sent for Adiaha (for that was the name of the spider's daughter), she began to get tired, and went back to her parents. Her father, the spider, then took her to another Ju Ju man, who, by making spells and casting lots, very soon discovered that it was the king's head wife who had made the Ju Ju and had enchanted the king so that he would not look at Adiaha. He therefore told the spider that Adiaha should give the king some medicine which he would prepare, which would make the king remember her. He prepared the medicine, for which the spider had to pay a large sum of money; and that very day Adiaha made a small dish of food, into which she had placed the medicine, and presented it to the king. Directly he had eaten the dish his eyes were opened and he recognised his wife, and told her to come to him that very evening. So in the afternoon, being very joyful, she went down to the river and washed, and when she returned she put on her best cloth and went to the king's palace.

Directly it was dark and all the lights were out she pulled off her ugly skin, and the king saw how beautiful she was, and was very pleased with her; but when the cock crowed Adiaha pulled on her ugly skin again, and went back to her own house.

This she did for four nights running, always taking the ugly skin off in the dark, and leaving before daylight in the morning. In course of time, to the great surprise of all the people, and particularly of the king's two hundred wives, she gave birth to a son; but what surprised them most of all was that only one son was born, whereas her mother had always had a great many children at a time, generally about fifty.

The king's head wife became more jealous than ever when Adiaha had a son; so she went again to the Ju Ju man, and by giving him a large present induced him to give her some medicine which would make the king sick and forget his son. And the medicine would then make the king go to the Ju Ju man, who would tell him that it was his son who had made him sick, as he wanted to reign instead of his father. The Ju Ju man would also tell the king that if he wanted to recover he must throw his son away into the water.

And the king, when he had taken the medicine, went to the Ju Ju man, who told him everything as had been arranged with the head wife. But at first the king did not want to destroy his son. Then his chief subjects begged him to throw his son away, and said that perhaps in a year's time he might get another son. So the king at last agreed, and threw his son into the river, at which the mother grieved and cried bitterly.

Then the head wife went again to the Ju Ju man and got more medicine, which made the king forget Adiaha for three years, during which time she was in mourning for her son. She then returned to her father, and he got some more medicine from his Ju Ju man, which Adiaha gave to the king. And the king knew her and called her to him again, and she lived with him as before. Now the Ju Ju who had helped Adiaha's father, the spider, was a Water Ju Ju, and he was ready when the king threw his son into the water, and saved his life and took him home and kept him alive. And the boy grew up very strong.

After a time Adiaha gave birth to a daughter, and her the jealous wife also persuaded the king to throw away. It took a longer time to persuade him, but at last he agreed, and threw his daughter into the water too, and forgot Adiaha again. But the Water Ju Ju was ready again, and when he had saved the little girl, he thought the time had arrived to punish the action of the jealous wife;

so he went about amongst the head young men and persuaded them to hold a wrestling match in the market place every week. This was done, and the Water Ju Ju told the king's son, who had become very strong, and was very like to his father in appearance, that he should go and wrestle, and that no one would be able to stand up before him. It was then arranged that there should be a grand wrestling match, to which all the strongest men in the country were invited, and the king promised to attend with his head wife.

On the day of the match the Water Ju Ju told the king's son that he need not be in the least afraid, and that his Ju Ju was so powerful, that even the strongest and best wrestlers in the country would not be able to stand up against him for even a few minutes. All the people of the country came to see the great contest, to the winner of which the king had promised to present prizes of cloth and money, and all the strongest men came. When they saw the king's son, whom nobody knew, they laughed and said, "Who is this small boy? He can have no chance against us." But when they came to wrestle, they very soon found that they were no match for him. The boy was very strong indeed, beautifully made and good to look upon, and all the people were surprised to see how like he was to the king.

After wrestling for the greater part of the day the king's son was declared the winner, having thrown everyone who had stood up against him; in fact, some of his opponents had been badly hurt, and had their arms or ribs broken owing to the tremendous strength of the boy. After the match was over the king presented him with cloth and money, and invited him to dine with him in the evening. The boy gladly accepted his father's invitation; and after he had had a good wash in the river, put on his cloth and went up to the palace, where he found the head chiefs of the country and some of the king's most favoured wives. They then sat down to their meal, and the king had his own son, whom he did not know, sitting next to him. On the other side of the boy sat the jealous wife, who had been the cause of all the trouble. All through the dinner this woman did her best to make friends with the boy, with whom she had fallen violently in love on account of his beautiful appearance, his strength, and his being the best wrestler in the country. The woman thought to herself, "I will have this boy as my husband, as my husband is now an old man and will surely soon die." The boy, however, who was as wise as he was strong, was quite aware of everything the jealous woman had done, and although he pretended to be very flattered at the advances of the king's head wife, he did not respond very readily, and went home as soon as he could.

When he returned to the Water Ju Ju's house he told him everything that had happened, and the Water Ju Ju said –

"As you are now in high favour with the king, you must go to him tomorrow and beg a favour from him. The favour you will ask is that all the country shall be called together, and that a certain case shall be tried, and that when the case is finished, the man or woman who is found to be in the wrong shall be killed by the Egbos before all the people."

So the following morning the boy went to the king, who readily granted his request, and at once sent all round the country appointing a day for all the people to come in and hear the case tried. Then the boy went back to the Water Ju Ju, who told him to go to his mother and tell her who he was, and that when the day of the trial arrived, she was to take off her ugly skin and appear in all her beauty, for the time had come when she need no longer wear it. This the son did.

When the day of trial arrived, Adiaha sat in a corner of the square, and nobody recognised the beautiful stranger as the spider's daughter. Her son then sat down next to her, and brought his sister with him. Immediately his mother saw her she said –

"This must be my daughter, whom I have long mourned as dead," and embraced her most affectionately.

The king and his head wife then arrived and sat on their stones in the middle of the square, all the people saluting them with the usual greetings. The king then addressed the people, and said that he had called them together to hear a strong palaver at the request of the young man who had been the victor of the wrestling, and who had promised that if the case went against him he would offer up his life to the Egbo. The king also said that if, on the other hand, the case was decided in the boy's favour, then the other party would be killed, even though it were himself or one of his wives; whoever it was would have to take his or her place on the killing-stone and have their heads cut off by the Egbos. To this all the people agreed, and said they would like to hear what the young man had to say. The young man then walked round the square, and bowed to the king and the people, and asked the question, "Am I not worthy to be the son of any chief in the country?" And all the people answered "Yes!"

The boy then brought his sister out into the middle, leading her by the hand. She was a beautiful girl and well made. When everyone had looked at her he said, "Is not my sister worthy to be any chief's daughter?" And the people replied that she was worthy of being anyone's daughter, even the king's. Then he called his mother Adiaha, and she came out, looking very beautiful with her best cloth and beads on, and all the people cheered, as they had never seen a finer woman. The boy then asked them, "Is this woman worthy of being the king's wife?" And a shout went up from everyone present that she would be a proper wife for the king, and looked as if she would be the mother of plenty of fine healthy sons.

Then the boy pointed out the jealous woman who was sitting next to the king, and told the people his story, how that his mother, who had two skins, was the spider's daughter; how she had married the king, and how the head wife was jealous and had made a bad Ju Ju for the king, which made him forget his wife; how she had persuaded the king to throw himself and his sister into the river, which, as they all knew, had been done, but the Water Ju Ju had saved both of them, and had brought them up.

Then the boy said: "I leave the king and all of you people to judge my case. If I have done wrong, let me be killed on the stone by the Egbos; if, on the other hand, the woman has done evil, then let the Egbos deal with her as you may decide."

When the king knew that the wrestler was his son he was very glad, and told the Egbos to take the jealous woman away, and punish her in accordance with their laws. The Egbos decided that the woman was a witch; so they took her into the forest and tied her up to a stake, and gave her two hundred lashes with a whip made from hippopotamus hide, and then burnt her alive, so that she should not make any more trouble, and her ashes were thrown into the river. The king then embraced his wife and daughter, and told all the people that she, Adiaha, was his proper wife, and would be the queen for the future.

When the palaver was over, Adiaha was dressed in fine clothes and beads, and carried back in state to the palace by the king's servants.

That night the king gave a big feast to all his subjects, and told them how glad he was to get back his beautiful wife whom he had never known properly before, also his son who was stronger than all men, and his fine daughter. The feast continued for a hundred and sixty-six days; and the king made a law that if any woman was found out getting medicine against her husband, she should be killed at once. Then the king built three new compounds, and placed many slaves in them, both men and women. One compound he gave to his wife, another to his son, and the third he gave to his daughter. They all lived together quite happily for some years until the king died, when his son came to the throne and ruled in his stead.

The Orphan Boy and the Magic Stone

A CHIEF OF INDE NAMED INKITA had a son named Ayong Kita, whose mother had died at his birth.

The old chief was a hunter, and used to take his son out with him when he went into the bush. He used to do most of his hunting in the long grass which grows over nearly all the Inde country, and used to kill plenty of bush buck in the dry season.

In those days the people had no guns, so the chief had to shoot everything he got with his bow and arrows, which required a lot of skill.

When his little son was old enough, he gave him a small bow and some small arrows, and taught him how to shoot. The little boy was very quick at learning, and by continually practising at lizards and small birds, soon became expert in the use of his little bow, and could hit them almost every time he shot at them.

When the boy was ten years old his father died, and as he thus became the head of his father's house, and was in authority over all the slaves, they became very discontented, and made plans to kill him, so he ran away into the bush.

Having nothing to eat, he lived for several days on the nuts which fell from the palm trees. He was too young to kill any large animals, and only had his small bow and arrows, with which he killed a few squirrels, bush rats, and small birds, and so managed to live.

Now once at night, when he was sleeping in the hollow of a tree, he had a dream in which his father appeared, and told him where there was plenty of treasure buried in the earth, but, being a small boy, he was frightened, and did not go to the place.

One day, some time after the dream, having walked far and being very thirsty, he went to a lake, and was just going to drink, when he heard a hissing sound, and heard a voice tell him not to drink. Not seeing anyone, he was afraid, and ran away without drinking.

Early next morning, when he was out with his bow trying to shoot some small animal, he met an old woman with quite long hair. She was so ugly that he thought she must be a witch, so he tried to run, but she told him not to fear, as she wanted to help him and assist him to rule over his late father's house. She also told him that it was she who had called out to him at the lake not to drink, as there was a bad Ju Ju in the water which would have killed him. The old woman then took Ayong to a stream some little distance from the lake, and bending down, took out a small shining stone from the water, which she gave to him, at the same time telling him to go to the place which his father had advised him to visit in his dream. She then said, "When you get there you must dig, and you will find plenty of money; you must then go and buy two strong slaves, and when you have got them, you must take them into the forest, away from the town, and get them to build you a house with several rooms in it. You must then place the stone in one of the rooms, and whenever you want anything, all you have to do is to go into the room and tell the stone what you want, and your wishes will be at once gratified."

Ayong did as the old woman told him, and after much difficulty and danger bought the two slaves and built a house in the forest, taking great care of the precious stone, which he placed in an inside room. Then for some time, whenever he wanted anything, he used to go into the room and ask for a sufficient number of rods to buy what he wanted, and they were always brought at once.

This went on for many years, and Ayong grew up to be a man, and became very rich, and bought many slaves, having made friends with the Aro men, who in those days used to do a big traffic in slaves. After ten years had passed Ayong had quite a large town and many slaves, but one night the old woman appeared to him in a dream and told him that she thought that he was sufficiently wealthy, and that it was time for him to return the magic stone to the small stream from whence it came. But Ayong, although he was rich, wanted to rule his father's house and be a head chief for all the Inde country, so he sent for all the Ju Ju men in the country and two witch men, and marched with all his slaves to his father's town. Before he started he held a big palaver, and told them to point out any slave who had a bad heart, and who might kill him when he came to rule the country. Then the Ju Ju men consulted together, and pointed out fifty of the slaves who, they said, were witches, and would try to kill Ayong. He at once had them made prisoners, and tried them by the ordeal of Esere bean to see whether they were witches or not. As none of them could vomit the beans they all died, and were declared to be witches. He then had them buried at once. When the remainder of his slaves saw what had happened, they all came to him and begged his pardon, and promised to serve him faithfully. Although the fifty men were buried they could not rest, and troubled Ayong very much, and after a time he became very sick himself, so he sent again for the Ju Ju men, who told him that it was the witch men who, although they were dead and buried, had power to come out at night and used to suck Ayong's blood, which was the cause of his sickness. They then said, "We are only three Ju Ju men; you must get seven more of us, making the magic number of ten." When they came they dug up the bodies of the fifty witches, and found they were quite fresh. Then Ayong had big fires made, and burned them one after the other, and gave the Ju Ju men a big present. He soon after became quite well again, and took possession of his father's property, and ruled over all the country.

Ever since then, whenever anyone is accused of being a witch, they are tried by the ordeal of the poisonous Esere bean, and if they can vomit they do not die, and are declared innocent, but if they cannot do so, they die in great pain.

The Goblin of Adachigahara

LONG, LONG AGO there was a large plain called Adachigahara, in the province of Mutsu in Japan. This place was said to be haunted by a cannibal goblin who took the form of an old woman. From time to time many travelers disappeared and were never heard of more, and the old women round the charcoal braziers in the evenings, and the girls washing the household rice at the wells in the mornings, whispered dreadful stories of how the missing folk had been lured to the goblin's cottage and devoured, for the goblin lived only on human flesh. No one dared to venture near the haunted spot after sunset, and all those who could, avoided it in the daytime, and travelers were warned of the dreaded place.

One day as the sun was setting, a priest came to the plain. He was a belated traveler, and his robe showed that he was a Buddhist pilgrim walking from shrine to shrine to pray for some blessing or to crave for forgiveness of sins. He had apparently lost his way, and as it was late he met no one who could show him the road or warn him of the haunted spot.

He had walked the whole day and was now tired and hungry, and the evenings were chilly, for it was late autumn, and he began to be very anxious to find some house where he could obtain a night's lodging. He found himself lost in the midst of the large plain, and looked about in vain for some sign of human habitation.

At last, after wandering about for some hours, he saw a clump of trees in the distance, and through the trees he caught sight of the glimmer of a single ray of light. He exclaimed with joy:

"Oh. surely that is some cottage where I can get a night's lodging!"

Keeping the light before his eyes he dragged his weary, aching feet as quickly as he could towards the spot, and soon came to a miserable-looking little cottage. As he drew near he saw that it was in a tumble-down condition, the bamboo fence was broken and weeds and grass pushed their way through the gaps. The paper screens which serve as windows and doors in Japan were full of holes, and the posts of the house were bent with age and seemed scarcely able to support the old thatched roof. The hut was open, and by the light of an old lantern an old woman sat industriously spinning.

The pilgrim called to her across the bamboo fence and said:

"O Baa San (old woman), good evening! I am a traveler! Please excuse me, but I have lost my way and do not know what to do, for I have nowhere to rest tonight. I beg you to be good enough to let me spend the night under your roof."

The old woman as soon as she heard herself spoken to stopped spinning, rose from her seat and approached the intruder.

"I am very sorry for you. You must indeed be distressed to have lost your way in such a lonely spot so late at night. Unfortunately I cannot put you up, for I have no bed to offer you, and no accommodation whatsoever for a guest in this poor place!"

"Oh, that does not matter," said the priest; "all I want is a shelter under some roof for the night, and if you will be good enough just to let me lie on the kitchen floor I shall be grateful. I am too tired to walk further tonight, so I hope you will not refuse me, otherwise I shall have to sleep out on the cold plain." And in this way he pressed the old woman to let him stay.

She seemed very reluctant, but at last she said:

"Very well, I will let you stay here. I can offer you a very poor welcome only, but come in now and I will make a fire, for the night is cold."

The pilgrim was only too glad to do as he was told. He took off his sandals and entered the hut. The old woman then brought some sticks of wood and lit the fire, and bade her guest draw near and warm himself.

"You must be hungry after your long tramp," said the old woman. "I will go and cook some supper for you." She then went to the kitchen to cook some rice.

After the priest had finished his supper the old woman sat down by the fire-place, and they talked together for a long time. The pilgrim thought to himself that he had been very lucky to come across such a kind, hospitable old woman. At last the wood gave out, and as the fire died slowly down he began to shiver with cold just as he had done when he arrived.

"I see you are cold," said the old woman; "I will go out and gather some wood, for we have used it all. You must stay and take care of the house while I am gone."

"No, no," said the pilgrim, "let me go instead, for you are old, and I cannot think of letting you go out to get wood for me this cold night!"

The old woman shook her head and said:

"You must stay quietly here, for you are my guest." Then she left him and went out.

In a minute she came back and said:

"You must sit where you are and not move, and whatever happens don't go near or look into the inner room. Now mind what I tell you!"

"If you tell me not to go near the back room, of course I won't," said the priest, rather bewildered.

The old woman then went out again, and the priest was left alone. The fire had died out, and the only light in the hut was that of a dim lantern. For the first time that night he began to feel that he was in a weird place, and the old woman's words, "Whatever you do don't peep into the back room," aroused his curiosity and his fear.

What hidden thing could be in that room that she did not wish him to see? For some time the remembrance of his promise to the old woman kept him still, but at last he could no longer resist his curiosity to peep into the forbidden place.

He got up and began to move slowly towards the back room. Then the thought that the old woman would be very angry with him if he disobeyed her made him come back to his place by the fireside.

As the minutes went slowly by and the old woman did not return, he began to feel more and more frightened, and to wonder what dreadful secret was in the room behind him. He must find out.

"She will not know that I have looked unless I tell her. I will just have a peep before she comes back," said the man to himself.

With these words he got up on his feet (for he had been sitting all this time in Japanese fashion with his feet under him) and stealthily crept towards the forbidden spot. With trembling hands he pushed back the sliding door and looked in. What he saw froze the blood in his veins. The room was full of dead men's bones and the walls were splashed and the floor was covered with human blood. In one corner skull upon skull rose to the ceiling, in another was a heap of arm bones, in another a heap of leg bones. The sickening smell made him faint. He fell backwards with horror, and for some time lay in a heap with fright on the floor, a pitiful sight. He trembled all over and his teeth chattered, and he could hardly crawl away from the dreadful spot.

"How horrible!" he cried out. "What awful den have I come to in my travels? May Buddha help me or I am lost. Is it possible that that kind old woman is really the cannibal goblin? When she comes back she will show herself in her true character and eat me up at one mouthful!"

With these words his strength came back to him and, snatching up his hat and staff, he rushed out of the house as fast as his legs could carry him. Out into the night he ran, his one thought to get as far as he could from the goblin's haunt. He had not gone far when he heard steps behind him and a voice crying: "Stop! stop!"

He ran on, redoubling his speed, pretending not to hear. As he ran he heard the steps behind him come nearer and nearer, and at last he recognized the old woman's voice which grew louder and louder as she came nearer.

"Stop! stop, you wicked man, why did you look into the forbidden room?"

The priest quite forgot how tired he was and his feet flew over the ground faster than ever. Fear gave him strength, for he knew that if the goblin caught him he would soon be one of her victims. With all his heart he repeated the prayer to Buddha:

"Namu Amida Butsu, Namu Amida Butsu."

And after him rushed the dreadful old hag, her hair flying in the wind, and her face changing with rage into the demon that she was. In her hand she carried a large blood-stained knife, and she still shrieked after him, "Stop! stop!"

At last, when the priest felt he could run no more, the dawn broke, and with the darkness of night the goblin vanished and he was safe. The priest now knew that he had met the Goblin of Adachigahara, the story of whom he had often heard but never believed to be true. He felt that he owed his wonderful escape to the protection of Buddha to whom he had prayed for help, so he took out his rosary and bowing his head as the sun rose he said his prayers and made his thanksgiving earnestly. He then set forward for another part of the country, only too glad to leave the haunted plain behind him.

A Bell and the Power of Karma

NEAR THE BANKS OF THE HIDAKA there once stood a far-famed tea-house nestling amid lovely scenery beside a hill called the Dragon's Claw. The fairest girl in this tea-house was Kiyo, for she was like "the fragrance of white lilies, when the wind, sweeping down the mountain heights, comes perfume-laden to the traveller."

Across the river stood a Buddhist temple where the abbot and a number of priests lived a simple and devout life. In the belfry of this temple reposed a great bell, six inches thick and weighing several tons. It was one of the monastery rules that none of the priests should eat fish or meat or drink *sake*, and they were especially forbidden to stop at tea-houses, lest they should lose their spirituality and fall into the sinful ways of the flesh.

One of the priests, however, on returning from a certain shrine, happened to see the pretty Kiyo, flitting hither and thither in the tea-garden, like a large, bright-winged butterfly. He stood and watched her for a moment, sorely tempted to enter the garden and speak to this beautiful creature, but, remembering his priestly calling, he crossed the river and entered his temple. That night, however, he could not sleep. The fever of a violent love had come upon him. He fingered his rosary and repeated passages from the Buddhist Scriptures, but these things brought him no peace of mind. Through all his pious thoughts there ever shone the winsome face of Kiyo, and it seemed to him that she was calling from that fair garden across the river.

His burning love grew so intense that it was not long before he stifled his religious feelings, broke one of the temple rules, and entered the forbidden tea-house. Here he entirely forgot his religion, or found a new one in contemplating the beautiful Kiyo, who brought him refreshment. Night after night he crept across the river and fell under the spell of this woman. She returned his love with equal passion, so that for the moment it appeared to this erring priest that he had found in a woman's charms something far sweeter than the possibility of attaining Nirvana.

After the priest had seen Kiyo on many nights conscience began to stir within him and to do battle with his unholy love. The power of Karma and the teaching of the Lord Buddha struggled within his breast. It was a fierce conflict, but in the end passion was vanquished, though, as we shall learn, not its awful consequences. The priest, having stamped out his carnal love, deemed it wise to deal with Kiyo as circumspectly as possible, lest his sudden change should make her angry.

When Kiyo saw the priest after his victory over the flesh she observed the far-away look in his eyes and the ascetic calm that now rested upon his face. She redoubled her feminine wiles, determined either to make the priest love her again, or, failing that, to put him to a cruel death by sorcery.

All Kiyo's blandishments failed to awaken love within the priest's heart, and, thinking only of vengeance, she set out, arrayed in a white robe, and went to a certain mountain where there was a Fudo shrine. Fudo sat, surrounded by fire, a sword in one hand and a small coil of rope in the other. Here Kiyo prayed with fearful vehemence that this hideous-looking God would show her how to kill the priest who had once loved her.

From Fudo she went to the shrine of Kompira, who has the knowledge of magic and is able to teach sorcery. Here she begged that she might have the power to turn herself at will into a dragon-serpent. After many visits a long-nosed sprite (probably a *tengu*), who waited upon Kompira, taught Kiyo all the mysteries of magic and sorcery. He taught this once sweet girl how to change herself into the awful creature she desired to be for the purpose of a cruel vengeance.

Still the priest visited Kiyo; but no longer was he the lover. By many exhortations he tried to stay the passion of this maiden he once loved; but these priestly discourses only made Kiyo more determined to win the victory in the end. She wept, she pleaded, she wound her fair arms about him; but none of her allurements had the slightest effect, except to drive away the priest for the last time.

Just as the priest was about to take his departure he was horrified to see Kiyo's eyes suddenly turn into those of a serpent. With a shriek of fear he ran out of the tea-garden, swam across the river, and hid himself inside the great temple bell.

Kiyo raised her magic wand, murmured a certain incantation, and in a moment the sweet face and form of this lovely maiden became transformed into that of a dragon-serpent, hissing and spirting fire. With eyes as large and luminous as moons she crawled over the garden, swam across the river, and entered the belfry. Her weight broke down the supporting columns, and the bell, with the priest inside, fell with a deafening crash to the ground.

Kiyo embraced the bell with a terrible lust for vengeance. Her coils held the metal as in a vice; tighter and tighter she hugged the bell, till the metal became red-hot. All in vain was the prayer of the captive priest; all in vain, too, were the earnest entreaties of his fellow brethren, who implored that Buddha would destroy the demon. Hotter and hotter grew the bell, and it rang with the piteous shrieks of the priest within. Presently his voice was stilled, and the bell melted and ran down into a pool of molten metal. The great power of Karma had destroyed it, and with it the priest and the dragon-serpent that was once the beautiful Kiyo.

The Soul of a Mirror

HE SHRINE OF OGAWACHI-MYOJIN fell into decay, and the Shinto priest in charge, Matsumura, journeyed to Kyoto in the hope of successfully appealing to the Shogun for a grant for the restoration of the temple.

Matsumura and his family resided in a house in Kyoto, said to be extremely unlucky, and many tenants had thrown themselves into the well on the north-east side of the dwelling. But Matsumura took no notice of these tales, and was not the least afraid of evil spirits.

During the summer of that year there was a great drought in Kyoto. Though the river-beds dried up and many wells failed for want of rain, the well in Matsumura's garden was full to overflowing. The distress elsewhere, owing to want of water, forced many poor people to beg for it, and for all their drawing the water in this particular well did not diminish.

One day, however, a dead body was found lying in the well, that of a servant who had come to fetch water. In his case suicide was out of the question, and it seemed impossible that he should have accidentally fallen in. When Matsumura heard of the fatality he went to inspect the well. To his surprise the water stirred with a strange rocking movement. When the motion lessened he saw reflected in the clear water the form of a fair young woman. She was touching her lips with *beni*. At length she smiled upon him. It was a strange smile that made Matsumura feel dizzy, a smile that blotted out everything else save the beautiful woman's face. He felt an almost irresistible desire to fling himself into the water in order that he might reach and hold this enchanting woman. He struggled against this strange feeling, however, and was able after a while to enter the house, where he gave orders that a fence should be built round the well, and that from thenceforth no one, on any pretext whatever, should draw water there.

Shortly afterwards the drought came to an end. For three days and nights there was a continuous downpour of rain, and the city shook with an earthquake. On the third night of the storm there was a loud knocking at Matsumura's door. The priest himself inquired who his visitor might be. He half opened the door, and saw once more the woman he had seen in the well. He refused her admission, and asked why she had been guilty of taking the lives of so many harmless and innocent people.

Thus the woman made answer: "Alas! good priest, I have never desired to lure human beings to their death. It is the Poison Dragon, who lived in that well, who forced me against my will to entice people to death. But now the Gods have compelled the Poison Dragon to live elsewhere, so that tonight I was able to leave my place of captivity. Now there is but little water in the well, and if you will search there you will find my body. Take care of it for me and I shall not fail to reward your goodness." With these words she vanished as suddenly as she had appeared.

Next day well-cleaners searched the well, and discovered some ancient hair ornaments and an old metal mirror.

Matsumura, being a wise man, took the mirror and cleaned it, believing that it might reveal a solution to the mystery.

Upon the back of the mirror he discovered several characters. Many of the ideographs were too blurred to be legible, but he managed to make out "third month, the third day." In ancient time the third month used to be called *Yayoi*, or Month of Increase, and remembering that the woman had called herself Yayoi, Matsumura realised that he had probably received a visit from the Soul of the Mirror.

Matsumura took every care of the mirror. He ordered it to be resilvered and polished, and when this had been done he laid it in a box specially made for it, and mirror and box were placed in a particular room in the house.

One day, when Matsumura was sitting in the apartment where the mirror reposed, he once more saw Yayoi standing before him, looking more beautiful than ever, and the refulgence of her beauty was like summer moonlight. After she had saluted Matsumura she explained that she was indeed the Soul of the Mirror, and narrated how she had fallen into the possession of Lady Kamo, of the Imperial Court, and how she had become an heirloom of the Fujiwara House, until during the period of Hogen, when the Taira and Minamoto clans were engaged in conflict, she was thrown into a well, and there forgotten. Having narrated these things, and all the horrors she had gone through under the tyranny of the Poison Dragon, Yayoi begged that Matsumura would present the mirror to the Shogun, the Lord Yoshimasa, who was a descendant of her former possessors, promising the priest considerable good fortune if he did so. Before Yayoi departed she advised Matsumura to leave his home immediately, as it was about to be washed away by a great storm.

On the following day Matsumura left the house, and, as Yayoi had prophesied, almost immediately afterwards his late dwelling was swept away.

At length Matsumura was able to present, the mirror to the Shogun Yoshimasa, together with a written account of its strange history. The Shogun was so pleased with the gift that he not only gave Matsumura many personal presents, but he also presented the priest with a considerable sum of money for the rebuilding of his temple.

The Honest Witch

THERE WAS A KOREAN ONCE, called Song Sang-in, whose mind was upright and whose spirit was true. He hated witches with all his might, and regarded them as deceivers of the people. "By their so-called prayers," said he, "they devour the people's goods. There is no limit to the foolishness and extravagance that accompanies them. This doctrine of theirs is all nonsense. Would that I could rid the earth of them and wipe out their names for ever."

Some time later Song was appointed magistrate of Nam Won County in Chulla Province. On his arrival he issued the following order: "If any witch is found in this county, let her be beaten to death." The whole place was so thoroughly spied upon that all the witches made their escape to other prefectures. The magistrate thought, "Now we are rid of them, and that ends the matter for this county at any rate."

On a certain day he went out for a walk, and rested for a time at Kwang-han Pavilion. As he looked out from his coign of vantage, he saw a woman approaching on horseback with a witch's drum on her head. He looked intently to make sure, and to his astonishment he saw that she was indeed a mutang (witch). He sent a yamen-runner to have her arrested, and when she was brought before him he asked, "Are you a mutang?"

She replied, "Yes, I am."

"Then," said he, "you did not know of the official order issued?"

"Oh yes, I heard of it," was her reply.

He then asked, "Are you not afraid to die, that you stay here in this county?"

The mutang bowed, and made answer, "I have a matter of complaint to lay before your Excellency to be put right; please take note of it and grant my request. It is this: There are true mutangs and false mutangs. False mutangs ought to be killed, but you would not kill an honest mutang, would you? Your orders pertain to false mutangs; I do not understand them as pertaining to those who are true. I am an honest mutang; I knew you would not kill me, so I remained here in peace."

The magistrate asked, "How do you know that there are honest mutangs?"

The woman replied, "Let's put the matter to the test and see. If I am not proven honest, let me die."

"Very well," said the magistrate; "but can you really make good, and do you truly know how to call back departed spirits?"

The mutang answered, "I can."

The magistrate suddenly thought of an intimate friend who had been dead for some time, and he said to her, "I had a friend of such and such rank in Seoul; can you call his spirit back to me?"

The mutang replied, "Let me do so; but first you must prepare food, with wine, and serve it properly."

The magistrate thought for a moment, and then said to himself, "It is a serious matter to take a person's life; let me find out first if she is true or not, and then decide." So he had the food brought.

The mutang said also, "I want a suit of your clothes, too, please." This was brought, and she spread her mat in the courtyard, placed the food in order, donned the dress, and so made all preliminary arrangements. She then lifted her eyes toward heaven and uttered the strange magic sounds by which spirits are called, meanwhile shaking a tinkling bell. In a little she turned and said, "I've come." Then she began telling the sad story of his sickness and death and their separation. She reminded the magistrate of how they had played together, and of things that had happened when they were at school at their lessons; of the difficulties they had met in the examinations; of experiences that had come to them during their terms of office. She told secrets that they had confided to each other as intimate friends, and many matters most definitely that only they two knew. Not a single mistake did she make, but told the truth in every detail.

The magistrate, when he heard these things, began to cry, saying, "The soul of my friend is really present; I can no longer doubt or deny it." Then he ordered the choicest fare possible to be prepared as a sacrifice to his friend. In a little the friend bade him farewell and took his departure.

The magistrate said, "Alas! I thought mutangs were a brood of liars, but now I know that there are true mutangs as well as false." He gave her rich rewards, sent her away in safety, recalled his order against witches, and refrained from any matters pertaining to them for ever after.

The House Dew and the Witch

ONCE A PADISHAH had three daughters. Before setting out on a journey he called his daughters before him and instructed them to feed his favourite horse personally, and not to entrust that duty to any other, as he would allow no stranger near it. The Padishah went away, and the eldest daughter carried food to the stable: the horse, however, would not permit her to approach him. The second daughter made the attempt, with no better result. Then the youngest went to the horse, who was perfectly quiet, and willingly received the food and drink from her hands. The two eldest sisters were glad thus to be relieved of an irksome and disagreeable duty.

When the Padishah returned home his first inquiry was as to whether his horse had been properly attended to during his absence. "He would not allow us even to go near him," answered the two elder daughters, "but our youngest sister has fed him."

On hearing this the monarch said that she should be wife to the horse, his other daughters being given in marriage to the Vezir and Sheik-ul-Islam respectively, The triple wedding festivities lasted forty days, and the youngest then went to her stable, while her sisters were taken to their splendid palaces,

Only in the daytime, how ever, had the youngest sister a horse for a husband and a stable for a dwelling. By night the stable was transformed into a rose garden and the horse into a handsome youth. Thus they lived in the utmost felicity, no one except themselves knowing their secret.

It came to pass that the Padishah arranged a tournament in the court yard of the palace, and the bravest of all the knights who took part therein were the husbands of the monarch's eldest daughters, "Look!" said they to their sister of the stable, "our husbands are like lions: see how beautifully they throw their lances. Where is your horse-husband?" At this the horse shook himself, changed into human form, mounted a steed, and begging his wife not to reveal his identity, he plunged into the fray. He overcame all the combatants, unhorsed his brothers-in-law, then vanished as completely as though he had never been there.

Next day the tournament was continued, and the elder sisters treated the youngest with scorn and contempt; but again the unknown hero appeared, struck down all his opponents, and vanished as before.

On the third day the horse-knight said to his wife: "If at any time I am in danger, or you are in need of help, burn these three hairs, and wherever you may be, I will come to you." Then he hastened to the tournament and fought again with his brothers-in-law. His prowess evoked universal admiration even his sisters-in-law could not withhold their tribute of praise; but in ill-natured raillery they said to their youngest sister: "See how these knights understand the tournament; they are not like your horse-husband."

The poor woman could no longer forbear to answer that the beautiful and valiant knight was her husband; but even as she turned to point him out, he vanished. This reminded her that he had warned her never to divulge the secret. Overcome with remorse, she awaited eagerly his return to the stable, but in vain; neither horse nor man came – neither roses nor garden were to be hers that night.

"Woe is me!" she groaned, "I have betrayed my husband; I have broken my promise; thus am I punished!" She did not close her eyes all night, but wept until morning. When it was daylight she went to her father the Padishah, and with tears told him what had happened, vowing that she would go in search of her husband even if she journeyed to the ends of the earth. In vain her father attempted to dissuade her. He reminded her that her husband was a Dew and consequently she would never find him; but all his arguments failed to shake her resolution.

Grief stricken she set out on her quest, and walked so long that at last she sank exhausted at the foot of a mountain. Here, remembering the three hairs, she burned one of them, and the next instant her husband enfolded her in his arms. Both were almost speechless with joy.

"Did I not counsel you never to betray our secret to anyone?" gently chided the youth. "If my mother sees us now she will separate us immediately. This mountain is our abode; my mother will be here directly, and woe to us if she catch sight of us."

The poor girl was terrified at these words, grieving bitterly that no sooner had she found her husband than she must lose him again. The Dew-son pitied her, gave her a light blow and changed her into an apple, which he put upon a shelf. Shrieking loudly, the witch flew down from the mountain, crying that she could smell human flesh and that human flesh she must have. In vain her son denied it – she refused to believe him.

"If you will swear on the egg to do it no harm, I will show you what I have hidden," said the youth. The witch accordingly promised, whereon the youth gave the apple a light blow and the beautiful maiden appeared. "Behold my wife!" said he. The old woman said nothing, but set her daughter-in-law some simple tasks, and went back to her work.

For a few days the husband and wife were allowed to live in peace, but the old witch was only waiting till her son went away from home to wreak her vengeance on his wife. At last she found an opportunity. "Sweep and don't sweep," she commanded the maiden, and went away. The poor girl was perplexed to know what she must "sweep" and what "not sweep." Recollecting the hairs, she took one and burnt it. Instantly her husband appeared, and she told him her difficulty. He explained that she must "sweep" the room and "not sweep" the courtyard.

The maiden acted accordingly. Towards evening the witch came in and asked whether the work was done. "I have swept and not swept," answered the daughter-in-law. "You deceitful thing!" scolded the old woman, "you have not thought that out for yourself; my son has certainly taught you."

Next day the old witch came again and gave the maiden three bowls, which she ordered her to fill with her tears. The maid wept and wept continually, but failed to fill even one of the vessels. In her difficulty she burnt the third hair, whereupon her husband appeared and advised her to fill the bowls with water and add a quantity of salt thereto. This the maiden did, and when the old woman came home in the evening, she was shown the three vessels duly filled. "You cunning creature!" stormed the witch, "that is not your own work; but you and my son shall not cheat me again."

On the following day she ordered her daughter-in-law to make a pancake. But though the maiden sought everywhere, not a single ingredient for the purpose could she find. This time she could expect no help, for her husband was away, and the three magic hairs had all been burned. The youth, however, suspecting his mother's wicked intentions, returned home unexpectedly to his wife, and seeing her in such grief he suggested that they should flee. "My mother will not rest until she has wrought your ruin," he said. "Let us escape before she returns." So they went together out into the wide world.

In the evening the witch came home, and saw that both her daughter-in-law and son were missing. "The wretches have abandoned me!" she shrieked, and calling her witch-sister to her, she sent her to follow the fugitives and bring them back. The second witch got into a bowl, made a whip out of snakes, and was off like a lightning-flash. But the Dew-son, seeing his aunt behind them in the distance, gave the maiden a light blow and changed her into a swimming-bath. He transformed himself into a bath attendant, and stood before the door. The witch came up, alighted from the bowl, and inquired of him whether he had seen a youth and a maiden. "I am just warming the bath," answered the youth; "there is no one in; if you do not believe me, go in and see for yourself." The woman, perceiving she could do nothing with him, reentered the bowl, went back to her sister, and reported the failure of her errand.

The witch asked her whether she had met anyone on the way. "Oh yes," answered she, "I spoke to the attendant at the door of a swimming bath, but he was either deaf or stupid, for I could get nothing out of him." "You were even more stupid," scolded the witch, "not to recognize that the bath and the attendant were my daughter-in-law and son." Now she called another sister and sent her after the fugitives.

The Dew-son looking back, saw his other aunt coming towards them in a bowl. He knocked his wife gently and she became a spring; he himself stood beside and drew water. The witch came up and asked whether he had seen anything of a youth and a maiden. "This spring has excellent drinking-water," the fellow answered with an air of simplicity. The woman, thinking he was too stupid to understand her questions, hurried back to her sister with the intelligence that she could see nothing of the missing couple. The witch inquired whether she had seen anyone on the way. "Only an imbecile drawing water from a spring," was the answer. "That imbecile was my son," exclaimed the witch in a great rage, "and the spring was his wife. I see I shall have to go myself." So she stepped into the bowl, made a whip out of snakes, and set off.

Looking back the youth now saw that his mother herself was coming. Striking the maid gently he turned her into a tree, and himself into a snake coiled round it. The witch knew them, and would have torn the tree to pieces if she could have done so without harming her son. So she said to the snake, "My son, at least show me the little finger of the maid and then I will leave you in peace."

The son saw that the only way to get rid of his mother was to do as she asked. He therefore allowed one of the maid's fingers to become visible this his mother immediately devoured, and then vanished.

At another gentle blow from her husband the maid again resumed her human form; and the two went home to her father, the Padishah. His talisman having been destroyed, the youth became a mortal, and as he was no longer a Dew, his witch-mother had no more power over him. The Padishah rejoiced in the return of his lost children, their marriage was again celebrated with great pomp, and after the old monarch's decease they reigned in his stead.

The Dead Witch

THERE WAS ONCE AN OLD WOMAN who was a terrible witch, and she had a daughter and a granddaughter. The time came for the old crone to die, so she summoned her daughter and gave her these instructions:

"Mind, daughter! when I'm dead, don't you wash my body with lukewarm water; but fill a cauldron, make it boil its very hottest, and then with that boiling water regularly scald me all over."

After saying this, the witch lay ill two or three days, and then died. The daughter ran round to all her neighbors, begging them to come and help her to wash the old woman, and meantime the little granddaughter was left all alone in the cottage. And this is what she saw there. All of a sudden there crept out from beneath the stove two demons – a big one and a tiny one – and they ran up to the dead witch. The old demon seized her by the feet, and tore away at her so that he stripped off all her skin at one pull. Then he said to the little demon:

"Take the flesh for yourself, and lug it under the stove."

So the little demon flung his arms round the carcase, and dragged it under the stove. Nothing was left of the old woman but her skin. Into it the old demon inserted himself, and then he lay down just where the witch had been lying.

Presently the daughter came back, bringing a dozen other women with her, and they all set to work laying out the corpse.

"Mammy," says the child, "they've pulled granny's skin off while you were away."

"What do you mean by telling such lies?"

"It's quite true, Mammy! There was ever such a blackie came from under the stove, and he pulled the skin off, and got into it himself."

"Hold your tongue, naughty child! you're talking nonsense!" cried the old crone's daughter; then she fetched a big cauldron, filled it with cold water, put it on the stove, and heated it till it boiled furiously. Then the women lifted up the old crone, laid her in a trough, took hold of the cauldron, and poured the whole of the boiling water over her at once. The demon couldn't stand it. He leaped out of the trough, dashed through the doorway, and disappeared, skin and all. The women stared:

"What marvel is this?" they cried. "Here was the dead woman, and now she isn't here. There's nobody left to lay out or to bury. The demons have carried her off before our very eyes!"

The Witch and Ivashko

THERE ONCE LIVED AN OLD COUPLE who had one son called Ivashko; no one can tell how fond they were of him!

Well, one day, Ivashko said to his father and mother:

"I'll go out fishing if you'll let me."

"What are you thinking about! you're still very small; suppose you get drowned, what good will there be in that?"

"No, no, I shan't get drowned. I'll catch you some fish; do let me go!"

So his mother put a white shirt on him, tied a red girdle round him, and let him go. Out in a boat he sat and said:

> *"Canoe, canoe, float a little farther,*
> *Canoe, canoe, float a little farther!"*

Then the canoe floated on farther and farther, and Ivashko began to fish. When some little time had passed by, the old woman hobbled down to the river side and called to her son:

> *"Ivashechko, Ivashechko, my boy,*
> *Float up, float up, unto the waterside;*
> *I bring thee food and drink."*

And Ivashko said:

> *"Canoe, canoe, float to the waterside;*
> *That is my mother calling me."*

The boat floated to the shore: the woman took the fish, gave her boy food and drink, changed his shirt for him and his girdle, and sent him back to his fishing. Again he sat in his boat and said:

> *"Canoe, canoe, float a little farther,*
> *Canoe, canoe, float a little farther."*

Then the canoe floated on farther and farther, and Ivashko began to fish. After a little time had passed by, the old man also hobbled down to the bank and called to his son:

"Ivashechko, Ivashechko, my boy,
Float up, float up, unto the waterside;
I bring thee food and drink."

And Ivashko replied:

"Canoe, canoe, float to the waterside;
That is my father calling me."

The canoe floated to the shore. The old man took the fish, gave his boy food and drink, changed his shirt for him and his girdle, and sent him back to his fishing.

Now a certain witch had heard what Ivashko's parents had cried aloud to him, and she longed to get hold of the boy. So she went down to the bank and cried with a hoarse voice:

"Ivashechko, Ivashechko, my boy,
Float up, float up, unto the waterside;
I bring thee food and drink."

Ivashko perceived that the voice was not his mother's, but was that of a witch, and he sang:

"Canoe, canoe, float a little farther,
Canoe, canoe, float a little farther;
That is not my mother, but a witch who calls me."

The witch saw that she must call Ivashko with just such a voice as his mother had.

So she hastened to a smith and said to him:

"Smith, smith! make me just such a thin little voice as Ivashko's mother has: if you don't, I'll eat you." So the smith forged her a little voice just like Ivashko's mother's. Then the witch went down by night to the shore and sang:

"Ivashechko, Ivashechko, my boy,
Float up, float up, unto the waterside;
I bring thee food and drink."

Ivashko came, and she took the fish, and seized the boy and carried him home with her. When she arrived she said to her daughter Alenka, "Heat the stove as hot as you can, and bake Ivashko well, while I go and collect my friends for the feast." So Alenka heated the stove hot, ever so hot, and said to Ivashko:

"Come here and sit on this shovel!"

"I'm still very young and foolish," answered Ivashko: "I haven't yet quite got my wits about me. Please teach me how one ought to sit on a shovel."

"Very good," said Alenka; "it won't take long to teach you."

But the moment she sat down on the shovel, Ivashko instantly pitched her into the oven, slammed to the iron plate in front of it, ran out of the hut, shut the door, and hurriedly climbed up ever so high an oak-tree [which stood close by].

Presently the witch arrived with her guests and knocked at the door of the hut. But nobody opened it for her.

"Ah! that cursed Alenka!" she cried. "No doubt she's gone off somewhere to amuse herself." Then she slipped in through the window, opened the door, and let in her guests. They all sat down to table, and the witch opened the oven, took out Alenka's baked body, and served it up. They all ate their fill and drank their fill, and then they went out into the courtyard and began rolling about on the grass.

"I turn about, I roll about, having fed on Ivashko's flesh," cried the witch. "I turn about, I roll about, having fed on Ivashko's flesh."

But Ivashko called out to her from the top of the oak:

"Turn about, roll about, having fed on Alenka's flesh!"

"Did I hear something?" said the witch. "No it was only the noise of the leaves." Again the witch began:

"I turn about, I roll about, having fed on Ivashko's flesh!"

And Ivashko repeated:

"Turn about, roll about, having fed on Alenka's flesh!"

Then the witch looked up and saw Ivashko, and immediately rushed at the oak on which Ivashko was seated, and began to gnaw away at it. And she gnawed, and gnawed, and gnawed, until at last she smashed two front teeth. Then she ran to a forge, and when she reached it she cried, "Smith, smith! make me some iron teeth; if you don't I'll eat you!"

So the smith forged her two iron teeth.

The witch returned and began gnawing the oak again.

She gnawed, and gnawed, and was just on the point of gnawing it through, when Ivashko jumped out of it into another tree which stood beside it. The oak that the witch had gnawed through fell down to the ground; but then she saw that Ivashko was sitting up in another tree, so she gnashed her teeth with spite and set to work afresh, to gnaw that tree also. She gnawed, and gnawed, and gnawed – broke two lower teeth, and ran off to the forge.

"Smith, smith!" she cried when she got there, "make me some iron teeth; if you don't I'll eat you!"

The smith forged two more iron teeth for her. She went back again, and once more began to gnaw the oak.

Ivashko didn't know what he was to do now. He looked out, and saw that swans and geese were flying by, so he called to them imploringly:

> "Oh, my swans and geese,
> Take me on your pinions,
> Bear me to my father and my mother,
> To the cottage of my father and my mother,
> There to eat, and drink, and live in comfort."

"Let those in the centre carry you," said the birds.

Ivashko waited; a second flock flew past, and he again cried imploringly:

> "Oh, my swans and geese!
> Take me on your pinions,
> Bear me to my father and my mother,
> To the cottage of my father and my mother,
> There to eat, and drink, and live in comfort."

"Let those in the rear carry you!" said the birds.

Again Ivashko waited. A third flock came flying up, and he cried:

"Oh, my swans and geese!
Take me on your pinions,
Bear me to my father and my mother,
To the cottage of my father and my mother,
There to eat, and drink, and live in comfort."

And those swans and geese took hold of him and carried him back, flew up to the cottage, and dropped him in the upper room.

Early the next morning his mother set to work to bake pancakes, baked them, and all of a sudden fell to thinking about her boy. "Where is my Ivashko?" she cried; "would that I could see him, were it only in a dream!"

Then his father said, "I dreamed that swans and geese had brought our Ivashko home on their wings."

And when she had finished baking the pancakes, she said, "Now, then, old man, let's divide the cakes: there's for you, father! there's for me! There's for you, father! there's for me."

"And none for me?" called out Ivashko.

"There's for you, father!" went on the old woman, "there's for me."

"And none for me!" [repeated the boy.]

"Why, old man," said the wife, "go and see whatever that is up there."

The father climbed into the upper room and there he found TIvashko. The old people were delighted, and asked their boy about everything that had happened. And after that he and they lived on happily together.

The Witch

ONCE UPON A TIME there was a peasant whose wife died, leaving him with two children – twins – a boy and a girl. For some years the poor man lived on alone with the children, caring for them as best he could; but everything in the house seemed to go wrong without a woman to look after it, and at last he made up his mind to marry again, feeling that a wife would bring peace and order to his household and take care of his motherless children. So he married, and in the following years several children were born to him; but peace and order did not come to the household. For the step-mother was very cruel to the twins, and beat them, and half-starved them, and constantly drove them out of the house; for her one idea was to get them out of the way. All day she thought of nothing but how she should get rid of them; and at last an evil idea came into her head, and she determined to send them out into the great gloomy wood where a wicked witch lived. And so one morning she spoke to them, saying:

"You have been such good children that I am going to send you to visit my granny, who lives in a dear little hut in the wood. You will have to wait upon her and serve her, but you will be well rewarded, for she will give you the best of everything."

So the children left the house together; and the little sister, who was very wise for her years, said to the brother:

"We will first go and see our own dear grandmother, and tell her where our step-mother is sending us."

And when the grandmother heard where they were going, she cried and said:

"You poor motherless children! How I pity you; and yet I can do nothing to help you! Your step-mother is not sending you to her granny, but to a wicked witch who lives in that great gloomy wood. Now listen to me, children. You must be civil and kind to everyone, and never say a cross word to anyone, and never touch a crumb belonging to anyone else. Who knows if, after all, help may not be sent to you?"

And she gave her grandchildren a bottle of milk and a piece of ham and a loaf of bread, and they set out for the great gloomy wood. When they reached it they saw in front of them, in the thickest of the trees, a queer little hut, and when they looked into it, there lay the witch, with her head on the threshold of the door, with one foot in one corner and the other in the other corner, and her knees cocked up, almost touching the ceiling.

"Who's there?" she snarled, in an awful voice, when she saw the children.

And they answered civilly, though they were so terrified that they hid behind one another, and said:

"Good-morning, granny; our step-mother has sent us to wait upon you, and serve you."

"See that you do it well, then," growled the witch. "If I am pleased with you, I'll reward you; but if I am not, I'll put you in a pan and fry you in the oven – that's what I'll do with you, my pretty dears! You have been gently reared, but you'll find my work hard enough. See if you don't."

And, so saying, she set the girl down to spin yarn, and she gave the boy a sieve in which to carry water from the well, and she herself went out into the wood. Now, as the girl was sitting at her distaff, weeping bitterly because she could not spin, she heard the sound of hundreds of little feet, and from every hole and corner in the hut mice came pattering along the floor, squeaking and saying:

> *"Little girl, why are your eyes so red?*
> *If you want help, then give us some bread."*

And the girl gave them the bread that her grandmother had given her. Then the mice told her that the witch had a cat, and the cat was very fond of ham; if she would give the cat her ham, it would show her the way out of the wood, and in the meantime they would spin the yarn for her. So the girl set out to look for the cat, and, as she was hunting about, she met her brother, in great trouble because he could not carry water from the well in a sieve, as it came pouring out as fast as he put it in. And as she was trying to comfort him they heard a rustling of wings, and a flight of wrens alighted on the ground beside them. And the wrens said:

> *"Give us some crumbs, then you need not grieve.*
> *For you'll find that water will stay in the sieve."*

Then the twins crumbled their bread on the ground, and the wrens pecked it, and chirruped and chirped. And when they had eaten the last crumb they told the boy to fill up the holes of the sieve with clay, and then to draw water from the well. So he did what they said, and carried the sieve full of water into the hut without spilling a drop. When they entered the hut the cat was curled up on the floor. So they stroked her, and fed her with ham, and said to her:

"Pussy, grey pussy, tell us how we are to get away from the witch?"

Then the cat thanked them for the ham, and gave them a pocket-handkerchief and a comb, and told them that when the witch pursued them, as she certainly would, all they had to do was to throw the handkerchief on the ground and run as fast as they could. As soon as the handkerchief touched the ground a deep, broad river would spring up, which would hinder the witch's progress. If she managed to get across it, they must throw the comb behind them and run for their lives, for where the comb fell a dense forest would start up, which would delay the witch so long that they would be able to get safely away. The cat had scarcely finished speaking when the witch returned to see if the children had fulfilled their tasks.

"Well, you have done well enough for to-day," she grumbled; "but to-morrow you'll have something more difficult to do, and if you don't do it well, you pampered brats, straight into the oven you go."

Half-dead with fright, and trembling in every limb, the poor children lay down to sleep on a heap of straw in the corner of the hut; but they dared not close their eyes, and scarcely ventured to breathe. In the morning the witch gave the girl two pieces of linen to weave before night, and the boy a pile of wood to cut into chips. Then the witch left them to their tasks, and went out into the wood. As soon as she had gone out of sight the children took the comb and the handkerchief, and, taking one another by the hand, they started and ran, and ran, and ran. And first they met the watch-dog, who was going to leap on them and tear them to pieces; but they threw the remains of their bread to him, and he ate them and wagged his tail. Then they were hindered by the birch-trees, whose branches almost put their eyes out. But the little sister tied the twigs together with a piece of ribbon, and they got past safely, and, after running through the wood, came out on to the open fields.

In the meantime in the hut the cat was busy weaving the linen and tangling the threads as it wove. And the witch returned to see how the children were getting on; and she crept up to the window, and whispered:

"Are you weaving, my little dear?"

"Yes, granny, I am weaving," answered the cat.

When the witch saw that the children had escaped her, she was furious, and, hitting the cat with a porringer, she said: "Why did you let the children leave the hut? Why did you not scratch their eyes out?"

But the cat curled up its tail and put its back up, and answered: "I have served you all these years and you never even threw me a bone, but the dear children gave me their own piece of ham."

Then the witch was furious with the watch-dog and with the birch-trees, because they had let the children pass. But the dog answered:

"I have served you all these years and you never gave me so much as a hard crust, but the dear children gave me their own loaf of bread."

And the birch rustled its leaves, and said: "I have served you longer than I can say, and you never tied a bit of twine even round my branches; and the dear children bound them up with their brightest ribbons."

So the witch saw there was no help to be got from her old servants, and that the best thing she could do was to mount on her broom and set off in pursuit of the children. And as the children ran they heard the sound of the broom sweeping the ground close behind them, so instantly they threw the handkerchief down over their shoulder, and in a moment a deep, broad river flowed behind them.

When the witch came up to it, it took her a long time before she found a place which she could ford over on her broom-stick; but at last she got across, and continued the chase faster than before. And as the children ran they heard a sound, and the little sister put her ear to the ground, and heard the broom sweeping the earth close behind them; so, quick as thought, she threw the comb down on the ground, and in an instant, as the cat had said, a dense forest sprung up, in which the roots and branches were so closely intertwined, that it was impossible to force a way through it. So when the witch came up to it on her broom she found that there was nothing for it but to turn round and go back to her hut.

But the twins ran straight on till they reached their own home. Then they told their father all that they had suffered, and he was so angry with their step-mother that he drove her out of the house, and never let her return; but he and the children lived happily together; and he took care of them himself, and never let a stranger come near them.

The Wonderful Birch

ONCE UPON A TIME there were a man and a woman, who had an only daughter. Now it happened that one of their sheep went astray, and they set out to look for it, and searched and searched, each in a different part of the wood. Then the good wife met a witch, who said to her:

"If you spit, you miserable creature, if you spit into the sheath of my knife, or if you run between my legs, I shall change you into a black sheep."

The woman neither spat, nor did she run between her legs, but yet the witch changed her into a sheep. Then she made herself look exactly like the woman, and called out to the good man:

"Ho, old man, halloa! I have found the sheep already!"

The man thought the witch was really his wife, and he did not know that his wife was the sheep; so he went home with her, glad at heart because his sheep was found. When they were safe at home the witch said to the man:

"Look here, old man, we must really kill that sheep lest it run away to the wood again."

The man, who was a peaceable quiet sort of fellow, made no objections, but simply said: "Good, let us do so."

The daughter, however, had overheard their talk, and she ran to the flock and lamented aloud: "Oh, dear little mother, they are going to slaughter you!"

"Well, then, if they do slaughter me," was the black sheep's answer, "eat you neither the meat nor the broth that is made of me, but gather all my bones, and bury them by the edge of the field."

Shortly after this they took the black sheep from the flock and slaughtered it. The witch made pease-soup of it, and set it before the daughter. But the girl remembered her mother's warning. She did not touch the soup, but she carried the bones to the edge of the field and buried them there; and there sprang up on the spot a birch tree – a very lovely birch tree.

Some time had passed away – who can tell how long they might have been living there? – when the witch, to whom a child had been born in the meantime, began to take an ill-will to the man's daughter, and to torment her in all sorts of ways.

Now it happened that a great festival was to be held at the palace, and the King had commanded that all the people should be invited, and that this proclamation should be made:

"Come, people all! Poor and wretched, one and all! Blind and crippled though ye be, Mount your steeds or come by sea."

And so they drove into the King's feast all the outcasts, and the maimed, and the halt, and the blind. In the good man's house, too, preparations were made to go to the palace. The witch said to the man:

"Go you on in front, old man, with our youngest; I will give the elder girl work to keep her from being dull in our absence."

So the man took the child and set out. But the witch kindled a fire on the hearth, threw a potful of barleycorns among the cinders, and said to the girl:

"If you have not picked the barley out of the ashes, and put it all back in the pot before nightfall, I shall eat you up!"

Then she hastened after the others, and the poor girl stayed at home and wept. She tried to be sure to pick up the grains of barley, but she soon saw how useless her labour was; and so she went in her sore trouble to the birch tree on her mother's grave, and cried and cried, because her mother lay dead beneath the sod and could help her no longer. In the midst of her grief she suddenly heard her mother's voice speak from the grave, and say to her:

"Why do you weep, little daughter?"

"The witch has scattered barleycorns on the hearth, and bid me pick them out of the ashes," said the girl; "that is why I weep, dear little mother."

"Do not weep," said her mother consolingly. "Break off one of my branches, and strike the hearth with it crosswise, and all will be put right." The girl did so. She struck the hearth with the birchen branch, and lo! the barleycorns flew into the pot, and the hearth was clean. Then she went back to the birch tree and laid the branch upon the grave. Then her mother bade her bathe on one side of the stem, dry herself on another, and dress on the third. When the girl had done all that, she had grown so lovely that no one on earth could rival her. Splendid clothing was given to her, and a horse, with hair partly of gold, partly of silver, and partly of something more precious still. The girl sprang into the saddle, and rode as swift as an arrow to the palace. As she turned into the courtyard of the castle the King's son came out to meet her, tied her steed to a pillar, and led her in. He never left her side as they passed through the castle rooms; and all the people gazed at her, and wondered who the lovely maiden was, and from what castle she came; but no one knew her – no one knew anything about her. At the banquet the Prince invited her to sit next him in the place of honour; but the witch's daughter gnawed the bones under the table. The Prince did not see her, and thinking it was a dog, he gave her such a push with his foot that her arm was broken. Are you not sorry for the witch's daughter? It was not her fault that her mother was a witch.

Towards evening the good man's daughter thought it was time to go home; but as she went, her ring caught on the latch of the door, for the King's son had had it smeared with tar. She did not take time to pull it off, but, hastily unfastening her horse from the pillar, she rode away beyond the castle walls as swift as an arrow. Arrived at home, she took off her clothes by the birch tree, left her horse standing there, and hastened to her place behind the stove. In a short time the man and the woman came home again too, and the witch said to the girl:

"Ah! you poor thing, there you are to be sure! You don't know what fine times we have had at the palace! The King's son carried my daughter about, but the poor thing fell and broke her arm."

The girl knew well how matters really stood, but she pretended to know nothing about it, and sat dumb behind the stove.

The next day they were invited again to the King's banquet.

"Hey! old man," said the witch, "get on your clothes as quick as you can; we are bidden to the feast. Take you the child; I will give the other one work, lest she weary."

She kindled the fire, threw a potful of hemp seed among the ashes, and said to the girl:

"If you do not get this sorted, and all the seed back into the pot, I shall kill you!"

The girl wept bitterly; then she went to the birch tree, washed herself on one side of it and dried herself on the other; and this time still finer clothes were given to her, and a very beautiful steed. She broke off a branch of the birch tree, struck the hearth with it, so that the seeds flew into the pot, and then hastened to the castle.

Again the King's son came out to meet her, tied her horse to a pillar, and led her into the banqueting hall. At the feast the girl sat next to him in the place of honour, as she had done the day before. But the witch's daughter gnawed bones under the table, and the Prince gave her a push by mistake, which broke her leg – he had never noticed her crawling about among the people's feet. She was VERY unlucky!

The good man's daughter hastened home again betimes, but the King's son had smeared the door-posts with tar, and the girl's golden circlet stuck to it. She had not time to look for it, but sprang to the saddle and rode like an arrow to the birch tree. There she left her horse and her fine clothes, and said to her mother:

"I have lost my circlet at the castle; the door-post was tarred, and it stuck fast."

"And even had you lost two of them," answered her mother, "I would give you finer ones."

Then the girl hastened home, and when her father came home from the feast with the witch, she was in her usual place behind the stove. Then the witch said to her:

"You poor thing! what is there to see here compared with what WE have seen at the palace? The King's son carried my daughter from one room to another; he let her fall, 'tis true, and my child's foot was broken."

The man's daughter held her peace all the time, and busied herself about the hearth.

The night passed, and when the day began to dawn, the witch awakened her husband, crying:

"Hi! get up, old man! We are bidden to the royal banquet."

So the old man got up. Then the witch gave him the child, saying:

"Take you the little one; I will give the other girl work to do, else she will weary at home alone."

She did as usual. This time it was a dish of milk she poured upon the ashes, saying:

"If you do not get all the milk into the dish again before I come home, you will suffer for it."

How frightened the girl was this time! She ran to the birch tree, and by its magic power her task was accomplished; and then she rode away to the palace as before. When she got to the courtyard she found the Prince waiting for her. He led her into the hall, where she was highly honoured; but the witch's daughter sucked the bones under the table, and crouching at the people's feet she got an eye knocked out, poor thing! Now no one knew any more than before about the good man's daughter, no one knew whence she came; but the Prince had had the threshold smeared with tar, and as she fled her gold slippers stuck to it. She reached the birch tree, and laying aside her finery, she said:

"Alas I dear little mother, I have lost my gold slippers!"

"Let them be," was her mother's reply; "if you need them I shall give you finer ones."

Scarcely was she in her usual place behind the stove when her father came home with the witch. Immediately the witch began to mock her, saying:

"Ah! you poor thing, there is nothing for you to see here, and WE – ah: what great things we have seen at the palace! My little girl was carried about again, but had the ill-luck to fall and get her eye knocked out. You stupid thing, you, what do you know about anything?"

"Yes, indeed, what can I know?" replied the girl; "I had enough to do to get the hearth clean."

Now the Prince had kept all the things the girl had lost, and he soon set about finding the owner of them. For this purpose a great banquet was given on the fourth day, and all the people were invited to the palace. The witch got ready to go too. She tied a wooden beetle on where her child's foot should have been, a log of wood instead of an arm, and stuck a bit of dirt in the empty socket for an eye, and took the child with her to the castle. When all the people were gathered together, the King's son stepped in among the crowd and cried:

"The maiden whose finger this ring slips over, whose head this golden hoop encircles, and whose foot this shoe fits, shall be my bride."

What a great trying on there was now among them all! The things would fit no one, however.

"The cinder wench is not here," said the Prince at last; "go and fetch her, and let her try on the things."

So the girl was fetched, and the Prince was just going to hand the ornaments to her, when the witch held him back, saying: "Don't give them to her; she soils everything with cinders; give them to my daughter rather."

Well, then the Prince gave the witch's daughter the ring, and the woman filed and pared away at her daughter's finger till the ring fitted. It was the same with the circlet and the shoes of gold. The witch would not allow them to be handed to the cinder wench; she worked at her own daughter's head and feet till she got the things forced on. What was to be done now? The Prince had to take the witch's daughter for his bride whether he would or no; he sneaked away to her father's house with her, however, for he was ashamed to hold the wedding festivities at the palace with so strange a bride. Some days passed, and at last he had to take his bride home to the palace, and he got ready to do so. Just as they were taking leave, the kitchen wench sprang down from her place by the stove, on the pretext of fetching something from the cowhouse, and in going by she whispered in the Prince's ear as he stood in the yard:

"Alas! dear Prince, do not rob me of my silver and my gold."

Thereupon the King's son recognised the cinder wench; so he took both the girls with him, and set out. After they had gone some little way they came to the bank of a river, and the Prince threw the witch's daughter across to serve as a bridge, and so got over with the cinder wench. There lay the witch's daughter then, like a bridge over the river, and could not stir, though her heart was consumed with grief. No help was near, so she cried at last in her anguish:

"May there grow a golden hemlock out of my body! perhaps my mother will know me by that token."

Scarcely had she spoken when a golden hemlock sprang up from her, and stood upon the bridge.

Now, as soon as the Prince had got rid of the witch's daughter he greeted the cinder wench as his bride, and they wandered together to the birch tree which grew upon the mother's grave. There they received all sorts of treasures and riches, three sacks full of gold, and as much silver, and a splendid steed, which bore them home to the palace. There they lived a long time together, and the young wife bore a son to the Prince. Immediately word was brought to the witch that her daughter had borne a son – for they all believed the young King's wife to be the witch's daughter.

"So, so," said the witch to herself; "I had better away with my gift for the infant, then."

And so saying she set out. Thus it happened that she came to the bank of the river, and there she saw the beautiful golden hemlock growing in the middle of the bridge, and when she began to cut it down to take to her grandchild, she heard a voice moaning:

"Alas! dear mother, do not cut me so!"

"Are you here?" demanded the witch.

"Indeed I am, dear little mother," answered the daughter "They threw me across the river to make a bridge of me."

In a moment the witch had the bridge shivered to atoms, and then she hastened away to the palace. Stepping up to the young Queen's bed, she began to try her magic arts upon her, saying:

"Spit, you wretch, on the blade of my knife; bewitch my knife's blade for me, and I shall change you into a reindeer of the forest."

"Are you there again to bring trouble upon me?" said the young woman.

She neither spat nor did anything else, but still the witch changed her into a reindeer, and smuggled her own daughter into her place as the Prince's wife. But now the child grew restless and cried, because it missed its mother's care. They took it to the court, and tried to pacify it in every conceivable way, but its crying never ceased.

"What makes the child so restless?" asked the Prince, and he went to a wise widow woman to ask her advice.

"Ay, ay, your own wife is not at home," said the widow woman; "she is living like a reindeer in the wood; you have the witch's daughter for a wife now, and the witch herself for a mother-in-law."

"Is there any way of getting my own wife back from the wood again?" asked the Prince.

"Give me the child," answered the widow woman. "I'll take it with me to-morrow when I go to drive the cows to the wood. I'll make a rustling among the birch leaves and a trembling among the aspens – perhaps the boy will grow quiet when he hears it."

"Yes, take the child away, take it to the wood with you to quiet it," said the Prince, and led the widow woman into the castle.

"How now? you are going to send the child away to the wood?" said the witch in a suspicious tone, and tried to interfere.

But the King's son stood firm by what he had commanded, and said:

"Carry the child about the wood; perhaps that will pacify it."

So the widow woman took the child to the wood. She came to the edge of a marsh, and seeing a herd of reindeer there, she began all at once to sing –

> "Little Bright-eyes, little Redskin,
> Come nurse the child you bore!
> That bloodthirsty monster,
> That man-eater grim,
> Shall nurse him, shall tend him no more.
> They may threaten and force as they will,
> He turns from her, shrinks from her still,"

and immediately the reindeer drew near, and nursed and tended the child the whole day long; but at nightfall it had to follow the herd, and said to the widow woman:

"Bring me the child to-morrow, and again the following day; after that I must wander with the herd far away to other lands."

The following morning the widow woman went back to the castle to fetch the child. The witch interfered, of course, but the Prince said:

"Take it, and carry it about in the open air; the boy is quieter at night, to be sure, when he has been in the wood all day."

So the widow took the child in her arms, and carried it to the marsh in the forest. There she sang as on the preceding day –

> "Little Bright-eyes, little Redskin,
> Come nurse the child you bore!
> That bloodthirsty monster,
> That man-eater grim,
> Shall nurse him, shall tend him no more.
> They may threaten and force as they will,
> He turns from her, shrinks from her still,"

and immediately the reindeer left the herd and came to the child, and tended it as on the day before. And so it was that the child throve, till not a finer boy was to be seen anywhere. But the King's son had been pondering over all these things, and he said to the widow woman:

"Is there no way of changing the reindeer into a human being again?"

"I don't rightly know," was her answer. "Come to the wood with me, however; when the woman puts off her reindeer skin I shall comb her head for her; whilst I am doing so you must burn the skin."

Thereupon they both went to the wood with the child; scarcely were they there when the reindeer appeared and nursed the child as before. Then the widow woman said to the reindeer:

"Since you are going far away to-morrow, and I shall not see you again, let me comb your head for the last time, as a remembrance of you."

Good; the young woman stript off the reindeer skin, and let the widow woman do as she wished. In the meantime the King's son threw the reindeer skin into the fire unobserved.

"What smells of singeing here?" asked the young woman, and looking round she saw her own husband. "Woe is me! you have burnt my skin. Why did you do that?"

"To give you back your human form again."

"Alack-a-day! I have nothing to cover me now, poor creature that I am!" cried the young woman, and transformed herself first into a distaff, then into a wooden beetle, then into a spindle, and into all imaginable shapes. But all these shapes the King's son went on destroying till she stood before him in human form again.

"Alas! wherefore take me home with you again," cried the young woman, "since the witch is sure to eat me up?"

"She will not eat you up," answered her husband; and they started for home with the child.

But when the witch wife saw them she ran away with her daughter, and if she has not stopped she is running still, though at a great age. And the Prince, and his wife, and the baby lived happy ever afterwards.

The Wicked Stepmother

ONCE UPON A TIME, in Armenia, there was a noted hunter, who was a widower. He had a son by a former wife. He married another wife, but soon was taken mortally sick. On his deathbed he said to his wife:

"Wife, I am dying, and I know that when my son grows up he will follow my profession. Take care and do not let him go to the Black Mountains to hunt."

After the death of the hunter, the son growing up, began to follow his father's profession, and became a hunter. One day his stepmother said:

"Son, your father, when dying, said that after you grew up, if you followed his profession, you should not go to the Black Mountains to hunt."

But the lad, paying no attention to what his father had advised him, one day took his bow and arrow, mounted his horse and hastened to the Black Mountains to hunt. As soon as he reached them, lo, a giant made his appearance on the back of his horse of lightning, and exclaimed:

"How now! Have you never heard my name, that you have dared to come and hunt on my ground?" And he threw three terrible maces at the lad, who very cleverly avoided them, hiding himself under the belly of his horse.

Now it was his turn; he drew his bow and arrow, took aim and shot the giant, who was nailed to the ground. He at once mounted the giant's horse of lightning, which galloping, soon brought him to a magnificent palace, gilded all over with gold and decorated with precious jewels. Lo, a maiden as beautiful as the sun appeared in the window, saying:

"Human being, the snake upon its belly and the bird with its wing could not come here; how could you venture to come?"

"Your love brought me hither, fair creature," answered the lad, who had already fallen in love with the charming maiden.

"But the giant will come and tear you into pieces," said the maiden, who also had fallen in love with the lad.

"I have killed him, and there lies his carcass," answered the lad.

The door of the palace was opened, and the lad was received by the maiden, who told him that she was the daughter of a Prince, and that the giant had stolen her and kept her in that palace, where she had forty beautiful handmaids serving her.

"And as you have killed the giant," she added, "I, who am a virgin, shall be your wife, and all these maidens will serve us." And they accepted one another as husband and wife.

Opening the treasures of the giant, they found innumerable jewels, gold, silver, and all kinds of wealth. The lad thought such a beautiful palace, with so many treasures worthy of a prince, and the most beautiful wife in the world, things that he could hardly have dreamed of, and he decided to live there, going to hunt every day as usual.

One day, however, he came home sighing, "Ah! alas! alas!"

"How now, what is the matter?" said the beautiful bride. "Am I and my forty handmaids not enough to please you? Why did you sigh?"

"You are sweet, my love," said the lad, "but my mother also is sweet. You have your place in my heart, but my mother also has her place. I remembered her, therefore I sighed."

"Well," said the young bride, "take a horseload of gold to your mother, let her live in abundance and be happy."

"No," said the lad, "let me go and bring her here."

"Very well, go, then," said the young bride.

The lad went to his stepmother and telling her all that he had done, brought her to the palace of the Black Mountains. There she was the mother-in-law of the fair bride, and therefore the superior of the whole palace. Both the bride and the maidens had to submit to her.

The lad used to go out hunting. The stepmother, being well versed in witchcraft and medicine, went secretly, and administered some remedy to the corpse of the giant, so that he was soon healed. Falling in love with the giant, she took him to the palace and hid him in the cellar, where she secretly paid him daily visits, as she was afraid of her stepson. Wishing, however, to have none to oppose her, the witch one day said to the giant:

"Giant, you must advise me of a way by which I may send my son on an errand, and from which he may never come back."

Upon the advice of the giant, she entered her room and putting under her bed pieces of very thin and dry Oriental bread, lay down upon the bed and feigned sickness. In the evening the lad returned from hunting, and hearing that his stepmother was ill, hastened to her side, and asked:

"What is the matter, mother?"

"O, son," exclaimed the witch, with a sickly voice, "I am very sick. I shall die," and as she turned from one side to the other the dry bread began to crackle.

"Hark!" exclaimed the witch, "how my bones are crackling!"

"What is the remedy, mother, what can I do for you?" asked the lad.

"O, my son," said the witch, "there is only one remedy for my sickness, and that is the Melon of Life. I shall never be healed, if I do not eat one of that fruit which you could bring to me."

"All right, mother," said the lad, "I will bring to you the Melon of Life."

He at once started upon the expedition, and after a long journey was guest in the house of an old woman who asked him where he was going. When she heard of the errand, she said to the lad:

"Son, you are deceived; the expedition is a fatal one – do not go."

But as the lad insisted, the old woman said:

"Well, then, let me advise you. On your way you will soon come to a mansion, which is the abode of forty giants, who in the day-time go out hunting. But you will find their dame there kneading dough. If you are agile enough to run and suck the nipples of the open breast of that giantess without being seen by her, you are safe; if not, she will make one mouthful of you and devour you."

The lad went and found as foretold by the old woman. He was clever enough to suck the nipples of the giantess without being seen by her.

"A plague on her who advised you!" exclaimed the angry giantess, "else I would make a good morsel of you. But now having sucked of my breast, you are like one of my own sons. Let me hide you in a box, lest the forty giants should come in the evening and finding you here, devour you."

And she shut the lad in a box. In the evening the forty giants came, and smelling a human being, said:

"O mother, all the year long we hunt beasts and fowls which we bring home to eat together, and now we smell a human being, whom no doubt you have devoured to-day. Have you not preserved for us at least a few bones which we might chew?"

"It is you," answered the dame, "that are coming from mountains and plains where no doubt you have found human beings, and the smell comes out of your own mouths. I have eaten no human being."

"Yes, mother, you have," exclaimed the giants.

"How if my nephew, the son of my human sister, has come to pay me a visit!" answered the giantess.

"O mother," exclaimed the giants, "show us our human cousin; we will not hurt him, but talk with him."

The giantess took the lad out of the box and brought him to the giants, who were very much pleased to see a human being so small, but so beautiful and manly. Holding him up like a toy, the giants handed him to one another to gratify their curiosity by looking at him.

"Mother, what has our cousin come for?" inquired the giants.

"He has come," answered the giantess, "to pick a Melon of Life, and carry it to his mother who is sick. You must go and get the Melon of Life for him."

"Not we," exclaimed the forty giants, "it is above our ability."

The youngest of the forty brothers, however, who was lame, said to the lad:

"Cousin, I will go with you and get the Melon of Life for you. You must only take with you a jug, a comb, and a razor."

On the following day the lad took what was necessary and followed the lame giant, who soon brought him to the garden of the Melon of Life, which was guarded by fifty giants. The guards being asleep, the lad and his companion entered the garden without being perceived, and picking the Melon began to run. But they were just crossing the hedges, when the lame leg of the giant was caught by the fence, and in his haste to release it he shook the hedges which crackled like thunder and, lo, all the fifty giants awoke crying:

"Thieves! human beings! a good prey for us!" and began to pursue the lad and his lame companion.

"Throw the jug behind you, cousin," exclaimed the lame giant.

The lad did so, and lo, plains and mountains behind them were covered by an immense sea which the fifty giants had to cross in order to reach them. By this means they gained quite a distance till the fifty crossed the sea.

"Now, cousin, throw the comb behind you," exclaimed the lame giant.

The lad did so, and lo, an extensive jungle between them and the fifty giants. They gained another great distance before the giants finished crossing the jungle.

"Throw the razor now, cousin," exclaimed the lame giant.

The lad did so, and lo, all the country between them and the fifty giants was covered with pieces of glass, sharp as razors. Before the fifty could cross the distance the thirty-nine giants came to the rescue of the two and took them, safely to their borders.

The lad took leave of his adopted aunt and cousins, find taking the Melon of Life with him, returned home. On his way, however, he was again the guest of the old woman, who seeing him come safely, asked if he had succeeded in bringing the precious fruit.

"Yes, I have brought it, auntie," answered the lad, and told her his tale.

In the middle of the night, when the lad was sound asleep, the old woman took the Melon of Life out of the lad's saddle bag and put a common melon in its place. In the morning the lad brought the melon to his stepmother, who eating it exclaimed:

"O, happy! I am healed."

The lad again went hunting, and the witch said to the giant:

"Look here, giant; this enterprise did not prove fatal to my stepson. Advise me of another more dangerous journey on which I may send him, and from which he shall surely not return."

Upon the advice of the giant she once more placed some thin and dry loaves of bread under her bed and lay down feigning sickness. In the evening when the lad came she said in a weak voice:

"O, son, I am dying, you will not see me any more."

"Why, mother," exclaimed the lad, "what is the matter? What can I do for you?"

"The only remedy for my sickness," answered the witch, "is the milk of the Fairy Lioness. If you bring it for me I shall live; if not, I must die."

The lad started, and again was the guest of the old woman, who asked where he was going.

"I am going this time to bring a skinful of the milk of the Fairy Lioness for my mother," answered the lad.

The old dame again importuned him not to go, but as he insisted she said:

"Well, as you are resolved to go, let me advise you. On the other side of yonder mountain is the den of the Fairy Lioness, which is at this moment very much troubled by a pustule on her paw, and you will find her at the entrance of her den, holding her pustulous paw above her head and roaring. Now, you must approach her cleverly without being noticed by her, and taking aim with your bow and arrow, shoot into the pustule, which, being wounded, will at first cause her great pain and make her roar. But soon the pain being past, she will feel comfortable and give you whatever you demand of her."

The lad went, and found the Fairy Lioness, as foretold by the old dame, standing at the entrance of her cave, and roaring on account of her pain. The lad at once taking aim, shot and wounded the pustule. The pain of the Lioness increasing she exclaimed:

"Oh! who was it that shot this arrow? I would I could find him and devour him. Oh! Oh! Oh!"

But soon, the matter of the wound coming out, she felt comfortable, and said:

"Who was it that shot this arrow? By Heaven, I would give him whatever he demanded."

The lad at once jumping out from his concealment stood before the Lioness, who seeing him exclaimed:

"Was it you, young hero, that healed me of my pain which was troubling me so long?"

"Yes, it was I," answered the lad.

"Demand of me whatever you please," said the Lioness, "I am ready to give to such a hero as you anything that you may ask."

"Give me," said the lad, "some milk of your own udders, which is the only remedy to heal my sick mother."

"In yonder cave," said the Lioness, "there are two orphan cubs; go kill them, and flaying them, bring the skins to me."

The lad did so and brought her the two whole skins. The Lioness milked her udders into them until they were filled.

"Here," said the Lioness, "take these and go, and be careful not to harm my little cubs on your way."

The lad took the two cubs' skins full of milk and thanking the Lioness, departed. On his way, however, he slily stole two beautiful cubs and began to run. But the mother Lioness smelling her young ones, pursued the lad, and overtaking him, exclaimed:

"How now, human being! is this the way you reward kindness done to you? Why did you steal my two cubs?"

"I humbly beg your pardon," answered the lad. "I was so much pleased with your kindness that I wanted to have a permanent keepsake from you, and what better thing could I carry with me than a brace of your cubs, which I will nourish on princely diet and keep as faithful friends."

The Lioness, being much pleased with this answer, gave him leave to carry the cubs. He soon came to his hostess, who asked if he brought the Fairy Lioness's milk.

"Yes, auntie, I have brought it," answered the lad, presenting the two skins full of milk.

During the night, however, when the lad was sound asleep, the old woman poured out the Lioness's milk from the skins into a cask and filled them with common goat's milk. On the following day, the lad, loading the skins on the back of his horse, took the cubs and went home. The stepmother, drinking the milk, exclaimed:

"O good! I am healed."

The lad again went hunting as usual. The witch said to the giant:

"Giant, did I not tell you to advise me and name a task from which my stepson would never return? Why are you devising only light tasks which he can so easily accomplish? Now you must either advise me as to the most dangerous expedition in which he will surely lose his life, or I will betray you to him and he will cut you into pieces."

"What can I do?" replied the giant, "your son is the bravest hero that ever lived; no mortal can vanquish him. He will return from any expedition, no matter how dangerous it may be. Let him go this time and bring you a jug full of the Water of Life."

The witch again feigned sickness, and when the lad came to see her she said:

"O my son, I am dying, my bones are breaking," and the crackling of the dry bread under the bed was heard when she turned from one side to the other.

"What shall I do for you, mother?" asked the lad sadly.

"The only remedy for me this time," answered the witch, "is the Water of Life, and you must go and bring to me a jug full, else I shall die."

The lad at once mounted his horse and taking with him the two cubs, which by that time had grown up to be a pair of fine young lions, he went to his hostess and explained the object of his expedition.

"O son," exclaimed the good woman, "I see plainly that you are employed for some wicked purpose; there must be a detestable plot against your life. This is the most dangerous expedition that ever human being has undertaken, and no one has ever returned from the task you have started upon. Be advised, go back; your mother is surely false."

"Not I," said the lad, "I will certainly go."

The old woman said, "As soon as you place your jug in the fountain to receive the water, which oozes out only in the thickness of a hair, a heavy sleep will fall upon you, and you will remain there benumbed for seven days and nights. First, scorpions will assail you; then serpents; then beasts of prey, and at last all kinds of genii. You will surely be devoured by them."

"Let come what may, I will go," said the lad, and taking the two lions with him, he started for the fountain of the Water of Life.

He came to the fountain and found the water oozing out in a tiny stream. As soon as he placed his jug under it, a sound sleep overpowered his senses and he remained there benumbed for seven days and seven nights. Soon innumerable large scorpions began to attack the sleeping hero. But the lions destroyed all of them. Then thousands of terrible serpents made their appearance and assailed the lad, hissing and striking with their forked tongues. The lions, after a bloody fight, destroyed them also. Soon a whole army of voracious beasts surrounded the fountain in search of the lad. The lions, after a sanguinary strife, succeeded in destroying them also.

At the end of the seven days and nights, the lad awoke, and to his great horror saw that he was surrounded by a high wall which the lions had built of the carcasses of the beasts and serpents they had killed. The two faithful guardians were now sitting on either side of their master and were watching his every motion. The lad, seeing them stained with blood from head to foot, understood how much he owed to them in the preservation of his life. He then washed them clean with the Water of Life and taking the jug, which by that time was filled, he returned to his hostess.

"Did you bring the Water of Life?" asked the old dame.

"Yes, auntie, I did," answered the lad, presenting her the jug full of water.

"It was not you that succeeded," returned the old woman, "but Heaven and your faithful lions that preserved your life."

During the night, as the lad was sleeping, the old woman poured the Water of Life into another vase, and filled the jug with common water, which the lad in the morning took to his stepmother, who drinking it said:

"O, happy! I am healed."

The following day the lad again went hunting. The witch said to the giant:

"Can you not devise some means to destroy my stepson? By Heaven, I will destroy you this time if you do not tell me how to destroy him."

"Your stepson is brave," answered the giant, "he is a unique hero, and no one can kill him but yourself."

"How! how!" exclaimed the witch with great joy, "tell me and I will do it."

"Do you not remember the three red hairs among his black hairs on his head? As soon as they are picked, your son dies."

On the following day the witch said to the lad:

"Come, son, lay your head in my lap and take a nap."

The lad did so and soon slept. The witch immediately took hold of the three red hairs and picked them out. A spasm or two, and the hero died.

"Now, giant," said the witch, "take that sword and chop this corpse into small pieces."

"Not I," answered the giant, "my hand will not be lifted to chop such a hero."

"You coward!" exclaimed the witch, and taking the sword she chopped the corpse into small pieces, put these into a sack, and threw them over the garden wall. One of the little fingers, however, fell into the garden.

The lions learned that their master was killed, and that his chopped body had been put into the bag. They immediately took hold of the bag and carried it to the old woman, the hostess of the hero. Opening the bag, she took out the body, and putting every part in its proper place made a whole; only the little finger was missing. She explained to the lions what was missing, and they at once went, and smelling their master's finger in the garden, found it and brought it to the old woman, who put it in its proper place. Now she brought the milk of the Fairy Lioness, which she had secretly preserved, and poured it over the body. Immediately all the broken bones, muscles and sinews came together, and all the members being united, the body became as sound and delicate as that of a newborn babe. Then she brought the Melon of Life, and put it before his nostrils. As soon as the lad smelt it, he sneezed seven times. Then she poured the Water of Life down his throat. At once the lad opened his eyes, and jumped up, saying:

"O, what a sound sleep was this that overpowered my senses!"

"Sleep!" exclaimed the kind woman. "Yes, a sleep out of which you would never have awaked had not Providence preserved you." And she told him what had happened.

"Now, my good hostess," said the lad, "you have done me a very great kindness – a kindness that I can never reward. May Heaven reward you!"

He brought her from his treasures a horseload of gold and a horseload of silver, saying:

"These are for you; spend as much as you like and pray for me as long as you live."

The lad came to his palace and found that his beautiful bride was imprisoned in a dark cellar, where she was left to starve, while the witch, his stepmother, was in an excess of merriment with the giant and half a dozen younglings around her. They were all amazed to see the hero enter, and the giant was about to make his exit through a secret door in the wall when the lad seized hold of him, saying:

"How now, coward, are you running? Stop and solve this puzzle for me; whose are these ugly younglings that are infecting the very air of my palace?"

"They are my children out of yonder woman, your mother," answered the giant.

"Mother! I have no mother," exclaimed the lad. "You increase so soon, do you? Now we are going to have great merriment. Go and bring me from yonder mountain, wood enough to build a large pile."

The giant obeyed, and soon a large pile of wood was built in the courtyard of the palace. The lad struck a flint and lighted the wood. Soon the whole pile was on fire, burning like a furnace.

"Now, giant," said the lad, "take hold of these bastards, and throw them into the fire, one by one."

The giant obeyed, and all the younglings were burned on the pile.

"Bring now yonder witch, and throw her into the fire," ordered the lad. She also shared the fate of the bastard children.

"Now, shall I throw you also?" asked the lad of the giant.

"Hero," exclaimed the giant, "I honor you, I will obey you."

"Well, then," said the lad, "I will not kill you. Come, pass under my sword and swear obedience to me."

The giant kissed the sword, and passing under it became the bondman of the lad.

The lad then released his beautiful wife from the dark prison. They celebrated anew their nuptials for forty days and forty nights, and enjoyed a happy life thereafter.

Thus they attained their wishes. May Heaven grant that you may attain your wishes!

Three apples fell from heaven; one for me, one for the story-teller, and one for him who entertained the company

The Witch in the Stone Boat

THERE WERE ONCE A KING AND A QUEEN, and they had a son called Sigurd, who was very strong and active, and good-looking. When the King came to be bowed down with the weight of years he spoke to his son, and said that now it was time for him to look out for a fitting match for himself, for he did not know how long he might last now, and he would like to see him married before he died.

Sigurd was not averse to this, and asked his father where he thought it best to look for a wife. The King answered that in a certain country there was a King who had a beautiful daughter, and he thought it would be most desirable if Sigurd could get her. So the two parted, and Sigurd prepared for the journey, and went to where his father had directed him.

He came to the King and asked his daughter's hand, which he readily granted him, but only on the condition that he should remain there as long as he could, for the King himself was not strong and not very able to govern his kingdom. Sigurd accepted this condition, but added that he would have to get leave to go home again to his own country when he heard news of his father's death. After that Sigurd married the Princess, and helped his father-in-law to govern the kingdom. He and the Princess loved each other dearly, and after a year a son came to them, who was two years old when word came to Sigurd that his father was dead. Sigurd now prepared to return home with his wife and child, and went on board ship to go by sea.

They had sailed for several days, when the breeze suddenly fell, and there came a dead calm, at a time when they needed only one day's voyage to reach home. Sigurd and his Queen were one day on deck, when most of the others on the ship had fallen asleep. There they sat and talked for a while, and had their little son along with them. After a time Sigurd became so heavy with sleep that he could no longer keep awake, so he went below and lay down, leaving the Queen alone on the deck, playing with her son.

A good while after Sigurd had gone below the Queen saw something black on the sea, which seemed to be coming nearer. As it approached she could make out that it was a boat, and could see the figure of someone sitting in it and rowing it. At last the boat came alongside the ship, and now the Queen saw that it was a stone boat, out of which there came up on board the ship a fearfully ugly Witch. The Queen was more frightened than words can describe, and could neither speak a word nor move from the place so as to awaken the King or the sailors. The Witch came right up to the Queen, took the child from her and laid it on the deck; then she took the Queen, and stripped her of all her fine clothes, which she proceeded to put on herself, and looked then like a human being. Last of all she took the Queen, put her into the boat, and said –

"This spell I lay upon you, that you slacken not your course until you come to my brother in the Under-world."

The Queen sat stunned and motionless, but the boat at once shot away from the ship with her, and before long she was out of sight.

When the boat could no longer be seen the child began to cry, and though the Witch tried to quiet it she could not manage it; so she went below to where the King was sleeping with the child on her arm, and awakened him, scolding him for leaving them alone on deck, while he and all the crew were asleep. It was great carelessness of him, she said, to leave no one to watch the ship with her.

Sigurd was greatly surprised to hear his Queen scold him so much, for she had never said an angry word to him before; but he thought it was quite excusable in this case, and tried to quiet the child along with her, but it was no use. Then he went and wakened the sailors, and bade them hoist the sails, for a breeze had sprung up and was blowing straight towards the harbour.

They soon reached the land which Sigurd was to rule over, and found all the people sorrowful for the old King's death, but they became glad when they got Sigurd back to the Court, and made him King over them.

The King's son, however, hardly ever stopped crying from the time he had been taken from his mother on the deck of the ship, although he had always been such a good child before, so that at last the King had to get a nurse for him – one of the maids of the Court. As soon as the child got into her charge he stopped crying, and behaved well as before.

After the sea-voyage it seemed to the King that the Queen had altered very much in many ways, and not for the better. He thought her much more haughty and stubborn and difficult to deal with than she used to be. Before long others began to notice this as well as the King. In the Court there were two young fellows, one of eighteen years old, the other of nineteen, who were very fond of playing chess, and often sat long inside playing at it. Their room was next the Queen's, and often during the day they heard the Queen talking.

One day they paid more attention than usual when they heard her talk, and put their ears close to a crack in the wall between the rooms, and heard the Queen say quite plainly, "When I yawn a little, then I am a nice little maiden; when I yawn half-way, then I am half a troll; and when I yawn fully, then I am a troll altogether."

As she said this she yawned tremendously, and in a moment had put on the appearance of a fearfully ugly troll. Then there came up through the floor of the room a three-headed Giant with a trough full of meat, who saluted her as his sister and set down the trough before her. She began to eat out of it, and never stopped till she had finished it. The young fellows saw all this going on, but did not hear the two of them say anything to each other. They were astonished though at how greedily the Queen devoured the meat, and how much she ate of it, and were no longer surprised that she took so little when she sat at table with the King. As soon as she had finished it the Giant disappeared with the trough by the same way as he had come, and the Queen returned to her human shape.

Now we must go back to the King's son after he had been put in charge of the nurse. One evening, after she had lit a candle and was holding the child, several planks sprang up in the floor of the room, and out at the opening came a beautiful woman dressed in white, with an iron belt round her waist, to which was fastened an iron chain that went down into the ground. The woman came up to the nurse, took the child from her, and pressed it to her breast; then she gave it back to the nurse and returned by the same way as she had come, and the floor closed over her again. Although the woman had not spoken a single word to her, the nurse was very much frightened, but told no one about it.

Next evening the same thing happened again, just as before, but as the woman was going away she said in a sad tone, "Two are gone, and one only is left," and then disappeared as before. The nurse was still more frightened when she heard the woman say this, and thought that perhaps some danger was hanging over the child, though she had no ill-opinion of the unknown woman, who, indeed, had behaved towards the child as if it were her own. The most mysterious thing was the woman saying "and only one is left;" but the nurse guessed that this must mean that only one day was left, since she had come for two days already.

At last the nurse made up her mind to go to the King, and told him the whole story, and asked him to be present in person next day about the time when the woman usually came. The King promised to do so, and came to the nurse's room a little before the time, and sat down on a chair with his drawn sword in his hand. Soon after the planks in the floor sprang up as before, and the woman came up, dressed in white, with the iron belt and chain. The King saw at once that it was his own Queen, and immediately hewed asunder the iron chain that was fastened to the belt. This was followed by such noises and crashings down in the earth that all the King's Palace shook, so that no one expected anything else than to see every bit of it shaken to pieces. At last, however, the noises and shaking stopped, and they began to come to themselves again.

The King and Queen embraced each other, and she told him the whole story – how the Witch came to the ship when they were all asleep and sent her off in the boat. After she had gone so far that she could not see the ship, she sailed on through darkness until she landed beside a three-headed Giant. The Giant wished her to marry him, but she refused; whereupon he shut her up by herself, and told her she would never get free until she consented. After a time she began to plan how to get her freedom, and at last told him that she would consent if he would allow her to visit her son on earth three days on end. This he agreed to, but put on her this iron belt and chain, the other end of which he fastened round his own waist, and the great noises that were heard when the King cut the chain must have been caused by the Giant's falling down the underground passage when the chain gave way so suddenly. The Giant's dwelling, indeed, was right under the Palace, and the terrible shakings must have been caused by him in his death-throes.

The King now understood how the Queen he had had for some time past had been so ill-tempered. He at once had a sack drawn over her head and made her be stoned to death, and after that torn in pieces by untamed horses. The two young fellows also told now what they had heard and seen in the Queen's room, for before this they had been afraid to say anything about it, on account of the Queen's power.

The real Queen was now restored to all her dignity, and was beloved by all. The nurse was married to a nobleman, and the King and Queen gave her splendid presents.

Esben and the Witch

THERE WAS ONCE A MAN who had twelve sons: the eleven eldest were both big and strong, but the twelfth, whose name was Esben, was only a little fellow. The eleven eldest went out with their father to field and forest, but Esben preferred to stay at home with his mother, and so he was never reckoned at all by the rest, but was a sort of outcast among them.

When the eleven had grown up to be men they decided to go out into the world to try their fortune, and they plagued their father to give them what they required for the journey. The father was not much in favour of this, for he was now old and weak, and could not well spare them from helping him with his work, but in the long run he had to give in. Each one of the eleven got a fine white horse and money for the journey, and so they said farewell to their father and their home, and rode away.

As for Esben, no one had ever thought about him; his brothers had not even said farewell to him.

After the eleven were gone Esben went to his father and said, "Father, give me also a horse and money; I should also like to see round about me in the world."

"You are a little fool," said his father. "If I could have let you go, and kept your eleven brothers at home, it would have been better for me in my old age."

"Well, you will soon be rid of me at any rate," said Esben.

As he could get no other horse, he went into the forest, broke off a branch, stripped the bark off it, so that it became still whiter than his brothers' horses, and, mounted on this, rode off after his eleven brothers.

The brothers rode on the whole day, and towards evening they came to a great forest, which they entered. Far within the wood they came to a little house, and knocked at the door. There came an old, ugly, bearded hag, and opened it, and they asked her whether all of them could get quarters for the night.

"Yes," said the old, bearded hag, "you shall all have quarters for the night, and, in addition, each of you shall have one of my daughters."

The eleven brothers thought that they had come to very hospitable people. They were well attended to, and when they went to bed, each of them got one of the hag's daughters.

Esben had been coming along behind them, and had followed the same way, and had also found the same house in the forest. He slipped into this, without either the witch or her daughters noticing him, and hid himself under one of the beds. A little before midnight he crept quietly out and wakened his brothers. He told these to change night-caps with the witch's daughters. The brothers saw no reason for this, but, to get rid of Esben's persistence, they made the exchange, and slept soundly again.

When midnight came Esben heard the old witch come creeping along. She had a broad-bladed axe in her hand, and went over all the eleven beds. It was so dark that she could not see a hand's breadth before her, but she felt her way, and hacked the heads off all the sleepers who had the men's night-caps on – and these were her own daughters. As soon as she had gone her way Esben wakened his brothers, and they hastily took their horses and rode off from the witch's house, glad that they had escaped so well. They quite forgot to thank Esben for what he had done for them.

When they had ridden onwards for some time they reached a king's palace, and inquired there whether they could be taken into service. Quite easily, they were told, if they would be stablemen, otherwise the king had no use for them. They were quite ready for this, and got the task of looking after all the king's horses.

Long after them came Esben riding on his stick, and he also wanted to get a place in the palace, but no one had any use for him, and he was told that he could just go back the way he had come. However, he stayed there and occupied himself as best he could. He got his food, but nothing more, and by night he lay just where he could.

At this time there was in the palace a knight who was called Sir Red. He was very well liked by the king, but hated by everyone else, for he was wicked both in will and deed. This Sir Red became angry with the eleven brothers, because they would not always stand at attention for him, so he determined to avenge himself on them.

One day, therefore, he went to the king, and said that the eleven brothers who had come to the palace a little while ago, and served as stablemen, could do a great deal more than they pretended. One day he had heard them say that if they liked they could get for the king a wonderful dove which had a feather of gold and a feather of silver time about. But they would not procure it unless they were threatened with death.

The king then had the eleven brothers called before him, and said to them, "You have said that you can get me a dove which has feathers of gold and silver time about."

All the eleven assured him that they had never said anything of the kind, and they did not believe that such a dove existed in the whole world.

"Take your own mind of it," said the king; "but if you don't get that dove within three days you shall lose your heads, the whole lot of you."

With that the king let them go, and there was great grief among them; some wept and others lamented.

At that moment Esben came along, and, seeing their sorrowful looks, said to them, "Hello, what's the matter with you?"

"What good would it do to tell you, you little fool? You can't help us."

"Oh, you don't know that," answered Esben. "I have helped you before."

In the end they told him how unreasonable the king was, and how he had ordered them to get for him a dove with feathers of gold and silver time about.

"Give me a bag of peas" said Esben, "and I shall see what I can do for you."

Esben got his bag of peas; then he took his white stick, and said,

"Fly quick, my little stick, Carry me across the stream."

Straightway the stick carried him across the river and straight into the old witch's courtyard. Esben had noticed that she had such a dove; so when he arrived in the courtyard he shook the peas out of the bag, and the dove came fluttering down to pick them up. Esben caught it at once, put it into the bag, and hurried off before the witch caught sight of him; but the next moment she came running, and shouted after him, "I Hey is that you, Esben?"

"Ye-e-s!"

"Is it you that has taken my dove?"

"Ye-e-s!"

"Was it you that made me kill my eleven daughters?"

"Ye-e-s!"

"Are you coming back again?"

"That may be," said Esben.

"Then you'll catch it," shouted the witch.

The stick carried Esben with the dove back to the king's palace, and his brothers were greatly delighted. The king thanked them many times for the dove, and gave them in return both silver and gold. At this Sir Red became still more embittered, and again thought of how to avenge himself on the brothers.

One day he went to the king and told him that the dove was by no means the best thing that the brothers could get for him; for one day he had heard them talking quietly among themselves, and they had said that they could procure a boar whose bristles were of gold and silver time about.

The king again summoned the brothers before him, and asked whether it was true that they had said that they could get for him a boar whose bristles were of gold and silver time about.

"No," said the brothers; they had never said nor thought such a thing, and they did not believe that there was such a boar in the whole world.

"You must get me that boar within three days," said the king, "or it will cost you your heads."

With that they had to go. This was still worse than before, they thought. Where could they get such a marvellous boar? They all went about hanging their heads; but when only one day remained of the three Esben came along. When he saw his brothers' sorrowful looks he cried, "Hallo, what's the matter now?"

"Oh, what's the use of telling you?" said his brothers. "You can't help us, at any rate."

"Ah, you don't know that," said Esben; "I've helped you before."

In the end they told him how Sir Red had stirred up the king against them, so that he had ordered them to get for him a boar with bristles of gold and silver time about.

"That's all right," said Esben; "give me a sack of malt, and it is not quite impossible that I may be able to help you."

Esben got his sack of malt; then he took his little white stick, set himself upon it, and said,

"Fly quick, my little stick, Carry me across the stream."

Off went the stick with him, and very soon he was again in the witch's courtyard. There he emptied out the malt, and next moment came the boar, which had every second bristle of gold and of silver. Esben at once put it into his sack and hurried off before the witch should catch sight of him; but the next moment she came running, and shouted after him, "Hey! is that you, Esben?"

"Ye-e-s!"

"Is it you that has taken my pretty boar?"

"Ye-e-s!"

"It was also you that took my dove?"

"Ye-e-s!"

"And it was you that made me kill my eleven daughters?"

"Ye-e-s!"

"Are you coming back again?"

"That may be," said Esben.

"Then you'll catch it," said the witch.

Esben was soon back at the palace with the boar, and his brothers scarcely knew which leg to stand on, so rejoiced were they that they were safe again. Not one of them, however, ever thought of thanking Esben for what he had done for them.

The king was still more rejoiced over the boar than he had been over the dove, and did not know what to give the brothers for it. At this Sir Red was again possessed with anger and envy, and again he went about and planned how to get the brothers into trouble.

One day he went again to the king and said, "These eleven brothers have now procured the dove and the boar, but they can do much more than that; I know they have said that if they liked they could get for the king a lamp that can shine over seven kingdoms."

"'If they have said that," said the king, "they shall also be made to bring it to me. That would be a glorious lamp for me."

Again the king sent a message to the brothers to come up to the palace. They went accordingly, although very unwillingly, for they suspected that Sir Red had fallen on some new plan to bring them into trouble.

As soon as they came before the king he said to them,

"You brothers have said that you could, if you liked, get for me a lamp that can shine over seven kingdoms. That lamp must be mine within three days, or it will cost you your lives."

The brothers assured him that they had never said so, and they were sure that no such lamp existed, but their words were of no avail.

"The lamp!" said the king, "or it will cost you your heads."

The brothers were now in greater despair than ever. They did not know what to do, for such a lamp no one had ever heard of. But just as things looked their worst along came Esben.

"Something wrong again?" said he. "What's the matter with you now?"

"Oh, it's no use telling you," said they. "You can't help us, at any rate."

"Oh, you might at least tell me," said Esben; "I have helped you before."

In the end they told him that the king had ordered them to bring him a lamp which could shine over seven kingdoms, but such a lamp no one had ever heard tell of.

"Give me a bushel of salt," said Esben, "and we shall see how matters go."

He got his bushel of salt, and then mounted his little white stick, and said,

"Fly quick, my little stick, Carry me across the stream."

With that both he and his bushel of salt were over beside the witch's courtyard. But now matters were less easy, for he could not get inside the yard, as it was evening and the gate was locked. Finally he hit upon a plan; he got up on the roof and crept down the chimney.

He searched all round for the lamp, but could find it nowhere, for the witch always had it safely guarded, as it was one of her most precious treasures. When he became tired of searching for it he crept into the baking-oven, intending to lie down there and sleep till morning; but just at that moment he heard the witch calling from her bed to one of her daughters, and telling her to make some porridge for her. She had grown hungry, and had taken such a fancy to some porridge. The daughter got out of bed, kindled the fire, and put on a pot with water in it.

"You mustn't put any salt in the porridge, though," cried the witch.

"No, neither will I," said the daughter; but while she was away getting the meal Esben slipped out of the oven and emptied the whole bushel of salt into the pot. The daughter came back then and put in the meal, and after it had boiled a little she took it in to her mother. The witch took a spoonful and tasted it.

"Uh!" said she; "didn't I tell you not to put any salt in it, and it's just as salt as the sea."

So the daughter had to go and make new porridge, and her mother warned her strictly not to put any salt in it. But now there was no water in the house, so she asked her mother to give her the lamp, so that she could go to the well for more.

"There you have it, then," said the witch; "but take good care of it."

The daughter took the lamp which shone over seven kingdoms, and went out to the well for water, while Esben slipped out after her. When she was going to draw the water from the well she set the lamp down on a stone beside her. Esben watched his chance, seized the lamp, and gave her a push from behind, so that she plumped head first into the well. Then he made off with the lamp. But the witch got out of her bed and ran after him, crying:

"Hey! is that you again, Esben?"

"Ye-e-s!"

"Was it you that took my dove?"

"Ye-e-s!"

"Was it also you that took my boar?"

"Ye-e-s!"

"And it was you that made me kill my eleven daughters?"

"Ye-e-s!"

"And now you have taken my lamp, and drowned my twelfth daughter in the well?"

"Ye-e-s!"

"Are you coming back again?"

"That may be," said Esben.

"Then you'll catch it," said the witch.

It was only a minute before the stick had again landed Esben at the king's palace, and the brothers were then freed from their distress. The king gave them many fine presents, but Esben did not get even so much as thanks from them.

Never had Sir Red been so eaten up with envy as he was now, and he racked his brain day and night to find something quite impossible to demand from the brothers.

One day he went to the king and told him that the lamp the brothers had procured was good enough, but they could still get for him something that was far better. The king asked what that was.

"It is," said Sir Red, "the most beautiful coverlet that any mortal ever heard tell of. It also has the property that, when anyone touches it, it sounds so that it can be heard over eight kingdoms."

"That must be a splendid coverlet," said the king, and he at once sent for the brothers.

"You have said that you know of a coverlet, the most beautiful in the whole world, and which sounds over eight kingdoms when anyone touches it. You shall procure it for me, or else lose your lives," said he.

The brothers answered him that they had never said a word about such a coverlet, did not believe it existed, and that it was quite impossible for them to procure it. But the king would not hear a word; he drove them away, telling them that if they did not get it very soon it would cost them their heads.

Things looked very black again for the brothers, for they were sure there was no escape for them. The youngest of them, indeed, asked where Esben was, but the others said that that little fool could scarcely keep himself in clothes, and it was not to be expected that he could help them. Not one of them thought it worth while to look for Esben, but he soon came along of himself.

"Well, what's the matter now?" said he.

"Oh, what's the use of telling you?" said the brothers. "You can't help us, at any rate."

"Ah! who knows that?" said Esben. "I have helped you before."

In the end the brothers told him about the coverlet which, when one touched it, sounded so that it could be heard over eight kingdoms. Esben thought that this was the worst errand that he had had yet, but he could not do worse than fail, and so he would make the attempt.

He again took his little white stick, set himself on it, and said,

"Fly quick, my little stick, Carry me across the stream."

Next moment he was across the river and beside the witch's house. It was evening, and the door was locked, but he knew the way down the chimney. When he had got into the house, however, the worst yet remained to do, for the coverlet was on the bed in which the witch lay and slept. He slipped into the room without either she or her daughter wakening; but as soon as he touched the coverlet to take it it sounded so that it could be heard over eight kingdoms. The witch awoke, sprang out of bed, and caught hold of Esben. He struggled with her, but could not free himself, and the witch called to her daughter, "Come and help me; we shall put him into the little dark room to be fattened. Ho, ho! now I have him!"

Esben was now put into a little dark hole, where he neither saw sun nor moon, and there he was fed on sweet milk and nut-kernels. The daughter had enough to do cracking nuts for him, and at the end of fourteen days she had only one tooth left in her mouth; she had broken all the rest with the nuts. In this time however, she had taken a liking to Esben, and would willingly have set him free, but could not.

When some time had passed the witch told her daughter to go and cut a finger off Esben, so that she could see whether he was nearly fat enough yet. The daughter went and told Esben, and asked him what she should do. Esben told her to take an iron nail and wrap a piece of skin round it: she could then give her mother this to bite at.

The daughter did so, but when the witch bit it she cried, "Uh! no, no! This is nothing but skin and bone; he must be fattened much longer yet."

So Esben was fed for a while longer on sweet milk and nut-kernels, until one day the witch thought that now he must surely be fat enough, and told her daughter again to go and cut a finger off him. By this time Esben was tired of staying in the dark hole, so he told her to go and cut a teat off a cow, and give it to the witch to bite at. This the daughter did, and the witch cried, "Ah! now he is fat – so fat that one can scarcely feel the bone in him. Now he shall be killed."

Now this was just the very time that the witch had to go to Troms Church, where all the witches gather once every year, so she had no time to deal with Esben herself. She therefore told her daughter to heat up the big oven while she was away, take Esben out of his prison, and roast him in there before she came back. The daughter promised all this, and the witch went off on her journey.

The daughter then made the oven as hot as could be, and took Esben out of his prison in order to roast him. She brought the oven spade, and told Esben to seat himself on it, so that she could shoot him into the oven. Esben accordingly took his seat on it, but when she had got him to the mouth of the oven he spread his legs out wide, so that she could not get him pushed in.

"You mustn't sit like that," said she.

"How then?" said Esben.

"You must cross your legs," said the daughter; but Esben could not understand what she meant by this.

"Get out of the way," said she, "and I will show you how to place yourself."

She seated herself on the oven spade, but no sooner had she done so than Esben laid hold of it, shot her into the oven, and fastened the door of it. Then he ran and seized the coverlet, but as soon as he did so it sounded so that it could be heard over eight kingdoms, and the witch, who was at Troms Church, came flying home, and shouted, "Hey! is that you again, Esben?"

"Ye-e-s!"

"It was you that made me kill my eleven daughters?"

"Ye-e-s!"

"And took my dove?"

"Ye-e-s!"

"And my beautiful boar?"

"Ye-e-s!"

"And drowned my twelfth daughter in the well, and took my lamp?"

"Ye-e-s!"

"And now you have roasted my thirteenth and last daughter in the oven, and taken my coverlet?"

"Ye-e-s!"

"Are you coming back again?"

"No, never again," said Esben.

At this the witch became so furious that she sprang into numberless pieces of flint, and from this come all the flint stones that one finds about the country.

Esben had found again his little stick, which the witch had taken from him, so he said,

"Fly quick, my little stick, Carry me across the stream."

Next moment he was back at the king's palace. Here things were in a bad way, for the king had thrown all the eleven brothers into prison, and they were to be executed very shortly because they had not brought him the coverlet. Esben now went up to the king and gave him the coverlet, with which the king was greatly delighted. When he touched it it could be heard over eight kingdoms, and all the other kings sat and were angry because they had not one like it.

Esben also told how everything had happened, and how Sir Red had done the brothers all the ill he could devise because he was envious of them. The brothers were at once set at liberty, while Sir Red, for his wickedness, was hanged on the highest tree that could be found, and so he got the reward he deserved.

Much was made of Esben and his brothers, and these now thanked him for all that he had done for them. The twelve of them received as much gold and silver as they could carry, and betook themselves home to their old father. When he saw again his twelve sons, whom he had never expected to see more, he was so glad that he wept for joy. The brothers told him how much Esben had done, and how he had saved their lives, and from that time forward he was no longer the butt of the rest at home.

Ottar and Angantyr

THE NORTHERN PEOPLE were wont to invoke Freyia [the Northern Goddess of beauty and love] not only for success in love, prosperity, and increase, but also, at times, for aid and protection. This she vouchsafed to all who served her truly, as appeared in the story of Ottar and Angantyr, two men who, after disputing for some time concerning their rights to a certain piece of property, laid their quarrel before the Thing. That popular assembly decreed that the man who could prove that he had the longest line of noble ancestors should be declared the winner, and a special day was appointed to investigate the genealogy of each claimant.

Ottar, unable to remember the names of more than a few of his progenitors, offered sacrifices to Freyia, entreating her aid. The goddess graciously heard his prayer, and appearing before him, she changed him into a boar, and rode off upon his back to the dwelling of the sorceress Hyndla, a most renowned witch. By threats and entreaties, Freyia compelled the old woman to trace Ottar's genealogy back to Odin, and to name every individual in turn, with a synopsis of his achievements. Then, fearing lest her votary's memory should be unable to retain so many details, Freyia further compelled Hyndla to brew a potion of remembrance, which she gave him to drink.

Thus prepared, Ottar presented himself before the Thing on the appointed day, and glibly reciting his pedigree, he named so many more ancestors than Angantyr could recollect, that he was easily awarded possession of the property he coveted.

Hansel and Grethel

HARD BY A GREAT FOREST dwelt a poor wood-cutter with his wife and his two children. The boy was called Hansel and the girl Grethel. He had little to bite and to break, and once when great scarcity fell on the land, he could no longer procure daily bread. Now when he thought over this by night in his bed, and tossed about in his anxiety, he groaned and said to his wife, "What is to become of us? How are we to feed our poor children, when we no longer have anything even for ourselves?" "I'll tell you what, husband," answered the woman, "early to-morrow morning we will take the children out into the forest to where it is the thickest, there we will light a fire for them, and give each of them one piece of bread more, and then we will go to our work and leave them alone. They will not find the way home again, and we shall be rid of them." "No, wife," said the man, "I will not do that; how can I bear to leave my children alone in the forest? - the wild animals would soon come and tear them to pieces." "O, thou fool!" said she, "then we must all four die of hunger, thou mayest as well plane the planks for our coffins," and she left him no peace until he consented. "But I feel very sorry for the poor children, all the same," said the man.

The two children had also not been able to sleep for hunger, and had heard what their step-mother had said to their father. Grethel wept bitter tears, and said to Hansel, "Now all is over with us." "Be quiet, Grethel," said Hansel, "do not distress thyself, I will soon find a way to help us." And when the old folks had fallen asleep, he got up, put on his little coat, opened the door below, and crept outside. The moon shone brightly, and the white pebbles which lay in front of the house glittered like real silver pennies. Hansel stooped and put as many of them in the little pocket of his coat as he could possibly get in. Then he went back and said to Grethel, "Be comforted, dear little sister, and sleep in peace, God will not forsake us," and he lay down again in his bed. When day dawned, but before the sun had risen, the woman came and awoke the two children, saying, "Get up, you sluggards! we are going into the forest to fetch wood." She gave each a little piece of bread, and said, "There is something for your dinner, but do not eat it up before then, for you will get nothing else." Grethel took the bread under her apron, as Hansel had the stones in his pocket. Then they all set out together on the way to the forest. When they had walked a short time, Hansel stood still and peeped back at the house, and did so again and again. His father said, "Hansel, what art thou looking at there and staying behind for? Mind what thou art about, and do not forget how to use thy legs." "Ah, father," said Hansel, "I am looking at my little white cat, which is sitting up on the roof, and wants to say good-bye to me." The wife said, "Fool, that is not thy little cat, that is the morning sun which is shining on the chimneys." Hansel, however, had not been looking back at the cat, but had been constantly throwing one of the white pebble-stones out of his pocket on the road.

When they had reached the middle of the forest, the father said, "Now, children, pile up some wood, and I will light a fire that you may not be cold." Hansel and Grethel gathered brushwood together, as high as a little hill. The brushwood was lighted, and when the flames were burning very high the woman said, "Now, children, lay yourselves down by the fire and rest, we will go into the forest and cut some wood. When we have done, we will come back and fetch you away."

Hansel and Grethel sat by the fire, and when noon came, each ate a little piece of bread, and as they heard the strokes of the woodaxe they believed that their father was near. It was, however, not the axe, it was a branch which he had fastened to a withered tree which the wind was blowing backwards and forwards. And as they had been sitting such a long time, their eyes shut with fatigue, and they fell fast asleep. When at last they awoke, it was already dark night. Grethel began to cry and said, "How are we to get out of the forest now?" But Hansel comforted her and said, "Just wait a little, until the moon has risen, and then we will soon find the way." And when the full moon had risen, Hansel took his little sister by the hand, and followed the pebbles which shone like newlycoined silver pieces, and showed them the way.

They walked the whole night long, and by break of day came once more to their father's house. They knocked at the door, and when the woman opened it and saw that it was Hansel and Grethel, she said, "You naughty children, why have you slept so long in the forest? - we thought you were never coming back at all!" The father, however, rejoiced, for it had cut him to the heart to leave them behind alone.

Not long afterwards, there was once more great scarcity in all parts, and the children heard their mother saying at night to their father, "Everything is eaten again, we have one half loaf left, and after that there is an end. The children must go, we will take them farther into the wood, so that they will not find their way out again; there is no other means of saving ourselves!" The man's heart was heavy, and he thought "it would be better for thee to share the last mouthful with thy children." The woman, however, would listen to nothing that he had to say, but scolded and reproached him. He who says A must say B, likewise, and as he had yielded the first time, he had to do so second time also.

The children were, however, still awake and had heard the conversation. When the old folks were asleep, Hansel again got up, and wanted to go out and pick up pebbles, but the woman had locked the door, and Hansel could not get out. Nevertheless he comforted his little sister, and said, "Do not cry, Grethel, go to sleep quietly, the good God will help us."

Early in the morning came the woman, and took the children out of their beds. Their bit of bread was given to them, but it was still smaller than the time before. On the way into the forest Hansel crumbled his in his pocket, and often stood still and threw a morsel on the ground. "Hansel, why dost thou stop and look around?" said the father, "go on." "I am looking back at my little pigeon which is sitting on the roof, and wants to say good-bye to me," answered Hansel. "Simpleton!" said the woman, "that is not thy little pigeon, that is the morning sun that is shining on the chimney." Hansel, however, little by little, threw all the crumbs on the path.

The woman led the children still deeper into the forest, where they had never in their lives been before. Then a great fire was again made, and the mother said, "Just sit there, you children, and when you are tired you may sleep a little; we are going into the forest to cut wood, and in the evening when we are done, we will come and fetch you away." When it was noon, Grethel shared her piece of bread with Hansel, who had scattered his by the way. Then they fell asleep and evening came and went, but no one came to the poor children. They did not awake until it was dark night, and Hansel comforted his little sister and said, "Just wait, Grethel, until the moon rises, and then we shall see the crumbs of bread which I have strewn about, they will show us our way home again." When the moon came they set out, but they found no crumbs, for the many thousands of birds which fly about in the woods and fields had picked them all up. Hansel said to Grethel, "We shall soon find the way," but they did not find it. They walked the whole night and all the next day too from morning till evening, but they did not get out of the forest, and were very hungry, for they had nothing to eat but two or three berries, which grew on the ground. And as they were so weary that their legs would carry them no longer, they lay down beneath a tree and fell asleep.

It was now three mornings since they had left their father's house. They began to walk again, but they always got deeper into the forest, and if help did not come soon, they must die of hunger and weariness. When it was mid – day, they saw a beautiful snow-white bird sitting on a bough, which sang so delightfully that they stood still and listened to it. And when it had finished its song, it spread its wings and flew away before them, and they followed it until they reached a little house, on the roof of which it alighted; and when they came quite up to the little house they saw that it was built of bread and covered with cakes, but that the windows were of clear sugar. "We will set to work on that," said Hansel, "and have a good meal. I will eat a bit of the roof, and thou, Grethel, canst eat some of the window, it will taste sweet." Hansel reached up above, and broke off a little of the roof to try how it tasted, and Grethel leant against the window and nibbled at the panes. Then a soft voice cried from the room,

"Nibble, nibble, gnaw,
Who is nibbling at my little house?"

The children answered,

"The wind, the wind,
the heaven-born wind,"

and went on eating without disturbing themselves. Hansel, who thought the roof tasted very nice, tore down a great piece of it, and Grethel pushed out the whole of one round window-pane, sat down, and enjoyed herself with it. Suddenly the door opened, and a very, very old woman, who supported herself on crutches, came creeping out. Hansel and Grethel were so terribly frightened that they let fall what they had in their hands. The old woman, however, nodded her head, and said, "Oh, you dear children, who has brought you here? Do come in, and stay with me. No harm shall happen to you." She took them both by the hand, and led them into her little house. Then good food was set before them, milk and pancakes, with sugar, apples, and nuts. Afterwards two pretty little beds were covered with clean white linen, and Hansel and Grethel lay down in them, and thought they were in heaven.

The old woman had only pretended to be so kind; she was in reality a wicked witch, who lay in wait for children, and had only built the little bread house in order to entice them there. When a child fell into her power, she killed it, cooked and ate it, and that was a feast day with her. Witches have red eyes, and cannot see far, but they have a keen scent like the beasts, and are aware when human beings draw near. When Hansel and Grethel came into her neighbourhood, she laughed maliciously, and said mockingly, "I have them, they shall not escape me again!" Early in the morning before the children were awake, she was already up, and when she saw both of them sleeping and looking so pretty, with their plump red cheeks, she muttered to herself, "That will be a dainty mouthful!" Then she seized Hansel with her shrivelled hand, carried him into a little stable, and shut him in with a grated door. He might scream as he liked, that was of no use. Then she went to Grethel, shook her till she awoke, and cried, "Get up, lazy thing, fetch some water, and cook something good for thy brother, he is in the stable outside, and is to be made fat. When he is fat, I will eat him." Grethel began to weep bitterly, but it was all in vain, she was forced to do what the wicked witch ordered her.

And now the best food was cooked for poor Hansel, but Grethel got nothing but crab-shells. Every morning the woman crept to the little stable, and cried, "Hansel, stretch out thy finger that I may feel if thou wilt soon be fat." Hansel, however, stretched out a little bone to her, and the old woman, who had dim eyes, could not see it, and thought it was Hansel's finger, and was astonished that there was no way of fattening him. When four weeks had gone by, and Hansel still continued thin, she was seized with impatience and would not wait any longer, "Hola, Grethel," she cried to the girl, "be active, and bring some water. Let Hansel be fat or lean, tomorrow I will kill him, and cook him." Ah, how the poor little sister did lament when she had to fetch the water, and how her tears did flow down over her cheeks! "Dear God, do help us," she cried. "If the wild beasts in the forest had but devoured us, we should at any rate have died together." "Just keep thy noise to thyself," said the old woman, "all that won't help thee at all."

Early in the morning, Grethel had to go out and hang up the cauldron with the water, and light the fire. "We will bake first," said the old woman, "I have already heated the oven, and kneaded the dough." She pushed poor Grethel out to the oven, from which flames of fire were already darting. "Creep in," said the witch, "and see if it is properly heated, so that we can shut the bread in." And when once Grethel was inside, she intended to shut the oven and let her bake in it, and then she would eat her, too. But Grethel saw what she had in her mind, and said, "I do not know how I am to do it; how do you get in?" "Silly goose," said the old woman. "The door is big enough; just look, I can get in myself!" and she crept up and thrust her head into the oven. Then Grethel gave her a push that drove her far into it, and shut the iron door, and fastened the bolt. Oh! then she began to howl quite horribly, but Grethel ran away, and the godless witch was miserably burnt to death.

Grethel, however, ran as quick as lightning to Hansel, opened his little stable, and cried, "Hansel, we are saved! The old witch is dead!" Then Hansel sprang out like a bird from its cage when the door is opened for it. How they did rejoice and embrace each other, and dance about and kiss each other! And as they had no longer any need to fear her, they went into the witch's house, and in every corner there stood chests full of pearls and jewels. "These are far better than pebbles!" said Hansel, and thrust into his pockets whatever could be got in, and Grethel said, "I, too, will take something home with me," and filled her pinafore full. "But now we will go away," said Hansel, "that we may get out of the witch's forest."

When they had walked for two hours, they come to a great piece of water. "We cannot get over," said Hansel, "I see no foot-plank, and no bridge." "And no boat crosses either," answered Grethel, "but a white duck is swimming there; if I ask her, she will help us over." Then she cried,

> "Little duck, little duck, dost thou see,
> Hansel and Grethel are waiting for thee?
> There's never a plank, or bridge in sight,
> Take us across on thy back so white."

The duck came to them, and Hansel seated himself on its back, and told his sister to sit by him. "No," replied Grethel, "that will be too heavy for the little duck; she shall take us across, one after the other." The good little duck did so, and when they were once safely across and had walked for a short time, the forest seemed to be more and more familiar to them, and at length they saw from afar their father's house. Then they began to run, rushed into the parlour, and threw themselves into their father's arms. The man had not known one happy hour since he had left the children in the forest; the woman, however, was dead. Grethel emptied her pinafore until pearls and precious stones ran about the room, and Hansel threw one handful after another out of his pocket to add to them. Then all anxiety was at an end, and they lived together in perfect happiness. My tale is done, there runs a mouse, whosoever catches it, may make himself a big fur cap out of it.

Rapunzel

ONCE UPON A TIME there lived a man and his wife who were very unhappy because they had no children. These good people had a little window at the back of their house, which looked into the most lovely garden, full of all manner of beautiful flowers and vegetables; but the garden was surrounded by a high wall, and no one dared to enter it, for it belonged to a Witch of great power, who was feared by the whole world. One day the woman stood at the window overlooking the garden, and saw there a bed full of the finest rampion: the leaves looked so fresh and green that she longed to eat them. The desire grew day by day, and just because she knew she couldn't possibly get any, she pined away and became quite pale and wretched. Then her husband grew alarmed and said:

"What ails you, dear wife?"

"Oh," she answered, "if I don't get some rampion to eat out of the garden behind the house, I know I shall die."

The man, who loved her dearly, thought to himself, "Come! rather than let your wife die you shall fetch her some rampion, no matter the cost." So at dusk he climbed over the wall into the Witch's garden, and, hastily gathering a handful of rampion leaves, he returned with them to his wife. She made them into a salad, which tasted so good that her longing for the forbidden food was greater than ever. If she were to know any peace of mind, there was nothing for it but that her husband should climb over the garden wall again, and fetch her some more. So at dusk over he got, but when he reached the other side he drew back in terror, for there, standing before him, was the old Witch.

"How dare you," she said, with a wrathful glance, "climb into my garden and steal my rampion like a common thief? You shall suffer for your foolhardiness."

"Oh!" he implored, "pardon my presumption; necessity alone drove me to the deed. My wife saw your rampion from her window, and conceived such a desire for it that she would certainly have died if her wish had not been gratified." Then the Witch's anger was a little appeased, and she said:

"If it's as you say, you may take as much rampion away with you as you like, but on one condition only – that you give me the child your wife will shortly bring into the world. All shall go well with it, and I will look after it like a mother."

The man in his terror agreed to everything she asked, and as soon as the child was born the Witch appeared, and having given it the name of Rapunzel, which is the same as rampion, she carried it off with her.

Rapunzel was the most beautiful child under the sun. When she was twelve years old the Witch shut her up in a tower, in the middle of a great wood, and the tower had neither stairs nor doors, only high up at the very top a small window. When the old Witch wanted to get in she stood underneath and called out:

"Rapunzel, Rapunzel, Let down your golden hair," for Rapunzel had wonderful long hair, and it was as fine as spun gold. Whenever she heard the Witch's voice she unloosed her plaits, and let her hair fall down out of the window about twenty yards below, and the old Witch climbed up by it.

After they had lived like this for a few years, it happened one day that a Prince was riding through the wood and passed by the tower. As he drew near it he heard someone singing so sweetly that he stood still spell-bound, and listened. It was Rapunzel in her loneliness trying to while away the time by letting her sweet voice ring out into the wood. The Prince longed to see the owner of the voice, but he sought in vain for a door in the tower. He rode home, but he was so haunted by the song he had heard that he returned every day to the wood and listened. One day, when he was standing thus behind a tree, he saw the old Witch approach and heard her call out:

"Rapunzel, Rapunzel, Let down your golden hair."

Then Rapunzel let down her plaits, and the Witch climbed up by them.

"So that's the staircase, is it?" said the Prince. "Then I too will climb it and try my luck."

So on the following day, at dusk, he went to the foot of the tower and cried:

"Rapunzel, Rapunzel, Let down your golden hair," and as soon as she had let it down the Prince climbed up.

At first Rapunzel was terribly frightened when a man came in, for she had never seen one before; but the Prince spoke to her so kindly, and told her at once that his heart had been so touched by her singing, that he felt he should know no peace of mind till he had seen her. Very soon Rapunzel forgot her fear, and when he asked her to marry him she consented at once. "For," she thought, "he is young and handsome, and I'll certainly be happier with him than with the old Witch." So she put her hand in his and said:

"Yes, I will gladly go with you, only how am I to get down out of the tower? Every time you come to see me you must bring a skein of silk with you, and I will make a ladder of them, and when it is finished I will climb down by it, and you will take me away on your horse."

They arranged that till the ladder was ready, he was to come to her every evening, because the old woman was with her during the day. The old Witch, of course, knew nothing of what was going on, till one day Rapunzel, not thinking of what she was about, turned to the Witch and said:

"How is it, good mother, that you are so much harder to pull up than the young Prince? He is always with me in a moment."

"Oh! you wicked child," cried the Witch. "What is this I hear? I thought I had hidden you safely from the whole world, and in spite of it you have managed to deceive me."

In her wrath she seized Rapunzel's beautiful hair, wound it round and round her left hand, and then grasping a pair of scissors in her right, snip snap, off it came, and the beautiful plaits lay on the ground. And, worse than this, she was so hard-hearted that she took Rapunzel to a lonely desert place, and there left her to live in loneliness and misery.

But on the evening of the day in which she had driven poor Rapunzel away, the Witch fastened the plaits on to a hook in the window, and when the Prince came and called out:

"Rapunzel, Rapunzel, Let down your golden hair," she let them down, and the Prince climbed up as usual, but instead of his beloved Rapunzel he found the old Witch, who fixed her evil, glittering eyes on him, and cried mockingly:

"Ah, ah! you thought to find your lady love, but the pretty bird has flown and its song is dumb; the cat caught it, and will scratch out your eyes too. Rapunzel is lost to you for ever – you will never see her more."

The Prince was beside himself with grief, and in his despair he jumped right down from the tower, and, though he escaped with his life, the thorns among which he fell pierced his eyes out. Then he wandered, blind and miserable, through the wood, eating nothing but roots and berries, and weeping and lamenting the loss of his lovely bride. So he wandered about for some years, as wretched and unhappy as he could well be, and at last he came to the desert place where Rapunzel was living. Of a sudden he heard a voice which seemed strangely familiar to him. He walked eagerly in the direction of the sound, and when he was quite close, Rapunzel recognised him and fell on his neck and wept. But two of her tears touched his eyes, and in a moment they became quite clear again, and he saw as well as he had ever done. Then he led her to his kingdom, where they were received and welcomed with great joy, and they lived happily ever after.

Great Head and the Ten Brothers

IN A REMOTE INDIAN VILLAGE at the edge of the forest, an orphaned family of ten boys lived in a small lodge with their uncle. The five elder brothers went out to hunt every day, but the younger ones, not yet ready for so rigorous a life, remained at home with their uncle, never daring to venture too far from their home.

One day, the group of elder brothers, who had been away deer-hunting, failed to return at the usual hour. As the evening wore on, there was still no sign of them, and by nightfall their uncle had become extremely worried for their safety. It was agreed among the remaining family that the eldest boy should go out on the following morning in search of his brothers. He readily accepted the challenge and he set off after sunrise, confident that he would locate them before long. But the boy did not return, and his disappearance caused even greater consternation among the household.

"We must find out what is happening to them," said the next in line. "Though I am young and ill-prepared for adventure, I cannot bear to picture any of my family lying wounded in some fearful, hostile place."

And so, having obtained his uncle's permission, he too set off enthusiastically, though he was not so self-assured as his brother before him. Just like the others, however, the youth failed to reappear, and an identical fate awaited the two more after him who took it upon themselves to go out in search of the lost hunters. At length, only one small brother remained with his uncle at the lodge, and fearing he might lose the last of his young nephews, the old man became very protective of him, turning a deaf ear to his persistent pleas to be allowed take his turn in the search.

The youngest brother was now obliged to accompany his uncle everywhere. He was even forced to walk with the old man the short distance to the wood-pile, and he longed for the day when adventure would come knocking on his door. He had almost resigned himself to the fact that this would never happen when, one morning, as the pair stooped to gather firewood, the young boy imagined he heard a deep groan coming from the earth beneath his feet. He called upon his uncle to listen and the sound, unmistakably a human groan, soon repeated itself. Both were deeply shocked by the discovery and began clawing frantically at the earth with their bare hands. Shortly afterwards, a human face revealed itself and before long, they had uncovered the entire body of a man, caked in mould and scarcely able to breathe.

Carefully, they lifted the unfortunate creature from the soil and carried him into their lodge where they rubbed his skin down with bear oil until he slowly began to revive. It was several hours before the man could bring himself to speak, but then, at last, he began mouthing a few words, informing his hosts that he had been out hunting when his mind had suddenly become entirely blank. He could remember nothing more, he told them, neither his name, nor the village he had come from. The old man and his nephew begged the stranger to stay with them, hoping that soon his memory would be restored and that then, perhaps, he could help them in their own search.

The days passed by, but after only a very short time, the young boy and his uncle began to observe that the person they had rescued was no ordinary mortal like themselves. He did not eat any of the food they served him, but his strength increased daily none the less. He had no need of sleep, and often when it rained he behaved very strangely, tossing restlessly in his chair and calling aloud in a curious language.

One night, a particularly violent storm raged outside. As the rain pelted down and the winds howled fiercely, the boy and his uncle were awoken by the loud cries of their guest:

"Do you hear that noise?" he yelled. "That is my brother, Great Head, riding on the wind. Can you not hear him wailing?"

"Yes, we can," said the old man. "Would you like us to invite him here? Would he come if you sent for him?"

"I would certainly like to see him," replied the strange guest, "but he will not come unless I bring him here by magic. You should prepare for him a welcoming meal, ten large blocks of maple-wood, for that is the food he lives on." And saying this, the stranger departed in search of his brother, taking with him his bow and a selection of arrows, carved from the roots of a hickory-tree.

At about midday, he drew near to Great Head's dwelling and quickly transformed himself into a mole, so that his brother would not notice his approach. Silently, he crept through the grass until he spotted Great Head up ahead, perched on a cliff-face, glowering fiercely at an owl.

"I see you!" shouted Great Head, "now you shall die." And he lunged forward, ready to devour the helpless creature.

Just at that moment, the mole stood up, and taking aim with his bow, shot an arrow in Great Head's direction. The arrow became larger and larger as it sped through the air towards the monstrous creature, but then, when it had almost reached its target, it turned back on itself and returned to the mole, regaining its normal size. Great Head was soon in pursuit, puffing and snorting like a hurricane as he trampled through the trees. Once more, the mole shot an arrow and again it returned to him, luring Great Head further and further onwards towards the lodge where the young boy and his uncle nervously awaited their arrival.

As soon as the door to their house burst open, its terrified occupants began attacking Great Head with wooden mallets. But the more vigorously they struck him, the more Great Head broke into peals of laughter, for he was not only impervious to pain, but the sight of his brother standing before him had put him in the best of moods. The two embraced warmly and Great Head sat down to his meal of maple-blocks which he devoured with great relish.

When he had done, he thanked his hosts for their hospitality and enquired of them how he might return their kindness. They began telling him the story of their missing relatives, but had only uttered a few words before Great Head interrupted them:

"You need tell me no more," he said to them, "I know precisely what has become of them. They have fallen into the hands of a woodland witch. Now if this boy will accompany me, I will point out her dwelling and show him the bones of his brothers."

Although reluctant to release him, the uncle perceived how anxious his nephew was to learn the fate of his brothers. Finally, he gave his consent, and the young boy started off with Great Head, smiling broadly at the thought of the adventure which lay ahead.

They did not once pause for rest and after a time they came upon a ramshackle hut, in front of which were strewn dry bones of every size and description. In the doorway sat a crooked old witch, rocking back and forth, singing to herself. When she looked up and saw her visitors, she flew into a rage and began chanting her spell to change the living into dry bones. But her magic had no effect on Great Head, and because his companion stood in his shadow, he too was protected from the charm. The youth sprang forward and began to attack the frail, old witch, beating her with his fists until she fell lifeless to the ground. As soon as she lay dead, a loud shriek pierced the silence, and her flesh was transformed into black-feathered birds that rose squawking into the air.

The young boy now set about the task of selecting the bones of his brothers. It was slow and difficult work, but, at last, he had gathered together nine white mounds. Great Head came forward to examine each of them and when he was satisfied that no bone was missing he spoke to his young companion:

"I am going back to my rock," he told him. "But do not despair or think I have abandoned you, for soon you will see me again."

The boy stood alone, guarding the heaps of bones, trying to decide whether he should make his way back home before daylight faded. Looking upwards, he noticed that a huge storm was gathering and began walking towards the hut for shelter. The hail beat on his back even as he walked the short distance and soon sharp needles of rain pricked his skin all over. The thunder now clashed and lightning struck the ground wherever he attempted to step. The young boy grew fearful and flung himself to the earth, but suddenly he heard a familiar voice calling to him, and lifting his eyes, he saw Great Head riding at the centre of the storm.

"Arise you bones," Great Head yelled, "I bid you come to life." The hurricane passed overhead in an instant, as rapidly as it had first appeared. The young boy felt certain that he must have been dreaming, but then, he observed that the mounds had disappeared. In a moment he was surrounded by his brothers and huge tears of relief and joy flooded down his cheeks.

The Raven Mocker

OF ALL THE CHEROKEE WIZARDS or witches the most dreaded is the Raven Mocker (Kâ'lanû Ahkyeli'skï), the one that robs the dying man of life. They are of either sex and there is no sure way to know one, though they usually look withered and old, because they have added so many lives to their own.

At night, when some one is sick or dying in the settlement, the Raven Mocker goes to the place to take the life. He flies through the air in fiery shape, with arms outstretched like wings, and sparks trailing behind, and a rushing sound like the noise of a strong wind. Every little while as he flies he makes a cry like the cry of a raven when it 'dives' in the air – not like the common raven cry – and those who hear are afraid, because they know that some man's life will soon go out. When the Raven Mocker comes to the house he finds others of his kind waiting there, and unless there is a doctor on guard who knows how to drive them away they go inside, all invisible, and frighten and torment the sick man until they kill him. Sometimes to do this they even lift him from the bed and throw him on the floor, but his friends who are with him think he is only struggling for breath.

After the witches kill him they take out his heart and eat it, and so add to their own lives as many days or years as they have taken from his. No one in the room can see them, and there is no sear where they take out the heart, but yet there is no heart left in the body. Only one who has the right medicine can recognize a Raven Mocker, and if such a man stays in the room with the sick person these witches are afraid to come in, and retreat as soon as they see him, because when one of them is recognized in his right shape he must die within seven days. There was once a man named Gûñskäli'skï, who had this medicine and used to hunt for Raven Mockers, and killed several. When the friends of a dying person know that there is no more hope they always try to have one of these medicine men stay in the house and watch the body until it is buried, because after burial the witches do not steal the heart.

The other witches are jealous of the Raven Mockers and afraid to come into the same house with one. Once a man who had the witch medicine was watching by a sick man and saw these other witches outside trying to get in. All at once they heard a Raven Mocker cry overhead and the others scattered 'like a flock of pigeons when the hawk swoops.' When at last a Raven Mocker dies these other witches sometimes take revenge by digging up the body and abusing it.

The following is told on the reservation as an actual happening:

A young man had been out on a hunting trip and was on his way home when night came on while he was still a long distance from the settlement. He knew of a house not far off the trail where an old man and his wife lived, so he turned in that direction to look for a place to sleep until morning. When he got to the house there was nobody in it. He looked into the âsï and found no one there either. He thought maybe they had gone after water, and so stretched himself out in the farther corner to sleep. Very soon he heard a raven cry outside, and in a little while afterwards the old man came into the âsï and sat down by the fire without noticing the young man, who kept still in the dark corner. Soon there was another raven cry outside, and the old man said to himself, "Now my wife is coming," and sure enough in a little while the old woman came in and sat down by her husband. Then the young man knew they were Raven Mockers and he was frightened and kept very quiet.

Said the old man to his wife, "Well, what luck did you have?" "None," said the old woman, "there were too many doctors watching. What luck did you have?" "I got what I went for," said the old man, "there is no reason to fail, but you never have luck. Take this and cook it and have something to eat." She fixed the fire and then the young man smelled meat roasting and thought it smelled sweeter than any meat he had ever tasted. He peeped out from one eye, and it looked like a man's heart roasting on a stick.

Suddenly the old woman said to her husband, "Who is over in the corner?" "Nobody," said the old man. "Yes, there is," said the old woman, "I hear him snoring," and she stirred the fire until it blazed and lighted up the whole place, and there was the young man lying in the corner. He kept quiet and pretended to be asleep. The old man made a noise at the fire to wake him, but still he pretended to sleep. Then the old man came over and shook him, and he sat up and rubbed his eyes as if he had been asleep all the time.

Now it was near daylight and the old woman was out in the other house getting breakfast ready, but the hunter could hear her crying to herself. "Why is your wife crying?" he asked the old man. "Oh, she has lost some of her friends lately and feels lonesome," said her husband; but the young man knew that she was crying because he had heard them talking.

When they came out to breakfast the old man put a bowl of corn mush before him and said, "This is all we have – we have had no meat for a long time." After breakfast the young man started on again, but when he had gone a little way the old man ran after him with a fine piece of beadwork and gave it to him, saying, "Take this, and don't tell anybody what you heard last, night, because my wife and I are always quarrelling that way." The young man took the piece, but when he came to the first creek he threw it into the water and then went on to the settlement. There he told the whole story, and a party of warriors started back with him to kill the Raven Mockers. When they reached the place it was seven days after the first night. They found the old man and his wife lying dead in the house, so they set fire to it and burned it and the witches together.

Turtle-Dove, Sage Cock, and the Witch

TURTLE-DOVE WAS A WIDOW with two children – Yellow-bird, a girl eleven years of age, and Sage-cock, a baby boy. The girl was big, awkward and stupid; but the boy, though only a baby, gave signs of being a remarkably bright child.

Turtle-dove was always anxious about him, for an old witch who lived in that part of the country stole every little boy that she could find.

One day Turtle-dove went down to the valley to gather seeds and herbs. She carried her baby on her back, but he was heavy, and after a time she grew tired from the weight and constant stooping. So she took the baby and laid him under a sage-brush, telling his sister to watch him.

Presently the old witch came that way, and going up to the bundle, felt it all over, and asked Yellow-bird what it contained.

"It is my sister," said she, for she thought the witch would not want to steal a girl.

Then the old witch scolded her, growing more and more loud and angry in her speech and manner until her eyes stood out, glaring at the girl, and her grizzled locks rattled like the naked branches of the trees. Yellow-bird grew cold as ice and could not even scream, she was so frightened.

The old witch, seeing that she was not likely to be attacked, seized the little pappoose and flew away with him on her bat-like wings to the distant mountain, which no man can climb by reason of the rattlesnake forest at its base.

When she reached her den, which was a hollow place black with cinders and hidden from sight by a clump of hemlock trees, she laid the boy on the ground, broke the strips of deer skin that held his fur blanket over him and stretched his legs till he became a man.

"Now," said she, "I shall have a husband."

Although Sage-cock had suddenly grown to a man's size, he had only a baby's heart and knew no better than to marry an ugly old witch.

When Turtle-dove returned and heard Yellow-bird's story she was very angry and would not forgive the girl for not calling her. She spent day after day searching among the rocks and wherever a wild beast or a witch might have a hiding-place. She left no clump of bushes, however small, unexplored, but all to no purpose. At last she went to her brother, the Eagle, and told him her story.

Eagle was keen of sight and a swift hunter. He put on his war feathers and his war paint and set out in search of the boy.

One day he heard a baby crying, but he did not recognize its voice. He told his sister, and she begged him to take her to the place, for she felt sure that she would know the child's voice and he would know hers.

They went towards the witch's mountain. Before they reached it they heard the child cry; but did not know how to get to him because of the rattlesnake forest.

Eagle thought he would try his magic, for he was one of the wizards of the tribe. He took two feathers from his head dress and spread them out into wings, which he fastened upon his shoulders. He then placed Turtle Dove on his back and flew with her over the forest of rattlesnakes.

He hid in some bushes while the mother called, "Sage-cock, Sage-cock."

The child cried and strove to get out of the den. He did struggle through the bushes, but the witch caught him. Then with one blow of her stick she killed a mountain sheep near by, and taking the boy in her arms, jumped into its stomach. She pulled the wool about them and lay very still.

Meanwhile Eagle killed a rabbit and put it on the top of a tall pine tree, then peeled the bark so that it would be hard to climb. They watched for days but with no success.

At last the old woman grew hungry, and Sage-cock cried for food. So she crept out, and seeing the rabbit, tried to get it.

When Eagle saw her he knew that the baby could not be far off. He stretched himself full length on the ground and listened, with his ear to the earth.

First he heard a faint cry which seemed to come from the sheep, then, as he went nearer, he heard the boy's heart thumping and knew just where to go. He found the baby, caught him up in his arms and ran quickly with him down to the edge of the rattlesnake forest.

Knowing the old witch would follow him, he raised a great snow-storm, that covered all his tracks, so that she should not know in what direction he had gone.

But in his haste he dropped two eagle's feathers, and the witch knew at once who had stolen her husband. She went to her brother, one of the chiefs of the rattlesnakes, and asked him to take her part. He hated her, for she was always getting him into trouble; but she was his sister, and he could not refuse.

Just then, Eagle's war-whoop was heard; and, having no place in which to hide her, he opened his mouth, and let her jump down his throat. She would not be still and bothered him so much that after Eagle had passed he tried to throw her off. But he could not rid himself of her, and at last he wrenched himself so hard that he jumped out of his own skin.

The witch still lives in it and rolls about among the rocks to this day, mocking all who pass, though no one can ever lay hold of her. The Pale-faces call her Echo.

Sage-cock became a little boy again and grew to be a mighty chief, succeeding his uncle, the Eagle, as a warrior and magician.

Pah-hah-undootah, or The Red Head

AS SPRING APPROACHES, the Indians return from their wintering grounds to their villages, engage in feasting, soon exhaust their stock of provisions, and begin to suffer for the want of food. Such of the hunters as are of an active and enterprising cast of character, take the occasion to separate from the mass of the population, and remove to some neighboring locality in the forest, which promises the means of subsistence during this season of general lassitude and enjoyment.

Among the families who thus separated themselves, on a certain occasion, there was a man called Odshedoph Waucheentongah, or the Child of Strong Desires, who had a wife and one son. After a day's travel he reached an ample wood with his family, which was thought to be a suitable place to encamp. The wife fixed the lodge, while the husband went out to hunt. Early in the evening he returned with a deer. Being tired and thirsty he asked his son to go to the river for some water. The son replied that it was dark and he was afraid. He urged him to go, saying that his mother, as well as himself, was tired, and the distance to the water was very short. But no persuasion was of any avail. He refused to go. "Ah, my son," said the father, at last, "if you are afraid to go to the river, you will never kill the Red Head."

The boy was deeply mortified by this observation. It seemed to call up all his latent energies. He mused in silence. He refused to eat, and made no reply when spoken to.

The next day he asked his mother to dress the skin of the deer, and make it into moccasins for him, while he busied himself in preparing a bow and arrows. As soon as these things were done, he left the lodge one morning at sunrise, without saying a word to his father or mother. He fired one of his arrows into the air, which fell westward. He took that course, and at night coming to the spot where the arrow had fallen, was rejoiced to find it piercing the heart of a deer. He refreshed himself with a meal of the venison, and the next morning fired another arrow. After travelling all day, he found it also in another deer. In this manner he fired four arrows, and every evening found that he had killed a deer. What was very singular, however, was, that he left the arrows sticking in the carcasses, and passed on without withdrawing them. In consequence of this, he had no arrow for the fifth day, and was in great distress at night for the want of food. At last he threw himself upon the ground in despair, concluding that he might as well perish there as go further. But he had not lain long before he heard a hollow, rumbling noise, in the ground beneath him. He sprang up, and discovered at a distance the figure of a human being, walking with a stick. He looked attentively and saw that the figure was walking in a wide beaten path, in a prairie, leading from a lodge to a lake. To his surprise, this lodge was at no great distance. He approached a little nearer and concealed himself. He soon discovered that the figure was no other than that of the terrible witch, Wok-on-kahtohn-zooeyah-pee-kah-haitchee, or the little old woman who makes war. Her path to the lake was perfectly smooth and solid, and the noise our adventurer had heard, was caused by the striking of her walking staff upon the ground. The top of this staff was decorated with a string of the toes and bills of birds of every kind, who at every stroke of the stick, fluttered and sung their various notes in concert.

She entered her lodge and laid off her mantle, which was entirely composed of the scalps of women. Before folding it, she shook it several times, and at every shake the scalps uttered loud shouts of laughter, in which the old hag joined. Nothing could have frightened him more than this horrific exhibition. After laying by the cloak she came directly to him. She informed him that she had known him from the time he left his father's lodge, and watched his movements. She told him not to fear or despair, for she would be his friend and protector. She invited him into her lodge, and gave him a supper. During the repast, she inquired of him his motives for visiting her. He related his history, stated the manner in which he had been disgraced, and the difficulties he labored under. She cheered him with the assurance of her friendship, and told him he would be a brave man yet.

She then commenced the exercise of her power upon him. His hair being very short, she took a large leaden comb, and after drawing it through his hair several times, it became of a handsome feminine length. She then proceeded to dress him as a female, furnishing him with the necessary garments, and decorated his face with paints of the most beautiful dye. She gave him a bowl of shining metal. She directed him to put in his girdle a blade of scented sword-grass, and to proceed the next morning to the banks of the lake, which was no other than that over which the Red Head reigned. Now Pah-hah-undootah, or the Red Head, was a most powerful sorcerer and the terror of all the country, living upon an island in the centre of the lake.

She informed him that there would be many Indians on the island, who, as soon as they saw him use the shining bowl to drink with, would come and solicit him to be their wife, and to take him over to the island. These offers he was to refuse, and say that he had come a great distance to be the wife of the Red Head, and that if the chief could not come for her in his own canoe, she should return to her village. She said that as soon as the Red Head heard of this, he would come for her in his own canoe, in which she must embark. On reaching the island he must consent to be his wife, and in the evening induce him to take a walk out of the village, when he was to take the first opportunity to cut off his head with the blade of grass. She also gave him general advice how he was to conduct himself to sustain his assumed character of a woman. His fear would scarcely permit him to accede to this plan, but the recollection of his father's words and looks decided him.

Early in the morning, he left the witch's lodge, and took the hard beaten path to the banks of the lake. He reached the water at a point directly opposite the Red Head's village. It was a beautiful day. The heavens were clear, and the sun shone out in the greatest effulgence. He had not been long there, having sauntered along the beach, when he displayed the glittering bowl, by dipping water from the lake. Very soon a number of canoes came off from the island. The men admired his dress, and were charmed with his beauty, and a great number made proposals of marriage. These he promptly declined, agreeably to the concerted plan. When the facts were reported to the Red Head, he ordered his canoe to be put in the water by his chosen men, and crossed over to see this wonderful girl. As he came near the shore, he saw that the ribs of the sorcerer's canoe were formed of living rattlesnakes, whose heads pointed outward to guard him from enemies. Our adventurer had no sooner stepped into the canoe than they began to hiss and rattle, which put him in a great fright. But the magician spoke to them, after which they became pacified and quiet, and all at once they were at the landing upon the island. The marriage immediately took place, and the bride made presents of various valuables which had been furnished by the old witch.

As they were sitting in the lodge surrounded by friends and relatives, the mother of the Red Head regarded the face of her new daughter-in-law for a long time with fixed attention. From this scrutiny she was convinced that this singular and hasty marriage augured no good to her son. She drew her husband aside and disclosed to him her suspicions: "This can be no female," said she; "the figure and manners, the countenance, and more especially the expression of the eyes, are, beyond a doubt, those of a man." Her husband immediately rejected her suspicions, and rebuked her severely for the indignity offered to her daughter-in-law. He became so angry, that seizing the first thing that came to hand, which happened to be his pipe stem, he beat her unmercifully. This act requiring to be explained to the spectators, the mock bride immediately rose up, and assuming an air of offended dignity, told the Red Head that after receiving so gross an insult from his relatives he could not think of remaining with him as his wife, but should forthwith return to his village and friends. He left the lodge followed by the Red Head, and walked until he came upon the beach of the island, near the spot where they had first landed. Red Head entreated him to remain. He pressed him by every motive which he thought might have weight, but they were all rejected. During this conference they had seated themselves upon the ground, and Red Head, in great affliction, reclined his head upon his fancied wife's lap. This was the opportunity ardently sought for, and it was improved to the best advantage. Every means was taken to lull him to sleep, and partly by a soothing manner, and partly by a seeming compliance with his request, the object was at last attained. Red Head fell into a sound sleep. Our aspirant for the glory of a brave man then drew his blade of grass, and drawing it once across the neck of the Red Head completely severed the head from the body.

He immediately stripped off his dress, seized the bleeding head, and plunging into the lake, swam safely over to the main shore. He had scarcely reached it, when, looking back, he saw amid the darkness the torches of persons come out in search of the new-married couple. He listened till they had found the headless body, and he heard their piercing shrieks of sorrow, as he took his way to the lodge of his kind adviser.

She received him with rejoicing. She admired his prudence, and told him his bravery could never be questioned again. Lifting up the head, she said he need only have brought the scalp. She cut off a small piece for herself, and told him he might now return with the head, which would be evidence of an achievement that would cause the Indians to respect him. In your way home, she said, you will meet with but one difficulty. Maunkah Keesh Woccaung, or the spirit of the Earth, requires an offering from those who perform extraordinary achievements. As you walk along in a prairie, there will be an earthquake. The earth will open and divide the prairie in the middle. Take this partridge and throw it into the opening, and instantly spring over it. All this happened precisely as it had been foretold. He cast the partridge into the crevice and leapt over it. He then proceeded without obstruction to a place near his village, where he secreted his trophy. On entering the village he found his parents had returned from the place of their spring encampment, and were in great sorrow for their son, whom they supposed to be lost. One and another of the young men had presented themselves to the disconsolate parents, and said, "Look up, I am your son." Having been often deceived in this manner, when their own son actually presented himself, they sat with their heads down, and with their eyes nearly blinded with weeping. It was some time before they could be prevailed upon to bestow a glance upon him. It was still longer before they recognized him for their son; when he recounted his adventures they believed him mad. The young men laughed at him. He left the lodge and soon returned with his trophy. It was soon recognized. All doubts of the reality of his adventures now vanished. He was greeted with joy and placed among the first warriors of the nation. He finally became a chief, and his family were ever after respected and esteemed.

The Catskill Witch

WHEN THE DUTCH gave the name of Katzbergs to the mountains west of the Hudson, by reason of the wild-cats and panthers that ranged there, they obliterated the beautiful Indian Ontiora, "mountains of the sky." In one tradition of the red men these hills were bones of a monster that fed on human beings until the Great Spirit turned it into stone as it was floundering toward the ocean to bathe. The two lakes near the summit were its eyes. These peaks were the home of an Indian witch, who adjusted the weather for the Hudson Valley with the certainty of a signal service bureau. It was she who let out the day and night in blessed alternation, holding back the one when the other was at large, for fear of conflict. Old moons she cut into stars as soon as she had hung new ones in the sky, and she was often seen perched on Round Top and North Mountain, spinning clouds and flinging them to the winds. Woe betide the valley residents if they showed irreverence, for then the clouds were black and heavy, and through them she poured floods of rain and launched the lightnings, causing disastrous freshets in the streams and blasting the wigwams of the mockers. In a frolic humor she would take the form of a bear or deer and lead the Indian hunters anything but a merry dance, exposing them to tire and peril, and vanishing or assuming some terrible shape when they had overtaken her. Sometimes she would lead them to the cloves and would leap into the air with a mocking "Ho, ho!" just as they stopped with a shudder at the brink of an abyss. Garden Rock was a spot where she was often found, and at its foot a lake once spread. This was held in such awe that an Indian would never wittingly pursue his quarry there; but once a hunter lost his way and emerged from the forest at the edge of the pond. Seeing a number of gourds in crotches of the trees he took one, but fearing the spirit he turned to leave so quickly that he stumbled and it fell. As it broke, a spring welled from it in such volume that the unhappy man was gulfed in its waters, swept to the edge of Kaaterskill clove and dashed on the rocks two hundred and sixty feet below. Nor did the water ever cease to run, and in these times the stream born of the witch's revenge is known as Catskill Creek.

The Brownie

IN SCOTLAND THERE'S A CREATURE that's not a witch, or a warlock, or even really a fairy. He's a brownie, and he's ugly so he's not often seen by mortal eyes. For brownies are small creatures, with great bulging eyes, and faces that are furred like the backside of a donkey. Their teeth are like battered stones, and when they smile they set fear in the hearts of all men. But a brownie is a helpful soul, and although they are not often wanted round about a house or a farm, they work a kind of magic, and help to clean and to tend the farm or run the mill, for just the price of a bowl of cream, and the odd bit of oatmeal.

There once was a brownie who lived round about a house on a farm in Wester Ross in Kintail. The house on the farm was empty, so the brownie had made himself a happy home there. In this same village, near the house on the farm, lived a young miller, who shared a house with his mother. Now his mother was a greedy woman, and she dabbled in magic of all sorts, not all of it white to be sure, and she had set her sights on the young lassie at the big house on the hill, to be the wife of her young miller son.

The lassie was pretty, and her nature was kind, but the young miller was already in love with another, a servant girl who went by the name of Katie. Now Katie was as fair as the morning sky, and her cheeks were flushed with roses. She was a bonnie lass, and she would work hard with her husband to tend a mill and to make him into something grand.

Now the young miller's mother would have nothing of it: "Look, ye must marry this farmer's daughter, with a big farm and everything, and it would be yours because her father's getting on."

But the miller was stubborn, and he cared only for Katie.

"I can't help it mother, I love Katie, and I am gonna marry her," he said firmly, to which his mother replied, "You're not gonna marry Katie, because Katie is gonna die."

But the miller's will was stronger than his love for his mother, and he married Katie in secret and took her to live in a deserted house on a farm. Now there were stories told in those parts about the brownie who had made his home there, but the miller was a friendly sort, and not easily scared, and so he convinced young Katie that it would be safe and together they went to meet with the brownie. Katie was a fair lass, and she could see that an appearance did not make a man, and although the brownie frightened her, she could sense his good nature and agreed to live there.

They settled in happily, in the house on the farm, and the brownie was made a fine bed of straw and bracken, and fed all the best bit of oatmeal and cream. For that he tended their mill, and each day new sacks of grain were laid neatly against the mill walls. He interfered not at all in their lives, but they came to love his quiet presence, his charming ways. For he would slip down the chimney as they slept and lay things just right, so that when they woke, the wee house gleamed from every corner.

As is wont to happen, especially with those who are young and in love, the young lady of the house became heavy with child, and as she grew more and more tired, the brownie would work harder, until he spent many a day in the house of the miller and Katie. He became a friend to Katie, and she became accustomed to his horrible face, warmed by his quiet presence, his charming ways. And when the baby was due to come, it was the brownie who she called to fetch her husband the miller, and he scampered with glee down the path to the mill.

Now the miller too had grown fond of the brownie, but he was more traditional than wee Katie, and he felt that the presence of his mother was necessary for that bairn to be born. And so he left Katie with the brownie, who mopped her brow as she called out with pain, and who stroked her face with his own furred hand. But as soon as the footfall of the miller's mother was heard on the path, he leapt up the chimney and disappeared from the room. For brownies are magic beings themselves and they know the dangers of a witch, especially those who dabble in magic that is not all white.

The miller's mother was friendly and calm, and in her pain and distress, Katie could not help but trust her. She allowed her mother-in-law to braid her hair, and to set her back against pillows that were freshly stuffed. A tiny black kitten was set by her side to keep company with her and the new baby. Then, turning the lassie's bed towards the door, she bid her farewell and left.

Now Katie was soothed by the presence of the witch, but when she left the pains began again in earnest and she moaned and writhed for two whole days before the miller was forced to go for help. He went first to his mother, but she feigned an illness and said she could not come back with him. And so he returned to the farm where he found poor Katie sick with exhaustion and great pain.

"I'll go for the howdie woman," he said, for the howdie woman delivered most of the babies in the village, having the gift for midwifery. But Katie would not hear of it, so frightened she had become.

"Don't leave me here," she sobbed. "Send the brownie." And that thought stopped them short, for many folk were frightened to visit them at their home because of that same brownie, and they wondered now if the howdie woman would fear to come as well.

But Katie's pain was dragging her deeper into a dreadful state, and the roses had disappeared from her cheeks. There was no sight of the bairn and there was nothing for it but to call the brownie to help.

The brownie was only too glad to help, and in the cover of darkness, with a great cloak wrapped across his hideous face, he rode off across the hills to fetch the howdie woman. And she came at once, for her calling was stronger than her fear, and she sat herself behind the brownie and wrapped her arms about him for warmth and for safety. And she whispered in his ear as they rode, "Katie will be well again, no doubt, but I hope I don't see that brownie. I am terrified of that brownie!"

But the brownie said, "No, don't worry, I can assure you for certain that you'll not see anything worse than what you're cuddling now." And he drove the howdie woman to the door of the house and made off with the horse, into the darkness.

The howdie woman had seen no birth like this, and for four more days she sat with Katie, who was expiring quickly now, torn by pains that wracked her thin frame, and struggling to keep sane as they plunged her into a burning hell with every contraction.

The miller sat brooding in a chair, helpless against this pain he could not understand, and suddenly he sat up and snapped his fingers. "I'll bet a shilling," he said then, "that this is the work of my mother."

So he rode straight to the house of his mother and shouted at her, "Take that spell off my Katie. I know you've done something."

And his mother shook her head, and said, "I will not. I told you she is gonna die, and you are gonna marry the farmer's daughter." She stood firm then and would not help his poor Katie.

So poor Katie seemed destined to die in agony, and he ran away then into the night, straight to the wee brownie, for he had no one else to whom he could turn. And the brownie thought for a while, and said, "I'll tell you what you can do. Take me down to your mother."

"Oh, no," said the miller, "that wouldn't help us at all. God himself couldn't help me against my mother."

"Ah," said the brownie, "but you take me down because I can become invisible, and if you were to rush in and tell your mother, "Oh, mother, mother, you've got a beautiful grandson!" and then run off again, I will stay behind to see what happens. And I'll be invisible."

And so it was decided that the brownie would come along, and when they reached the house of his mother, the miller ran in and cried, "Mother, you have got a beautiful grandson."

And she said, "What?" her face a mask of alarm and fury.

"Oh yes," shouted the miller, "But I can't stop, I must see Katie." And with that he ran back over the hills to wait for the brownie.

And as he went out the door, the woman stamped her feet and pulled at her hair, cursing all the time, "Who told him about the witches' knots in Katie's hair? How did he know about the black cat? Who told him about the raven's feathers in those great white pillows? And who told them that I'd turned her feet to the door?"

And then the brownie skipped away, as fast as his legs would carry him, over the hills to greet the miller, and together they ran back to the house on the farm where Katie lay with the howdie woman.

Now the howdie woman had only to set eyes on the grinning brownie when she was up and out the door in a flash, but the brownie set himself to work, stroking the poor lass's cheek and mopping her brow, warming her with his quiet presence and his charming ways. He untied her head, and brushed it down around her shoulders, crooning softly in her ears. Then he took those great new pillows and set them aflame in the hearth until only dust remained of those evil black feathers. And then, with one angry twist, he took the head from the kitten and burnt her too, out of sight, of course, of poor Katie. And so it was, when the brownie moved the bed round, so that her feet faced the door no longer, that the cry of an infant was heard in that house on the farm. Katie slept then, and when she woke, her baby was cleaned and swaddled, and the roses returned to her cheeks once more.

But the brownie had gone, for brownies often do that, just disappear, never to be seen again. They missed the wee man's quiet presence and his charming ways, but he had milled enough grain for twenty odd years, and they lived on that house on the farm with their new baby in comfort and in good fortune.

The Three Knots

THERE ONCE WAS A FAMILY on the island of Heisker in Ulst. They were farm people and worked hard all the year, but when the harvest was over, and the grain tucked safely away for the frosty months ahead, they took it upon themselves to plan a little trip to Lewis, to visit some friends there.

It was the same every year, they crossed the sea and got to Lewis where they had a grand time of it, and then they went home again, to cosy themselves away for the long frosty months. And so it was this time, that they gathered an able crew and set off.

At Lewis things seemed much the same as they ever had. The man of the family went to greet the woman of the house they were visiting, and they talked for many hours, of days of old, and of good friends and family. And just as he made preparations to get off to bed, a tall lithe woman entered the room, with hair as black as a raven's back. Her eyes were cool and dark, and she whispered something to the woman of the house, and then she left, stopping only to stroke the woman's hair.

"Who's that ugly black thing," asked the man, curious about the familiarity between the two women.

And the woman sighed and replied, "Is that what you say? Ugly, is she? Woe betide you, man, but you'll be lost in love with her before you leave Lewis; if you can, of course." And with that she rose and went off to bed.

Now the man scowled with the thought of it, for he had three great strong bairns and a lovely wife, as fair and pink and white as this thing was black. "Indeed," he muttered to himself, "I won't fall in love with her." He spat a bit of the old tobacco into the iron sink and prepared to retire himself.

Now he rose in the morning and the first thing that ate at his mind was the thought of that tall lithe girl, with hair as black as a raven's back, and he went downstairs, stormy as the North Sea waters. That night the girl came again to the house, though she'd not been out of his mind since her last visit, and he hated her even more, all tall and lithe and black, with those cool dark eyes. But when she left he longed for her like he'd longed for no other, and he grew black himself with rage and with desire.

Now this went on every day for a week, with the man from Heisker growing silent and cold, so his wife felt afraid and begged him to take leave of that house.

"We've had a good visit now, and it's time for us to be making for home," she said firmly to her husband, and with the last tiny shred of rational thought left in his mind, which longed for the tall, lithe girl, with hair as black as a raven's back, he agreed.

And so it was that their belongings were packed, and their big strong boat made good, and they arrived at the sea to leave. But as the first foot was set inside that big boat, a great black gale was brewed and flung at them, and they could go no further. There was nothing for it but to return to the house from which they'd come, and to that tall, lithe woman.

And again the next morning they set out, but the mists drew around them then, cool and dark, and they could go no further. There was nothing for it but to return to the house from which they'd come, and to the cool dark eyes of that woman.

But as they walked away from the coast, they met a wee old witch, with hair that was whiter than the down of a thistle, and a small wrinkled face that spoke of great wisdom. And she stopped them there and beckoned them aside.

"Well, my good folks," she said, "you've a bit of trouble leaving this dark place."

They nodded, and listened intently.

"It's no wonder," said the wee old witch, "seeing the kind of place you've been staying. What will you give to me for fine weather to go tomorrow?"

"Anything, anything we'll give to you," said the wife earnestly, and looked to her husband, but his eyes were trained on the hill, on the house with the tall, lithe woman, with the cool dark eyes, and his face was rent by a longing such as she'd never seen before. "We'll do anything," she said again firmly.

"A pound of snuff," said the old witch. "And I'll need to have a word with the skipper. Send him by this evening." And with that she showed them to the door.

So later that night the skipper of the big strong boat was sent to see the old witch, and there she handed him a rope with three big knots.

"Here you are," she said. "You take this aboard and you'll have a good day for sailing tomorrow. It'll not be long before you're at Lewis harbour. Now if you haven't enough wind, just open one of these knots. And then if that is not enough still, untie the second. But whatever you do, by God, don't untie the third."

And so it happened that on that next morning, the day dawned clear and bright, with a fresh puff of wind to set them on their course. They loaded the boat, and without a backward glance, they headed to sea. And the man of the family let out a sigh of relief so long and frenzied that the others averted their eyes. His thoughts were once again pure, and the magic of that old witch had set him free. He called to the skipper.

"Untie a knot," he said grandly, "let's get us home at once." And so a knot was untied, and a swift breeze blew up that sent them cutting through the waves.

"And again," he cried, the wind cold on his body, his soul cleansed and clear. And another knot was untied, so that a great wind was let loose on the tiny ship, and they flew across the water now, the sails stretched to the limit.

And the man of the family settled himself on deck, and with the sea air licking his face, he felt safe from all danger, and perhaps a little too confident. For he called out then, "Let's test that old woman's magic. What means that third knot?"

And his crew cowered away from him, and his wife shook her head, but he insisted, and being the man of the family, and in charge of his boat and his own fate, he had his way and the knot was untied.

What happened then is a story for the ears of the fearless only, for from the sea rose a sight that clamped shut the mouths of the men, and the wife and their children until their dying day. It was a shape, tall and lithe, with a face of sorts, from which shone cold dark eyes. And a hand was reached down, and the man of the family plucked from amongst them, and into the sea. And then the boat itself was lifted high above the waves, placed on the sands of Heisker from where she'd never move again.

She's still there, a warning to all who think that magic can be tested, and the land there has come to be called Port Eilein na Culaigh, or Port of the Island of the Boat.

The Cauldron

THE LITTLE ISLAND OF SANDRAY juts firmly through the waves of the Atlantic Ocean, which spits and surges around it. No human lives there, although sheep graze calmly on the succulent green grass, freshened by the moist salt air, and kept company by the fairy folk who live in a verdant knoll. But once upon a time there were men and women on the island of Sandray, and one was a herder's wife, called Mairearad, who kept a tiny cottage on the northernmost tip.

She had in her possession a large copper cauldron, blackened with age and with use. One day, as she wiped it clean of the evening meal, she was visited by a Woman of Peace, a fairy woman who tiptoed quietly into the cottage and asked to take away the cauldron for a short time. Now this was an older fairy, with a nature that was gentle and kind, and she presented little danger to Mairearad. She had a wizened fairy face, and features as tiny as the markings of a butterfly, and she moved swiftly and silently, advising no one of her coming or going. Mairearad passed her the cauldron, and as the Woman of Peace retreated down the cottage path, towards the twin hills that marked the fairy's Land of Light, she said to the fairy,

> *"A smith is able to make*
> *Cold iron hot with a coal;*
> *The due of the kettle is bones,*
> *And to bring it back again whole."*

And so it was that the cauldron was returned that evening, left quietly on the cottage doorstop, filled with juicy bones.

The Woman of Peace came again, later that day, and without saying a word, indicated the cauldron. And as days turned into years, an unspoken relationship developed between the two women, fairy and mortal. Mairearad would loan her cauldron, and in exchange she would have it filled with delicious bones. She never forgot to whisper, as the fairy drew out of sight,

> *"A smith is able to make*
> *Cold iron hot with a coal;*
> *The due of the kettle is bones,*
> *And to bring it back again whole."*

Then one day, Mairearad had to leave her cottage for a day, to travel to Castlebay, across the sea on Barra.

She said to her husband before she left, "When the Woman of Peace comes to the doorstep, you must let her take the cauldron, but do not forget to say to her what I always say."

And so her husband worked his field, as he always did, and as he returned for his midday meal he met with a curious sight, for scurrying along the path in front of him was a wee woman, her face gnarled with age, her eyes bright and shrewd. Suddenly he felt an inexplicable fear, for most men have had fed to them as bairns the tales of fairies and the cruel tricks they play, their enchantments and their evil spells. He remembered them all now in a rush of tortuous thought, and pushed past the fairy woman to slam the cottage door. She knocked firmly, but he refused to answer, panting with terror on the other side of the door.

At last there was silence, and then, a weird howl echoed around the cottage walls and there was a scrambling on the roof. Through the chimney was thrust the long brown arm of the fairy woman, and she reached straight down to the fire upon which the cauldron sat, and pulled it with a rush of air, through the cottage roof.

Mairearad's husband was still pressed against the door when she returned that evening, and she looked curiously at the empty hearth, remarking, "The Woman of Peace always returns the cauldron before darkness falls."

Then her husband hung his head in shame and told her how he'd barred the door, and when the fairy had taken the cauldron, he'd forgotten to ask for its return. Well Mairearad scolded her husband, and putting on her overcoat and boots, she left the cottage, lantern in hand.

Darkness can play tricks as devilish as those of the fairies themselves, and it was not long before the dancing shadows, and whispering trees sent a shiver along the spine of the fierce wife Mairearad, but still she pressed on, safe in the knowledge that the Woman of Peace was her friend. She reached the threshold of the Land of Light and saw on a fire, just inside the door, her cauldron, filled as usual with tender bones. And so she grabbed it, and half-fearing where she was, began to ran, exciting the attention of the black fairy dogs that slept beside an old man who guarded the entrance.

Up they jumped, and woke the old man, who cried out,

> *"Silent woman, dumb woman,*
> *Who has come to us from the Land of the Dead*
> *Since you have not blessed the brugh –*
> *Unleash Black and let go Fierce."*

And he let the dogs free to chase the terrified woman right back to the door of her cottage, baying and howling, spitting with determination and hunger. As she ran she dropped the tasty bones, buying herself a moment or two's respite from the snarling dogs. For fairy dogs are faster than any dogs on earth, and will devour all human flesh that comes across their paths. Mairearad fled down the path, finally reaching her door and slamming it shut behind her. There she told her breathless story to her husband, and they held one another's ears against the painful wailing of the hounds. Finally there was silence.

Never again did the fairy Woman of Peace come to Mairearad's cottage, nor did she borrow the cauldron. Mairearad and her husband missed the succulent bones, but never again did they trouble the fairy folk. They are long dead now, buried on the grassy verge on the island of Sandray, where the sheep graze calmly on the succulent green grass, freshened by the moist salt air, kept company by the fairy folk who live in a verdant knoll.

The Horned Women

A RICH WOMAN SAT UP LATE ONE NIGHT carding and preparing wool, while all the family and servants were asleep. Suddenly a knock was given at the door, and a voice called, "Open! open!"

"Who is there?" said the woman of the house.

"I am the Witch of one Horn," was answered.

The mistress, supposing that one of her neighbours had called and required assistance, opened the door, and a woman entered, having in her hand a pair of wool-carders, and bearing a horn on her forehead, as if growing there. She sat down by the fire in silence, and began to card the wool with violent haste. Suddenly she paused, and said aloud: "Where are the women? they delay too long."

Then a second knock came to the door, and a voice called as before,
"Open! open!"

The mistress felt herself obliged to rise and open to the call, and immediately a second witch entered, having two horns on her forehead, and in her hand a wheel for spinning wool.

"Give me place," she said; "I am the Witch of the two Horns," and she began to spin as quick as lightning.

And so the knocks went on, and the call was heard, and the witches entered, until at last twelve women sat round the fire – the first with one horn, the last with twelve horns.

And they carded the thread, and turned their spinning-wheels, and wound and wove, all singing together an ancient rhyme, but no word did they speak to the mistress of the house. Strange to hear, and frightful to look upon, were these twelve women, with their horns and their wheels; and the mistress felt near to death, and she tried to rise that she might call for help, but she could not move, nor could she utter a word or a cry, for the spell of the witches was upon her.

Then one of them called to her in Irish, and said, "Rise, woman, and make us a cake."

Then the mistress searched for a vessel to bring water from the well that she might mix the meal and make the cake, but she could find none.

And they said to her, "Take a sieve and bring water in it."

And she took the sieve and went to the well; but the water poured from it, and she could fetch none for the cake, and she sat down by the well and wept.

Then a voice came by her and said, "Take yellow clay and moss, and bind them together, and plaster the sieve so that it will hold."

This she did, and the sieve held the water for the cake; and the voice said again:

"Return, and when thou comest to the north angle of the house, cry aloud three times and say, 'The mountain of the Fenian women and the sky over it is all on fire.'"

And she did so.

When the witches inside heard the call, a great and terrible cry broke from their lips, and they rushed forth with wild lamentations and shrieks, and fled away to Slievenamon, where was their chief abode. But the Spirit of the Well bade the mistress of the house to enter and prepare her home against the enchantments of the witches if they returned again.

And first, to break their spells, she sprinkled the water in which she had washed her child's feet, the feet-water, outside the door on the threshold; secondly, she took the cake which in her absence the witches had made of meal mixed with the blood drawn from the sleeping family, and she broke the cake in bits, and placed a bit in the mouth of each sleeper, and they were restored; and she took the cloth they had woven, and placed it half in and half out of the chest with the padlock; and lastly, she secured the door with a great crossbeam fastened in the jambs, so that the witches could not enter, and having done these things she waited.

Not long were the witches in coming back, and they raged and called for vengeance.

"Open! open!" they screamed; "open, feet-water!"

"I cannot," said the feet-water; "I am scattered on the ground, and my path is down to the Lough."

"Open, open, wood and trees and beam!" they cried to the door.

"I cannot," said the door, "for the beam is fixed in the jambs and I have no power to move."

"Open, open, cake that we have made and mingled with blood!" they cried again.

"I cannot," said the cake, "for I am broken and bruised, and my blood is on the lips of the sleeping children."

Then the witches rushed through the air with great cries, and fled back to Slievenamon, uttering strange curses on the Spirit of the Well, who had wished their ruin; but the woman and the house were left in peace, and a mantle dropped by one of the witches in her flight was kept hung up by the mistress in memory of that night; and this mantle was kept by the same family from generation to generation for five hundred years after.

Paddy O'Kelly and the Weasel

A LONG TIME AGO there was once a man of the name of Paddy O'Kelly, living near Tuam, in the county Galway. He rose up one morning early, and he did not know what time of day it was, for there was fine light coming from the moon. He wanted to go to the fair of Cauher-na-mart to sell a *sturk* of an ass that he had.

He had not gone more than three miles of the road when a great darkness came on, and a shower began falling. He saw a large house among trees about five hundred yards in from the road, and he said to himself that he would go to that house till the shower would be over. When he got to the house he found the door open before him, and in with him. He saw a large room to his left, and a fine fire in the grate. He sat down on a stool that was beside the wall, and began falling asleep, when he saw a big weasel coming to the fire with something yellow in his mouth, which it dropped on the hearth-stone, and then it went away. She soon came back again with the same thing in her mouth, and he saw that it was a guinea she had. She dropped it on the hearth-stone, and went away again. She was coming and going, until there was a great heap of guineas on the hearth. But at last, when she got her gone, Paddy rose up, thrust all the gold she had gathered into his pockets, and out with him.

He had not gone far till he heard the weasel coming after him, and she screeching as loud as a bag-pipes. She went before Paddy and got on the road, and she was twisting herself back and forwards, and trying to get a hold of his throat. Paddy had a good oak stick, and he kept her from him, until two men came up who were going to the same fair, and one of them had a good dog, and it routed the weasel into a hole in the wall.

Paddy went to the fair, and instead of coming home with the money he got for his old ass, as he thought would be the way with him in the morning, he went and bought a horse with some of the money he took from the weasel, and he came home riding. When he came to the place where the dog had routed the weasel into the hole in the wall, she came out before him, gave a leap, and caught the horse by the throat. The horse made off, and Paddy could not stop him, till at last he gave a leap into a big drain that was full up of water and black mud, and he was drowning and choking as fast as he could, until men who were coming from Galway came up and drove away the weasel.

Paddy brought the horse home with him, and put him into the cow's byre and fell asleep.

Next morning, the day on the morrow, Paddy rose up early, and went out to give his horse hay and oats. When he got to the door he saw the weasel coming out of the byre and she covered with blood.

"My seven thousand curses on you," said Paddy, "but I'm afraid you've done harm."

He went in and found the horse, a pair of milch cows, and two calves dead. He came out and set a dog he had after the weasel. The dog got a hold of her, and she got a hold of the dog. The dog was a good one, but he was forced to loose his hold of her before Paddy could come up. He kept his eye on her, however, all through, until he saw her creeping into a little hovel that was on the brink of a lake. Paddy came running, and when he got to the little hut he gave the dog a shake to rouse him up and put anger on him, and then he sent him in. When the dog went in he began barking. Paddy went in after him, and saw an old hag in the corner. He asked her if she saw a weasel coming in there.

"I did not," said she; "I'm all destroyed with a plague of sickness, and if you don't go out quick, you'll catch it from me."

While Paddy and the hag were talking, the dog kept moving in all the time, till at last he gave a leap and caught the hag by the throat. She screeched and said:

"Paddy Kelly, take off your dog, and I'll make you a rich man."

Paddy made the dog loose his hold, and said:

"Tell me who you are, or why did you kill my horse and my cows?"

"And why did you bring away my gold that I was gathering for five hundred years throughout the hills and hollows of the world?"

"I thought you were a weasel," said Paddy, "or I wouldn't touch your gold; and another thing," says he, "if you're for five hundred years in this world, it's time for you to go to rest now."

"I committed a great crime in my youth," said the hag, "and now I am to be released from my sufferings if you can pay twenty pounds for a hundred and three-score masses for me."

"Where's the money?" said Paddy.

"Go and dig under a bush that's over a little well in the corner of that field there without, and you'll get a pot filled with gold. Pay the twenty pounds for the masses, and yourself shall have the rest. When you'll lift the flag off the pot, you'll see a big black dog coming out; but don't be afraid before him; he is a son of mine. When you get the gold, buy the house in which you saw me at first. You'll get it cheap, for it has the name of there being a ghost in it. My son will be down in the cellar. He'll do you no harm, but he'll be a good friend to you. I shall be dead a month from this day, and when you get me dead, put a coal under this little hut and burn it. Don't tell a living soul anything about me – and the luck will be on you."

"What is your name?" said Paddy.

"Mary Kerwan," said the hag.

Paddy went home, and when the darkness of the night came on, he took with him a spade and went to the bush that was in the corner of the field, and began digging. It was not long till he found the pot, and when he took the flag off of it a big black dog leaped out, and off and away with him, and Paddy's dog after him.

Paddy brought home the gold, and hid it in the cow-house. About a month after that he went to the fair of Galway, and bought a pair of cows, a horse, and a dozen sheep. The neighbours did not know where he had got all the money; they said that he had a share with the good people.

One day Paddy dressed himself, and went to the gentleman who owned the large house where he first saw the weasel, and asked to buy the house of him, and the land that was round about.

"You can have the house without paying any rent at all; but there is a ghost in it, and I wouldn't like you to go to live in it without my telling you, but I couldn't part with the land without getting a hundred pounds more than you have to offer me."

"Perhaps I have as much as you have yourself," said Paddy. "I'll be here tomorrow with the money, if you're ready to give me possession."

"I'll be ready," said the gentleman.

Paddy went home and told his wife that he had bought a large house and a holding of land.

"Where did you get the money?" says the wife.

"Isn't it all one to you where I got it?" says Paddy.

The day on the morrow Paddy went to the gentleman, gave him the money, and got possession of the house and land; and the gentleman left him the furniture and everything that was in the house, into the bargain.

Paddy remained in the house that night, and when darkness came he went down to the cellar, and he saw a little man with his two legs spread on a barrel.

"God save you, honest man," says he to Paddy.

"The same to you," says Paddy.

"Don't be afraid of me, at all," says the little man. "I'll be a friend to you, if you are able to keep a secret."

"I am able, indeed; I kept your mother's secret, and I'll keep yours as well."

"Maybe you're thirsty?" said the little man.

"I'm not free from it," said Paddy.

The little man put a hand in his bosom and drew out a gold goblet. He gave it to Paddy, and said: "Draw wine out of that barrel under me."

Paddy drew the full up of the goblet, and handed it to the little man.

"Drink yourself first," says he.

Paddy drank, drew another goblet, and handed it to the little man, and he drank it.

"Fill up and drink again," said the little man. "I have a mind to be merry tonight."

The pair of them sat there drinking until they were half drunk. Then the little man gave a leap down to the floor, and said to Paddy:

"Don't you like music?"

"I do, surely," said Paddy, "and I'm a good dancer, too."

"Lift up the big flag over there in the corner, and you'll get my pipes under it."

Paddy lifted the flag, got the pipes, and gave them to the little man. He squeezed the pipes on him, and began playing melodious music. Paddy began dancing till he was tired. Then they had another drink, and the little man said:

"Do as my mother told you, and I'll show you great riches. You can bring your wife in here, but don't tell her that I'm there, and she won't see me. Any time at all that ale or wine are wanting, come here and draw. Farewell, now; go to sleep, and come again to me tomorrow night."

Paddy went to bed, and it wasn't long till he fell asleep.

On the morning of the day on the morrow, Paddy went home, and brought his wife and children to the big house, and they were very comfortable. That night Paddy went down to the cellar; the little man welcomed him and asked him did he wish to dance?

"Not till I get a drink," said Paddy.

"Drink your fill," said the little man; "that barrel will never be empty as long as you live."

Paddy drank the full of the goblet, and gave a drink to the little man. Then the little man said to him:

"I am going to the Fortress of the Fairies tonight, to play music for the good people, and if you come with me you'll see fine fun. I'll give you a horse that you never saw the like of him before."

"I'll go with you, and welcome," said Paddy; "but what excuse will I make to my wife?"

"I'll bring you away from her side without her knowing it, when you are both asleep together, and I'll bring you back to her the same way," said the little man.

"I'm obedient," says Paddy; "we'll have another drink before I leave you."

He drank drink after drink, till he was half drunk, and he went to bed with his wife.

When he awoke he found himself riding on a broom near Doon-na-shee, and the little man riding on another besom by his side. When they came as far as the green hill of the Doon, the little man said a couple of words that Paddy did not understand. The green hill opened, and the pair went into a fine chamber.

Paddy never saw before a gathering like that which was in the Doon. The whole place was full up of little people, men and women, young and old. They all welcomed little Donal – that was the name of the piper – and Paddy O'Kelly. The king and queen of the fairies came up to them, and said:

"We are all going on a visit tonight to Cnoc Matha, to the high king and queen of our people."

They all rose up then and went out. There were horses ready for each one of them, and the *coash-t'ya bower* for the king and queen. The king and queen got into the coach, each man leaped on his own horse, and be certain that Paddy was not behind. The piper went out before them, and began playing them music, and then off and away with them. It was not long till they came to Cnoc Matha. The hill opened, and the king of the fairy host passed in.

Finvara and Nuala were there, the arch-king and queen of the fairy host of Connacht, and thousands of little persons. Finvara came up and said:

"We are going to play a hurling match tonight against the fairy host of Munster, and unless we beat them our fame is gone for ever. The match is to be fought out on Moytura, under Slieve Belgadaun."

The Connacht host cried out: "We are all ready, and we have no doubt but we'll beat them."

"Out with ye all," cried the high king; "the men of the hill of Nephin will be on the ground before us."

They all went out, and little Donal and twelve pipers more before them, playing melodious music. When they came to Moytura, the fairy host of Munster and the fairy men of the hill of Nephin were there before them.

Now it is necessary for the fairy host to have two live men beside them when they are fighting or at a hurling match, and that was the reason that little Donal took Paddy O'Kelly with him. There was a man they called the 'Yellow Stongirya' with the fairy host of Munster, from Ennis, in the County Clare.

It was not long till the two hosts took sides; the ball was thrown up between them, and the fun began in earnest. They were hurling away, and the pipers playing music, until Paddy O'Kelly saw the host of Munster getting the strong hand, and he began helping the fairy host of Connacht. The *Stongirya* came up and he made at Paddy O'Kelly, but Paddy turned him head over heels. From hurling the two hosts began at fighting, but it was not long until the host of Connacht beat the other host. Then the host of Munster made flying beetles of themselves, and they began eating every green thing that they came up to. They were destroying the country before them until they came as far as Cong. Then there rose up thousands of doves out of the hole, and they swallowed down the beetles. That hole has no other name until this day but Pull-na-gullam, the dove's hole.

When the fairy host of Connacht won their battle, they came back to Cnoc Matha joyous enough, and the king Finvara gave Paddy O'Kelly a purse of gold, and the little piper brought him home, and put him into bed beside his wife, and left him sleeping there.

A month went by after that without anything worth mentioning, until one night Paddy went down to the cellar, and the little man said to him: "My mother is dead; burn the house over her."

"It is true for you," said Paddy. "She told me that she hadn't but a month to be in the world, and the month was up yesterday."

On the next morning of the next day Paddy went to the hut and he found the hag dead. He put a coal under the hut and burned it. He came home and told the little man that the hag was burnt. The little man gave him a purse and said to him: "This purse will never be empty as long as you are alive. Now, you will never see me more; but have a loving remembrance of the weasel.

She was the beginning and the prime cause of your riches." Then he went away and Paddy never saw him again.

Paddy O'Kelly and his wife lived for years after this in the large house, and when he died he left great wealth behind him, and a large family to spend it.

There now is the story for you, from the first word to the last, as I heard it from my grandmother.

Morraha

MORRAHA ROSE IN THE MORNING and washed his hands and face, and said his prayers, and ate his food; and he asked God to prosper the day for him. So he went down to the brink of the sea, and he saw a currach, short and green, coming towards him; and in it there was but one youthful champion, and he was playing hurly from prow to stern of the currach. He had a hurl of gold and a ball of silver; and he stopped not till the currach was in on the shore; and he drew her up on the green grass, and put fastenings on her for a year and a day, whether he should be there all that time or should only be on land for an hour by the clock. And Morraha saluted the young man courteously; and the other saluted him in the same fashion, and asked him would he play a game of cards with him; and Morraha said that he had not the wherewithal; and the other answered that he was never without a candle or the making of it; and he put his hand in his pocket and drew out a table and two chairs and a pack of cards, and they sat down on the chairs and went to card-playing. The first game Morraha won, and the Slender Red Champion bade him make his claim; and he asked that the land above him should be filled with stock of sheep in the morning. It was well; and he played no second game, but home he went.

The next day Morraha went to the brink of the sea, and the young man came in the currach and asked him would he play cards; they played, and Morraha won. The young man bade him make his claim; and he asked that the land above should be filled with cattle in the morning. It was well; and he played no other game, but went home.

On the third morning Morraha went to the brink of the sea, and he saw the young man coming. He drew up his boat on the shore and asked him would he play cards. They played, and Morraha won the game; and the young man bade him give his claim. And he said he would have a castle and a wife, the finest and fairest in the world; and they were his. It was well; and the Red Champion went away.

On the fourth day his wife asked him how he had found her. And he told her. "And I am going out," said he, "to play again today."

"I forbid you to go again to him. If you have won so much, you will lose more; have no more to do with him."

But he went against her will, and he saw the currach coming; and the Red Champion was driving his balls from end to end of the currach; he had balls of silver and a hurl of gold, and he stopped not till he drew his boat on the shore, and made her fast for a year and a day. Morraha and he saluted each other; and he asked Morraha if he would play a game of cards, and they played, and he won. Morraha said to him, "Give your claim now."

Said he, "You will hear it too soon. I lay on you bonds of the art of the Druid, not to sleep two nights in one house, nor finish a second meal at the one table, till you bring me the sword of light and news of the death of Anshgayliacht."

He went home to his wife and sat down in a chair, and gave a groan, and the chair broke in pieces.

"That is the groan of the son of a king under spells," said his wife; "and you had better have taken my counsel than that the spells should be on you."

He told her he had to bring news of the death of Anshgayliacht and the sword of light to the Slender Red Champion.

"Go out," said she, "in the morning of the morrow, and take the bridle in the window, and shake it; and whatever beast, handsome or ugly, puts its head in it, take that one with you. Do not speak a word to her till she speaks to you; and take with you three pint bottles of ale and three sixpenny loaves, and do the thing she tells you; and when she runs to my father's land, on a height above the castle, she will shake herself, and the bells will ring, and my father will say, "Brown Allree is in the land. And if the son of a king or queen is there, bring him to me on your shoulders; but if it is the son of a poor man, let him come no further.""

He rose in the morning, and took the bridle that was in the window, and went out and shook it; and Brown Allree came and put her head in it. He took the three loaves and three bottles of ale, and went riding; and when he was riding she bent her head down to take hold of her feet with her mouth, in hopes he would speak in ignorance; but he spoke not a word during the time, and the mare at last spoke to him, and told him to dismount and give her her dinner. He gave her the sixpenny loaf toasted, and a bottle of ale to drink.

"Sit up now riding, and take good heed of yourself: there are three miles of fire I have to clear at a leap."

She cleared the three miles of fire at a leap, and asked if he were still riding, and he said he was. Then they went on, and she told him to dismount and give her a meal; and he did so, and gave her a sixpenny loaf and a bottle; she consumed them and said to him there were before them three miles of hill covered with steel thistles, and that she must clear it. She cleared the hill with a leap, and she asked him if he were still riding, and he said he was. They went on, and she went not far before she told him to give her a meal, and he gave her the bread and the bottleful. She went over three miles of sea with a leap, and she came then to the land of the King of France; she went up on a height above the castle, and she shook herself and neighed, and the bells rang; and the king said that it was Brown Allree was in the land.

"Go out," said he; "and if it is the son of a king or queen, carry him in on your shoulders; if it is not, leave him there."

They went out; and the stars of the son of a king were on his breast; they lifted him high on their shoulders and bore him in to the king. They passed the night cheerfully, playing and drinking with sport and with diversion, till the whiteness of the day came upon the morrow morning.

Then the young king told the cause of his journey, and he asked the queen to give him counsel and good luck, and she told him everything he was to do.

"Go now," said she, "and take with you the best mare in the stable, and go to the door of Rough Niall of the Speckled Rock, and knock, and call on him to give you news of the death of Anshgayliacht and the sword of light: and let the horse's back be to the door, and apply the spurs and away with you."

In the morning he did so, and he took the best horse from the stable and rode to the door of Niall, and turned the horse's back to the door, and demanded news of the death of Anshgayliacht and the sword of light; then he applied the spurs, and away with him. Niall followed him hard, and as he was passing the gate, cut the horse in two. His wife was there with a dish of puddings and flesh, and she threw it in his eyes and blinded him, and said, "Fool! whatever kind of man it is that's mocking you, isn't that a fine condition you have got your father's horse into?"

On the morning of the next day Morraha rose, and took another horse from the stable, and went again to the door of Niall, and knocked and demanded news of the death of Anshgayliacht and the sword of light, and applied the spurs to the horse and away with him. Niall followed, and as Morraha was passing, the gate cut the horse in two and took half the saddle with him; but his wife met him and threw flesh in his eyes and blinded him.

On the third day, Morraha went again to the door of Niall; and Niall followed him, and as he was passing the gate, cut away the saddle from under him and the clothes from his back. Then his wife said to Niall:

"The fool that's mocking you, is out yonder in the little currach, going home; and take good heed to yourself, and don't sleep one wink for three days."

For three days the little currach kept in sight, but then Niall's wife came to him and said:

"Sleep as much as you want now. He is gone."

He went to sleep, and there was heavy sleep on him, and Morraha went in and took hold of the sword that was on the bed at his head. And the sword thought to draw itself out of the hand of Morraha; but it failed. Then it gave a cry, and it wakened Niall, and Niall said it was a rude and rough thing to come into his house like that; and said Morraha to him:

"Leave your much talking, or I will cut the head off you. Tell me the news of the death of Anshgayliacht."

"Oh, you can have my head."

"But your head is no good to me; tell me the story."

"Oh," said Niall's wife, "you must get the story."

"Well," said Niall, "let us sit down together till I tell the story. I thought no one would ever get it; but now it will be heard by all."

The Story

When I was growing up, my mother taught me the language of the birds; and when I got married, used to be listening to their conversation; and I would be laughing; and my wife would be asking me what was the reason of my laughing, but I did not like to tell her, as women are always asking questions. We went out walking one fine morning, and the birds were arguing with one another. One of them said to another:

"Why should you be comparing yourself with me, when there is not a king nor knight that does not come to look at my tree?"

"What advantage has your tree over mine, on which there are three rods of magic mastery growing?"

When I heard them arguing, and knew that the rods were there, I began to laugh.

"Oh," asked my wife, "why are you always laughing? I believe it is at myself you are jesting, and I'll walk with you no more."

"Oh, it is not about you I am laughing. It is because I understand the language of the birds."

Then I had to tell her what the birds were saying to one another; and she was greatly delighted, and she asked me to go home, and she gave orders to the cook to have breakfast ready at six o'clock in the morning. I did not know why she was going out early, and breakfast was ready in the morning at the hour she appointed. She asked me to go out walking. I went with her. She went to the tree, and asked me to cut a rod for her.

"Oh, I will not cut it. Are we not better without it?"

"I will not leave this until I get the rod, to see if there is any good in it."

I cut the rod and gave it to her. She turned from me and struck a blow on a stone, and changed it; and she struck a second blow on me, and made of me a black raven, and she went home and left me after her. I thought she would come back; she did not come, and I had to go into a tree till morning. In the morning, at six o'clock, there was a bellman out, proclaiming that every one who killed a raven would get a fourpenny-bit. At last you could not find man or boy without a gun, nor, if you were to walk three miles, a raven that was not killed. I had to make a nest in the top of the parlour chimney, and hide myself all day till night came, and go out to pick up a bit to support me, till I spent a month. Here she is herself to say if it is a lie I am telling.

"It is not," said she.

Then I saw her out walking. I went up to her, and I thought she would turn me back to my own shape, and she struck me with the rod and made of me an old white horse, and she ordered me to be put to a cart with a man, to draw stones from morning till night. I was worse off then. She spread abroad a report that I had died suddenly in my bed, and prepared a coffin, and waked and buried me. Then she had no trouble. But when I got tired I began to kill every one who came near me, and I used to go into the haggard every night and destroy the stacks of corn; and when a man came near me in the morning I would follow him till I broke his bones. Every one got afraid of me. When she saw I was doing mischief she came to meet me, and I thought she would change me. And she did change me, and made a fox of me. When I saw she was doing me every sort of damage I went away from her. I knew there was a badger's hole in the garden, and I went there till night came, and I made great slaughter among the geese and ducks. There she is herself to say if I am telling a lie.

"Oh! you are telling nothing but the truth, only less than the truth."

When she had enough of my killing the fowl she came out into the garden, for she knew I was in the badger's hole. She came to me and made me a wolf. I had to be off, and go to an island where no one at all would see me, and now and then I used to be killing sheep, for there were no many of them, and I was afraid of being seen and hunted; and so I passed a year, till a shepherd saw me among the sheep and a pursuit was made after me. And when the dogs came near me there was no place for me to escape to from them; but I recognised the sign of the king among the men, and I made for him, and the king cried out to stop the hounds. I took a leap upon the front of the king's saddle, and the woman behind cried out, "My king and my lord, kill him, or he will kill you!"

"Oh! he will not kill me. He knew me; he must be pardoned."

The king took me home with him, and gave orders I should be well cared for. I was so wise when I got food, I would not eat one morsel until I got a knife and fork. The man told the king and the king came to see if it was true, and I got a knife and fork, and I took the knife in one paw and the fork in the other, and I bowed to the king. The king gave orders to bring him drink, and came; and the king filled a glass of wine and gave it to me.

I took hold of it in my paw and drank it, and thanked the king.

"On my honour," said he, "it is some king or other has lost him, when he came on the island and I will keep him, as he is trained; and perhaps he will serve us yet."

And this is the sort of king he was, – a king who had not a child living. Eight sons were born him and three daughters, and they were stolen the same night they were born. No matter what guard was placed over them, the child would be gone in the morning. A twelfth child now came to the queen, and the king took me with him to watch the baby. The women were not satisfied with me.

"Oh," said the king, "what was all your watching ever good for? One that was born to me I have not; I will leave this one in the dog's care, and he will not let it go."

A coupling was put between me and the cradle, and when every one went to sleep I was watching till the person woke who attended in the daytime; but I was there only two nights; when it was near the day, I saw a hand coming down through the chimney, and the hand was so big that it took round the child altogether, and thought to take him away. I caught hold of the hand above the wrist, and as I was fastened to the cradle, I did not let go my hold till I cut the hand from the wrist, and there was a howl from the person without. I laid the hand in the cradle with the child, and as I was tired I fell asleep; and when I awoke, I had neither child nor hand; and I began to howl, and the king heard me, and he cried out that something was wrong with me, and he sent servants to see what was the matter with me, and when the messenger came he saw me covered with blood, and he could not see the child; and he went to the king and told him the child was not to be got. The king came and saw the cradle coloured with the blood, and he cried out "where was the child gone?" and every one said it was the dog had eaten it.

The king said: "It is not: loose him, and he will get the pursuit himself."

When I was loosed, I found the scent of the blood till I came to a door of the room in which the child was. I went back to the king and took hold of him, and went back again and began to tear at the door. The king followed me and asked for the key. The servant said it was in the room of the stranger woman. The king caused search to be made for her, and she was not to be found. "I will break the door," said the king, "as I can't get the key." The king broke the door, and I went in, and went to the trunk, and the king asked for a key to unlock it. He got no key, and he broke the lock. When he opened the trunk, the child and the hand were stretched side by side, and the child was asleep. The king took the hand and ordered a woman to come for the child, and he showed the hand to every one in the house. But the stranger woman was gone, and she did not see the king; – and here she is herself to say if I am telling lies of her.

"Oh, it's nothing but the truth you have!"

The king did not allow me to be tied any more. He said there was nothing so much to wonder at as that I cut the hand off, as I was tied.

The child was growing till he was a year old. He was beginning to walk, and no one cared for him more than I did. He was growing till he was three, and he was running out every minute; so the king ordered a silver chain to be put between me and the child, that he might not go away from me. I was out with him in the garden every day, and the king was as proud as the world of the child. He would be watching him everywhere we went, till the child grew so wise that he would loose the chain and get off. But one day that he loosed it I failed to find him; and I ran into the house and searched the house, but there was no getting him for me. The king cried to go out and find the child, that had got loose from the dog. They went searching for him, but could not find him. When they failed altogether to find him, there remained no more favour with the king towards me, and every one disliked me, and I grew weak, for I did not get a morsel to eat half the time. When summer came, I said I would try and go home to my own country. I went away one fine morning, and I went swimming, and God helped me till I came home. I went into the garden, for I knew there was a place in the garden where I could hide myself, for fear my wife should see me. In the morning I saw her out walking, and the child with her, held by the hand. I pushed out to see the child, and as he was looking about him everywhere, he saw me and called out, "I see my shaggy papa. Oh!" said he; "oh, my heart's love, my shaggy papa, come here till I see you!"

I was afraid the woman would see me, as she was asking the child where he saw me, and he said I was up in a tree; and the more the child called me, the more I hid myself. The woman took the child home with her, but I knew he would be up early in the morning.

I went to the parlour-window, and the child was within, and he playing. When he saw me he cried out, "Oh! my heart's love, come here till I see you, shaggy papa." I broke the window and went in, and he began to kiss me. I saw the rod in front of the chimney, and I jumped up at the rod and knocked it down. "Oh! my heart's love, no one would give me the pretty rod," said he. I hoped he would strike me with the rod, but he did not. When I saw the time was short I raised my paw, and I gave him a scratch below the knee. "Oh! you naughty, dirty, shaggy papa, you have hurt me so much, I'll give you a blow of the rod." He struck me a light blow, and so I came back to my own shape again. When he saw a man standing before him he gave a cry, and I took him up in my arms. The servants heard the child. A maid came in to see what was the matter with him. When she saw me she gave a cry out of her, and she said, "Oh, if the master isn't come to life again!"

Another came in, and said it was he really. When the mistress heard of it, she came to see with her own eyes, for she would not believe I was there; and when she saw me she said she'd drown herself. But I said to her, "If you yourself will keep the secret, no living man will ever get the story from me until I lose my head." Here she is herself to say if I am telling the truth. "Oh, it's nothing but truth you are telling."

When I saw I was in a man's shape, I said I would take the child back to his father and mother, as I knew the grief they were in after him. I got a ship, and took the child with me; and as I journeyed I came to land on an island, and I saw not a living soul on it, only a castle dark and gloomy. I went in to see was there any one in it. There was no one but an old hag, tall and frightful, and she asked me, "What sort of person are you?" I heard some one groaning in another room, and I said I was a doctor, and I asked her what ailed the person who was groaning.

"Oh," said she, "it is my son, whose hand has been bitten from his wrist by a dog."

I knew then that it was he who had taken the child from me, and I said I would cure him if I got a good reward.

"I have nothing; but there are eight young lads and three young women, as handsome as any one ever laid eyes on, and if you cure him I will give you them."

"Tell me first in what place his hand was cut from him?"

"Oh, it was out in another country, twelve years ago."

"Show me the way, that I may see him."

She brought me into a room, so that I saw him, and his arm was swelled up to the shoulder. He asked me if I would cure him; and I said I would cure him if he would give me the reward his mother promised.

"Oh, I will give it; but cure me."

"Well, bring them out to me."

The hag brought them out of the room. I said I should burn the flesh that was on his arm. When I looked on him he was howling with pain. I said that I would not leave him in pain long. The wretch had only one eye in his forehead. I took a bar of iron, and put it in the fire till it was red, and I said to the hag, "He will be howling at first, but will fall asleep presently, and do not wake him till he has slept as much as he wants. I will close the door when I am going out." I took the bar with me, and I stood over him, and I turned it across through his eye as far as I could. He began to bellow, and tried to catch me, but I was out and away, having closed the door. The hag asked me, "Why is he bellowing?"

"Oh, he will be quiet presently, and will sleep for a good while, and I'll come again to have look at him; but bring me out the young men and the young women."

I took them with me, and I said to her, "Tell me where you got them."

"My son brought them with him, and they are all the children of one king."

I was well satisfied, and I had no wish for delay to get myself free from the hag, so I took them on board the ship, and the child I had myself. I thought the king might leave me the child I nursed myself; but when I came to land, and all those young people with me, the king and queen were out walking. The king was very aged, and the queen aged likewise. When I came to converse with them, and the twelve with me, the king and queen began to cry. I asked, "Why are you crying?"

"It is for good cause I am crying. As many children as these I should have, and now I am withered, grey, at the end of my life, and I have not one at all."

I told him all I went through, and I gave him the child in his hand, and "These are your other children who were stolen from you, whom I am giving to you safe. They are gently reared."

When the king heard who they were he smothered them with kisses and drowned them with tears, and dried them with fine cloths silken and the hair of his own head, and so also did their mother, and great was his welcome for me, as it was I who found them all. The king said to me, "I will give you the last child, as it is you who have earned him best; but you must come to my court every year, and the child with you, and I will share with you my possessions."

"I have enough of my own, and after my death I will leave it to the child."

I spent a time, till my visit was over, and I told the king all the troubles I went through, only I said nothing about my wife. And now you have the story.

And now when you go home, and the Slender Red Champion asks you for news of the death of Anshgayliacht and for the sword of light, tell him the way in which his brother was killed, and say you have the sword; and he will ask the sword from you. Say you to him, "If I promised to bring it to you, I did not promise to bring it for you;" and then throw the sword into the air and it will come back to me.

He went home, and he told the story of the death of Anshgayliacht to the Slender Red Champion, "And here," said he, "is the sword." The Slender Red Champion asked for the sword; but he said: "If I promised to bring it to you, I did not promise to bring it for you;" and he threw it into the air and it returned to Blue Niall.

The Wisdom of the King

THE HIGH-QUEEN of the Island of Woods had died in childbirth, and her child was put to nurse with a woman who lived in a hut of mud and wicker, within the border of the wood. One night the woman sat rocking the cradle, and pondering over the beauty of the child, and praying that the gods might grant him wisdom equal to his beauty. There came a knock at the door, and she got up, not a little wondering, for the nearest neighbours were in the dun of the High-King a mile away; and the night was now late. "Who is knocking?" she cried, and a thin voice answered, "Open! for I am a crone of the grey hawk, and I come from the darkness of the great wood." In terror she drew back the bolt, and a grey-clad woman, of a great age, and of a height more than human, came in and stood by the head of the cradle. The nurse shrank back against the wall, unable to take her eyes from the woman, for she saw by the gleaming of the firelight that the feathers of the grey hawk were upon her head instead of hair. But the child slept, and the fire danced, for the one was too ignorant and the other too full of gaiety to know what a dreadful being stood there. "Open!" cried another voice, "for I am a crone of the grey hawk, and I watch over his nest in the darkness of the great wood." The nurse opened the door again, though her fingers could scarce hold the bolts for trembling, and another grey woman, not less old than the other, and with like feathers instead of hair, came in and stood by the first. In a little, came a third grey woman, and after her a fourth, and then another and another and another, until the hut was full of their immense bodies. They stood a long time in perfect silence and stillness, for they were of those whom the dropping of the sand has never troubled, but at last one muttered in a low thin voice: "Sisters, I knew him far away by the redness of his heart under his silver skin;" and then another spoke: "Sisters, I knew him because his heart fluttered like a bird under a net of silver cords;" and then another took up the word: "Sisters, I knew him because his heart sang like a bird that is happy in a silver cage." And after that they sang together, those who were nearest rocking the cradle with long wrinkled fingers; and their voices were now tender and caressing, now like the wind blowing in the great wood, and this was their song:

"Out of sight is out of mind:
Long have man and woman-kind,
Heavy of will and light of mood,
Taken away our wheaten food,
Taken away our Altar stone;
Hail and rain and thunder alone,
And red hearts we turn to grey,
Are true till Time gutter away."

When the song had died out, the crone who had first spoken, said: "We have nothing more to do but to mix a drop of our blood into his blood." And she scratched her arm with the sharp point of a spindle, which she had made the nurse bring to her, and let a drop of blood, grey as the mist, fall upon the lips of the child; and passed out into the darkness. Then the others passed out in silence one by one; and all the while the child had not opened his pink eyelids or the fire ceased to dance, for the one was too ignorant and the other too full of gaiety to know what great beings had bent over the cradle.

When the crones were gone, the nurse came to her courage again, and hurried to the dun of the High-King, and cried out in the midst of the assembly hall that the Sidhe, whether for good or evil she knew not, had bent over the child that night; and the king and his poets and men of law, and his huntsmen, and his cooks, and his chief warriors went with her to the hut and gathered about the cradle, and were as noisy as magpies, and the child sat up and looked at them.

Two years passed over, and the king died fighting against the Fer Bolg; and the poets and the men of law ruled in the name of the child, but looked to see him become the master himself before long, for no one had seen so wise a child, and tales of his endless questions about the household of the gods and the making of the world went hither and thither among the wicker houses of the poor. Everything had been well but for a miracle that began to trouble all men; and all women, who, indeed, talked of it without ceasing. The feathers of the grey hawk had begun to grow in the child's hair, and though, his nurse cut them continually, in but a little while they would be more numerous than ever. This had not been a matter of great moment, for miracles were a little thing in those days, but for an ancient law of Eri that none who had any blemish of body could sit upon the throne; and as a grey hawk was a wild thing of the air which had never sat at the board, or listened to the songs of the poets in the light of the fire, it was not possible to think of one in whose hair its feathers grew as other than marred and blasted; nor could the people separate from their admiration of the wisdom that grew in him a horror as at one of unhuman blood. Yet all were resolved that he should reign, for they had suffered much from foolish kings and their own disorders, and moreover they desired to watch out the spectacle of his days; and no one had any other fear but that his great wisdom might bid him obey the law, and call some other, who had but a common mind, to reign in his stead.

When the child was seven years old the poets and the men of law were called together by the chief poet, and all these matters weighed and considered. The child had already seen that those about him had hair only, and, though they had told him that they too had had feathers but had lost them because of a sin committed by their forefathers, they knew that he would learn the truth when he began to wander into the country round about. After much consideration they decreed a new law commanding every one upon pain of death to mingle artificially the feathers of the grey hawk into his hair; and they sent men with nets and slings and bows into the countries round about to gather a sufficiency of feathers. They decreed also that any who told the truth to the child should be flung from a cliff into the sea.

The years passed, and the child grew from childhood into boyhood and from boyhood into manhood, and from being curious about all things he became busy with strange and subtle thoughts which came to him in dreams, and with distinctions between things long held the same and with the resemblance of things long held different. Multitudes came from other lands to see him and to ask his counsel, but there were guards set at the frontiers, who compelled all that came to wear the feathers of the grey hawk in their hair. While they listened to him his words seemed to make all darkness light and filled their hearts like music; but, alas, when they returned to their own lands his words seemed far off, and what they could remember too strange and subtle to help them to live out their hasty days. A number indeed did live differently afterwards, but their new life was less excellent than the old: some among them had long served a good cause, but when they heard him praise it and their labour, they returned to their own lands to find what they had loved less lovable and their arm lighter in the battle, for he had taught them how little a hair divides the false and true; others, again, who had served no cause, but wrought in peace the welfare of their own households, when he had expounded the meaning of their purpose, found their bones softer and their will less ready for toil, for he had shown them greater purposes; and numbers of the young, when they had heard him upon all these things, remembered certain words that became like a fire in their hearts, and made all kindly joys and traffic between man and man as nothing, and went different ways, but all into vague regret.

When any asked him concerning the common things of life; disputes about the mear of a territory, or about the straying of cattle, or about the penalty of blood; he would turn to those nearest him for advice; but this was held to be from courtesy, for none knew that these matters were hidden from him by thoughts and dreams that filled his mind like the marching and counter-marching of armies. Far less could any know that his heart wandered lost amid throngs of overcoming thoughts and dreams, shuddering at its own consuming solitude.

Among those who came to look at him and to listen to him was the daughter of a little king who lived a great way off; and when he saw her he loved, for she was beautiful, with a strange and pale beauty unlike the women of his land; but Dana, the great mother, had decreed her a heart that was but as the heart of others, and when she considered the mystery of the hawk feathers she was troubled with a great horror. He called her to him when the assembly was over and told her of her beauty, and praised her simply and frankly as though she were a fable of the bards; and he asked her humbly to give him her love, for he was only subtle in his dreams. Overwhelmed with his greatness, she half consented, and yet half refused, for she longed to marry some warrior who could carry her over a mountain in his arms. Day by day the king gave her gifts; cups with ears of gold and findrinny wrought by the craftsmen of distant lands; cloth from over sea, which, though woven with curious figures, seemed to her less beautiful than the bright cloth of her own country; and still she was ever between a smile and a frown; between yielding and withholding. He laid down his wisdom at her feet, and told how the heroes when they die return to the world and begin their labour anew; how the kind and mirthful Men of Dea drove out the huge and gloomy and misshapen People from Under the Sea; and a multitude of things that even the Sidhe have forgotten, either because they happened so long ago or because they have not time to think of them; and still she half refused, and still he hoped, because he could not believe that a beauty so much like wisdom could hide a common heart.

There was a tall young man in the dun who had yellow hair, and was skilled in wrestling and in the training of horses; and one day when the king walked in the orchard, which was between the foss and the forest, he heard his voice among the salley bushes which hid the waters of the foss. "My blossom," it said, "I hate them for making you weave these dingy feathers into your beautiful hair, and all that the bird of prey upon the throne may sleep easy o' nights; and then the low, musical voice he loved answered: "My hair is not beautiful like yours; and now that I have plucked the feathers out of your hair I will put my hands through it, thus, and thus, and thus; for it casts no shadow of terror and darkness upon my heart." Then the king remembered many things that he had forgotten without understanding them, doubtful words of his poets and his men of law, doubts that he had reasoned away, his own continual solitude; and he called to the lovers in a trembling voice. They came from among the salley bushes and threw themselves at his feet and prayed for pardon, and he stooped down and plucked the feathers out of the hair of the woman and then turned away towards the dun without a word. He strode into the hall of assembly, and having gathered his poets and his men of law about him, stood upon the dais and spoke in a loud, clear voice: "Men of law, why did you make me sin against the laws of Eri? Men of verse, why did you make me sin against the secrecy of wisdom, for law was made by man for the welfare of man, but wisdom the gods have made, and no man shall live by its light, for it and the hail and the rain and the thunder follow a way that is deadly to mortal things? Men of law and men of verse, live according to your kind, and call Eocha of the Hasty Mind to reign over you, for I set out to find my kindred." He then came down among them, and drew out of the hair of first one and then another the feathers of the grey hawk, and, having scattered them over the rushes upon the floor, passed out, and none dared to follow him, for his eyes gleamed like the eyes of the birds of prey; and no man saw him again or heard his voice. Some believed that he found his eternal abode among the demons, and some that he dwelt henceforth with the dark and dreadful goddesses, who sit all night about the pools in the forest watching the constellations rising and setting in those desolate mirrors.

MacCodrum's Seal Wife

DEEP IN THE COLD SEA, long before men chanced the waves for the first time, there lived a king and his queen, and their lovely sea-children. The children were elegant, graceful creatures, with deep brown eyes and voices that filled the sea with laughter and song. They dwelt deep in that sea, in happiness and in comfort, and spent days chasing one another through the schools of fish, catching a ride on a tail, hiding in a murky cave, frolicking in the waves that caressed their young bodies and made them strong.

And so their days were spent, and they were fed and loved by the kindly queen and her husband, who brushed their hair, and stroked their heads, and gave them a home like none other. Until the sad day when the queen became ill and died, and left her children forlorn and lonely, but still with the sea as their home, and the fish, and the warm waves to comfort them. Their voices were softer now, and their music still sweet, but the king was concerned about their uncombed hair, and their unstroked heads, and he began to search for a mother for the sea-children.

The king found them a mother in a darker part of the sea, where the sun could not light the coral reefs, or dance upon the weeds and the shimmering scales of the fish. The mother was in fact a witch, and she charmed the king with a magic potion that put him under her spell. She came with him to the lighter part of the sea, where the sun kissed the elegant bodies of the sea-children, glowed in their soft brown eyes, and she made her home there, combing their hair, and stroking their heads, but never loving them, and so the friendly waters grew cold, and although the light continued to dance, and the waves lapped at their bodies, the children were sad and downcast.

And so it was that the witch decided to dispose of these sea-children, and from the depths of her wicked being she created a cruel spell that would rid the sea-children of their elegance and their beauty. She turned them to seals, who could live no longer in the marine palace of their father the king, their graceful limbs replaced by heavy bodies and sleek dark fur. They were to live in the sea for all but one day each year when they could find a secluded shore and transform, for just that day, into children once more.

But the witch could not rob the children of everything, and although their bodies were ungainly, and they were beautiful children no longer, they re-tained their soft brown eyes, and their music was as pure and mellifluous as the wind in the trees, as the birds who flew above the water.

Time went on, and the seals grew used to their shiny coats, and to the sea, where they played once again in the waves, and fished, and sang, but they loved too becoming children again, that one day each year, and it was when they had shed their coats, beautiful children once more, that they were seen for the first time by human eyes, those belonging to a fisherman who lived on an isolated rock, a man called Roderic MacCodrum, of the Clan Donald, in the Outer Hebrides.

On this fateful day he walked to the beach to rig his boat when he heard the sound of exquisite singing, and he hid himself behind some driftwood and watched the delightful dance of the sea-children, who waved arms that were no longer clumsy seal flippers, and who ran with legs that were long and lean. Their soft brown eyes were alight with happiness and never before had Roderic MacCodrum seen such a sight.

His eyes sparkled. He must have one. And so it was that Roderic MacCodrum stole one of the glistening pelts that lay cast to the side of the beach, and put it above the rafters in his barn, safe from the searching eyes of the young seal woman who came to call.

The seal woman was elegant and beautiful, her long hair hiding her comely nakedness. She implored him to return her coat to her, but he feigned concern and told her that he knew not where it was. In despair she sat down on his doorstep, her head in her hands, and it was then that he offered her a life on land, as his wife and lover. Because she had no seal skin like her brothers and sisters, and no place to go, she agreed, and so it was that the seal woman came to live with Roderic MacCodrum, where she lived happily, or so it was thought, and bore him many children.

But the seal woman, or Selkie as she came to be called, had a cold, lonely heart, and although she loved and nurtured her children, and grew to find a kind of peace with her husband, she longed for the waves, for the cold fresh waters of the sea. And she would sit on its shores and she would sing a song that was so haunting, so melancholy that the seals would come to her here and cease their frolicking to return her unhappy song, to sing with her of times gone by when the waves and the water comforted them and made them strong, when the sun in the lighter part of the sea kissed their elegant bodies and made them gleam with light.

And then at night she would return to her cottage, and light the peat in the hearth, and make a home for her family, all the while living her life in her dreams of the sea.

It was her unknowing child who found the beautiful fur coat, fallen from its hiding place in the rafters, where it had remained unseen for all those years, and she brought it to her mother whose eyes glowed with a warmth that none had seen before. Her mother kissed her then, and all her brothers and sisters, and whispered that they must look out for her, for she would be back.

Roderic MacCodrum of the Seals, as he had come to be known, returned to his cottage that night to find it empty and cold, like the heart of the seal woman he had married, and his children were lined on the beaches, bereft and alone, for their mother had left for the chill waters and she had not come back.

Their mother never came back, for she had gone with that lustrous fur coat, that gleamed in the light like her soft brown eyes when she saw it. They heard her, though, for from the sea came those same lilting melodies, happier now, to be sure. And they often saw a graceful seal, who came closer to shore than the others, and who seemed to beckon, and in whose presence they felt a strange comfort, a familiar warmth, especially when the sun caught those soft brown eyes they knew so well.

The Thirsty Ploughman

IT WAS IN BERNERAY that two men from Brusda walked along a hot and sun-burnt field, parched from the fiery sun, from a long day of ploughing. Sweat glistened on their brows and they talked little, saving words for a time when their tongues were moister. Their feet were bare and despite the great heat they moved quickly, thirsting for a drink, for cool refreshment.

They passed across a rocky knoll and then they heard a woman, working at a churn. They looked at one another with relief.

"Ah, Donald," said Ewan, the slighter of the two men, "if the milkmaid had my thirst, what a drink of buttermilk she would drink."

Donald was not sure. "Ah, it's not buttermilk I would care for," he said.

As they carried on over the dry brush that lined the hillock, the sound of the fresh milk splashing in the churn grew louder, more enticing, and both men licked their lips at the thought of it. There before them stood a fair maiden, her apron starched crisp white, holding a jug that foamed with pure butter-milk. She offered it to them then, Ewan first because he was the smaller of the two.

Ewan refused to drink because he knew neither the maiden nor the source of the buttermilk. He was afraid of what he did not know and though he thirsted for the cool milk, he would allow none to pass his lips.

Donald, who cared not for buttermilk, drank deeply from the jug, and wiping the frosting of white lather from his lip, he declared it the best he had ever tasted.

"Ah," said the bonny maiden, whose face was cool with contempt, "you who asked for the drink and did not accept it will have a short life. And you," she gestured to Donald, "you who took the drink, but did not ask for it, a long life and good living."

She turned on her heel, and apron bright in the sunlight, left the men, one thirsty and one sated.

And so it was that Ewan returned home that night and took to his bed, never to waken, for the fear of God had been put into him that day by the maiden on the hill, who could be none other than a witch. And Donald lived a long and prosperous life, ploughing his field alone, but reaping better crops, and amassing great riches. He looked always across the knoll, listened intently for the sound of milk in the churn, but never again did he see the witch, or fairy, though he blessed her often.

Murtough and the Witch Woman

IN THE DAYS WHEN Murtough Mac Erca was in the High Kingship of Ireland, the country was divided between the old beliefs of paganism and the new doctrines of the Christian teaching. Part held with the old creed and part with the new, and the thought of the people was troubled between them, for they knew not which way to follow and which to forsake. The faith of their forefathers clung close around them, holding them by many fine and tender threads of memory and custom and tradition; yet still the new faith was making its way, and every day it spread wider and wider through the land.

The family of Murtough had joined itself to the Christian faith, and his three brothers were bishops and abbots of the Church, but Murtough himself remained a pagan, for he was a wild and lawless prince, and the peaceful teachings of the Christian doctrine, with its forgiveness of enemies, pleased him not at all. Fierce and cruel was his life, filled with dark deeds and bloody wars, and savage and tragic was his death, as we shall hear.

Now Murtough was in the sunny summer palace of Cletty, which Cormac, son of Art, had built for a pleasure house on the brink of the slow-flowing Boyne, near the Fairy Brugh of Angus the Ever Young, the God of Youth and Beauty. A day of summer was that day, and the King came forth to hunt on the borders of the Brugh, with all his boon companions around him. But when the high-noon came the sun grew hot, and the King sat down to rest upon the fairy mound, and the hunt passed on beyond him, and he was left alone.

There was a witch woman in that country whose name was 'Sigh, Sough, Storm, Rough Wind, Winter Night, Cry, Wail, and Groan.' Star-bright and beautiful was she in face and form, but inwardly she was cruel as her names. And she hated Murtough because he had scattered and destroyed the Ancient Peoples of the Fairy Tribes of Erin, her country and her fatherland, and because in the battle which he fought at Cerb on the Boyne her father and her mother and her sister had been slain. For in those days women went to battle side by side with men.

She knew, too, that with the coming of the new faith trouble would come upon the fairy folk, and their power and their great majesty would depart from them, and men would call them demons, and would drive them out with psalm-singing and with the saying of prayers, and with the sound of little tinkling bells. So trouble and anger wrought in the witch woman, and she waited the day to be revenged on Murtough, for he being yet a pagan, was still within her power to harm.

So when Sheen (for Sheen or 'Storm' was the name men gave to her) saw the King seated on the fairy mound and all his comrades parted from him, she arose softly, and combed her hair with her comb of silver adorned with little ribs of gold, and she washed her hands in a silver basin wherein were four golden birds sitting on the rim of the bowl, and little bright gems of carbuncle set round about the rim. And she donned her fairy mantle of flowing green, and her cloak, wide and hooded, with silvery fringes, and a brooch of fairest gold. On her head were tresses yellow like to gold, plaited in four locks, with a golden drop at the end of each long tress. The hue of her hair was like the flower of the iris in summer or like red gold after the burnishing thereof. And she wore on her breasts and at her shoulders marvellous clasps of gold, finely worked with the tracery of the skilled craftsman, and a golden twisted torque around her throat. And when she was decked she went softly and sat down beside Murtough on the turfy hunting mound. And after a space Murtough perceived her sitting there, and the sun shining upon her, so that the glittering of the gold and of her golden hair and the bright shining of the green silk of her garments, was like the yellow iris-beds upon the lake on a sunny summer's day. Wonder and terror seized on Murtough at her beauty, and he knew not if he loved her or if he hated her the most; for at one moment all his nature was filled with longing and with love of her, so that it seemed to him that he would give the whole of Ireland for the loan of one hour's space of dalliance with her; but after that he felt a dread of her, because he knew his fate was in her hands, and that she had come to work him ill. But he welcomed her as if she were known to him and he asked her wherefore she was come. "I am come," she said, "because I am beloved of Murtough, son of Erc, King of Erin, and I come to seek him here." Then Murtough was glad, and he said, "Dost thou not know me, maiden?"

"I do," she answered, "for all secret and mysterious things are known to me and thou and all the men of Erin are well known."

After he had conversed with her awhile, she appeared to him so fair that the King was ready to promise her anything in life she wished, so long as she would go with him to Cletty of the Boyne. "My wish," she said, "is that you take me to your house, and that you put out from it your wife and your children because they are of the new faith, and all the clerics that are in your house, and that neither your wife nor any cleric be permitted to enter the house while I am there."

"I will give you," said the King, "a hundred head of every herd of cattle that is within my kingdom, and a hundred drinking horns, and a hundred cups, and a hundred rings of gold, and a feast every other night in the summer palace of Cletty. But I pledge thee my word, oh, maiden, it were easier for me to give thee half of Ireland than to do this thing that thou hast asked." For Murtough feared that when those that were of the Christian faith were put out of his house, she would work her spells upon him, and no power would be left with him to resist those spells.

"I will not take thy gifts," said the damsel, "but only those things that I have asked; moreover, it is thus, that my name must never be uttered by thee, nor must any man or woman learn it."

"What is thy name," said Murtough, "that it may not come upon my lips to utter it?"

And she said, "Sigh, Sough, Storm, Rough Wind, Winter Night, Cry, Wail, Groan, this is my name, but men call me Sheen, for 'Storm' or Sheen is my chief name, and storms are with me where I come."

Nevertheless, Murtough was so fascinated by her that he brought her to his home, and drove out the clerics that were there, with his wife and children along with them, and drove out also the nobles of his own clan, the children of Niall, two great and gallant battalions. And Duivsech, his wife, went crying along the road with her children around her to seek Bishop Cairnech, the half-brother of her husband, and her own soul-friend, that she might obtain help and shelter from him.

But Sheen went gladly and light-heartedly into the House of Cletty, and when she saw the lovely lightsome house and the goodly nobles of the clan of Niall, and the feasting and banqueting and the playing of the minstrels and all the joyous noise of that kingly dwelling, her heart was lifted within her, and "Fair as a fairy palace is this house of Cletty," said she.

"Fair, indeed, it is," replied the King; "for neither the Kings of Leinster nor the Kings of mighty Ulster, nor the lords of the clans of Owen or of Niall, have such a house as this; nay, in Tara of the Kings itself, no house to equal this house of mine is found." And that night the King robed himself in all the splendour of his royal dignity, and on his right hand he seated Sheen, and a great banquet was made before them, and men said that never on earth was to be seen a woman more goodly of appearance than she. And the King was astonished at her, and he began to ask her questions, for it seemed to him that the power of a great goddess of the ancient time was in her; and he asked her whence she came, and what manner was the power that he saw in her. He asked her, too, did she believe in the God of the clerics, or was she herself some goddess of the older world? For he feared her, feeling that his fate was in her hands.

She laughed a careless and a cruel laugh, for she knew that the King was in their power, now that she was there alone with him, and the clerics and the Christian teachers gone.

"Fear me not, O Murtough," she cried; "I am, like thee, a daughter of the race of men of the ancient family of Adam and of Eve; fit and meet my comradeship with thee; therefore, fear not nor regret. And as to that true God of thine, worker of miracles and helper of His people, no miracle in all the world is there that I, by mine own unaided power, cannot work the like. I can create a sun and moon; the heavens I can sprinkle with radiant stars of night. I can call up to life men fiercely fighting in conflict, slaughtering one another. Wine I could make of the cold water of the Boyne, and sheep of lifeless stones, and swine of ferns. In the presence of the hosts I can make gold and silver, plenty and to spare; and hosts of famous fighting men I can produce from naught. Now, tell me, can thy God work the like?"

"Work for us," says the King, "some of these great wonders." Then Sheen went forth out of the house, and she set herself to work spells on Murtough, so that he knew not whether he was in his right mind or no. She took of the water of the Boyne and made a magic wine thereout, and she took ferns and spiked thistles and light puff-balls of the woods, and out of them she fashioned magic swine and sheep and goats, and with these she fed Murtough and the hosts. And when they had eaten, all their strength went from them, and the magic wine sent them into an uneasy sleep and restless slumbers. And out of stones and sods of earth she fashioned three battalions, and one of the battalions she placed at one side of the house, and the other at the further side beyond it, and one encircling the rest southward along the hollow windings of the glen. And thus were these battalions, one of them all made of men stark-naked and their colour blue, and the second with heads of goats with shaggy beards and horned; but the third, more terrible than they, for these were headless men, fighting like human beings, yet finished at the neck; and the sound of heavy shouting as of hosts and multitudes came from the first and the second battalion, but from the third no sound save only that they waved their arms and struck their weapons together, and smote the ground with their feet impatiently. And though terrible was the shout of the blue men and the bleating of the goats with human limbs, more horrible yet was the stamping and the rage of those headless men, finished at the neck.

And Murtough, in his sleep and in his dreams, heard the battle-shout, and he rose impetuously from off his bed, but the wine overcame him, and his strength departed from him, and he fell helplessly upon the floor. Then he heard the challenge a second time, and the stamping of the feet without, and he rose again, and madly, fiercely, he set on them, charging the hosts and scattering them before him, as he thought, as far as the fairy palace of the Brugh. But all his strength was lost in fighting phantoms, for they were but stones and sods and withered leaves of the forest that he took for fighting men.

Now Duivsech, Murtough's wife, knew what was going on. She called upon Cairnech to arise and to gather together the clans of the children of his people, the men of Owen and of Niall, and together they went to the fort; but Sheen guarded it well, so that they could by no means find an entrance. Then Cairnech was angry, and he cursed the place, and he dug a grave before the door, and he stood up upon the mound of the grave, and rang his bells and cursed the King and his house, and prophesied his downfall. But he blessed the clans of Owen and of Niall, and they returned to their own country.

Then Cairnech sent messengers to seek Murtough and to draw him away from the witch woman who sought his destruction, but because she was so lovely the King would believe no evil of her; and whenever he made any sign to go to Cairnech, she threw her spell upon the King, so that he could not break away. When he was so weak and faint that he had no power left, she cast a sleep upon him, and she went round the house, putting everything in readiness. She called upon her magic host of warriors, and set them round the fortress, with their spears and javelins pointed inwards towards the house, so that the King would not dare to go out amongst them. And that night was a night of Samhain-tide, the eve of Wednesday after All Souls' Day.

Then she went everywhere throughout the house, and took lighted brands and burning torches, and scattered them in every part of the dwelling. And she returned into the room wherein Murtough slept, and lay down by his side. And she caused a great wind to spring up, and it came soughing through the house from the north-west; and the King said, "This is the sigh of the winter night." And Sheen smiled, because, unwittingly, the King had spoken her name, for she knew by that that the hour of her revenge had come. "'Tis I myself that am Sigh and Winter Night," she said, "and I am Rough Wind and Storm, a daughter of fair nobles; and I am Cry and Wail, the maid of elfin birth, who brings ill-luck to men."

After that she caused a great snowstorm to come round the house; and like the noise of troops and the rage of battle was the storm, beating and pouring in on every side, so that drifts of deep snow were piled against the walls, blocking the doors and chilling the folk that were feasting within the house. But the King was lying in a heavy, unresting sleep, and Sheen was at his side. Suddenly he screamed out of his sleep and stirred himself, for he heard the crash of falling timbers and the noise of the magic hosts, and he smelled the strong smell of fire in the palace.

He sprang up. "It seems to me," he cried, "that hosts of demons are around the house, and that they are slaughtering my people, and that the house of Cletty is on fire."

"It was but a dream," the witch maiden said. Then he slept again, and he saw a vision, to wit, that he was tossing in a ship at sea, and the ship floundered, and above his head a griffin, with sharp beak and talons, sailed, her wings outspread and covering all the sun, so that it was dark as middle-night; and lo! As she rose on high, her plumes quivered for a moment in the air; then down she swooped and picked him from the waves, carrying him to her eyrie on the dismal cliff outhanging o'er the ocean; and the griffin began to pierce him and to prod him with her talons, and to pick out pieces of his flesh with her beak; and this went on awhile, and then a flame, that came he knew not whence, rose from the nest, and he and the griffin were enveloped in the flame. Then in her beak the griffin picked him up, and together they fell downward over the cliff's edge into the seething ocean; so that, half by fire and half by water, he died a miserable death.

When the King saw that vision, he rose screaming from his sleep, and donned his arms; and he made one plunge forward seeking for the magic hosts, but he found no man to answer him. The damsel went forth from the house, and Murtough made to follow her, but as he turned the flames leaped out, and all between him and the door was one vast sheet of flame. He saw no way of escape, save the vat of wine that stood in the banqueting hall, and into that he got; but the burning timbers of the roof fell upon his head and the hails of fiery sparks rained on him, so that half of him was burned and half was drowned, as he had seen in his dream.

The next day, amid the embers, the clerics found his corpse, and they took it up and washed it in the Boyne, and carried it to Tuilen to bury it. And they said, "Alas! That Mac Erca, High King of Erin, of the noble race of Conn and of the descendants of Ugaine the Great, should die fighting with sods and stones! Alas! That the Cross of Christ was not signed upon his face that he might have known the witchdoms of the maiden what they were."

As they went thus, bewailing the death of Murtough and bearing him to his grave, Duivsech, wife of Murtough, met them, and when she found her husband dead, she struck her hands together and she made a great and mournful lamentation; and because weakness came upon her she leaned her back against the ancient tree that is in Aenech Reil; and a burst of blood broke from her heart, and there she died, grieving for her husband. And the grave of Murtough was made wide and deep, and there they laid the Queen beside him, two in the one grave, near the north side of the little church that is in Tuilen.

Now, when the burial was finished, and the clerics were reciting over his grave the deeds of the King, and were making prayers for Murtough's soul that it might be brought out of hell, for Cairnech showed great care for this, they saw coming towards them across the sward a lonely woman, star-bright and beautiful, and a kirtle of priceless silk upon her, and a green mantle with its fringes of silver thread flowing to the ground. She reached the place where the clerics were, and saluted them, and they saluted her. And they marvelled at her beauty, but they perceived on her an appearance of sadness and of heavy grief. They asked of her, "Who art thou, maiden, and wherefore art thou come to the house of mourning? For a king lies buried here."

"A king lies buried here, indeed," said she, "and I it was who slew him, Murtough of the many deeds, of the race of Conn and Niall, High King of Ireland and of the West. And though it was I who wrought his death, I myself will die for grief of him."

And they said, "Tell us, maiden, why you brought him to his death, if so be that he was dear to thee?" And she said, "Murtough was dear to me, indeed, dearest of the men of the whole world; for I am Sheen, the daughter of Sige, the son of Dian, from whom Ath Sigi or the 'Ford of Sige' is called today. But Murtough slew my father, and my mother and sister were slain along with him, in the battle of Cerb upon the Boyne, and there was none of my house to avenge their death, save myself alone. Moreover, in his time the Ancient Peoples of the Fairy Tribes of Erin were scattered and destroyed, the folk of the underworld and of my fatherland; and to avenge the wrong and loss he wrought on them I slew the man I loved. I made poison for him; alas! I made for him magic drink and food which took his strength away, and out of the sods of earth and puff-balls that float down the wind, I wrought men and armies of headless, hideous folk, till all his senses were distraught. And, now, take me to thee, O Cairnech, in fervent and true repentance, and sign the Cross of Christ upon my brow, for the time of my death is come." Then she made penitence for the sin that she had sinned, and she died there upon the grave of grief and of sorrow after the King. And they digged a grave lengthways across the foot of the wide grave of Murtough and his spouse, and there they laid the maiden who had wrought them woe. And the clerics wondered at those things, and they wrote them and revised them in a book.

The Witches' Excursion

SHEMUS (RED JAMES) AWAKENED from his sleep one night by noises in his kitchen. Stealing to the door, he saw half-a-dozen old women sitting round the fire, jesting and laughing, his old housekeeper, Madge, quite frisky and gay, helping her sister crones to cheering glasses of punch. He began to admire the impudence and imprudence of Madge, displayed in the invitation and the riot, but recollected on the instant her officiousness in urging him to take a comfortable posset, which she had brought to his bedside just before he fell asleep. Had he drunk it, he would have been just now deaf to the witches' glee. He heard and saw them drink his health in such a mocking style as nearly to tempt him to charge them, besom in hand, but he restrained himself.

The jug being emptied, one of them cried out, "Is it time to be gone?" and at the same moment, putting on a red cap, she added –

> *"By yarrow and rue,*
> *And my red cap too,*
> *Hie over to England."*

Making use of a twig which she held in her hand as a steed, she gracefully soared up the chimney, and was rapidly followed by the rest. But when it came to the housekeeper, Shemus interposed. "By your leave, ma'am," said he, snatching twig and cap. "Ah, you desateful ould crocodile! If I find you here on my return, there'll be wigs on the green –

> *'By yarrow and rue,*
> *And my red cap too,*
> *Hie over to England.'"*

The words were not out of his mouth when he was soaring above the ridge pole, and swiftly ploughing the air. He was careful to speak no word (being somewhat conversant with witch-lore), as the result would be a tumble, and the immediate return of the expedition.

In a very short time they had crossed the Wicklow hills, the Irish Sea, and the Welsh mountains, and were charging, at whirlwind speed, the hall door of a castle. Shemus, only for the company in which he found himself, would have cried out for pardon, expecting to be mummy against the hard oak door in a moment; but, all bewildered, he found himself passing through the key-hole, along a passage, down a flight of steps, and through a cellar-door key-hole before he could form any clear idea of his situation.

Waking to the full consciousness of his position, he found himself sitting on a stillion, plenty of lights glimmering round, and he and his companions, with full tumblers of frothing wine in hand, hob-nobbing and drinking healths as jovially and recklessly as if the liquor was honestly come by, and they were sitting in Shemus's own kitchen. The red birredh had assimilated Shemus's nature for the time being to that of his unholy companions. The heady liquors soon got into their brains, and a period of unconsciousness succeeded the ecstasy, the head-ache, the turning round of the barrels, and the 'scattered sight' of poor Shemus. He woke up under the impression of being roughly seized, and shaken, and dragged upstairs, and subjected to a disagreeable examination by the lord of the castle, in his state parlour. There was much derision among the whole company, gentle and simple, on hearing Shemus's explanation, and, as the thing occurred in the dark ages, the unlucky Leinster man was sentenced to be hung as soon as the gallows could be prepared for the occasion.

The poor Hibernian was in the cart proceeding on his last journey, with a label on his back, and another on his breast, announcing him as the remorseless villain who for the last month had been draining the casks in my lord's vault every night. He was surprised to hear himself addressed by his name, and in his native tongue, by an old woman in the crowd.

"Ach, Shemus, alanna! Is it going to die you are in a strange place without your cappeen d'yarrag?" These words infused hope and courage into the poor victim's heart. He turned to the lord and humbly asked leave to die in his red cap, which he supposed had dropped from his head in the vault. A servant was sent for the head-piece, and Shemus felt lively hope warming his heart while placing it on his head. On the platform he was graciously allowed to address the spectators, which he proceeded to do in the usual formula composed for the benefit of flying stationers –

"Good people all, a warning take by me;" but when he had finished the line, "My parents reared me tenderly," he unexpectedly added – "By yarrow and rue," etc., and the disappointed spectators saw him shoot up obliquely through the air in the style of a sky-rocket that had missed its aim. It is said that the lord took the circumstance much to heart, and never afterwards hung a man for twenty-four hours after his offence.

A Queen's County Witch

IT WAS ABOUT EIGHTY YEARS AGO, in the month of May, that a Roman Catholic clergyman, near Rathdowney, in the Queen's County, was awakened at midnight to attend a dying man in a distant part of the parish. The priest obeyed without a murmur, and having performed his duty to the expiring sinner, saw him depart this world before he left the cabin. As it was yet dark, the man who had called on the priest offered to accompany him home, but he refused, and set forward on his journey alone. The grey dawn began to appear over the hills. The good priest was highly enraptured with the beauty of the scene, and rode on, now gazing intently at every surrounding object, and again cutting with his whip at the bats and big beautiful night-flies which flitted ever and anon from hedge to hedge across his lonely way. Thus engaged, he journeyed on slowly, until the nearer approach of sunrise began to render objects completely discernible, when he dismounted from his horse, and slipping his arm out of the rein, and drawing forth his 'Breviary' from his pocket, he commenced reading his 'morning office' as he walked leisurely along.

He had not proceeded very far, when he observed his horse, a very spirited animal, endeavouring to stop on the road, and gazing intently into a field on one side of the way where there were three or four cows grazing. However, he did not pay any particular attention to this circumstance, but went on a little farther, when the horse suddenly plunged with great violence, and endeavoured to break away by force. The priest with great difficulty succeeded in restraining him, and, looking at him more closely, observed him shaking from head to foot, and sweating profusely. He now stood calmly, and refused to move from where he was, nor could threats or entreaty induce him to proceed. The father was greatly astonished, but recollecting to have often heard of horses labouring under affright being induced to go by blindfolding them, he took out his handkerchief and tied it across his eyes. He then mounted, and, striking him gently, he went forward without reluctance, but still sweating and trembling violently. They had not gone far, when they arrived opposite a narrow path or bridle-way, flanked at either side by a tall, thick hedge, which led from the high road to the field where the cows were grazing. The priest happened by chance to look into the lane, and saw a spectacle which made the blood curdle in his veins. It was the legs of a man from the hips downwards, without head or body, trotting up the avenue at a smart pace. The good father was very much alarmed, but, being a man of strong nerve, he resolved, come what might, to stand, and be further acquainted with this singular spectre. He accordingly stood, and so did the headless apparition, as if afraid to approach him. The priest observing this, pulled back a little from the entrance of the avenue, and the phantom again resumed its progress. It soon arrived on the road, and the priest now had sufficient opportunity to view it minutely. It wore yellow buckskin breeches, tightly fastened at the knees with green ribbon; it had neither shoes nor stockings on, and its legs were covered with long, red hairs, and all full of wet, blood, and clay, apparently contracted in its progress through the thorny hedges. The priest, although very much alarmed, felt eager to examine the phantom, and for this purpose summoned all his philosophy to enable him to speak to it. The ghost was now a little ahead, pursuing its march at its usual brisk trot, and the priest urged on his horse speedily until he came up with it, and thus addressed it –

"Hilloa, friend! who art thou, or whither art thou going so early?"

The hideous spectre made no reply, but uttered a fierce and superhuman growl, or "Umph."

"A fine morning for ghosts to wander abroad," again said the priest.

Another "Umph" was the reply.

"Why don't you speak?"

"Umph."

"You don't seem disposed to be very loquacious this morning."

"Umph," again.

The good man began to feel irritated at the obstinate silence of his unearthly visitor, and said, with some warmth –

"In the name of all that's sacred, I command you to answer me, Who art thou, or where art thou travelling?"

Another "Umph," more loud and more angry than before, was the only reply.

'Perhaps," said the father, "a taste of whipcord might render you a little more communicative;" and so saying, he struck the apparition a heavy blow with his whip on the breech.

The phantom uttered a wild and unearthly yell, and fell forward on the road, and what was the priest's astonishment when he perceived the whole place running over with milk. He was struck dumb with amazement; the prostrate phantom still continued to eject vast quantities of milk from every part; the priest's head swam, his eyes got dizzy; a stupor came all over him for some minutes, and on his recovering, the frightful spectre had vanished, and in its stead he found stretched on the road, and half drowned in milk, the form of Sarah Kennedy, an old woman of the neighbourhood, who had been long notorious in that district for her witchcraft and superstitious practices, and it was now discovered that she had, by infernal aid, assumed that monstrous shape, and was employed that morning in sucking the cows of the village. Had a volcano burst forth at his feet, he could not be more astonished; he gazed awhile in silent amazement – the old woman groaning, and writhing convulsively.

"Sarah," said he, at length, "I have long admonished you to repent of your evil ways, but you were deaf to my entreaties; and now, wretched woman, you are surprised in the midst of your crimes."

"Oh, father, father," shouted the unfortunate woman, "can you do nothing to save me? I am lost; hell is open for me, and legions of devils surround me this moment, waiting to carry my soul to perdition."

The priest had not power to reply; the old wretch's pains increased; her body swelled to an immense size; her eyes flashed as if on fire, her face was black as night, her entire form writhed in a thousand different contortions; her outcries were appalling, her face sunk, her eyes closed, and in a few minutes she expired in the most exquisite tortures.

The priest departed homewards, and called at the next cabin to give notice of the strange circumstances. The remains of Sarah Kennedy were removed to her cabin, situate at the edge of a small wood at a little distance. She had long been a resident in that neighbourhood, but still she was a stranger, and came there no one knew from whence. She had no relation in that country but one daughter, now advanced in years, who resided with her. She kept one cow, but sold more butter, it was said, than any farmer in the parish, and it was generally suspected that she acquired it by devilish agency, as she never made a secret of being intimately acquainted with sorcery and fairyism. She professed the Roman Catholic religion, but never complied with the practices enjoined by that church, and her remains were denied Christian sepulture, and were buried in a sand-pit near her own cabin.

On the evening of her burial. the villagers assembled and burned her cabin to the earth. Her daughter made her escape, and never after returned.

The Lady Witch

ABOUT A HUNDRED YEARS AGO there lived a woman in Joyce County, of whom all the neighbours were afraid, for she had always plenty of money, though no one knew how she came by it; and the best of eating and drinking went on at her house, chiefly at night – meat and fowls and Spanish wines in plenty for all comers. And when people asked how it all came, she laughed and said, "I have paid for it," but would tell them no more.

So the word went through the county that she had sold herself to the Evil One, and could have everything she wanted by merely wishing and willing, and because of her riches they called her "The Lady Witch."

She never went out but at night, and then always with a bridle and whip in her hand; and the sound of a horse galloping was heard often far on in the night along the roads near her house.

Then a strange story was whispered about, that if a young man drank of her Spanish wines at supper and afterwards fell asleep, she would throw the bridle over him and change him to a horse, and ride him all over the country, and whatever she touched with her whip became hers. Fowls, or butter, or wine, or the new-made cakes – she had but to wish and will and they were carried by spirit hands to her house, and laid in her larder. Then when the ride was done, and she had gathered enough through the country of all she wanted, she took the bridle off the young man, and he came back to his own shape and fell asleep; and when he awoke he had no knowledge of all that had happened, and the Lady Witch bade him come again and drink of her Spanish wines as often as it pleased him.

Now there was a fine brave young fellow in the neighbourhood, and he determined to make out the truth of the story. So he often went back and forwards, and made friends with the Lady Witch, and sat down to talk to her, but always on the watch. And she took a great fancy to him and told him he must come to supper some night, and she would give him the best of everything, and he must taste her Spanish wine.

So she named the night, and he went gladly, for he was filled with curiosity. And when he arrived there was a beautiful supper laid, and plenty of wine to drink; and he ate and drank, but was cautious about the wine, and spilled it on the ground from his glass when her head was turned away. Then he pretended to be very sleepy, and she said –

"My son, you are weary. Lie down there on the bench and sleep, for the night is far spent, and you are far from your home."

So he lay down as if he were quite dead with sleep, and closed his eyes, but watched her all the time.

And she came over in a little while and looked at him steadily, but he never stirred, only breathed the more heavily.

Then she went softly and took the bridle from the wall, and stole over to fling it over his head; but he started up, and, seizing the bridle, threw it over the woman, who was immediately changed into a spanking grey mare. And he led her out and jumped on her back and rode away as fast as the wind till he came to the forge.

"Ho, smith," he cried, "rise up and shoe my mare, for she is weary after the journey."

And the smith got up and did his work as he was bid, well and strong. Then the young man mounted again, and rode back like the wind to the house of the Witch; and there he took off the bridle, and she immediately regained her own form, and sank down in a deep sleep.

But as the shoes had been put on at the forge without saying the proper form of words, they remained on her hands and feet, and no power on earth could remove them.

So she never rose from her bed again, and died not long after of grief and shame. And not one in the whole country would follow the coffin of the Lady Witch to the grave; and the bridle was burned with fire, and of all her riches nothing was left but a handful of ashes, and this was flung to the four points of earth and the four winds of heaven; so the enchantment was broken and the power of the Evil One ended.

The Witch of Slieu Whallian

IT WAS MIDSUMMER DAY, and the Peel Herring Fleet, with sails half set, was ready for sea. The men had their barley sown, and their potatoes down, and now their boats were rigged and nets stowed on board and they were ready for the harvest of the sea. It was a fine day, the sky was clear and the wind was in the right airt, being from the north. But, as they say, "If custom will not get custom, custom will weep." A basinful of water was brought from the Holy Well and given to the Wise Woman that sold fair winds, as she stood on the harbour-side with the women and children to watch the boats off. They told her to look and tell of the luck of the Herring Fleet. She bent over the water and, as she looked, her face grew pale with fear, and she gasped: "Hurroose, hurroose! An' do ye know what I'm seeing?"

"Let us hear," said they.

> I'm seeing the wild waves lashed to foam away by great Bradda Head,
> I'm seeing the surge round the Chicken's Rock an' the breaker's lip is red;
> I'm seeing where corpses toss in the Sound, with nets an' gear an' spars,
> An' never a one of the Fishing Fleet is riding under the stars.

There was a dead hush, and the men gathered close together, muttering, till Gorry, the Admiral of the Fishing Fleet, stepped forward, caught the basin out of her hands and flung it out to sea, growling:

"Sure as I'm alive, sure as I'm alive, woman, I've more than half a mind to heave you in after it. If I had my way, the like of you an' your crew would be run into the sea. Boys, are we goin' to lose a shot for that bleb? Come on, let's go an' chonce it with the help of God."

"Aye, no herring, no wedding. Let's go an' chonce it," said young Cashen.

So hoisting sails they left the port and when the land was fairly opened out, so that they could see the Calf, they headed for the south and stood out for the Shoulder. Soon a fine breeze put them in the fishing-ground, and every man was looking out for signs of herring – perkins, gannets, fish playing on the surface, oily water, and such like. When the sun was set and the evening was too dark to see the Admiral's Flag, the skipper of each lugger held his arm out at full length, and when he could no longer see the black in his thumb-nail he ordered the men to shoot their nets. And as they lay to their trains it all fell out as the witch had said. Soon the sea put on another face, the wind from westward blew a sudden gale and swelled up the waves with foam. The boats were driven hither and thither, and the anchors dragged quickly behind them. Then the men hoisted sail before the wind and struggled to get back to land, and the lightning was all the light they had. It was so black dark that they could see no hill, and above the uproar of the sea they could hear the surges pounding on the rocky coast. The waves were rising like mountains, breaking over the boats and harrying them from stem to stern. They were dashed to pieces on the rocks of the Calf, and only two men escaped with their lives.

But there was one boat that had got safe back to port before the storm, and that was the boat of the Seven Boys. She was a Dalby boat and belonged to seven young men who were all unmarried. They were always good to the Dooinney Marrey, the Merman, and when they were hauling their nets they would throw him a dishful of herring, and in return they had always good luck with their fishing. This night, after the Fleet had shot their nets sometime, the night being still fine and calm, the Seven Boys heard the voice of the Merman hailing them and saying:

"It is calm and fine now; there will be storm enough soon!"

When the Skipper heard this he said: "Every herring must hang by its own gills," and he and his crew at once put their nets on board and gained the harbour. And it was given for law ever after that no crew was to be made up of single men only; there was to be at least one married man on board and no man was bound by his hiring to fish in this same south sea, which was called 'The Sea of Blood' from that day.

As for the witch, they said she had raised the storm by her spells and they took her to the top of the great mountain Slieu Whallian, put her into a spiked barrel and rolled her from the top to the bottom, where the barrel sank into the bog. For many and many a long year there was a bare track down the steep mountain-side, where grass would never grow, nor ling, nor gorse. They called it 'The Witch's Way,' and they say that her screams are heard in the air every year on the day she was put to death.

The Witches of Delnabo

IN THE TIME OF MY GRANDMOTHER, the farm of Delnabo was proportionally divided between three tenants. At first equally comfortable in their circumstances, it was in the course of some time remarked by all, and by none more forcibly than by one of the said three portioners, that, although superior in point of industry and talent to his two fellow-portioners, one of the tenants was daily lapsing into poverty, while his two neighbours were daily improving in estate. Amazed and grieved at the adverse fortune which thus attended his family, compared to the prosperous condition of his neighbours, the wife of the poor man was in the habit of expressing her astonishment at the circumstance, not only to her own particular friends, but likewise to the wives of her neighbours themselves.

On one of these occasions, the other two wives asked her what would she do to ameliorate her condition, if it were in her power? She answered them she would do anything whatever. (Here the other wives thought they had got a gudgeon that would snap at any bait, and immediately resolved to make her their confidante.) "Well, then," says one of the other two wives, "if you agree to keep our communications strictly secret, and implicitly obey our instructions, neither poverty nor want shall ever assail you more." This speech of the other wife immediately impressed the poor man's wife with a strong suspicion of their real character. Dissembling all surprise at the circumstance, she promised to agree to all their conditions. She was then directed, when she went to bed that night, to carry along with her the floor broom, well known for its magical properties, which she was to leave by her husband's side in the course of the night, and which would represent her so exactly that the husband could not distinguish the difference in the morning. They at the same time enjoined her to discard all fears of detection, as their own husbands had been satisfied with those lovely substitutes (the brooms) for a great number of years. Matters being thus arranged, she was desired to join them at the hour of midnight, in order to accompany them to that scene which was to realise her future happiness.

Promising to attend to their instructions, the poor man's wife took leave of her neighbours, full of those sensations of horror which the discovery of such depravity was calculated to produce in a virtuous mind. Hastening home to her husband, she thought it no crime to break her promise to her wicked neighbours, and, like a dutiful and prudent wife, to reveal to the husband of her bosom the whole particulars of their interview. The husband greatly commended his wife's fidelity, and immediately entered into a collusion with her, which displays no ordinary degree of ingenuity. It was agreed that the husband should exchange apparel with the wife, and that he should, in this disguise, accompany the wives to the place appointed, to see what cantrips they intended to perform.

He accordingly arrayed himself in his wife's habiliments, and, at the hour of midnight, joined the party at the place appointed. The "bride," as they called him, was most cordially received by the two Ladies of the Broom, who warmly congratulated the "bride" upon her good fortune, and the speedy consummation of her happiness. He was then presented with a fir torch, a broom, and a riddle, articles with which they themselves were furnished. They directed their course along the banks of the rolling Avon, until they reached Craic-pol-nain, or the Craig of the Birdspool. Here, in consequence of the steepness of the craig, they found it convenient to pass to the other side of the river. This passage they effected without the use of the navy, the river being fordable at the place. They then came in sight of Pol-nain, and lo! what human eye ever witnessed such a scene before! The pool appeared as if actually enveloped in a flame of fire. A hundred torches blazed aloft, reflecting their beams on the towering woods of Loynchork. And what ear ever beard such shrieks and yells as proceeded from the horrid crew engaged at their hellish orgies on Pol-nain? Those cries were, however, sweet music to the two wives of Delnabo. Every yell produced from them a burst of unrestrained pleasure, and away they frisked, leaving the amiable bride a considerable way behind. For the fact is, that he was in no hurry to reach the scene, and when he did reach it, it was with a determination to be only a spectator, and not a participator in the night's performance. On reaching the pool's side he saw what was going on – he saw abundance of hags steering themselves to and fro in their riddles, by means of their oars (the brooms), hallooing and skirling worse than the bogles, and each holding in her left hand a torch of fir – whilst at other times they would swirl themselves into a row, and make profound obeisance to a large black ugly tyke, perched on a lofty rock, and who was no doubt the "muckle thief" himself, and who was pleased to acknowledge most graciously those expressions of their loyalty and devotion, by bowing, grinning, and clapping his paws. Having administered to the bride some preliminary instructions, the impatient wives desired him to remain by the pool's side until they should commune with his Satanic Highness on the subject of her inauguration, directing her, as they proceeded on their voyage across the pool, to speed them in their master's name. To this order of the black pair the bride was resolved to pay particular attention. As soon as they were embarked in their riddles, and had wriggled themselves, by means of their brooms, into a proper depth of water, "Go," says he, "in the name of the Best." A horrid yell from the witches announced their instant fate – the magic spell was now dissolved – crash went the riddles, and down sank the two witches, never more to rise, amidst the shrieks and lamentations of the Old Thief and all his infernal crew, whose combined power and policy could not save them from a watery end. All the torches were extinguished in an instant, and the affrighted company fled in different directions, in such forms and similitudes as they thought most convenient for them to adopt; and the wily bride returned home at his leisure, enjoying himself vastly at the clever manner in which he had executed the instructions of his deceased friends. On arriving at his house, he dressed himself in his own clothes, and, without immediately satisfying his wife's curiosity at the result of his excursion, he yoked his cattle, and commenced his morning labours with as little concern as usual. His two neighbours, who were not even conscious of the absence of their wives (so ably substituted were they by the brooms), did the same. Towards breakfast-time, however, the two neighbours were not a little astonished that they observed no signs of their wives having risen from bed – notwithstanding their customary earliness – and this surprise they expressed to the late bride, their neighbour. The latter archly remarked that he had great suspicions, in his own mind, of their rising even that day. "What mean you by that?" replied they. "We left our wives apparently in good health when we ourselves arose." "Find them now," was the reply – the bride, setting up as merry a whistle as before. Running each to his bed, what was the astonishment of the husbands, when, instead of his wife, he only found an old broom? Their neighbour then told them that, if they chose to examine Pol-nain well, they would find both their dear doxies there. The grieving husbands accordingly proceeded thither, and with the necessary instruments dragged their late worthy partners to dry land, and afterwards privately interred them. The shattered vessels and oars of those unfortunate navigators, whirling about the pool, satisfied their lords of the manner by which they came to their ends; and their names were no longer mentioned by their kindred in the land. It need scarcely be added that the poor man gradually recovered his former opulence; and that, in the course of a short time, he was comparatively as rich as he was formerly poor.

The Old Witch

ONCE UPON A TIME there were two girls who lived with their mother and father. Their father had no work, and the girls wanted to go away and seek their fortunes. Now one girl wanted to go to service, and her mother said she might if she could find a place. So she started for the town. Well, she went all about the town, but no one wanted a girl like her. So she went on farther into the country, and she came to the place where there was an oven where there was lots of bread baking. And the bread said, "Little girl, little girl, take us out, take us out. We have been baking seven years, and no one has come to take us out." So the girl took out the bread, laid it on the ground, and went on her way. Then she met a cow, and the cow said, "Little girl, little girl, milk me, milk me! Seven years have I been waiting, and no one has come to milk me." The girl milked the cow into the pails that stood by. As she was thirsty she drank some, and left the rest in the pails by the cow. Then she went on a little bit farther, and came to an apple tree, so loaded with fruit that its branches were breaking down, and the tree said, "Little girl, little girl, help me shake my fruit. My branches are breaking, it is so heavy." And the girl said, "Of course I will, you poor tree." So she shook the fruit all off, propped up the branches, and left the fruit on the ground under the tree. Then she went on again till she came to a house. Now in this house there lived a witch, and this witch took girls into her house as servants. And when she heard that this girl had left her home to seek service, she said that she would try her, and give her good wages. The witch told the girl what work she was to do. "You must keep the house clean and tidy, sweep the floor and the fireplace; but there is one thing you must never do. You must never look up the chimney, or something bad will befall you."

So the girl promised to do as she was told, but one morning as she was cleaning, and the witch was out, she forgot what the witch said, and looked up the chimney. When she did this a great bag of money fell down in her lap. This happened again and again. So the girl started to go off home.

When she had gone some way she heard the witch coming after her. So she ran to the apple tree and cried:

> "Apple-tree, apple-tree hide me,
> So the old witch can't find me;
> If she does she'll pick my bones,
> And bury me under the marble stones."

So the apple-tree hid her. When the witch came up she said:

> *"Tree of mine, tree of mine,*
> *Have you seen a girl*
> *With a willy-willy wag, and a long-tailed bag,*
> *Who's stole my money, all I had?"*

And the apple-tree said, "No, mother; not for seven year."

When the witch had gone down another way, the girl went on again, and just as she got to the cow heard the witch coming after her again, so she ran to the cow and cried:

> *"Cow, cow, hide me,*
> *So the old witch can't find me;*
> *If she does she'll pick my bones,*
> *And bury me under the marble stones."*

So the cow hid her.

When the old witch came up, she looked about and said to the cow:

> *"Cow of mine, cow of mine,*
> *Have you seen a girl*
> *With a willy-willy wag, and a long-tailed bag,*
> *Who's stole my money, all I had?"*

And the cow said, "No, mother, not for seven year."

When the witch had gone off another way, the little girl went on again, and when she was near the oven she heard the witch coming after her again, so she ran to the oven and cried:

> *"Oven, oven, hide me,*
> *So the old witch can't find me;*
> *If she does she'll break my bones,*
> *And bury me under the marble stones."*

And the oven said, "I've no room, ask the baker," and the baker hid her behind the oven.

When the witch came up she looked here and there and everywhere, and then said to the baker:

> *"Man of mine, man of mine,*
> *Have you seen a girl,*
> *With a willy-willy wag, and a long-tailed bag,*
> *Who's stole my money, all I had?"*

So the baker said, "Look in the oven." The old witch went to look, and the oven said, "Get in and look in the furthest corner." The witch did so, and when she was inside the oven shut her door, and the witch was kept there for a very long time.

The girl then went off again, and reached her home with her money bags, married a rich man, and lived happy ever afterwards.

The other sister then thought she would go and do the same. And she went the same way. But when she reached the oven, and the bread said, "Little girl, little girl, take us out. Seven years have we been baking, and no one has come to take us out," the girl said, "No, I don't want to burn my fingers." So she went on till she met the cow, and the cow said, "Little girl, little girl, milk me, milk me, do. Seven years have I been waiting, and no one has come to milk me." But the girl said, "No, I can't milk you, I'm in a hurry," and went on faster. Then she came to the apple-tree, and the apple-tree asked her to help shake the fruit. "No, I can't; another day p'raps I may," and went on till she came to the witch's house. Well, it happened to her just the same as to the other girl – she forgot what she was told, and one day when the witch was out, looked up the chimney, and down fell a bag of money. Well, she thought she would be off at once. When she reached the apple-tree, she heard the witch coming after her, and she cried:

"Apple-tree, apple-tree, hide me,
So the old witch can't find me;
If she does she'll break my bones,
And bury me under the marble stones."

But the tree didn't answer, and she ran on further. Presently the witch came up and said:

"Tree of mine, tree of mine,
Have you seen a girl,
With a willy-willy wag, and a long-tailed bag,
Who's stole my money, all I had?"

The tree said, "Yes, mother; she's gone down that way."

So the old witch went after her and caught her, she took all the money away from her, beat her, and sent her off home just as she was.

Circe and the Island of Aeaea

IN GREEK MYTHOLOGY, the Odyssey describes Odysseus's voyage back to Ithaca following the Trojan War. Odysseus and his men faced numerous challenges on their epic journey home, including an attack by the cannibalistic Laestrygonians that destroyed eleven of their twelve ships. Odysseus and his remaining men fled to safety aboard the sole surviving vessel, rowing furiously for two days in search of safe harbour. Eventually they reached the shores of another island, where they collapsed, and it is here that we pick up their story...

For nearly two days the men slept on the shores of the unknown island, drinking in the peacefulness which covered them like a blanket, coming to terms with the loss of their comrades in their dreams. They woke freshened, but wary, eager to explore the land, but made prudent by their misadventures. In the distance, smoke curled lethargically into the windless sky. The island was inhabited, but by whom?

Odysseus divided the group into two camps, one taken by himself, the other led by his lieutenant, the courageous and loyal warrior Eurylochus. They drew lots from a helmet, and so it was decreed that Eurylochus would lead his party into the forest, towards the signs of life. His men gathered themselves up, and brushed off their clothes, trembling with anticipation and fear. They moved off.

The path wound its way through the tree-clad island, drawing the men into the bosom of the hills. There, at its centre, was a roughly hewn cottage, chimney smoking, and no sign of danger. Its fine stone walls were guarded by wolves and lions, but they leapt playfully towards the explorers, licking them and wagging their tails. Confused but comforted by the welcome, the men drew forward, and soon were enticed by the exquisite melody which drifted from the cottage. A woman's voice rang out, pure and sweet, calming their hearts, and drying the sweat on their brows. They moved forward confidently, only Eurylochus hanging back in caution.

They were greeted by the figure of a beautiful woman, whose hair tumbled to her heels, whose eyes were two green jewels in an ivory facade. Her smile was benevolent, welcoming, her arms outstretched. The men stumbled over one another to greet her, and were led into the cavernous depths of the cottage, where tables groaned with luxurious morsels of food – candied fruits, roasted spiced meats, plump vegetables and glazed breads, tumbling from platters of silver and gold. Wines and juices glistened in frosted glasses, and a barrel of fine brandy dripped into platinum goblets. It was a feast beyond compare, and the aroma enveloped the men, drawing them forward. They ate and drank while Eurylochus waited uncomfortably, outside the gates. And after many hours, when the men had taken their fill, they sat back with smiles of contentment, of satisfied gluttony, and raised their eyes in gratitude to their hostess.

"Who are you, fine woman?" slurred one of the crewman, made bold by the spirits.

"I am Circe," she whispered back. And with a broad sweep of her hand, and a cry of laughter which startled her guests, drawing them from their stupor, she shouted, "And you are but swine, like all men."

Circe was a great and beautiful enchantress, living alone on this magical island where all visitors were pampered and fed with a charmed repast until Circe grew bored with them. And then, stroking their stupid heads, Circe would make them beasts. Now, she raised her mighty hands and laid them down upon the heads of Eurylochus's men and turned them to swine, corralling them snuffling and grunting through the door. Eurylochus peered round a tree in dismay. Ten men had entered, and now ten pigs left. The enchantress followed them, penning them in sties and stopping to speak gently to the other beasts, who had once been men. Happily she returned to her cottage and took up her loom once more.

Eurylochus sprinted through the forest, breathless with fear and disbelief as he rejoined Odysseus and the crew. Odysseus drew himself up, and a determined look transformed his distinguished features. He reached for his sword, and thrusting a dagger in his belt he set off to rescue his men, turning his head heavenwards and praying for assistance from the very gods who had spurned him. Odysseus had suffered the insults of war, and the tortures of their perilous journey. He would fight for his men, for his depleted crew. No woman, enchantress or not, would outwit him, would take from him his few remaining men.

As he struggled through the forest, a youth stumbled across his path.

"Here," he whispered. "Take this." And he thrust into the hands of Odysseus a divine herb known as Moly, a plant with black roots and a snow white flower so beautiful that only those with celestial hands had the strength to pluck it. Moly was an antidote against the spells of Circe, and with this in his possession, Odysseus would be safe. The boy, who was really the god Hermes, sent by the goddess Athene, warned Odysseus of Circe's magical powers, and offered him a plan.

And so it was that Odysseus reached the cottage of Circe, and entered its welcoming gates. There the same feast greeted him, and he partook of the food until he lay sleepy and sated. Circe could hardly disguise her glee at the ease with which she had trapped this new traveller, and as she waved her wand to change him into a pig, Odysseus rose and spoke.

"Your magic has no power over me," he said, and he thrust her to the ground at the point of his sword. She trembled with fear, and with longing.

"You," she breathed, "you must be the brave Odysseus, come from far to be my loving friend." And she threw down her wand and took the soldier into her warm embrace. They lay together for a night of love, and in the morning, spent yet invigorated by their carnal feast they rose to set free Odysseus's men.

And there, on the enchanted island of Circe, Odysseus and his men spent days which stretched into golden weeks and then years, fed from the platters laden with food, their glasses poured over with drink, resting and growing fat, until they had forgotten the tortures of their journey. Odysseus was charmed by the lovely Circe, and all thoughts of Penelope and Telemachus were chased from his mind. His body was numbed by the pleasures inflicted upon it.

But the great Odysseus was a supreme leader, and even pure indulgence could not blunt his keen mind forever. As his senses gradually cleared, as Circe's powers over his body, over his soul began to wane, he felt the first rush of homesickness, of longing for Ithaca and his family. And in his heart he began to feel the weight of his responsibilities, the burden of his obligations to his country, to his men and to the gods.

With that, he made secret plans for their escape, and as the enchantment began also to wear at the sanity of his men, as they grew tired of the hedonism which filled their every waking hour, they became party to his strategy. With that, he went in search of Circe.

The House of Hades

Odysseus found the enchantress Circe in a calm and equable mood. She loved Odysseus, who had warmed her heart and her bed, but she had known since first setting eyes on the great warrior that he could never be completely hers. This day had been long in coming, but now that it was upon her, she gave him her blessing.

There were, however, tasks to be undertaken before Odysseus could be freed. He and his men could not voyage to Ithaca until they had met with the ghost of the blind prophet Tiresias, wiser than any dead or alive. They must travel to him at Hades, bringing gifts to sacrifice to the powers of the Underworld. Whitened by fear the men agreed to journey with Odysseus, to learn their fate and to receive instructions for their return to Ithaca.

All his men, spare one, prepared themselves for the voyage, but Elpenor, the youngest of the crew, lay sleeping on the roof of the cottage, where he'd stumbled in a drunken stupor the previous night. He woke to see the ship and his comrades setting sail from the island of Circe, and forgetting himself, he tumbled to the ground where he met an instant and silent death.

The men pressed on, unaware that one of their lot was missing. They sailed through a fair wind, raised by Circe, and as darkness drew itself around them, they entered the deep waters of Oceanus, where the Cimmerians lived in eternal night. There the rivers Phlegethon, Cocytus and Styx converged beneath a great rock, and Odysseus and his men drew aground. Following Circe's instructions, they dug a deep well in the earth beside the rock, then they cut the throats of a ram and a ewe, allowing their virgin blood to fill the trough.

The ghosts of the departed began to gather round the blood, some in battle-stained garb, others lost and confused; they struggled up to the pit and fought for a drink. Odysseus drew his sword to hold back the swelling crowd, startled as Elpenor, pale and blood-spattered, greeted his former master. He pressed forward, moaning and reaching greedily for the mortals.

"I have no grave," he uttered. "I cannot rest." He clung to Odysseus whose cold stare belied the anxiety that pressed down on his heart. He was too close to the wretched creatures of the Underworld, near enough to be dragged down with them. He shook Elpenor loose.

"I will build you a grave," he said gruffly. "A fine grave with a tomb. There your ashes will lay and you shall have peace."

Elpenor pulled back at once, a bemused expression crossing his pale face. He slid away, as reaching arms grappled into the space he left. Faces blended together in a grotesque dance of the macabre, writhing bodies struggling to catch a glimpse of mortals, of the other side. Familiar features appeared and then disappeared, as Odysseus fought to keep control of his senses.

"Odysseus," the voice was soft, crooning. How often he'd heard it, sheltered in the tender arms of its bearer, rocked, adored. Mother.

Anticleia had been alive when he'd sailed for Troy and until this moment he knew not of her death. He longed to reach out for her, to take her pale and withered body against his own, to provide her with the comfort she had so tenderly invested in him.

But his duties prodded at his conscience, and he pricked his sword at her, edging her away from him, searching the tumultuous mass for Tiresias. At last he appeared from the shadowy depths, stopping to drink deeply from the bloody sacrifice. He leaned against his golden staff, and spoke slowly, in a language mellowed with age.

"Odysseus," Tiresias said. "Thy homecoming will not be easy. Poseidon bears spite against thee for blinding his Cyclops son Polyphemus. Yet you have guardians, and all may go well still, if, when you reach the hallowed shores of Trinacrian, ye harm not the herds of the Sun that pasture there. Control thy men, Odysseus. Allow not the greed that has tainted their hearts, that has led you astray, to shadow your journey."

He paused, drinking again from the trenches and shrugging aside the groping arms of his comrades. He spat into the pool of blood.

"If you slay them, Odysseus, you will bring death upon your men, wreckage to your ships, and if you do escape, you will find thy house in trouble, no glory in your homecoming. And in the end, death will come to thee from the sea, from the great Poseidon." With that, Tiresias leaned heavily on his staff and stumbled away, calling out as he left, "Mark my words, brave Odysseus. My sight is not hampered by the darkness."

Odysseus sat down and pondered the blind man's words. Anticleia appeared once again and he beckoned her closer, coaxed her to drink, and with the power invested in her by the blood, she drew a deep breath and spoke. She asked eagerly of his news, and told of her own, how she had died of grief thinking him dead at Troy. But his father, Laertes, she said, was still alive, though weakened by despair and feeble in his old age. Penelope his wife waited for him, loyal despite the attentions of many suitors. And Telemachus had become a man, grown tall and strong like his father.

Odysseus was torn by the sight of his mother, knowing not when he would set eyes on her again. He reached out to touch her, but she shrank from his embrace, a vision only, no substance, no warm blood coursing through her veins. He stood abruptly and was thronged by the clambering dead, as his mother drifted from his sight. He called after her, but she had gone.

Many of his comrades from Troy appeared now, eager to see the fine Odysseus, curious about his presence in Hades without having suffered the indignity of death. There was Agamemnon, and again, Achilles, whose stature was diminished, whose glory had tarnished. Ajax was there, and Tantalus and Sisyphus reached out to him, howling with anguish. And then there was

Minos, and Orion, and Heracles, great men once, ghostly spectres now. They circled him and he felt chilled by their emptiness, by their singleness, by their determination to possess him. He turned away and strode from the group, shaking with the effort.

And his men joined him there, as they rowed away from that perilous island, down the Ocean river and back to the open sea. The friendly winds tossed them back to Circe's island, where the enchantress awaited them. Their belongings were ready, and she had resigned herself to the loss of her great love. She pulled Odysseus to one side, stroking him until he stiffened with pleasure, tempted as always to remain with her, enjoyed and enjoying. She whispered in his ear, warning him of the hazards which stood between Aeaea and Ithaca, the perils of his course. And he kissed her deeply and with a great surge of confidence, pushed her aside and went to meet his men.

Together they uncovered the body of poor Elpenor, and burned it with great ceremony, placing his ashes in a grand and sturdy tomb. Their duty done, they looked towards home.

And so it was that Odysseus escaped the fires of Hades, and the clutches of the shrewd Circe, and found himself heading once more towards Ithaca and home, the warnings of Circe and Tiresias echoing in his ears. As chance would have it, the first of the dangers lay just across the shimmering sea.

Calypso's Island

LATER IN ITS JOURNEY BACK TO ITHACA, Odysseus's ship was destroyed by a violent tempest created by Poseidon. Odysseus was the sole survivor of the great storm and was left clinging to the wreckage of the ship for nine days before eventually being washed ashore on the island of Ogygia…

Odysseus could see land and in the distance a beautiful nymph, the most beautiful woman on whom he had ever laid eyes. Her milk-white skin was gleaming in the moonlight, and the wrathful winds tossed her silken hair. Her voice was soft, inviting above the raging storms.

"Come to me, Odysseus," she whispered. "Here you will find love, and eternal life."

Odysseus struggled for breath, filled with longing and wonder. She reached a slender hand towards him, across the expanse of water, and lifted him from its depths, the strength of her grip, the length of her reach inhuman. He shuddered at her touch.

"You have come to join me," she said calmly, as Odysseus laid restless and dripping beneath her.

Odysseus nodded, his passion spent. He was alive. The others had been clutched by the revengeful Poseidon. He was grateful to this nymph. He would plan his escape later.

"I have asked for you, and you have come," she intoned quietly, settling herself at his side. Odysseus felt the first stirring of fear, but dismissed it as the lovely maiden smiled down on him.

She was Calypso, the lovely daughter of Thetis, and like Circe she was an enchantress. She lived alone on the island, in a comfortable cavern overhung by vines and fragrant foliage. She was gentle, and quiet, tending to Odysseus's every need, feeding him with morsels of delicious foods, warming him with handspun garments which clung to his body like a new skin, and she welcomed him in her bed, running his body over with hot hands that explored and relaxed the beaten hero until he grew to love her, and to build his life with her on the idyllic island.

For seven years he lived with Calypso, drunk with luxury and love. She was more beautiful than any he had seen before, and her island was dripping with pleasures. And as his happiness grew deeper, his fire and fervour spent to become a peaceful equilibrium, he felt the jab of conscience, of something untoward eating at the corners of his idyll, and he realized that he was living in a numb oblivion, that his passion to return home, to see his family, to take up the responsibilities of his leadership, were as strong in him as they had ever been and that he must allow them to surge forth, to fill him again with fiery ambition.

And in that seventh year he spent more and more time seated on the banks of the island, gazing towards his own land where time did not stand still and where his wife's suitors were threatening to take over his country, his rule. He came eventually to the notice of Athene, whose favour he had kept despite the outrage of the other gods, and she went at once to Zeus on his behalf. Zeus was fair and kind, and he balanced the sins of Odysseus against his innate good will, and the struggles to keep in check his unruly crews, all of which were lost to him now. Poseidon was away from Olympus and the time seemed right to set Odysseus free, for he had lived long enough in an enchanted purgatory.

Calypso reluctantly agreed to allow him his freedom, and she provided him with the tools to create a sturdy boat, and with provisions of food and drink enough to last the entire journey. She bathed him, dressed him in fine silks and jewels, as befitted a returning warrior, and kissing him gently but with all the fire of her love for him, she bade him go, with a tear-stained farewell. She had provided him with instructions which would see him round the dangers, across the perils that could beset him. He set sail for Ithaca.

Perseus and the Gorgon

THERE ONCE WAS A TROUBLED KING who learned, through an Oracle, that he would reach his death through the hand of his own grandson. This king was Acrisius, king of Argos, and he had only one child, the fair Danae. Acrisius shut her away in a cave, in order to keep her unwedded, and there she grew older, and more beautiful, as time passed. No man could reach her, although many tried, and eventually word of her beauty reached the gods, and finally the king of the Gods himself, Zeus.

He entered her prison in a cascade of light, and planted in her womb the seed of the gods, and from this the infant Perseus was spawned. Acrisius heard the infant's cries, and unable to kill him outright, he released Danae from her prison, and with her child she was placed on a raft, and sent out on the stormy seas to meet their death.

Now Poseidon knew of Zeus's child, and calmed the seas, lifting the mother and child carefully to the island of Seriphos, where they washed onto safe shores. They were discovered there by a kind fisherman, who brought them to his home. It was in this humble and peaceful abode that Perseus grew up, a boy of effortless intelligence, cunning and nobility. He was a sportsman beyond compare, and a hero among his playmates. He was visited in his dreams by Athene, the goddess of war, who filled his head with lusty ambition and inspired him to seek danger and excitement.

The fisherman became a father figure to Perseus, but another schemed to take his place. The fisherman's brother Polydectes, chief of the island, was besotted by the beautiful Danae, and longed to have her for his wife. He showered her with priceless jewels, succulent morsels of food, rich fabrics and furs, but her heart belonged to Perseus, and she refused his attentions. Embittered, he resolved to dispose of the youth, and set Perseus a task at which he could not help but fail, and from which no mortal man could ever return.

The task was to slay the creature Medusa, one of the three Gorgon sisters. Medusa was the only mortal of the Gorgons, with a face so hideous, so repulsive, that any man who laid eyes on her would be turned to stone before he could attack. Her hair was a nest of vipers, which writhed around that flawed and fatal face. Perseus was enthralled by the idea of performing an act of such bravery and that night, as he slept, he summoned again the goddess Athene, who provided him with the tools by which the task could be shouldered.

Athene came to him, a glorious figure of war, and with her she brought Hermes, her brother, who offered the young man powerful charms with which he could make his way. Perseus was provided with Hermes own crooked sword, sturdy enough to cut through even the strongest armour, and Perseus's feet were fitted with winged sandals, by which he could make his escape. From Hades he received a helmet which had the power to make its wearer invisible. Athene offered her mirrored shield, which would allow Perseus to strike Medusa without seeing her horrible face. Finally, he was given a skin bag, to carry the Gorgon's head from the site.

Perseus set out the next morning, his first assignment to find the half-sisters of the Gorgons, in the icy wilderness of the northern steppes of Graiae. They alone could provide him with the whereabouts of Medusa. With the aid of his winged sandals, Perseus flew north, till he came to the frosted mists of the mountains. There the earth was so cold, a fabulous crack was rent across her surface. The land was barren, icy, empty, and although he felt no fear, Perseus had to struggle to carry on, his breath frozen on his lips. There, on the edge of the Hyperborean sea were the Gray Sisters, witches from another era who had come there to end their days, wreaking a wretched existence from the snow-capped mountains, toothless and haggard with age. They had but one eye between them, and one tooth, without which they would surely have died.

Perseus chose his moment carefully, and lunged into their midst, grasping their single eye, and stepping out of reach.

"I require your assistance," he said firmly. "I must know the way to the Gorgons. If you cannot help me I shall take your tooth as well, and you shall starve in this wilderness."

The Gray Sisters swayed and muttered, lolling upon the snow and fumbling across its icy surface towards the awe-inspiring voice.

A cry rose up when they realized that he had their eye, and they threatened and cursed Perseus, their howls echoing in the blackness of the wasteland. Finally, they succumbed, the fear of blindness in that empty place enlivening their tongues, loosening their resolve. Perseus graciously returned their eye, and on a breath of Arctic air, he rose and headed southwards, out of sight of the sisters, who struggled to see their tormentor.

Back through the mists he flew, where the sea sent spirals of spray that lashed at his heels and tried to drag him down. On he went, and the snows melted away into a sea so blue he seemed enveloped in it. The sky grew bright, the grass of the fields green and inviting, and as he flew he grew hotter, his eyes heavy with exhaustion, his perfect skin dripping with effort. The other end of the world rose up, a land and a sea where no human dared enter, a land of burning heat, of fiery hatred and fear, where none lived but the Gorgons themselves, surrounded by the hapless stone statues of man and beast who had dared to look upon them.

He came across the sisters as they slept in the midday sun. Medusa lay between her sisters, who protectively laid their arms across her mass. Her body was scaled and repellent, her limbs clawed and gnarled. Perseus dared look no further, but from the corner of his eye he saw the coiling vipers, and the serpent's tongue which even in sleep darted from her razor-sharp lips. Her fearsome eyes were shut. He was safe.

With one decisive movement he plunged himself and his sword towards this creature, Athene's shield held high. And Medusa's answering howl pierced the air, ripping the breath from his lungs, and dragging him down towards her. He struggled to maintain his composure, shivering and drawn to look at the source of this violent cry. He fell on her, shaking his head to clear it, fighting the temptation to give in. And then the courage that was deep inside him, born within him, the gift of his father Zeus, redeemed him. He lifted his head, and with shield held high, thrust his sword in one wild swoop that lopped off the head of Medusa.

He packed it hastily in his bag, and leapt up, away from the arms of the Sisters Gorgon who had woken abruptly, and now hissed and struck out at him. The Gorgons were not human, and could not, like Medusa, be slain by humans. They rose on wings, like murderous vultures, yowling and gnashing their teeth, screaming of revenge.

But Perseus had disappeared. His helmet took him from their side, enshrouded him with a curtain that protected him from their eyes. He was safe.

For days on end he flew with his booty, across the desert, where the dripping blood of Medusa hit the sand and bred evil vipers and venomous snakes, ever to populate the sunburnt earth. The Gorgons flew behind him, a whirlwind of hatred and revenge, but Perseus soared above them, until he was safe, at the edge of his world.

He came to rest at the home of Atlas, the giant, who held up with great pillars the weight of the sky. He begged for a place to lay his weary head, for sustenance and water. But the giant refused him. Tired and angry, Perseus thrust his hand into his bag and drew out the monstrous head. To this day, Atlas stands, a stone giant holding up the skies, his head frosted with snow, his face frozen with horror.

And Perseus flew on, although it was several months and many more challenges before he was able to present his trophy. But his travels are another story, involving passion, bravery and an ultimate battle. He would meet Polydectes once again, would defend his hostage mother, and face his long-lost grandfather. He would make his own mark at Olympus, and become, eventually, a bright star, a divine beacon which would guide courageous wanderers, as he had once been.

How the Argonauts Sailed to Colchis

N THE STORY OF JASON AND THE ARGONAUTS, Jason was charged with a quest to find he Golden Fleece. Along with his gallant crew, who are named the Argonauts after the ship upon which they sailed, the adventurers would face great foes and tremendous adversities as they sought the fabled fleece. We pick up their story shortly after the Argo is launched from Iolcos...

And what happened next, whether it be true or not, stands written in ancient songs. And grand old songs they are, written in grand old rolling verse; and they call them the Songs of Orpheus, or the Orphics, to this day. And they tell how the heroes came to Aphetai, across the bay, and waited for the south-west wind, and chose themselves a captain from their crew: and how all called for Heracles, because he was the strongest and most huge; but Heracles refused, and called for Jason, because he was the wisest of them all. So Jason was chosen captain; and Orpheus heaped a pile of wood, and slew a bull, and offered it to Hera, and called all the heroes to stand round, each man's head crowned with olive, and to strike their swords into the bull. Then he filled a golden goblet with the bull's blood, and with wheaten flour, and honey, and wine, and the bitter salt-sea water, and bade the heroes taste. So each tasted the goblet, and passed it round, and vowed an awful vow: and they vowed before the sun, and the night, and the blue-haired sea who shakes the land, to stand by Jason faithfully in the adventure of the golden fleece; and whosoever shrank back, or disobeyed, or turned traitor to his vow, then justice should minister against him, and the Erinnues who track guilty men.

Then Jason lighted the pile, and burnt the carcase of the bull; and they went to their ship and sailed eastward, like men who have a work to do; and the place from which they went was called Aphetai, the sailing-place, from that day forth. Three thousand years and more they sailed away, into the unknown Eastern seas; and great nations have come and gone since then, and many a storm has swept the earth; and many a mighty armament, to which *Argo* would be but one small boat; English and French, Turkish and Russian, have sailed those waters since; yet the fame of that small *Argo* lives for ever, and her name is become a proverb among men.

So they sailed past the Isle of Sciathos, with the Cape of Sepius on their left, and turned to the northward toward Pelion, up the long Magnesian shore. On their right hand was the open sea, and on their left old Pelion rose, while the clouds crawled round his dark pine-forests, and his caps of summer snow. And their hearts yearned for the dear old mountain, as they thought of pleasant days gone by, and of the sports of their boyhood, and their hunting, and their schooling in the cave beneath the cliff. And at last Peleus spoke, "Let us land here, friends, and climb the dear old hill once more. We are going on a fearful journey; who knows if we shall see Pelion again? Let us go up to Cheiron our master, and ask his blessing ere we start. And I have a boy, too, with him, whom he trains as he trained me once – the son whom Thetis brought me, the silver-footed lady of the sea, whom I caught in the cave, and tamed her, though she changed her shape seven times. For she changed, as I held her, into water, and to vapour, and to burning flame, and to a rock, and to a black-maned lion, and to a tall and stately tree. But I held her and held her ever, till she took her own shape again, and led her to my father's house, and won her for my bride. And all the rulers of Olympus came to our wedding, and the heavens and the earth rejoiced together, when an Immortal wedded mortal man. And now let me see my son; for it is not often I shall see him upon earth: famous he will be, but short-lived, and die in the flower of youth."

So Tiphys the helmsman steered them to the shore under the crags of Pelion; and they went up through the dark pine-forests towards the Centaur's cave.

And they came into the misty hall, beneath the snow-crowned crag; and saw the great Centaur lying, with his huge limbs spread upon the rock; and beside him stood Achilles, the child whom no steel could wound, and played upon his harp right sweetly, while Cheiron watched and smiled.

Then Cheiron leapt up and welcomed them, and kissed them every one, and set a feast before them of swine's flesh, and venison, and good wine; and young Achilles served them, and carried the golden goblet round. And after supper all the heroes clapped their hands, and called on Orpheus to sing; but he refused, and said, "How can I, who am the younger, sing before our ancient host?" So they called on Cheiron to sing, and Achilles brought him his harp; and he began a wondrous song; a famous story of old time, of the fight between the Centaurs and the Lapithai, which you may still see carved in stone. He sang how his brothers came to ruin by their folly, when they were mad with wine; and how they and the heroes fought, with fists, and teeth, and the goblets from which they drank; and how they tore up the pine-trees in their fury, and hurled great crags of stone, while the mountains thundered with the battle, and the land was wasted far and wide; till the Lapithai drove them from their home in the rich Thessalian plains to the lonely glens of Pindus, leaving Cheiron all alone. And the heroes praised his song right heartily; for some of them had helped in that great fight.

Then Orpheus took the lyre, and sang of Chaos, and the making of the wondrous World, and how all things sprang from Love, who could not live alone in the Abyss. And as he sang, his voice rose from the cave, above the crags, and through the tree-tops, and the glens of oak and pine. And the trees bowed their heads when they heard it, and the grey rocks cracked and rang, and the forest beasts crept near to listen, and the birds forsook their nests and hovered round. And old Cheiron claps his hands together, and beat his hoofs upon the ground, for wonder at that magic song.

Then Peleus kissed his boy, and wept over him, and they went down to the ship; and Cheiron came down with them, weeping, and kissed them one by one, and blest them, and promised to them great renown. And the heroes wept when they left him, till their great hearts could weep no more; for he was kind and just and pious, and wiser than all beasts and men. Then he went up to a cliff, and prayed for them, that they might come home safe and well; while the heroes rowed away, and watched him standing on his cliff above the sea, with his great hands raised toward heaven, and his white locks waving in the wind; and they strained their eyes to watch him to the last, for they felt that they should look on him no more.

So they rowed on over the long swell of the sea, past Olympus, the seat of the Immortals, and past the wooded bays of Athos, and Samothrace the sacred isle; and they came past Lemnos to the Hellespont, and through the narrow strait of Abydos, and so on into the Propontis, which we call Marmora now. And there they met with Cyzicus, ruling in Asia over the Dolions, who, the songs say, was the son of Aeneas, of whom you will hear many a tale some day. For Homer tells us how he fought at Troy, and Virgil how he sailed away and founded Rome; and men believed until late years that from him sprang our old British kings. Now Cyzicus, the songs say, welcomed the heroes, for his father had been one of Cheiron's scholars; so he welcomed them, and feasted them, and stored their ship with corn and wine, and cloaks and rugs, the songs say, and shirts, of which no doubt they stood in need.

But at night, while they lay sleeping, came down on them terrible men, who lived with the bears in the mountains, like Titans or giants in shape; for each of them had six arms, and they fought with young firs and pines. But Heracles killed them all before morn with his deadly poisoned arrows; but among them, in the darkness, he slew Cyzicus the kindly prince.

Then they got to their ship and to their oars, and Tiphys bade them cast off the hawsers and go to sea. But as he spoke a whirlwind came, and spun the *Argo* round, and twisted the hawsers together, so that no man could loose them. Then Tiphys dropped the rudder from his hand, and cried, "This comes from the Gods above." But Jason went forward, and asked counsel of the magic bough.

Then the magic bough spoke, and answered, "This is because you have slain Cyzicus your friend. You must appease his soul, or you will never leave this shore."

Jason went back sadly, and told the heroes what he had heard. And they leapt on shore, and searched till dawn; and at dawn they found the body, all rolled in dust and blood, among the corpses of those monstrous beasts. And they wept over their kind host, and laid him on a fair bed, and heaped a huge mound over him, and offered black sheep at his tomb, and Orpheus sang a magic song to him, that his spirit might have rest. And then they held games at the tomb, after the custom of those times, and Jason gave prizes to each winner. To Ancaeus he gave a golden cup, for he wrestled best of all; and to Heracles a silver one, for he was the strongest of all; and to Castor, who rode best, a golden crest; and Polydeuces the boxer had a rich carpet, and to Orpheus for his song a sandal with golden wings. But Jason himself was the best of all the archers, and the Minuai crowned him with an olive crown; and so, the songs say, the soul of good Cyzicus was appeased and the heroes went on their way in peace.

But when Cyzicus' wife heard that he was dead she died likewise of grief; and her tears became a fountain of clear water, which flows the whole year round.

Then they rowed away, the songs say, along the Mysian shore, and past the mouth of Rhindacus, till they found a pleasant bay, sheltered by the long ridges of Arganthus, and by high walls of basalt rock. And there they ran the ship ashore upon the yellow sand, and furled the sail, and took the mast down, and lashed it in its crutch. And next they let down the ladder, and went ashore to sport and rest.

And there Heracles went away into the woods, bow in hand, to hunt wild deer; and Hylas the fair boy slipt away after him, and followed him by stealth, until he lost himself among the glens, and sat down weary to rest himself by the side of a lake; and there the water nymphs came up to look at him, and loved him, and carried him down under the lake to be their playfellow, for ever happy and young. And Heracles sought for him in vain, shouting his name till all the mountains rang; but Hylas never heard him, far down under the sparkling lake. So while Heracles wandered searching for him, a fair breeze sprang up, and Heracles was nowhere to be found; and the *Argo* sailed away, and Heracles was left behind, and never saw the noble Phasian stream.

Then the Minuai came to a doleful land, where Amycus the giant ruled, and cared nothing for the laws of Zeus, but challenged all strangers to box with him, and those whom he conquered he slew. But Polydeuces the boxer struck him a harder blow than he ever felt before, and slew him; and the Minuai went on up the Bosphorus, till they came to the city of Phineus, the fierce Bithynian king; for Zetes and Calais bade Jason land there, because they had a work to do.

And they went up from the shore toward the city, through forests white with snow; and Phineus came out to meet them with a lean and woful face, and said, "Welcome, gallant heroes to the land of bitter blasts, the land of cold and misery; yet I will feast you as best I can." And he led them in, and set meat before them; but before they could put their hands to their mouths down came two fearful monsters, the like of whom man never saw; for they had the faces and the hair of fair maidens, but the wings and claws of hawks; and they snatched the meat from off the table, and flew shrieking out above the roofs.

Then Phineus beat his breast and cried, "These are the Harpies, whose names are the Whirlwind and the Swift, the daughters of Wonder and of the Amber-nymph, and they rob us night and day. They carried off the daughters of Pandareus, whom all the Gods had blest; for Aphrodite fed them on Olympus with honey and milk and wine; and Hera gave them beauty and wisdom, and Athene skill in all the arts; but when they came to their wedding, the Harpies snatched them both away, and gave them to be slaves to the Erinnues, and live in horror all their days. And now they haunt me, and my people, and the Bosphorus, with fearful storms; and sweep away our food from off our tables, so that we starve in spite of all our wealth."

Then up rose Zetes and Calais, the winged sons of the North-wind, and said, "Do you not know us, Phineus, and these wings which grow upon our backs?" And Phineus hid his face in terror; but he answered not a word.

"Because you have been a traitor, Phineus, the Harpies haunt you night and day. Where is Cleopatra our sister, your wife, whom you keep in prison? And where are her two children, whom you blinded in your rage, at the bidding of an evil woman, and cast them out upon the rocks? Swear to us that you will right our sister, and cast out that wicked woman; and then we will free you from your plague, and drive the whirlwind maidens to the south; but if not, we will put out your eyes, as you put out the eyes of your own sons."

Then Phineus swore an oath to them, and drove out the wicked woman; and Jason took those two poor children, and cured their eyes with magic herbs.

But Zetes and Calais rose up sadly and said, "Farewell now, heroes all; farewell, our dear companions, with whom we played on Pelion in old times; for a fate is laid upon us, and our day is come at last, in which we must hunt the whirlwinds over land and sea for ever; and if we catch them they die, and if not, we die ourselves."

At that all the heroes wept; but the two young men sprang up, and aloft into the air after the Harpies, and the battle of the winds began.

The heroes trembled in silence as they heard the shrieking of the blasts; while the palace rocked and all the city, and great stones were torn from the crags, and the forest pines were hurled earthward, north and south and east and west, and the Bosphorus boiled white with foam, and the clouds were dashed against the cliffs.

But at last the battle ended, and the Harpies fled screaming toward the south, and the sons of the North-wind rushed after them, and brought clear sunshine where they passed. For many a league they followed them, over all the isles of the Cyclades, and away to the south-west across Hellas, till they came to the Ionian Sea, and there they fell upon the Echinades, at the mouth of the Achelous; and those isles were called the Whirlwind Isles for many a hundred years. But what became of Zetes and Calais I know not, for the heroes never saw them again: and some say that Heracles met them, and quarrelled with them, and slew them with his arrows; and some say that they fell down from weariness and the heat of the summer sun, and that the Sun-god buried them among the Cyclades, in the pleasant Isle of Tenos; and for many hundred years their grave was shown there, and over it a pillar, which turned to every wind. But those dark storms and whirlwinds haunt the Bosphorus until this day.

But the Argonauts went eastward, and out into the open sea, which we now call the Black Sea, but it was called the Euxine then. No Hellen had ever crossed it, and all feared that dreadful sea, and its rocks, and shoals, and fogs, and bitter freezing storms; and they told strange stories of it, some false and some half-true, how it stretched northward to the ends of the earth, and the sluggish Putrid Sea, and the everlasting night, and the regions of the dead. So the heroes trembled, for all their courage, as they came into that wild Black Sea, and saw it stretching out before them, without a shore, as far as eye could see.

And first Orpheus spoke, and warned them, "We shall come now to the wandering blue rocks; my mother warned me of them, Calliope, the immortal muse."

And soon they saw the blue rocks shining like spires and castles of grey glass, while an ice-cold wind blew from them and chilled all the heroes' hearts. And as they neared they could see them heaving, as they rolled upon the long sea-waves, crashing and grinding together, till the roar went up to heaven. The sea sprang up in spouts between them, and swept round them in white sheets of foam; but their heads swung nodding high in air, while the wind whistled shrill among the crags.

The heroes' hearts sank within them, and they lay upon their oars in fear; but Orpheus called to Tiphys the helmsman, "Between them we must pass; so look ahead for an opening, and be brave, for Hera is with us."

But Tiphys the cunning helmsman stood silent, clenching his teeth, till he saw a heron come flying mast-high toward the rocks, and hover awhile before them, as if looking for a passage through. Then he cried, "Hera has sent us a pilot; let us follow the cunning bird."

Then the heron flapped to and fro a moment, till he saw a hidden gap, and into it he rushed like an arrow, while the heroes watched what would befall.

And the blue rocks clashed together as the bird fled swiftly through; but they struck but a feather from his tail, and then rebounded apart at the shock.

Then Tiphys cheered the heroes, and they shouted; and the oars bent like withes beneath their strokes as they rushed between those toppling ice-crags and the cold blue lips of death. And ere the rocks could meet again they had passed them, and were safe out in the open sea.

And after that they sailed on wearily along the Asian coast, by the Black Cape and Thyneis, where the hot stream of Thymbris falls into the sea, and Sangarius, whose waters float on the Euxine, till they came to Wolf the river, and to Wolf the kindly king. And there died two brave heroes, Idmon and Tiphys the wise helmsman: one died of an evil sickness, and one a wild boar slew. So the heroes heaped a mound above them, and set upon it an oar on high, and left them there to sleep together, on the far-off Lycian shore. But Idas killed the boar, and avenged Tiphys; and Ancaios took the rudder and was helmsman, and steered them on toward the east.

And they went on past Sinope, and many a mighty river's mouth, and past many a barbarous tribe, and the cities of the Amazons, the warlike women of the East, till all night they heard the clank of anvils and the roar of furnace-blasts, and the forge-fires shone like sparks through the darkness in the mountain glens aloft; for they were come to the shores of the Chalybes, the smiths who never tire, but serve Ares the cruel War-god, forging weapons day and night.

And at day-dawn they looked eastward, and midway between the sea and the sky they saw white snow-peaks hanging, glittering sharp and bright above the clouds. And they knew that they were come to Caucasus, at the end of all the earth: Caucasus the highest of all mountains, the father of the rivers of the East. On his peak lies chained the Titan, while a vulture tears his heart; and at his feet are piled dark forests round the magic Colchian land.

And they rowed three days to the eastward, while Caucasus rose higher hour by hour, till they saw the dark stream of Phasis rushing headlong to the sea, and, shining above the tree-tops, the golden roofs of King Aeetes, the child of the Sun.

Then out spoke Ancaios the helmsman, "We are come to our goal at last, for there are the roofs of Aeetes, and the woods where all poisons grow; but who can tell us where among them is hid the golden fleece? Many a toil must we bear ere we find it, and bring it home to Greece."

But Jason cheered the heroes, for his heart was high and bold; and he said, "I will go alone up to Aeetes, though he be the child of the Sun, and win him with soft words. Better so than to go altogether, and to come to blows at once."

But the Minuai would not stay behind, so they rowed boldly up the stream.

And a dream came to Aeetes, and filled his heart with fear. He thought he saw a shining star, which fell into his daughter's lap; and that Medea his daughter took it gladly, and carried it to the river-side, and cast it in, and there the whirling river bore it down, and out into the Euxine Sea.

Then he leapt up in fear, and bade his servants bring his chariot, that he might go down to the river-side and appease the nymphs, and the heroes whose spirits haunt the bank. So he went down in his golden chariot, and his daughters by his side, Medea the fair witch-maiden, and Chalciope, who had been Phrixus' wife, and behind him a crowd of servants and soldiers, for he was a rich and mighty prince.

And as he drove down by the reedy river he saw *Argo* sliding up beneath the bank, and many a hero in her, like Immortals for beauty and for strength, as their weapons glittered round them in the level morning sunlight, through the white mist of the stream. But Jason was the noblest of all; for Hera, who loved him, gave him beauty and tallness and terrible manhood.

And when they came near together and looked into each other's eyes the heroes were awed before Aeetes as he shone in his chariot, like his father the glorious Sun; for his robes were of rich gold tissue, and the rays of his diadem flashed fire; and in his hand he bore a jewelled sceptre, which glittered like the stars; and sternly he looked at them under his brows, and sternly he spoke and loud:

"Who are you, and what want you here, that you come to the shore of Cutaia? Do you take no account of my rule, nor of my people the Colchians who serve me, who never tired yet in the battle, and know well how to face an invader?"

And the heroes sat silent awhile before the face of that ancient king. But Hera the awful goddess put courage into Jason's heart, and he rose and shouted loudly in answer, "We are no pirates nor lawless men. We come not to plunder and to ravage, or carry away slaves from your land; but my uncle, the son of Poseidon, Pelias the Minuan king, he it is who has set me on a quest to bring home the golden fleece. And these too, my bold comrades, they are no nameless men; for some are the sons of Immortals, and some of heroes far renowned. And we too never tire in battle, and know well how to give blows and to take: yet we wish to be guests at your table: it will be better so for both."

Then Aeetes' race rushed up like a whirlwind, and his eyes flashed fire as he heard; but he crushed his anger down in his breast, and spoke mildly a cunning speech –

"If you will fight for the fleece with my Colchians, then many a man must die. But do you indeed expect to win from me the fleece in fight? So few you are that if you be worsted I can load your ship with your corpses. But if you will be ruled by me, you will find it better far to choose the best man among you, and let him fulfil the labours which I demand. Then I will give him the golden fleece for a prize and a glory to you all."

So saying, he turned his horses and drove back in silence to the town. And the Minuai sat silent with sorrow, and longed for Heracles and his strength; for there was no facing the thousands of the Colchians and the fearful chance of war.

But Chalciope, Phrixus' widow, went weeping to the town; for she remembered her Minuan husband, and all the pleasures of her youth, while she watched the fair faces of his kinsmen, and their long locks of golden hair. And she whispered to Medea her sister, "Why should all these brave men die? Why does not my father give them up the fleece, that my husband's spirit may have rest?"

And Medea's heart pitied the heroes, and Jason most of all; and she answered, "Our father is stern and terrible, and who can win the golden fleece?"

But Chalciope said, "These men are not like our men; there is nothing which they cannot dare nor do."

And Medea thought of Jason and his brave countenance, and said, "If there was one among them who knew no fear, I could show him how to win the fleece."

So in the dusk of evening they went down to the river-side, Chalciope and Medea the witch-maiden, and Argus, Phrixus' son. And Argus the boy crept forward, among the beds of reeds, till he came where the heroes were sleeping, on the thwarts of the ship, beneath the bank, while Jason kept ward on shore, and leant upon his lance full of thought. And the boy came to Jason, and said:

"I am the son of Phrixus, your Cousin; and Chalciope my mother waits for you, to talk about the golden fleece."

Then Jason went boldly with the boy, and found the two princesses standing; and when Chalciope saw him she wept, and took his hands, and cried: "O cousin of my beloved, go home before you die!"

"It would be base to go home now, fair princess, and to have sailed all these seas in vain." Then both the princesses besought him; but Jason said, "It is too late."

"But you know not," said Medea, "what he must do who would win the fleece. He must tame the two brazen-footed bulls, who breathe devouring flame; and with them he must plough ere nightfall four acres in the field of Ares; and he must sow them with serpents' teeth, of which each tooth springs up into an armed man. Then he must fight with all those warriors; and little will it profit him to conquer them, for the fleece is guarded by a serpent, more huge than any mountain pine; and over his body you must step if you would reach the golden fleece."

Then Jason laughed bitterly. "Unjustly is that fleece kept here, and by an unjust and lawless king; and unjustly shall I die in my youth, for I will attempt it ere another sun be set."

Then Medea trembled, and said, "No mortal man can reach that fleece unless I guide him through. For round it, beyond the river, is a wall full nine ells high, with lofty towers and buttresses, and mighty gates of threefold brass; and over the gates the wall is arched, with golden battlements above. And over the gateway sits Brimo, the wild witch-huntress of the woods, brandishing a pine-torch in her hands, while her mad hounds howl around. No man dare meet her or look on her, but only I her priestess, and she watches far and wide lest any stranger should come near."

"No wall so high but it may be climbed at last, and no wood so thick but it may be crawled through; no serpent so wary but he may be charmed, or witch-queen so fierce but spells may soothe her; and I may yet win the golden fleece, if a wise maiden help bold men."

And he looked at Medea cunningly, and held her with his glittering eye, till she blushed and trembled, and said:

"Who can face the fire of the bulls' breath, and fight ten thousand armed men?"

"He whom you help," said Jason, flattering her, "for your fame is spread over all the earth. Are you not the queen of all enchantresses, wiser even than your sister Circe, in her fairy island in the West?"

"Would that I were with my sister Circe in her fairy island in the West, far away from sore temptation and thoughts which tear the heart! But if it must be so – for why should you die? – I have an ointment here; I made it from the magic ice-flower which sprang from Prometheus' wound, above the clouds on Caucasus, in the dreary fields of snow. Anoint yourself with that, and you shall have in you seven men's strength; and anoint your shield with it, and neither fire nor sword can harm you. But what you begin you must end before sunset, for its virtue lasts only one day. And anoint your helmet with it before you sow the serpents' teeth; and when the sons of earth spring up, cast your helmet among their ranks, and the deadly crop of the War-god's field will mow itself, and perish."

Then Jason fell on his knees before her, and thanked her and kissed her hands; and she gave him the vase of ointment, and fled trembling through the reeds. And Jason told his comrades what had happened, and showed them the box of ointment; and all rejoiced but Idas, and he grew mad with envy.

And at sunrise Jason went and bathed, and anointed himself from head to foot, and his shield, and his helmet, and his weapons, and bade his comrades try the spell. So they tried to bend his lance, but it stood like an iron bar; and Idas in spite hewed at it with his sword, but the blade flew to splinters in his face. Then they hurled their lances at his shield, but the spear-points turned like lead; and Caineus tried to throw him, but he never stirred a foot; and Polydeuces struck him with his fist a blow which would have killed an ox, but Jason only smiled, and the heroes danced about him with delight; and he leapt, and ran, and shouted in the joy of that enormous strength, till the sun rose, and it was time to go and to claim Aeetes' promise.

So he sent up Telamon and Aithalides to tell Aeetes that he was ready for the fight; and they went up among the marble walls, and beneath the roofs of gold, and stood in Aeetes' hall, while he grew pale with rage.

"Fulfil your promise to us, child of the blazing Sun. Give us the serpents' teeth, and let loose the fiery bulls; for we have found a champion among us who can win the golden fleece."

And Aeetes bit his lips, for he fancied that they had fled away by night: but he could not go back from his promise; so he gave them the serpents' teeth.

Then he called for his chariot and his horses, and sent heralds through all the town; and all the people went out with him to the dreadful War-god's field.

And there Aeetes sat upon his throne, with his warriors on each hand, thousands and tens of thousands, clothed from head to foot in steel chain-mail. And the people and the women crowded to every window and bank and wall; while the Minuai stood together, a mere handful in the midst of that great host.

And Chalciope was there and Argus, trembling, and Medea, wrapped closely in her veil; but Aeetes did not know that she was muttering cunning spells between her lips.

Then Jason cried, "Fulfil your promise, and let your fiery bulls come forth."

Then Aeetes bade open the gates, and the magic bulls leapt out. Their brazen hoofs rang upon the ground, and their nostrils sent out sheets of flame, as they rushed with lowered heads upon Jason; but he never flinched a step. The flame of their breath swept round him, but it singed not a hair of his head; and the bulls stopped short and trembled when Medea began her spell.

Then Jason sprang upon the nearest and seized him by the horn; and up and down they wrestled, till the bull fell grovelling on his knees; for the heart of the brute died within him, and his mighty limbs were loosed, beneath the steadfast eye of that dark witch-maiden and the magic whisper of her lips.

So both the bulls were tamed and yoked; and Jason bound them to the plough, and goaded them onward with his lance till he had ploughed the sacred field.

And all the Minuai shouted; but Aeetes bit his lips with rage, for the half of Jason's work was over, and the sun was yet high in heaven.

Then he took the serpents' teeth and sowed them, and waited what would befall. But Medea looked at him and at his helmet, lest he should forget the lesson she had taught.

And every furrow heaved and bubbled, and out of every clod arose a man. Out of the earth they rose by thousands, each clad from head to foot in steel, and drew their swords and rushed on Jason, where he stood in the midst alone.

Then the Minuai grew pale with fear for him; but Aeetes laughed a bitter laugh. "See! If I had not warriors enough already round me, I could call them out of the bosom of the earth."

But Jason snatched off his helmet, and hurled it into the thickest of the throng. And blind madness came upon them, suspicion, hate, and fear; and one cried to his fellow, "Thou didst strike me!" and another, "Thou art Jason; thou shalt die!"

So fury seized those earth-born phantoms, and each turned his hand against the rest; and they fought and were never weary, till they all lay dead upon the ground. Then the magic furrows opened, and the kind earth took them home into her breast and the grass grew up all green again above them, and Jason's work was done.

Then the Minuai rose and shouted, till Prometheus heard them from his crag. And Jason cried, "Lead me to the fleece this moment, before the sun goes down."

But Aeetes thought, "He has conquered the bulls, and sown and reaped the deadly crop. Who is this who is proof against all magic? He may kill the serpent yet."

So he delayed, and sat taking counsel with his princes till the sun went down and all was dark. Then he bade a herald cry, "Every man to his home for tonight. Tomorrow we will meet these heroes, and speak about the golden fleece."

Then he turned and looked at Medea. "This is your doing, false witch-maid! You have helped these yellow-haired strangers, and brought shame upon your father and yourself!"

Medea shrank and trembled, and her face grew pale with fear; and Aeetes knew that she was guilty, and whispered, "If they win the fleece, you die!"

But the Minuai marched toward their ship, growling like lions cheated of their prey; for they saw that Aeetes meant to mock them, and to cheat them out of all their toil. And Oileus said, "Let us go to the grove together, and take the fleece by force."

And Idas the rash cried, "Let us draw lots who shall go in first; for, while the dragon is devouring one, the rest can slay him and carry off the fleece in peace." But Jason held them back, though he praised them; for he hoped for Medea's help.

And after awhile Medea came trembling, and wept a long while before she spoke. And at last – "My end is come, and I must die; for my father has found out that I have helped you. You he would kill if he dared; but he will not harm you, because you have been his guests. Go then, go, and remember poor Medea when you are far away across the sea."

But all the heroes cried: "If you die, we die with you; for without you we cannot win the fleece, and home we will not go without it, but fall here fighting to the last man."

"You need not die," said Jason. "Flee home with us across the sea. Show us first how to win the fleece; for you can do it. Why else are you the priestess of the grove? Show us but how to win the fleece, and come with us, and you shall be my queen, and rule over the rich princes of the Minuai, in Iolcos by the sea."

And all the heroes pressed round, and vowed to her that she should be their queen.

Medea wept, and shuddered, and hid her face in her hands; for her heart yearned after her sisters and her playfellows, and the home where she was brought up as a child. But at last she looked up at Jason, and spoke between her sobs:

"Must I leave my home and my people, to wander with strangers across the sea? The lot is cast, and I must endure it. I will show you how to win the golden fleece. Bring up your ship to the wood-side, and moor her there against the bank; and let Jason come up at midnight, and one brave comrade with him, and meet me beneath the wall."

Then all the heroes cried together, "I will go!" "and I!" "and I!"

And Idas the rash grew mad with envy; for he longed to be foremost in all things. But Medea calmed them, and said, "Orpheus shall go with Jason, and bring his magic harp; for I hear of him that he is the king of all minstrels, and can charm all things on earth."

And Orpheus laughed for joy, and clapped his hands, because the choice had fallen on him; for in those days poets and singers were as bold warriors as the best.

So at midnight they went up the bank, and found Medea; and beside came Absyrtus her young brother, leading a yearling lamb.

Then Medea brought them to a thicket beside the War-god's gate; and there she bade Jason dig a ditch, and kill the lamb, and leave it there, and strew on it magic herbs and honey from the honeycomb.

Then sprang up through the earth, with the red fire flashing before her, Brimo the wild witch-huntress, while her mad hounds howled around. She had one head like a horse's, and another like a ravening hound's, and another like a hissing snake's, and a sword in either hand. And she leapt into the ditch with her hounds, and they ate and drank their fill, while Jason and Orpheus trembled, and Medea hid her eyes. And at last the witch-queen vanished, and fled with her hounds into the woods; and the bars of the gates fell down, and the brazen doors flew wide, and Medea and the heroes ran forward and hurried through the poison wood, among the dark stems of the mighty beeches, guided by the gleam of the golden fleece, until they saw it hanging on one vast tree in the midst. And Jason would have sprung to seize it; but Medea held him back, and pointed, shuddering, to the tree-foot, where the mighty serpent lay, coiled in and out among the roots, with a body like a mountain pine. His coils stretched many a fathom, spangled with bronze and gold; and half of him they could see, but no more, for the rest lay in the darkness far beyond.

And when he saw them coming he lifted up his head, and watched them with his small bright eyes, and flashed his forked tongue, and roared like the fire among the woodlands, till the forest tossed and groaned. For his cries shook the trees from leaf to root, and swept over the long reaches of the river, and over Aeetes' hall, and woke the sleepers in the city, till mothers clasped their children in their fear.

But Medea called gently to him, and he stretched out his long spotted neck, and licked her hand, and looked up in her face, as if to ask for food. Then she made a sign to Orpheus, and he began his magic song.

And as he sung, the forest grew calm again, and the leaves on every tree hung still; and the serpent's head sank down, and his brazen coils grew limp, and his glittering eyes closed lazily, till he breathed as gently as a child, while Orpheus called to pleasant Slumber, who gives peace to men, and beasts, and waves.

Then Jason leapt forward warily, and stepped across that mighty snake, and tore the fleece from off the tree-trunk; and the four rushed down the garden, to the bank where the *Argo* lay.

There was a silence for a moment, while Jason held the golden fleece on high. Then he cried, "Go now, good *Argo*, swift and steady, if ever you would see Pelion more."

And she went, as the heroes drove her, grim and silent all, with muffled oars, till the pine-wood bent like willow in their hands, and stout *Argo* groaned beneath their strokes.

On and on, beneath the dewy darkness, they fled swiftly down the swirling stream; underneath black walls, and temples, and the castles of the princes of the East; past sluice-mouths, and fragrant gardens, and groves of all strange fruits; past marshes where fat kine lay sleeping, and long beds of whispering reeds; till they heard the merry music of the surge upon the bar, as it tumbled in the moonlight all alone.

Into the surge they rushed, and *Argo* leapt the breakers like a horse; for she knew the time was come to show her mettle, and win honour for the heroes and herself.

Into the surge they rushed, and *Argo* leapt the breakers like a horse, till the heroes stopped all panting, each man upon his oar, as she slid into the still broad sea.

Then Orpheus took his harp and sang a paean, till the heroes' hearts rose high again; and they rowed on stoutly and steadfastly, away into the darkness of the West.

How the Argonauts Were Driven into the Unknown Sea

SO THEY FLED AWAY in haste to the westward; but Aeetes manned his fleet and followed them. And Lynceus the quick-eyed saw him coming, while he was still many a mile away, and cried, "I see a hundred ships, like a flock of white swans, far in the east." And at that they rowed hard, like heroes; but the ships came nearer every hour.

Then Medea, the dark witch-maiden, laid a cruel and a cunning plot; for she killed Absyrtus her young brother, and cast him into the sea, and said, "Ere my father can take up his corpse and bury it, he must wait long, and be left far behind."

And all the heroes shuddered, and looked one at the other for shame; yet they did not punish that dark witch-woman, because she had won for them the golden fleece.

And when Aeetes came to the place he saw the floating corpse; and he stopped a long while, and bewailed his son, and took him up, and went home. But he sent on his sailors toward the westward, and bound them by a mighty curse: "Bring back to me that dark witch-woman, that she may die a dreadful death. But if you return without her, you shall die by the same death yourselves."

So the Argonauts escaped for that time: but Father Zeus saw that foul crime; and out of the heavens he sent a storm, and swept the ship far from her course. Day after day the storm drove her, amid foam and blinding mist, till they knew no longer where they were, for the sun was blotted from the skies. And at last the ship struck on a shoal, amid low isles of mud and sand, and the waves rolled over her and through her, and the heroes lost all hope of life.

Then Jason cried to Hera, "Fair queen, who hast befriended us till now, why hast thou left us in our misery, to die here among unknown seas? It is hard to lose the honour which we have won with such toil and danger, and hard never to see Hellas again, and the pleasant bay of Pagasai."

Then out and spoke the magic bough which stood upon the *Argo's* beak, "Because Father Zeus is angry, all this has fallen on you; for a cruel crime has been done on board, and the sacred ship is foul with blood."

At that some of the heroes cried, "Medea is the murderess. Let the witch-woman bear her sin, and die!" And they seized Medea, to hurl her into the sea, and atone for the young boy's death; but the magic bough spoke again, "Let her live till her crimes are full. Vengeance waits for her, slow and sure; but she must live, for you need her still. She must show you the way to her sister Circe, who lives among the islands of the West. To her you must sail, a weary way, and she shall cleanse you from your guilt."

Then all the heroes wept aloud when they heard the sentence of the oak; for they knew that a dark journey lay before them, and years of bitter toil. And some upbraided the dark witch-woman, and some said, "Nay, we are her debtors still; without her we should never have won the fleece." But most of them bit their lips in silence, for they feared the witch's spells.

And now the sea grew calmer, and the sun shone out once more, and the heroes thrust the ship off the sand-bank, and rowed forward on their weary course under the guiding of the dark witch-maiden, into the wastes of the unknown sea.

Whither they went I cannot tell, nor how they came to Circe's isle. Some say that they went to the westward, and up the Ister stream, and so came into the Adriatic, dragging their ship over the snowy Alps. And others say that they went southward, into the Red Indian Sea, and past the sunny lands where spices grow, round Aethiopia toward the West; and that at last they came to Libya, and dragged their ship across the burning sands, and over the hills into the Syrtes, where the flats and quicksands spread for many a mile, between rich Cyrene and the Lotus-eaters' shore. But all these are but dreams and fables, and dim hints of unknown lands.

But all say that they came to a place where they had to drag their ship across the land nine days with ropes and rollers, till they came into an unknown sea. And the best of all the old songs tells us how they went away toward the North, till they came to the slope of Caucasus, where it sinks into the sea; and to the narrow Cimmerian Bosphorus, where the Titan swam across upon the bull; and thence into the lazy waters of the still Maeotid lake. And thence they went northward ever, up the Tanais, which we call Don, past the Geloni and Sauromatai, and many a wandering shepherd-tribe, and the one-eyed Arimaspi, of whom old Greek poets tell, who steal the gold from the Griffins, in the cold Riphaian hills.

And they passed the Scythian archers, and the Tauri who eat men, and the wandering Hyperboreai, who feed their flocks beneath the pole-star, until they came into the northern ocean, the dull dead Cronian Sea. And there *Argo* would move on no longer; and each man clasped his elbow, and leaned his head upon his hand, heart-broken with toil and hunger, and gave himself up to death. But brave Ancaios the helmsman cheered up their hearts once more, and bade them leap on land, and haul the ship with ropes and rollers for many a weary day, whether over land, or mud, or ice, I know not, for the song is mixed and broken like a dream. And it says next, how they came to the rich nation of the famous long-lived men; and to the coast of the Cimmerians, who never saw the sun, buried deep in the glens of the snow mountains; and to the fair land of Hermione, where dwelt the most righteous of all nations; and to the gates of the world below, and to the dwelling-place of dreams.

And at last Ancaios shouted, "Endure a little while, brave friends, the worst is surely past; for I can see the pure west wind ruffle the water, and hear the roar of ocean on the sands. So raise up the mast, and set the sail, and face what comes like men."

Then out spoke the magic bough, "Ah, would that I had perished long ago, and been whelmed by the dread blue rocks, beneath the fierce swell of the Euxine! Better so, than to wander for ever, disgraced by the guilt of my princes; for the blood of Absyrtus still tracks me, and woe follows hard upon woe. And now some dark horror will clutch me, if I come near the Isle of Ierne. Unless you will cling to the land, and sail southward and southward for ever, I shall wander beyond the Atlantic, to the ocean which has no shore."

Then they blest the magic bough, and sailed southward along the land. But ere they could pass Ierne, the land of mists and storms, the wild wind came down, dark and roaring, and caught the sail, and strained the ropes. And away they drove twelve nights, on the wide wild western sea, through the foam, and over the rollers, while they saw neither sun nor stars. And they cried again, "We shall perish, for we know not where we are. We are lost in the dreary damp darkness, and cannot tell north from south."

But Lynceus the long-sighted called gaily from the bows, "Take heart again, brave sailors; for I see a pine-clad isle, and the halls of the kind Earth-mother, with a crown of clouds around them."

But Orpheus said, "Turn from them, for no living man can land there: there is no harbour on the coast, but steep-walled cliffs all round."

So Ancaios turned the ship away; and for three days more they sailed on, till they came to Aiaia, Circe's home, and the fairy island of the West.

And there Jason bid them land, and seek about for any sign of living man. And as they went inland Circe met them, coming down toward the ship; and they trembled when they saw her, for her hair, and face, and robes shone like flame.

And she came and looked at Medea; and Medea hid her face beneath her veil.

And Circe cried, "Ah, wretched girl, have you forgotten all your sins, that you come hither to my island, where the flowers bloom all the year round? Where is your aged father, and the brother whom you killed? Little do I expect you to return in safety with these strangers whom you love. I will send you food and wine: but your ship must not stay here, for it is foul with sin, and foul with sin its crew."

And the heroes prayed her, but in vain, and cried, "Cleanse us from our guilt!" But she sent them away, and said, "Go on to Malea, and there you may be cleansed, and return home."

Then a fair wind rose, and they sailed eastward by Tartessus on the Iberian shore, till they came to the Pillars of Hercules, and the Mediterranean Sea. And thence they sailed on through the deeps of Sardinia, and past the Ausonian islands, and the capes of the Tyrrhenian shore, till they came to a flowery island, upon a still bright summer's eve. And as they neared it, slowly and wearily, they heard sweet songs upon the shore. But when Medea heard it, she started, and cried, "Beware, all heroes, for these are the rocks of the Sirens. You must pass close by them, for there is no other channel; but those who listen to that song are lost."

Then Orpheus spoke, the king of all minstrels, "Let them match their song against mine. I have charmed stones, and trees, and dragons, how much more the hearts of men!" So he caught up his lyre, and stood upon the poop, and began his magic song.

And now they could see the Sirens on Anthemousa, the flowery isle; three fair maidens sitting on the beach, beneath a red rock in the setting sun, among beds of crimson poppies and golden asphodel. Slowly they sung and sleepily, with silver voices, mild and clear, which stole over the golden waters, and into the hearts of all the heroes, in spite of Orpheus' song.

And all things stayed around and listened; the gulls sat in white lines along the rocks; on the beach great seals lay basking, and kept time with lazy heads; while silver shoals of fish came up to hearken, and whispered as they broke the shining calm. The Wind overhead hushed his whistling, as he shepherded his clouds toward the west; and the clouds stood in mid blue, and listened dreaming, like a flock of golden sheep.

And as the heroes listened, the oars fell from their hands, and their heads drooped on their breasts, and they closed their heavy eyes; and they dreamed of bright still gardens, and of slumbers under murmuring pines, till all their toil seemed foolishness, and they thought of their renown no more.

Then one lifted his head suddenly, and cried, "What use in wandering for ever? Let us stay here and rest awhile." And another, "Let us row to the shore, and hear the words they sing." And another, "I care not for the words, but for the music. They shall sing me to sleep, that I may rest."

And Butes, the son of Pandion, the fairest of all mortal men, leapt out and swam toward the shore, crying, "I come, I come, fair maidens, to live and die here, listening to your song."

Then Medea clapped her hands together, and cried, "Sing louder, Orpheus, sing a bolder strain; wake up these hapless sluggards, or none of them will see the land of Hellas more."

Then Orpheus lifted his harp, and crashed his cunning hand across the strings; and his music and his voice rose like a trumpet through the still evening air; into the air it rushed like thunder, till the rocks rang and the sea; and into their souls it rushed like wine, till all hearts beat fast within their breasts.

And he sung the song of Perseus, how the Gods led him over land and sea, and how he slew the loathly Gorgon, and won himself a peerless bride; and how he sits now with the Gods upon Olympus, a shining star in the sky, immortal with his immortal bride, and honoured by all men below.

So Orpheus sang, and the Sirens, answering each other across the golden sea, till Orpheus' voice drowned the Sirens', and the heroes caught their oars again.

And they cried, "We will be men like Perseus, and we will dare and suffer to the last. Sing us his song again, brave Orpheus, that we may forget the Sirens and their spell."

And as Orpheus sang, they dashed their oars into the sea, and kept time to his music, as they fled fast away; and the Sirens' voices died behind them, in the hissing of the foam along their wake.

But Butes swam to the shore, and knelt down before the Sirens, and cried, "Sing on! Sing on!"

But he could say no more, for a charmed sleep came over him, and a pleasant humming in his ears; and he sank all along upon the pebbles, and forgot all heaven and earth, and never looked at that sad beach around him, all strewn with the bones of men.

Then slowly rose up those three fair sisters, with a cruel smile upon their lips; and slowly they crept down towards him, like leopards who creep upon their prey; and their hands were like the talons of eagles as they stepped across the bones of their victims to enjoy their cruel feast.

But fairest Aphrodite saw him from the highest Idalian peak, and she pitied his youth and his beauty, and leapt up from her golden throne; and like a falling star she cleft the sky, and left a trail of glittering light, till she stooped to the Isle of the Sirens, and snatched their prey from their claws. And she lifted Butes as he lay sleeping, and wrapped him in golden mist; and she bore him to the peak of Lilybaeum, and he slept there many a pleasant year.

But when the Sirens saw that they were conquered, they shrieked for envy and rage, and leapt from the beach into the sea, and were changed into rocks until this day.

Then they came to the straits by Lilybaeum, and saw Sicily, the three-cornered island, under which Enceladus the giant lies groaning day and night, and when he turns the earth quakes, and his breath bursts out in roaring flames from the highest cone of Etna, above the chestnut woods. And there Charybdis caught them in its fearful coils of wave, and rolled mast-high about them, and spun them round and round; and they could go neither back nor forward, while the whirlpool sucked them in.

And while they struggled they saw near them, on the other side the strait, a rock stand in the water, with its peak wrapped round in clouds – a rock which no man could climb, though he had twenty hands and feet, for the stone was smooth and slippery, as if polished by man's hand; and halfway up a misty cave looked out toward the west.

And when Orpheus saw it he groaned, and struck his hands together. And "Little will it help us," he cried, "to escape the jaws of the whirlpool; for in that cave lives Scylla, the sea-hag with a young whelp's voice; my mother warned me of her ere we sailed away from Hellas; she has six heads, and six long necks, and hides in that dark cleft. And from her cave she fishes for all things which pass by – for sharks, and seals, and dolphins, and all the herds of Amphitrite. And never ship's crew boasted that they came safe by her rock, for she bends her long necks down to them, and every mouth takes up a man. And who will help us now? For Hera and Zeus hate us, and our ship is foul with guilt; so we must die, whatever befalls."

Then out of the depths came Thetis, Peleus' silver-footed bride, for love of her gallant husband, and all her nymphs around her; and they played like snow-white dolphins, diving on from wave to wave, before the ship, and in her wake, and beside her, as dolphins play. And they caught the ship, and guided her, and passed her on from hand to hand, and tossed her through the billows, as maidens toss the ball. And when Scylla stooped to seize her, they struck back her ravening heads, and foul Scylla whined, as a whelp whines, at the touch of their gentle hands.

But she shrank into her cave affrighted – for all bad things shrink from good – and *Argo* leapt safe past her, while a fair breeze rose behind. Then Thetis and her nymphs sank down to their coral caves beneath the sea, and their gardens of green and purple, where live flowers bloom all the year round; while the heroes went on rejoicing, yet dreading what might come next.

After that they rowed on steadily for many a weary day, till they saw a long high island, and beyond it a mountain land. And they searched till they found a harbour, and there rowed boldly in. But after awhile they stopped, and wondered, for there stood a great city on the shore, and temples and walls and gardens, and castles high in air upon the cliffs. And on either side they saw a harbour, with a narrow mouth, but wide within; and black ships without number, high and dry upon the shore.

Then Ancaios, the wise helmsman, spoke, "What new wonder is this? I know all isles, and harbours, and the windings of all seas; and this should be Corcyra, where a few wild goat-herds dwell. But whence come these new harbours and vast works of polished stone?"

But Jason said, "They can be no savage people. We will go in and take our chance."

So they rowed into the harbour, among a thousand black-beaked ships, each larger far than *Argo*, toward a quay of polished stone. And they wondered at that mighty city, with its roofs of burnished brass, and long and lofty walls of marble, with strong palisades above. And the quays were full of people, merchants, and mariners, and slaves, going to and fro with merchandise among the crowd of ships. And the heroes' hearts were humbled, and they looked at each other and said, "We thought ourselves a gallant crew when we sailed from Iolcos by the sea; but how small we look before this city, like an ant before a hive of bees."

Then the sailors hailed them roughly from the quay, "What men are you? – We want no strangers here, nor pirates. We keep our business to ourselves."

But Jason answered gently, with many a flattering word, and praised their city and their harbour, and their fleet of gallant ships. "Surely you are the children of Poseidon, and the masters of the sea; and we are but poor wandering mariners, worn out with thirst and toil. Give us but food and water, and we will go on our voyage in peace."

Then the sailors laughed, and answered, "Stranger, you are no fool; you talk like an honest man, and you shall find us honest too. We are the children of Poseidon, and the masters of the sea; but come ashore to us, and you shall have the best that we can give."

So they limped ashore, all stiff and weary, with long ragged beards and sunburnt cheeks, and garments torn and weather-stained, and weapons rusted with the spray, while the sailors laughed at them (for they were rough-tongued, though their hearts were frank and kind). And one said, "These fellows are but raw sailors; they look as if they had been sea-sick all the day." And another, "Their legs have grown crooked with much rowing, till they waddle in their walk like ducks."

At that Idas the rash would have struck them; but Jason held him back, till one of the merchant kings spoke to them, a tall and stately man.

"Do not be angry, strangers; the sailor boys must have their jest. But we will treat you justly and kindly, for strangers and poor men come from God; and you seem no common sailors by your strength, and height, and weapons. Come up with me to the palace of Alcinous, the rich sea-going king, and we will feast you well and heartily; and after that you shall tell us your name."

But Medea hung back, and trembled, and whispered in Jason's ear, "We are betrayed, and are going to our ruin, for I see my countrymen among the crowd; dark-eyed Colchi in steel mail-shirts, such as they wear in my father's land."

"It is too late to turn," said Jason. And he spoke to the merchant king, "What country is this, good sir; and what is this new-built town?"

'This is the land of the Phaeaces, beloved by all the Immortals; for they come hither and feast like friends with us, and sit by our side in the hall. Hither we came from Liburnia to escape the unrighteous Cyclopes; for they robbed us, peaceful merchants, of our hard-earned wares and wealth. So Nausithous, the son of Poseidon, brought us hither, and died in peace; and now his son Alcinous rules us, and Arete the wisest of queens."

So they went up across the square, and wondered still more as they went; for along the quays lay in order great cables, and yards, and masts, before the fair temple of Poseidon, the blue-haired king of the seas. And round the square worked the ship-wrights, as many in number as ants, twining ropes, and hewing timber, and smoothing long yards and oars. And the Minuai went on in silence through clean white marble streets, till they came to the hall of Alcinous, and they wondered then still more. For the lofty palace shone aloft in the sun, with walls of plated brass, from the threshold to the innermost chamber, and the doors were of silver and gold. And on each side of the doorway sat living dogs of gold, who never grew old or died, so well Hephaestus had made them in his forges in smoking Lemnos, and gave them to Alcinous to guard his gates by night. And within, against the walls, stood thrones on either side, down the whole length of the hall, strewn with rich glossy shawls; and on them the merchant kings of those crafty sea-roving Phaeaces sat eating and drinking in pride, and feasting there all the year round. And boys of molten gold stood each on a polished altar, and held torches in their hands, to give light all night to the guests. And round the house sat fifty maid-servants, some grinding the meal in the mill, some turning the spindle, some weaving at the loom, while their hands twinkled as they passed the shuttle, like quivering aspen leaves.

And outside before the palace a great garden was walled round, filled full of stately fruit-trees, grey olives and sweet figs, and pomegranates, pears, and apples, which bore the whole year round. For the rich south-west wind fed them, till pear grew ripe on pear, fig on fig, and grape on grape, all the winter and the spring. And at the farther end gay flower-beds bloomed through all seasons of the year; and two fair fountains rose, and ran, one through the garden grounds, and one beneath the palace gate, to water all the town. Such noble gifts the heavens had given to Alcinous the wise.

So they went in, and saw him sitting, like Poseidon, on his throne, with his golden sceptre by him, in garments stiff with gold, and in his hand a sculptured goblet, as he pledged the merchant kings; and beside him stood Arete, his wise and lovely queen, and leaned against a pillar as she spun her golden threads.

Then Alcinous rose, and welcomed them, and bade them sit and eat; and the servants brought them tables, and bread, and meat, and wine.

But Medea went on trembling toward Arete the fair queen, and fell at her knees, and clasped them, and cried, weeping, as she knelt:

"I am your guest, fair queen, and I entreat you by Zeus, from whom prayers come. Do not send me back to my father to die some dreadful death; but let me go my way, and bear my burden. Have I not had enough of punishment and shame?"

"Who are you, strange maiden? And what is the meaning of your prayer?"

"I am Medea, daughter of Aeetes, and I saw my countrymen here today; and I know that they are come to find me, and take me home to die some dreadful death."

Then Arete frowned, and said, "Lead this girl in, my maidens; and let the kings decide, not I."

And Alcinous leapt up from his throne, and cried, "Speak, strangers, who are you? And who is this maiden?"

"We are the heroes of the Minuai," said Jason; "and this maiden has spoken truth. We are the men who took the golden fleece, the men whose fame has run round every shore. We came hither out of the ocean, after sorrows such as man never saw before. We went out many, and come back few, for many a noble comrade have we lost. So let us go, as you should let your guests go, in peace; that the world may say, 'Alcinous is a just king.'"

But Alcinous frowned, and stood deep in thought; and at last he spoke:

"Had not the deed been done which is done, I should have said this day to myself, 'It is an honour to Alcinous, and to his children after him, that the far-famed Argonauts are his guests.' But these Colchi are my guests, as you are; and for this month they have waited here with all their fleet, for they have hunted all the seas of Hellas, and could not find you, and dared neither go farther, nor go home."

"Let them choose out their champions, and we will fight them, man for man."

"No guests of ours shall fight upon our island, and if you go outside they will outnumber you. I will do justice between you, for I know and do what is right."

Then he turned to his kings, and said, "This may stand over till tomorrow. Tonight we will feast our guests, and hear the story of all their wanderings, and how they came hither out of the ocean."

So Alcinous bade the servants take the heroes in, and bathe them, and give them clothes. And they were glad when they saw the warm water, for it was long since they had bathed. And they washed off the sea-salt from their limbs, and anointed themselves from head to foot with oil, and combed out their golden hair. Then they came back again into the hall, while the merchant kings rose up to do them honour. And each man said to his neighbour, "No wonder that these men won fame. How they stand now like Giants, or Titans, or Immortals come down from Olympus, though many a winter has worn them, and many a fearful storm. What must they have been when they sailed from Iolcos, in the bloom of their youth, long ago?"

Then they went out to the garden; and the merchant princes said, "Heroes, run races with us. Let us see whose feet are nimblest."

"We cannot race against you, for our limbs are stiff from sea; and we have lost our two swift comrades, the sons of the north wind. But do not think us cowards: if you wish to try our strength, we will shoot, and box, and wrestle, against any men on earth."

And Alcinous smiled, and answered, "I believe you, gallant guests; with your long limbs and broad shoulders, we could never match you here. For we care nothing here for boxing, or for shooting with the bow; but for feasts, and songs, and harping, and dancing, and running races, to stretch our limbs on shore."

So they danced there and ran races, the jolly merchant kings, till the night fell, and all went in.

And then they ate and drank, and comforted their weary souls, till Alcinous called a herald, and bade him go and fetch the harper.

The herald went out, and fetched the harper, and led him in by the hand; and Alcinous cut him a piece of meat, from the fattest of the haunch, and sent it to him, and said, "Sing to us, noble harper, and rejoice the heroes' hearts."

So the harper played and sang, while the dancers danced strange figures; and after that the tumblers showed their tricks, till the heroes laughed again.

Then, "Tell me, heroes," asked Alcinous, "you who have sailed the ocean round, and seen the manners of all nations, have you seen such dancers as ours here, or heard such music and such singing? We hold ours to be the best on earth."

"Such dancing we have never seen," said Orpheus; "and your singer is a happy man, for Phoebus himself must have taught him, or else he is the son of a Muse, as I am also, and have sung once or twice, though not so well as he."

"Sing to us, then, noble stranger," said Alcinous; "and we will give you precious gifts."

So Orpheus took his magic harp, and sang to them a stirring song of their voyage from Iolcos, and their dangers, and how they won the golden fleece; and of Medea's love, and how she helped them, and went with them over land and sea; and of all their fearful dangers, from monsters, and rocks, and storms, till the heart of Arete was softened, and all the women wept. And the merchant kings rose up, each man from off his golden throne, and clapped their hands, and shouted, "Hail to the noble Argonauts, who sailed the unknown sea!"

Then he went on, and told their journey over the sluggish northern main, and through the shoreless outer ocean, to the fairy island of the west; and of the Sirens, and Scylla, and Charybdis, and all the wonders they had seen, till midnight passed and the day dawned; but the kings never thought of sleep. Each man sat still and listened, with his chin upon his hand.

And at last, when Orpheus had ended, they all went thoughtful out, and the heroes lay down to sleep, beneath the sounding porch outside, where Arete had strewn them rugs and carpets, in the sweet still summer night.

But Arete pleaded hard with her husband for Medea, for her heart was softened. And she said, "The Gods will punish her, not we. After all, she is our guest and my suppliant, and prayers are the daughters of Zeus. And who, too, dare part man and wife, after all they have endured together?"

And Alcinous smiled. "The minstrel's song has charmed you: but I must remember what is right, for songs cannot alter justice; and I must be faithful to my name. Alcinous I am called, the man of sturdy sense; and Alcinous I will be." But for all that Arete besought him, until she won him round.

So next morning he sent a herald, and called the kings into the square, and said, "This is a puzzling matter: remember but one thing. These Minuai live close by us, and we may meet them often on the seas; but Aeetes lives afar off, and we have only heard his name. Which, then, of the two is it safer to offend – the men near us, or the men far off?"

The princes laughed, and praised his wisdom; and Alcinous called the heroes to the square, and the Colchi also; and they came and stood opposite each other, but Medea stayed in the palace. Then Alcinous spoke, "Heroes of the Colchi, what is your errand about this lady?"

"To carry her home with us, that she may die a shameful death; but if we return without her, we must die the death she should have died."

"What say you to this, Jason the Aeolid?" said Alcinous, turning to the Minuai.

"I say," said the cunning Jason, "that they are come here on a bootless errand. Do you think that you can make her follow you, heroes of the Colchi – her, who knows all spells and charms? She will cast away your ships on quicksands, or call down on you Brimo the wild huntress; or the chains will fall from off her wrists, and she will escape in her dragon-car; or if not thus, some other way, for she has a thousand plans and wiles. And why return home at all, brave heroes, and face the long seas again, and the Bosphorus, and the stormy Euxine, and double all your toil? There is many a fair land round these coasts, which waits for gallant men like you. Better to settle there, and build a city, and let Aeetes and Colchis help themselves."

Then a murmur rose among the Colchi, and some cried "He has spoken well;" and some, "We have had enough of roving, we will sail the seas no more!" And the chief said at last, "Be it so, then; a plague she has been to us, and a plague to the house of her father, and a plague she will be to you. Take her, since you are no wiser; and we will sail away toward the north."

Then Alcinous gave them food, and water, and garments, and rich presents of all sorts; and he gave the same to the Minuai, and sent them all away in peace.

So Jason kept the dark witch-maiden to breed him woe and shame; and the Colchi went northward into the Adriatic, and settled, and built towns along the shore.

Then the heroes rowed away to the eastward, to reach Hellas, their beloved land; but a storm came down upon them, and swept them far away toward the south. And they rowed till they were spent with struggling, through the darkness and the blinding rain; but where they were they could not tell, and they gave up all hope of life. And at last touched the ground, and when daylight came waded to the shore; and saw nothing round but sand and desolate salt pools, for they had come to the quicksands of the Syrtis, and the dreary treeless flats which lie between Numidia and Cyrene, on the burning shore of Africa. And there they wandered starving for many a weary day, ere they could launch their ship again, and gain the open sea. And there Canthus was killed, while he was trying to drive off sheep, by a stone which a herdsman threw.

And there too Mopsus died, the seer who knew the voices of all birds; but he could not foretell his own end, for he was bitten in the foot by a snake, one of those which sprang from the Gorgon's head when Perseus carried it across the sands.

At last they rowed away toward the northward, for many a weary day, till their water was spent, and their food eaten; and they were worn out with hunger and thirst. But at last they saw a long steep island, and a blue peak high among the clouds; and they knew it for the peak of Ida, and the famous land of Crete. And they said, "We will land in Crete, and see Minos the just king, and all his glory and his wealth; at least he will treat us hospitably, and let us fill our water-casks upon the shore."

But when they came nearer to the island they saw a wondrous sight upon the cliffs. For on a cape to the westward stood a giant, taller than any mountain pine, who glittered aloft against the sky like a tower of burnished brass. He turned and looked on all sides round him, till he saw the *Argo* and her crew; and when he saw them he came toward them, more swiftly than the swiftest horse, leaping across the glens at a bound, and striding at one step from down to down. And when he came abreast of them he brandished his arms up and down, as a ship hoists and lowers her yards, and shouted with his brazen throat like a trumpet from off the hills, "You are pirates, you are robbers! If you dare land here, you die."

Then the heroes cried, "We are no pirates. We are all good men and true, and all we ask is food and water;" but the giant cried the more:

"You are robbers, you are pirates all; I know you; and if you land, you shall die the death."

Then he waved his arms again as a signal, and they saw the people flying inland, driving their flocks before them, while a great flame arose among the hills. Then the giant ran up a valley and vanished, and the heroes lay on their oars in fear.

But Medea stood watching all from under her steep black brows, with a cunning smile upon her lips, and a cunning plot within her heart. At last she spoke, "I know this giant. I heard of him in the East. Hephaestus the Fire King made him in his forge in Etna beneath the earth, and called him Talus, and gave him to Minos for a servant, to guard the coast of Crete. Thrice a day he walks round the island, and never stops to sleep; and if strangers land he leaps into his furnace, which flames there among the hills; and when he is red-hot he rushes on them, and burns them in his brazen hands."

Then all the heroes cried, "What shall we do, wise Medea? We must have water, or we die of thirst. Flesh and blood we can face fairly; but who can face this red-hot brass?"

"I can face red-hot brass, if the tale I hear be true. For they say that he has but one vein in all his body, filled with liquid fire; and that this vein is closed with a nail: but I know not where that nail is placed. But if I can get it once into these hands, you shall water your ship here in peace."

Then she bade them put her on shore, and row off again, and wait what would befall.

And the heroes obeyed her unwillingly, for they were ashamed to leave her so alone; but Jason said, "She is dearer to me than to any of you, yet I will trust her freely on shore; she has more plots than we can dream of in the windings of that fair and cunning head."

So they left the witch-maiden on the shore; and she stood there in her beauty all alone, till the giant strode back red-hot from head to heel, while the grass hissed and smoked beneath his tread.

And when he saw the maiden alone, he stopped; and she looked boldly up into his face without moving, and began her magic song:

"Life is short, though life is sweet; and even men of brass and fire must die. The brass must rust, the fire must cool, for time gnaws all things in their turn. Life is short, though life is sweet: but sweeter to live for ever; sweeter to live ever youthful like the Gods, who have ichor in their veins – ichor which gives life, and youth, and joy, and a bounding heart."

Then Talus said, "Who are you, strange maiden, and where is this ichor of youth?"

Then Medea held up a flask of crystal, and said, "Here is the ichor of youth. I am Medea the enchantress; my sister Circe gave me this, and said, 'Go and reward Talus, the faithful servant, for his fame is gone out into all lands.' So come, and I will pour this into your veins, that you may live for ever young."

And he listened to her false words, that simple Talus, and came near; and Medea said, "Dip yourself in the sea first, and cool yourself, lest you burn my tender hands; then show me where the nail in your vein is, that I may pour the ichor in."

Then that simple Talus dipped himself in the sea, till it hissed, and roared, and smoked; and came and knelt before Medea, and showed her the secret nail.

And she drew the nail out gently, but she poured no ichor in; and instead the liquid fire spouted forth, like a stream of red-hot iron. And Talus tried to leap up, crying, "You have betrayed me, false witch-maiden!" But she lifted up her hands before him, and sang, till he sank beneath her spell. And as he sank, his brazen limbs clanked heavily, and the earth groaned beneath his weight; and the liquid fire ran from his heel, like a stream of lava, to the sea; and Medea laughed, and called to the heroes, "Come ashore, and water your ship in peace."

So they came, and found the giant lying dead; and they fell down, and kissed Medea's feet; and watered their ship, and took sheep and oxen, and so left that inhospitable shore.

At last, after many more adventures, they came to the Cape of Malea, at the south-west point of the Peloponnese. And there they offered sacrifices, and Orpheus purged them from their guilt. Then they rode away again to the northward, past the Laconian shore, and came all worn and tired by Sunium, and up the long Euboean Strait, until they saw once more Pelion, and Aphetai, and Iolcos by the sea.

And they ran the ship ashore; but they had no strength left to haul her up the beach; and they crawled out on the pebbles, and sat down, and wept till they could weep no more. For the houses and the trees were all altered; and all the faces which they saw were strange; and their joy was swallowed up in sorrow, while they thought of their youth, and all their labour, and the gallant comrades they had lost.

And the people crowded round, and asked them "Who are you, that you sit weeping here?"

"We are the sons of your princes, who sailed out many a year ago. We went to fetch the golden fleece, and we have brought it, and grief therewith. Give us news of our fathers and our mothers, if any of them be left alive on earth."

Then there was shouting, and laughing, and weeping; and all the kings came to the shore, and they led away the heroes to their homes, and bewailed the valiant dead.

Then Jason went up with Medea to the palace of his uncle Pelias. And when he came in Pelias sat by the hearth, crippled and blind with age; while opposite him sat Aeson, Jason's father, crippled and blind likewise; and the two old men's heads shook together as they tried to warm themselves before the fire.

And Jason fell down at his father's knees, and wept, and called him by his name. And the old man stretched his hands out, and felt him, and said, "Do not mock me, young hero. My son Jason is dead long ago at sea."

"I am your own son Jason, whom you trusted to the Centaur upon Pelion; and I have brought home the golden fleece, and a princess of the Sun's race for my bride. So now give me up the kingdom, Pelias my uncle, and fulfil your promise as I have fulfilled mine."

Then his father clung to him like a child, and wept, and would not let him go; and cried, "Now I shall not go down lonely to my grave. Promise me never to leave me till I die."

MAGIC, SPELLS, ENCHANTMENTS & CURSES

Introduction

WORLD MYTHOLOGY, WE HAVE SEEN, abounds in captivating stories of enchantment and all the wonders that it can work. The stories in this section take us a little deeper into the kind of spells that are cast and the curses that are imposed.

Not that they actually explain these things. After all, if it's explicable, it isn't magic. But they introduce us to some of the stranger spells, like the ju ju used by 'The Slave Girl Who Tried to Kill her Mistress' in the Nigerian myth. And to some of the props and paraphernalia of enchantment: the 'Magic Book' with which alarmed apprentices end up cooking up a storm in the English story. They could have done with the mysterious 'Magic Circle' into which the Babylonian wizard and his associates were able safely to withdraw. Then there's the special talisman, inscribed in cinnabar with magic signs, which the dying Laotsze spontaneously spits out before his astonished followers in Chinese legend. From Japanese myth we meet a wonder-working kettle which becomes a tanuki – a raccoon-dog – with special powers; from Ireland the dancing pudding that livens up a dismal wedding.

The Disobedient Daughter Who Married a Skull

EFFIONG EDEM WAS A NATIVE of Cobham Town. He had a very fine daughter, whose name was Afiong. All the young men in the country wanted to marry her on account of her beauty; but she refused all offers of marriage in spite of repeated entreaties from her parents, as she was very vain, and said she would only marry the best-looking man in the country, who would have to be young and strong, and capable of loving her properly. Most of the men her parents wanted her to marry, although they were rich, were old men and ugly, so the girl continued to disobey her parents, at which they were very much grieved. The skull who lived in the spirit land heard of the beauty of this Calabar virgin, and thought he would like to possess her; so he went about amongst his friends and borrowed different parts of the body from them, all of the best. From one he got a good head, another lent him a body, a third gave him strong arms, and a fourth lent him a fine pair of legs. At last he was complete, and was a very perfect specimen of manhood.

He then left the spirit land and went to Cobham market, where he saw Afiong, and admired her very much.

About this time Afiong heard that a very fine man had been seen in the market, who was better-looking than any of the natives. She therefore went to the market at once, and directly she saw the Skull in his borrowed beauty, she fell in love with him, and invited him to her house. The Skull was delighted, and went home with her, and on his arrival was introduced by the girl to her parents, and immediately asked their consent to marry their daughter. At first they refused, as they did not wish her to marry a stranger, but at last they agreed.

He lived with Afiong for two days in her parents' house, and then said he wished to take his wife back to his country, which was far off. To this the girl readily agreed, as he was such a fine man, but her parents tried to persuade her not to go. However, being very headstrong, she made up her mind to go, and they started off together. After they had been gone a few days the father consulted his Ju Ju man, who by casting lots very soon discovered that his daughter's husband belonged to the spirit land, and that she would surely be killed. They therefore all mourned her as dead.

After walking for several days, Afiong and the Skull crossed the border between the spirit land and the human country. Directly they set foot in the spirit land, first of all one man came to the Skull and demanded his legs, then another his head, and the next his body, and so on, until in a few minutes the skull was left by itself in all its natural ugliness. At this the girl was very frightened, and wanted to return home, but the skull would not allow this, and ordered her to go with him. When they arrived at the skull's house they found his mother, who was a very old woman quite incapable of doing any work, who could only creep about. Afiong tried her best to help her, and cooked her food, and brought water and firewood for the old woman. The old creature was very grateful for these attentions, and soon became quite fond of Afiong.

One day the old woman told Afiong that she was very sorry for her, but all the people in the spirit land were cannibals, and when they heard there was a human being in their country, they would come down and kill her and eat her. The skull's mother then hid Afiong, and as she had looked after her so well, she promised she would send her back to her country as soon as possible, providing that she promised for the future to obey her parents. This Afiong readily consented to do. Then the old woman sent for the spider, who was a very clever hairdresser, and made him dress Afiong's hair in the latest fashion. She also presented her with anklets and other things on account of her kindness. She then made a Ju Ju and called the winds to come and convey Afiong to her home. At first a violent tornado came, with thunder, lightning and rain, but the skull's mother sent him away as unsuitable. The next wind to come was a gentle breeze, so she told the breeze to carry Afiong to her mother's house, and said goodbye to her. Very soon afterwards the breeze deposited Afiong outside her home, and left her there.

When the parents saw their daughter they were very glad, as they had for some months given her up as lost. The father spread soft animals' skins on the ground from where his daughter was standing all the way to the house, so that her feet should not be soiled. Afiong then walked to the house, and her father called all the young girls who belonged to Afiong's company to come and dance, and the feasting and dancing was kept up for eight days and nights. When the rejoicing was over, the father reported what had happened to the head chief of the town. The chief then passed a law that parents should never allow their daughters to marry strangers who came from a far country. Then the father told his daughter to marry a friend of his, and she willingly consented, and lived with him for many years, and had many children.

Of the Pretty Girl and the Seven Jealous Women

THERE WAS ONCE A VERY BEAUTIFUL GIRL called Akim. She was a native of Ibibio, and the name was given to her on account of her good looks, as she was born in the spring-time. She was an only daughter, and her parents were extremely fond of her. The people of the town, and more particularly the young girls, were so jealous of Akim's good looks and beautiful form – for she was perfectly made, very strong, and her carriage, bearing, and manners were most graceful – that her parents would not allow her to join the young girls' society in the town, as is customary for all young people to do, both boys and girls belonging to a company according to their age; a company consisting, as a rule, of all the boys or girls born in the same year.

Akim's parents were rather poor, but she was a good daughter, and gave them no trouble, so they had a happy home. One day as Akim was on her way to draw water from the spring she met the company of seven girls, to which in an ordinary way she would have belonged, if her parents had not forbidden her. These girls told her that they were going to hold a play in the town in three days' time, and asked her to join them. She said she was very sorry, but that her parents were poor, and only had herself to work for them, she therefore had no time to spare for dancing and plays. She then left them and went home.

In the evening the seven girls met together, and as they were very envious of Akim, they discussed how they should be revenged upon her for refusing to join their company, and they talked for a long time as to how they could get Akim into danger or punish her in some way.

At last one of the girls suggested that they should all go to Akim's house every day and help her with her work, so that when they had made friends with her they would be able to entice her away and take their revenge upon her for being more beautiful than themselves. Although they went every day and helped Akim and her parents with their work, the parents knew that they were jealous of their daughter, and repeatedly warned her not on any account to go with them, as they were not to be trusted.

At the end of the year there was going to be a big play, called the new yam play, to which Akim's parents had been invited. The play was going to be held at a town about two hours' march from where they lived. Akim was very anxious to go and take part in the dance, but her parents gave her plenty of work to do before they started, thinking that this would surely prevent her going, as she was a very obedient daughter, and always did her work properly.

On the morning of the play the jealous seven came to Akim and asked her to go with them, but she pointed to all the water pots she had to fill, and showed them where her parents had told her to polish the walls with a stone and make the floor good; and after that she had to pull up all the weeds round the house and clean up all round. She therefore said it was impossible for her to leave the house until all the work was finished. When the girls heard this they took up the water pots, went to the spring, and quickly returned with them full; they placed them in a row, and then they got stones, and very soon had the walls polished and the floor made good; after that they did the weeding outside and the cleaning up, and when everything was completed they said to Akim, "Now then, come along; you have no excuse to remain behind, as all the work is done."

Akim really wanted to go to the play; so as all the work was done which her parents had told her to do, she finally consented to go. About half-way to the town, where the new yam play was being held, there was a small river, about five feet deep, which had to be crossed by wading, as there was no bridge. In this river there was a powerful Ju Ju, whose law was that whenever anyone crossed the river and returned the same way on the return journey, whoever it was, had to give some food to the Ju Ju. If they did not make the proper sacrifice the Ju Ju dragged them down and took them to his home, and kept them there to work for him. The seven jealous girls knew all about this Ju Ju, having often crossed the river before, as they walked about all over the country, and had plenty of friends in the different towns. Akim, however, who was a good girl, and never went anywhere, knew nothing about this Ju Ju, which her companions had found out.

When the work was finished they all started off together, and crossed the river without any trouble. When they had gone a small distance on the other side they saw a small bird, perched on a high tree, who admired Akim very much, and sang in praise of her beauty, much to the annoyance of the seven girls; but they walked on without saying anything, and eventually arrived at the town where the play was being held. Akim had not taken the trouble to change her clothes, but when she arrived at the town, although her companions had on all their best beads and their finest clothes, the young men and people admired Akim far more than the other girls, and she was declared to be the finest and most beautiful woman at the dance. They gave her plenty of palm wine, foo-foo, and everything she wanted, so that the seven girls became more angry and jealous than before. The people danced and sang all that night, but Akim managed to keep out of the sight of her parents until the following morning, when they asked her how it was that she had disobeyed them and neglected her work; so Akim told them that the work had all been done by her friends, and they had enticed her to come to the play with them. Her mother then told her to return home at once, and that she was not to remain in the town any longer.

When Akim told her friends this they said, "Very well, we are just going to have some small meal, and then we will return with you." They all then sat down together and had their food, but each of the seven jealous girls hid a small quantity of foo-foo and fish in her clothes for the Water

Ju Ju. However Akim, who knew nothing about this, as her parents had forgotten to tell her about the Ju Ju, never thinking for one moment that their daughter would cross the river, did not take any food as a sacrifice to the Ju Ju with her.

When they arrived at the river Akim saw the girls making their small sacrifices, and begged them to give her a small share so that she could do the same, but they refused, and all walked across the river safely. Then when it was Akim's turn to cross, when she arrived in the middle of the river, the Water Ju Ju caught hold of her and dragged her underneath the water, so that she immediately disappeared from sight. The seven girls had been watching for this, and when they saw that she had gone they went on their way, very pleased at the success of their scheme, and said to one another, "Now Akim is gone forever, and we shall hear no more about her being better-looking than we are."

As there was no one to be seen at the time when Akim disappeared they naturally thought that their cruel action had escaped detection, so they went home rejoicing; but they never noticed the little bird high up in the tree who had sung of Akim's beauty when they were on their way to the play. The little bird was very sorry for Akim, and made up his mind that, when the proper time came, he would tell her parents what he had seen, so that perhaps they would be able to save her. The bird had heard Akim asking for a small portion of the food to make a sacrifice with, and had heard all the girls refusing to give her any.

The following morning, when Akim's parents returned home, they were much surprised to find that the door was fastened, and that there was no sign of their daughter anywhere about the place, so they inquired of their neighbours, but no one was able to give them any information about her. They then went to the seven girls, and asked them what had become of Akim. They replied that they did not know what had become of her, but that she had reached their town safely with them, and then said she was going home. The father then went to his Ju Ju man, who, by casting lots, discovered what had happened, and told him that on her way back from the play Akim had crossed the river without making the customary sacrifice to the Water Ju Ju, and that, as the Ju Ju was angry, he had seized Akim and taken her to his home. He therefore told Akim's father to take one goat, one basketful of eggs, and one piece of white cloth to the river in the morning, and to offer them as a sacrifice to the Water Ju Ju; then Akim would be thrown out of the water seven times, but that if her father failed to catch her on the seventh time, she would disappear forever.

Akim's father then returned home, and, when he arrived there, the little bird who had seen Akim taken by the Water Ju Ju, told him everything that had happened, confirming the Ju Ju's words. He also said that it was entirely the fault of the seven girls, who had refused to give Akim any food to make the sacrifice with.

Early the following morning the parents went to the river, and made the sacrifice as advised by the Ju Ju. Immediately they had done so, the Water Ju Ju threw Akim up from the middle of the river. Her father caught her at once, and returned home very thankfully.

He never told anyone, however, that he had recovered his daughter, but made up his mind to punish the seven jealous girls, so he dug a deep pit in the middle of his house, and placed dried palm leaves and sharp stakes in the bottom of the pit. He then covered the top of the pit with new mats, and sent out word for all people to come and hold a play to rejoice with him, as he had recovered his daughter from the spirit land. Many people came, and danced and sang all the day and night, but the seven jealous girls did not appear, as they were frightened. However, as they were told that everything had gone well on the previous day, and that there had been no trouble, they went to the house the following morning and mixed with the dancers; but they were ashamed to look Akim in the face, who was sitting down in the middle of the dancing ring.

When Akim's father saw the seven girls he pretended to welcome them as his daughter's friends, and presented each of them with a brass rod, which he placed round their necks. He also gave them tombo to drink.

He then picked them out, and told them to go and sit on mats on the other side of the pit he had prepared for them. When they walked over the mats which hid the pit they all fell in, and Akim's father immediately got some red-hot ashes from the fire and threw them in on top of the screaming girls, who were in great pain. At once the dried palm leaves caught fire, killing all the girls at once.

When the people heard the cries and saw the smoke, they all ran back to the town.

The next day the parents of the dead girls went to the head chief, and complained that Akim's father had killed their daughters, so the chief called him before him, and asked him for an explanation.

Akim's father went at once to the chief, taking the Ju Ju man, whom everybody relied upon, and the small bird, as his witnesses.

When the chief had heard the whole case, he told Akim's father that he should only have killed one girl to avenge his daughter, and not seven. So he told the father to bring Akim before him.

When she arrived, the head chief, seeing how beautiful she was, said that her father was justified in killing all the seven girls on her behalf, so he dismissed the case, and told the parents of the dead girls to go away and mourn for their daughters, who had been wicked and jealous women, and had been properly punished for their cruel behaviour to Akim.

Moral: Never kill a man or a woman because you are envious of their beauty, as if you do, you will surely be punished.

The Slave Girl Who Tried to Kill Her Mistress

A MAN CALLED AKPAN, who was a native of Oku, a town in the Ibibio country, admired a girl called Emme very much, who lived at Ibibio, and wished to marry her, as she was the finest girl in her company. It was the custom in those days for the parents to demand such a large amount for their daughters as dowry, that if after they were married they failed to get on with their husbands, as they could not redeem themselves, they were sold as slaves. Akpan paid a very large sum as dowry for Emme, and she was put in the fatting-house until the proper time arrived for her to marry.

Akpan told the parents that when their daughter was ready they must send her over to him. This they promised to do. Emme's father was a rich man, and after seven years had elapsed, and it became time for her to go to her husband, he saw a very fine girl, who had also just come out of the fatting-house, and whom the parents wished to sell as a slave. Emme's father therefore bought her, and gave her to his daughter as her handmaiden.

The next day Emme's little sister, being very anxious to go with her, obtained the consent of her mother, and they started off together, the slave girl carrying a large bundle containing clothes and presents from Emme's father. Akpan's house was a long day's march from where they lived. When they arrived just outside the town they came to a spring, where the people used to get their drinking water from, but no one was allowed to bathe there. Emme, however, knew nothing about this. They took off their clothes to wash close to the spring, and where there was a deep hole which led to the Water Ju Ju's house. The slave girl knew of this Ju Ju, and thought if she could get her mistress to bathe, she would be taken by the Ju Ju, and she would then be able to take her place and marry Akpan. So they went down to bathe, and when they were close to the water the slave girl pushed her mistress in, and she at once disappeared. The little girl then began to cry, but the slave girl said, "If you cry any more I will kill you at once, and throw your body into the hole after your sister." And she told the child that she must never mention what had happened to anyone, and particularly not to Akpan, as she was going to represent her sister and marry him, and that if she ever told anyone what she had seen, she would be killed at once. She then made the little girl carry her load to Akpan's house.

When they arrived, Akpan was very much disappointed at the slave girl's appearance, as she was not nearly as pretty and fine as he had expected her to be; but as he had not seen Emme for seven years, he had no suspicion that the girl was not really Emme, for whom he had paid such a large dowry. He then called all his company together to play and feast, and when they arrived they were much astonished, and said, "Is this the fine woman for whom you paid so much dowry, and whom you told us so much about?" And Akpan could not answer them.

The slave girl was then for some time very cruel to Emme's little sister, and wanted her to die, so that her position would be more secure with her husband. She beat the little girl every day, and always made her carry the largest water pot to the spring; she also made the child place her finger in the fire to use as firewood. When the time came for food, the slave girl went to the fire and got a burning piece of wood and burned the child all over the body with it. When Akpan asked her why she treated the child so badly, she replied that she was a slave that her father had bought for her. When the little girl took the heavy water pot to the river to fill it there was no one to lift it up for her, so that she could not get it on to her head; she therefore had to remain a long time at the spring, and at last began calling for her sister Emme to come and help her.

When Emme heard her little sister crying for her, she begged the Water Ju Ju to allow her to go and help her, so he told her she might go, but that she must return to him again immediately. When the little girl saw her sister she did not want to leave her, and asked to be allowed to go into the hole with her. She then told Emme how very badly she had been treated by the slave girl, and her elder sister told her to have patience and wait, that a day of vengeance would arrive sooner or later. The little girl went back to Akpan's house with a glad heart as she had seen her sister, but when she got to the house, the slave girl said, "Why have you been so long getting the water?" and then took another stick from the fire and burnt the little girl again very badly, and starved her for the rest of the day.

This went on for some time, until, one day, when the child went to the river for water, after all the people had gone, she cried out for her sister as usual, but she did not come for a long time, as there was a hunter from Akpan's town hidden near watching the hole, and the Water Ju Ju told Emme that she must not go; but, as the little girl went on crying bitterly, Emme at last persuaded the Ju Ju to let her go, promising to return quickly. When she emerged from the water, she looked very beautiful with the rays of the setting sun shining on her glistening body. She helped her little sister with her water pot, and then disappeared into the hole again.

The hunter was amazed at what he had seen, and when he returned, he told Akpan what a beautiful woman had come out of the water and had helped the little girl with her water pot. He also told Akpan that he was convinced that the girl he had seen at the spring was his proper wife, Emme, and that the Water Ju Ju must have taken her.

Akpan then made up his mind to go out and watch and see what happened, so, in the early morning the hunter came for him, and they both went down to the river, and hid in the forest near the water-hole.

When Akpan saw Emme come out of the water, he recognised her at once, and went home and considered how he should get her out of the power of the Water Ju Ju. He was advised by some of his friends to go to an old woman, who frequently made sacrifices to the Water Ju Ju, and consult her as to what was the best thing to do.

When he went to her, she told him to bring her one white slave, one white goat, one piece of white cloth, one white chicken, and a basket of eggs. Then, when the great Ju Ju day arrived, she would take them to the Water Ju Ju, and make a sacrifice of them on his behalf. The day after the sacrifice was made, the Water Ju Ju would return the girl to her, and she would bring her to Akpan.

Akpan then bought the slave, and took all the other things to the old woman, and, when the day of the sacrifice arrived, he went with his friend the hunter and witnessed the old woman make the sacrifice. The slave was bound up and led to the hole, then the old woman called to the Water Ju Ju and cut the slave's throat with a sharp knife and pushed him into the hole. She then did the same to the goat and chicken, and also threw the eggs and cloth in on top of them.

After this had been done, they all returned to their homes. The next morning at dawn the old woman went to the hole, and found Emme standing at the side of the spring, so she told her that she was her friend, and was going to take her to her husband. She then took Emme back to her own home, and hid her in her room, and sent word to Akpan to come to her house, and to take great care that the slave woman knew nothing about the matter.

So Akpan left the house secretly by the back door, and arrived at the old woman's house without meeting anybody.

When Emme saw Akpan, she asked for her little sister, so he sent his friend, the hunter, for her to the spring, and he met her carrying her water pot to get the morning supply of water for the house, and brought her to the old woman's house with him.

When Emme had embraced her sister, she told her to return to the house and do something to annoy the slave woman, and then she was to run as fast as she could back to the old woman's house, where, no doubt, the slave girl would follow her, and would meet them all inside the house, and see Emme, who she believed she had killed.

The little girl did as she was told, and, directly she got into the house, she called out to the slave woman: "Do you know that you are a wicked woman, and have treated me very badly? I know you are only my sister's slave, and you will be properly punished." She then ran as hard as she could to the old woman's house. Directly the slave woman heard what the little girl said, she was quite mad with rage, and seized a burning stick from the fire, and ran after the child; but the little one got to the house first, and ran inside, the slave woman following close upon her heels with the burning stick in her hand.

Then Emme came out and confronted the slave woman, and she at once recognised her mistress, whom she thought she had killed, so she stood quite still.

Then they all went back to Akpan's house, and when they arrived there, Akpan asked the slave woman what she meant by pretending that she was Emme, and why she had tried to kill her. But, seeing she was found out, the slave woman had nothing to say.

Many people were then called to a play to celebrate the recovery of Akpan's wife, and when they had all come, he told them what the slave woman had done.

After this, Emme treated the slave girl in the same way as she had treated her little sister. She made her put her fingers in the fire, and burnt her with sticks. She also made her beat foo-foo with her head in a hollowed-out tree, and after a time she was tied up to a tree and starved to death.

Ever since that time, when a man marries a girl, he is always present when she comes out of the fatting-house and takes her home himself, so that such evil things as happened to Emme and her sister may not occur again.

The Fate of Essido and His Evil Companions

CHIEF OBORRI lived at a town called Adiagor, which is on the right bank of the Calabar River. He was a wealthy chief, and belonged to the Egbo Society. He had many large canoes, and plenty of slaves to paddle them. These canoes he used to fill up with new yams – each canoe being under one head slave and containing eight paddles; the canoes were capable of holding three puncheons of palm oil, and cost eight hundred rods each. When they were full, about ten of them used to start off together and paddle to Rio del Rey. They went through creeks all the way, which run through mangrove swamps, with palm oil trees here and there. Sometimes in the tornado season it was very dangerous crossing the creeks, as the canoes were so heavily laden, having only a few inches above the water, that quite a small wave would fill the canoe and cause it to sink to the bottom. Although most of the boys could swim, it often happened that some of them were lost, as there are many large alligators in these waters. After four days' hard paddling they would arrive at Rio del Rey, where they had very little difficulty in exchanging their new yams for bags of dried shrimps and sticks with smoked fish on them.

Chief Oborri had two sons, named Eyo I. and Essido. Their mother having died when they were babies, the children were brought up by their father. As they grew up, they developed entirely different characters. The eldest was very hard-working and led a solitary life; but the younger son was fond of gaiety and was very lazy, in fact, he spent most of his time in the neighbouring towns playing and dancing. When the two boys arrived at the respective ages of eighteen and twenty their father died, and they were left to look after themselves. According to native custom, the elder son, Eyo I., was entitled to the whole of his father's estate; but being very fond of his younger brother, he gave him a large number of rods and some land with a house. Immediately Essido became possessed of the money he became wilder than ever, gave big feasts to his companions, and always had his house full of women, upon whom he spent large sums. Although the amount his brother had given him on his father's death was very large, in the course of a few years Essido had spent it all. He then sold his house and effects, and spent the proceeds on feasting.

While he had been living this gay and unprofitable life, Eyo I. had been working harder than ever at his father's old trade, and had made many trips to Rio del Rey himself. Almost every week he had canoes laden with yams going down river and returning after about twelve days with shrimps and fish, which Eyo I. himself disposed of in the neighbouring markets, and he very rapidly became a rich man. At intervals he remonstrated with Essido on his extravagance, but his warnings had no effect; if anything, his brother became worse. At last the time arrived when all his money was spent, so Essido went to his brother and asked him to lend him two thousand rods, but Eyo refused, and told Essido that he would not help him in any way to continue his present life of debauchery, but that if he liked to work on the farm and trade, he would give him a fair share of the profits. This Essido indignantly refused, and went back to the town and consulted some of the very few friends he had left as to what was the best thing to do.

The men he spoke to were thoroughly bad men, and had been living upon Essido for a long time. They suggested to him that he should go round the town and borrow money from the people he had entertained, and then they would run away to Akpabryos town, which was about four days' march from Calabar. This Essido did, and managed to borrow a lot of money, although many people refused to lend him anything. Then at night he set off with his evil companions, who carried his money, as they had not been able to borrow any themselves, being so well known. When they arrived at Akpabryos town they found many beautiful women and graceful dancers. They then started the same life again, until after a few weeks most of the money had gone. They then met and consulted together how to get more money, and advised Essido to return to his rich brother, pretending that he was going to work and give up his old life; he should then get poison from a man they knew of, and place it in his brother's food, so that he would die, and then Essido would become possessed of all his brother's wealth, and they would be able to live in the same way as they had formerly. Essido, who had sunk very low, agreed to this plan, and they left Akpabryos town the next morning. After marching for two days, they arrived at a small hut in the bush where a man who was an expert poisoner lived, called Okponesip. He was the head Ju Ju man of the country, and when they had bribed him with eight hundred rods he swore them to secrecy, and gave Essido a small parcel containing a deadly poison which he said would kill his brother in three months. All he had to do was to place the poison in his brother's food.

When Essido returned to his brother's house he pretended to be very sorry for his former mode of living, and said that for the future he was going to work. Eyo I. was very glad when he heard this, and at once asked his brother in, and gave him new clothes and plenty to eat.

In the evening, when supper was being prepared, Essido went into the kitchen, pretending he wanted to get a light from the fire for his pipe. The cook being absent and no one about, he put the poison in the soup, and then returned to the living-room. He then asked for some tombo, which was brought, and when he had finished it, he said he did not want any supper, and went to sleep. His brother, Eyo I., had supper by himself and consumed all the soup. In a week's time he began to feel very ill, and as the days passed he became worse, so he sent for his Ju Ju man.

When Essido saw him coming, he quietly left the house; but the Ju Ju man, by casting lots, very soon discovered that it was Essido who had given poison to his brother. When he told Eyo I. this, he would not believe it, and sent him away. However, when Essido returned, his elder brother told him what the Ju Ju man had said, but that he did not believe him for one moment, and had sent him away. Essido was much relieved when he heard this, but as he was anxious that no suspicion of the crime should be attached to him, he went to the Household Ju Ju, and having first sworn that he had never administered poison to his brother, he drank out of the pot.

Three months after he had taken the poison Eyo I. died, much to the grief of everyone who knew him, as he was much respected, not only on account of his great wealth, but because he was also an upright and honest man, who never did harm to anyone.

Essido kept his brother's funeral according to the usual custom, and there was much playing and dancing, which was kept up for a long time. Then Essido paid off his old creditors in order to make himself popular, and kept open house, entertaining most lavishly, and spending his money in many foolish ways. All the bad women about collected at his house, and his old evil companions went on as they had done before.

Things got so bad that none of the respectable people would have anything to do with him, and at last the chiefs of the country, seeing the way Essido was squandering his late brother's estate, assembled together, and eventually came to the conclusion that he was a witch man, and had poisoned his brother in order to acquire his position. The chiefs, who were all friends of the late Eyo, and who were very sorry at the death, as they knew that if he had lived he would have become a great and powerful chief, made up their minds to give Essido the Ekpawor Ju Ju, which is a very strong medicine, and gets into men's heads, so that when they have drunk it they are compelled to speak the truth, and if they have done wrong they die very shortly. Essido was then told to dress himself and attend the meeting at the palaver house, and when he arrived the chiefs charged him with having killed his brother by witchcraft. Essido denied having done so, but the chiefs told him that if he were innocent he must prove it by drinking the bowl of Ekpawor medicine which was placed before him. As he could not refuse to drink, he drank the bowl off in great fear and trembling, and very soon the Ju Ju having got hold of him, he confessed that he had poisoned his brother, but that his friends had advised him to do so. About two hours after drinking the Ekpawor, Essido died in great pain.

The friends were then brought to the meeting and tied up to posts, and questioned as to the part they had taken in the death of Eyo. As they were too frightened to answer, the chiefs told them that they knew from Essido that they had induced him to poison his brother. They were then taken to the place where Eyo was buried, the grave having been dug open, and their heads were cut off and fell into the grave, and their bodies were thrown in after them as a sacrifice for the wrong they had done. The grave was then filled up again.

Ever since that time, whenever anyone is suspected of being a witch, he is tried by the Ekpawor Ju Ju.

The Story of the Drummer and the Alligators

THERE WAS ONCE A WOMAN named Affiong Any who lived at Nsidung, a small town to the south of Calabar. She was married to a chief of Hensham Town called Etim Ekeng. They had lived together for several years, but had no children. The chief was very anxious to have a child during his lifetime, and made sacrifices to his Ju Ju, but they had no effect. So he went to a witch man, who told him that the reason he had no children was that he was too rich. The chief then asked the witch man how he should spend his money in order to get a child, and he was told to make friends with everybody, and give big feasts, so that he should get rid of some of his money and become poorer.

The chief then went home and told his wife. The next day his wife called all her company together and gave them a big dinner, which cost a lot of money; much food was consumed, and large quantities of tombo were drunk. Then the chief entertained his company, which cost a lot more money. He also wasted a lot of money in the Egbo house. When half of his property was wasted, his wife told him that she had conceived. The chief, being very glad, called a big play for the next day.

In those days all the rich chiefs of the country belonged to the Alligator Company, and used to meet in the water. The reason they belonged to the company was, first of all, to protect their canoes when they went trading, and secondly, to destroy the canoes and property of the people who did not belong to their company, and to take their money and kill their slaves.

Chief Etim Ekeng was a kind man, and would not join this society, although he was repeatedly urged to do so. After a time a son was born to the chief, and he called him Edet Etim. The chief then called the Egbo society together, and all the doors of the houses in the town were shut, the markets were stopped, and the women were not allowed to go outside their houses while the Egbo was playing. This was kept up for several days, and cost the chief a lot of money. Then he made up his mind that he would divide his property, and give his son half when he became old enough. Unfortunately after three months the chief died, leaving his sorrowing wife to look after their little child.

The wife then went into mourning for seven years for her husband, and after that time she became entitled to all his property, as the late chief had no brothers. She looked after the little boy very carefully until he grew up, when he became a very fine, healthy young man, and was much admired by all the pretty girls of the town; but his mother warned him strongly not to go with them, because they would make him become a bad man. Whenever the girls had a play they used to invite Edet Etim, and at last he went to the play, and they made him beat the drum for them to dance to. After much practice he became the best drummer in the town, and whenever the girls had a play they always called him to drum for them. Plenty of the young girls left their husbands, and went to Edet and asked him to marry them. This made all the young men of the town very jealous, and when they met together at night they considered what would be the best way to kill him. At last they decided that when Edet went to bathe they would induce the alligators to take him. So one night, when he was washing, one alligator seized him by the foot, and others came and seized him round the waist. He fought very hard, but at last they dragged him into the deep water, and took him to their home.

When his mother heard this, she determined to do her best to recover her son, so she kept quite quiet until the morning.

When the young men saw that Edet's mother remained quiet, and did not cry, they thought of the story of the hawk and the owl, and determined to keep Edet alive for a few months.

At cockcrow the mother raised a cry, and went to the grave of her dead husband in order to consult his spirit as to what she had better do to recover her lost son. After a time she went down to the beach with small young green branches in her hands, with which she beat the water, and called upon all the Ju Jus of the Calabar River to help her to recover her son. She then went home and got a load of rods, and took them to a Ju Ju man in the farm. His name was Ininen Okon; he was so called because he was very artful, and had plenty of strong Ju Jus.

When the young boys heard that Edet's mother had gone to Ininen Okon, they all trembled with fear, and wanted to return Edet, but they could not do so, as it was against the rules of their society. The Ju Ju man having discovered that Edet was still alive, and was being detained in the alligators' house, told the mother to be patient. After three days Ininen himself joined another alligators' society, and went to inspect the young alligators' house. He found a young man whom he knew, left on guard when all the alligators had gone to feed at the ebb of the tide, and came back and told the mother to wait, as he would make a Ju Ju which would cause them all to depart in seven days, and leave no one in the house. He made his Ju Ju, and the young alligators said that as no one had come for Edet, they would all go at the ebb tide to feed, and leave no one in charge of the house. When they returned they found Edet still there, and everything as they had left it, as Ininen had not gone that day.

Three days afterwards they all went away again, and this time went a long way off, and did not return quickly. When Ininen saw that the tide was going down he changed himself into an alligator, and swam to the young alligators' home, where he found Edet chained to a post. He then found an axe and cut the post, releasing the boy. But Edet, having been in the water so long, was deaf and dumb. He then found several loin cloths which had been left behind by the young alligators, so he gathered them together and took them away to show to the king, and Ininen left the place, taking Edet with him.

He then called the mother to see her son, but when she came the boy could only look at her, and could not speak. The mother embraced her boy, but he took no notice, as he did not seem capable of understanding anything, but sat down quietly. Then the Ju Ju man told Edet's mother that he would cure her son in a few days, so he made several Ju Jus, and gave her son medicine, and after a time the boy recovered his speech and became sensible again.

Then Edet's mother put on a mourning cloth, and pretended that her son was dead, and did not tell the people he had come back to her. When the young alligators returned, they found that Edet was gone, and that someone had taken their loin cloths. They were therefore much afraid, and made inquiries if Edet had been seen, but they could hear nothing about him, as he was hidden in a farm, and the mother continued to wear her mourning cloth in order to deceive them.

Nothing happened for six months, and they had quite forgotten all about the matter. Affiong, the mother, then went to the chiefs of the town, and asked them to hold a large meeting of all the people, both young and old, at the palaver house, so that her late husband's property might be divided up in accordance with the native custom, as her son had been killed by the alligators.

The next day the chiefs called all the people together, but the mother in the early morning took her son to a small room at the back of the palaver house, and left him there with the seven loin cloths which the Ju Ju man had taken from the alligators' home. When the chiefs and all the people were seated, Affiong stood up and addressed them, saying –

"Chiefs and young men of my town, eight years ago my husband was a fine young man. He married me, and we lived together for many years without having any children. At last I had a son, but my husband died a few months afterwards. I brought my boy up carefully, but as he was a good drummer and dancer the young men were jealous, and had him caught by the alligators. Is there anyone present who can tell me what my son would have become if he had lived?" She then asked them what they thought of the alligator society, which had killed so many young men.

The chiefs, who had lost a lot of slaves, told her that if she could produce evidence against any members of the society they would destroy it at once. She then called upon Ininen to appear with her son Edet. He came out from the room leading Edet by the hand, and placed the bundle of loin cloths before the chiefs.

The young men were very much surprised when they saw Edet, and wanted to leave the palaver house; but when they stood up to go the chiefs told them to sit down at once, or they would receive three hundred lashes. They then sat down, and the Ju Ju man explained how he had gone to the alligators' home, and had brought Edet back to his mother. He also said that he had found the seven loin cloths in the house, but he did not wish to say anything about them, as the owners of some of the cloths were sons of the chiefs.

The chiefs, who were anxious to stop the bad society, told him, however, to speak at once and tell them everything. Then he undid the bundle and took the cloths out one by one, at the same time calling upon the owners to come and take them. When they came to take their cloths, they were told to remain where they were; and they were then told to name their company. The seven young men then gave the names of all the members of their society, thirty-two in all. These men were all placed in a line, and the chiefs then passed sentence, which was that they should all be killed the next morning on the beach. So they were then all tied together to posts, and seven men were placed as a guard over them. They made fires and beat drums all the night.

Early in the morning, at about 4am, the big wooden drum was placed on the roof of the palaver house, and beaten to celebrate the death of the evildoers, which was the custom in those days.

The boys were then unfastened from the posts, and had their hands tied behind their backs, and were marched down to the beach. When they arrived there, the head chief stood up and addressed the people. "This is a small town of which I am chief, and I am determined to stop this bad custom, as so many men have been killed." He then told a man who had a sharp matchet to cut off one man's head. He then told another man who had a sharp knife to skin another young man alive. A third man who had a heavy stick was ordered to beat another to death, and so the chief went on and killed all the thirty-two young men in the most horrible ways he could think of. Some of them were tied to posts in the river, and left there until the tide came up and drowned them. Others were flogged to death.

After they had all been killed, for many years no one was killed by alligators, but some little time afterwards on the road between the beach and the town the land fell in, making a very large and deep hole, which was said to be the home of the alligators, and the people have ever since tried to fill it up, but have never yet been able to do so.

The Magic Circle

THE MAGIC CIRCLE, as in use among the Chaldean sorcerers, bears many points of resemblance to that described in mediaeval works on magic. The Babylonian magician, when describing the circle, made seven little winged figures, which he set before an image of the god Nergal. After doing so he stated that he had covered them with a dark robe and bound them with a coloured cord, setting beside them tamarisk and the heart of the palm, that he had completed the magic circle and had surrounded them with a sprinkling of lime and flour.

That the magic circle of mediaeval times must have been evolved from the Chaldean is plain from the strong resemblance between the two. Directions for the making of a mediaeval magic circle are as follows:

In the first place the magician is supposed to fix upon a spot proper for such a purpose, which must be either in a subterranean vault, hung round with black, and lighted by a magical torch, or else in the centre of some thick wood or desert, or upon some extensive unfrequented plain, where several roads meet, or amidst the ruins of ancient castles, abbeys, or monasteries, or amongst the rocks on the seashore, in some private detached churchyard, or any other melancholy place between the hours of twelve and one in the night, either when the moon shines very bright, or else when the elements are disturbed with storms of thunder, lightning, wind, and rain; for, in these places, times, and seasons, it is contended that spirits can with less difficulty manifest themselves to mortal eyes, and continue visible with the least pain.

When the proper time and place are fixed upon, a magic circle is to be formed within which the master and his associates are carefully to retire. The reason assigned by magicians and others for the institution and use of the circles is, that so much ground being blessed and consecrated by holy words and ceremonies has a secret force to expel all evil spirits from the bounds thereof, and, being sprinkled with sacred water, the ground is purified from all uncleanness; beside the holy names of God being written over every part of it, its force becomes proof against all evil spirits.

Snorter and Blower

AT THE TIME of the overthrow of the Shang and establishment of the Chou dynasty in 1122 BC there lived two marshals, Cheng Lung and Ch'en Ch'i. These were Heng and Ha, the Snorter and Blower respectively. The former was the chief superintendent of supplies for the armies of the tyrant emperor Chou, the Nero of China. The latter was in charge of obtaining food for the same army.

Legend has it that from his master, Tu O, the celebrated Taoist magician of the K'un-lun Mountains, Heng acquired a marvellous power. When he snorted, his nostrils emitted two white columns of light, which destroyed his enemies, body and soul. It was through him the Chou gained numerous victories. One day he was captured, bound and taken to the general of Chou. His life was spared and he was made general superintendent of army stores as well as generalissimo of five army corps.

Later on he found himself face to face with the Blower. The latter had learned from the magician how to store a supply of yellow gas in his chest which, when he blew it out, annihilated anyone it struck. By this means he caused large gaps to be made in the ranks of the enemy.

Being opposed to each other, one snorting out great streaks of white light, the other blowing streams of yellow gas, the battle continued until the Blower was wounded in the shoulder by No-cha, of the Chou army, and pierced in the stomach with a spear by Huang Fei-hu, Yellow Flying Tiger.

The Snorter in turn was slain in this fight by Marshal Chin Ta-sheng, 'Golden Big Pint', an ox spirit who was blessed with the mysterious power of producing the celebrated niu huang, ox-yellow, or bezoar. Facing the Snorter, with a noise like thunder he spat a piece of bezoar as large as a rice bowl in his face. It struck him on the nose and split his nostrils. He fell to the earth and was cut in two by a blow from his victor's sword.

After the Chou dynasty had been fully established Chiang Tzu-ya canonized the two marshals Heng and Ha, and granted them the offices of guardians of the Buddhist temple gates, where their gigantic images may be seen.

The God of Riches

AS WITH MANY OTHER CHINESE GODS, the God of Wealth, Ts'ai Shen, has been ascribed to several different people. The original and best known until later times was Chao Kung-ming. The accounts of him also differ but the following is the most popular.

When Chiang Tzu-ya was fighting for the Chou dynasty against the last of the Shang emperors, Chao Kung-ming, then a hermit on Mount O-mei, took the part of the latter.

He performed many wonderful feats. He could ride a black tiger and hurl pearls which burst like bombshells. But he was eventually overcome by the form of witchcraft known in Wales as Ciurp Creadh. Chiang Tzu-ya made a straw image of him, wrote his name on it, burned incense and worshipped before it for twenty days. On the twenty-first day he shot arrows made of peach wood into its eyes and heart. At that same moment Kung-ming, then in the enemy's camp, felt ill and fainted, and uttering a cry gave up the ghost.

Later on Chiang Tzu-ya persuaded Yuan-shih T'ien-tsun to release the spirits of the heroes who had died in battle from the Otherworld, and when Chao Kung-ming was led into his presence he praised his bravery and canonized him as President of the Ministry of Riches and Prosperity.

The God of Riches is universally worshipped in China. Talismans, trees of which the branches are strings of cash, and the fruits ingots of gold, to be obtained merely by shaking them down, a magic inexhaustible casket full of gold and silver – these and other spiritual sources of wealth are associated with this much-adored deity. He is represented in the guise of a visitor accompanied by a crowd of attendants laden down with all the treasures that the hearts of men, women and children could desire.

Yang Oerlang

THE SECOND DAUGHTER of the Ruler of Heaven once came down upon the earth and secretly became the wife of a mortal man named Yang. And when she returned to Heaven she was blessed with a son. But the Ruler of Heaven was very angry at this desecration of the heavenly halls. He banished her to earth and covered her with the Wu-I hills. Her son, however, Oerlang by name, the nephew of the Ruler of Heaven, was extraordinarily gifted by nature. By the time he was full grown he had learned the magic art of being able to control eight times nine transformations. He could make himself invisible, or could assume the shape of birds and beasts, grasses, flowers, snakes and fishes, as he chose. He also knew how to empty out seas and remove mountains from one place to another. So he went to the Wu-I hills and rescued his mother, whom he took on his back and carried away. They stopped to rest on a flat ledge of rock.

Then the mother said: "I am very thirsty!"

Oerlang climbed down into the valley in order to fetch her water, and some time passed before he returned. When he did his mother was no longer there. He searched eagerly, but on the rock lay only her skin and bones, and a few blood-stains. Now you must know that at that time there were still ten suns in the heavens, glowing and burning like fire. The Daughter of Heaven, it is true, was divine by nature; yet because she had incurred the anger of her father and had been banished to earth, her magic powers had failed her. Then, too, she had been imprisoned so long beneath the hills in the dark that, coming out suddenly into the sunlight, she had been devoured by its blinding radiance.

When Oerlang thought of his mother's sad end, his heart ached. He took two mountains on his shoulders, pursued the suns and crushed them to death between the mountains. And whenever he had crushed another sun-disk, he picked up a fresh mountain. In this way he had already slain nine of the ten suns, and there was but one left. And as Oerlang pursued him relentlessly, he hid himself in his distress beneath the leaves of the portulacca plant. But there was a rainworm close by who betrayed his hiding-place, and kept repeating: "There he is! There he is!"

Oerlang was about to seize him, when a messenger from the Ruler of the Heaven suddenly descended from the skies with a command: "Sky, air and earth need the sunshine. You must allow this one sun to live, so that all created beings may live. Yet, because you rescued your mother, and showed yourself to be a good son, you shall be a god, and be my bodyguard in the Highest Heaven, and shall rule over good and evil in the mortal world, and have power over devils and demons." When Oerlang received this command he ascended to Heaven.

Then the sun-disk came out again from beneath the portulacca leaves, and out of gratitude, since the plant had saved him, he bestowed upon it the gift of a free-blooming nature, and ordained that it never need fear the sunshine. To this very day one may see on the lower side of the portulacca leaves quite delicate little white pearls. They are the sunshine that remained hanging to the leaves when the sun hid under them. But the sun pursues the rainworm, when he ventures forth out of the ground, and dries him up as a punishment for his treachery.

Since that time Yang Oerlang has been honored as a god. He has oblique, sharply marked eyebrows, and holds a double-bladed, three-pointed sword in his hand. Two servants stand beside him, with a falcon and a hound; for Yang Oerlang is a great hunter. The falcon is the falcon of the gods, and the hound is the hound of the gods. When brute creatures gain possession of magic powers or demons oppress men, he subdues them by means of the falcon and hound.

Laotsze

LAOTSZE IS REALLY OLDER than heaven and earth put together. He is the Yellow Lord or Ancient, who created this world together with the other four. At various times he has appeared on earth, under various names. His most celebrated incarnation, however, is that of Laotsze, "The Old Child", which name he was given because he made his appearance on earth with white hair.

He acquired all sorts of magic powers by means of which he extended his life-span. Once he hired a servant to do his bidding. He agreed to give him a hundred pieces of copper daily; yet he did not pay him, and finally he owed him seven million, two hundred thousand pieces of copper. Then he mounted a black steer and rode to the West. He wanted to take his servant along. But when they reached the Han-Gu pass, the servant refused to go further, and insisted on being paid. Yet Laotsze gave him nothing.

When they came to the house of the guardian of the pass, red clouds appeared in the sky. The guardian understood this sign and knew that a holy man was drawing near. So he went out to meet him and took him into his house. He questioned him with regard to hidden knowledge, but Laotsze only stuck out his tongue at him and would not say a word. Nevertheless, the guardian of the pass treated him with the greatest respect in his home. Laotsze's servant told the servant of the guardian that his master owed him a great deal of money, and begged the latter to put in a good word for him. When the guardian's servant heard how large a sum it was, he was tempted to win so wealthy a man for a son-in-law, and he married him to his daughter. Finally the guardian heard of the matter and came to Laotsze together with the servant. Then Laotsze said to his servant: "You rascally servant. You really should have been dead long ago. I hired you, and since I was poor and could give you no money, I gave you a life-giving talisman to eat. That is how you still happen to be alive. I said to you: 'If you will follow me into the West, the land of Blessed Repose, I will pay you your wages in yellow gold. But you did not wish to do this.'" And with that he patted his servant's neck. Thereupon the latter opened his mouth, and spat out the life-giving talisman. The magic signs written on it with cinnabar, quite fresh and well-preserved, might still be seen. But the servant suddenly collapsed and turned into a heap of dry bones. Then the guardian of the pass cast himself to earth and pleaded for him. He promised to pay the servant for Laotsze and begged the latter to restore him to life. So Laotsze placed the talisman among the bones and at once the servant came to life again. The guardian of the pass paid him his wages and dismissed him. Then he adored Laotsze as his master, and the latter taught him the art of eternal life, and left him his teachings, in five thousand words, which the guardian wrote down. The book which thus came into being is the Tao Teh King, "The Book of the Way and Life." Laotsze then disappeared from the eyes of men. The guardian of the pass however, followed his teachings, and was given a place among the immortals.

The Ape Sun Wu King

FAR, FAR AWAY to the East, in the midst of the Great Sea there is an island called the Mountain of Flowers and Fruits. And on this mountain there is a high rock. Now this rock, from the very beginning of the world, had absorbed all the hidden seed power of heaven and earth and sun and moon, which endowed it with supernatural creative gifts. One day the rock burst, and out came an egg of stone. And out of this stone egg a stone ape was hatched by magic power. When he broke the shell he bowed to all sides. Then he gradually learned to walk and to leap, and two streams of golden radiance broke from his eyes which shot up to the highest of the castles of heaven, so that the Lord of the Heavens was frightened. So he sent out the two gods, Thousandmile-Eye and Fine-Ear, to find out what had happened. The two gods came back and reported: "The rays shine from the eyes of the stone ape who was hatched out of the egg which came from the magic rock. There is no reason for uneasiness."

Little by little the ape grew up, ran and leaped about, drank from the springs in the valleys, ate the flowers and fruits, and time went by in unconstrained play.

One day, during the summer, when he was seeking coolness, together with the other apes on the island, they went to the valley to bathe. There they saw a waterfall which plunged down a high cliff. Said the apes to each other: "Whoever can force his way through the waterfall, without suffering injury, shall be our king." The stone ape at once leaped into the air with joy and cried: "I will pass through!" Then he closed his eyes, bent down low and leaped through the roar and foam of the waters. When he opened his eyes once more he saw an iron bridge, which was shut off from the outer world by the waterfall as though by a curtain.

At its entrance stood a tablet of stone on which were graven the words: "This is the heavenly cave behind the water-curtain on the Blessed Island of Flowers and Fruits." Filled with joy, the stone ape leaped out again through the waterfall and told the other apes what he had found. They received the news with great content, and begged the stone ape to take them there. So the tribe of apes leaped through the water on the iron bridge, and then crowded into the cave castle where they found a hearth with a profusion of pots, cups and platters. But all were made of stone. Then the apes paid homage to the stone ape as their king, and he was given the name of Handsome King of the Apes. He appointed long-tailed, ring-tailed and other monkeys to be his officials and counselors, servants and retainers, and they led a blissful life on the Mountain, sleeping by night in their cave castle, keeping away from birds and beasts, and their king enjoyed untroubled happiness. In this way some three hundred years went by.

One day, when the King of the Apes sat with his subjects at a merry meal, he suddenly began to weep. Frightened, the apes asked him why he so suddenly grew sad amid all his bliss. Said the King: "It is true that we are not subject to the law and rule of man, that birds and beasts do not dare attack us, yet little by little we grow old and weak, and some day the hour will strike when Death, the Ancient, will drag us off! Then we are gone in a moment, and can no longer dwell upon earth!" When the apes heard these words, they hid their faces and sobbed. But an old ape, whose arms were connected in such a way that he could add the length of one to that of the other, stepped forth from the ranks. In a loud tone of voice he said: "That you have hit upon this thought, O King, shows the desire to search for truth has awakened you! Among all living creatures, there are but three kinds who are exempt from Death's power: the Buddhas, the blessed spirits and the gods. Whoever attains one of these three grades escapes the rod of re-birth, and lives as long as the Heavens themselves."

The King of the Apes said: "Where do these three kinds of beings live?" And the old ape replied: "They live in caves and on holy mountains in the great world of mortals." The King was pleased when he heard this, and told his apes that he was going to seek out gods and sainted spirits in order to learn the road to immortality from them. The apes dragged up peaches and other fruits and sweet wine to celebrate the parting banquet, and all made merry together.

On the following morning the Handsome King of the Apes rose very early, built him a raft of old pine trees and took a bamboo staff for a pole. Then he climbed on the raft, quite alone, and poled his way through the Great Sea. Wind and waves were favorable and he reached Asia. There he went ashore. On the strand he met a fisherman. He at once stepped up to him, knocked him down, tore off his clothes and put them on himself. Then he wandered around and visited all famous spots, went into the market-places, the densely populated cities, learned how to conduct himself properly, and how to speak and act like a well-bred human being. Yet his heart was set on learning the teaching of the Buddhas, the blessed spirits and the holy gods. But the people of the country in which he was were only concerned with honors and wealth. Not one of them seemed to care for life. Thus he went about until nine years had passed by unnoticed. Then he came to the strand of the Western Sea and it occurred to him: "No doubt there are gods and saints on the other side of the sea!" So he built another raft, floated it over the Western Sea and reached the land of the West. There he let his raft drift, and went ashore. After he had searched for many days, he suddenly saw a high mountain with deep, quiet valleys. As the Ape King went toward it, he heard a man singing in the woods, and the song sounded like one the blessed spirits might sing. So he hastily entered the wood to see who might be singing. There he met a wood-chopper at work. The Ape King bowed to him and said: "Venerable, divine master, I fall down and worship at your feet!" Said the wood-chopper: "I am only a workman; why do you call me divine master?" "Then, if you are no blessed god, how comes it you sing that divine song?" The wood-chopper laughed and said: "You are at home in music. The song I was singing was really taught me by a saint." "If you are acquainted with a saint," said the Ape King, "he surely cannot live far from here. I beg of you to show me the way to his dwelling." The wood-chopper replied: "It is not far from here. This mountain is known as the Mountain of the Heart. In it is a cave where dwells a saint who is called 'The Discerner'. The number of his disciples who have attained blessedness is countless. He still has some thirty to forty disciples gathered about him. You need only follow this path which leads to the South, and you cannot miss his dwelling." The Ape King thanked the wood-chopper and, sure enough, he came to the cave which the latter had described to him. The gate was locked and he did not venture to knock. So he leaped up into a pine tree, picked pine-cones and devoured the seed. Before long one of the saint's disciples came and opened the door and said: "What sort of a beast is it that is making such a noise?" The Ape King leaped down from his tree, bowed, and said: "I have come in search of truth. I did not venture to knock." Then the disciple had to laugh and said: "Our master was seated lost in meditation, when he told me to lead in the seeker after truth who stood without the gate, and here you really are. Well, you may come along with me!" The Ape King smoothed his clothes, put his hat on straight, and stepped in. A long passage led past magnificent buildings and quiet hidden huts to the place where the master was sitting upright on a seat of white marble. At his right and left stood his disciples, ready to serve him. The Ape King flung himself down on the ground and greeted the master humbly. In answer to his questions he told him how he had found his way to him. And when he was asked his name, he said: "I have no name. I am the ape who came out of the stone." So the master said: "Then I will give you a name. I name you Sun Wu Kung." The Ape King thanked him, full of joy, and thereafter he was called Sun Wu Kung. The master ordered his oldest disciple to instruct Sun Wu Kung in sweeping and cleaning, in going in and out, in good manners, how to labor in the field and how to water the gardens. In the course of time he learned to write, to burn incense and read the sutras. And in this way some six or seven years went by.

One day the master ascended the seat from which he taught, and began to speak regarding the great truth. Sun Wu Kung understood the hidden meaning of his words, and commenced to jerk about and dance in his joy. The master reproved him: "Sun Wu Kung, you have still not laid aside your wild nature! What do you mean by carrying on in such an unfitting manner?" Sun Wu Kung bowed and answered: "I was listening attentively to you when the meaning of your words was disclosed to my heart, and without thinking I began to dance for joy. I was not giving way to my wild nature." Said the master: "If your spirit has really awakened, then I will announce the great truth to you. But there are three hundred and sixty ways by means of which one may reach this truth. Which way shall I teach you?" Said Sun Wu Kung: "Whichever you will, O Master!" Then the Master asked: "Shall I teach you the way of magic?" Said Sun Wu Kung: "What does magic teach one?" The Master replied: "It teaches one to raise up spirits, to question oracles, and to foretell fortune and misfortune." "Can one secure eternal life by means of it?" inquired Sun Wu Kung. "No," was the answer. "Then I will not learn it." "Shall I teach you the sciences?" "What are the sciences?" "They are the nine schools of the three faiths. You learn how to read the holy books, pronounce incantations, commune with the gods, and call the saints to you." "Can one gain eternal life by means of them?" "No." "Then I will not learn them." "The way of repose is a very good way." "What is the way of repose?" "It teaches how to live without nourishment, how to remain quiescent in silent purity, and sit lost in meditation." "Can one gain eternal life in this way?" "No." "Then I will not learn it." "The way of deeds is also a good way." "What does that teach?" "It teaches one to equalize the vital powers, to practise bodily exercise, to prepare the elixir of life and to hold one's breath." "Will it give one eternal life?" "Not so." "Then I will not learn it! I will not learn it!" Thereupon the Master pretended to be angry, leaped down from his stand, took his cane and scolded: "What an ape! This he will not learn, and that he will not learn! What are you waiting to learn, then?" With that he gave him three blows across the head, retired to his inner chamber, and closed the great door after him.

The disciples were greatly excited, and overwhelmed Sun Wu Kung with reproaches. Yet the latter paid no attention to them, but smiled quietly to himself, for he had understood the riddle which the Master had given him to solve. And in his heart he thought: "His striking me over the head three times meant that I was to be ready at the third watch of the night. His withdrawing to his inner chamber and closing the great door after him, meant that I was to go in to him by the back door, and that he would make clear the great truth to me in secret." Accordingly he waited until evening, and made a pretense of lying down to sleep with the other disciples. But when the third watch of the night had come he rose softly and crept to the back door. Sure enough it stood ajar. He slipped in and stepped before the Master's bed. The Master was sleeping with his face turned toward the wall, and the ape did not venture to wake him, but knelt down in front of the bed. After a time the Master turned around and hummed a stanza to himself:

"A hard, hard grind,Truth's lesson to expound.One talks oneself deaf, dumb and blind,Unless the right man's found."

Then Sun Wu Kung replied: "I am waiting here reverentially!"

The Master flung on his clothes, sat up in bed and said harshly: "Accursed ape! Why are you not asleep? What are you doing here?"

Sun Wu Kung answered: "Yet you pointed out to me yesterday that I was to come to you at the third watch of the night, by the back door, in order to be instructed in the truth. Therefore I have ventured to come. If you will teach me in the fulness of your grace, I will be eternally grateful to you."

Thought the Master to himself: "There is real intelligence in this ape's head, to have made him understand me so well." Then he replied: "Sun Wu Kung, it shall be granted you! I will speak freely with you. Come quite close to me, and then I will show you the way to eternal life."

With that he murmured into his ear a divine, magical incantation to further the concentration of his vital powers, and explained the hidden knowledge word for word. Sun Wu Kung listened to him eagerly, and in a short time had learned it by heart. Then he thanked his teacher, went out again and lay down to sleep. From that time forward he practised the right mode of breathing, kept guard over his soul and spirit, and tamed the natural instincts of his heart. And while he did so three more years passed by. Then the task was completed.

One day the Master said to him: "Three great dangers still threaten you. Everyone who wishes to accomplish something out of the ordinary is exposed to them, for he is pursued by the envy of demons and spirits. And only those who can overcome these three great dangers live as long as the heavens."

Then Sun Wu Kung was frightened and asked: "Is there any means of protection against these dangers?"

Then the Master again murmured a secret incantation into his ear, by means of which he gained the power to transform himself seventy-two times.

And when no more than a few days had passed Sun Wu Kung had learned the art.

One day the Master was walking before the cave in the company of his disciples. He called Sun Wu Kung up to him and asked: "What progress have you made with your art? Can you fly already?"

"Yes, indeed," said the ape.

"Then let me see you do so."

The ape leaped into the air to a distance of five or six feet from the ground. Clouds formed beneath his feet, and he was able to walk on them for several hundred yards. Then he was forced to drop down to earth again.

The Master said with a smile: "I call that crawling around on the clouds, not floating on them, as do the gods and saints who fly over the whole world in a single day. I will teach you the magic incantation for turning somersaults on the clouds. If you turn one of those somersaults you advance eighteen thousand miles at a clip."

Sun Wu Kung thanked him, full of joy, and from that time on he was able to move without limitation of space in any direction.

One day Sun Wu Kung was sitting together with the other disciples under the pine-tree by the gate, discussing the secrets of their teachings. Finally they asked him to show them some of his transforming arts. Sun Wu Kung could not keep his secret to himself, and agreed to do so.

With a smile he said: "Just set me a task! What do you wish me to change myself into?"

They said: "Turn yourself into a pine-tree."

So Sun Wu Kung murmured a magic incantation, turned around – and there stood a pine-tree before their very eyes. At this they all broke out into a horse-laugh. The Master heard the noise and came out of the gate, dragging his cane behind him.

"Why are you making such a noise?" he called out to them harshly.

Said they: "Sun Wu Kung has turned himself into a pine-tree, and this made us laugh."

"Sun Wu Kung, come here!" said the Master. "Now just tell me what tricks you are up to? Why do you have to turn yourself into a pine-tree? All the work you have done means nothing more to you than a chance to make magic for your companions to wonder at. That shows that your heart is not yet under control."

Humbly Sun Wu Kung begged his forgiveness.

But the Master said: "I bear you no ill will, but you must go away."

With tears in his eyes Sun Wu Kung asked him: "But where shall I go?"

"You must go back again whence you came," said the Master. And when Sun Wu Kung sadly bade him farewell, he threatened him: "Your savage nature is sure to bring down evil upon you some time. You must tell no one that you are my pupil. If you so much as breathe a word about it, I will fetch your soul and lock it up in the nethermost hell, so that you cannot escape for a thousand eternities."

Sun Wu Kung replied: "I will not say a word! I will not say a word!"

Then he once more thanked him for all the kindness shown him, turned a somersault and climbed up to the clouds.

Within the hour he had passed the seas, and saw the Mountain of Flowers and Fruits lying before him. Then he felt happy and at home again, let his cloud sink down to earth and cried: "Here I am back again, children!" And at once, from the valley, from behind the rocks, out of the grass and from amid the trees came his apes. They came running up by thousands, surrounded and greeted him, and inquired as to his adventures. Sun Wu Kung said: "I have now found the way to eternal life, and need fear Death the Ancient no longer." Then all the apes were overjoyed, and competed with each other in bringing flowers and fruits, peaches and wine, to welcome him. And again they honored Sun Wu Kung as the Handsome Ape King.

Sun Wu Kung now gathered the apes about him and questioned them as to how they had fared during his absence.

Said they: "It is well that you have come back again, great king! Not long ago a devil came here who wanted to take possession of our cave by force. We fought with him, but he dragged away many of your children and will probably soon return."

Sun Wu Kung grew very angry and said: "What sort of a devil is this who dares be so impudent?"

The apes answered: "He is the Devil-King of Chaos. He lives in the North, who knows how many miles away. We only saw him come and go amid clouds and mist."

Sun Wu Kung said: "Wait, and I will see to him!" With that he turned a somersault and disappeared without a trace.

In the furthest North rises a high mountain, upon whose slope is a cave above which is the inscription: "The Cave of the Kidneys." Before the door little devils were dancing. Sun Wu Kung called harshly to them: "Tell your Devil-King quickly that he had better give me my children back again!" The little devils were frightened, and delivered the message in the cave. Then the Devil-King reached for his sword and came out. But he was so large and broad that he could not even see Sun Wu Kung. He was clad from head to foot in black armor, and his face was as black as the bottom of a kettle. Sun Wu Kung shouted at him: "Accursed devil, where are your eyes, that you cannot see the venerable Sun?" Then the devil looked to the ground and saw a stone ape standing before him, bare-headed, dressed in red, with a yellow girdle and black boots. So the Devil-King laughed and said: "You are not even four feet high, less than thirty years of age, and weaponless, and yet you venture to make such a commotion." Said Sun Wu Kung: "I am not too small for you; and I can make myself large at will. You scorn me because I am without a weapon, but my two fists can thresh to the very skies." With that he stooped, clenched his fists and began to give the devil a beating. The devil was large and clumsy, but Sun Wu Kung leaped about nimbly. He struck him between the ribs and between the wind and his blows fell ever more fast and furious. In his despair the devil raised his great knife and aimed a blow at Sun Wu Kung's head. But the latter avoided the blow, and fell back on his magic powers of transformation. He pulled out a hair, put it in his mouth, chewed it, spat it out into the air and said: "Transform yourself!" And at once it turned into many hundreds of little apes who began to attack the devil. Sun Wu Kung, be it said, had eighty-four thousand hairs on his body, every single one of which he could transform. The little apes with their sharp eyes, leaped around with the greatest rapidity. They surrounded the Devil-King on all sides, tore at his clothes, and pulled at his legs, until he finally measured his length on the ground. Then Sun Wu Kung stepped up, tore his knife from his hand, and put an end to him. After that he entered the cave and released his captive children, the apes. The transformed hairs he drew to him again, and making a fire, he burned the evil cave to the ground. Then he gathered up those he had released, and flew back with them like a storm-wind to his cavern on the Mountain of Flowers and Fruits, joyfully greeted by all the apes.

After Sun Wu Kung had obtained possession of the Devil-King's great knife, he exercised his apes every day. They had wooden swords and lances of bamboo, and played their martial music on reed pipes. He had them build a camp so that they would be prepared for all dangers. Suddenly the thought came to Sun Wu Kung: "If we go on this way, perhaps we may incite some human or animal king to fight with us, and then we would not be able to withstand him with our wooden swords and bamboo lances!" And to his apes he said: "What should be done?" Four baboons stepped forward and said: "In the capital city of the Aulai empire there are warriors without number. And there coppersmiths and steelsmiths are also to be found. How would it be if we were to buy steel and iron and have those smiths weld weapons for us?"

A somersault and Sun Wu Kung was standing before the city moat. Said he to himself: "To first buy the weapons would take a great deal of time. I would rather make magic and take some." So he blew on the ground. Then a tremendous storm-wind arose which drove sand and stones before it, and caused all the soldiers in the city to run away in terror. Then Sun Wu Kung went to the armory, pulled out one of his hairs, turned it into thousands of little apes, cleared out the whole supply of weapons, and flew back home on a cloud.

Then he gathered his people about him and counted them. In all they numbered seventy-seven thousand. They held the whole Mountain in terror, and all the magic beasts and spirit princes who dwelt on it. And these came forth from seventy-two caves and honored Sun Wu Kung as their head.

One day the Ape King said: "Now you all have weapons; but this knife which I took from the Devil-King is too light, and no longer suits me. What should be done?"

Then the four baboons stepped forward and said: "In view of your spirit powers, O king, you will find no weapon fit for your use on all the earth! Is it possible for you to walk through the water?"

The Ape King answered: "All the elements are subject to me and there is no place where I cannot go."

Then the baboons said: "The water at our cave here flows into the Great Sea, to the castle of the Dragon-King of the Eastern Sea. If your magic power makes it possible, you could go to the Dragon-King and let him give you a weapon."

This suited the Ape King. He leaped on the iron bridge and murmured an incantation. Then he flung himself into the waves, which parted before him and ran on till he came to the palace of water-crystal. There he met a Triton who asked who he was. He mentioned his name and said: "I am the Dragon-King's nearest neighbor, and have come to visit him." The Triton took the message to the castle, and the Dragon-King of the Eastern Sea came out hastily to receive him. He bade him be seated and served him with tea.

Sun Wu Kung said: "I have learned the hidden knowledge and gained the powers of immortality. I have drilled my apes in the art of warfare in order to protect our mountain; but I have no weapon I can use, and have therefore come to you to borrow one."

The Dragon-King now had General Flounder bring him a great spear. But Sun Wu Kung was not satisfied with it. Then he ordered Field-Marshal Eel to fetch in a nine-tined fork, which weighed three thousand six hundred pounds. But Sun Wu Kung balanced it in his hand and said: "Too light! Too light! Too light!"

Then the Dragon-King was frightened, and had the heaviest weapon in his armory brought in. It weighed seven thousand two hundred pounds. But this was still too light for Sun Wu Kung. The Dragon-King assured him that he had nothing heavier, but Sun Wu Kung would not give in and said: "Just look around!"

Finally the Dragon-Queen and her daughter came out, and said to the Dragon-King: "This saint is an unpleasant customer with whom to deal. The great iron bar is still lying here in our sea; and not so long ago it shone with a red glow, which is probably a sign it is time for it to be taken away."

Said the Dragon-King: "But that is the rod which the Great Yu used when he ordered the waters, and determined the depth of the seas and rivers. It cannot be taken away."

The Dragon-Queen replied: "Just let him see it! What he then does with it is no concern of ours."

So the Dragon-King led Sun Wu Kung to the measuring rod. The golden radiance that came from it could be seen some distance off. It was an enormous iron bar, with golden clamps on either side.

Sun Wu Kung raised it with the exertion of all his strength, and then said: "It is too heavy, and ought to be somewhat shorter and thinner!"

No sooner had he said this than the iron rod grew less. He tried it again, and then he noticed that it grew larger or smaller at command. It could be made to shrink to the size of a pin. Sun Wu Kung was overjoyed and beat about in the sea with the rod, which he had let grow large again, till the waves spurted mountain-high and the dragon-castle rocked on its foundations. The Dragon-King trembled with fright, and all his tortoises, fishes and crabs drew in their heads.

Sun Wu Kung laughed, and said: "Many thanks for the handsome present!" Then he continued: "Now I have a weapon, it is true, but as yet I have no armor. Rather than hunt up two or three other households, I think you will be willing to provide me with a suit of mail."

The Dragon-King told him that he had no armor to give him.

Then the ape said: "I will not leave until you have obtained one for me." And once more he began to swing his rod.

"Do not harm me!" said the terrified Dragon-King, "I will ask my brothers."

And he had them beat the iron drum and strike the golden gong, and in a moment's time all the Dragon-King's brothers came from all the other seas. The Dragon-King talked to them in private and said: "This is a terrible fellow, and we must not rouse his anger! First he took the rod with the golden clamps from me, and now he also insists on having a suit of armor. The best thing to do would be to satisfy him at once, and complain of him to the Lord of the Heavens later."

So the brothers brought a magic suit of golden mail, magic boots and a magic helmet.

Then Sun Wu Kung thanked them and returned to his cave. Radiantly he greeted his children, who had come to meet him, and showed them the rod with the golden clamps. They all crowded up and wished to pick it up from the ground, if only a single time; but it was just as though a dragon-fly had attempted to overthrow a stone column, or an ant were trying to carry a great mountain. It would not move a hair's breadth. Then the apes opened their mouths and stuck out their tongues, and said: "Father, how is it possible for you to carry that heavy thing?" So he told them the secret of the rod and showed them its effects. Then he set his empire in order, and appointed the four baboons field-marshals; and the seven beast-spirits, the ox-spirit, the dragon-spirit, the bird-spirit, the lion-spirit and the rest also joined him.

One day he took a nap after dinner. Before he did so he had let the bar shrink, and had stuck it in his ear. While he was sleeping he saw two men come along in his dream, who had a card on which was written "Sun Wu Kung." They would not allow him to resist, but fettered him and led his spirit away. And when they reached a great city the Ape King gradually came to himself. Over the city gate he saw a tablet of iron on which was engraved in large letters: "The Nether World."

Then all was suddenly clear to him and he said: "Why, this must be the dwelling-place of Death! But I have long since escaped from his power, and how dare he have me dragged here!" The more he reflected the wilder he grew. He drew out the golden rod from his ear, swung it and let it grow large. Then he crushed the two constables to mush, burst his fetters, and rolled his bar before him into the city. The ten Princes of the Dead were frightened, bowed before him and asked: "Who are you?"

Sun Wu Kung answered: "If you do not know me then why did you send for me and have me dragged to this place? I am the heaven-born saint Sun Wu Kung of the Mountain of Flowers and Fruits. And now, who are you? Tell me your names quickly or I will strike you!"

The ten Princes of the Dead humbly gave him their names.

Sun Wu Kung said: "I, the Venerable Sun, have gained the power of eternal life! You have nothing to say to me! Quick, let me have the Book of Life!"

They did not dare defy him, and had the scribe bring in the Book. Sun Wu Kung opened it. Under the head of "Apes," No. 1350, he read: "Sun Wu Kung, the heaven-born stone ape. His years shall be three hundred and twenty-four. Then he shall die without illness."

Sun Wu Kung took the brush from the table and struck out the whole ape family from the Book of Life, threw the Book down and said: "Now we are even! From this day on I will suffer no impertinences from you!"

With that he cleared a way for himself out of the Nether World by means of his rod, and the ten Princes of the Dead did not venture to stay him, but only complained of him afterward to the Lord of the Heavens.

When Sun Wu Kung had left the city he slipped and fell to the ground. This caused him to wake, and he noticed he had been dreaming. He called his four baboons to him and said: "Splendid, splendid! I was dragged to Death's castle and I caused considerable uproar there. I had them give me the Book of Life, and I struck out the mortal hour of all the apes!" And after that time the apes on the Mountain no longer died, because their names had been stricken out in the Nether World.

But the Lord of the Heavens sat in his castle, and had all his servants assembled about him. And a saint stepped forward and presented the complaint of the Dragon-King of the Eastern Sea. And another stepped forward and presented the complaint of the ten Princes of the Dead. The Lord of the Heavens glanced through the two memorials. Both told of the wild, unmannerly conduct of Sun Wu Kung. So the Lord of the Heavens ordered a god to descend to earth and take him prisoner. The Evening Star came forward, however, and said: "This ape was born of the purest powers of heaven and earth and sun and moon. He has gained the hidden knowledge and has become an immortal. Recall, O Lord, your great love for all that which has life, and forgive him his sin! Issue an order that he be called up to the heavens, and be given a charge here, so that he may come to his senses. Then, if he again oversteps your commands, let him be punished without mercy." The Lord of the Heavens was agreeable, had the order issued, and told the Evening Star to take it to Sun Wu Kung. The Evening Star mounted a colored cloud and descended on the Mountain of Flowers and Fruits.

He greeted Sun Wu Kung and said to him: "The Lord had heard of your actions and meant to punish you. I am the Evening Star of the Western Skies, and I spoke for you. Therefore he has commissioned me to take you to the skies, so that you may be given a charge there."

Sun Wu Kung was overjoyed and answered: "I had just been thinking I ought to pay Heaven a visit some time, and sure enough, Old Star, here you have come to fetch me!"

Then he had his four baboons come and said to them impressively: "See that you take good care of our Mountain! I am going up to the heavens to look around there a little!"

Then he mounted a cloud together with the Evening Star and floated up. But he kept turning his somersaults, and advanced so quickly that the Evening Star on his cloud was left behind. Before he knew it he had reached the Southern Gate of Heaven and was about to step carelessly through. The gate-keeper did not wish to let him enter, but he did not let this stop him. In the midst of their dispute the Evening Star came up and explained matters, and then he was allowed to enter the heavenly gate. When he came to the castle of the Lord of the Heavens, he stood upright before it, without bowing his head.

The Lord of the Heavens asked: "Then this hairy face with the pointed lips is Sun Wu Kung?"

He replied: "Yes, I am the Venerable Sun!"

All the servants of the Lord of the Heavens were shocked and said: "This wild ape does not even bow, and goes so far as to call himself the Venerable Sun. His crime deserves a thousand deaths!"

But the Lord said: "He has come up from the earth below, and is not as yet used to our rules. We will forgive him."

Then he gave orders that a charge be found for him. The marshal of the heavenly court reported: "There is no charge vacant anywhere, but an official is needed in the heavenly stables." Thereupon the Lord made him stablemaster of the heavenly steeds. Then the servants of the

Lord of the Heavens told him he should give thanks for the grace bestowed on him. Sun Wu Kung called out aloud: "Thanks to command!" took possession of his certificate of appointment, and went to the stables in order to enter upon his new office.

Sun Wu Kung attended to his duties with great zeal. The heavenly steeds grew sleek and fat, and the stables were filled with young foals. Before he knew it half a month had gone by. Then his heavenly friends prepared a banquet for him.

While they were at table Sun Wu Kung asked accidentally: "Stablemaster? What sort of a title is that?"

"Why, that is an official title," was the reply.

"What rank has this office?"

"It has no rank at all," was the answer.

"Ah," said the ape, "is it so high that it outranks all other dignities?"

"No, it is not high, it is not high at all," answered his friends. "It is not even set down in the official roster, but is quite a subordinate position. All you have to do is to attend to the steeds. If you see to it that they grow fat, you get a good mark; but if they grow thin or ill, or fall down, your punishment will be right at hand."

Then the Ape King grew angry: "What, they treat me, the Venerable Sun, in such a shameful way!" and he started up. "On my Mountain I was a king, I was a father! What need was there for him to lure me into his heaven to feed horses? I'll do it no longer! I'll do it no longer!"

Hola, and he had already overturned the table, drawn the rod with the golden clamps from his ear, let it grow large and beat a way out for himself to the Southern gate of Heaven. And no one dared stop him.

Already he was back in his island Mountain and his people surrounded him and said: "You have been gone for more than ten years, great king! How is it you do not return to us until now?"

The Ape King said: "I did not spend more than about ten days in Heaven. This Lord of the Heavens does not know how to treat his people. He made me his stablemaster, and I had to feed his horses. I am so ashamed that I am ready to die. But I did not put up with it, and now I am here once more!"

His apes eagerly prepared a banquet to comfort him. While they sat at table two horned devil-kings came and brought him a yellow imperial robe as a present. Filled with joy he slipped into it, and appointed the two devil-kings leaders of the vanguard. They thanked him and began to flatter him: "With your power and wisdom, great king, why should you have to serve the Lord of the Heavens? To call you the Great Saint who is Heaven's Equal would be quite in order."

The ape was pleased with this speech and said: "Good, good!" Then he ordered his four baboons to have a flag made quickly, on which was to be inscribed: "The Great Saint Who Is Heaven's Equal." And from that time on he had himself called by that title.

When the Lord of the Heavens learned of the flight of the ape, he ordered Li Dsing,[2] the pagoda-bearing god, and his third son, Notscha, to take the Ape King prisoner. They sallied forth at the head of a heavenly warrior host, laid out a camp before his cave, and sent a brave warrior to challenge him to single combat. But he was easily beaten by Sun Wu Kung and obliged to flee, and Sun Wu Kung even shouted after him, laughing: "What a bag of wind! And he calls himself a heavenly warrior! I'll not slay you. Run along quickly and send me a better man!"

When Notscha saw this he himself hurried up to do battle.

Said Sun Wu Kung to him: "To whom do you belong, little one? You must not play around here, for something might happen to you!"

But Notscha cried out in a loud voice: "Accursed ape! I am Prince Notscha, and have been ordered to take you prisoner!" And with that he swung his sword in the direction of Sun Wu Kung.

"Very well," said the latter, "I will stand here and never move."

Then Notscha grew very angry, and turned into a three-headed god with six arms, in which he held six different weapons. Thus he rushed on to the attack.

Sun Wu Kung laughed. "The little fellow knows the trick of it! But easy, wait a bit! I will change shape, too!"

And he also turned himself into a figure with three heads and with six arms, and swung three gold-clamp rods. And thus they began to fight. Their blows rained down with such rapidity that it seemed as though thousands of weapons were flying through the air. After thirty rounds the combat had not yet been decided. Then Sun Wu Kung hit upon an idea. He secretly pulled out one of his hairs, turned it into his own shape, and let it continue the fight with Notscha. He himself, however, slipped behind Notscha, and gave him such a blow on the left arm with his rod that his knees gave way beneath him with pain, and he had to withdraw in defeat.

So Notscha told his father Li Dsing: "This devil-ape is altogether too powerful! I cannot get the better of him!" There was nothing left to do but to return to the Heavens and admit their overthrow. The Lord of the Heavens bowed his head, and tried to think of some other hero whom he might send out.

Then the Evening Star once more came forward and said: "This ape is so strong and so courageous, that probably not one of us here is a match for him. He revolted because the office of stablemaster appeared too lowly for him. The best thing would be to temper justice with mercy, let him have his way, and appoint him Great Saint Who Is Heaven's Equal. It will only be necessary to give him the empty title, without combining a charge with it, and then the matter would be settled." The Lord of the Heavens was satisfied with this suggestion, and once more sent the Evening Star to summon the new saint. When Sun Wu Kung heard that he had arrived, he said: "The old Evening Star is a good fellow!" and he had his army draw up in line to give him a festive reception. He himself donned his robes of ceremony and politely went out to meet him.

Then the Evening Star told him what had taken place in the Heavens, and that he had his appointment as Great Saint Who Is Heaven's Equal with him.

Thereupon the Great Saint laughed and said: "You also spoke in my behalf before, Old Star! And now you have again taken my part. Many thanks! Many thanks!"

Then when they appeared together in the presence of the Lord of the Heavens the latter said: "The rank of Great Saint Who Is Heaven's Equal is very high. But now you must not cut any further capers."

The Great Saint expressed his thanks, and the Lord of the Heavens ordered two skilled architects to build a castle for him East of the peach-garden of the Queen-Mother of the West. And he was led into it with all possible honors.

Now the Saint was in his element. He had all that heart could wish for, and was untroubled by any work. He took his ease, walked about in the Heavens as he chose, and paid visits to the gods. The Three Pure Ones and the Four Rulers he treated with some little respect; but the planetary gods and the lords of the twenty-eight houses of the moon, and of the twelve zodiac signs, and the other stars he addressed familiarly with a "Hey, you!" Thus he idled day by day, without occupation among the clouds of the Heavens. On one occasion one of the wise said to the Lord of the Heavens: "The holy Sun is idle while day follows day. It is to be feared that some mischievous thoughts may occur to him, and it might be better to give him some charge."

So the Lord of the Heavens summoned the Great Saint and said to him: "The life-giving peaches in the garden of the Queen-Mother will soon be ripe. I give you the charge of watching over them. Do your duty conscientiously!"

This pleased the Saint and he expressed his thanks. Then he went to the garden, where the caretakers and gardeners received him on their knees.

He asked them: "How many trees in all are there in the garden?"

"Three thousand six hundred," replied the gardener. "There are twelve-hundred trees in the foremost row. They have red blossoms and bear small fruit, which ripens every three thousand years. Whoever eats it grows bright and healthy. The twelve hundred trees in the middle row have double blossoms and bear sweet fruit, which ripens every six thousand years. Whoever eats of it is able to float in the rose-dawn without aging. The twelve hundred trees in the last row bear red-striped fruit with small pits. They ripen every nine thousand years. Whoever eats their fruit lives eternally, as long as the Heavens themselves, and remains untouched for thousands of eons."

The Saint heard all this with pleasure. He checked up the lists and from that time on appeared every day or so to see to things. The greater part of the peaches in the last row were already ripe. When he came to the garden, he would on each occasion send away the caretakers and gardeners under some pretext, leap up into the trees, and gorge himself to his heart's content with the peaches.

At that time the Queen-Mother of the West was preparing the great peach banquet to which she was accustomed to invite all the gods of the Heavens. She sent out the fairies in their garments of seven colors with baskets, that they might pick the peaches. The caretaker said to them: "The garden has now been entrusted to the guardianship of the Great Saint Who is Heaven's Equal, so you will first have to announce yourselves to him." With that he led the seven fairies into the garden. There they looked everywhere for the Great Saint, but could not find him. So the fairies said: "We have our orders and must not be late. We will begin picking the peaches in the meantime!" So they picked several baskets full from the foremost row. In the second row the peaches were already scarcer. And in the last row there hung only a single half-ripe peach. They bent down the bough and picked it, and then allowed it to fly up again.

Now it happened that the Great Saint, who had turned himself into a peach-worm, had just been taking his noon-day nap on this bough. When he was so rudely awakened, he appeared in his true form, seized his rod and was about to strike the fairies.

But the fairies said: "We have been sent here by the Queen-Mother. Do not be angry, Great Saint!"

Said the Great Saint: "And who are all those whom the Queen-Mother has invited?"

They answered: "All the gods and saints in the Heavens, on the earth and under the earth."

"Has she also invited me?" said the Saint.

"Not that we know of," said the fairies.

Then the Saint grew angry, murmured a magic incantation and said: "Stay! Stay! Stay!"

With that the seven fairies were banned to the spot. The Saint then took a cloud and sailed away on it to the palace of the Queen-Mother.

On the way he met the Bare-Foot God and asked him: "Where are you going?"

"To the peach banquet," was the answer.

Then the Saint lied to him, saying: "I have been commanded by the Lord of the Heavens to tell all the gods and saints that they are first to come to the Hall of Purity, in order to practise the rites, and then go together to the Queen-Mother."

Then the Great Saint changed himself into the semblance of the Bare-Foot God and sailed to the palace of the Queen-Mother. There he let his cloud sink down and entered quite unconcerned. The meal was ready, yet none of the gods had as yet appeared. Suddenly the Great Saint caught the aroma of wine, and saw well-nigh a hundred barrels of the precious nectar standing in a room to one side. His mouth watered. He tore a few hairs out and turned them into sleep-worms. These worms crept into the nostrils of the cup-bearers so that they all fell asleep. Thereupon he enjoyed the delicious viands to the full, opened the barrels and drank until he was nearly stupefied. Then he said to himself: "This whole affair is beginning to make me feel creepy. I had better go home first of all and sleep a bit." And he stumbled out of the garden with uncertain steps. Sure enough, he missed his way, and came to the dwelling of Laotzse. There he regained consciousness. He arranged his clothing and went in. There was no one to be seen in the place, for at the moment Laotzse was at the God of Light's abode, talking to him, and with him were all his servants, listening. Since he found no one at home the Great Saint went as far as the inner chamber, where Laotzse was in the habit of brewing the elixir of life. Beside the stove stood five gourd containers full of the pills of life which had already been rolled. Said the Great Saint: "I had long since intended to prepare a couple of these pills. So it suits me very well to find them here." He poured out the contents of the gourds, and ate up all the pills of life. Since he had now had enough to eat and drink he thought to himself: "Bad, bad! The mischief I have done cannot well be repaired. If they catch me my life will be in danger. I think I had better go down to earth again and remain a king!" With that he made himself invisible, went out at the Western Gate of Heaven, and returned to the Mountain of Flowers and Fruits, where he told his people who received him the story of his adventures.

When he spoke of the wine-nectar of the peach garden, his apes said: "Can't you go back once more and steal a few bottles of the wine, so that we too may taste of it and gain eternal life?"

The Ape King was willing, turned a somersault, crept into the garden unobserved, and picked up four more barrels. Two of them he took under his arms and two he held in his hands. Then he disappeared with them without leaving a trace and brought them to his cave, where he enjoyed them together with his apes.

In the meantime the seven fairies, whom the Great Saint had banned to the spot, had regained their freedom after a night and a day. They picked up their baskets and told the Queen-Mother what had happened to them. And the cup-bearers, too, came hurrying up and reported the destruction which someone unknown had caused among the eatables and drinkables. The Queen-Mother went to the Lord of the Heavens to complain. Shortly afterward Laotzse also came to him to tell about the theft of the pills of life. And the Bare-Foot God came along and reported that he had been deceived by the Great Saint Who Is Heaven's Equal; and from the Great Saint's palace the servants came running and said that the Saint had disappeared and was nowhere to be found. Then the Lord of the Heavens was frightened, and said: "This whole mess is undoubtedly the work of that devilish ape!"

Now the whole host of Heaven, together with all the star-gods, the time-gods and the mountain-gods was called out in order to catch the ape. Li Dsing once more was its commander-in-chief. He invested the entire Mountain, and spread out the sky-net and the earth-net, so that no one could escape. Then he sent his bravest heroes into battle. Courageously the ape withstood all attacks from early morn till sundown. But by that time his most faithful followers had been captured. That was too much for him. He pulled out a hair and turned it into thousands of Ape-Kings, who all hewed about them with golden-clamped iron rods. The heavenly host was vanquished, and the ape withdrew to his cave to rest.

Now it happened that Guan Yin[4] had also gone to the peach banquet in the garden, and had found out what Sun Wu Kung had done. When she went to visit the Lord of the Heavens, Li Dsing was just coming in, to report the great defeat which he had suffered on the Mountain of Flowers and Fruits. Then Guan Yin said to the Lord of the Heavens: "I can recommend a hero to you who will surely get the better of the ape. It is your grandson Yang Oerlang. He has conquered all the beast and bird spirits, and overthrown the elves in the grass and the brush. He knows what has to be done to get the better of such devils."

So Yang Oerlang was brought in, and Li Dsing led him to his camp. Li Dsing asked Yang Oerlang how he would go about getting the better of the ape.

Yang Oerlang laughed and said: "I think I will have to go him one better when it comes to changing shapes. It would be best for you to take away the sky-net so that our combat is not disturbed." Then he requested Li Dsing to post himself in the upper air with the magic spirit mirror in his hand, so that when the ape made himself invisible, he might be found again by means of the mirror. When all this had been arranged, Yang Oerlang went out in front of the cave with his spirits to give battle.

The ape leaped out, and when he saw the powerful hero with the three-tined sword standing before him he asked: "And who may you be?"

The other said: "I am Yang Oerlang, the grandson of the Lord of the Heavens!"

Then the ape laughed and said: "Oh yes, I remember! His daughter ran away with a certain Sir Yang, to whom heaven gave a son. You must be that son!"

Yang Oerlang grew furious, and advanced upon him with his spear. Then a hot battle began. For three hundred rounds they fought without decisive results. Then Yang Oerlang turned himself into a giant with a black face and red hair.

"Not bad," said the ape, "but I can do that too!"

So they continued to fight in that form. But the ape's baboons were much frightened. The beast and planet spirits of Yang Oerlang pressed the apes hard. They slew most of them and the others hid away. When the ape saw this his heart grew uneasy. He drew the magic giant-likeness in again, took his rod and fled. But Yang Oerlang followed hard on his heels. In his urgent need the ape thrust the rod, which he had turned into a needle, into his ear, turned into a sparrow, and flew up into the crest of a tree. Yang Oerlang who was following in his tracks, suddenly lost sight of him. But his keen eyes soon recognized that he had turned himself into a sparrow. So he flung away spear and crossbow, turned himself into a sparrow-hawk, and darted down on the sparrow. But the latter soared high into the air as a cormorant. Yang Oerlang shook his plumage, turned into a great sea-crane, and shot up into the clouds to seize the cormorant. The latter dropped, flew into a valley and dove beneath the waters of a brook in the guise of a fish. When Yang Oerlang reached the edge of the valley, and had lost his trail he said to himself: "This ape has surely turned himself into a fish or a crab! I will change my form as well in order to catch him." So he turned into a fish-hawk and floated above the surface of the water. When the ape in the water caught sight of the fish-hawk, he saw that he was Yang Oerlang. He swiftly swung around and fled, Yang Oerlang in pursuit. When the latter was no further away than the length of a beak, the ape turned, crept ashore as a water-snake and hid in the grass. Yang Oerlang, when he saw the water-snake creep from the water, turned into an eagle and spread his claws to seize the snake. But the water-snake sprang up and turned into the lowest of all birds, a speckled buzzard, and perched on the steep edge of a cliff. When Yang Oerlang saw that the ape had turned himself into so contemptible a creature as a buzzard, he would no longer play the game of changing form with him. He reappeared in his original form, took up his crossbow and shot at the bird. The buzzard slipped and fell down the side of the cliff. At its foot the ape turned himself into the chapel of a field-god. He opened his mouth for a gate, his teeth became the two wings of the door, his tongue the image of the god, and his eyes the windows. His tail was the only thing he did not know what to do with. So he let it stand up stiffly behind him in the shape of a flagpole. When Yang Oerlang reached the foot of the hill he saw the chapel, whose flagpole stood in the rear. Then he laughed and said: "That ape is really a devil of an ape! He wants to lure me into the chapel in order to bite me. But I will not go in. First I will break his windows for him, and then I will stamp down the wings of his door!" When the ape heard this he was much frightened. He made a bound like a tiger, and disappeared without a trace in the air. With a single somersault he reached Yang Oerlang's own temple. There he assumed Yang Oerlang's own form and stepped in. The spirits who were on guard were unable to recognize him. They received him on their knees. So the ape then seated himself on the god's throne, and had the prayers which had come in submitted to him.

When Yang Oerlang no longer saw the ape, he rose in the air to Li Dsing and said: "I was vying with the ape in changing shape. Suddenly I could no longer find him. Take a look in the mirror!" Li Dsing took a look in the magic spirit mirror and then he laughed and said: "The ape has turned himself into your likeness, is sitting in your temple quite at home there, and making mischief." When Yang Oerlang heard this he took his three-tined spear, and hastened to his temple. The door-spirits were frightened and said: "But father came in only this very minute! How is it that another one comes now?" Yang Oerlang, without paying attention to them, entered the temple and aimed his spear at Sun Wu Kung. The latter resumed his own shape, laughed and said: "Young sir, you must not be angry! The god of this place is now Sun Wu Kung." Without uttering a word Yang Oerlang assailed him. Sun Wu Kung took up his rod and returned the blows. Thus they crowded out of the temple together, fighting, and wrapped in mists and clouds once more gained the Mountain of Flowers and Fruits.

In the meantime Guan Yin was sitting with Laotzse, the Lord of the Heavens and the Queen-Mother in the great hall of Heaven, waiting for news. When none came she said: "I will go with Laotzse to the Southern Gate of Heaven and see how matters stand." And when they saw that the struggle had still not come to an end she said to Laotzse: "How would it be if we helped Yang Oerlang a little? I will shut up Sun Wu Kung in my vase."

But Laotzse said: "Your vase is made of porcelain. Sun Wu Kung could smash it with his iron rod. But I have a circlet of diamonds which can enclose all living creatures. That we can use!" So he flung his circlet through the air from the heavenly gate, and struck Sun Wu Kung on the head with it. Since he had his hands full fighting, the latter could not guard himself against it, and the blow on the forehead caused him to slip. Yet he rose again and tried to escape. But the heavenly hound of Yang Oerlang bit his leg until he fell to the ground. Then Yang Oerlang and his followers came up and tied him with thongs, and thrust a hook through his collar-bone so that he could no longer transform himself. And Laotzse took possession of his diamond circlet again, and returned with Guan Yin to the hall of Heaven. Sun Wu Kung was now brought in in triumph, and was condemned to be beheaded. He was then taken to the place of execution and bound to a post. But all efforts to kill him by means of ax and sword, thunder and lightning were vain. Nothing so much as hurt a hair on his head.

Said Laotzse: "It is not surprising. This ape has eaten the peaches, has drunk the nectar and also swallowed the pills of life. Nothing can harm him. The best thing would be for me to take him along and thrust him into my stove in order to melt the elixir of life out of him again. Then he will fall into dust and ashes."

So Sun Wu Kung's fetters were loosed, and Laotzse took him with him, thrust him into his oven, and ordered the boy to keep up a hot fire.

But along the edge of the oven were graven the signs of the eight elemental forces.[5] And when the ape was thrust into the oven he took refuge beneath the sign of the wind, so that the fire could not injure him; and the smoke only made his eyes smart. He remained in the oven seven times seven days. Then Laotzse had it opened to take a look. As soon as Sun Wu Kung saw the light shine in, he could no longer bear to be shut up, but leaped out and upset the magic oven. The guards and attendants he threw to the ground and Laotzse himself, who tried to seize him, received such a push that he stuck his legs up in the air like an onion turned upside down. Then Sun Wu Kung took his rod out of his ear, and without looking where he struck, hewed everything to bits, so that the star-gods closed their doors and the guardians of the Heavens ran away. He came to the castle of the Lord of the Heavens, and the guardian of the gate with his steel whip was only just in time to hold him back. Then the thirty-six thunder gods were set at him, and surrounded him, though they could not seize him.

The Lord of the Heavens said: "Buddha[6] will know what is to be done. Send for him quickly!"

So Buddha came up out of the West with Ananada and Kashiapa, his disciples. When he saw the turmoil he said: "First of all, let weapons be laid aside and lead out the Saint. I wish to speak with him!" The gods withdrew. Sun Wu Kung snorted and said: "Who are you, who dare to speak to me?" Buddha smiled and replied: "I have come out of the blessed West, Shakiamuni Amitofu. I have heard of the revolt you have raised, and am come to tame you!"

Said Sun Wu Kung: "I am the stone ape who has gained the hidden knowledge. I am master of seventy-two transformations, and will live as long as Heaven itself. What has the Lord of the Heavens accomplished that entitles him to remain eternally on his throne? Let him make way for me, and I will be satisfied!"

Buddha replied with a smile: "You are a beast which has gained magic powers. How can you expect to rule here as Lord of the Heavens? Be it known to you that the Lord of the Heavens has toiled for eons in perfecting his virtues. How many years would you have to pass before you could attain the dignity he has gained? And then I must ask you whether there is anything else you can do, aside from playing your tricks of transformation?"

Said Sun Wu Kung: "I can turn cloud somersaults. Each one carries me eighteen thousand miles ahead. Surely that is enough to entitle me to be the Lord of the Heavens?"

Buddha answered with a smile: "Let us make a wager. If you can so much as leave my hand with one of your somersaults, then I will beg the Lord of the Heavens to make way for you. But if you are not able to leave my hand, then you must yield yourself to my fetters."

Sun Wu Kung suppressed his laughter, for he thought: "This Buddha is a crazy fellow! His hand is not a foot long; how could I help but leap out of it?" So he opened his mouth wide and said: "Agreed!"

Buddha then stretched out his right hand. It resembled a small lotus-leaf. Sun Wu Kung leaped up into it with one bound. Then he said: "Go!" And with that he turned one somersault after another, so that he flew along like a whirlwind. And while he was flying along he saw five tall, reddish columns towering to the skies. Then he thought: "That is the end of the world! Now I will turn back and become Lord of the Heavens. But first I will write down my name to prove that I was there." He pulled out a hair, turned it into a brush, and wrote with great letters on the middle column: "The Great Saint Who Is Heaven's Equal." Then he turned his somersaults again until he had reached the place whence he had come. He leaped down from the Buddha's hand laughing and cried: "Now hurry, and see to it that the Lord of the Heavens clears his heavenly castle for me! I have been at the end of the world and have left a sign there!"

Buddha scolded: "Infamous ape! How dare you claim that you have left my hand? Take a look and see whether or not 'The Great Saint Who Is Heaven's Equal', is written on my middle finger!"

Sun Wu Kung was terribly frightened, for at the first glance he saw that this was the truth. Yet outwardly he pretended that he was not convinced, said he would take another look, and tried to make use of the opportunity to escape. But Buddha covered him with his hand, shoved him out of the gate of Heaven, and formed a mountain of water, fire, wood, earth and metal, which he softly set down on him to hold him fast. A magic incantation pasted on the mountain prevented his escape.

Here he was obliged to lie for hundreds of years, until he finally reformed and was released, in order to help the Monk of the Yangtze-kiang[7] fetch the holy writings from out of the West. He honored the Monk as his master, and thenceforward was known as the Wanderer. Guan Yin, who had released him, gave the Monk a golden circlet. Sun Wu Kung was induced to put it on, and it at once grew into his flesh so that he could not remove it. And Guan Yin gave the Monk a magic formula by means of which the ring could be tightened, should the ape grow disobedient. But from that time on he was always polite and well-mannered.

Sky O'Dawn

ONCE UPON A TIME there was a man who took a child to a woman in a certain village, and told her to take care of him. Then he disappeared. And because the dawn was just breaking in the sky when the woman took the child into her home, she called him Sky O'Dawn. When the child was three years old, he would often look up to the heavens and talk with the stars. One day he ran away and many months passed before he came home again. The woman gave him a whipping. But he ran away again, and did not return for a year. His foster-mother was frightened, and asked: "Where have you been all year long?" The boy answered: "I only made a quick trip to the Purple Sea. There the water stained my clothes red. So I went to the spring at which the sun turns in, and washed them. I went away in the morning and I came back at noon. Why do you speak about my having been gone a year?"

Then the woman asked: "And where did you pass on your way?"

The boy answered: "When I had washed my clothes, I rested for a while in the City of the Dead and fell asleep. And the King-Father of the East gave me red chestnuts and rosy dawn-juice to eat, and my hunger was stilled. Then I went to the dark skies and drank the yellow dew, and my thirst was quenched. And I met a black tiger and wanted to ride home on his back. But I whipped him too hard, and he bit me in the leg. And so I came back to tell you about it."

Once more the boy ran away from home, thousands of miles, until he came to the swamp where dwelt the Primal Mist. There he met an old man with yellow eyebrows and asked him how old he might be. The old man said: "I have given up the habit of eating, and live on air. The pupils of my eyes have gradually acquired a green glow, which enables me to see all hidden things. Whenever a thousand years have passed I turn around my bones and wash the marrow. And every two thousand years I scrape my skin to get rid of the hair. I have already washed my bones thrice and scraped my skin five times."

Afterward Sky O'Dawn served the Emperor Wu of the Han dynasty. The Emperor, who was fond of the magic arts, was much attached to him. One day he said to him: "I wish that the empress might not grow old. Can you prevent it?"

Sky O'Dawn answered: "I know of only one means to keep from growing old."

The Emperor asked what herbs one had to eat. Sky O'Dawn replied: "In the North-East grow the mushrooms of life. There is a three-legged crow in the sun who always wants to get down and eat them. But the Sun-God holds his eyes shut and does not let him get away. If human beings eat them they become immortal, when animals eat them they grow stupefied."

"And how do you know this?" asked the Emperor.

"When I was a boy I once fell into a deep well, from which I could not get out for many decades. And down there was an immortal who led me to this herb. But one has to pass through a red river whose water is so light that not even a feather can swim on it. Everything that touches its surface sinks to the depths. But the man pulled off one of his shoes and gave it to me. And I crossed the water on the shoe, picked the herb and ate it. Those who dwell in that place weave mats of pearls and precious stones. They led me to a spot before which hung a curtain of delicate, colored skin. And they gave me a pillow carved of black jade, on which were graven sun and moon, clouds and thunder. They covered me with a dainty coverlet spun of the hair of a hundred gnats. A cover of that kind is very cool and refreshing in summer. I felt of it with my hands, and it seemed to be formed of water; but when I looked at it more closely, it was pure light."

Once the Emperor called together all his magicians in order to talk with them about the fields of the blessed spirits. Sky O'Dawn was there, too, and said: "Once I was wandering about the North Pole and I came to the Fire-Mirror Mountain. There neither sun nor moon shines. But there is a dragon who holds a fiery mirror in his jaws in order to light up the darkness. On the mountain is a park, and in the park is a lake. By the lake grows the glimmer-stalk grass, which shines like a lamp of gold. If you pluck it and use it for a candle, you can see all things visible, and the shapes of the spirits as well. It even illuminates the interior of a human being."

Once Sky O'Dawn went to the East, into the country of the fortunate clouds. And he brought back with him from that land a steed of the gods, nine feet high. The Emperor asked him how he had come to find it.

So he told him: "The Queen-Mother of the West had him harnessed to her wagon when she went to visit the King-Father of the East. The steed was staked out in the field of the mushrooms of life. But he trampled down several hundred of them. This made the King-Father angry, and he drove the steed away to the heavenly river. There I found him and rode him home. I rode three times around the sun, because I had fallen asleep on the steed's back. And then, before I knew it, I was here. This steed can catch up with the sun's shadow. When I found him he was quite thin and as sad as an aged donkey. So I mowed the grass of the country of the fortunate clouds, which grows once every two-thousand years on the Mountain of the Nine Springs and fed it to the horse; and that made him lively again."

The Emperor asked what sort of a place the country of the fortunate clouds might be. Sky O'Dawn answered: "There is a great swamp there. The people prophesy fortune and misfortune by the air and the clouds. If good fortune is to befall a house, clouds of five colors form in the rooms, which alight on the grass and trees and turn into a colored dew. This dew tastes as sweet as cider."

The Emperor asked whether he could obtain any of this dew. Sky O'Dawn replied: "My steed could take me to the place where it falls four times in the course of a single day!"

And sure enough he came back by evening, and brought along dew of every color in a crystal flask. The Emperor drank it and his hair grew black again. He gave it to his highest officials to drink, and the old grew young again and the sick became well.

Once, when a comet appeared in the heavens, Sky O'Dawn gave the Emperor the astrologer's wand. The Emperor pointed it at the comet and the comet was quenched.

Sky O'Dawn was an excellent whistler. And whenever he whistled in full tones, long drawn out, the motes in the sunbeams danced to his music.

Once he said to a friend: "There is not a soul on earth who knows who I am with the exception of the astrologer!"

When Sky O'Dawn had died, the Emperor called the astrologer to him and asked: "Did you know Sky O'Dawn?"

He replied: "No!"

The Emperor said: "What do you know?"

The astrologer answered: "I know how to gaze on the stars."

"Are all the stars in their places?" asked the Emperor.

"Yes, but for eighteen years I have not seen the Star of the Great Year. Now it is visible once more."

Then the Emperor looked up towards the skies and sighed: "For eighteen years Sky O'Dawn kept me company, and I did not know that he was the Star of the Great Year!"

Tales of Kobo Daishi

KOBO DAISHI ('Glory to the Great Teacher'), who was born AD 774, was the most holy and most famous of the Japanese Buddhist saints. He founded the Shingon-shu, a Buddhist sect remarkable for its magical formulae and for its abstruse and esoteric teachings, and he is also said to have invented the *Hiragana* syllabary, a form of running script.

In the *Namudaishi*, which is a Japanese poem on the life of this great saint, we are informed that Kobo Daishi brought back with him from China a millstone and some seeds of the tea-plant, and thus revived the drinking of this beverage, which had fallen into disuse. We are also told in the same poem that it was Kobo Daishi who "demonstrated to the world the use of coal." He was renowned as a great preacher, but was not less famous as a calligraphist, painter, sculptor, and traveller.

'A Divine Prodigy'

Kobo Daishi, however, is essentially famous for the extraordinary miracles which he performed, and numerous are the legends associated with him. His conception was miraculous, for when he was born in the Baron's Hall, on the shore of Byobu, a bright light shone, and he came into the world with his hands folded as if in prayer. When but five years of age he would sit among the lotuses and converse with Buddhas, and he kept secret all the wisdom he thus obtained. His heart was troubled by the sorrow and pain of humanity. While on Mount Shashin he sought to sacrifice his own life by way of propitiation, but he was prevented from doing so by a number of angels who would not allow this ardent soul to suffer death until he had fulfilled his destiny. His very games were of a religious nature. On one occasion he built a clay pagoda, and he was immediately surrounded by the Four Heavenly Kings (originally Hindu deities). The Imperial Messenger, who happened to pass by when this miracle took place, was utterly amazed, and described the young Kobo Daishi as 'a divine prodigy'. While at Muroto, in Tosa, performing his devotions, we are told in the *Namu-daishi* that a bright star fell from Heaven and entered his mouth, while at midnight an evil dragon came forth against him, "but he spat upon it, and with his saliva he killed it."

In his nineteenth year he wore the black silk robes of a Buddhist priest, and with a zeal that never failed him sought for enlightenment. "Many are the ways," he said; "but Buddhism is the best of all." During his mystical studies he came across a book containing the Shingon doctrine, a doctrine that closely resembles the old Egyptian speculations. The book was so abstruse that even Kobo Daishi failed to master it; but, nothing daunted, he received permission from the Emperor to visit China, where he ultimately unravelled its profound mysteries, and attained to that degree of saintship associated with the miraculous.

Gohitsu-Osho

When Kobo Daishi was in China the Emperor, hearing of his fame, sent for him and bade him rewrite the name of a certain room in the royal palace, a name that had become obliterated by the effacing finger of Time. Kobo Daishi, with a brush in each hand, another in his mouth, and two others between the toes, wrote the characters required upon the wall, and for this extraordinary performance the Emperor named him Gohitsu-Osho ('The Priest who writes with Five Brushes').

Writing on Sky and Water

While still in China Kobo Daishi met a boy standing by the side of a river. "If you be Kobo Daishi," said he, "be honourably pleased to write upon the sky, for I have heard that no wonder is beyond your power."

Kobo Daishi raised his brush; it moved quickly in the air, and writing appeared in the blue sky, characters that were perfectly formed and wonderfully beautiful.

When the boy had also written upon the sky with no less skill, he said to Kobo Daishi: "We have both written upon the sky. Now I beg that you will write upon this flowing river."

Kobo Daishi readily complied. Once again his brush moved, and this time a poem appeared on the water, a poem written in praise of that particular river. The letters lingered for a moment, and then were carried away by the swift current.

There seems to have been a contest in magical power between these two workers of marvels, for no sooner had the letters passed out of sight than the boy also wrote upon the running water the character of the Dragon, and it remained stationary.

Kobo Daishi, who was a great scholar, at once perceived that the boy had omitted the *ten*, a dot which rightly belonged to this character. When Kobo Daishi pointed out the error, the boy told him that he had forgotten to insert the *ten*, and begged that the famous saint would put it in for him. No sooner had Kobo Daishi done so than the Dragon character became a Dragon. Its tail lashed the waters, thunder-clouds sped across the sky, and lightning flashed. In another moment the Dragon arose from the water and ascended to heaven.

Though Kobo Daishi's powers of magic excelled those of the boy, he inquired who this youth might be, and the boy replied: "I am Monju Bosatsu, the Lord of Wisdom." Having spoken these words, he became illumined by a radiant light; the beauty of the Gods shone upon his countenance, and, like the Dragon, he ascended into heaven.

How Kobo Daishi Painted the Ten

On one occasion Kobo Daishi omitted the *ten* on a tablet placed above one of the gates of the Emperor's palace. The Emperor commanded that ladders should be brought; but Kobo Daishi, without making use of them, stood upon the ground, and threw up his brush, which, after making the *ten*, fell into his hand.

Kino Momoye and Onomo Toku

Kino Momoye once ridiculed some of Kobo Daishi's characters, and said that one of them resembled a conceited wrestler. On the night he made this foolish jest Momoye dreamed that a wrestler struck him blow upon blow – moreover, that his antagonist leapt upon his body, causing him considerable pain. Momoye awoke, and cried aloud in his agony, and as he cried he saw the wrestler suddenly change into the character he had so unwisely jeered at. It rose into the air, and went back to the tablet from whence it had come.

Momoye was not the only man who imprudently scoffed at the great Kobo Daishi's work. Legend records that one named Onomo Toku said that the saint's character *Shu* was far more like the character 'rice'. That night Onomo Toku had good reason to regret his folly, for in a dream the character *Shu* took bodily form and became a rice-cleaner, who moved up and down the offender's body after the manner of hammers that were used in beating this grain. When Onomo Toku awoke it was to find that his body was covered with bruises and that his flesh was bleeding in many places.

Kobo Daishi's Return

When Kobo Daishi was about to leave China and return to his own country he went down to the seashore and threw his *vajra* across the ocean waves, and it was afterwards found hanging on the branch of a pine-tree at Takano, in Japan.

We are not told anything about Kobo Daishi's voyage to his own land; but directly he arrived in Japan he gave thanks for the divine protection he had received during his travels. On the Naked Mountain he offered incantations of so powerful a nature that the once barren mountain became covered with flowers and trees.

Kobo Daishi, as time advanced, became still more holy. During a religious discussion the Divine Light streamed from him, and he continued to perform many great marvels. He made brackish water pure, raised the dead to life, and continued to commune with certain gods. On one occasion Inari, the God of Rice, appeared on Mount Fushime and took from the great saint the sacrifice he offered. "Together, you and I," said Kobo Daishi, "we will protect this people."

The Death of Kobo Daishi

In AD 834 this remarkable saint died, and we are told that a very great gathering, both lay and priestly, wept at the graveyard of Okunoin, in Koya, where he was buried. His death, however, by no means meant a sudden cessation of miracles on his part, for when the Emperor Saga died "his coffin was mysteriously borne through the air to Koya, and Kobo himself, coming forth from his grave, performed the funeral obsequies." Nor did the wonders cease with this incident, for the Emperor Uda received from Kobo

Daishi the sacred Baptism. When the Imperial Messenger to the temple where Kobo Daishi was worshipped was unable to see the face of this great saint, Kobo "guided the worshipper's hand to touch his knee. Never, as long as he lived, did the Messenger forget that feeling!"

Kadzutoyo and the Badger

ON ONE OCCASION Kadzutoyo and his retainer went fishing. They had had excellent sport, and were about to return home, when a violent shower came on, and they were forced to take shelter under a willow-tree. After waiting for some time the rain showed no sign of abating, and as it was already growing dark they decided to continue their journey in spite of the inclement weather. They had not proceeded far when they perceived a young girl weeping bitterly. Kadzutoyo regarded her with suspicion, but his retainer was charmed by the maiden's great beauty, and inquired who she was and why she lingered on such a stormy night.

"Alas! good sir," said the maiden, still weeping, "my tale is a sad one. I have long endured the taunts and cruelties of my wicked stepmother, who hates me. Tonight she spat upon me and beat me. I could bear the bitter humiliation no longer, and I was on the way to my aunt, who lives in yonder village, there to receive peace and shelter, when I was stricken down with a strange malady, and compelled to remain here until the pain subsided."

These words much affected the kind-hearted retainer, and he fell desperately in love with this fair maiden; but Kadzutoyo, after carefully considering the matter, drew his sword and cut off her head.

"Oh! my lord," said the retainer, "what awful deed is this? How can you kill a harmless girl? Believe me, you will have to pay for your folly."

"You do not understand," replied Kadzutoyo, "but all I ask is that you keep silence in the matter."

When they reached home Kadzutoyo soon fell asleep; but his retainer, after brooding over the murder of the fair maiden, went to his lord's parents and told them the whole pitiful story.

Kadzutoyo's father was stricken with anger when he heard the dreadful tale. He at once went to his son's room, roused him, and said: "Oh, miserable murderer! How could you slay an innocent girl without the least provocation? You have shamed the honourable name of *samurai*, a name that stands for true chivalry and for the defence of the weak and helpless. You have brought dishonour upon our house, and it is my duty to take your life." Having said these words, he drew his sword.

"Sir," replied Kadzutoyo, without flinching at the shining weapon, "you, like my retainer, do not understand. It has been given me to solve certain mysteries, and with that knowledge I assure you that I have not been guilty of so foul a crime as you suppose, but have been loyal to the fair calling of a *samurai*. The girl I cut down with my sword was no mortal. Be pleased to go tomorrow with your retainers to the spot where this scene occurred. If you find the corpse of a girl you will have no need to take my life, for I will disembowel myself."

Early next day, when the sun had scarce risen in the sky, Kadzutoyo's father, together with his retainers, set out upon the journey. When they reached the place where the tragedy had taken place the father saw lying by the roadside, not the corpse of a fair maiden as he had feared, but the body of a great headless badger.

When the father reached home again he questioned his son: "How is it," said he, "that what appeared to be a girl to your retainer seemed to you to be a badger?"

"Sir," replied Kadzutoyo, "the creature I saw last night appeared to me as a girl; but her beauty was strange, and not like the beauty of earthly women. Moreover, although it was raining hard, I observed that the garments of this being did not get wet, and having noticed this weird occurrence, I knew at once that the woman was none other than some wicked goblin. The creature took the form of a lovely maiden with the idea of bewitching us with her many charms, in the hope that she might get our fish."

The old Prince was filled with admiration for his son's cleverness. Having discovered so much foresight and prudence, he resolved to abdicate, and proclaim Kadzutoyo Prince of Tosa in his stead.

How a Man Was Bewitched and Had His Head Shaved by the Foxes

IN THE VILLAGE OF IWAHARA, in the province of Shinshiu, there dwelt a family which had acquired considerable wealth in the wine trade. On some auspicious occasion it happened that a number of guests were gathered together at their house, feasting on wine and fish; and as the wine-cup went round, the conversation turned upon foxes. Among the guests was a certain carpenter, Tokutaro by name, a man about thirty years of age, of a stubborn and obstinate turn, who said:

"Well, sirs, you've been talking for some time of men being bewitched by foxes; surely you must be under their influence yourselves, to say such things. How on earth can foxes have such power over men? At any rate, men must be great fools to be so deluded. Let's have no more of this nonsense."

Upon this a man who was sitting by him answered:

"Tokutaro little knows what goes on in the world, or he would not speak so. How many myriads of men are there who have been bewitched by foxes? Why, there have been at least twenty or thirty men tricked by the brutes on the Maki Moor alone. It's hard to disprove facts that have happened before our eyes."

"You're no better than a pack of born idiots," said Tokutaro. "I will engage to go out to the Maki Moor this very night and prove it. There is not a fox in all Japan that can make a fool of Tokutaro."

Thus he spoke in his pride; but the others were all angry with him for boasting, and said:

"If you return without anything having happened, we will pay for five measures of wine and a thousand copper cash worth of fish; and if you are bewitched, you shall do as much for us."

Tokutaro took the bet, and at nightfall set forth for the Maki Moor by himself. As he neared the moor, he saw before him a small bamboo grove, into which a fox ran; and it instantly occurred to him that the foxes of the moor would try to bewitch him. As he was yet looking, he suddenly saw the daughter of the headman of the village of Upper Horikane, who was married to the headman of the village of Maki.

"Pray, where are you going to, Master Tokutaro?" said she.

"I am going to the village hard by."

"Then, as you will have to pass my native place, if you will allow me, I will accompany you so far."

Tokutaro thought this very odd, and made up his mind that it was a fox trying to make a fool of him; he accordingly determined to turn the tables on the fox, and answered – "It is a long time since I have had the pleasure of seeing you; and as it seems that your house is on my road, I shall be glad to escort you so far."

With this he walked behind her, thinking he should certainly see the end of a fox's tail peeping out; but, look as he might, there was nothing to be seen. At last they came to the village of Upper Horikane; and when they reached the cottage of the girl's father, the family all came out, surprised to see her.

"Oh dear! oh dear! here is our daughter come: I hope there is nothing the matter."

And so they went on, for some time, asking a string of questions.

In the meanwhile, Tokutaro went round to the kitchen door, at the back of the house, and, beckoning out the master of the house, said:

"The girl who has come with me is not really your daughter. As I was going to the Maki Moor, when I arrived at the bamboo grove, a fox jumped up in front of me, and when it had dashed into the grove it immediately took the shape of your daughter, and offered to accompany me to the village; so I pretended to be taken in by the brute, and came with it so far."

On hearing this, the master of the house put his head on one side, and mused a while; then, calling his wife, he repeated the story to her, in a whisper.

But she flew into a great rage with Tokutaro, and said:

"This is a pretty way of insulting people's daughters. The girl is our daughter, and there's no mistake about it. How dare you invent such lies?"

"Well," said Tokutaro, "you are quite right to say so; but still there is no doubt that this is a case of witchcraft."

Seeing how obstinately he held to his opinion, the old folks were sorely perplexed, and said:

"What do you think of doing?"

"Pray leave the matter to me: I'll soon strip the false skin off, and show the beast to you in its true colours. Do you two go into the store-closet, and wait there."

With this he went into the kitchen, and, seizing the girl by the back of the neck, forced her down by the hearth.

"Oh! Master Tokutaro, what means this brutal violence? Mother! father! help!"

So the girl cried and screamed; but Tokutaro only laughed, and said:

"So you thought to bewitch me, did you? From the moment you jumped into the wood, I was on the look-out for you to play me some trick. I'll soon make you show what you really are;" and as he said this, he twisted her two hands behind her back, and trod upon her, and tortured her; but she only wept, and cried:

"Oh! it hurts, it hurts!"

"If this is not enough to make you show your true form, I'll roast you to death;" and he piled firewood on the hearth, and, tucking up her dress, scorched her severely.

"Oh! oh! this is more than I can bear;" and with this she expired.

The two old people then came running in from the rear of the house, and, pushing aside Tokutaro, folded their daughter in their arms, and put their hands to her mouth to feel whether she still breathed; but life was extinct, and not the sign of a fox's tail was to be seen about her. Then they seized Tokutaro by the collar, and cried:

"On pretence that our true daughter was a fox, you have roasted her to death. Murderer! Here, you there, bring ropes and cords, and secure this Tokutaro!"

So the servants obeyed, and several of them seized Tokutaro and bound him to a pillar. Then the master of the house, turning to Tokutaro, said:

"You have murdered our daughter before our very eyes. I shall report the matter to the lord of the manor, and you will assuredly pay for this with your head. Be prepared for the worst."

And as he said this, glaring fiercely at Tokutaro, they carried the corpse of his daughter into the store-closet. As they were sending to make the matter known in the village of Maki, and taking other measures, who should come up but the priest of the temple called Anrakuji, in the village of Iwahara, with an acolyte and a servant, who called out in a loud voice from the front door:

"Is all well with the honourable master of this house? I have been to say prayers today in a neighbouring village, and on my way back I could not pass the door without at least inquiring after your welfare. If you are at home, I would fain pay my respects to you."

As he spoke thus in a loud voice, he was heard from the back of the house; and the master got up and went out, and, after the usual compliments on meeting had been exchanged, said:

"I ought to have the honour of inviting you to step inside this evening; but really we are all in the greatest trouble, and I must beg you to excuse my impoliteness."

"Indeed! Pray, what may be the matter?" replied the priest. And when the master of the house had told the whole story, from beginning to end, he was thunderstruck, and said:

"Truly, this must be a terrible distress to you." Then the priest looked on one side, and saw Tokutaro bound, and exclaimed, "Is not that Tokutaro that I see there?"

"Oh, your reverence," replied Tokutaro, piteously, "it was this, that, and the other: and I took it into my head that the young lady was a fox, and so I killed her. But I pray your reverence to intercede for me, and save my life;" and as he spoke, the tears started from his eyes.

"To be sure," said the priest, "you may well bewail yourself; however, if I save your life, will you consent to become my disciple, and enter the priesthood?"

"Only save my life, and I'll become your disciple with all my heart."

When the priest heard this, he called out the parents, and said to them:

"It would seem that, though I am but a foolish old priest, my coming here today has been unusually well timed. I have a request to make of you. Your putting Tokutaro to death won't bring your daughter to life again. I have heard his story, and there certainly was no malice prepense on his part to kill your daughter. What he did, he did thinking to do a service to your family; and it would surely be better to hush the matter up. He wishes, moreover, to give himself over to me, and to become my disciple."

"It is as you say," replied the father and mother, speaking together. "Revenge will not recall our daughter. Please dispel our grief, by shaving his head and making a priest of him on the spot."

"I'll shave him at once, before your eyes," answered the priest, who immediately caused the cords which bound Tokutaro to be untied, and, putting on his priest's scarf, made him join his hands together in a posture of prayer. Then the reverend man stood up behind him, razor in hand, and, intoning a hymn, gave two or three strokes of the razor, which he then handed to his acolyte, who made a clean shave of Tokutaro's hair. When the latter had finished his obeisance to the priest, and the ceremony was over, there was a loud burst of laughter; and at the same moment the day broke, and Tokutaro found himself alone, in the middle of a large moor. At first, in his surprise, he thought that it was all a dream, and was much annoyed at having been tricked by the foxes. He then passed his hand over his head, and found that he was shaved quite bald. There was nothing for it but to get up, wrap a handkerchief round his head, and go back to the place where his friends were assembled.

"Hallo, Tokutaro! so you've come back. Well, how about the foxes?"

"Really, gentlemen," replied he, bowing, "I am quite ashamed to appear before you."

Then he told them the whole story, and, when he had finished, pulled off the kerchief, and showed his bald pate.

"What a capital joke!" shouted his listeners, and amid roars of laughter, claimed the bet of fish, and wine. It was duly paid; but Tokutaro never allowed his hair to grow again, and renounced the world, and became a priest under the name of Sainen.

The Vampire Cat

THE PRINCE OF HIZEN, a distinguished member of the Nabeshima family, lingered in the garden with O Toyo, the favourite among his ladies. When the sun set they retired to the palace, but failed to notice that they were being followed by a large cat.

O Toyo went to her room and fell asleep. At midnight she awoke and gazed about her, as if suddenly aware of some dreadful presence in the apartment. At length she saw, crouching close beside her, a gigantic cat, and before she could cry out for assistance the animal sprang upon her and strangled her. The animal then made a hole under the verandah, buried the corpse, and assumed the form of the beautiful O Toyo.

The Prince, who knew nothing of what had happened, continued to love the false O Toyo, unaware that in reality he was caressing a foul beast. He noticed, little by little, that his strength failed, and it was not long before he became dangerously ill. Physicians were summoned, but they could do nothing to restore the royal patient. It was observed that he suffered most during the night, and was troubled by horrible dreams. This being so his councillors arranged that a hundred retainers should sit with their lord and keep watch while he slept.

The watch went into the sick-room, but just before ten o'clock it was overcome by a mysterious drowsiness. When all the men were asleep the false O Toyo crept into the apartment and disturbed the Prince until sunrise. Night after night the retainers came to guard their master, but always they fell asleep at the same hour, and even three loyal councillors had a similar experience.

During this time the Prince grew worse, and at length a priest named Ruiten was appointed to pray on his behalf. One night, while he was engaged in his supplications, he heard a strange noise proceeding from the garden. On looking out of the window he saw a young soldier washing himself. When he had finished his ablutions he stood before an image of Buddha, and prayed most ardently for the recovery of the Prince.

Ruiten, delighted to find such zeal and loyalty, invited the young man to enter his house, and when he had done so inquired his name.

"I am Ito Soda," said the young man, "and serve in the infantry of Nabeshima. I have heard of my lord's sickness and long to have the honour of nursing him; but being of low rank it is not meet that I should come into his presence. I have, nevertheless, prayed to the Buddha that my lord's life may be spared. I believe that the Prince of Hizen is bewitched, and if I might remain with him I would do my utmost to find and crush the evil power that is the cause of his illness."

Ruiten was so favourably impressed with these words that he went the next day to consult with one of the councillors, and after much discussion it was arranged that Ito Soda should keep watch with the hundred retainers.

When Ito Soda entered the royal apartment he saw that his master slept in the middle of the room, and he also observed the hundred retainers sitting in the chamber quietly chatting together in the hope that they would be able to keep off approaching drowsiness. By ten o'clock all the retainers, in spite of their efforts, had fallen asleep. Ito Soda tried to keep his eyes open, but a heaviness was gradually overcoming him, and he realised that if he wished to keep awake he must resort to extreme measures. When he had carefully spread oil-paper over the mats he stuck his dirk into his thigh. The sharp pain he experienced warded off sleep for a time, but eventually he felt his eyes closing once more. Resolved to outwit the spell which had proved too much for the retainers, he twisted the knife in his thigh, and thus increased the pain and kept his loyal watch, while blood continually dripped upon the oil-paper.

While Ito Soda watched he saw the sliding doors drawn open and a beautiful woman creep softly into the apartment. With a smile she noticed the sleeping retainers, and was about to approach the Prince when she observed Ito Soda. After she had spoken curtly to him she approached the Prince and inquired how he fared, but the Prince was too ill to make a reply. Ito Soda watched every movement, and believed she tried to bewitch the Prince, but she was always frustrated in her evil purpose by the dauntless eyes of Ito Soda, and at last she was compelled to retire.

In the morning the retainers awoke, and were filled with shame when they learnt how Ito Soda had kept his vigil. The councillors loudly praised the young soldier for his loyalty and enterprise, and he was commanded to keep watch again that night. He did so, and once more the false O Toyo entered the sick-room, and, as on the previous night, she was compelled to retreat without being able to cast her spell over the Prince.

It was discovered that immediately the faithful Soda had kept guard the Prince was able to obtain peaceful slumber, and, moreover, that he began to get better, for the false O Toyo, having been frustrated on two occasions, now kept away altogether, and the guard was not troubled with mysterious drowsiness. Soda, impressed by these strange circumstances, went to one of the councillors and informed him that the so-called O Toyo was a goblin of some kind.

That night Soda planned to go to the creature's room and try to kill her, arranging that in case she should escape there should be eight retainers outside waiting to capture her and despatch her immediately.

At the appointed hour Soda went to the creature's apartment, pretending that he bore a message from the Prince.

"What is your message?" inquired the woman.

"Kindly read this letter," replied Soda, and with these words he drew his dirk and tried to kill her.

The false O Toyo seized a halberd and endeavoured to strike her adversary. Blow followed blow, but at last perceiving that flight would serve her better than battle she threw away her weapon, and in a moment the lovely maiden turned into a cat and sprang on to the roof. The eight men waiting outside in case of emergency shot at the animal, but the creature succeeded in eluding them.

The cat made all speed for the mountains, and caused trouble among the people who lived in the vicinity, but was finally killed during a hunt ordered by the Prince Hizen. The Prince became well again, and Ito Soda received the honour and reward he so richly deserved.

Jiraiya, or The Magic Frog

OGATA was the name of a castle-lord who lived in the Island of the Nine Provinces, (Kiushiu). He had but one son, an infant, whom the people in admiration nicknamed Jiraiya (Young Thunder.) During one of the civil wars, this castle was taken, and Ogata was slain; but by the aid of a faithful retainer, who hid Jiraiya in his bosom, the boy escaped and fled northward to Echigo. There he lived until he grew up to manhood.

At that time Echigo was infested with robbers. One day the faithful retainer of Jiraiya being attacked, made resistance, and was slain by the robbers. Jiraiya now left alone in the world went out from Echigo and led a wandering life in several provinces.

All this time he was consumed with the desire to revive the name of his father, and restore the fortunes of his family. Being exceedingly brave, and an expert swordsman, he became chief of a band of robbers and plundered many wealthy merchants, and in a short time he was rich in men, arms and booty. He was accustomed to disguise himself, and go in person into the houses and presence of men of wealth, and thus learn all about their gates and guards, where they slept, and in what rooms their treasures were stored, so that success was easy.

Hearing of an old man who lived in Shinano, he started to rob him, and for this purpose put on the disguise of a pilgrim. Shinano is a very high table-land, full of mountains, and the snow lies deep in winter. A great snow storm coming on, Jiraiya took refuge in a humble house by the way. Entering, he found a very beautiful woman, who treated him with great kindness. This, however, did not change the robber's nature. At midnight, when all was still, he unsheathed his sword, and going noiselessly to her room, he found the lady absorbed in reading.

Lifting his sword, he was about to strike at her neck, when, in a flash, her body changed into that of a very old man, who seized the heavy steel blade and broke it in pieces as though it were a stick. Then he tossed the bits of steel away, and thus spoke to Jiraiya, who stood amazed but fearless:

"I am a man named Senso Dojin, and I have lived in these mountains many hundred years, though my true body is that of a huge frog. I can easily put you to death but I have another purpose. So I shall pardon you and teach you magic instead."

Then the youth bowed his head to the floor, poured out his thanks to the old man and begged to be received as his pupil.

Remaining with the old man of the mountain for several weeks, Jiraiya learned all the arts of the mountain spirits; how to cause a storm of wind and rain, to make a deluge, and to control the elements at will.

He also learned how to govern the frogs, and at his bidding they assumed gigantic size, so that on their backs he could stand up and cross rivers and carry enormous loads.

When the old man had finished instructing him he said "Henceforth cease from robbing, or in any way injuring the poor. Take from the wicked rich, and those who acquire money dishonestly, but help the needy and the suffering." Thus speaking, the old man turned into a huge frog and hopped away.

What this old mountain spirit bade him do, was just what Jiraiya wished to accomplish. He set out on his journey with a light heart. "I can now make the storm and the waters obey me, and all the frogs are at my command; but alas! the magic of the frog cannot control that of the serpent. I shall beware of his poison."

From that time forth the oppressed poor people rejoiced many a time as the avaricious merchants and extortionate money lenders lost their treasures. For when a poor farmer, whose crops failed, could not pay his rent or loan on the date promised, these hard-hearted money lenders would turn him out of his house, seize his beds and mats and rice-tub, and even the shrine and images on the god-shelf, to sell them at auction for a trifle, to their minions, who resold them at a high price for the money-lender, who thus got a double benefit. Whenever a miser was robbed, the people said, "The young thunder has struck," and then they were glad, knowing that it was Jiraiya, (Young Thunder.) In this manner his name soon grew to be the poor people's watchword in those troublous times.

Yet Jiraiya was always ready to help the innocent and honest, even if they were rich. One day a merchant named Fukutaro was sentenced to death, though he was really not guilty. Jiraiya hearing of it, went to the magistrate and said that he himself was the very man who committed the robbery. So the man's life was saved, and Jiraiya was hanged on a large oak tree. But during the night, his dead body changed into a bull-frog which hopped away out of sight, and off into the mountains of Shinano.

At this time, there was living in this province, a young and beautiful maiden named Tsunade. Her character was very lovely. She was always obedient to her parents and kind to her friends. Her daily task was to go to the mountains and cut brushwood for fuel. One day while thus busy singing at the task, she met a very old man, with a long white beard sweeping his breast, who said to her:

"Do not fear me. I have lived in this mountain many hundred years, but my real body is that of a snail. I will teach you the powers of magic, so that you can walk on the sea, or cross a river however swift and deep, as though it were dry land."

Gladly the maiden took daily lessons of the old man, and soon was able to walk on the waters as on the mountain paths. One day the old man said, "I shall now leave you and resume my former shape. Use your power to destroy wicked robbers. Help those who defend the poor. I advise you to marry the celebrated man Jiraiya, and thus you will unite your powers."

Thus saying, the old man shrivelled up into a snail and crawled away.

"I am glad," said the maiden to herself, "for the magic of the snail can overcome that of the serpent. When Jiraiya, who has the magic of the frog, shall marry me, we can then destroy the son of the serpent, the robber named Dragon-coil (Orochimaru)."

By good fortune, Jiraiya met the maiden Tsunade, and being charmed with her beauty, and knowing her power of magic, sent a messenger with presents to her parents, asking them to give him their daughter to wife. The parents agreed, and so the young and loving couple were married.

Hitherto when Jiraiya wished to cross a river he changed himself into a frog and swam across; or, he summoned a bull-frog before him, which increased in size until as large as an elephant. Then standing erect on his warty back, even though the wind blew his garments wildly, Jiraiya reached the opposite shore in safety. But now, with his wife's powers, the two, without any delay, walked over as though the surface was a hard floor.

Soon after their marriage, war broke out in Japan between the two famous clans of Tsukikage and Inukage. To help them fight their battles, and capture the castles of their enemies, the Tsukikage family besought the aid of Jiraiya, who agreed to serve them and carried their banner in his back. Their enemies, the Inukage, then secured the services of Dragon-coil.

This Orochimaru, or Dragon-coil, was a very wicked robber whose father was a man, and whose mother was a serpent that lived in the bottom of Lake Takura. He was perfectly skilled in the magic of the serpent, and by spurting venom on his enemies, could destroy the strongest warriors.

Collecting thousands of followers, he made great ravages in all parts of Japan, robbing and murdering good and bad, rich and poor alike. Loving war and destruction he joined his forces with the Inukage family.

Now that the magic of the frog and snail was joined to the one army, and the magic of the serpent aided the other, the conflicts were bloody and terrible, and many men were slain on both sides.

On one occasion, after a hard fought battle, Jiraiya fled and took refuge in a monastery, with a few trusty vassals, to rest a short time. In this retreat a lovely princess named Tagoto was dwelling. She had fled from Orochimaru, who wished her for his bride. She hated to marry the offspring of a serpent, and hoped to escape him. She lived in fear of him continually. Orochimaru hearing at one time that both Jiraiya and the princess were at this place, changed himself into a serpent, and distilling a large mouthful of poisonous venom, crawled up to the ceiling in the room where Jiraiya and his wife were sleeping, and reaching a spot directly over them, poured the poisonous venom on the heads of his rivals. The fumes of the prison so stupefied Jiraiya's followers, and even the monks, that Orochimaru, instantly changing himself to a man, profited by the opportunity to seize the princess Tagoto, and make off with her.

Gradually the faithful retainers awoke from their stupor to find their master and his beloved wife delirious, and near the point of death, and the princess gone.

"What can we do to restore our dear master to life?" This was the question each one asked of the others, as with sorrowful faces and weeping eyes they gazed at the pallid forms of their unconscious master and his consort. They called in the venerable abbot of the monastery to see if he could suggest what could be done.

"Alas!" said the aged priest, "there is no medicine in Japan to cure your lord's disease, but in India there is an elixir which is a sure antidote. If we could get that, the master would recover."

"Alas! alas!" and a chorus of groans showed that all hope had fled, for the mountain in India, where the elixir was made, lay five thousand miles from Japan.

Just then a youth named Rikimatsu, one of the pages of Jiraiya, arose to speak. He was but fourteen years old, and served Jiraiya out of gratitude, for he had rescued his father from many dangers and saved his life. He begged permission to say a word to the abbot, who, seeing the lad's eager face, motioned to him with his fan to speak.

"How long can our lord live," asked the youth.

"He will be dead in thirty hours," answered the abbot, with a sigh.

"I'll go and procure the medicine, and if our master is still living when I come back, he will get well."

Now Rikimatsu had learned magic and sorcery from the Tengus, or long-nosed elves of the mountains, and could fly high in the air with incredible swiftness. Speaking a few words of incantation, he put on the wings of a Tengu, mounted a white cloud and rode on the east wind to India, bought the elixir of the mountain spirits, and returned to Japan in one day and a night.

On the first touch of the elixir on the sick man's face he drew a deep breath, perspiration glistened on his forehead, and in a few moments more he sat up.

Jiraiya and his wife both got well, and the war broke out again. In a great battle Dragon-coil was killed and the princess rescued. For his prowess and aid Jiraiya was made daimyo of Idzu.

Being now weary of war and the hardships of active life, Jiraiya was glad to settle down to tranquil life in the castle and rear his family in peace. He spent the remainder of his days in reading the books of the sages, in composing verses, in admiring the flowers, the moon and the landscape, and occasionally going out hawking or fishing. There, amid his children and children's children, he finished his days in peace.

The Magic Kettle

RIGHT IN THE MIDDLE OF JAPAN, high up among the mountains, an old man lived in his little house. He was very proud of it, and never tired of admiring the whiteness of his straw mats, and the pretty papered walls, which in warm weather always slid back, so that the smell of the trees and flowers might come in.

One day he was standing looking at the mountain opposite, when he heard a kind of rumbling noise in the room behind him. He turned round, and in the corner he beheld a rusty old iron kettle, which could not have seen the light of day for many years. How the kettle got there the old man did not know, but he took it up and looked it over carefully, and when he found that it was quite whole he cleaned the dust off it and carried it into his kitchen.

"That was a piece of luck," he said, smiling to himself; "a good kettle costs money, and it is as well to have a second one at hand in case of need; mine is getting worn out, and the water is already beginning to come through its bottom."

Then he took the other kettle off the fire, filled the new one with water, and put it in its place.

No sooner was the water in the kettle getting warm than a strange thing happened, and the man, who was standing by, thought he must be dreaming. First the handle of the kettle gradually changed its shape and became a head, and the spout grew into a tail, while out of the body sprang four paws, and in a few minutes the man found himself watching, not a kettle, but a tanuki! The creature jumped off the fire, and bounded about the room like a kitten, running up the walls and over the ceiling, till the old man was in an agony lest his pretty room should be spoilt. He cried to a neighbour for help, and between them they managed to catch the tanuki, and shut him up safely in a wooden chest. Then, quite exhausted, they sat down on the mats, and consulted together what they should do with this troublesome beast. At length they decided to sell him, and bade a child who was passing send them a certain tradesman called Jimmu.

When Jimmu arrived, the old man told him that he had something which he wished to get rid of, and lifted the lid of the wooden chest, where he had shut up the tanuki. But, to his surprise, no tanuki was there, nothing but the kettle he had found in the corner. It was certainly very odd, but the man remembered what had taken place on the fire, and did not want to keep the kettle any more, so after a little bargaining about the price, Jimmu went away carrying the kettle with him.

Now Jimmu had not gone very far before he felt that the kettle was getting heavier and heavier, and by the time he reached home he was so tired that he was thankful to put it down in the corner of his room, and then forgot all about it. In the middle of the night, however, he was awakened by a loud noise in the corner where the kettle stood, and raised himself up in bed to see what it was. But nothing was there except the kettle, which seemed quiet enough. He thought that he must have been dreaming, and fell asleep again, only to be roused a second time by the same disturbance. He jumped up and went to the corner, and by the light of the lamp that he always kept burning he saw that the kettle had become a tanuki, which was running round after his tail. After he grew weary of that, he ran on the balcony, where he turned several somersaults, from pure gladness of heart. The tradesman was much troubled as to what to do with the animal, and it was only towards morning that he managed to get any sleep; but when he opened his eyes again there was no tanuki, only the old kettle he had left there the night before.

As soon as he had tidied his house, Jimmu set off to tell his story to a friend next door. The man listened quietly, and did not appear so surprised as Jimmu expected, for he recollected having heard, in his youth, something about a wonder-working kettle. "Go and travel with it, and show it off," said he, "and you will become a rich man; but be careful first to ask the tanuki's leave, and also to perform some magic ceremonies to prevent him from running away at the sight of the people."

Jimmu thanked his friend for his counsel, which he followed exactly. The tanuki's consent was obtained, a booth was built, and a notice was hung up outside it inviting the people to come and witness the most wonderful transformation that ever was seen.

They came in crowds, and the kettle was passed from hand to hand, and they were allowed to examine it all over, and even to look inside. Then Jimmu took it back, and setting it on the platform, commanded it to become a tanuki. In an instant the handle began to change into a head, and the spout into a tail, while the four paws appeared at the sides. "Dance," said Jimmu, and the tanuki did his steps, and moved first on one side and then on the other, till the people could not stand still any longer, and began to dance too. Gracefully he led the fan dance, and glided without a pause into the shadow dance and the umbrella dance, and it seemed as if he might go on dancing for ever. And so very likely he would, if Jimmu had not declared he had danced enough, and that the booth must now be closed.

Day after day the booth was so full it was hardly possible to enter it, and what the neighbour foretold had come to pass, and Jimmu was a rich man. Yet he did not feel happy. He was an honest man, and he thought that he owed some of his wealth to the man from whom he had bought the kettle. So, one morning, he put a hundred gold pieces into it, and hanging the kettle once more on his arm, he returned to the seller of it. "I have no right to keep it any longer," he added when he had ended his tale, "so I have brought it back to you, and inside you will find a hundred gold pieces as the price of its hire."

The man thanked Jimmu, and said that few people would have been as honest as he. And the kettle brought them both luck, and everything went well with them till they died, which they did when they were very old, respected by everyone.

The Wizard Dervish

A LONG TIME AGO lived a Padishah who had no son.

As he was taking a walk with his lala one day, they came to a well, near which they stopped to wish. A dervish suddenly appeared and cried: "All hail, my Padishah!" upon which the latter made answer: "If you know that I am the Padishah, then can you tell me the cause of my sorrow." The dervish drew an apple from his breast and said: "Your sorrow is that you have no son. Take this apple; eat half yourself and give the other half to your wife; then in due time you shall have a son. He shall belong to you till his twentieth year afterwards he is mine." With these words he vanished.

The Padishah went home to his palace, and cut the apple, sharing it with his wife according to the instructions of the dervish. Some time later, as the wizard had promised, a little prince came to the palace and the Padishah, in his great joy, ordered the happy event to be celebrated throughout his dominions.

When the boy was five years old a tutor was appointed to teach him reading and writing. In his thirteenth year he began to take walks and go on journeys, and soon after wards he took part in the hunting excursions also. When he was nearing his twentieth year his father began to think of finding him a wife. A suitable maiden being discovered, the young couple were betrothed, but on the very day of the wedding, when all the guests had assembled in readiness for the ceremony, the dervish came and carried off the bridegroom to the foot of a mountain. With the words "Remain in peace" he went away. In great fear the young Prince looked around him, but saw nothing more alarming than three white doves flying towards the river on whose bank he was resting.

As they alighted, they were transformed into three beautiful maidens, who entered the water to bathe. Presently two of them came out, resumed their bird forms, and flew away. As the third maiden left the water, she caught sight of the young Prince. Much astonished at his presence, she inquired how he had come there.

"A dervish carried me hither," he answered, whereon the girl rejoined: "That dervish is my father. When he comes, he will take you by your hair, hang you on that tree, and flog you with a whip. 'Dost know? he will ask, and to this question you must answer, 'I know not.'" Having given this advice, the girl, transforming herself into a white dove, flew quickly away.

Presently the young Prince saw the dervish approaching with a whip in his hand. He hung the youth by his hair to a tree; flogged him soundly, and asked, "Dost know?" When the young Prince answered "I know not" the dervish went away. For three days in succession the youth was beaten black and blue; but when the dervish had satisfied himself that his victim under stood nothing at all, he set him free.

When the youth was out walking one day the dove came to him and said: "Take this bird and hide it. When my father asks which of the three maidens you desire, point to me; if, however, you do not recognise me, produce the bird and answer: 'I desire the maiden to whom this bird shall fly.'"

Saying this the dove flew away.

The next day the dervish brought with him the three maidens and asked the youth which of them pleased him best. The youth accordingly produced the bird and said that he desired her to whom the bird should fly. The bird was set free and alighted on the maiden who had instructed him. She was given in marriage to the youth, but without the consent of her mother, who was a witch.

While the youth and the maiden were walking together, they saw the mother coming after them. The maiden, giving the youth a knock, changed him into a large garden, and by another knock changed herself into a gardener. When the woman came up she inquired: "Gardener, did not a maiden and a youth pass this way?" The gardener answered: "My red turnips are not yet ripe – they are still small." The witch retorted: "My dear Gardener, I do not ask about your turnips, but about a youth and a maiden." But the gardener only replied: "I have set no spinach, it will not be up for a month or two." Seeing she was not understood, the woman turned and went away. When the woman was no longer in sight, the gardener knocked the garden, which became a youth again, and knocked herself and became a maiden once more.

They now walked on. The woman turning back and seeing them together, hastened to overtake them. The maiden also turned round and saw her mother hurrying after them. Quickly she gave the youth a knock and turned him into an oven, knocked herself and became a baker. The mother came up and asked: "Baker, have not a youth and a maiden passed this way?" "The bread is not yet baked – I have just put it in; come again in half an hour, then you may have some," was the answer. At this the woman said: "I did not ask you for bread; I inquired whether a youth and a maiden had passed this way." The reply was as little to the point as before. "Wait a while; when the bread is ready we will eat" When the woman saw she was not understood she went away again. As soon as the coast was clear the baker knocked the oven, which became a youth, and knocked herself back into a maiden; then they pursued their way.

Looking back once more the woman again saw the youth and the maiden.

She now realised that the oven and the baker were the runaways in disguise, and hurried after them. Seeing that her mother was coming, the maiden again knocked the youth and changed him into a pond; herself she changed into a duck swimming upon the water. When the woman arrived at the pond she ran to and fro seeking a place whence she could reach the opposite side. At length, seeing she could go no further, she turned round and went home again. The danger over, the duck struck the pond and changed it into the youth; and transformed herself into a maiden as before; upon which they resumed their journey.

Wandering onward they came at length to the birthplace of the youth, where they entered an inn. Then said he to the maiden: "Remain here while I fetch a carriage to take you away." On the road he encountered the dervish, who seized him and transported him immediately to his father's palace, and set him down in the great hall where the wedding-guests were still waiting. The Prince looked round at them all, and rubbed his eyes, Had he been dreaming? "What can it all mean?" he said to himself.

Meanwhile, the maiden at the inn, seeing that the youth returned not, said to herself: "The faithless one has forsaken me." Then she transformed herself into a dove, and flew to the palace. Through an open window she entered the great hall, and alighted on the Prince's shoulder. "Faithless one!" she said reproachfully, "to leave me alone at the inn whilst you are making merry here!" Saying this, she flew back immediately to the inn.

When the youth realised that it was no dream, but fact, he took a carriage and returned without delay to the inn, put the maiden into the coach, and took her to the palace. By this time the first bride had grown tired of waiting for so eccentric a bridegroom and had gone home. So the Prince married the dervish's daughter, and the wedding festivities lasted forty days and forty nights.

The Enchanted Princess

IN A CERTAIN KINGDOM a soldier served in the mounted guard of the king. He served twenty-five years in faithfulness and truth; and for his good conduct the king gave orders to discharge him with honor, and give him as reward the same horse on which he had ridden in the regiment, with all the caparison.

The soldier took farewell of his comrades and set out for his native place. He travelled a day, a second, and a third. Behold, a whole week had gone; a second and third week! The soldier had no money; he had nothing to eat himself, nothing to give his horse, and his home was far, far away. He saw that the affair was a very bad one; he wanted terribly to eat, began to look in one direction and another, and saw on one side a great castle. "Well," thought he, "better go there; maybe they will take me even for a time to serve – I'll earn something."

He turned to the castle, rode into the court, put his horse in the stable, gave him hay, and entered the castle. In the castle a table was set with food and wine – with everything that the soul could wish for.

The soldier ate and drank. "Now," thought he, "I may sleep."

All at once a bear came in. "Fear me not, brave hero; thou hast come in good time. I am not a savage bear, but a fair maiden, an enchanted princess. If thou canst endure and pass three nights in this place, the enchantment will be broken, I shall be a princess as before, and will marry thee."

The soldier consented. Now, there fell upon him such a sadness that he could not look on the world, and every moment the sadness increased; if there had been no wine he could not have held out a single night, as it seemed. The second night it went so far that the soldier resolved to leave everything and run away; but no matter how he struggled, no matter how he tried, he found no way out of the castle. There was no help for it, he had to stay in spite of himself.

He passed the third night. In the morning there stood before him a princess of unspeakable beauty. She thanked him for his service, and told him to make ready for the crown (marriage). Straightway they had the wedding, and began to live together without care or trouble. After a time the soldier remembered his native place; he wanted to spend some time there. The princess tried to dissuade him.

"Remain, stay here, my friend, go not away. What is lacking to thee?"

No, she could not dissuade him. She took farewell of her husband, gave him a sack filled with seeds, and said: "On whatever road thou mayest travel, throw these seeds on both sides. Wherever they fall, that moment trees will spring up; on the trees precious fruit will be hanging in beauty, various birds will sing songs, and tom-cats from over the sea will tell tales."

The good hero sat on his horse of service and went his way. Wherever he journeyed he cast seeds on both sides, and after him forests were rising, just creeping out of the damp earth. He rode one day, he rode a second, a third, and saw in the open field a caravan. On the grass merchants were sitting playing cards, near them a great kettle was hanging, and, though there was no fire under the kettle, it was boiling like a fountain within the pot. "What a wonder!" thought the soldier; "there is no fire to be seen, and in the kettle it is boiling like a fountain – let me look at it more closely." He turned his horse to the place and rode up to the merchants.

"Hail, honorable gentlemen!" He had no suspicion that these were not merchants, but all unclean. "That is a good trick of yours – a kettle boiling without fire; but I have a better one."

He took out a seed and threw it on the ground – that moment a full-grown tree came up; on the tree were precious fruits in their beauty, various birds were singing songs, and tom-cats from over the sea were telling tales. From this boast the unclean knew him.

"Ah," said they among themselves, "this is the man who liberated the princess! Come, brothers, let us drug him with a weed, and let him sleep half a year."

They went to entertaining him, and drugged him with the magic weed. The soldier dropped on the grass and fell into deep sleep from which he could not be roused. The merchants, the caravan, and the kettle vanished in a twinkle.

Soon after the princess went out in her garden and saw that the tops of all the trees had begun to wither. "This is not for good," thought she; "it is evident that evil has come to my husband."

Three months passed. It was time for his return, and there was nothing of him, nothing. The princess made ready and went to search for him. She went by that road along which he had travelled – on both sides forests were growing, birds were singing, and tom-cats from over the sea were purring their tales. She reached the spot where there were no more trees, the road wound out into the open field; she thought, "Where has he gone to? Of course he has not sunk through the earth."

She looked, aside by itself was one of the wonderful trees, and under it her dear husband. She ran to him, pushed, and tried to rouse him. No, he did not wake. She pinched him, stuck pins in his side, pricked and pricked him. He did not feel even the pain – lay like a corpse without motion.

The princess grew angry, and in her anger pronounced the spell: "Mayest thou be caught by the stormy whirlwind, thou good-for-nothing sleepy head, and be borne to places unknown!"

She had barely uttered these words when the wind began to whistle, to sound, and in one flash the soldier was caught up by a boisterous whirlwind and borne away from the eyes of the princess. She saw too late that she had spoken an evil speech. She shed bitter tears, went home, lived alone and lonely.

The poor soldier was borne by the whirlwind far, far away beyond the thrice-ninth land, to the thirtieth kingdom, and thrown on a point between two seas; he fell on the very narrowest little wedge. If the sleeping man were to turn to the right, or roll to the left, that moment he would tumble into the sea, and then remember his name.

The good hero slept out his half year – moved not a finger; and when he woke he sprang straight to his feet, looked on both sides. The waves are rolling; no end can be seen to the broad sea. He stands in doubt, asking himself, "By what miracle have I come to this place? Who dragged me hither?" He turned back from the point and came out on an island; on that island was a mountain steep and lofty, touching the clouds with its peak, and on the mountain a great stone. He came near this mountain and saw three devils fighting; blood was just flowing from them, and bits of flesh flying.

"Stop, ye outcasts! What are ye fighting for?"

"But seest thou our father died three days ago and left three wonderful things – a flying carpet, swift-moving boots, and a cap of invisibility; and we cannot divide them."

"Oh, ye cursed fellows, to fight for such trifles! If ye wish I'll divide them between you, and ye shall be satisfied; I'll offend no one."

"Well then, countryman, divide between us if it please thee."

"Very good. Run quickly through the pine woods and gather one hundred poods of pitch, and bring it here."

The devils rushed through the pine woods, collected three hundred poods of pitch, and brought it to the soldier.

"Now bring me from your own kingdom the very largest kettle that is in it." The devils brought the very largest kettle – one holding forty barrels – and put the pitch into it. The soldier made a fire, and when the pitch was boiling he ordered the devils to take it on the mountain and pour it out from the top to the bottom. The devils did this in a flash. "Now," said the soldier, "push that stone there; let it roll from the mountain, and follow it. Whoever comes up with it first may take any of the three things; whoever comes up second will choose from the two remaining ones whichever he likes; and the last wonder will go to the third." The devils pushed the stone, and it rolled from the mountain quickly, quickly. One devil caught up, seized the stone, the stone turned, and in a flash put him under it, crushed him into the pitch. The second devil caught up, and then the third; and with them it happened as with the first – they were driven firmly into the pitch.

The soldier took under his arm the swift boots and the cap of invisibility, sat on the flying carpet, and flew off to look for his own country. Whether it was long or short, he came to a hut, went in. In the hut was sitting a Baba-Yaga, boneleg, old and toothless. "Greetings to thee, grandmother! Tell how I am to find my fair princess."

"I have not seen her with sight, I have not heard of her with hearing; but pass over so many seas and so many lands, and there lives my second sister. She knows more than I do; mayhap she can tell thee."

The soldier sat on his carpet and flew away. He had to wander long over the white world. Whenever he wanted to eat or drink, he put on the cap of invisibility, let himself down, entered a shop, and took what his heart desired; then to the carpet and off on his journey. He came to the second hut, entered; inside was sitting Baba-Yaga, boneleg, old and toothless. "Greetings to thee, grandmother! Dost thou know how I can find my fair princess?"

"No, my dove, I do not know."

"Ah, thou old hag! how many years art thou living in the world? All thy teeth are out, and thou knowest no good."

He sat on the flying carpet and flew toward the eldest sister. Long did he wander, many seas and many lands did he see. At last he flew to the end of the world, where there was a hut and no road beyond – nothing but outer darkness, nothing to be seen.

"Well," thought he, "if I can get no account here, there is nowhere else to fly to." He went into the hut; there a Baba-Yaga was sitting, gray, toothless.

"Greetings to thee, grandmother! Tell me where must I seek my princess."

"Wait a little; I will call all my winds together and ask them. They blow over all the world, so they must know where she is living at present."

The old woman went out on the porch, cried with a loud voice, whistled with a hero's whistle. Straightway the stormy winds rose and blew from every side; the hut just quivered.

"Quieter, quieter!" cried Baba-Yaga; and as soon as the winds had assembled, she said: "My stormy winds, ye blow through all the world. Have ye seen the beautiful princess anywhere?"

"We have not seen her anywhere," answered the winds in one voice.

"But are ye all here?"

"All but South Wind."

After waiting a little, South Wind flew up. The old woman asked: "Where hast thou been lost to this moment? I could hardly wait for thee."

"Pardon, grandmother; I went into a new kingdom, where the beautiful princess is living. Her husband has vanished without tidings, so now various Tsars and Tsars' sons, kings and kings' sons are paying court to her."

"And how far is it to the new kingdom?"

"For a man on foot thirty-five years, ten years on wings; but if I blow I can put a man there in three hours."

The soldier implored South Wind tearfully to take him and bear him to the new kingdom.

"I will, if it please thee," said South Wind, "provided thou wilt let me run around in thy kingdom three days and three nights as I like."

"Frolic three weeks if thou choosest."

"Well, I will rest for two or three days, collect my forces and my strength, and then for the road!"

South Wind rested, collected his strength, and said to the soldier: "Well, brother, make ready, we'll go straightway; but look out, have no fear, thou wilt arrive in safety."

All at once a mighty whirlwind whistled and roared, caught the soldier into the air, and bore him over mountains and seas up to the very clouds; and in three hours exactly he was in the new kingdom, where his beautiful princess was living. South Wind said –

"Farewell, good hero; out of compassion for thee I will not frolic in thy kingdom."

"Why is that?"

"Because if I frolic, not one house will be standing in the town, not one tree in the gardens; I should put everything bottom upward."

"Farewell then; God save thee!" said the soldier, who put on his cap of invisibility and went to the white-walled castle. Behold, while he was absent from the kingdom all the trees in the garden had stood with withered tops, and the moment he appeared they came to life and began to bloom. He entered the great hall; there were sitting at the table various Tsars and Tsars' sons, kings and kings' sons who had come to pay court to the beautiful princess. They were sitting and entertaining themselves with sweet wines. Whoever filled a glass and raised it to his lips, the soldier that moment struck it with his fist and knocked it from his hand. All the guests wondered at this; but the beautiful princess understood in a moment the reason.

"Surely," thought she, "my friend is here." She looked through the window; all the tree-tops in the garden had come to life, and she gave a riddle to the guests. "I had a home-made casket with a golden key; I lost this key, and did not think to find it: but now this key has found itself. Who guesses the riddle, him will I marry."

The Tsars and Tsars' sons, the kings and kings' sons were long breaking their wise heads over this riddle, and could not solve it in any way.

The princess said: "Show thyself, dear friend."

The soldier removed his cap of invisibility, took her by the white hand, and began to kiss her on the sweet mouth.

"Here is the riddle for you," said the fair princess: "I am the home-made casket, and the golden key is my faithful husband."

The wooers had to turn their wagon-shafts around. They all drove home, and the princess began to live with her husband, to live and win wealth.

The Magic Ring

ONCE UPON A TIME there lived an old couple who had one son called Martin. Now when the old man's time had come, he stretched himself out on his bed and died. Though all his life long he had toiled and moiled, he only left his widow and son two hundred florins. The old woman determined to put by the money for a rainy day; but alas! the rainy day was close at hand, for their meal was all consumed, and who is prepared to face starvation with two hundred florins at their disposal? So the old woman counted out a hundred of her florins, and giving them to Martin, told him to go into the town and lay in a store of meal for a year.

So Martin started off for the town. When he reached the meat-market he found the whole place in turmoil, and a great noise of angry voices and barking of dogs. Mixing in the crowd, he noticed a stag-hound which the butchers had caught and tied to a post, and which was being flogged in a merciless manner. Overcome with pity, Martin spoke to the butchers, saying:

"Friends, why are you beating the poor dog so cruelly?"

"We have every right to beat him," they replied; "he has just devoured a newly-killed pig."

"Leave off beating him," said Martin, "and sell him to me instead."

"If you choose to buy him," answered the butchers derisively; "but for such a treasure we won't take a penny less than a hundred florins."

"A hundred!" exclaimed Martin. "Well, so be it, if you will not take less;" and, taking the money out of his pocket, he handed it over in exchange for the dog, whose name was Schurka.

When Martin got home, his mother met him with the question:

"Well, what have you bought?"

"Schurka, the dog," replied Martin, pointing to his new possession. Whereupon his mother became very angry, and abused him roundly. He ought to be ashamed of himself, when there was scarcely a handful of meal in the house, to have spent the money on a useless brute like that. On the following day she sent him back to the town, saying, "Here, take our last hundred florins, and buy provisions with them. I have just emptied the last grains of meal out of the chest, and baked a bannock; but it won't last over to-morrow."

Just as Martin was entering the town he met a rough-looking peasant who was dragging a cat after him by a string which was fastened round the poor beast's neck.

"Stop," cried Martin; "where are you dragging that poor cat?"

"I mean to drown him," was the answer.

"What harm has the poor beast done?" said Martin.

"It has just killed a goose," replied the peasant.

"Don't drown him, sell him to me instead," begged Martin.

"Not for a hundred florins," was the answer.

"Surely for a hundred florins you'll sell it?" said Martin. "See! here is the money;" and, so saying, he handed him the hundred florins, which the peasant pocketed, and Martin took possession of the cat, which was called Waska.

When he reached his home his mother greeted him with the question:

"Well, what have you brought back?"

"I have brought this cat, Waska," answered Martin.

"And what besides?"

"I had no money over to buy anything else with," replied Martin.

"You useless ne'er-do-weel!" exclaimed his mother in a great passion. "Leave the house at once, and go and beg your bread among strangers;" and as Martin did not dare to contradict her, he called Schurka and Waska and started off with them to the nearest village in search of work. On the way he met a rich peasant, who asked him where he was going.

"I want to get work as a day labourer," he answered.

"Come along with me, then. But I must tell you I engage my labourers without wages. If you serve me faithfully for a year, I promise you it shall be for your advantage."

So Martin consented, and for a year he worked diligently, and served his master faithfully, not sparing himself in any way. When the day of reckoning had come the peasant led him into a barn, and pointing to two full sacks, said: "Take whichever of these you choose."

Martin examined the contents of the sacks, and seeing that one was full of silver and the other of sand, he said to himself:

"There must be some trick about this; I had better take the sand." And throwing the sack over his shoulders he started out into the world, in search of fresh work. On and on he walked, and at last he reached a great gloomy wood. In the middle of the wood he came upon a meadow, where a fire was burning, and in the midst of the fire, surrounded by flames, was a lovely damsel, more beautiful than anything that Martin had ever seen, and when she saw him she called to him:

"Martin, if you would win happiness, save my life. Extinguish the flames with the sand that you earned in payment of your faithful service."

"Truly," thought Martin to himself, "it would be more sensible to save a fellow-being's life with this sand than to drag it about on one's back, seeing what a weight it is." And forthwith he lowered the sack from his shoulders and emptied its contents on the flames, and instantly the fire was extinguished; but at the same moment lo! and behold the lovely damsel turned into a Serpent, and, darting upon him, coiled itself round his neck, and whispered lovingly in his ear:

"Do not be afraid of me, Martin; I love you, and will go with you through the world. But first you must follow me boldly into my Father's Kingdom, underneath the earth; and when we get there, remember this – he will offer you gold and silver, and dazzling gems, but do not touch them. Ask him, instead, for the ring which he wears on his little finger, for in that ring lies a magic power; you have only to throw it from one hand to the other, and at once twelve young men will appear, who will do your bidding, no matter how difficult, in a single night."

So they started on their way, and after much wandering they reached a spot where a great rock rose straight up in the middle of the road. Instantly the Serpent uncoiled itself from his neck, and, as it touched the damp earth, it resumed the shape of the lovely damsel. Pointing to the rock, she showed him an opening just big enough for a man to wriggle through. Passing into it, they entered a long underground passage, which led out on to a wide field, above which spread a blue sky. In the middle of the field stood a magnificent castle, built out of porphyry, with a roof of gold and with glittering battlements. And his beautiful guide told him that this was the palace in which her father lived and reigned over his kingdom in the Under-world.

Together they entered the palace, and were received by the King with great kindness. Turning to his daughter, he said:

"My child, I had almost given up the hope of ever seeing you again. Where have you been all these years?"

"My father," she replied, "I owe my life to this youth, who saved me from a terrible death."

Upon which the King turned to Martin with a gracious smile, saying: "I will reward your courage by granting you whatever your heart desires. Take as much gold, silver, and precious stones as you choose."

"I thank you, mighty King, for your gracious offer," answered Martin, "but I do not covet either gold, silver, or precious stones; yet if you will grant me a favour, give me, I beg, the ring from off the little finger of your royal hand. Every time my eye falls on it I shall think of your gracious Majesty, and when I marry I shall present it to my bride."

So the King took the ring from his finger and gave it to Martin, saying: "Take it, good youth; but with it I make one condition – you are never to confide to anyone that this is a magic ring. If you do, you will straightway bring misfortune on yourself."

Martin took the ring, and, having thanked the King, he set out on the same road by which he had come down into the Under-world. When he had regained the upper air he started for his old home, and having found his mother still living in the old house where he had left her, they settled down together very happily. So uneventful was their life that it almost seemed as if it would go on in this way always, without let or hindrance. But one day it suddenly came into his mind that he would like to get married, and, moreover, that he would choose a very grand wife – a King's daughter, in short. But as he did not trust himself as a wooer, he determined to send his old mother on the mission.

"You must go to the King," he said to her, "and demand the hand of his lovely daughter in marriage for me."

"What are you thinking of, my son?" answered the old woman, aghast at the idea. "Why cannot you marry someone in your own rank? That would be far more fitting than to send a poor old woman like me a-wooing to the King's Court for the hand of a Princess. Why, it is as much as our heads are worth. Neither my life nor yours would be worth anything if I went on such a fool's errand."

"Never fear, little mother," answered Martin. "Trust me; all will be well. But see that you do not come back without an answer of some kind."

And so, obedient to her son's behest, the old woman hobbled off to the palace, and, without being hindered, reached the courtyard, and began to mount the flight of steps leading to the royal presence chamber. At the head of the landing rows of courtiers were collected in magnificent attire, who stared at the queer old figure, and called to her, and explained to her, with every kind of sign, that it was strictly forbidden to mount those steps. But their stern words and forbidding gestures made no impression whatever on the old woman, and she resolutely continued to climb the stairs, bent on carrying out her son's orders. Upon this some of the courtiers seized her by the arms, and held her back by sheer force, at which she set up such a yell that the King himself heard it, and stepped out on to the balcony to see what was the matter. When he beheld the old woman flinging her arms wildly about, and heard her scream that she would not leave the place till she had laid her case before the King, he ordered that she should be brought into his presence. And forthwith she was conducted into the golden presence chamber, where, leaning back amongst cushions of royal purple, the King sat, surrounded by his counsellors and courtiers. Courtesying low, the old woman stood silent before him. "Well, my good old dame, what can I do for you?" asked the King.

"I have come," replied Martin's mother – "and your Majesty must not be angry with me – I have come a-wooing."

"Is the woman out of her mind?" said the King, with an angry frown.

But Martin's mother answered boldly: "If the King will only listen patiently to me, and give me a straightforward answer, he will see that I am not out of my mind. You, O King, have a lovely daughter to give in marriage. I have a son – a wooer – as clever a youth and as good a son-in-law as you will find in your whole kingdom. There is nothing that he cannot do. Now tell me, O King, plump and plain, will you give your daughter to my son as wife?" The King listened to the end of the old woman's strange request, but every moment his face grew blacker, and his features sterner; till all at once he thought to himself, "Is it worth while that I, the King, should be angry with this poor old fool?" And all the courtiers and counsellors were amazed when they saw the hard lines round his mouth and the frown on his brow grow smooth, and heard the mild but mocking tones in which he answered the old woman, saying:

"If your son is as wonderfully clever as you say, and if there is nothing in the world that he cannot do, let him build a magnificent castle, just opposite my palace windows, in four and twenty hours. The palace must be joined together by a bridge of pure crystal. On each side of the bridge there must be growing trees, having golden and silver apples, and with birds of Paradise among the branches. At the right of the bridge there must be a church, with five golden cupolas; in this church your son shall be wedded to my daughter, and we will keep the wedding festivities in the new castle. But if he fails to execute this my royal command, then, as a just but mild monarch, I shall give orders that you and he are taken, and first dipped in tar and then in feathers, and you shall be executed in the market-place for the entertainment of my courtiers."

And a smile played round the King's lips as he finished speaking, and his courtiers and counsellors shook with laughter when they thought of the old woman's folly, and praised the King's wise device, and said to each other, "What a joke it will be when we see the pair of them tarred and feathered! The son is just as able to grow a beard on the palm of his hand as to execute such a task in twenty-four hours."

Now the poor old woman was mortally afraid and, in a trembling voice she asked:

"Is that really your royal will, O King? Must I take this order to my poor son?"

"Yes, old dame; such is my command. If your son carries out my order, he shall be rewarded with my daughter; but if he fails, away to the tar-barrel and the stake with you both!"

On her way home the poor old woman shed bitter tears, and when she saw Martin she told him what the King had said, and sobbed out:

"Didn't I tell you, my son, that you should marry someone of your own rank? It would have been better for us this day if you had. As I told you, my going to Court has been as much as our lives are worth, and now we will both be tarred and feathered, and burnt in the public market-place. It is terrible!" and she moaned and cried.

"Never fear, little mother," answered Martin; "trust me, and you will see all will be well. You may go to sleep with a quiet mind."

And, stepping to the front of the hut, Martin threw his ring from the palm of one hand into the other, upon which twelve youths instantly appeared, and demanded what he wanted them to do. Then he told them the King's commands, and they answered that by next morning all should be accomplished exactly as the King had ordered.

Next morning when the King awoke, and looked out of his window, to his amazement he beheld a magnificent castle, just opposite his own palace, and joined to it a bridge of pure crystal.

At each side of the bridge trees were growing, from whose branches hung golden and silver apples, among which birds of Paradise perched. At the right, gleaming in the sun, were the five golden cupolas of a splendid church, whose bells rang out, as if they would summon people from all corners of the earth to come and behold the wonder. Now, though the King would much rather have seen his future son-in-law tarred, feathered, and burnt at the stake, he remembered his royal oath, and had to make the best of a bad business. So he took heart of grace, and made Martin a Duke, and gave his daughter a rich dowry, and prepared the grandest wedding-feast that had ever been seen, so that to this day the old people in the country still talk of it.

After the wedding Martin and his royal bride went to dwell in the magnificent new palace, and here Martin lived in the greatest comfort and luxury, such luxury as he had never imagined. But though he was as happy as the day was long, and as merry as a grig, the King's daughter fretted all day, thinking of the indignity that had been done her in making her marry Martin, the poor widow's son, instead of a rich young Prince from a foreign country. So unhappy was she that she spent all her time wondering how she should get rid of her undesirable husband. And first she determined to learn the secret of his power, and, with flattering, caressing words, she tried to coax him to tell her how he was so clever that there was nothing in the world that he could not do. At first he would tell her nothing; but once, when he was in a yielding mood, she approached him with a winning smile on her lovely face, and, speaking flattering words to him, she gave him a potion to drink, with a sweet, strong taste. And when he had drunk it Martin's lips were unsealed, and he told her that all his power lay in the magic ring that he wore on his finger, and he described to her how to use it, and, still speaking, he fell into a deep sleep. And when she saw that the potion had worked, and that he was sound asleep, the Princess took the magic ring from his finger, and, going into the courtyard, she threw it from the palm of one hand into the other.

On the instant the twelve youths appeared, and asked her what she commanded them to do. Then she told them that by the next morning they were to do away with the castle, and the bridge, and the church, and put in their stead the humble hut in which Martin used to live with his mother, and that while he slept her husband was to be carried to his old lowly room; and that they were to bear her away to the utmost ends of the earth, where an old King lived who would make her welcome in his palace, and surround her with the state that befitted a royal Princess.

"You shall be obeyed," answered the twelve youths at the same moment. And lo and behold! the following morning, when the King awoke and looked out of his window he beheld to his amazement that the palace, bridge, church, and trees had all vanished, and there was nothing in their place but a bare, miserable-looking hut.

Immediately the King sent for his son-in-law, and commanded him to explain what had happened. But Martin looked at his royal father-in-law, and answered never a word. Then the King was very angry, and, calling a council together, he charged Martin with having been guilty of witchcraft, and of having deceived the King, and having made away with the Princess; and he was condemned to imprisonment in a high stone tower, with neither meat nor drink, till he should die of starvation.

Then, in the hour of his dire necessity, his old friends Schurka (the dog) and Waska (the cat) remembered how Martin had once saved them from a cruel death; and they took counsel together as to how they should help him. And Schurka growled, and was of opinion that he would like to tear everyone in pieces; but Waska purred meditatively, and scratched the back of her ear with a velvet paw, and remained lost in thought. At the end of a few minutes she had made up her mind, and, turning to Schurka, said: "Let us go together into the town, and the moment we meet a baker you must make a rush between his legs and upset the tray from off his head; I will lay hold of the rolls, and will carry them off to our master." No sooner said than done. Together the two faithful creatures trotted off into the town, and very soon they met a baker bearing a tray on his head, and looking round on all sides, while he cried:

> "Fresh rolls, sweet cake,
> Fancy bread of every kind.
> Come and buy, come and take,
> Sure you'll find it to your mind."

At that moment Schurka made a rush between his legs – the baker stumbled, the tray was upset, the rolls fell to the ground, and, while the man angrily pursued Schurka, Waska managed to drag the rolls out of sight behind a bush. And when a moment later Schurka joined her, they set off at full tilt to the stone tower where Martin was a prisoner, taking the rolls with them. Waska, being very agile, climbed up by the outside to the grated window, and called in an anxious voice:

"Are you alive, master?"

"Scarcely alive – almost starved to death," answered Martin in a weak voice. "I little thought it would come to this, that I should die of hunger."

"Never fear, dear master. Schurka and I will look after you," said Waska. And in another moment she had climbed down and brought him back a roll, and then another, and another, till she had brought him the whole tray-load. Upon which she said: "Dear master, Schurka and I are going off to a distant kingdom at the utmost ends of the earth to fetch you back your magic ring. You must be careful that the rolls last till our return."

And Waska took leave of her beloved master, and set off with Schurka on their journey. On and on they travelled, looking always to right and left for traces of the Princess, following up every track, making inquiries of every cat and dog they met, listening to the talk of every wayfarer they passed; and at last they heard that the kingdom at the utmost ends of the earth where the twelve youths had borne the Princess was not very far off. And at last one day they reached that distant kingdom, and, going at once to the palace, they began to make friends with all the dogs and cats in the place, and to question them about the Princess and the magic ring; but no one could tell them much about either. Now one day it chanced that Waska had gone down to the palace cellar to hunt for mice and rats, and seeing an especially fat, well-fed mouse, she pounced upon it, buried her claws in its soft fur, and was just going to gobble it up, when she was stopped by the pleading tones of the little creature, saying, "If you will only spare my life I may be of great service to you. I will do everything in my power for you; for I am the King of the Mice, and if I perish the whole race will die out."

"So be it," said Waska. "I will spare your life; but in return you must do something for me. In this castle there lives a Princess, the wicked wife of my dear master. She has stolen away his magic ring. You must get it away from her at whatever cost; do you hear? Till you have done this I won't take my claws out of your fur."

"Good!" replied the mouse; "I will do what you ask." And, so saying, he summoned all the mice in his kingdom together. A countless number of mice, small and big, brown and grey, assembled, and formed a circle round their king, who was a prisoner under Waska's claws. Turning to them he said: "Dear and faithful subjects, who ever among you will steal the magic ring from the strange Princess will release me from a cruel death; and I shall honour him above all the other mice in the kingdom."

Instantly a tiny mouse stepped forward and said: "I often creep about the Princess's bedroom at night, and I have noticed that she has a ring which she treasures as the apple of her eye. All day she wears it on her finger, and at night she keeps it in her mouth. I will undertake, sire, to steal away the ring for you."

And the tiny mouse tripped away into the bedroom of the Princess, and waited for nightfall; then, when the Princess had fallen asleep, it crept up on to her bed, and gnawed a hole in the pillow, through which it dragged one by one little down feathers, and threw them under the Princess's nose. And the fluff flew into the Princess's nose, and into her mouth, and starting up she sneezed and coughed, and the ring fell out of her mouth on to the coverlet. In a flash the tiny mouse had seized it, and brought it to Waska as a ransom for the King of the Mice. Thereupon Waska and Schurka started off, and travelled night and day till they reached the stone tower where Martin was imprisoned; and the cat climbed up the window, and called out to him:

"Martin, dear master, are you still alive?"

"Ah! Waska, my faithful little cat, is that you?" replied a weak voice. "I am dying of hunger. For three days I have not tasted food."

"Be of good heart, dear master," replied Waska; "from this day forth you will know nothing but happiness and prosperity. If this were a moment to trouble you with riddles, I would make you guess what Schurka and I have brought you back. Only think, we have got you your ring!"

At these words Martin's joy knew no bounds, and he stroked her fondly, and she rubbed up against him and purred happily, while below Schurka bounded in the air, and barked joyfully. Then Martin took the ring, and threw it from one hand into the other, and instantly the twelve youths appeared and asked what they were to do.

"Fetch me first something to eat and drink, as quickly as possible; and after that bring musicians hither, and let us have music all day long."

Now when the people in the town and palace heard music coming from the tower they were filled with amazement, and came to the King with the news that witchcraft must be going on in Martin's Tower, for, instead of dying of starvation, he was seemingly making merry to the sound of music, and to the clatter of plates, and glass, and knives and forks; and the music was so enchantingly sweet that all the passers-by stood still to listen to it. On this the King sent at once a messenger to the Starvation Tower, and he was so astonished with what he saw that he remained rooted to the spot. Then the King sent his chief counsellors, and they too were transfixed with wonder. At last the King came himself, and he likewise was spellbound by the beauty of the music.

Then Martin summoned the twelve youths, spoke to them, saying, "Build up my castle again, and join it to the King's Palace with a crystal bridge; do not forget the trees with the golden and silver apples, and with the birds of Paradise in the branches; and put back the church with the five cupolas, and let the bells ring out, summoning the people from the four corners of the kingdom. And one thing more: bring back my faithless wife, and lead her into the women's chamber."

And it was all done as he commanded, and, leaving the Starvation Tower, he took the King, his father-in-law, by the arm, and led him into the new palace, where the Princess sat in fear and trembling, awaiting her death. And Martin spoke to the King, saying, "King and royal father, I have suffered much at the hands of your daughter. What punishment shall be dealt to her?"

Then the mild King answered: "Beloved Prince and son-in-law, if you love me, let your anger be turned to grace – forgive my daughter, and restore her to your heart and favour."

And Martin's heart was softened and he forgave his wife, and they lived happily together ever after. And his old mother came and lived with him, and he never parted with Schurka and Waska; and I need hardly tell you that he never again let the ring out of his possession.

Prince Hyacinth and the Dear Little Princess

ONCE UPON A TIME there lived a king who was deeply in love with a princess, but she could not marry anyone, because she was under an enchantment. So the King set out to seek a fairy, and asked what he could do to win the Princess's love. The Fairy said to him:

"You know that the Princess has a great cat which she is very fond of. Whoever is clever enough to tread on that cat's tail is the man she is destined to marry."

The King said to himself that this would not be very difficult, and he left the Fairy, determined to grind the cat's tail to powder rather than not tread on it at all.

You may imagine that it was not long before he went to see the Princess, and puss, as usual, marched in before him, arching his back. The King took a long step, and quite thought he had the tail under his foot, but the cat turned round so sharply that he only trod on air. And so it went on for eight days, till the King began to think that this fatal tail must be full of quicksilver – it was never still for a moment.

At last, however, he was lucky enough to come upon puss fast asleep and with his tail conveniently spread out. So the King, without losing a moment, set his foot upon it heavily.

With one terrific yell the cat sprang up and instantly changed into a tall man, who, fixing his angry eyes upon the King, said:

"You shall marry the Princess because you have been able to break the enchantment, but I will have my revenge. You shall have a son, who will never be happy until he finds out that his nose is too long, and if you ever tell anyone what I have just said to you, you shall vanish away instantly, and no one shall ever see you or hear of you again."

Though the King was horribly afraid of the enchanter, he could not help laughing at this threat.

"If my son has such a long nose as that," he said to himself, "he must always see it or feel it; at least, if he is not blind or without hands."

But, as the enchanter had vanished, he did not waste any more time in thinking, but went to seek the Princess, who very soon consented to marry him. But after all, they had not been married very long when the King died, and the Queen had nothing left to care for but her little son, who was called Hyacinth. The little Prince had large blue eyes, the prettiest eyes in the world, and a sweet little mouth, but, alas! his nose was so enormous that it covered half his face. The Queen was inconsolable when she saw this great nose, but her ladies assured her that it was not really as large as it looked; that it was a Roman nose, and you had only to open any history to see that every hero has a large nose. The Queen, who was devoted to her baby, was pleased with what they told her, and when she looked at Hyacinth again, his nose certainly did not seem to her quite so large.

The Prince was brought up with great care; and, as soon as he could speak, they told him all sorts of dreadful stories about people who had short noses. No one was allowed to come near him whose nose did not more or less resemble his own, and the courtiers, to get into favor with the Queen, took to pulling their babies' noses several times every day to make them grow long. But, do what they would, they were nothing by comparison with the Prince's.

When he grew sensible he learned history; and whenever any great prince or beautiful princess was spoken of, his teachers took care to tell him that they had long noses.

His room was hung with pictures, all of people with very large noses; and the Prince grew up so convinced that a long nose was a great beauty, that he would not on any account have had his own a single inch shorter!

When his twentieth birthday was passed the Queen thought it was time that he should be married, so she commanded that the portraits of several princesses should be brought for him to see, and among the others was a picture of the Dear Little Princess!

Now, she was the daughter of a great king, and would some day possess several kingdoms herself; but Prince Hyacinth had not a thought to spare for anything of that sort, he was so much struck with her beauty. The Princess, whom he thought quite charming, had, however, a little saucy nose, which, in her face, was the prettiest thing possible, but it was a cause of great embarrassment to the courtiers, who had got into such a habit of laughing at little noses that they sometimes found themselves laughing at hers before they had time to think; but this did not do at all before the Prince, who quite failed to see the joke, and actually banished two of his courtiers who had dared to mention disrespectfully the Dear Little Princess's tiny nose!

The others, taking warning from this, learned to think twice before they spoke, and one even went so far as to tell the Prince that, though it was quite true that no man could be worth anything unless he had a long nose, still, a woman's beauty was a different thing; and he knew a learned man who understood Greek and had read in some old manuscripts that the beautiful Cleopatra herself had a "tip-tilted" nose!

The Prince made him a splendid present as a reward for this good news, and at once sent ambassadors to ask the Dear Little Princess in marriage. The King, her father, gave his consent; and Prince Hyacinth, who, in his anxiety to see the Princess, had gone three leagues to meet her was just advancing to kiss her hand when, to the horror of all who stood by, the enchanter appeared as suddenly as a flash of lightning, and, snatching up the Dear Little Princess, whirled her away out of their sight!

The Prince was left quite unconsolable, and declared that nothing should induce him to go back to his kingdom until he had found her again, and refusing to allow any of his courtiers to follow him, he mounted his horse and rode sadly away, letting the animal choose his own path.

So it happened that he came presently to a great plain, across which he rode all day long without seeing a single house, and horse and rider were terribly hungry, when, as the night fell, the Prince caught sight of a light, which seemed to shine from a cavern.

He rode up to it, and saw a little old woman, who appeared to be at least a hundred years old.

She put on her spectacles to look at Prince Hyacinth, but it was quite a long time before she could fix them securely because her nose was so very short.

The Prince and the Fairy (for that was who she was) had no sooner looked at one another than they went into fits of laughter, and cried at the same moment, "Oh, what a funny nose!"

"Not so funny as your own," said Prince Hyacinth to the Fairy, "but, madam, I beg you to leave the consideration of our noses – such as they are – and to be good enough to give me something to eat, for I am starving, and so is my poor horse."

"With all my heart," said the Fairy. "Though your nose is so ridiculous you are, nevertheless, the son of my best friend. I loved your father as if he had been my brother. Now he had a very handsome nose!"

"And pray what does mine lack?" said the Prince.

"Oh! it doesn't lack anything," replied the Fairy. "On the contrary quite, there is only too much of it. But never mind, one may be a very worthy man though his nose is too long. I was telling you that I was your father's friend; he often came to see me in the old times, and you must know that I was very pretty in those days; at least, he used to say so. I should like to tell you of a conversation we had the last time I ever saw him."

"Indeed," said the Prince, "when I have supped it will give me the greatest pleasure to hear it; but consider, madam, I beg of you, that I have had nothing to eat to-day."

"The poor boy is right," said the Fairy; "I was forgetting. Come in, then, and I will give you some supper, and while you are eating I can tell you my story in a very few words – for I don't like endless tales myself. Too long a tongue is worse than too long a nose, and I remember when I was young that I was so much admired for not being a great chatterer. They used to tell the Queen, my mother, that it was so. For though you see what I am now, I was the daughter of a great king. My father –"

"Your father, I dare say, got something to eat when he was hungry!" interrupted the Prince.

"Oh! certainly," answered the Fairy, "and you also shall have supper directly. I only just wanted to tell you –"

"But I really cannot listen to anything until I have had something to eat," cried the Prince, who was getting quite angry; but then, remembering that he had better be polite as he much needed the Fairy's help, he added:

"I know that in the pleasure of listening to you I should quite forget my own hunger; but my horse, who cannot hear you, must really be fed!"

The Fairy was very much flattered by this compliment, and said, calling to her servants:

"You shall not wait another minute, you are so polite, and in spite of the enormous size of your nose you are really very agreeable."

"Plague take the old lady! How she does go on about my nose!" said the Prince to himself. "One would almost think that mine had taken all the extra length that hers lacks! If I were not so hungry I would soon have done with this chatterpie who thinks she talks very little! How stupid people are not to see their own faults! That comes of being a princess: she has been spoiled by flatterers, who have made her believe that she is quite a moderate talker!"

Meanwhile the servants were putting the supper on the table, and the prince was much amused to hear the Fairy who asked them a thousand questions simply for the pleasure of hearing herself speak; especially he noticed one maid who, no matter what was being said, always contrived to praise her mistress's wisdom.

"Well!" he thought, as he ate his supper, "I'm very glad I came here. This just shows me how sensible I have been in never listening to flatterers. People of that sort praise us to our faces without shame, and hide our faults or change them into virtues. For my part I never will be taken in by them. I know my own defects, I hope."

Poor Prince Hyacinth! He really believed what he said, and hadn't an idea that the people who had praised his nose were laughing at him, just as the Fairy's maid was laughing at her; for the Prince had seen her laugh slyly when she could do so without the Fairy's noticing her.

However, he said nothing, and presently, when his hunger began to be appeased, the Fairy said:

"My dear Prince, might I beg you to move a little more that way, for your nose casts such a shadow that I really cannot see what I have on my plate. Ah! thanks. Now let us speak of your father. When I went to his Court he was only a little boy, but that is forty years ago, and I have been in this desolate place ever since. Tell me what goes on nowadays; are the ladies as fond of amusement as ever? In my time one saw them at parties, theatres, balls, and promenades every day. Dear me! what a long nose you have! I cannot get used to it!"

"Really, madam," said the Prince, "I wish you would leave off mentioning my nose. It cannot matter to you what it is like. I am quite satisfied with it, and have no wish to have it shorter. One must take what is given one."

"Now you are angry with me, my poor Hyacinth," said the Fairy, "and I assure you that I didn't mean to vex you; on the contrary, I wished to do you a service. However, though I really cannot help your nose being a shock to me, I will try not to say anything about it. I will even try to think that you have an ordinary nose. To tell the truth, it would make three reasonable ones."

The Prince, who was no longer hungry, grew so impatient at the Fairy's continual remarks about his nose that at last he threw himself upon his horse and rode hastily away. But wherever he came in his journeyings he thought the people were mad, for they all talked of his nose, and yet he could not bring himself to admit that it was too long, he had been so used all his life to hear it called handsome.

The old Fairy, who wished to make him happy, at last hit upon a plan. She shut the Dear Little Princess up in a palace of crystal, and put this palace down where the Prince would not fail to find it. His joy at seeing the Princess again was extreme, and he set to work with all his might to try to break her prison; but in spite of all his efforts he failed utterly. In despair he thought at least that he would try to get near enough to speak to the Dear Little Princess, who, on her part, stretched out her hand that he might kiss it; but turn which way he might, he never could raise it to his lips, for his long nose always prevented it. For the first time he realized how long it really was, and exclaimed:

"Well, it must be admitted that my nose is too long!"

In an instant the crystal prison flew into a thousand splinters, and the old Fairy, taking the Dear Little Princess by the hand, said to the Prince:

"Now, say if you are not very much obliged to me. Much good it was for me to talk to you about your nose! You would never have found out how extraordinary it was if it hadn't hindered you from doing what you wanted to. You see how self-love keeps us from knowing our own defects of mind and body. Our reason tries in vain to show them to us; we refuse to see them till we find them in the way of our interests."

Prince Hyacinth, whose nose was now just like anyone's else, did not fail to profit by the lesson he had received. He married the Dear Little Princess, and they lived happily ever after.

An Impossible Enchantment

THERE ONCE LIVED A KING who was much loved by his people, and he, too, loved them warmly. He led a very happy life, but he had the greatest dislike to the idea of marrying, nor had he ever felt the slightest wish to fall in love. His subjects begged him to marry, and at last he promised to try to do so. But as, so far, he had never cared for any woman he had seen, he made up his mind to travel in hopes of meeting some lady he could love.

So he arranged all the affairs of state in an orderly manner, and set out, attended by only one equerry, who, though not very clever, had most excellent good sense. These people indeed generally make the best fellow travellers.

The king explored several countries, doing all he could to fall in love, but in vain; and at the end of two years' journeys he turned his face towards home, with as free a heart as when he set out.

As he was riding along through a forest he suddenly heard the most awful miawing and shrieking of cats you can imagine. The noise drew nearer, and nearer, and at last they saw a hundred huge Spanish cats rush through the trees close to them. They were so closely packed together that you could easily have covered them with a large cloak, and all were following the same track. They were closely pursued by two enormous apes, dressed in purple suits, with the prettiest and best made boots you ever saw.

The apes were mounted on superb mastiffs, and spurred them on in hot haste, blowing shrill blasts on little toy trumpets all the time.

The king and his equerry stood still to watch this strange hunt, which was followed by twenty or more little dwarfs, some mounted on wolves, and leading relays, and others with cats in leash. The dwarfs were all dressed in purple silk liveries like the apes.

A moment later a beautiful young woman mounted on a tiger came in sight. She passed close to the king, riding at full speed, without taking any notice of him; but he was at once enchanted by her, and his heart was gone in a moment.

To his great joy he saw that one of the dwarfs had fallen behind the rest, and at once began to question him.

The dwarf told him that the lady he had just seen was the Princess Mutinosa, the daughter of the king in whose country they were at that moment. He added that the princess was very fond of hunting, and that she was now in pursuit of rabbits.

The king then asked the way to the court, and having been told it, hurried off, and reached the capital in a couple of hours.

As soon as he arrived, he presented himself to the king and queen, and on mentioning his own name and that of his country, was received with open arms. Not long after, the princess returned, and hearing that the hunt had been very successful, the king complimented her on it, but she would not answer a word.

Her silence rather surprised him, but he was still more astonished when he found that she never spoke once all through supper-time. Sometimes she seemed about to speak, but whenever this was the case her father or mother at once took up the conversation. However, this silence did not cool the king's affection, and when he retired to his rooms at night he confided his feelings to his faithful equerry. But the equerry was by no means delighted at his king's love affair, and took no pains to hide his disappointment.

"But why are you vexed?" asked the king. "Surely the princess is beautiful enough to please anyone?"

"She is certainly very handsome," replied the equerry, "but to be really happy in love something more than beauty is required. To tell the truth, sire," he added, "her expression seems to me hard."

"That is pride and dignity," said the king, "and nothing can be more becoming."

"Pride or hardness, as you will," said the equerry; "but to my mind the choice of so many fierce creatures for her amusements seems to tell of a fierce nature, and I also think there is something suspicious in the care taken to prevent her speaking."

The equerry's remarks were full of good sense; but as opposition is only apt to increase love in the hearts of men, and especially of kings who hate being contradicted, this king begged, the very next day, for the hand of the Princess Mutinosa. It was granted him on two conditions.

The first was that the wedding should take place the very next day; and the second, that he should not speak to the princess till she was his wife; to all of which the king agreed, in spite of his equerry's objections, so that the first word he heard his bride utter was the "Yes" she spoke at their marriage.

Once married, however, she no longer placed any check on herself, and her ladies-in-waiting came in for plenty of rude speeches – even the king did not escape scolding; but as he was a good-tempered man, and very much in love, he bore it patiently. A few days after the wedding the newly married pair set out for their kingdom without leaving many regrets behind.

The good equerry's fears proved only too true, as the king found out to his cost. The young queen made herself most disagreeable to all her court, her spite and bad temper knew no bounds, and before the end of a month she was known far and wide as a regular vixen.

One day, when riding out, she met a poor old woman walking along the road, who made a curtsy and was going on, when the queen had her stopped, and cried: "You are a very impertinent person; don't you know that I am the queen? And how dare you not make me a deeper curtsy?"

"Madam," said the old woman, "I have never learnt how to measure curtsies; but I had no wish to fail in proper respect."

"What!" screamed the queen; "'she dares to answer! Tie her to my horse's tail and I'll just carry her at once to the best dancing-master in the town to learn how to curtsy."

The old woman shrieked for mercy, but the queen would not listen, and only mocked when she said she was protected by the fairies. At last the poor old thing submitted to be tied up, but when the queen urged her horse on he never stirred. In vain she spurred him, he seemed turned to bronze. At the same moment the cord with which the old woman was tied changed into wreaths of flowers, and she herself into a tall and stately lady.

Looking disdainfully at the queen, she said, "Bad woman, unworthy of your crown; I wished to judge for myself whether all I heard of you was true. I have now no doubt of it, and you shall see whether the fairies are to be laughed at."

So saying the fairy Placida (that was her name) blew a little gold whistle, and a chariot appeared drawn by six splendid ostriches. In it was seated the fairy queen, escorted by a dozen other fairies mounted on dragons.

All having dismounted, Placida told her adventures, and the fairy queen approved all she had done, and proposed turning Mutinosa into bronze like her horse.

Placida, however, who was very kind and gentle, begged for a milder sentence, and at last it was settled that Mutinosa should become her slave for life unless she should have a child to take her place.

The king was told of his wife's fate and submitted to it, which, as he could do nothing to help it, was the only course open to him.

The fairies then all dispersed, Placida taking her slave with her, and on reaching her palace she said: "You ought by rights to be scullion, but as you have been delicately brought up the change might be too great for you. I shall therefore only order you to sweep my rooms carefully, and to wash and comb my little dog.'

Mutinosa felt there was no use in disobeying, so she did as she was bid and said nothing.

After some time she gave birth to a most lovely little girl, and when she was well again the fairy gave her a good lecture on her past life, made her promise to behave better in future, and sent her back to the king, her husband.

Placida now gave herself up entirely to the little princess who was left in her charge. She anxiously thought over which of the fairies she would invite to be godmothers, so as to secure the best gift, for her adopted child.

At last she decided on two very kindly and cheerful fairies, and asked them to the christening feast. Directly it was over the baby was brought to them in a lovely crystal cradle hung with red silk curtains embroidered with gold.

The little thing smiled so sweetly at the fairies that they decided to do all they could for her. They began by naming her Graziella, and then Placida said: "You know, dear sisters, that the commonest form of spite or punishment amongst us consists of changing beauty to ugliness, cleverness to stupidity, and oftener still to change a person's form altogether. Now, as we can only each bestow one gift, I think the best plan will be for one of you to give her beauty, the other good understanding, whilst I will undertake that she shall never be changed into any other form."

The two godmothers quite agreed, and as soon as the little princess had received their gifts, they went home, and Placida gave herself up to the child's education. She succeeded so well with it, and little Graziella grew so lovely, that when she was still quite a child her fame was spread abroad only too much, and one day Placida was surprised by a visit from the Fairy Queen, who was attended by a very grave and severe-looking fairy.

The queen began at once: "I have been much surprised by your behaviour to Mutinosa; she had insulted our whole race, and deserved punishment. You might forgive your own wrongs if you chose, but not those of others. You treated her very gently whilst she was with you, and I come now to avenge our wrongs on her daughter. You have ensured her being lovely and clever, and not subject to change of form, but I shall place her in an enchanted prison, which she shall never leave till she finds herself in the arms of a lover whom she herself loves. It will be my care to prevent anything of the kind happening."

The enchanted prison was a large high tower in the midst of the sea, built of shells of all shapes and colours. The lower floor was like a great bathroom, where the water was let in or off at will. The first floor contained the princess's apartments, beautifully furnished. On the second was a library, a large wardrobe-room filled with beautiful clothes and every kind of linen, a music-room, a pantry with bins full of the best wines, and a store-room with all manner of preserves, bonbons, pastry and cakes, all of which remained as fresh as if just out of the oven.

The top of the tower was laid out like a garden, with beds of the loveliest flowers, fine fruit trees, and shady arbours and shrubs, where many birds sang amongst the branches.

The fairies escorted Graziella and her governess, Bonnetta, to the tower, and then mounted a dolphin which was waiting for them. At a little distance from the tower the queen waved her wand and summoned two thousand great fierce sharks, whom she ordered to keep close guard, and not to let a soul enter the tower

The good governess took such pains with Graziella's education that when she was nearly grown up she was not only most accomplished, but a very sweet, good girl.

One day, as the princess was standing on a balcony, she saw the most extraordinary figure rise out of the sea. She quickly called Bonnetta to ask her what it could be. It looked like some kind of man, with a bluish face and long sea-green hair. He was swimming towards the tower, but the sharks took no notice of him.

"It must be a merman," said Bonnetta.

"A man, do you say?" cried Graziella; "let us hurry down to the door and see him nearer."

When they stood in the doorway the merman stopped to look at the princess and made many signs of admiration. His voice was very hoarse and husky, but when he found that he was not understood he took to signs. He carried a little basket made of osiers and filled with rare shells, which he presented to the princess.

She took it with signs of thanks; but as it was getting dusk she retired, and the merman plunged back into the sea.

When they were alone, Graziella said to her governess: "What a dreadful-looking creature that was! Why do those odious sharks let him come near the tower? I suppose all men are not like him?"

"No, indeed," replied Bonnetta. "I suppose the sharks look on him as a sort of relation, and so did not attack him."

A few days later the two ladies heard a strange sort of music, and looking out of the window, there was the merman, his head crowned with water plants, and blowing a great sea-shell with all his might.

They went down to the tower door, and Graziella politely accepted some coral and other marine curiosities he had brought her. After this he used to come every evening, and blow his shell, or dive and play antics under tile princess's window. She contented herself with bowing to him from the balcony, but she would not go down to the door in spite of all his signs.

Some days later he came with a person of his own kind, but of another sex. Her hair was dressed with great taste, and she had a lovely voice. This new arrival induced the ladies to go down to the door. They were surprised to find that, after trying various languages, she at last spoke to them in their own, and paid Graziella a very pretty compliment on her beauty. The mermaid noticed that the lower floor was full of water. "Why," cried she, "that is just the place for us, for we can't live quite out of water." So saying, she and her brother swam in and took up a position in the bathroom, the princess and her governess seating themselves on the steps which ran round the room.

"No doubt, madam," said the mermaid, "you have given up living on land so as to escape from crowds of lovers; but I fear that even here you cannot avoid them, for my brother is already dying of love for you, and I am sure that once you are seen in our city he will have many rivals."

She then went on to explain how grieved her brother was not to be able to make himself understood, adding: "I interpret for him, having been taught several languages by a fairy."

"Oh, then, you have fairies, too?" asked Graziella, with a sigh.

"Yes, we have," replied the mermaid; "but if I am not mistaken you have suffered from the fairies on earth."

The princess, on this, told her entire history to the mermaid, who assured her how sorry she felt for her, but begged her not to lose courage; adding, as she took her leave: Perhaps, some day, you may find a way out of your difficulties.'

The princess was delighted with this visit and with the hopes the mermaid held out. It was something to meet someone fresh to talk to.

"We will make acquaintance with several of these people," she said to her governess, "and I dare say they are not all as hideous as the first one we saw. Anyhow, we shan't be so dreadfully lonely."

"Dear me," said Bonnetta, "how hopeful young people are to be sure! As for me I feel afraid of these folk. But what do you think of the lover you have captivated?"

"Oh, I could never love him," cried the princess; "I can't bear him. But, perhaps, as his sister says they are related to the fairy Marina, they may be of some use to us."

The mermaid often returned, and each time she talked of her brother's love, and each time Graziella talked of her longing to escape from her prison, till at length the mermaid promised to bring the fairy Marina to see her, in hopes she might suggest something.

Next day the fairy came with the mermaid, and the princess received her with delight. After a little talk she begged Graziella to show her the inside of the tower and let her see the garden on the top, for with the help of crutches she could manage to move about, and being a fairy could live out of water for a long time, provided she wetted her forehead now and then.

Graziella gladly consented, and Bonnetta stayed below with the mermaid.

When they were in the garden the fairy said: "Let us lose no time, but tell me how I can be of use to you." Graziella then told all her story and Marina replied: "My dear princess, I can do nothing for you as regards dry land, for my power does not reach beyond my own element. I can only say that if you will honour my cousin by accepting his hand, you could then come and live amongst us. I could teach you in a moment to swim and dive with the best of us. I can harden your skin without spoiling its colour. My cousin is one of the best matches in the sea, and I will bestow so many gifts on him that you will be quite happy."

The fairy talked so well and so long that the princess was rather impressed, and promised to think the matter over.

Just as they were going to leave the garden they saw a ship sailing nearer the tower than any other had done before. On the deck lay a young man under a splendid awning, gazing at the tower through a spy-glass; but before they could see anything clearly the ship moved away, and the two ladies parted, the fairy promising to return shortly.

As soon as she was gone Graziella told her governess what she had said. Bonnetta was not at all pleased at the turn matters were taking, for she did not fancy being turned into a mermaid in her old age. She thought the matter well over, and this was what she did. She was a very clever artist, and next morning she began to paint a picture of a handsome young man, with beautiful curly hair, a fine complexion, and lovely blue eyes. When it was finished she showed it to Graziella, hoping it would show her the difference there was between a fine young man and her marine suitor.

The princess was much struck by the picture, and asked anxiously whether there could be any man so good looking in the world. Bonnetta assured her that there were plenty of them; indeed, many far handsomer.

"I can hardly believe that," cried the princess; "but, alas! If there are, I don't suppose I shall ever see them or they me, so what is the use? Oh, dear, how unhappy I am!"

She spent the rest of the day gazing at the picture, which certainly had the effect of spoiling all the merman's hopes or prospects.

After some days, the fairy Marina came back to hear what was decided; but Graziella hardly paid any attention to her, and showed such dislike to the idea of the proposed marriage that the fairy went off in a regular huff.

Without knowing it, the princess had made another conquest. On board the ship which had sailed so near was the handsomest prince in the world. He had heard of the enchanted tower, and determined to get as near it as he could. He had strong glasses on board, and whilst looking through them he saw the princess quite clearly, and fell desperately in love with her at once. He wanted to steer straight for the tower and to row off to it in a small boat, but his entire crew fell at his feet and begged him not to run such a risk. The captain, too, urged him not to attempt it. "You will only lead us all to certain death," he said. "Pray anchor nearer land, and I will then seek a kind fairy I know, who has always been most obliging to me, and who will, I am sure, try to help your Highness."

The prince rather unwillingly listened to reason. He landed at the nearest point, and sent off the captain in all haste to beg the fairy's advice and help. Meantime he had a tent pitched on the shore, and spent all his time gazing at the tower and looking for the princess through his spyglass.

After a few days the captain came back, bringing the fairy with him. The prince was delighted to see her, and paid her great attention. "I have heard about this matter," she said; "and, to lose no time, I am going to send off a trusty pigeon to test the enchantment. If there is any weak spot he is sure to find it out and get in. I shall bid him bring a flower back as a sign of success; and if he does so I quite hope to get you in too."

"But," asked the prince, "could I not send a line by the pigeon to tell the princess of my love?"

"Certainly," replied the fairy, "it would be a very good plan."

So the prince wrote as follows: –

'Lovely Princess – I adore you, and beg you to accept my heart, and to believe there is nothing I will not do to end your misfortunes – BLONDEL.'

This note was tied round the pigeon's neck, and he flew off with it at once. He flew fast till he got near the tower, when a fierce wind blew so hard against him that he could not get on. But he was not to be beaten, but flew carefully round the top of the tower till he came to one spot which, by some mistake, had not been enchanted like the rest. He quickly slipped into the arbour and waited for the princess.

Before long Graziella appeared alone, and the pigeon at once fluttered to meet her, and seemed so tame that she stopped to caress the pretty creature. As she did so she saw it had a pink ribbon round its neck, and tied to the ribbon was a letter. She read it over several times and then wrote this answer: –

'You say you love me; but I cannot promise to love you without seeing you. Send me your portrait by this faithful messenger. If I return it to you, you must give up hope; but if I keep it you will know that to help me will be to help yourself – GRAZIELA.'

Before flying back the pigeon remembered about the flower, so, seeing one in the princess's dress, he stole it and flew away.

The prince was wild with joy at the pigeon's return with the note. After an hour's rest the trusty little bird was sent back again, carrying a miniature of the prince, which by good luck he had with him.

On reaching the tower the pigeon found the princess in the garden. She hastened to untie the ribbon, and on opening the miniature case what was her surprise and delight to find it very like the picture her governess had painted for her. She hastened to send the pigeon back, and you can fancy the prince's joy when he found she had kept his portrait.

"Now," said the fairy, "let us lose no more time. I can only make you happy by changing you into a bird, but I will take care to give you back your proper shape at the right time."

The prince was eager to start, so the fairy, touching him with her wand, turned him into the loveliest humming-bird you ever saw, at the same time letting him keep the power of speech. The pigeon was told to show him the way.

Graziella was much surprised to see a perfectly strange bird, and still more so when it flew to her saying, "Good-morning, sweet princess."

She was delighted with the pretty creature, and let him perch on her finger, when he said, "Kiss, kiss, little birdie," which she gladly did, petting and stroking him at the same time.

After a time the princess, who had been up very early, grew tired, and as the sun was hot she went to lie down on a mossy bank in the shade of the arbour. She held the pretty bird near her breast, and was just falling asleep, when the fairy contrived to restore the prince to his own shape, so that as Graziella opened her eyes she found herself in the arms of a lover whom she loved in return!

At the same moment her enchantment came to an end. The tower began to rock and to split. Bonnetta hurried up to the top so that she might at least perish with her dear princess. Just as she reached the garden, the kind fairy who had helped the prince arrived with the fairy Placida, in a car of Venetian glass drawn by six eagles.

"Come away quickly," they cried, "the tower is about to sink!" The prince, princess, and Bonnetta lost no time in stepping into the car, which rose in the air just as, with a terrible crash, the tower sank into the depths of the sea, for the fairy Marina and the mermen had destroyed its foundations to avenge themselves on Graziella. Luckily their wicked plans were defeated, and the good fairies took their way to the kingdom of Graziella's parents.

They found that Queen Mutinosa had died some years ago, but her kind husband lived on peacefully, ruling his country well and happily. He received his daughter with great delight, and there were universal rejoicings at the return of the lovely princess.

The wedding took place the very next day, and, for many days after, balls, dinners, tournaments, concerts and all sorts of amusements went on all day and all night.

All the fairies were carefully invited, and they came in great state, and promised the young couple their protection and all sorts of good gifts. Prince Blondel and Princess Graziella lived to a good old age, beloved by every one, and loving each other more and more as time went on.

The Treasure-Bringer

ONCE UPON A TIME there lived a young farmer whose crops had totally failed. His harvest had been spoiled, his hay parched up, and all his cattle died, so that he was unable to perform his lawful obligations to his feudal superior. One Sunday he was sitting at his door in great trouble, just as the people were going to church. Presently Michel, an old fellow who used to wander about the country, came up. He had a bad reputation; people said that he was a wizard, and that he used to suck the milk from the cows, to bring storms and hail upon the crops, and diseases upon the people. So he was never allowed to depart without alms when he visited a farm.

"Good day, farmer," said Michel, advancing.

"God bless you," answered the other.

"What ails you?" said the old man. "You are looking very miserable."

"Alas! everything is going with me badly enough. But it is a good thing that you have come. People say that you have power to do much evil, but that you are a clever fellow. Perhaps you can help me."

"People talk evil of others because they themselves are evil," answered the old man. "But what is to be done?"

The farmer told him all his misfortunes, and Michel said, "Would you like to escape from all your troubles, and to become a rich man all at once?"

"With all my heart!" cried the other. Old Michel answered, with a smile, "If I were as young and strong as you, and if I had sufficient courage to face the darkness of night, and knew how to hold my tongue, I know what I'd do."

"Only tell me what you know. I will do anything if I can only become rich, for I am weary of my life at present."

Then the old man looked cautiously round on all sides, and then said in a whisper, "Do you know what a Kratt is?"

The farmer was startled, and answered, "I don't know exactly, but I have heard dreadful tales about it."

"I'll tell you," said the old man. "Mark you, it is a creature that anybody can make for himself, but it must be done so secretly that no human eye sees it. Its body is a broomstick, its head a broken jug, its nose a piece of glass, and its arms two reels which have been used by an old crone of a hundred years. All these things are easy to procure. You must set up this creature on three Thursday evenings at a cross-road, and animate it with the words which I will teach you. On the third Thursday the creature will come to life."

"God preserve us from the evil one!" cried the farmer.

"What! you are frightened? Have I told you too much already?"

"No, I'm not frightened at all. Go on."

The old man continued, "This creature is then your servant, for you have brought him to life at a cross-road. Nobody can see him but his master. He will bring him all kinds of money, corn, and hay, as often as he likes, but not more at once than a man's burden."

"But, old man, if you knew all this, why haven't you yourself made such a useful treasure-carrier, instead of which you have remained poor all your life?"

"I have been about to do it a hundred times, and have made a beginning a hundred times, but my courage always failed me. I had a friend who possessed such a treasure-carrier, and often told me about it, but I could not screw up courage to follow his example. My friend died, and the creature, left without a master, lived in the village for a long time, and wrought all manner of tricks among the people. He once tore all a woman's yarn to pieces; but when it was discovered, and they were going to remove it, they found a heap of money underneath. After this no more was seen of the creature. At that time I should have been glad enough to have a treasure-bringer, but I am now old and grey, and think no more of it."

"I've plenty of courage," said the farmer; "but wouldn't it be better for me to consult the parson about it?"

"No; you mustn't mention it to anybody, but least of all to the parson; for if you call the creature to life, you sell your soul to the devil."

The farmer started back in horror.

"Don't be frightened," said the old man. "You are sure of a long life in exchange, and of all your heart desires. And if you feel that your last hour is approaching, you can always escape from the clutches of the evil one, if you are clever enough to get rid of your familiar."

"But how can this be done?"

"If you give him a task which he is unable to perform, you are rid of him for the future. But you must set about it very circumspectly, for he is not easy to outwit. The peasant of whom I told you wanted to get rid of his familiar, and ordered him to fill a barrel of water with a sieve. But the creature fetched and spilled water, and did not rest till the barrel was filled with the drops which hung on the sieve."

"So he died, without getting rid of the creature?"

"Yes; why didn't he manage the affair better? But I have something more to tell you. The creature must be well fed, if he is to be kept in good-humour. A peasant once put a dish of broth under the roof for his familiar, as he was in the habit of doing. But a labourer saw it, so he ate the broth, and filled the dish with sand. The familiar came that night, and beat the farmer unmercifully, and continued to do so every night till he discovered the reason, and put a fresh dish of broth under the roof. After this, he let him alone. And now you know all," said the old man.

The farmer sat silent, and at last replied, "There is much about it that is unpleasant, Michel."

"You asked for my advice," answered the old man, "and I have given it you. You must make your own choice. Want and misery have come upon you. This is the only way in which you can save yourself and become a rich man; and if you are only a little prudent, you will cheat the devil out of your soul into the bargain."

After some reflection, the farmer answered, "Tell me the words which I am to repeat on the Thursdays."

"What will you give me, then?" said the old man.

"When I have the treasure-bringer, you shall live the life of a gentleman."

"Come, then," said the old man, and they entered the house together.

After this Sunday the young farmer was seen no more in the village. He neglected his work in the fields, and left what little was left there to waste, and his household management went all astray. His man loafed about the public-houses, and his maid-servant slept at home, for her master himself never looked after anything.

In the meantime the farmer sat in his smoky room. He kept the door locked, and the windows closely curtained. Here he worked hard day and night at the creature in a dark corner by the light of a pine-splinter. He had procured everything necessary, even the reels on which a crone of a hundred years old had spun. He put all the parts together carefully, fixed the old pot on the broomstick, made the nose of a bit of glass, and painted in the eyes and mouth red. He wrapped the body in coloured rags, according to his instructions, and all the time he thought with a shudder that it was now in his power to bring this uncanny creature to life, and that he must remain with him till his end. But when he thought of the riches and treasures, all his horror vanished. At length the creature was finished, and on the following Thursday the farmer carried it after nightfall to the cross-roads in the wood. There he put down the creature, seated himself on a stone, and waited. But every time he looked at the creature he nearly fell to the ground with terror. If only a breeze sprung up, it went through the marrow of his bones, and if only the screech-owl cried afar off, he thought he heard the croaking of the creature, and the blood froze in his veins. Morning came at last, and he seized the creature, and slunk away cautiously home.

On the second Thursday it was just the same. At length the night of the third Thursday came, and now he was to complete the charm. There was a howling wind, and the moon was covered with thick dark clouds, when the farmer brought the creature to the cross-roads at dead of night. Then he set it up as before, but he thought, "If I was now to smash it into a thousand pieces, and then go home and set hard at work, I need not then do anything wicked."

Presently, however, he reflected: "But I am so miserably poor, and this will make me rich. Let it go as it may, I can't be worse off than I am now."

He looked fearfully round him, turned towards the creature trembling, let three drops of blood fall on it from his finger, and repeated the magic words which the old man had taught him.

Suddenly the moon emerged from the clouds and shone upon the place where the farmer was standing before the figure. But the farmer stood petrified with terror when he saw the creature come to life. The spectre rolled his eyes horribly, turned slowly round, and when he saw his master again, he asked in a grating voice, "What do you want of me?"

But the farmer was almost beside himself with fear, and could not answer. He rushed away in deadly terror, not caring whither. But the creature ran after him, clattering and puffing, crying out all the time, "Why did you bring me to life if you desert me now?"

But the farmer ran on, without daring to look round.

Then the creature grasped his shoulder from behind with his wooden hand, and screamed out, "You have broken your compact by running away. You have sold your soul to the devil without gaining the least advantage for yourself. You have set me free. I am no longer your servant, but will be your tormenting demon, and will persecute you to your dying hour."

The farmer rushed madly to his house, but the creature followed him, invisible to every one else.

From this hour everything went wrong with the farmer which he undertook. His land produced nothing but weeds, his cattle all died, his sheds fell in, and if he took anything up, it broke in his hand. Neither man nor maid would work in his house, and at last all the people held aloof from him, as from an evil spirit who brought misfortune wherever he appeared.

Autumn came, and the farmer looked like a shadow, when one day he met old Michel, who saluted him, and looked scoffingly in his face.

"Oh, it's you," cried the farmer angrily. "It is good that I have met you, you hell-hound. Where are all your fine promises of wealth and good luck? I have sold myself to the devil, and I find a hell on earth already. But all this is your doing!"

"Quiet, quiet!" said the old man. "Who told you to meddle with evil things if you had not courage? I gave you fair warning. But you showed yourself a coward at the last moment, and released the creature from your service. If you had not done this, you might have become a rich and prosperous man, as I promised you."

"But you never saw the horrible face of the creature when he came to life," said the farmer in anguish. "Oh, what a fool I was to allow myself to be tempted by you!"

"I did not tempt you; I only told you what I knew."

"Help me now."

"Help yourself, for I can't. Haven't I more reason to complain of you than you of me? I have not deceived you; but where is my reward, and the fine life you promised me? You are the deceiver."

"All right! all right! Only tell me how I can save myself, and advise me what to do. I will perform everything."

"No," said the old man, "I have no further advice to give you. I am still a beggar, and it is all your fault;" and he turned round and left him.

"Curse upon you!" cried the farmer, whose last hope had vanished.

"But can't I save myself in any way?" said he to himself. "This creature who sits with the Devil on my neck is after all nothing but my own work, a thing of wood and potsherds. I must needs be able to destroy him, if I set about it right."

He ran to his house, where he now lived quite alone. There stood the creature in a corner, grinning, and asking, "Where's my dinner?"

"What shall I give you to get rid of you?"

"Where's my dinner? Get my dinner, quick. I'm hungry."

"Wait a little; you shall have it presently."

Then the farmer took up a pine-faggot which was burning in the stove, as if pondering, and then ran out, and locked all the doors on the outside.

It was a cold autumn night. The wind whistled through the neighbouring pine forest with a strange sighing sound.

"Now you may burn and roast, you spirit of hell!" cried the farmer, and cast the fire on the thatch. Presently the whole house was wrapped in bright flames.

Then the farmer laughed madly, and kept on calling out, "Burn and roast!"

The light of the fire roused the people of the village, and they crowded round the ill-starred spot. They wished to put out the fire and save the house, but the farmer pushed them back, saying, "Let it be. What does the house matter, if he only perishes? He has tormented me long enough, and I will plague him now, and all may yet be well with me."

The people stared at him in amazement as he spoke. But now the house fell in crashing, and the farmer shouted, "Now he's burnt!"

At this moment the creature, visible only to the farmer, rose unhurt from the smoking ruins with a threatening gesture. As soon as the farmer saw him, he fell on the ground with a loud shriek.

"What do you see?" asked old Michel, who had just arrived on the scene, and stood by smiling. But the farmer returned no answer. He had died of terror.

Long, Broad and Quickeye

ONCE UPON A TIME there lived a king who had an only son whom he loved dearly. Now one day the king sent for his son and said to him:

"My dearest child, my hair is grey and I am old, and soon I shall feel no more the warmth of the sun, or look upon the trees and flowers. But before I die I should like to see you with a good wife; therefore marry, my son, as speedily as possible."

"My father," replied the prince, "now and always, I ask nothing better than to do your bidding, but I know of no daughter-in-law that I could give you."

On hearing these words the old king drew from his pocket a key of gold, and gave it to his son, saying:

"Go up the staircase, right up to the top of the tower. Look carefully round you, and then come and tell me which you like best of all that you see."

So the young man went up. He had never before been in the tower, and had no idea what it might contain.

The staircase wound round and round and round, till the prince was almost giddy, and every now and then he caught sight of a large room that opened out from the side. But he had been told to go to the top, and to the top he went. Then he found himself in a hall, which had an iron door at one end. This door he unlocked with his golden key, and he passed through into a vast chamber which had a roof of blue sprinkled with golden stars, and a carpet of green silk soft as turf. Twelve windows framed in gold let in the light of the sun, and on every window was painted the figure of a young girl, each more beautiful than the last. While the prince gazed at them in surprise, not knowing which he liked best, the girls began to lift their eyes and smile at him. He waited, expecting them to speak, but no sound came.

Suddenly he noticed that one of the windows was covered by a curtain of white silk.

He lifted it, and saw before him the image of a maiden beautiful as the day and sad as the tomb, clothed in a white robe, having a girdle of silver and a crown of pearls. The prince stood and gazed at her, as if he had been turned into stone, but as he looked the sadness which, was on her face seemed to pass into his heart, and he cried out:

"This one shall be my wife. This one and no other."

As he said the words the young girl blushed and hung her head, and all the other figures vanished.

The young prince went quickly back to his father, and told him all he had seen and which wife he had chosen. The old man listened to him full of sorrow, and then he spoke:

"You have done ill, my son, to search out that which was hidden, and you are running to meet a great danger. This young girl has fallen into the power of a wicked sorcerer, who lives in an iron castle. Many young men have tried to deliver her, and none have ever come back. But what is done is done! You have given your word, and it cannot be broken. Go, dare your fate, and return to me safe and sound."

So the prince embraced his father, mounted his horse, and set forth to seek his bride. He rode on gaily for several hours, till he found himself in a wood where he had never been before, and soon lost his way among its winding paths and deep valleys. He tried in vain to see where he was: the thick trees shut out the sun, and he could not tell which was north and which was south, so that he might know what direction to make for. He felt in despair, and had quite given up all hope of getting out of this horrible place, when he heard a voice calling to him.

"Hey! hey! stop a minute!"

The prince turned round and saw behind him a very tall man, running as fast as his legs would carry him.

"Wait for me," he panted, "and take me into your service. If you do, you will never be sorry."

"Who are you?" asked the prince, "and what can you do?"

"Long is my name, and I can lengthen my body at will. Do you see that nest up there on the top of that pine-tree? Well, I can get it for you without taking the trouble of climbing the tree," and Long stretched himself up and up and up, till he was very soon as tall as the pine itself. He put the nest in his pocket, and before you could wink your eyelid he had made himself small again, and stood before the prince.

"Yes; you know your business," said he, "but birds' nests are no use to me. I am too old for them. Now if you were only able to get me out of this wood, you would indeed be good for something."

"Oh, there's no difficulty about that," replied Long, and he stretched himself up and up and up till he was three times as tall as the tallest tree in the forest. Then he looked all round and said, "We must go in this direction in order to get out of the wood," and shortening himself again, he took the prince's horse by the bridle, and led him along. Very soon they got clear of the forest, and saw before them a wide plain ending in a pile of high rocks, covered here and there with trees, and very much like the fortifications of a town.

As they left the wood behind, Long turned to the prince and said, "My lord, here comes my comrade. You should take him into your service too, as you will find him a great help."

"Well, call him then, so that I can see what sort of a man he is."

"He is a little too far off for that," replied Long. "He would hardly hear my voice, and he couldn't be here for some time yet, as he has so much to carry. I think I had better go and bring him myself," and this time he stretched himself to such a height that his head was lost in the clouds. He made two or three strides, took his friend on his back, and set him down before the prince. The new-comer was a very fat man, and as round as a barrel.

"Who are you?" asked the prince, "and what can you do?"

"Your worship, Broad is my name, and I can make myself as wide as I please."

"Let me see how you manage it."

"Run, my lord, as fast as you can, and hide yourself in the wood," cried Broad, and he began to swell himself out.

The prince did not understand why he should run to the wood, but when he saw Long flying towards it, he thought he had better follow his example. He was only just in time, for Broad had so suddenly inflated himself that he very nearly knocked over the prince and his horse too. He covered all the space for acres round. You would have thought he was a mountain!

At length Broad ceased to expand, drew a deep breath that made the whole forest tremble, and shrank into his usual size.

"You have made me run away," said the prince. "But it is not every day one meets with a man of your sort. I will take you into my service."

So the three companions continued their journey, and when they were drawing near the rocks they met a man whose eyes were covered by a bandage.

"Your excellency," said Long, "this is our third comrade. You will do well to take him into your service, and, I assure you, you will find him worth his salt."

"Who are you?" asked the prince. "And why are your eyes bandaged? You can never see your way!"

"It is just the contrary, my lord! It is because I see only too well that I am forced to bandage my eyes. Even so I see as well as people who have no bandage. When I take it off my eyes pierce through everything. Everything I look at catches fire, or, if it cannot catch fire, it falls into a thousand pieces. They call me Quickeye."

And so saying he took off his bandage and turned towards the rock. As he fixed his eyes upon it a crack was heard, and in a few moments it was nothing but a heap of sand. In the sand something might be detected glittering brightly. Quickeye picked it up and brought it to the prince. It turned out to be a lump of pure gold.

"You are a wonderful creature," said the prince, "and I should be a fool not to take you into my service. But since your eyes are so good, tell me if I am very far from the Iron Castle, and what is happening there just now."

"If you were travelling alone," replied Quickeye, "it would take you at least a year to get to it; but as we are with you, we shall arrive there to-night. Just now they are preparing supper."

"There is a princess in the castle. Do you see her?"

"A wizard keeps her in a high tower, guarded by iron bars."

"Ah, help me to deliver her!" cried the prince.

And they promised they would.

Then they all set out through the grey rocks, by the breach made by the eyes of Quickeye, and passed over great mountains and through deep woods. And every time they met with any obstacle the three friends contrived somehow to put it aside. As the sun was setting, the prince beheld the towers of the Iron Castle, and before it sank beneath the horizon he was crossing the iron bridge which led to the gates. He was only just in time, for no sooner had the sun disappeared altogether, than the bridge drew itself up and the gates shut themselves.

There was no turning back now!

The prince put up his horse in the stable, where everything looked as if a guest was expected, and then the whole party marched straight up to the castle. In the court, in the stables, and all over the great halls, they saw a number of men richly dressed, but every one turned into stone. They crossed an endless set of rooms, all opening into each other, till they reached the dining-hall. It was brilliantly lighted; the table was covered with wine and fruit, and was laid for four. They waited a few minutes expecting someone to come, but as nobody did, they sat down and began to eat and drink, for they were very hungry.

When they had done their supper they looked about for some place to sleep. But suddenly the door burst open, and the wizard entered the hall. He was old and hump-backed, with a bald head and a grey beard that fell to his knees. He wore a black robe, and instead of a belt three iron circlets clasped his waist. He led by the hand a lady of wonderful beauty, dressed in white, with a girdle of silver and a crown of pearls, but her face was pale and sad as death itself.

The prince knew her in an instant, and moved eagerly forward; but the wizard gave him no time to speak, and said:

"I know why you are here. Very good; you may have her if for three nights following you can prevent her making her escape. If you fail in this, you and your servants will all be turned into stone, like those who have come before you." And offering the princess a chair, he left the hall.

The prince could not take his eyes from the princess, she was so lovely! He began to talk to her, but she neither answered nor smiled, and sat as if she were made of marble. He seated himself by her, and determined not to close his eyes that night, for fear she should escape him. And in order that she should be doubly guarded, Long stretched himself like a strap all round the room, Broad took his stand by the door and puffed himself out, so that not even a mouse could slip by, and Quickeye leant against a pillar which stood in the middle of the floor and supported the roof. But in half a second they were all sound asleep, and they slept sound the whole night long.

In the morning, at the first peep of dawn, the prince awoke with a start. But the princess was gone. He aroused his servants and implored them to tell him what he must do.

"Calm yourself, my lord," said Quickeye. "I have found her already. A hundred miles from here there is a forest. In the middle of the forest, an old oak, and on the top of the oak, an acorn. This acorn is the princess. If Long will take me on his shoulders, we shall soon bring her back." And sure enough, in less time than it takes to walk round a cottage, they had returned from the forest, and Long presented the acorn to the prince.

"Now, your excellency, throw it on the ground."

The prince obeyed, and was enchanted to see the princess appear at his side. But when the sun peeped for the first time over the mountains, the door burst open as before, and the wizard entered with a loud laugh. Suddenly he caught sight of the princess; his face darkened, he uttered a low growl, and one of the iron circlets gave way with a crash. He seized the young girl by the hand and bore her away with him.

All that day the prince wandered about the castle, studying the curious treasures it contained, but everything looked as if life had suddenly come to a standstill. In one place he saw a prince who had been turned into stone in the act of brandishing a sword round which his two hands were clasped. In another, the same doom had fallen upon a knight in the act of running away. In a third, a serving man was standing eternally trying to convey a piece of beef to his mouth, and all around them were others, still preserving for evermore the attitudes they were in when the wizard had commanded "From henceforth be turned into marble." In the castle, and round the castle all was dismal and desolate. Trees there were, but without leaves; fields there were, but no grass grew on them. There was one river, but it never flowed and no fish lived in it. No flowers blossomed, and no birds sang.

Three times during the day food appeared, as if by magic, for the prince and his servants. And it was not until supper was ended that the wizard appeared, as on the previous evening, and delivered the princess into the care of the prince.

All four determined that this time they would keep awake at any cost. But it was no use. Off they went as they had done before, and when the prince awoke the next morning the room was again empty.

With a pang of shame, he rushed to find Quickeye. "Awake! Awake! Quickeye! Do you know what has become of the princess?"

Quickeye rubbed his eyes and answered: "Yes, I see her. Two hundred miles from here there is a mountain. In this mountain is a rock. In the rock, a precious stone. This stone is the princess. Long shall take me there, and we will be back before you can turn round."

So Long took him on his shoulders and they set out. At every stride they covered twenty miles, and as they drew near Quickeye fixed his burning eyes on the mountain; in an instant it split into a thousand pieces, and in one of these sparkled the precious stone. They picked it up and brought it to the prince, who flung it hastily down, and as the stone touched the floor the princess stood before him. When the wizard came, his eyes shot forth flames of fury. Cric-crac was heard, and another of his iron bands broke and fell. He seized the princess by the hand and led her off, growling louder than ever.

All that day things went on exactly as they had done the day before. After supper the wizard brought back the princess, and looking him straight in the eyes he said, "We shall see which of us two will gain the prize after all!"

That night they struggled their very hardest to keep awake, and even walked about instead of sitting down. But it was quite useless. One after another they had to give in, and for the third time the princess slipped through their fingers.

When morning came, it was as usual the prince who awoke the first, and as usual, the princess being gone, he rushed to Quickeye.

"Get up, get up, Quickeye, and tell me where is the princess?"

Quickeye looked about for some time without answering. 'Oh, my lord, she is far, very far. Three hundred miles away there lies a black sea. In the middle of this sea there is a little shell, and in the middle of the shell is fixed a gold ring. That gold ring is the princess. But do not vex your soul; we will get her. Only to-day, Long must take Broad with him. He will be wanted badly."

So Long took Quickeye on one shoulder, and Broad on the other, and they set out. At each stride they left thirty miles behind them. When they reached the black sea, Quickeye showed them the spot where they must seek the shell. But though Long stretched down his hand as far as it would go, he could not find the shell, for it lay at the bottom of the sea.

"Wait a moment, comrades, it will be all right. I will help you," said Broad.

Then he swelled himself out so that you would have thought the world could hardly have held him, and stooping down he drank. He drank so much at every mouthful, that only a minute or so passed before the water had sunk enough for Long to put his hand to the bottom. He soon found the shell, and pulled the ring out. But time had been lost, and Long had a double burden to carry. The dawn was breaking fast before they got back to the castle, where the prince was waiting for them in an agony of fear.

Soon the first rays of the sun were seen peeping over the tops of the mountains. The door burst open, and finding the prince standing alone the wizard broke into peals of wicked laughter. But as he laughed a loud crash was heard, the window fell into a thousand pieces, a gold ring glittered in the air, and the princess stood before the enchanter. For Quickeye, who was watching from afar, had told Long of the terrible danger now threatening the prince, and Long, summoning all his strength for one gigantic effort, had thrown the ring right through the window.

The wizard shrieked and howled with rage, till the whole castle trembled to its foundations. Then a crash was heard, the third band split in two, and a crow flew out of the window.

Then the princess at length broke the enchanted silence, and blushing like a rose, gave the prince her thanks for her unlooked-for deliverance.

But it was not only the princess who was restored to life by the flight of the wicked black crow. The marble figures became men once more, and took up their occupations just as they had left them off. The horses neighed in the stables, the flowers blossomed in the garden, the birds flew in the air, the fish darted in the water. Everywhere you looked, all was life, all was joy!

And the knights who had been turned into stone came in a body to offer their homage to the prince who had set them free.

"Do not thank me," he said, "for I have done nothing. Without my faithful servants, Long, Broad, and Quickeye, I should even have been as one of you."

With these words he bade them farewell, and departed with the princess and his faithful companions for the kingdom of his father.

The old king, who had long since given up all hope, wept for joy at the sight of his son, and insisted that the wedding should take place as soon as possible.

All the knights who had been enchanted in the Iron Castle were invited to the ceremony, and after it had taken place, Long, Broad, and Quickeye took leave of the young couple, saying that they were going to look for more work.

The prince offered them all their hearts could desire if they would only remain with him, but they replied that an idle life would not please them, and that they could never be happy unless they were busy, so they went away to seek their fortunes, and for all I know are seeking still.

Vali

BILLING, KING OF THE RUTHENES, was sorely dismayed when he heard that a great force was about to invade his kingdom, for he was too old to fight as of yore, and his only child, a daughter named Rinda, although she was of marriageable age, obstinately refused to choose a husband from among her many suitors, and thus give her father the help which he so sadly needed.

While Billing was musing disconsolately in his hall, a stranger suddenly entered his palace. Looking up, the king beheld a middle-aged man wrapped in a wide cloak, with a broad-brimmed hat drawn down over his forehead to conceal the fact that he had but one eye. The stranger courteously enquired the cause of his evident depression, and as there was that in his bearing that compelled confidence, the king told him all, and at the end of the relation he volunteered to command the army of the Ruthenes against their foe.

His services being joyfully accepted, it was not long ere Odin – for it was he – won a signal victory, and, returning in triumph, he asked permission to woo the king's daughter Rinda for his wife. Despite the suitor's advancing years, Billing hoped that his daughter would lend a favourable ear to a wooer who appeared to be very distinguished, and he immediately signified his consent. So Odin, still unknown, presented himself before the princess, but she scornfully rejected his proposal, and rudely boxed his ears when he attempted to kiss her.

Forced to withdraw, Odin nevertheless did not relinquish his purpose to make Rinda his wife, for he knew, thanks to Rossthiof's prophecy, that none but she could bring forth the destined avenger of his murdered son. His next step, therefore, was to assume the form of a smith, in which guise he came back to Billing's hall, and fashioning costly ornaments of silver and gold, he so artfully multiplied these precious trinkets that the king joyfully acquiesced when he inquired whether he might pay his addresses to the princess. The smith, Rosterus as he announced himself, was, however, as unceremoniously dismissed by Rinda as the successful general had been; but although his ear once again tingled with the force of her blow, he was more determined than ever to make her his wife.

The next time Odin presented himself before the capricious damsel, he was disguised as a dashing warrior, for, thought he, a young soldier might perchance touch the maiden's heart; but when he again attempted to kiss her, she pushed him back so suddenly that he stumbled and fell upon one knee.

This third insult so enraged Odin that he drew his magic rune stick out of his breast, pointed it at Rinda, and uttered such a terrible spell that she fell back into the arms of her attendants rigid and apparently lifeless.

When the princess came to life again, her suitor had disappeared, but the king discovered with great dismay that she had entirely lost her senses and was melancholy mad. In vain all the physicians were summoned and all their simples tried; the maiden remained passive and sad, and her distracted father had well-nigh abandoned hope when an old woman, who announced herself as Vecha, or Vak, appeared and offered to undertake the cure of the princess. The seeming old woman, who was Odin in disguise, first prescribed a foot-bath for the patient; but as this did not appear to have any very marked effect, she proposed to try a more drastic treatment. For this, Vecha declared, the patient must be entrusted to her exclusive care, securely bound so that she could not offer the least resistance. Billing, anxious to save his child, was ready to assent to anything; and having thus gained full power over Rinda, Odin compelled her to wed him, releasing her from bonds and spell only when she had faithfully promised to be his wife.

The prophecy of Rossthiof was now fulfilled, for Rinda duly bore a son named Vali (Ali, Bous, or Beav), a personification of the lengthening days, who grew with such marvellous rapidity that in the course of a single day he attained his full stature. Without waiting even to wash his face or comb his hair, this young god hastened to Asgard, bow and arrow in hand, to avenge the death of Balder upon his murderer, Hodur, the blind god of darkness.

In this myth, Rinda, a personification of the hard-frozen rind of the earth, resists the warm wooing of the sun, Odin, who vainly points out that spring is the time for warlike exploits, and offers the adornments of golden summer. She only yields when, after a shower (the footbath), a thaw sets in. Conquered then by the sun's irresistible might, the earth yields to his embrace, is freed from the spell (ice) which made her hard and cold, and brings forth Vali the nourisher, or Bous the peasant, who emerges from his dark hut when the pleasant days have come. The slaying of Hodur by Vali is therefore emblematical of 'the breaking forth of new light after wintry darkness.'

Vali, who ranked as one of the twelve deities occupying seats in the great hall of Gladsheim, shared with his father the dwelling called Valaskialf, and was destined, even before birth, to survive the last battle and twilight of the gods, and to reign with Vidar over the regenerated earth.

Aunt Rachel's Curse

ON A HEADLAND NEAR PLYMOUTH lived "Aunt Rachel," a reputed seer, who made a scant livelihood by forecasting the future for such seagoing people as had crossed her palm. The crew of a certain brig came to see her on the day before sailing, and she reproached one of the lads for keeping bad company. "Avast, there, granny," interrupted another, who took the chiding to himself. "None of your slack, or I'll put a stopper on your gab." The old woman sprang erect. Levelling her skinny finger at the man, she screamed, "Moon cursers! You have set false beacons and wrecked ships for plunder. It was your fathers and mothers who decoyed a brig to these sands and left me childless and a widow. He who rides the pale horse be your guide, and you be of the number who follow him!"

That night old Rachel's house was burned, and she barely escaped with her life, but when it was time for the brig to sail she took her place among the townfolk who were to see it off. The owner of the brig tried to console her for the loss of the house. "I need it no longer," she answered, "for the narrow house will soon be mine, and you wretches cannot burn that. But you! Who will console you for the loss of your brig?"

"My brig is stanch. She has already passed the worst shoal in the bay."

"But she carries a curse. She cannot swim long."

As each successive rock and bar was passed the old woman leaned forward, her hand shaking, her gray locks flying, her eyes starting, her lips mumbling maledictions, "like an evil spirit, chiding forth the storms as ministers of vengeance." The last shoal was passed, the merchant sighed with relief at seeing the vessel now safely on her course, when the woman uttered a harsh cry, and raised her hand as if to command silence until something happened that she evidently expected. For this the onlookers had not long to wait: the brig halted and trembled – her sails shook in the wind, her crew were seen trying to free the cutter – then she careened and sank until only her mast-heads stood out of the water. Most of the company ran for boats and lines, and few saw Rachel pitch forward on the earth-dead, with a fierce smile of exultation on her face. The rescuers came back with all the crew, save one – the man who had challenged the old woman and revengefully burned her cabin. Rachel's body was buried where her house had stood, and the rock – before unknown – where the brig had broken long bore the name of Rachel's Curse.

The Daughter of Duart

THERE ONCE WAS A MAN, MacLean of Duart, who sent his daughter to become a scholar. Now in those days, an education was a novelty for a lassie, but so highly did he think of his daughter that he found the money, and sent her away. And a long time she was away, too, for it was three or four years before her feet touched the MacLean soil once more.

While she was gone, the man, MacLean of Duart, would sit himself in her room, and look around him. It was a fine room, it was, for so highly did he think of his daughter that he found the money to buy her everything she ever wanted. There were books a plenty, but since MacLean of Duart could not read, they meant nothing to them, with their drawings of cats, and circles, and great long poems. There were pictures, too, on the walls of that room, and a soft cover on the bed, that made it look just so. For she was a clever girl, and she knew how to make a room feel warm.

MacLean of Duart was lonely without his daughter, but he carried on working his land, and the day came again when she returned home to him there. And so it was that he took his daughter on his arm, and led her up into the hills, where the clouds quivered around them, and the air shone bright and blue. Then they looked around them, at all the beauty of the land, and he turned to her, his eyes alight with pride and joy, and he said to his daughter, "How much have you learned?"

And his daughter stopped, and she looked about, across the mossy hills to the sea beyond, and there she pointed to a tall ship, which fought a course away from them against the waves.

"There," she said, "that ship. I have learned enough to bring it to shore."

And her father laughed warmly, and taking her arm again, he said, "Well, then, lass, bring her in."

The ship turned then, and made its way across the waters towards them. And it kept on coming, as the water grew shallow and the sands rose up to meet it, and then the rocks were there, thrusting their way through the waves as the prow of the ship drew nigh. And that ship kept on coming until it was about to be wrecked on the rocks.

MacLean of Duart looked at his daughter then, and he said with a soft voice, "Save them now, lass. Why don't you save them now."

And his daughter shrugged her shoulders, and she smiled an easy smile, then said, "But I can't. I don't know how to do that."

There was silence then, filled by the crash of the ship upon the rocks. He turned to her then, did MacLean of Duart, and he laid down her arm. He looked at his daughter with new eyes, and he said to her, "Well, then. If that is the education I have bought you, if that is what you have learned, then I would rather your room than your company."

He strode home, and built a great fire. And when his daughter came in after him, he cut her to bits and burnt her there, saying, as he poked the flames, "I will never have your sort in the same place as myself."

And he went to her room, and gathered together her books, and her pictures, and threw them on the fire. Then he took her soft cover from her bed and put that on, too, till there was no trace of the girl who was his daughter. For MacLean of Duart thought so highly of his daughter that he could not allow her to practise the education she'd gathered, for he would have nothing to do with black magic, and she had mastered the art.

The Greek Princess and the Young Gardener

THERE WAS ONCE A KING, but I didn't hear what country he was over, and he had one very beautiful daughter. Well, he was getting old and sickly, and the doctors found out that the finest medicine in the world for him was the apples of a tree that grew in the orchard just under his window. So you may be sure he had the tree well minded, and used to get the apples counted from the time they were the size of small marbles. One harvest, just as they were beginning to turn ripe, the king was awakened one night by the flapping of wings outside in the orchard; and when he looked out, what did he see but a bird among the branches of his tree. Its feathers were so bright that they made a light all round them, and the minute it saw the king in his night-cap and night-shirt it picked off an apple, and flew away. "Oh, botheration to that thief of a gardener!" says the king, "this is a nice way he's watching my precious fruit."

He didn't sleep a wink the rest of the night; and as soon as any one was stirring in the palace, he sent for the gardener, and abused him for his neglect.

"Please your Majesty!" says he, "not another apple you shall lose. My three sons are the best shots at the bow and arrow in the kingdom, and they and myself will watch in turn every night."

When the night came, the gardener's eldest son took his post in the garden, with his bow strung and his arrow between his fingers, and watched, and watched. But at the dead hour, the king, that was wide awake, heard the flapping of wings, and ran to the window. There was the bright bird in the tree, and the boy fast asleep, sitting with his back to the wall, and his bow on his lap.

"Rise, you lazy thief!" says the king, "there's the bird again, botheration to her!"

Up jumped the poor fellow; but while he was fumbling with the arrow and the string, away was the bird with the nicest apple on the tree. Well, to be sure, how the king fumed and fretted, and how he abused the gardener and the boy, and what a twenty-four hours he spent till midnight came again!

He had his eye this time on the second son of the gardener; but though he was up and lively enough when the clock began to strike twelve, it wasn't done with the last bang when he saw him stretched like one dead on the long grass, and saw the bright bird again, and heard the flap of her wings, and saw her carry away the third apple. The poor fellow woke with the roar the king let at him, and even was in time enough to let fly an arrow after the bird. He did not hit her, you may depend; and though the king was mad enough, he saw the poor fellows were under *pishtrogues*, and could not help it.

Well, he had some hopes out of the youngest, for he was a brave, active young fellow, that had everybody's good word. There he was ready, and there was the king watching him, and talking to him at the first stroke of twelve. At the last clang, the brightness coming before the bird lighted up the wall and the trees, and the rushing of the wings was heard as it flew into the branches; but at the same instant the crack of the arrow on her side might be heard a quarter of a mile off. Down came the arrow and a large bright feather along with it, and away was the bird, with a screech that was enough to break the drum of your ear. She hadn't time to carry off an apple; and bedad, when the feather was thrown up into the king's room it was heavier than lead, and turned out to be the finest beaten gold.

Well, there was great *cooramuch* made about the youngest boy next day, and he watched night after night for a week, but not a mite of a bird or bird's feather was to be seen, and then the king told him to go home and sleep. Every one admired the beauty of the gold feather beyond anything, but the king was fairly bewitched. He was turning it round and round, and rubbing it against his forehead and his nose the live-long day; and at last he proclaimed that he'd give his daughter and half his kingdom to whoever would bring him the bird with the gold feathers, dead or alive.

The gardener's eldest son had great conceit of himself, and away he went to look for the bird. In the afternoon he sat down under a tree to rest himself, and eat a bit of bread and cold meat that he had in his wallet, when up comes as fine a looking fox as you'd see in the burrow of Munfin. "Musha, sir," says he, "would you spare a bit of that meat to a poor body that's hungry?"

"Well," says the other, "you must have the divil's own assurance, you common robber, to ask me such a question. Here's the answer," and he let fly at the *moddhereen rua*.

The arrow scraped from his side up over his back, as if he was made of hammered iron, and stuck in a tree a couple of perches off.

"Foul play," says the fox; "but I respect your young brother, and will give a bit of advice. At nightfall you'll come into a village. One side of the street you'll see a large room lighted up, and filled with young men and women, dancing and drinking. The other side you'll see a house with no light, only from the fire in the front room, and no one near it but a man and his wife, and their child. Take a fool's advice, and get lodging there." With that he curled his tail over his crupper, and trotted off.

The boy found things as the fox said, but *begonies* he chose the dancing and drinking, and there we'll leave him. In a week's time, when they got tired at home waiting for him, the second son said he'd try his fortune, and off he set. He was just as ill-natured and foolish as his brother, and the same thing happened to him. Well, when a week was over, away went the youngest of all, and as sure as the hearth-money, he sat under the same tree, and pulled out his bread and meat, and the same fox came up and saluted him. Well, the young fellow shared his dinner with the *moddhereen*, and he wasn't long beating about the bush, but told the other he knew all about his business.

"I'll help you," says he, "if I find you're biddable. So just at nightfall you'll come into a village.... Goodbye till tomorrow."

It was just as the fox said, but the boy took care not to go near dancer, drinker, fiddler, or piper. He got welcome in the quiet house to supper and bed, and was on his journey next morning before the sun was the height of the trees.

He wasn't gone a quarter of a mile when he saw the fox coming out of a wood that was by the roadside.

"Good-morrow, fox," says one.

"Good-morrow, sir," says the other.

"Have you any notion how far you have to travel till you find the golden bird?"

"Dickens a notion have I; – how could I?"

"Well, I have. She's in the King of Spain's palace, and that's a good two hundred miles off."

"Oh, dear! we'll be a week going."

"No, we won't. Sit down on my tail, and we'll soon make the road short."

"Tail, indeed! that "ud be the droll saddle, my poor *moddhereen*."

"Do as I tell you, or I'll leave you to yourself."

Well, rather than vex him he sat down on the tail that was spread out level like a wing, and away they went like thought. They overtook the wind that was before them, and the wind that came after didn't overtake them. In the afternoon, they stopped in a wood near the King of Spain's palace, and there they stayed till nightfall.

"Now," says the fox, "I'll go before you to make the minds of the guards easy, and you'll have nothing to do but go from lighted hall to another lighted hall till you find the golden bird in the last. If you have a head on you, you'll bring himself and his cage outside the door, and no one then can lay hands on him or you. If you haven't a head I can't help you, nor no one else." So he went over to the gates.

In a quarter of an hour the boy followed, and in the first hall he passed he saw a score of armed guards standing upright, but all dead asleep. In the next he saw a dozen, and in the next half a dozen, and in the next three, and in the room beyond that there was no guard at all, nor lamp, nor candle, but it was as bright as day; for there was the golden bird in a common wood and wire cage, and on the table were the three apples turned into solid gold.

On the same table was the most lovely golden cage eye ever beheld, and it entered the boy's head that it would be a thousand pities not to put the precious bird into it, the common cage was so unfit for her. Maybe he thought of the money it was worth; anyhow he made the exchange, and he had soon good reason to be sorry for it. The instant the shoulder of the bird's wing touched the golden wires, he let such a *squawk* out of him as was enough to break all the panes of glass in the windows, and at the same minute the three men, and the half-dozen, and the dozen, and the score men, woke up and clattered their swords and spears, and surrounded the poor boy, and jibed, and cursed, and swore at home, till he didn't know whether it's his foot or head he was standing on. They called the king, and told him what happened, and he put on a very grim face. "It's on a gibbet you ought to be this moment," says he, "but I'll give you a chance of your life, and of the golden bird, too. I lay you under prohibitions, and restrictions, and death, and destruction, to go and bring me the King of Moróco's bay filly that outruns the wind, and leaps over the walls of castle-bawns. When you fetch her into the bawn of this palace, you must get the golden bird, and liberty to go where you please."

Out passed the boy, very down-hearted, but as he went along, who should come out of a brake but the fox again.

"Ah, my friend," says he, "I was right when I suspected you hadn't a head on you; but I won't rub your hair again' the grain. Get on my tail again, and when we come to the King of Moróco's palace, we'll see what we can do."

So away they went like thought. The wind that was before them they would overtake; the wind that was behind them would not overtake them.

Well, the nightfall came on them in a wood near the palace, and says the fox, "I'll go and make things easy for you at the stables, and when you are leading out the filly, don't let her touch the door, nor doorposts, nor anything but the ground, and that with her hoofs; and if you haven't a head on you once you are in the stable, you'll be worse off than before."

So the boy delayed for a quarter of an hour, and then he went into the big bawn of the palace. There were two rows of armed men reaching from the gate to the stable, and every man was in the depth of deep sleep, and through them went the boy till he got into the stable. There was the filly, as handsome a beast as ever stretched leg, and there was one stable-boy with a currycomb in his hand, and another with a bridle, and another with a sieve of oats, and another with an armful of hay, and all as if they were cut out of stone. The filly was the only live thing in the place except himself. She had a common wood and leather saddle on her back, but a golden saddle with the nicest work on it was hung from the post, and he thought it the greatest pity not to put it in place of the other. Well, I believe there was some *pishrogues* over it for a saddle; anyhow, he took off the other, and put the gold one in its place.

Out came a squeal from the filly's throat when she felt the strange article, that might be heard from Tombrick to Bunclody, and all as ready were the armed men and the stable-boys to run and surround the *omadhan* of a boy, and the King of Moróco was soon there along with the rest, with a face on him as black as the sole of your foot. After he stood enjoying the abuse the poor boy got from everybody for some time, he says to him, "You deserve high hanging for your impudence, but I'll give you a chance for your life and the filly, too. I lay on you all sorts of prohibitions, and restrictions, and death, and destruction to go bring me Princess Golden Locks, the King of Greek's daughter. When you deliver her into my hand, you may have the 'daughter of the wind,' and welcome. Come in and take your supper and your rest, and be off at the flight of night."

The poor boy was down in the mouth, you may suppose, as he was walking away next morning, and very much ashamed when the fox looked up in his face after coming out of the wood.

"What a thing it is," says he, "not to have a head when a body wants it worst; and here we have a fine long journey before us to the King of Greek's palace. The worse luck now, the same always. Here, get on my tail, and we'll be making the road shorter."

So he sat on the fox's tail, and swift as thought they went. The wind that was before them they would overtake it, the wind that was behind them would not overtake them, and in the evening they were eating their bread and cold meat in the wood near the castle.

"Now," says the fox, when they were done, "I'll go before you to make things easy. Follow me in a quarter of an hour. Don't let Princess Golden Locks touch the jambs of the doors with her hands, or hair, or clothes, and if you're asked any favour, mind how you answer. Once she's outside the door, no one can take her from you."

Into the palace walked the boy at the proper time, and there were the score, and the dozen, and the half-dozen, and the three guards all standing up or leaning on their arms, and all dead asleep, and in the farthest room of all was the Princess Golden Locks, as lovely as Venus herself. She was asleep in one chair, and her father, the King of Greek, in another. He stood before her for ever so long with the love sinking deeper into his heart every minute, till at last he went down on one knee, and took her darling white hand in his hand, and kissed it.

When she opened her eyes, she was a little frightened, but I believe not very angry, for the boy, as I call him, was a fine handsome young fellow, and all the respect and love that ever you could think of was in his face. She asked him what he wanted, and he stammered, and blushed, and began his story six times, before she understood it.

"And would you give me up to that ugly black King of Moróco?" says she.

"I am obliged to do so," says he, "by prohibitions, and restrictions, and death, and destruction, but I'll have his life and free you, or lose my own. If I can't get you for my wife, my days on the earth will be short."

"Well," says she, "let me take leave of my father at any rate."

"Ah, I can't do that," says he, "or they'd all waken, and myself would be put to death, or sent to some task worse than any I got yet."

But she asked leave at any rate to kiss the old man; that wouldn't waken him, and then she'd go. How could he refuse her, and his heart tied up in every curl of her hair? But, bedad, the moment her lips touched her father's, he let a cry, and every one of the score, the dozen guards woke up, and clashed their arms, and were going to make *gibbets* of the foolish boy.

But the king ordered them to hold their hands, till he'd be *insensed* of what it was all about, and when he heard the boy's story he gave him a chance for his life.

"There is," says he, "a great heap of clay in front of the palace, that won't let the sun shine on the walls in the middle of summer. Every one that ever worked at it found two shovelfuls added to it for every one they threw away. Remove it, and I'll let my daughter go with you. If you're the man I suspect you to be, I think she'll be in no danger of being wife to that yellow *Molott.*"

Early next morning was the boy tackled to his work, and for every shovelful he flung away two came back on him, and at last he could hardly get out of the heap that gathered round him. Well, the poor fellow scrambled out some way, and sat down on a sod, and he'd have cried only for the shame of it. He began at it in ever so many places, and one was still worse than the other, and in the heel of the evening, when he was sitting with his head between his hands, who should be standing before him but the fox.

"Well, my poor fellow," says he, "you're low enough. Go in: I won't say anything to add to your trouble. Take your supper and your rest: tomorrow will be a new day."

"How is the work going off?" says the king, when they were at supper.

"Faith, your Majesty," says the poor boy, "it's not going off, but coming on it is. I suppose you'll have the trouble of digging me out at sunset tomorrow, and waking me."

"I hope not," says the princess, with a smile on her kind face; and the boy was as happy as anything the rest of the evening.

He was wakened up next morning with voices shouting, and bugles blowing, and drums beating, and such a hullibulloo he never heard in his life before. He ran out to see what was the matter, and there, where the heap of clay was the evening before, were soldiers, and servants, and lords, and ladies, dancing like mad for joy that it was gone.

"Ah, my poor fox!" says he to himself, "this is your work."

Well, there was little delay about his return. The king was going to send a great retinue with the princess and himself, but he wouldn't let him take the trouble.

"I have a friend," says he, "that will bring us both to the King of Moróco's palace in a day, d– fly away with him!"

There was great crying when she was parting from her father.

"Ah!" says he, "what a lonesome life I'll have now! Your poor brother in the power of that wicked witch, and kept away from us, and now you taken from me in my old age!"

Well, they both were walking on through the wood, and he telling her how much he loved her; out walked the fox from behind a brake, and in a short time he and she were sitting on the brush, and holding one another fast for fear of slipping off, and away they went like thought.

The wind that was before them they would overtake it, and in the evening he and she were in the big bawn of the King of Morôco's castle.

"Well," says he to the boy, "you've done your duty well; bring out the bay filly. I'd give the full of the bawn of such fillies, if I had them, for this handsome princess. Get on your steed, and here is a good purse of guineas for the road."

"Thank you," says he. "I suppose you'll let me shake hands with the princess before I start."

"Yes, indeed, and welcome."

Well, he was some little time about the hand-shaking, and before it was over he had her fixed snug behind him; and while you could count three, he, and she, and the filly were through all the guards, and a hundred perches away. On they went, and next morning they were in the wood near the King of Spain's palace, and there was the fox before them.

"Leave your princess here with me," says he, "and go get the golden bird and the three apples. If you don't bring us back the filly along with the bird, I must carry you both home myself."

Well, when the King of Spain saw the boy and the filly in the bawn, he made the golden bird, and the golden cage, and the golden apples be brought out and handed to him, and was very thankful and very glad of his prize. But the boy could not part with the nice beast without petting it and rubbing it; and while no one was expecting such a thing, he was up on its back, and through the guards, and a hundred perches away, and he wasn't long till he came to where he left his princess and the fox.

They hurried away till they were safe out of the King of Spain's land, and then they went on easier; and if I was to tell you all the loving things they said to one another, the story wouldn't be over till morning. When they were passing the village of the dance house, they found his two brothers begging, and they brought them along. When they came to where the fox appeared first, he begged the young man to cut off his head and his tail. He would not do it for him; he shivered at the very thought, but the eldest brother was ready enough. The head and tail vanished with the blows, and the body changed into the finest young man you could see, and who was he but the princess's brother that was bewitched. Whatever joy they had before, they had twice as much now, and when they arrived at the palace bonfires were set blazing, oxes roasting, and puncheons of wine put out in the lawn. The young Prince of Greece was married to the king's daughter, and the prince's sister to the gardener's son. He and she went a shorter way back to her father's house, with many attendants, and the king was so glad of the golden bird and the golden apples, that he had sent a waggon full of gold and a waggon full of silver along with them.

Smallhead and the King's Son

LONG AGO THERE LIVED in Erin a woman who married a man of high degree and had one daughter. Soon after the birth of the daughter the husband died.

The woman was not long a widow when she married a second time, and had two daughters. These two daughters hated their half-sister, thought she was not so wise as another, and nicknamed her Smallhead. When the elder of the two sisters was fourteen years old their father died. The mother was in great grief then, and began to pine away. She used to sit at home in the corner and never left the house. Smallhead was kind to her mother, and the mother was fonder of her eldest daughter than of the other two, who were ashamed of her.

At last the two sisters made up in their minds to kill their mother. One day, while their half-sister was gone, they put the mother in a pot, boiled her, and threw the bones outside. When Smallhead came home there was no sign of the mother.

"Where is my mother?" asked she of the other two.

"She went out somewhere. How should we know where she is?"

"Oh, wicked girls! you have killed my mother," said Smallhead.

Smallhead wouldn't leave the house now at all, and the sisters were very angry.

"No man will marry either one of us," said they, "if he sees our fool of a sister."

Since they could not drive Smallhead from the house they made up their minds to go away themselves. One fine morning they left home unknown to their half-sister and travelled on many miles. When Smallhead discovered that her sisters were gone she hurried after them and never stopped till she came up with the two. They had to go home with her that day, but they scolded her bitterly.

The two settled then to kill Smallhead, so one day they took twenty needles and scattered them outside in a pile of straw. "We are going to that hill beyond," said they, "to stay till evening, and if you have not all the needles that are in that straw outside gathered and on the tables before us, we'll have your life."

Away they went to the hill. Smallhead sat down, and was crying bitterly when a short grey cat walked in and spoke to her.

"Why do you cry and lament so?" asked the cat.

"My sisters abuse me and beat me," answered Smallhead. "This morning they said they would kill me in the evening unless I had all the needles in the straw outside gathered before them."

"Sit down here," said the cat, "and dry your tears."

The cat soon found the twenty needles and brought them to Smallhead. "Stop there now," said the cat, "and listen to what I tell you. I am your mother; your sisters killed me and destroyed my body, but don't harm them; do them good, do the best you can for them, save them: obey my words and it will be better for you in the end."

The cat went away for herself, and the sisters came home in the evening. The needles were on the table before them. Oh, but they were vexed and angry when they saw the twenty needles, and they said some one was helping their sister!

One night when Smallhead was in bed and asleep they started away again, resolved this time never to return. Smallhead slept till morning. When she saw that the sisters were gone she followed, traced them from place to place, inquired here and there day after day, till one evening some person told her that they were in the house of an old hag, a terrible enchantress, who had one son and three daughters: that the house was a bad place to be in, for the old hag had more power of witchcraft than any one and was very wicked.

Smallhead hurried away to save her sisters, and facing the house knocked at the door, and asked lodgings for God's sake.

"Oh, then," said the hag, "it is hard to refuse any one lodgings, and besides on such a wild, stormy night. I wonder if you are anything to the young ladies who came the way this evening?"

The two sisters heard this and were angry enough that Smallhead was in it, but they said nothing, not wishing the old hag to know their relationship. After supper the hag told the three strangers to sleep in a room on the right side of the house. When her own daughters were going to bed Smallhead saw her tie a ribbon around the neck of each one of them, and heard her say:

"Do you sleep in the left-hand bed." Smallhead hurried and said to her sisters: "Come quickly, or I'll tell the woman who you are."

They took the bed in the left-hand room and were in it before the hag's daughters came.

"Oh," said the daughters, "the other bed is as good." So they took the bed in the right-hand room. When Smallhead knew that the hag's daughters were asleep she rose, took the ribbons off their necks, and put them on her sister's necks and on her own. She lay awake and watched them. After a while she heard the hag say to her son:

"Go, now, and kill the three girls; they have the clothes and money."

"You have killed enough in your life and so let these go," said the son.

But the old woman would not listen. The boy rose up, fearing his mother, and taking a long knife, went to the right-hand room and cut the throats of the three girls without ribbons. He went to bed then for himself, and when Smallhead found that the old hag was asleep she roused her sisters, told what had happened, made them dress quickly and follow her. Believe me, they were willing and glad to follow her this time.

The three travelled briskly and came soon to a bridge, called at that time 'The Bridge of Blood." Whoever had killed a person could not cross the bridge. When the three girls came to the bridge the two sisters stopped: they could not go a step further. Smallhead ran across and went back again.

"If I did not know that you killed our mother," said she, "I might know it now, for this is the Bridge of Blood.'

She carried one sister over the bridge on her back and then the other. Hardly was this done when the hag was at the bridge.

"Bad luck to you, Smallhead!" said she, "I did not know that it was you that was in it last evening. You have killed my three daughters."

"It wasn't I that killed them, but yourself," said Smallhead.

The old hag could not cross the bridge, so she began to curse, and she put every curse on Smallhead that she could remember. The sisters travelled on till they came to a King's castle. They heard that two servants were needed in the castle.

"Go now," said Smallhead to the two sisters, "and ask for service. Be faithful and do well. You can never go back by the road you came."

The two found employment at the King's castle. Smallhead took lodgings in the house of a blacksmith near by.

"I should be glad to find a place as kitchen-maid in the castle," said Smallhead to the blacksmith's wife.

"I will go to the castle and find a place for you if I can," said the woman.

The blacksmith's wife found a place for Smallhead as kitchen-maid in the castle, and she went there next day.

"I must be careful," thought Smallhead, "and do my best. I am in a strange place. My two sisters are here in the King's castle. Who knows, we may have great fortune yet."

She dressed neatly and was cheerful. Every one liked her, liked her better than her sisters, though they were beautiful. The King had two sons, one at home and the other abroad. Smallhead thought to herself one day: "It is time for the son who is here in the castle to marry. I will speak to him the first time I can." One day she saw him alone in the garden, went up to him, and said:

"Why are you not getting married, it is high time for you?"

He only laughed and thought she was too bold, but then thinking that she was a simple-minded girl who wished to be pleasant, he said:

"I will tell you the reason: My grandfather bound my father by an oath never to let his oldest son marry until he could get the Sword of Light, and I am afraid that I shall be long without marrying."

"Do you know where the Sword of Light is, or who has it?" asked Smallhead.

"I do," said the King's son, "an old hag who has great power and enchantment, and she lives a long distance from this, beyond the Bridge of Blood. I cannot go there myself, I cannot cross the bridge, for I have killed men in battle. Even if I could cross the bridge I would not go, for many is the King's son that hag has destroyed or enchanted."

"Suppose some person were to bring the Sword of Light, and that person a woman, would you marry her?"

"I would, indeed," said the King's son.

"If you promise to marry my elder sister I will strive to bring the Sword of Light."

"I will promise most willingly," said the King's son.

Next morning early, Smallhead set out on her journey. Calling at the first shop she bought a stone weight of salt, and went on her way, never stopping or resting till she reached the hag's house at nightfall. She climbed to the gable, looked down, and saw the son making a great pot of stirabout for his mother, and she hurrying him. "I am as hungry as a hawk!" cried she.

Whenever the boy looked away, Smallhead dropped salt down, dropped it when he was not looking, dropped it till she had the whole stone of salt in the stirabout. The old hag waited and waited till at last she cried out: "Bring the stirabout. I am starving! Bring the pot. I will eat from the pot. Give the milk here as well."

The boy brought the stirabout and the milk, the old woman began to eat, but the first taste she got she spat out and screamed: "You put salt in the pot in place of meal!"

"I did not, mother."

"You did, and it's a mean trick that you played on me. Throw this stirabout to the pig outside and go for water to the well in the field."

"I cannot go," said the boy, "the night is too dark; I might fall into the well."

"You must go and bring the water; I cannot live till morning without eating."

"I am as hungry as yourself," said the boy, "but how can I go to the well without a light? I will not go unless you give me a light."

"If I give you the Sword of Light there is no knowing who may follow you; maybe that devil of a Smallhead is outside."

But sooner than fast till morning the old hag gave the Sword of Light to her son, warning him to take good care of it. He took the Sword of Light and went out. As he saw no one when he came to the well he left the sword on the top of the steps going down to the water, so as to have good light. He had not gone down many steps when Smallhead had the sword, and away she ran over hills, dales, and valleys towards the Bridge of Blood.

The boy shouted and screamed with all his might. Out ran the hag. "Where is the sword?" cried she.

"Some one took it from the step."

Off rushed the hag, following the light, but she didn't come near Smallhead till she was over the bridge.

"Give me the Sword of Light, or bad luck to you," cried the hag.

"Indeed, then, I will not; I will keep it, and bad luck to yourself," answered Smallhead.

On the following morning she walked up to the King's son and said:

"I have the Sword of Light; now will you marry my sister?"

"I will," said he.

The King's son married Smallhead's sister and got the Sword of Light. Smallhead stayed no longer in the kitchen – the sister didn't care to have her in kitchen or parlour.

The King's second son came home. He was not long in the castle when Smallhead said to herself, "Maybe he will marry my second sister."

She saw him one day in the garden, went toward him; he said something, she answered, then asked: "Is it not time for you to be getting married like your brother?"

"When my grandfather was dying," said the young man, "he bound my father not to let his second son marry till he had the Black Book. This book used to shine and give brighter light than ever the Sword of Light did, and I suppose it does yet. The old hag beyond the Bridge of Blood has the book, and no one dares to go near her, for many is the King's son killed or enchanted by that woman."

"Would you marry my second sister if you were to get the Black Book?"

"I would, indeed; I would marry any woman if I got the Black Book with her. The Sword of Light and the Black Book were in our family till my grandfather's time, then they were stolen by that cursed old hag."

"I will have the book," said Smallhead, "or die in the trial to get it."

Knowing that stirabout was the main food of the hag, Smallhead settled in her mind to play another trick. Taking a bag she scraped the chimney, gathered about a stone of soot, and took it with her. The night was dark and rainy. When she reached the hag's house, she climbed up the gable to the chimney and found that the son was making stirabout for his mother. She dropped the soot down by degrees till at last the whole stone of soot was in the pot; then she scraped around the top of the chimney till a lump of soot fell on the boy's hand.

"Oh, mother," said he, "the night is wet and soft, the soot is falling."

"Cover the pot," said the hag. "Be quick with that stirabout, I am starving."

The boy took the pot to his mother.

"Bad luck to you," cried the hag the moment she tasted the stirabout, "this is full of soot; throw it out to the pig."

"If I throw it out there is no water inside to make more, and I'll not go in the dark and rain to the well."

"You must go!" screamed she.

"I'll not stir a foot out of this unless I get a light," said the boy.

"Is it the book you are thinking of, you fool, to take it and lose it as you did the sword? Smallhead is watching you."

"How could Smallhead, the creature, be outside all the time? If you have no use for the water you can do without it."

Sooner than stop fasting till morning, the hag gave her son the book, saying: "Do not put this down or let it from your hand till you come in, or I'll have your life."

The boy took the book and went to the well. Smallhead followed him carefully. He took the book down into the well with him, and when he was stooping to dip water she snatched the book and pushed him into the well, where he came very near drowning.

Smallhead was far away when the boy recovered, and began to scream and shout to his mother. She came in a hurry, and finding that the book was gone, fell into such a rage that she thrust a knife into her son's heart and ran after Smallhead, who had crossed the bridge before the hag could come up with her.

When the old woman saw Smallhead on the other side of the bridge facing her and dancing with delight, she screamed:

"You took the Sword of Light and the Black Book, and your two sisters are married. Oh, then, bad luck to you. I will put my curse on you wherever you go. You have all my children killed, and I a poor, feeble, old woman."

"Bad luck to yourself," said Smallhead. "I am not afraid of a curse from the like of you. If you had lived an honest life you wouldn't be as you are today."

"Now, Smallhead," said the old hag, "you have me robbed of everything, and my children destroyed. Your two sisters are well married. Your fortune began with my ruin. Come, now, and take care of me in my old age. I'll take my curse from you, and you will have good luck. I bind myself never to harm a hair of your head."

Smallhead thought awhile, promised to do this, and said: "If you harm me, or try to harm me, it will be the worse for yourself."

The old hag was satisfied and went home. Smallhead went to the castle and was received with great joy. Next morning she found the King's son in the garden, and said: "If you marry my sister tomorrow, you will have the Black Book."

"I will marry her gladly," said the King's son.

Next day the marriage was celebrated and the King's son got the book. Smallhead remained in the castle about a week, then she left good health with her sisters and went to the hag's house. The old woman was glad to see her and showed the girl her work. All Smallhead had to do was to wait on the hag and feed a large pig that she had.

"I am fatting that pig," said the hag; "he is seven years old now, and the longer you keep a pig the harder his meat is: we'll keep this pig a while longer, and then we'll kill and eat him."

Smallhead did her work; the old hag taught her some things, and Smallhead learned herself far more than the hag dreamt of. The girl fed the pig three times a day, never thinking that he could be anything but a pig. The hag had sent word to a sister that she had in the Eastern World, bidding her come and they would kill the pig and have a great feast. The sister came, and one day when the hag was going to walk with her sister she said to Smallhead:

"Give the pig plenty of meal today; this is the last food he'll have; give him his fill."

The pig had his own mind and knew what was coming. He put his nose under the pot and threw it on Smallhead's toes, and she barefoot. With that she ran into the house for a stick, and seeing a rod on the edge of the loft, snatched it and hit the pig.

That moment the pig was a splendid young man.

Smallhead was amazed.

"Never fear," said the young man, "I am the son of a King that the old hag hated, the King of Munster. She stole me from my father seven years ago and enchanted me – made a pig of me."

Smallhead told the King's son, then, how the hag had treated her. "I must make a pig of you again," said she, "for the hag is coming. Be patient and I'll save you, if you promise to marry me."

"I promise you," said the King's son.

With that she struck him, and he was a pig again. She put the switch in its place and was at her work when the two sisters came. The pig ate his meal now with a good heart, for he felt sure of rescue.

"Who is that girl you have in the house, and where did you find her?" asked the sister.

"All my children died of the plague, and I took this girl to help me. She is a very good servant."

At night the hag slept in one room, her sister in another, and Smallhead in a third. When the two sisters were sleeping soundly Smallhead rose, stole the hag's magic book, and then took the rod. She went next to where the pig was, and with one blow of the rod made a man of him.

With the help of the magic book Smallhead made two doves of herself and the King's son, and they took flight through the air and flew on without stopping. Next morning the hag called Smallhead, but she did not come. She hurried out to see the pig. The pig was gone. She ran to her book. Not a sign of it.

"Oh!" cried she, "that villain of a Smallhead has robbed me. She has stolen my book, made a man of the pig, and taken him away with her."

What could she do but tell her whole story to the sister. "Go you," said she, "and follow them. You have more enchantment than Smallhead has."

"How am I to know them?" asked the sister.

"Bring the first two strange things that you find; they will turn themselves into something wonderful."

The sister then made a hawk of herself and flew away as swiftly as any March wind.

"Look behind," said Smallhead to the King's son some hours later; "see what is coming."

"I see nothing," said he, "but a hawk coming swiftly."

"That is the hag's sister. She has three times more enchantment than the hag herself. But fly down on the ditch and be picking yourself as doves do in rainy weather, and maybe she'll pass without seeing us."

The hawk saw the doves, but thinking them nothing wonderful, flew on till evening, and then went back to her sister.

"Did you see anything wonderful?"

"I did not; I saw only two doves, and they picking themselves."

"You fool, those doves were Smallhead and the King's son. Off with you in the morning and don't let me see you again without the two with you."

Away went the hawk a second time, and swiftly as Smallhead and the King's son flew, the hawk was gaining on them. Seeing this Smallhead and the King's son dropped down into a large village, and, it being market-day, they made two heather brooms of themselves. The two brooms began to sweep the road without any one holding them, and swept toward each other. This was a great wonder. Crowds gathered at once around the two brooms.

The old hag flying over in the form of a hawk saw this and thinking that it must be Smallhead and the King's son were in it, came down, turned into a woman, and said to herself:

"I'll have those two brooms."

She pushed forward so quickly through the crowd that she came near knocking down a man standing before her. The man was vexed.

"You cursed old hag!" cried he, "do you want to knock us down?" With that he gave her a blow and drove her against another man, that man gave her a push that sent her spinning against a third man, and so on till between them all they came near putting the life out of her, and pushed her away from the brooms. A woman in the crowd called out then:

"It would be nothing but right to knock the head off that old hag, and she trying to push us away from the mercy of God, for it was God who sent the brooms to sweep the road for us."

"True for you," said another woman. With that the people were as angry as angry could be, and were ready to kill the hag. They were going to take the head off the hag when she made a hawk of herself and flew away, vowing never to do another stroke of work for her sister. She might do her own work or let it alone.

When the hawk disappeared the two heather brooms rose and turned into doves. The people felt sure when they saw the doves that the brooms were a blessing from heaven, and it was the old hag that drove them away.

On the following day Smallhead and the King's son saw his father's castle, and the two came down not too far from it in their own forms. Smallhead was a very beautiful woman now, and why not? She had the magic and didn't spare it. She made herself as beautiful as ever she could: the like of her was not to be seen in that kingdom or the next one.

The King's son was in love with her that minute, and did not wish to part with her, but she would not go with him.

"When you are at your father's castle," said Smallhead, "all will be overjoyed to see you, and the king will give a great feast in your honour. If you kiss any one or let any living thing kiss you, you'll forget me for ever."

"I will not let even my own mother kiss me," said he.

The King's son went to the castle. All were overjoyed; they had thought him dead, had not seen him for seven years. He would let no one come near to kiss him. "I am bound by oath to kiss no one," said he to his mother. At that moment an old grey hound came in, and with one spring was on his shoulder licking his face: all that the King's son had gone through in seven years was forgotten in one moment.

Smallhead went toward a forge near the castle. The smith had a wife far younger than himself, and a stepdaughter. They were no beauties. In the rear of the forge was a well and a tree growing over it. "I will go up in that tree," thought Smallhead, "and spend the night in it." She went up and sat just over the well. She was not long in the tree when the moon came out high above the hill tops and shone on the well. The blacksmith's stepdaughter, coming for water, looked down in the well, saw the face of the woman above in the tree, thought it her own face, and cried:

"Oh, then, to have me bringing water to a smith, and I such a beauty. I'll never bring another drop to him." With that she cast the pail in the ditch and ran off to find a king's son to marry.

When she was not coming with the water, and the blacksmith waiting to wash after his day's work in the forge, he sent the mother. The mother had nothing but a pot to get the water in, so off she went with that, and coming to the well saw the beautiful face in the water.

"Oh, you black, swarthy villain of a smith," cried she, "bad luck to the hour that I met you, and I such a beauty. I'll never draw another drop of water for the life of you!"

She threw the pot down, broke it, and hurried away to find some king's son.

When neither mother nor daughter came back with water the smith himself went to see what was keeping them. He saw the pail in the ditch, and, catching it, went to the well; looking down, he saw the beautiful face of a woman in the water. Being a man, he knew that it was not his own face that was in it, so he looked up, and there in the tree saw a woman. He spoke to her and said:

"I know now why my wife and her daughter did not bring water. They saw your face in the well, and, thinking themselves too good for me, ran away. You must come now and keep the house till I find them."

"I will help you," said Smallhead. She came down, went to the smith's house, and showed the road that the women took. The smith hurried after them, and found the two in a village ten miles away. He explained their own folly to them, and they came home.

The mother and daughter washed fine linen for the castle. Smallhead saw them ironing one day, and said:

"Sit down: I will iron for you."

She caught the iron, and in an hour had the work of the day done.

The women were delighted. In the evening the daughter took the linen to the housekeeper at the castle.

"Who ironed this linen?" asked the housekeeper.

"My mother and I."

"Indeed, then, you did not. You can't do the like of that work, and tell me who did it."

The girl was in dread now and answered:

"It is a woman who is stopping with us who did the ironing."

The housekeeper went to the Queen and showed her the linen.

"Send that woman to the castle," said the Queen.

Smallhead went: the Queen welcomed her, wondered at her beauty; put her over all the maids in the castle. Smallhead could do anything; everybody was fond of her. The King's son never knew that he had seen her before, and she lived in the castle a year; what the Queen told her she did.

The King had made a match for his son with the daughter of the King of Ulster. There was a great feast in the castle in honour of the young couple, the marriage, was to be a week later. The bride's father brought many of his people who were versed in all kinds of tricks and enchantment.

The King knew that Smallhead could do many things, for neither the Queen nor himself had asked her to do a thing that she did not do in a twinkle.

"Now," said the King to the Queen, "I think she can do something that his people cannot do." He summoned Smallhead and asked:

"Can you amuse the strangers?"

"I can if you wish me to do so."

When the time came and the Ulster men had shown their best tricks, Smallhead came forward and raised the window, which was forty feet from the ground. She had a small ball of thread in her hand; she tied one end of the thread to the window, threw the ball out and over a wall near the castle; then she passed out the window, walked on the thread and kept time to music from players that no man could see. She came in; all cheered her and were greatly delighted.

"I can do that," said the King of Ulster's daughter, and sprang out on the string; but if she did she fell and broke her neck on the stones below. There were cries, there was lamentation, and, in place of a marriage, a funeral.

The King's son was angry and grieved and wanted to drive Smallhead from the castle in some way.

"She is not to blame," said the King of Munster, who did nothing but praise her.

Another year passed: the King got the daughter of the King of Connacht for his son. There was a great feast before the wedding day, and as the Connacht people are full of enchantment and witchcraft, the King of Munster called Smallhead and said:

"Now show the best trick of any."

"I will," said Smallhead.

When the feast was over and the Connacht men had shown their tricks the King of Munster called Smallhead.

She stood before the company, threw two grains of wheat on the floor, and spoke some magic words. There was a hen and a cock there before her of beautiful plumage, she threw a grain of wheat between them; the hen sprang to eat the wheat, the cock gave her a blow of his bill, the hen drew back, looked at him, and said:

"Bad luck to you, you wouldn't do the like of that when I was serving the old hag and you her pig, and I made a man of you and gave you back your own form."

The King's son looked at her and thought, "There must be something in this."

Smallhead threw a second grain. The cock pecked the hen again. "Oh," said the hen, "you would not do that the day the hag's sister was hunting us, and we two doves."

The King's son was still more astonished.

She threw a third grain. The cock struck the hen, and she said, "You would not do that to me the day I made two heather brooms out of you and myself." She threw a fourth grain. The cock pecked the hen a fourth time. "You would not do that the day you promised not to let any living thing kiss you or kiss any one yourself but me – you let the hound kiss you and you forgot me."

The King's son made one bound forward, embraced and kissed Smallhead, and told the King his whole story from beginning to end.

"This is my wife," said he; "I'll marry no other woman."

"Whose wife will my daughter be?" asked the King of Connacht.

"Oh, she will be the wife of the man who will marry her," said the King of Munster, "my son gave his word to this woman before he saw your daughter, and he must keep it."

So Smallhead married the King of Munster's son.

The Curse of the Fires and of the Shadows

ONE SUMMER NIGHT, when there was peace, a score of Puritan troopers under the pious Sir Frederick Hamilton, broke through the door of the Abbey of the White Friars which stood over the Gara Lough at Sligo. As the door fell with a crash they saw a little knot of friars, gathered about the altar, their white habits glimmering in the steady light of the holy candles. All the monks were kneeling except the abbot, who stood upon the altar steps with a great brazen crucifix in his hand. "Shoot them!" cried Sir Frederick Hamilton, but none stirred, for all were new converts, and feared the crucifix and the holy candles. The white lights from the altar threw the shadows of the troopers up on to roof and wall. As the troopers moved about, the shadows began a fantastic dance among the corbels and the memorial tablets. For a little while all was silent, and then five troopers who were the body-guard of Sir Frederick Hamilton lifted their muskets, and shot down five of the friars. The noise and the smoke drove away the mystery of the pale altar lights, and the other troopers took courage and began to strike. In a moment the friars lay about the altar steps, their white habits stained with blood. "Set fire to the house!" cried Sir Frederick Hamilton, and at his word one went out, and came in again carrying a heap of dry straw, and piled it against the western wall, and, having done this, fell back, for the fear of the crucifix and of the holy candles was still in his heart. Seeing this, the five troopers who were Sir Frederick Hamilton's body-guard darted forward, and taking each a holy candle set the straw in a blaze. The red tongues of fire rushed up and flickered from corbel to corbel and from tablet to tablet, and crept along the floor, setting in a blaze the seats and benches. The dance of the shadows passed away, and the dance of the fires began. The troopers fell back towards the door in the southern wall, and watched those yellow dancers springing hither and thither.

For a time the altar stood safe and apart in the midst of its white light; the eyes of the troopers turned upon it. The abbot whom they had thought dead had risen to his feet and now stood before it with the crucifix lifted in both hands high above his head. Suddenly he cried with a loud voice, "Woe unto all who smite those who dwell within the Light of the Lord, for they shall wander among the ungovernable shadows, and follow the ungovernable fires!" And having so cried he fell on his face dead, and the brazen crucifix rolled down the steps of the altar. The smoke had now grown very thick, so that it drove the troopers out into the open air. Before them were burning houses. Behind them shone the painted windows of the Abbey filled with saints and martyrs, awakened, as from a sacred trance, into an angry and animated life. The eyes of the troopers were dazzled, and for a while could see nothing but the flaming faces of saints and martyrs. Presently, however, they saw a man covered with dust who came running towards them. "Two messengers," he cried, "have been sent by the defeated Irish to raise against you the whole country about Manor Hamilton, and if you do not stop them you will be overpowered in the woods before you reach home again! They ride north-east between Ben Bulben and Cashel-na-Gael."

Sir Frederick Hamilton called to him the five troopers who had first fired upon the monks and said, "Mount quickly, and ride through the woods towards the mountain, and get before these men, and kill them."

In a moment the troopers were gone, and before many moments they had splashed across the river at what is now called Buckley's Ford, and plunged into the woods. They followed a beaten track that wound along the northern bank of the river. The boughs of the birch and quicken trees mingled above, and hid the cloudy moonlight, leaving the pathway in almost complete darkness. They rode at a rapid trot, now chatting together, now watching some stray weasel or rabbit scuttling away in the darkness. Gradually, as the gloom and silence of the woods oppressed them, they drew closer together, and began to talk rapidly; they were old comrades and knew each other's lives. One was married, and told how glad his wife would be to see him return safe from this harebrained expedition against the White Friars, and to hear how fortune had made amends for rashness. The oldest of the five, whose wife was dead, spoke of a flagon of wine which awaited him upon an upper shelf; while a third, who was the youngest, had a sweetheart watching for his return, and he rode a little way before the others, not talking at all. Suddenly the young man stopped, and they saw that his horse was trembling. "I saw something," he said, "and yet I do not know but it may have been one of the shadows. It looked like a great worm with a silver crown upon his head." One of the five put his hand up to his forehead as if about to cross himself, but remembering that he had changed his religion he put it down, and said: "I am certain it was but a shadow, for there are a great many about us, and of very strange kinds." Then they rode on in silence. It had been raining in the earlier part of the day, and the drops fell from the branches, wetting their hair and their shoulders. In a little they began to talk again. They had been in many battles against many a rebel together, and now told each other over again the story of their wounds, and so awakened in their hearts the strongest of all fellowships, the fellowship of the sword, and half forgot the terrible solitude of the woods.

Suddenly the first two horses neighed, and then stood still, and would go no further. Before them was a glint of water, and they knew by the rushing sound that it was a river. They dismounted, and after much tugging and coaxing brought the horses to the river-side. In the midst of the water stood a tall old woman with grey hair flowing over a grey dress. She stood up to her knees in the water, and stooped from time to time as though washing. Presently they could see that she was washing something that half floated. The moon cast a flickering light upon it, and they saw that it was the dead body of a man, and, while they were looking at it, an eddy of the river turned the face towards them, and each of the five troopers recognised at the same moment his own face. While they stood dumb and motionless with horror, the woman began to speak, saying slowly and loudly: "Did you see my son? He has a crown of silver on his head, and there are rubies in the crown." Then the oldest of the troopers, he who had been most often wounded, drew his sword and cried: "I have fought for the truth of my God, and need not fear the shadows of Satan," and with that rushed into the water. In a moment he returned. The woman had vanished, and though he had thrust his sword into air and water he had found nothing.

The five troopers remounted, and set their horses at the ford, but all to no purpose. They tried again and again, and went plunging hither and thither, the horses foaming and rearing. "Let us," said the old trooper, "ride back a little into the wood, and strike the river higher up." They rode in under the boughs, the ground-ivy crackling under the hoofs, and the branches striking against their steel caps. After about twenty minutes' riding they came out again upon the river, and after another ten minutes found a place where it was possible to cross without sinking below the stirrups. The wood upon the other side was very thin, and broke the moonlight into long streams. The wind had arisen, and had begun to drive the clouds rapidly across the face of the moon, so that thin streams of light seemed to be dancing a grotesque dance among the scattered bushes and small fir-trees. The tops of the trees began also to moan, and the sound of it was like the voice of the dead in the wind; and the troopers remembered the belief that tells how the dead in purgatory are spitted upon the points of the trees and upon the points of the rocks. They turned a little to the south, in the hope that they might strike the beaten path again, but they could find no trace of it.

Meanwhile, the moaning grew louder and louder, and the dance of the white moon-fires more and more rapid. Gradually they began to be aware of a sound of distant music. It was the sound of a bagpipe, and they rode towards it with great joy. It came from the bottom of a deep, cup-like hollow. In the midst of the hollow was an old man with a red cap and withered face. He sat beside a fire of sticks, and had a burning torch thrust into the earth at his feet, and played an old bagpipe furiously. His red hair dripped over his face like the iron rust upon a rock. "Did you see my wife?" he cried, looking up a moment; "she was washing! she was washing!" "I am afraid of him," said the young trooper, "I fear he is one of the Sidhe." "No," said the old trooper, "he is a man, for I can see the sun-freckles upon his face. We will compel him to be our guide"; and at that he drew his sword, and the others did the same. They stood in a ring round the piper, and pointed their swords at him, and the old trooper then told him that they must kill two rebels, who had taken the road between Ben Bulben and the great mountain spur that is called Cashel-na-Gael, and that he must get up before one of them and be their guide, for they had lost their way. The piper turned, and pointed to a neighbouring tree, and they saw an old white horse ready bitted, bridled, and saddled. He slung the pipe across his back, and, taking the torch in his hand, got upon the horse, and started off before them, as hard as he could go.

The wood grew thinner and thinner, and the ground began to slope up toward the mountain. The moon had already set, and the little white flames of the stars had come out everywhere. The ground sloped more and more until at last they rode far above the woods upon the wide top of the mountain. The woods lay spread out mile after mile below, and away to the south shot up the red glare of the burning town. But before and above them were the little white flames. The guide drew rein suddenly, and pointing upwards with the hand that did not hold the torch, shrieked out, "Look; look at the holy candles!" and then plunged forward at a gallop, waving the torch hither and thither. "Do you hear the hoofs of the messengers?" cried the guide. "Quick, quick! or they will be gone out of your hands!" and he laughed as with delight of the chase. The troopers thought they could hear far off, and as if below them, rattle of hoofs; but now the ground began to slope more and more, and the speed grew more headlong moment by moment. They tried to pull up, but in vain, for the horses seemed to have gone mad. The guide had thrown the reins on to the neck of the old white horse, and was waving his arms and singing a wild Gaelic song. Suddenly they saw the thin gleam of a river, at an immense distance below, and knew that they were upon the brink of the abyss that is now called Lug-na-Gael, or in English the Stranger's Leap. The six horses sprang forward, and five screams went up into the air, a moment later five men and horses fell with a dull crash upon the green slopes at the foot of the rocks.

Dubh a' Ghiubhais

IT WAS MANY HUNDREDS OF YEARS AGO, long before the days when stories were written down, that Scotland was covered in a great dark forest. This was a forest of fir trees, tall and fine as any to be seen, and there lived there a colony of people who made the trees their friends. Trees can be good friends indeed, for they spread their arms across the land, protecting it from the wind that blows from the stormy coasts, and the rain which is carried on its back. And they make homes for the wee folk, and animals of the forest, and wood for the houses and fires of the men who live there.

Now this fine forest was much admired, and there was one in particular who was very envious of Scotland's great dark trees. He was the king of Lochlann and he wanted more than anything to destroy them. He would pace round his castle, overcast and gloomy as the winter sky, and he would lament his unhappy lot, ridden right through with jealousy as hot as any good peat fire.

It was his daughter, the princess, who had watched this curious pacing for years on end who finally came to find out the cause of his unhappiness. He explained that he wished to find a way to destroy the trees of the Scottish forest; and that wee princess, she was a practical lass, and she said there was nothing for it but to do it herself.

And so it was that she bade her father leave to find a witch to put her in the shape of a bird, and when he'd done that, and when she'd become a beautiful, pure white bird, she set out over the grassy hills of Lochlann to the deep fir forests that carpeted the Scottish land. On the west coast of Scotland she came down, and there she struck a tree with a wand she had under her wing. With that single motion the tree would burst into flames and burn there, and it was not long before this beautiful white bird had burnt a great number of trees in that forest.

Now this beautiful white bird was no longer fair or pure; indeed, the smoke of the pinewood had cast an ugly black shadow across her feathers and she came to be known by the people of the country as the Dubh a' Ghiubhais, or Fir Black. And so it was that this Dubh a' Ghiubhais flew across the land, causing damage that robbed the wee folk of their homes and sent the animals scattering for shelter, and the men had no wood for their homes or their fires, and the trees could no longer spread their comforting arms across the land, protecting it from the wind that blows from the stormy coasts, bringing the rain on its back. And it was for this reason that the men of the land grouped together and decided that this bird must be stopped, for the Dubh a' Ghiubhais had brought sadness and rain to their sheltered lives.

It was not easy to catch the Dubh a' Ghiubhais, but it was heard, somewhere on the west coast of Scotland, that the bird had a soft, sweet heart in that blackened breast, and that a plan could be made to capture it.

And so it was that a man at Loch Broom hatched the plan, and on the very next morning spent a day at work in his barnyard, taking mother from her young all across the barn. For the piglets were taken wailing from their sows, the puppies barked as they were snatched from their mothers' teats, the foals were taken from mares, the lambs from sheep, the calves from the cows, the chickens from the hens, the kittens from the cats, and even the kids from the goats that grazed on the tender shoots of grass on the verge. And the uproar that followed was enough to churn the stomach of any man alive, for there were cries so piteous, so plaintive, so needing that the men and women for miles around hid themselves under soft down pillows in order to block out that dreadful sound.

It was not long before it reached the ears of the Dubh a' Ghiubhais, who was passing on her fiery course of devastation. And her soft, sweet heart nearly burst with pity for these poor creatures. She flew at once to the ground, and drawing her wand from beneath her wing she made as if to set the animals free when a small sharp arrow stung her breast, piercing her heart and bringing a clean, cold death. And the man at Loch Broom picked up his quiver and slinging it over his shoulder, bent over to collect the dead bird.

And so it was that the Dubh a' Ghiubhais was hung from a tree, where folk gathered round to cheer her death. News of what had happened reached her father, the king of Lochlann, and he was torn with grief and guilt. He sent his hardiest crew in a great long boat to bring the body of his dear daughter home. But there were fearful gales which pitched and jolted the ships that carried the funeral pyre, and although the brave sailors tried three times, they could get no further than the mouth of the Little Loch Broom.

And so it was that the Dubh a' Ghiubhais was buried beneath the tree where she hung, at Kildonan, at the bend of the loch at Little Loch Broom. She rests there still, a single fir tree growing atop her grave, which lies beneath a grassy green hillock.

Bewitched Butter

NOT FAR from Rathmullen lived, last spring, a family called Hanlon; and in a farm-house, some fields distant, people named Dogherty. Both families had good cows, but the Hanlons were fortunate in possessing a Kerry cow that gave more milk and yellower butter than the others.

Grace Dogherty, a young girl, who was more admired than loved in the neighbourhood, took much interest in the Kerry cow, and appeared one night at Mrs. Hanlon's door with the modest request –

"Will you let me milk your Moiley cow?"

"An' why wad you wish to milk wee Moiley, Grace, dear?" inquired Mrs. Hanlon.

"Oh, just becase you're sae throng at the present time."

"Thank you kindly, Grace, but I'm no too throng to do my ain work. I'll no trouble you to milk."

The girl turned away with a discontented air; but the next evening, and the next, found her at the cow-house door with the same request.

At length Mrs. Hanlon, not knowing well how to persist in her refusal, yielded, and permitted Grace to milk the Kerry cow.

She soon had reason to regret her want of firmness. Moiley gave no more milk to her owner.

When this melancholy state of things lasted for three days, the Hanlons applied to a certain Mark McCarrion, who lived near Binion.

"That cow has been milked by someone with an evil eye," said he. "Will she give you a wee drop, do you think? The full of a pint measure wad do."

"Oh, ay, Mark, dear; I'll get that much milk frae her, any way."

"Weel, Mrs. Hanlon, lock the door, an' get nine new pins that was never used in clothes, an' put them into a saucepan wi' the pint o' milk. Set them on the fire, an' let them come to the boil."

The nine pins soon began to simmer in Moiley's milk.

Rapid steps were heard approaching the door, agitated knocks followed, and Grace Dogherty's high-toned voice was raised in eager entreaty.

"Let me in, Mrs. Hanlon!" she cried. "Tak off that cruel pot! Tak out them pins, for they're pricking holes in my heart, an' I'll never offer to touch milk of yours again."

The Pudding Bewitched

"MOLL ROE RAFFERTY was the son – daughter I mane – of ould Jack Rafferty, who was remarkable for a habit he had of always wearing his head undher his hat; but indeed the same family was a quare one, as everybody knew that was acquainted wid them. It was said of them – but whether it was thrue or not I won't undhertake to say, for 'fraid I'd tell a lie – that whenever they didn't wear shoes or boots they always went barefooted; but I heard afterwards that this was disputed, so rather than say anything to injure their character, I'll let that pass. Now, ould Jack Rafferty had two sons, Paddy and Molly – hut! what are you all laughing at? – I mane a son and daughter, and it was generally believed among the neighbours that they were brother and sisther, which you know might be thrue or it might not: but that's a thing that, wid the help o' goodness, we have nothing to say to. Troth there was many ugly things put out on them that I don't wish to repate, such as that neither Jack nor his son Paddy ever walked a perch widout puttin' one foot afore the other like a salmon; an' I know it was whispered about, that whinever Moll Roe slep', she had an out-of-the-way custom of keepin' her eyes shut. If she did, however, for that matther the loss was her own; for sure we all know that when one comes to shut their eyes they can't see as far before them as another.

"Moll Roe was a fine young bouncin' girl, large and lavish, wid a purty head o' hair on her like scarlet, that bein' one of the raisons why she was called *Roe*, or red; her arms an' cheeks were much the colour of the hair, an' her saddle nose was the purtiest thing of its kind that ever was on a face. Her fists – for, thank goodness, she was well sarved wid them too – had a strong simularity to two thumpin' turnips, reddened by the sun; an' to keep all right and tight, she had a temper as fiery as her head – for, indeed, it was well known that all the Rafferties were *warm*-hearted. Howandiver, it appears that God gives nothing in vain, and of coorse the same fists, big and red as they were, if all that is said about them is thrue, were not so much given to her for ornament as use. At laist, takin' them in connection wid her lively temper, we have it upon good authority, that there was no danger of their getting blue-moulded for want of practice. She had a twist, too, in one of her eyes that was very becomin' in its way, and made her poor husband, when she got him, take it into his head that she could see round a corner. She found him out in many quare things, widout doubt; but whether it was owin' to that or not, I wouldn't undertake to say *for fraid I'd tell a lie*.

"Well, begad, anyhow it was Moll Roe that was the *dilsy*. It happened that there was a nate vagabone in the neighbourhood, just as much overburdened wid beauty as herself, and he was named Gusty Gillespie. Gusty, the Lord guard us, was what they call a black-mouth Prosbytarian, and wouldn't keep Christmas-day, the blagard, except what they call 'ould style'. Gusty was rather good-lookin' when seen in the dark, as well as Moll herself; and, indeed, it was purty well known that – accordin' as the talk went – it was in nightly meetings that they had an opportunity of becomin' detached to one another. The quensequence was, that in due time both families began to talk very seriously as to what was to be done. Moll's brother, Pawdien O'Rafferty, gave Gusty the best of two choices. What they were it's not worth spakin' about; but at any rate *one* of them was a poser, an' as Gusty knew his man, he soon came to his senses. Accordianly everything was deranged for their marriage, and it was appointed that they should be spliced by the Rev. Samuel M'Shuttle, the Prosbytarian parson, on the following Sunday.

"Now this was the first marriage that had happened for a long time in the neighbourhood betune a black-mouth an' a Catholic, an' of coorse there was strong objections on both sides aginst it; an' begad, only for one thing, it would never 'a tuck place at all. At any rate, faix, there was one of the bride's uncles, ould Harry Connolly, a fairy-man, who could cure all complaints wid a secret he had, and as he didn't wish to see his niece married upon sich a fellow, he fought bitterly against the match. All Moll's friends, however, stood up for the marriage barrin' him, an' of coorse the Sunday was appointed, as I said, that they were to be dove-tailed together.

"Well, the day arrived, and Moll, as became her, went to mass, and Gusty to meeting, afther which they were to join one another in Jack Rafferty's, where the priest, Father M'Sorley, was to slip up afther mass to take his dinner wid them, and to keep Misther M'Shuttle, who was to marry them, company. Nobody remained at home but ould Jack Rafferty an' his wife, who stopped to dress the dinner, for, to tell the truth, it was to be a great let-out entirely. Maybe, if all was known, too, that Father M'Sorley was to give them a cast of his office over an' above the ministher, in regard that Moll's friends were not altogether satisfied at the kind of marriage which M'Shuttle could give them. The sorrow may care about that – splice here – splice there – all I can say is, that when Mrs. Rafferty was goin' to tie up a big bag pudden, in walks Harry Connolly, the fairy-man, in a rage, and shouts out – 'Blood and blunderbushes, what are yez here for?'

"'Arrah why, Harry? Why, avick?'

"'Why, the sun's in the suds and the moon in the high Horicks; there's a clipstick comin' an, an' there you're both as unconsarned as if it was about to rain mether. Go out and cross yourselves three times in the name o' the four Mandromarvins, for as prophecy says: – Fill the pot, Eddy, supernaculum – a blazing star's a rare spectaculum. Go out both of you and look at the sun, I say, an' ye'll see the condition he's in – off!'

"Begad, sure enough, Jack gave a bounce to the door, and his wife leaped like a two-year-ould, till they were both got on a stile beside the house to see what was wrong in the sky.

"'Arrah, what is it, Jack,' said she; 'can you see anything?'

"'No,' says he, 'sorra the full o' my eye of anything I can spy, barrin' the sun himself, that's not visible in regard of the clouds. God guard us! I doubt there's something to happen.'

"'If there wasn't, Jack, what 'ud put Harry, that knows so much, in the state he's in?'

"'I doubt it's this marriage,' said Jack: 'betune ourselves, it's not over an' above religious for Moll to marry a black-mouth, an' only for –; but it can't be helped now, though you see not a taste o' the sun is willin' to show his face upon it.'

"'As to that,' says the wife, winkin' wid both her eyes, 'if Gusty's satisfied wid Moll, it's enough. I know who'll carry the whip hand, anyhow; but in the manetime let us ax Harry 'ithin what ails the sun.'

"Well, they accordianly went in an' put the question to him:

"'Harry, what's wrong, ahagur? What is it now, for if anybody alive knows, 'tis yourself?'

"'Ah!' said Harry, screwin' his mouth wid a kind of a dhry smile, 'the sun has a hard twist o' the cholic; but never mind that, I tell you you'll have a merrier weddin' than you think, that's all'; and havin' said this, he put on his hat and left the house.

"Now, Harry's answer relieved them very much, and so, afther calling to him to be back for the dinner, Jack sat down to take a shough o' the pipe, and the wife lost no time in tying up the pudden and puttin' it in the pot to be boiled.

"In this way things went on well enough for a while, Jack smokin' away, an' the wife cookin' and dhressin' at the rate of a hunt. At last, Jack, while sittin', as I said, contentedly at the fire, thought he could persave an odd dancin' kind of motion in the pot that puzzled him a good deal.

"'Katty,' said he, 'what the dickens is in this pot on the fire?'

"'Nerra thing but the big pudden. Why do you ax?' says she.

"'Why,' said he, 'if ever a pot tuck it into its head to dance a jig, and this did. Thundher and sparbles, look at it!'

"Begad, it was thrue enough; there was the pot bobbin' up an' down and from side to side, jiggin' it away as merry as a grig; an' it was quite aisy to see that it wasn't the pot itself, but what was inside of it, that brought about the hornpipe.

"'Be the hole o' my coat,' shouted Jack, 'there's something alive in it, or it would never cut sich capers!'

"'Be gorra, there is, Jack; something sthrange entirely has got into it. Wirra, man alive, what's to be done?'

"Jist as she spoke, the pot seemed to cut the buckle in prime style, and afther a spring that 'ud shame a dancin'-masther, off flew the lid, and out bounced the pudden itself, hoppin', as nimble as a pea on a drum-head, about the floor. Jack blessed himself, and Katty crossed herself. Jack shouted, and Katty screamed. 'In the name of goodness, keep your distance; no one here injured you!'

"The pudden, however, made a set at him, and Jack lepped first on a chair and then on the kitchen table to avoid it. It then danced towards Kitty, who was now repatin' her prayers at the top of her voice, while the cunnin' thief of a pudden was hoppin' and jiggin' it round her, as if it was amused at her distress.

"'If I could get the pitchfork,' said Jack, 'I'd dale wid it – by goxty I'd thry its mettle.'

"'No, no,' shouted Katty, thinkin' there was a fairy in it; 'let us spake it fair. Who knows what harm it might do? Aisy now,' said she to the pudden, 'aisy, dear; don't harm honest people that never meant to offend you. It wasn't us – no, in troth, it was ould Harry Connolly that bewitched you; pursue *him* if you wish, but spare a woman like me; for, whisper, dear, I'm not in a condition to be frightened – troth I'm not.'

"The pudden, bedad, seemed to take her at her word, and danced away from her towards Jack, who, like the wife, believin' there was a fairy in it, an' that spakin' it fair was the best plan, thought he would give it a soft word as well as her.

"'Plase your honour,' said Jack, 'she only spaiks the truth; an', upon my voracity, we both feels much oblaiged to your honour for your quietness. Faith, it's quite clear that if you weren't a gentlemanly pudden all out, you'd act otherwise. Ould Harry, the rogue, is your mark; he's jist gone down the road there, and if you go fast you'll overtake him. Be me song, your dancin' masther did his duty, anyhow. Thank your honour! God speed you, an' may you never meet wid a parson or alderman in your thravels!'

"Jist as Jack spoke the pudden appeared to take the hint, for it quietly hopped out, and as the house was directly on the road-side, turned down towards the bridge, the very way that ould Harry went. It was very natural, of coorse, that Jack and Katty should go out to see how it intended to thravel; and, as the day was Sunday, it was but natural, too, that a greater number of people than usual were passin' the road. This was a fact; and when Jack and his wife were seen followin' the pudden, the whole neighbourhood was soon up and afther it.

"'Jack Rafferty, what is it? Katty, ahagur, will you tell us what it manes?'

"'Why,' replied Katty, 'it's my big pudden that's bewitched, an' it's now hot foot pursuin' –'; here she stopped, not wishin' to mention her brother's name – '*someone* or other that surely put *pishrogues* an it.'

"This was enough; Jack, now seein' that he had assistance, found his courage comin' back to him; so says he to Katty, 'Go home,' says he, 'an' lose no time in makin' another pudden as good, an' here's Paddy Scanlan's wife, Bridget, says she'll let you boil it on her fire, as you'll want our own to dress the rest o' the dinner: and Paddy himself will lend me a pitchfork, for purshuin to the morsel of that same pudden will escape till I let the wind out of it, now that I've the neighbours to back an' support me,' says Jack.

"This was agreed to, and Katty went back to prepare a fresh pudden, while Jack an' half the townland pursued the other wid spades, graips, pitchforks, scythes, flails, and all possible description of instruments. On the pudden went, however, at the rate of about six Irish miles an hour, an' sich a chase never was seen. Catholics, Prodestants, an' Prosbytarians, were all afther it, armed, as I said, an' bad end to the thing but its own activity could save it. Here it made a hop, and there a prod was made at it; but off it went, an' someone, as eager to get a slice at it on the other side, got the prod instead of the pudden. Big Frank Farrell, the miller of Ballyboulteen, got a prod backwards that brought a hullabaloo out of him you might hear at the other end of the parish. One got a slice of a scythe, another a whack of a flail, a third a rap of a spade that made him look nine ways at wanst.

"'Where is it goin'?' asked one. 'My life for you, it's on its way to Meeting. Three cheers for it if it turns to Carntaul.' 'Prod the sowl out of it, if it's a Prodestan',' shouted the others; 'if it turns to the left, slice it into pancakes. We'll have no Prodestan' puddens here.'

"Begad, by this time the people were on the point of beginnin' to have a regular fight about it, when, very fortunately, it took a short turn down a little by-lane that led towards the Methodist praichin-house, an' in an instant all parties were in an uproar against it as a Methodist pudden. 'It's a Wesleyan,' shouted several voices; 'an' by this an' by that, into a Methodist chapel it won't put a foot today, or we'll lose a fall. Let the wind out of it. Come, boys, where's your pitchforks?'

"The divle purshuin to the one of them, however, ever could touch the pudden, an' jist when they thought they had it up against the gavel of the Methodist chapel, begad it gave them the slip, and hops over to the left, clane into the river, and sails away before all their eyes as light as an egg-shell.

"Now, it so happened that a little below this place, the demesne-wall of Colonel Bragshaw was built up to the very edge of the river on each side of its banks; and so findin' there was a stop put to their pursuit of it, they went home again, every man, woman, and child of them, puzzled to think what the pudden was at all, what it meant, or where it was goin'! Had Jack Rafferty an' his wife been willin' to let out the opinion they held about Harry Connolly bewitchin' it, there is no doubt of it but poor Harry might be badly trated by the crowd, when their blood was up. They had sense enough, howandiver, to keep that to themselves, for Harry bein' an' ould bachelor, was a kind friend to the Raffertys. So, of coorse, there was all kinds of talk about it – some guessin' this, and some guessin' that –one party sayin' the pudden was of there side, another party denyin' it, an' insistin' it belonged to them, an' so on.

"In the manetime, Katty Rafferty, for 'fraid the dinner might come short, went home and made another pudden much about the same size as the one that had escaped, and bringin' it over to their next neighbour, Paddy Scanlan's, it was put into a pot and placed on the fire to boil, hopin' that it might be done in time, espishilly as they were to have the ministher, who loved a warm slice of a good pudden as well as e'er a gintleman in Europe.

"Anyhow, the day passed; Moll and Gusty were made man an' wife, an' no two could be more lovin'. Their friends that had been asked to the weddin' were saunterin' about in pleasant little groups till dinner-time, chattin' an' laughin'; but, above all things, sthrivin' to account for the figaries of the pudden; for, to tell the truth, its adventures had now gone through the whole parish.

"Well, at any rate, dinner-time was dhrawin' near, and Paddy Scanlan was sittin' comfortably wid his wife at the fire, the pudden boilen before their eyes, when in walks Harry Connolly, in a flutter, shoutin' – 'Blood an' blunderbushes, what are yez here for?'

"'Arra, why, Harry – why, avick?' said Mrs. Scanlan.

"'Why,' said Harry, 'the sun's in the suds an' the moon in the high Horicks! Here's a clipstick comin' an, an' there you sit as unconsarned as if it was about to rain mether! Go out both of you, an' look at the sun, I say, and ye'll see the condition he's in – off!'

"'Ay, but, Harry, what's that rowled up in the tail of your *cothamore* (big coat)?'

"'Out wid yez,' said Harry, 'an' pray aginst the clipstick – the sky's fallin'!'

"Begad, it was hard to say whether Paddy or the wife got out first, they were so much alarmed by Harry's wild thin face an' piercin' eyes; so out they went to see what was wondherful in the sky, an' kep' lookin' an' lookin' in every direction, but not a thing was to be seen, barrin' the sun shinin' down wid great good-humour, an' not a single cloud in the sky.

"Paddy an' the wife now came in laughin', to scould Harry, who, no doubt, was a great wag in his way when he wished. 'Musha, bad scran to you, Harry –.' They had time to say no more, howandiver, for, as they were goin' into the door, they met him comin' out of it wid a reek of smoke out of his tail like a lime-kiln.

"'Harry,' shouted Bridget, 'my sowl to glory, but the tail of your cothamore's a-fire – you'll be burned. Don't you see the smoke that's out of it?'

"'Cross yourselves three times,' said Harry, widout stoppin', or even lookin' behind him, 'for, as the prophecy says –Fill the pot, Eddy –' They could hear no more, for Harry appeared to feel like a man that carried something a great deal hotter than he wished, as anyone might see by the liveliness of his motions, and the quare faces he was forced to make as he went along.

"'What the dickens is he carryin' in the skirts of his big coat?' asked Paddy.

"'My sowl to happiness, but maybe he has stole the pudden,' said Bridget, 'for it's known that many a sthrange thing he does.'

"They immediately examined the pot, but found that the pudden was there as safe as tuppence, an' this puzzled them the more, to think what it was he could be carryin' about wid him in the manner he did. But little they knew what he had done while they were sky-gazin'!

"Well, anyhow, the day passed and the dinner was ready, an' no doubt but a fine gatherin' there was to partake of it. The Prosbytarian ministher met the Methodist praicher – a divilish stretcher of an appetite he had, in throth – on their way to Jack Rafferty's, an' as he knew he could take the liberty, why he insisted on his dinin' wid him; for, afther all, begad, in thim times the clargy of all descriptions lived upon the best footin' among one another, not all as one as now – but no matther. Well, they had nearly finished their dinner, when Jack Rafferty himself axed Katty for the pudden; but, jist as he spoke, in it came as big as a mess-pot.

"'Gintlemen,' said he, 'I hope none of you will refuse tastin' a bit of Katty's pudden; I don't mane the dancin' one that tuck to its thravels today, but a good solid fellow that she med since.'

"'To be sure we won't,' replied the priest; 'so, Jack, put a thrifle on them three plates at your right hand, and send them over here to the clargy, an' maybe,' he said, laughin' – for he was a droll good-humoured man – 'maybe, Jack, we won't set you a proper example.'

"'Wid a heart an' a half, yer reverence an' gintlemen; in throth, it's not a bad example ever any of you set us at the likes, or ever will set us, I'll go bail. An' sure I only wish it was betther fare I had for you; but we're humble people, gintlemen, and so you can't expect to meet here what you would in higher places.'

"'Betther a male of herbs,' said the Methodist praicher, 'where pace is –.' He had time to go no farther, however; for much to his amazement, the priest and the ministher started up from the table jist as he was goin' to swallow the first spoonful of the pudden, and before you could say Jack Robinson, started away at a lively jig down the floor.

"At this moment a neighbour's son came runnin' in, an' tould them that the parson was comin' to see the new-married couple, an' wish them all happiness; an' the words were scarcely out of his mouth when he made his appearance. What to think he knew not, when he saw the ministher footing it away at the rate of a weddin'. He had very little time, however, to think; for, before he could sit down, up starts the Methodist praicher, and clappin' his two fists in his sides chimes in in great style along wid him.

"'Jack Rafferty,' says he – and, by the way, Jack was his tenant – 'what the dickens does all this mane?' says he; 'I'm amazed!'

"'The not a particle o' me can tell you,' says Jack; 'but will your reverence jist taste a morsel o' pudden, merely that the young couple may boast that you ait at their weddin'; for sure if *you* wouldn't, *who* would?'

"'Well,' says he, 'to gratify them I will; so just a morsel. But, Jack, this bates Bannagher,' says he again, puttin' the spoonful o' pudden into his mouth; 'has there been dhrink here?'

"'Oh, the divle a *spudh*,' says Jack, 'for although there's plinty in the house, faith, it appears the gintlemen wouldn't wait for it. Unless they tuck it elsewhere, I can make nothin' of this.'

"He had scarcely spoken, when the parson, who was an active man, cut a caper a yard high, an' before you could bless yourself, the three clargy were hard at work dancin', as if for a wager. Begad, it would be unpossible for me to tell you the state the whole meetin' was in when they seen this. Some were hoarse wid laughin'; some turned up their eyes wid wondher; many thought them mad, an' others thought they had turned up their little fingers a thrifle too often.

"'Be goxty, it's a burnin' shame,' said one, 'to see three black-mouth clargy in sich a state at this early hour!' 'Thundher an' ounze, what's over them at all?' says others; 'why, one would think they're bewitched. Holy Moses, look at the caper the Methodis cuts! An' as for the Recther, who would think he could handle his feet at such a rate! Be this an' be that, he cuts the buckle, and does the threblin' step aiquil to Paddy Horaghan, the dancin'-masther himself? An' see! Bad cess to the morsel of the parson that's not hard at *Peace upon a trancher*, an' it of a Sunday too! Whirroo, gintlemen, the fun's in yez afther all – whish! more power to yez!'

"The sorra's own fun they had, an' no wondher; but judge of what they felt, when all at once they saw ould Jack Rafferty himself bouncin' in among them, and footing it away like the best o' them. Bedad, no play could come up to it, an' nothin' could be heard but laughin', shouts of encouragement, and clappin' of hands like mad. Now the minute Jack Rafferty left the chair where he had been carvin' the pudden, ould Harry Connolly comes over and claps himself down in his place, in ordher to send it round, of coorse; an' he was scarcely sated, when who should make his appearance but Barney Hartigan, the piper. Barney, by the way, had been sent for early in the day, but bein' from home when the message for him went, he couldn't come any sooner.

"'Begorra,' said Barney, 'you're airly at the work, gintlemen! But what does this mane? But, divle may care, yez shan't want the music while there's a blast in the pipes, anyhow!' So sayin' he gave them *Jig Polthogue*, an' after that *Kiss My Lady*, in his best style.

"In the manetime the fun went on thick an' threefold, for it must be remimbered that Harry, the ould knave, was at the pudden; an' maybe he didn't sarve it about in double quick time too. The first he helped was the bride, and, before you could say chopstick, she was at it hard an' fast before the Methodist praicher, who gave a jolly spring before her that threw them into convulsions. Harry liked this, and made up his mind soon to find partners for the rest; so he accordianly sent the pudden about like lightnin'; an' to make a long story short, barrin' the piper an' himself, there wasn't a pair o' heels in the house but was as busy at the dancin' as if their lives depinded on it.

"'Barney,' says Harry, 'just taste a morsel o' this pudden; divle the such a bully of a pudden ever you ett; here, your sowl! Thry a snig of it – it's beautiful.'

"'To be sure I will,' says Barney. 'I'm not the boy to refuse a good thing; but, Harry, be quick, for you know my hands is engaged, an' it would be a thousand pities not to keep them in music, an' they so well inclined. Thank you, Harry; begad that is a famous pudden; but blood an' turnips, what's this for?'

"The word was scarcely out of his mouth when he bounced up, pipes an' all, an' dashed into the middle of the party. 'Hurroo, your sowls, let us make a night of it! The Ballyboulteen boys for ever! Go it, your reverence – turn your partner – heel an' toe, ministher. Good! Well done again – Whish! Hurroo! Here's for Ballyboulteen, an' the sky over it!'

"Bad luck to the sich a set ever was seen together in this world, or will again, I suppose. The worst, however, wasn't come yet, for jist as they were in the very heat an' fury of the dance, what do you think comes hoppin' in among them but another pudden, as nimble an' merry as the first! That was enough; they all had heard of – the ministhers among the rest – an' most o' them had seen the other pudden, and knew that there must be a fairy in it, sure enough. Well, as I said, in it comes to the thick o' them; but the very appearance of it was enough. Off the three clargy danced, and off the whole weddiners danced afther them, everyone makin' the best of their way home; but not a sowl of them able to break out of the step, if they were to be hanged for it. Throth it wouldn't lave a laugh in you to see the parson dancin' down the road on his way home, and the ministher and Methodist praicher cuttin' the buckle as they went along in the opposite direction. To make short work of it, they all danced home at last, wid scarce a puff of wind in them, the bride and bridegroom danced away to bed; an' now, boys, come an' let us dance the *Horo Lheig* in the barn 'idout. But you see, boys, before we go, an' in ordher that I may make everything plain, I had as good tell you that Harry, in crossing the bridge of Ballyboulteen, a couple of miles below Squire Bragshaw's demense-wall, saw the pudden floatin' down the river – the truth is he was waitin' for it; but be this as it may, he took it out, for the wather had made it as clane as a new pin, and tuckin' it up in the tail of his big coat, contrived, as you all guess, I suppose, to change it while Paddy Scanlan an' the wife were examinin' the sky; an' for the other, he contrived to bewitch it in the same manner, by gettin' a fairy to go into it, for, indeed, it was purty well known that the same Harry was hand an' glove wid the *good people*. Others will tell you that it was half a pound of quicksilver he put into it; but that doesn't stand to raison. At any rate, boys, I have tould you the adventures of the Mad Pudden of Ballyboulteen; but I don't wish to tell you many other things about it that happened – *for fraid I'd tell a lie.*"

Princess Finola and the Dwarf

A LONG, LONG TIME AGO there lived in a little hut in the midst of a bare, brown, lonely moor an old woman and a young girl. The old woman was withered, sour-tempered, and dumb. The young girl was as sweet and as fresh as an opening rosebud, and her voice was as musical as the whisper of a stream in the woods in the hot days of summer. The little hut, made of branches woven closely together, was shaped like a beehive. In the centre of the hut a fire burned night and day from year's end to year's end, though it was never touched or tended by human hand. In the cold days and nights of winter it gave out light and heat that made the hut cosy and warm, but in the summer nights and days it gave out light only. With their heads to the wall of the hut and their feet towards the fire were two sleeping-couches – one of plain woodwork, in which slept the old woman; the other was Finola's. It was of bog-oak, polished as a looking-glass, and on it were carved flowers and birds of all kinds, that gleamed and shone in the light of the fire. This couch was fit for a princess, and a princess Finola was, though she did not know it herself.

Outside the hut the bare, brown, lonely moor stretched for miles on every side, but towards the east it was bounded by a range of mountains that looked to Finola blue in the daytime, but which put on a hundred changing colours as the sun went down. Nowhere was a house to be seen, nor a tree, nor a flower, nor sign of any living thing. From morning till night, nor hum of bee, nor song of bird, nor voice of man, nor any sound fell on Finola's ear. When the storm was in the air the great waves thundered on the shore beyond the mountains, and the wind shouted in the glens; but when it sped across the moor it lost its voice, and passed as silently as the dead. At first the silence frightened Finola, but she got used to it after a time, and often broke it by talking to herself and singing.

The only other person beside the old woman Finola ever saw was a dumb dwarf who, mounted on a broken-down horse, came once a month to the hut, bringing with him a sack of corn for the old woman and Finola. Although he couldn't speak to her, Finola was always glad to see the dwarf and his old horse, and she used to give them cake made with her own white hands. As for the dwarf he would have died for the little princess, he was so much in love with her, and often and often his heart was heavy and sad as he thought of her pining away in the lonely moor.

It chanced that he came one day, and she did not, as usual, come out to greet him. He made signs to the old woman, but she took up a stick and struck him, and beat his horse and drove him away; but as he was leaving he caught a glimpse of Finola at the door of the hut, and saw that she was crying. This sight made him so very miserable that he could think of nothing else but her sad face that he had always seen so bright, and he allowed the old horse to go on without minding where he was going. Suddenly he heard a voice saying: "It is time for you to come."

The dwarf looked, and right before him, at the foot of a green hill, was a little man not half as big as himself, dressed in a green jacket with brass buttons, and a red cap and tassel.

"It is time for you to come," he said the second time; "but you are welcome, anyhow. Get off your horse and come in with me, that I may touch your lips with the wand of speech, that we may have a talk together."

The dwarf got off his horse and followed the little man through a hole in the side of a green hill. The hole was so small that he had to go on his hands and knees to pass through it, and when he was able to stand he was only the same height as the little fairyman. After walking three or four steps they were in a splendid room, as bright as day. Diamonds sparkled in the roof as stars sparkle in the sky when the night is without a cloud. The roof rested on golden pillars, and between the pillars were silver lamps, but their light was dimmed by that of the diamonds. In the middle of the room was a table, on which were two golden plates and two silver knives and forks, and a brass bell as big as a hazelnut, and beside the table were two little chairs covered with blue silk and satin.

"Take a chair," said the fairy, "and I will ring for the wand of speech."

The dwarf sat down, and the fairyman rang the little brass bell, and in came a little weeny dwarf no bigger than your hand.

"Bring me the wand of speech," said the fairy, and the weeny dwarf bowed three times and walked out backwards, and in a minute he returned, carrying a little black wand with a red berry at the top of it, and, giving it to the fairy, he bowed three times and walked out backwards as he had done before.

The little man waved the rod three times over the dwarf, and struck him once on the right shoulder and once on the left shoulder, and then touched his lips with the red berry, and said: "Speak!"

The dwarf spoke, and he was so rejoiced at hearing the sound of his own voice that he danced about the room.

"Who are you at all, at all?" said he to the fairy.

"Who is yourself?" said the fairy. "But come, before we have any talk let us have something to eat, for I am sure you are hungry."

Then they sat down to table, and the fairy rang the little brass bell twice, and the weeny dwarf brought in two boiled snails in their shells, and when they had eaten the snails he brought in a dormouse, and when they had eaten the dormouse he brought in two wrens, and when they had eaten the wrens he brought in two nuts full of wine, and they became very merry, and the fairyman sang 'Cooleen dhas', and the dwarf sang 'The little blackbird of the glen'.

"Did you ever hear the 'Foggy Dew?'" said the fairy.

"No," said the dwarf.

"Well, then, I'll give it to you; but we must have some more wine."

And the wine was brought, and he sang the 'Foggy Dew', and the dwarf said it was the sweetest song he had ever heard, and that the fairyman's voice would coax the birds off the bushes.

"You asked me who I am?" said the fairy.

"I did," said the dwarf.

"And I asked you who is yourself?"

"You did," said the dwarf.

"And who are you, then?"

"Well, to tell the truth, I don't know," said the dwarf, and he blushed like a rose.

"Well, tell me what you know about yourself."

"I remember nothing at all," said the dwarf, "before the day I found myself going along with a crowd of all sorts of people to the great fair of the Liffey. We had to pass by the king's palace on our way, and as we were passing the king sent for a band of jugglers to come and show their tricks before him. I followed the jugglers to look on, and when the play was over the king called me to him, and asked me who I was and where I came from. I was dumb then, and couldn't answer; but even if I could speak I could not tell him what he wanted to know, for I remember nothing of myself before that day. Then the king asked the jugglers, but they knew nothing about me, and no one knew anything, and then the king said he would take me into his service; and the only work I have to do is to go once a month with a bag of corn to the hut in the lonely moor."

"And there you fell in love with the little princess," said the fairy, winking at the dwarf.

The poor dwarf blushed twice as much as he had done before.

"You need not blush," said the fairy; "it is a good man's case. And now tell me, truly, do you love the princess, and what would you give to free her from the spell of enchantment that is over her?"

"I would give my life," said the dwarf.

"Well, then, listen to me," said the fairy. "The Princess Finola was banished to the lonely moor by the king, your master. He killed her father, who was the rightful king, and would have killed Finola, only he was told by an old sorceress that if he killed her he would die himself on the same day, and she advised him to banish her to the lonely moor, and she said she would fling a spell of enchantment over it, and that until the spell was broken Finola could not leave the moor. And the sorceress also promised that she would send an old woman to watch over the princess by night and by day, so that no harm should come to her; but she told the king that he himself should select a messenger to take food to the hut, and that he should look out for someone who had never seen or heard of the princess, and whom he could trust never to tell anyone anything about her; and that is the reason he selected you."

"Since you know so much," said the dwarf, "can you tell me who I am, and where I came from?"

"You will know that time enough," said the fairy. "I have given you back your speech. It will depend solely on yourself whether you will get back your memory of who and what you were before the day you entered the king's service. But are you really willing to try and break the spell of enchantment and free the princess?"

"I am," said the dwarf.

"Whatever it will cost you?"

"Yes, if it cost me my life," said the dwarf; "but tell me, how can the spell be broken?"

"Oh, it is easy enough to break the spell if you have the weapons," said the fairy.

"And what are they, and where are they?" said the dwarf.

"The spear of the shining haft and the dark blue blade and the silver shield," said the fairy. "They are on the farther bank of the Mystic Lake in the Island of the Western Seas. They are there for the man who is bold enough to seek them. If you are the man who will bring them back to the lonely moor you will only have to strike the shield three times with the haft, and three times with the blade of the spear, and the silence of the moor will be broken for ever, the spell of enchantment will be removed, and the princess will be free."

"I will set out at once," said the dwarf, jumping from his chair.

"And whatever it cost you," said the fairy, "will you pay the price?"

"I will," said the dwarf.

"Well, then, mount your horse, give him his head, and he will take you to the shore opposite the Island of the Mystic Lake. You must cross to the island on his back, and make your way through the water-steeds that swim around the island night and day to guard it; but woe betide you if you attempt to cross without paying the price, for if you do the angry water-steeds will rend you and your horse to pieces. And when you come to the Mystic Lake you must wait until the waters are as red as wine, and then swim your horse across it, and on the farther side you will find the spear and shield; but woe betide you if you attempt to cross the lake before you pay the price, for if you do, the black Cormorants of the Western Seas will pick the flesh from your bones."

"What is the price?" said the dwarf.

"You will know that time enough," said the fairy; "but now go, and good luck go with you."

The dwarf thanked the fairy, and said goodbye! He then threw the reins on his horse's neck, and started up the hill, that seemed to grow bigger and bigger as he ascended, and the dwarf soon found that what he took for a hill was a great mountain. After travelling all the day, toiling up by steep crags and heathery passes, he reached the top as the sun was setting in the ocean, and he saw far below him out in the waters the island of the Mystic Lake.

He began his descent to the shore, but long before he reached it the sun had set, and darkness, unpierced by a single star, dropped upon the sea. The old horse, worn out by his long and painful journey, sank beneath him, and the dwarf was so tired that he rolled off his back and fell asleep by his side.

He awoke at the breaking of the morning, and saw that he was almost at the water's edge. He looked out to sea, and saw the island, but nowhere could he see the water-steeds, and he began to fear he must have taken a wrong course in the night, and that the island before him was not the one he was in search of. But even while he was so thinking he heard fierce and angry snortings, and, coming swiftly from the island to the shore, he saw the swimming and prancing steeds. Sometimes their heads and manes only were visible, and sometimes, rearing, they rose half out of the water, and, striking it with their hoofs, churned it into foam, and tossed the white spray to the skies. As they approached nearer and nearer their snortings became more terrible, and their nostrils shot forth clouds of vapour. The dwarf trembled at the sight and sound, and his old horse, quivering in every limb, moaned piteously, as if in pain. On came the steeds, until they almost touched the shore, then rearing, they seemed about to spring on to it. The frightened dwarf turned his head to fly, and as he did so he heard the twang of a golden harp, and right before him who should he see but the little man of the hills, holding a harp in one hand and striking the strings with the other.

"Are you ready to pay the price?" said he, nodding gaily to the dwarf.

As he asked the question, the listening water-steeds snorted more furiously than ever.

"Are you ready to pay the price?" said the little man a second time.

A shower of spray, tossed on shore by the angry steeds, drenched the dwarf to the skin, and sent a cold shiver to his bones, and he was so terrified that he could not answer.

"For the third and last time, are you ready to pay the price?" asked the fairy, as he flung the harp behind him and turned to depart.

When the dwarf saw him going he thought of the little princess in the lonely moor, and his courage came back, and he answered bravely:

"Yes, I am ready."

The water-steeds, hearing his answer, and snorting with rage, struck the shore with their pounding hoofs.

"Back to your waves!" cried the little harper; and as he ran his fingers across his lyre, the frightened steeds drew back into the waters.

"What is the price?" asked the dwarf.

"Your right eye," said the fairy; and before the dwarf could say a word, the fairy scooped out the eye with his finger, and put it into his pocket.

The dwarf suffered most terrible agony; but he resolved to bear it for the sake of the little princess. Then the fairy sat down on a rock at the edge of the sea, and, after striking a few notes, he began to play the 'Strains of Slumber'.

The sound crept along the waters, and the steeds, so ferocious a moment before, became perfectly still. They had no longer any motion of their own, and they floated on the top of the tide like foam before a breeze.

"Now," said the fairy, as he led the dwarf's horse to the edge of the tide.

The dwarf urged the horse into the water, and once out of his depth, the old horse struck out boldly for the island. The sleeping water-steeds drifted helplessly against him, and in a short time he reached the island safely, and he neighed joyously as his hoofs touched solid ground.

The dwarf rode on and on, until he came to a bridle-path, and following this, it led him up through winding lanes, bordered with golden furze that filled the air with fragrance, and brought him to the summit of the green hills that girdled and looked down on the Mystic Lake. Here the horse stopped of his own accord, and the dwarf's heart beat quickly as his eye rested on the lake, that, clipped round by the ring of hills, seemed in the breezeless and sunlit air –

> As still as death,
> And as bright as life can be.

After gazing at it for a long time, he dismounted, and lay at his ease in the pleasant grass. Hour after hour passed, but no change came over the face of the waters, and when the night fell sleep closed the eyelids of the dwarf.

The song of the lark awoke him in the early morning, and, starting up, he looked at the lake, but its waters were as bright as they had been the day before.

Towards midday he beheld what he thought was a black cloud sailing across the sky from east to west. It seemed to grow larger as it came nearer and nearer, and when it was high above the lake he saw it was a huge bird, the shadow of whose outstretched wings darkened the waters of the lake; and the dwarf knew it was one of the Cormorants of the Western Seas. As it descended slowly, he saw that it held in one of its claws a branch of a tree larger than a full-grown oak, and laden with clusters of ripe red berries. It alighted at some distance from the dwarf, and, after resting for a time, it began to eat the berries and to throw the stones into the lake, and wherever a stone fell a bright red stain appeared in the water. As he looked more closely at the bird the dwarf saw that it had all the signs of old age, and he could not help wondering how it was able to carry such a heavy tree.

Later in the day, two other birds, as large as the first, but younger, came up from the west and settled down beside him. They also ate the berries, and throwing the stones into the lake it was soon as red as wine.

When they had eaten all the berries, the young birds began to pick the decayed feathers off the old bird and to smooth his plumage. As soon as they had completed their task, he rose slowly from the hill and sailed out over the lake, and dropping down on the waters, dived beneath them. In a moment he came to the surface, and shot up into the air with a joyous cry, and flew off to the west in all the vigour of renewed youth, followed by the other birds.

When they had gone so far that they were like specks in the sky, the dwarf mounted his horse and descended towards the lake.

He was almost at the margin, and in another minute would have plunged in, when he heard a fierce screaming in the air, and before he had time to look up, the three birds were hovering over the lake.

The dwarf drew back frightened.

The birds wheeled over his head, and then, swooping down, they flew close to the water, covering it with their wings, and uttering harsh cries.

Then, rising to a great height, they folded their wings and dropped headlong, like three rocks, on the lake, crashing its surface, and scattering a wine-red shower upon the hills.

Then the dwarf remembered what the fairy told him, that if he attempted to swim the lake, without paying the price, the three Cormorants of the Western Seas would pick the flesh off his bones. He knew not what to do, and was about to turn away, when he heard once more the twang of the golden harp, and the little fairy of the hills stood before him.

"Faint heart never won fair lady," said the little harper. "Are you ready to pay the price? The spear and shield are on the opposite bank, and the Princess Finola is crying this moment in the lonely moor."

At the mention of Finola's name the dwarf's heart grew strong.

"Yes," he said; "I am ready – win or die. What is the price?"

"Your left eye," said the fairy. And as soon as said he scooped out the eye, and put it in his pocket. The poor blind dwarf almost fainted with pain.

"It's your last trial," said the fairy, "and now do what I tell you. Twist your horse's mane round your right hand, and I will lead him to the water. Plunge in, and fear not. I gave you back your speech. When you reach the opposite bank you will get back your memory, and you will know who and what you are."

Then the fairy led the horse to the margin of the lake.

"In with you now, and good luck go with you," said the fairy.

The dwarf urged the horse. He plunged into the lake, and went down and down until his feet struck the bottom. Then he began to ascend, and as he came near the surface of the water the dwarf thought he saw a glimmering light, and when he rose above the water he saw the bright sun shining and the green hills before him, and he shouted with joy at finding his sight restored.

But he saw more. Instead of the old horse he had ridden into the lake he was bestride a noble steed, and as the steed swam to the bank the dwarf felt a change coming over himself, and an unknown vigour in his limbs.

When the steed touched the shore he galloped up the hillside, and on the top of the hill was a silver shield, bright as the sun, resting against a spear standing upright in the ground.

The dwarf jumped off, and, running towards the shield, he saw himself as in a looking-glass.

He was no longer a dwarf, but a gallant knight. At that moment his memory came back to him, and he knew he was Conal, one of the Knights of the Red Branch, and he remembered now that the spell of dumbness and deformity had been cast upon him by the Witch of the Palace of the Quicken Trees.

Slinging his shield upon his left arm, he plucked the spear from the ground and leaped on to his horse. With a light heart he swam back over the lake, and nowhere could he see the black Cormorants of the Western Seas, but three white swans floating abreast followed him to the bank. When he reached the bank he galloped down to the sea, and crossed to the shore.

Then he flung the reins upon his horse's neck, and swifter than the wind the gallant horse swept on and on, and it was not long until he was bounding over the enchanted moor. Wherever his hoofs struck the ground, grass and flowers sprang up, and great trees with leafy branches rose on every side.

At last the knight reached the little hut. Three times he struck the shield with the haft and three times with the blade of his spear. At the last blow the hut disappeared, and standing before him was the little princess.

The knight took her in his arms and kissed her; then he lifted her on to the horse, and, leaping up before her, he turned towards the north, to the palace of the Red Branch Knights, and as they rode on beneath the leafy trees from every tree the birds sang out, for the spell of silence over the lonely moor was broken for ever.

The Wicked Widow

THE EVIL SPELLS OVER MILK AND BUTTER are generally practised by women, and arise from some feeling of malice or envy against a prosperous neighbour. But the spell will not work unless some portion of the milk is first given by consent. The people therefore are very reluctant to give away milk, unless to some friend that they could not suspect of evil. Tramps coming in to beg for a mug of milk should always be avoided, they may be witches in disguise; and even if milk is given, it must be drunk in the house, and not carried away out of it. In every case the person who enters must give a hand to the churn, and say, "God bless all here."

A young farmer, one of the fine handsome fellows of the West, named Hugh Connor, who was also well off and rich, took to wife a pretty young girl of the village called Mary, one of the Leydons, and there was no better girl in all the country round, and they were very comfortable and happy together. But Hugh Connor had been keeping company before his marriage with a young widow of the place, who had designs on him, and was filled with rage when Mary Leydon was selected for Connor's bride, in place of herself. Then a desire for vengeance rose up in her heart, and she laid her plans accordingly. First she got a fairy woman to teach her some witch secrets and spells, and then by great pretence of love and affection for Mary Connor, she got frequent admission to the house, soothing and flattering the young wife; and on churning days she would especially make it a point to come in and offer a helping hand, and if the cakes were on the griddle, she would sit down to watch and turn them. But it so happened that always on these days the cakes were sure to be burned and spoiled, and the butter would not rise in the churn, or if any did come, it was sour and bad, and of no use for the market. But still the widow kept on visiting, and soothing, and flattering, till Mary Connor thought she was the very best friend to her in the whole wide world, though it was true that whenever the widow came to the house something evil happened. The best dish fell down of itself off the dresser and broke; or the rain got in through the roof, and Mary's new cashmere gown, a present that had come to her all the way from Dublin, was quite ruined and spoiled. But worse came, for the cow sickened, and a fine young brood of turkeys walked straight into the lake and got drowned. And still worst of all, the picture of the Blessed Virgin Mother, that was pinned up to the wall, fell down one day, and was blown into the fire and burned.

After this, what luck could be on the house? and Mary's heart sank within her, and she fairly broke down, and cried her very life out in a torrent of tears.

Now it so happened that an old woman with a blue cloak, and the hood of it over her head, a stranger, was passing by at the time, and she stepped in and asked Mary kindly what ailed her. So Mary told her all her misfortunes, and how everything in the house seemed bewitched for evil.

"Now," said the stranger, "I see it all, for I am wise, and know the mysteries. Some one with the Evil Eye comes to your house. We must find out who it is."

Then Mary told her that the nearest friend she had was the widow, but she was so sweet and kind, no one could suspect her of harm.

"We'll see," said the stranger, "only do as I bid you, and have everything ready when she comes."

"She will be here soon," said Mary, "for it is churning day, and she always comes to help exactly at noon."

"Then I'll begin at once; and now close the door fast," said the stranger.

And with that, she threw some herbs on the fire, so that a great smoke arose. Then she took all the plough irons that were about, and one of them she drove into the ground close beside the churn, and put a live coal beside it; and the other irons she heated red-hot in the fire, and still threw on more herbs to make a thick smoke, which Mary thought smelt like the incense in the church. Then with a hot iron rod from the fire, the strange woman made the sign of the cross on the threshold, and another over the hearth. After which a loud roaring was heard outside, and the widow rushed in crying out that a hot stick was running through her heart, and all her body was on fire. And then she dropped down on the floor in a fit, and her face became quite black, and her limbs worked in convulsions.

"Now," said the stranger, "you see who it is put the Evil Eye on all your house; but the spell has been broken at last. Send for the men to carry her back to her own house, and never let that witch-woman cross your threshold again."

After this the stranger disappeared, and was seen no more in the village.

Now when all the neighbours heard the story, they would have no dealings with the widow. She was shunned and hated; and no respectable person would be seen talking to her, and she went by the name of the Evil Witch. So her life was very miserable, and not long after she died of sheer vexation and spite, all by herself alone, for no one would go near her; and the night of the wake no one went to offer a prayer, for they said the devil would be there in person to look after his own. And no one would walk with her coffin to the grave, for they said the devil was waiting at the churchyard gate for her; and they firmly believe to this day that her body was carried away on that night from the graveyard by the powers of darkness. But no one ventured to test the truth of the story by opening the coffin, so the weird legend remains still unsolved.

But as for Hugh Connor and the pretty Mary, they prospered after that in all things, and good luck and the blessing of God seemed to be evermore on them and their house, and their cattle, and their children. At the same time, Mary never omitted on churning days to put a red-hot horse-shoe under the churn according as the stranger had told her, who she firmly believed was a good fairy in disguise, who came to help her in the time of her sore trouble and anxiety.

The Hags of the Long Teeth

LONG AGO, IN THE OLD TIME, there came a party of gentlemen from Dublin to Loch Glynn a-hunting and a-fishing. They put up in the priest's house, as there was no inn in the little village.

The first day they went a-hunting, they went into the Wood of Driminuch, and it was not long till they routed a hare. They fired many a ball after him, but they could not bring him down. They followed him till they saw him going into a little house in the wood.

When they came to the door, they saw a great black dog, and he would not let them in.

"Put a ball through the beggar," said a man of them. He let fly a ball, but the dog caught it in his mouth, chewed it, and flung it on the ground. They fired another ball, and another, but the dog did the same thing with them. Then he began barking as loud as he could, and it was not long till there came out a hag, and every tooth in her head as long as the tongs. "What are you doing to my pup?" says the hag.

"A hare went into your house, and this dog won't let us in after him," says a man of the hunters.

"Lie down, pup," said the hag. Then she said: "Ye can come in if ye wish." The hunters were afraid to go in, but a man of them asked: "Is there any person in the house with you?"

"There are six sisters," said the old woman. "We should like to see them," said the hunters. No sooner had he said the word than the six old women came out, and each of them with teeth as long as the other. Such a sight the hunters had never seen before.

They went through the wood then, and they saw seven vultures on one tree, and they screeching. The hunters began cracking balls after them, but if they were in it ever since they would never bring down one of them.

There came a gray old man to them and said:

"Those are the hags of the long tooth that are living in the little house over there. Do ye not know that they are under enchantment? They are there these hundreds of years, and they have a dog that never lets in anyone to the little house. They have a castle under the lake, and it is often the people saw them making seven swans of themselves, and going into the lake."

When the hunters came home that evening they told everything they heard and saw to the priest, but he did not believe the story.

On the day on the morrow, the priest went with the hunters, and when they came near the little house they saw the big black dog at the door. The priest put his conveniencies for blessing under his neck, and drew out a book and began reading prayers. The big dog began barking loudly. The hags came out, and when they saw the priest they let a screech out of them that was heard in every part of Ireland. When the priest was a while reading, the hags made vultures of themselves and flew up into a big tree that was over the house.

The priest began pressing in on the dog until he was within a couple of feet of him.

The dog gave a leap up, struck the priest with its four feet, and put him head over heels.

When the hunters took him up he was deaf and dumb, and the dog did not move from the door.

They brought the priest home and sent for the bishop. When he came and heard the story there was great grief on him. The people gathered together and asked of him to banish the hags of enchantment out of the wood. There was fright and shame on him, and he did not know what he would do, but he said to them: "I have no means of banishing them till I go home, but I will come at the end of a month and banish them."

The priest was too badly hurt to say anything. The big black dog was father of the hags, and his name was Dermod O'Muloony. His own son killed him, because he found him with his wife the day after their marriage, and killed the sisters for fear they should tell on him.

One night the bishop was in his chamber asleep, when one of the hags of the long tooth opened the door and came in. When the bishop wakened up he saw the hag standing by the side of his bed. He was so much afraid he was not able to speak a word until the hag spoke and said to him: "Let there be no fear on you; I did not come to do you harm, but to give you advice. You promised the people of Loch Glynn that you would come to banish the hags of the long tooth out of the wood of Driminuch. If you come you will never go back alive."

His talk came to the bishop, and he said: "I cannot break my word."

"We have only a year and a day to be in the wood," said the hag, "and you can put off the people until then."

"Why are ye in the woods as ye are?" says the bishop.

"Our brother killed us," said the hag, "and when we went before the arch-judge, there was judgment passed on us, we to be as we are two hundred years. We have a castle under the lake, and be in it every night. We are suffering for the crime our father did." Then she told him the crime the father did.

"Hard is your case," said the bishop, "but we must put up with the will of the arch-judge, and I shall not trouble ye."

"You will get an account, when we are gone from the wood," said the hag. Then she went from him.

In the morning, the day on the morrow, the bishop came to Loch Glynn. He sent out notice and gathered the people. Then he said to them: "It is the will of the arch-king that the power of enchantment be not banished for another year and a day, and ye must keep out of the wood until then. It is a great wonder to me that ye never saw the hags of enchantment till the hunters came from Dublin. It's a pity they did not remain at home."

About a week after that the priest was one day by himself in his chamber alone. The day was very fine and the window was open. The robin of the red breast came in and a little herb in its mouth. The priest stretched out his hand, and she laid the herb down on it. "Perhaps it was God sent me this herb," said the priest to himself, and he ate it. He had not eaten it one moment till he was as well as ever he was, and he said: "A thousand thanks to Him who has power stronger than the power of enchantment."

Then said the robin: "Do you remember the robin of the broken foot you had, two years this last winter."

"I remember her, indeed," said the priest, "but she went from me when the summer came."

"I am the same robin, and but for the good you did me I would not be alive now, and you would be deaf and dumb throughout your life. Take my advice now, and do not go near the hags of the long tooth any more, and do not tell to any person living that I gave you the herb." Then she flew from him.

When the house-keeper came she wondered to find that he had both his talk and his hearing. He sent word to the bishop and he came to Loch Glynn. He asked the priest how it was that he got better so suddenly. "It is a secret," said the priest, "but a certain friend gave me a little herb and it cured me."

Nothing else happened worth telling, till the year was gone. One night after that the bishop was in his chamber when the door opened, and the hag of the long tooth walked in, and said: "I come to give you notice that we will be leaving the wood a week from to-day. I have one thing to ask of you if you will do it for me."

"If it is in my power, and it not to be against the faith," said the bishop.

"A week from to-day," said the hag, "there will be seven vultures dead at the door of our house in the wood. Give orders to bury them in the quarry that is between the wood and Ballyglas; that is all I am asking of you."

"I shall do that if I am alive," said the bishop. Then she left him, and he was not sorry she to go from him.

A week after that day, the bishop came to Loch Glynn, and the day after he took men with him and went to the hags' house in the wood of Driminuch.

The big black dog was at the door, and when he saw the bishop he began running and never stopped until he went into the lake.

He saw the seven vultures dead at the door, and he said to the men: "Take them with you and follow me."

They took up the vultures and followed him to the brink of the quarry. Then he said to them: "Throw them into the quarry. There is an end to the hags of the enchantment."

As soon as the men threw them down to the bottom of the quarry, there rose from it seven swans as white as snow, and flew out of their sight. It was the opinion of the bishop and of every person who heard the story that it was up to heaven they flew, and that the big black dog went to the castle under the lake.

At any rate, nobody saw the hags of the long tooth or the big black dog from that out, any more.

The Enchanted Hare

THERE WAS A STRONG FARMER one time and he had nine beautiful cows grazing on the best of land. Surely that was a great prosperity, and you'd be thinking him the richest man in all the countryside. But it was little milk he was getting from his nine lovely cows, and no butter from the milk. They'd be churning in that house for three hours or maybe for five hours of a morning, and at the end of all a few wee grains of butter, the dead spit of spiders' eggs, would be floating on the top of the milk. Evenly that much did not remain to it, for when herself ran the strainer in under them they melted from the churn.

There were great confabulations held about the loss of the yield, but the strength of the spoken word was powerless to restore what was gone. Herself allowed that her man be to have the evil eye, and it was overlooking his own cattle he was by walking through them and he fasting at the dawn of day. The notion didn't please him too well, indeed he was horrid vexed at her for saying the like, but he went no more among the cows until after his breakfast time. Sure that done no good at all – it was less and less milk came in each day. And butter going a lovely price in the market, to leave it a worse annoyance to have none for to sell.

The man of the house kept a tongue hound that was odious wise. The two walked the cattle together, and it happened one day that they came on a hare was running with the nine cows through the field. The hound gave tongue and away with him after the hare, she making a great offer to escape.

"Maybe there is something in it," says the man to himself. "I have heard my old grandfather tell that hares be's enchanted people; let it be true or no, I doubt they're not right things in any case."

With that he set out for to follow his tongue hound, and the hunt went over the ditches and through the quick hedges and down by the lake.

"Begob it's odious weighty I am to be diverting myself like a little gosoon," says the man. And indeed he was a big, hearty farmer was leaving powerful gaps behind him where he burst through the hedges.

There was a small, wee house up an old laneway, and that was where the hunt headed for. The hare came in on the street not a yard in front of the tongue hound, and she made a lep for to get into the cabin by a hole on the wall convenient to the door. The hound got a grip of her and she rising from the ground. But the farmer was coming up close behind them and didn't he let a great crow out of him.

"Hold your hold, my bully boy! Hold your hold!" The tongue hound turned at the voice of the master calling, and the hare contrived for to slip from between his teeth. One spring brought her in on the hole in the wall, but she splashed it with blood as she passed, and there was blood on the mouth of the hound.

The man came up, cursing himself for spoiling the diversion, but he was well determined to follow on. He took the coat off his back and he stuffed it into the opening the way the hare had no chance to get out where she was after entering, then he walked round the house for to see was there any means of escape for what was within. There wasn't evenly a space where a fly might contrive to slip through, and himself was satisfied the hunt was shaping well.

He went to the door, and it was there the tongue hound went wild to be making an entry, but a lock and a chain were upon it. The farmer took up a stone and he broke all before him to get in after the hare they followed so far.

"The old house is empty this long time," says he, "and evenly if I be to repair the destruction I make – sure what is the price of a chain and a lock to a fine, warm man like myself!"

With that he pushed into the kitchen, and there was neither sight nor sign of a hare to be found, but an old woman lay in a corner and she bleeding.

The tongue hound gave the mournfullest whine and he juked to his master's feet, it was easy knowing the beast was in odious dread. The farmer gave a sort of a groan and he turned for to go away home.

"It's a queer old diversion I'm after enjoying," says he. "Surely there's not a many in the world do be hunting hares through the fields and catching old women are bleeding to death."

When he came to his own place the wife ran out of the house.

"Will you look at the gallons of beautiful milk the cows are after giving this day," says she, pulling him in on the door.

Sure enough from that out there was a great plenty of milk and a right yield of butter on the churn.

Cucúlin

THERE WAS A KING in a land not far from Greece who had two daughters, and the younger was fairer than the elder daughter.

This old king made a match between the king of Greece and his own elder daughter; but he kept the younger one hidden away till after the marriage. Then the younger daughter came forth to view; and when the king of Greece saw her, he wouldn't look at his own wife. Nothing would do him but to get the younger sister and leave the elder at home with her father.

The king wouldn't listen to this, wouldn't agree to the change, so the king of Greece left his wife where she was, went home alone in a terrible rage and collected all his forces to march against the kingdom of his father-in-law.

He soon conquered the king and his army and, so far as he was able, he vexed and tormented him. To do this the more completely, he took from him a rod of Druidic spells, enchantment, and ring of youth which he had, and, striking the elder sister with the rod, he said: "You will be a serpent of the sea and live outside there in the bay by the castle."

Then turning to the younger sister, whose name was Gil an Og, he struck her, and said: "You'll be a cat while inside this castle, and have your own form only when you are outside the walls."

After he had done this, the king of Greece went home to his own country, taking with him the rod of enchantment and the ring of youth.

The king died in misery and grief, leaving his two daughters spellbound.

Now there was a Druid in that kingdom, and the younger sister went to consult him, and asked: "Shall I ever be released from the enchantment that's on me now?"

"You will not, unless you find the man to release you; and there is no man in the world to do that but a champion who is now with Fin MacCumhail in Erin."

"Well, how can I find that man?" asked she.

"I will tell you," said the Druid. "Do you make a shirt out of your own hair, take it with you; and never stop till you land in Erin and find Fin and his men; the man that the shirt will fit is the man who will release you."

She began to make the shirt and worked without stopping till it was finished. Then she went on her journey and never rested till she came to Erin in a ship. She went on shore and inquired where Fin and his men were to be found at that time of the year.

"You will find them at Knock an Ar," was the answer she got.

She went to Knock an Ar carrying the shirt with her. The first man she met was Conan Maol, and she said to him: "I have come to find the man this shirt will fit. From the time one man tries it all must try till I see the man it fits."

The shirt went from hand to hand till Cucúlin put it on. "Well," said she, "it fits as your own skin."

Now Gil an Og told Cucúlin all that had happened – how her father had forced her sister to marry the king of Greece, how this king had made war on her father, enchanted her sister and herself, and carried off the rod of enchantment with the ring of youth, and how the old Druid said the man this shirt would fit was the only man in the world who could release them.

Now Gil an Og and Cucúlin went to the ship and sailed across the seas to her country and went to her castle.

"You'll have no one but a cat for company tonight," said Gil an Og. "I have the form of a cat inside this castle, but outside I have my own appearance. Your dinner is ready, go in."

After the dinner Cucúlin went to another room apart, and lay down to rest after the journey. The cat came to his pillow, sat there and purred till he fell asleep and slept soundly till morning.

When he rose up, a basin of water, and everything he needed was before him, and his breakfast ready. He walked out after breakfast; Gil an Og was on the green outside before him and said:

"If you are not willing to free my sister and my-self, I shall not urge you; but if you do free us, I shall be glad and thankful. Many king's sons and champions before you have gone to recover the ring and the rod; but they have never come back."

"Well, whether I thrive or not, I'll venture," said Cucúlin.

"I will give you," said Gil an Og, "a present such as I have never given before to any man who ventured out on my behalf; I will give you the speckled boat."

Cucúlin took leave of Gil an Og and sailed away in the speckled boat to Greece, where he went to the king's court, and challenged him to combat.

The king of Greece gathered his forces and sent them out to chastise Cucúlin. He killed them all to the last man. Then Cucúlin challenged the king a second time.

"I have no one now to fight but myself," said the king; "and I don't think it becomes me to go out and meet the like of you."

"If you don't come out to me," said Cucúlin, "I'll go in to you and cut the head off you in your own castle."

"That's enough of impudence from you, you scoundrel," said the king of Greece "I won't have you come into my castle, but I'll meet you on the open plain."

The king went out, and they fought till Cucúlin got the better of him, bound him head and heels, and said: "I'll cut the head off you now unless you give me the ring of youth and the rod of enchantment that you took from the father of Gil an Og."

"Well, I did carry them away," said the king, "but it wouldn't be easy for me now to give them to you or to her; for there was a man who came and carried them away, who could take them from you and from me, and from as many more of us, if they were here."

"Who was that man?" asked Cucúlin.

"His name," said the king, "is Lug [pronounced 'Loog'] Longhand. And if I had known what you wanted, there would have been no difference between us. I'll tell you how I lost the ring and rod and I'll go with you and show you where Lug Longhand lives. But do you come to my castle. We'll have a good time together."

They set out next day, and never stopped till they came opposite Lug Longhand castle, and Cucúlin challenged his forces to combat.

"I have no forces," said Lug, "but I'll fight you myself." So the combat began, and they spent the whole day at one another, and neither gained the victory.

The king of Greece himself put up a tent on the green in front of the castle, and prepared everything necessary to eat and drink (there was no one else to do it). After breakfast next day, Cucúlin and Lug began fighting again. The king of Greece looked on as the day before.

They fought the whole day till near evening, when Cucúlin got the upper hand of Lug Longhand and bound him head and heels, saying: "I'll cut the head off you now unless you give me the rod and the ring that you carried away from the king of Greece."

"Oh, then," said Lug, "it would be hard for me to give them to you or to him; for forces came and took them from me; and they would have taken them from you and from him, if you had been here."

"Who in the world took them from you?" asked the king of Greece.

"Release me from this bond, and come to my castle, and I'll tell you the whole story," said Lug Longhand.

Cucúlin released him, and they went to the castle. They got good reception and entertainment from Lug that night, and the following morning as well. He said: "The ring and the rod were taken from me by the knight of the island of the Flood. This island is surrounded by a chain, and there is a ring of fire seven miles wide between the chain and the castle. No man can come near the island without breaking the chain, and the moment the chain is broken the fire stops burning at that place; and the instant the fire goes down the knight rushes out and attacks and slays every man that's before him."

The king of Greece, Cucúlin, and Lug Longhand now sailed on in the speckled boat towards the island of the Flood. On the following morning when the speckled boat struck the chain, she was thrown back three days' sail, and was near being sunk, and would have gone to the bottom of the sea but for her own goodness and strength.

As soon as Cucúlin saw what had happened, he took the oars, rowed on again, and drove the vessel forward with such venom that she cut through the chain and went one third of her length on to dry land. That moment the fire was quenched where the vessel struck, and when the knight of the Island saw the fire go out, he rushed to the shore and met Cucúlin, the king of Greece, and Lug Longhand.

When Cucúlin saw him, he threw aside his weapons, caught him, raised him above his head, hurled him down on the flat of his back, bound him head and heels, and said: "I'll cut the head off you unless you give me the ring and the rod that you carried away from Lug Longhand."

"I took them from him, it's true," said the knight; "but it would be hard for me to give them to you now; for a man came and took them from me, who would have taken them from you and all that are with you, and as many more if they had been here before him."

"Who in the world could that man be?" asked Cucúlin.

"The dark Gruagach of the Northern Island. Release me, and come to my castle. I'll tell you all and entertain you well."

He took them to his castle, gave them good cheer, and told them all about the Gruagach and his island. Next morning all sailed away in Cucúlin's vessel, which they had left at the shore of the island, and never stopped till they came to the Gruagach's castle, and pitched their tents in front of it.

Then Cucúlin challenged the Gruagach. The others followed after to know would he thrive. The Gruagach came out and faced Cucúlin, and they began and spent the whole day at one another and neither of them gained the upper hand. When evening came, they stopped and prepared for supper and the night.

Next day after breakfast Cucúlin challenged the Gruagach again, and they fought till evening; when Cucúlin got the better in the struggle, disarmed the Gruagach, bound him, and said: "Unless you give up the rod of enchantment and the ring of youth that you took from the knight of the island of the Flood, I'll cut the head off you now."

"I took them from him, 'tis true; but there was a man named Thin-in-Iron, who took them from me, and he would have taken them from you and from me, and all that are here, if there were twice as many. He is such a man that sword cannot cut him, fire cannot burn him, water cannot drown him, and 'tis no easy thing to get the better of him. But if you'll free me now and come to my castle, I'll treat you well and tell you all about him." Cucúlin agreed to this.

Next morning they would not stop nor be satisfied till they went their way. They found the castle of Thin-in-Iron, and Cucúlin challenged him to combat. They fought; and he was cutting the flesh from Cucúlin, but Cucúlin's sword cut no flesh from him. They fought till Cucúlin said:

"It is time now to stop till to-morrow."

Cucúlin was scarcely able to reach the tent. They had to support him and put him to bed. Now, who should come to Cucúlin that night but Gil an Og, and she said: "You have gone further than any man before you, and I'll cure you now, and you need go no further for the rod of enchantment and the ring of youth."

"Well," said Cucúlin, "I'll never give over till I knock another day's trial out of Thin-in-Iron."

When it was time for rest, Gil an Og went away, and Cucúlin fell asleep for himself. On the following morning all his comrades were up and facing his tent. They thought to see him dead, but he was in as good health as ever.

They prepared breakfast, and after breakfast Cucúlin went before the door of the castle to challenge his enemy.

Thin-in-Iron thrust his head out and said: "That man I fought yesterday has come again to-day. It would have been a good deed if I had cut the head off him last night. Then he wouldn't be here to trouble me this morning. I won't come home this day till I bring his head with me. Then I'll have peace."

They met in combat and fought till the night was coming. Then Thin-in-Iron cried out for a cessation, and if he did, Cucúlin was glad to give it; for his sword had no effect upon Thin-in-Iron except to tire and nearly kill him (he was enchanted and no arms could cut him). When Thin-in-Iron went to his castle, he threw up three sups of blood, and said to his housekeeper: "Though his sword could not penetrate me, he has nearly broken my heart."

Cucúlin had to be carried to his tent. His comrades laid him on his bed and said:

"Whoever came and healed him yesterday, may be the same will be here to-night."

They went away and were not long gone when Gil an Og came and said:

"Cucúlin, if you had done my bidding, you wouldn't be as you are to-night. But if you neglect my words now, you'll never see my face again. I'll cure you this time and make you as well as ever;" and whatever virtue she had she healed him so he was as strong as before.

"Oh, then," said Cucúlin, "whatever comes on me I'll never turn back till I knock another day's trial out of Thin-in-Iron."

"Well," said she, "you are a stronger man than he, but there is no good in working at him with a sword. Throw your sword aside to-morrow, and you'll get the better of him and bind him. You'll not see me again."

She went away and he fell asleep. His comrades came in the morning and found him sleeping. They got breakfast, and, after eating, Cucúlin went out and called a challenge.

"Oh, 'tis the same man as yesterday," said Thin-in-Iron, "and if I had cut the head off him then, it wouldn't be he that would trouble me to-day. If I live for it, I'll bring his head in my hand to-night, and he'll never disturb me again."

When Cucúlin saw Thin-in-Iron coming, he threw his sword aside, and facing him, caught him by the body, raised him up, then dashed him to the ground, and said, "If you don't give me what I want, I'll cut the head off you."

"What do you want of me?" asked Thin-in-Iron.

"I want the rod of enchantment and the ring of youth you carried from the Gruagach."

"I did indeed carry them from him, but it would be no easy thing for me to give them to you or any other man; for a force came which took them from me."

"What could take them from you?" asked Cucúlin.

"The queen of the Wilderness, an old hag that has them now. But release me from this bondage and I'll take you to my castle and entertain you well, and I'll go with you and the rest of the company to see how will you thrive."

So he took Cucúlin and his friends to the castle and entertained them joyously, and he said:

"The old hag, the queen of the Wilderness, lives in a round tower, which is always turning on wheels. There is but one entrance to the tower, and that high above the ground, and in the one chamber in which she lives, keeping the ring and the rod, is a chair, and she has but to sit on the chair and wish herself in any part of the world, and that moment she is there. She has six lines of guards protecting her tower, and if you pass all of these, you'll do what no man before you has done to this day. The first guards are two lions that rush out to know which of them will get the first bite out of the throat of any one that tries to pass. The second are seven men with iron hurlies and an iron ball, and with their hurlies they wallop the life out of any man that goes their way. The third is Hung-up-Naked, who hangs on a tree with his toes to the earth, his head cut from his shoulders and lying on the ground, and who kills every man who comes near him. The fourth is the bull of the Mist that darkens the woods for seven miles around, and destroys everything that enters the Mist. The fifth are seven cats with poison tails and one drop of their poison would kill the strongest man.

Next morning all went with Cucúlin as far as the lions who guarded the queen of the Wilderness, an old hag made young by the ring of youth. The two lions ran at Cucúlin to see which would have the first bite out of him.

Cucúlin wore a red silk scarf around his neck and had a fine head of hair. He cut the hair off his head and wound it around one hand, took his scarf and wrapped it around the other. Then rushing at the lions, he thrust a hand down the throat of each lion (for lions can bite neither silk nor hair). He pulled the livers and lights out of the two and they fell dead before him. His comrades looking on, said: "You'll thrive now since you have done this deed;" and they left him and went home, each to his own country.

Cucúlin went further. The next people he met were the seven men with the iron hurlies (ball clubs), and they said; "'Tis long since any man walked this way to us; we'll have sport now."

The first one said: "Give him a touch of the hurly and let the others do the same; and we'll wallop him till he is dead."

Now Cucúlin drew his sword and cut the head off the first man before he could make an offer of the hurly at him; and then he did the same to the other six.

He went on his way till he came to Hung-up-Naked, who was hanging from a tree, his head on the ground near him. The queen of the Wilderness had fastened him to the tree because he wouldn't marry her; and she said: "If any man comes who will put your head on you, you'll be free." And she laid the injunction on him to kill every man who tried to pass his way without putting the head on him.

Cucúlin went up, looked at him, and saw heaps of bones around the tree. The body said: "You can't go by here. I fight with every man who tries to pass."

"Well, I'm not going to fight with a man unless he has a head on him. Take your head." And Cucúlin, picking up the head, clapped it on the body, and said, "Now I'll fight with you!"

The man said: "I'm all right now. I know where you are going. I'll stay here till you come; if you conquer you'll not forget me. Take the head off me now; put it where you found it; and if you succeed, remember that I shall be here before you on your way home."

Cucúlin went on, but soon met the bull of the Mist that covered seven miles of the wood with thick mist. When the bull saw him, he made at him and stuck a horn in his ribs and threw him three miles into the wood, against a great oak tree and broke three ribs in his side.

"Well," said Cucúlin, when he recovered, "if I get another throw like that, I'll not be good for much exercise." He was barely on his feet when the bull was at him again; but when he came up he caught the bull by both horns and away they went wrestling and struggling. For three days and nights Cucúlin kept the bull in play, till the morning of the fourth day, when he put him on the flat of his back. Then he turned him on the side, and putting a foot on one horn and taking the other in his two hands, he said: "'Tis well I earned you; there is not a stitch on me that isn't torn to rags from wrestling with you." He pulled the bull asunder from his horns to his tail, into two equal parts, and said: "Now that I have you in two, it's in quarters I'll put you." He took his sword, and when he struck the backbone of the bull, the sword remained in the bone and he couldn't pull it out.

He walked away and stood awhile and looked. "'Tis hard to say," said he, "that any good champion would leave his sword behind him." So he went back and made another pull and took the hilt off his sword, leaving the blade in the back of the bull. Then he went away tattered and torn, the hilt in his hand, and he turned up towards the forge of the Strong Smith. One of the Smith's boys was out for coal at the time: he saw Cucúlin coming with the hilt in his hand, and ran in, saying: "There is a man coming up and he looks like a fool; we'll have fun!"

"Hold your tongue!" said the master. "Have you heard any account of the bull of the Mist these three days?"

"We have not," said the boys.

"Perhaps," said the Strong Smith, "that's a good champion that's coming, and do you mind yourselves."

At that moment Cucúlin walked in to the forge where twelve boys and the master were working. He saluted them and asked, "Can you put a blade in this hilt?"

"We can," said the master. They put in the blade, Cucúlin raised the sword and took a shake out of it and broke it to bits.

"This is a rotten blade," said he. "Go at it again."

They made a second blade. The boys were in dread of him now. He broke the second blade in the same way as the first. They made six blades, one stronger than the other. He did the same to them all.

"There is no use in talking," said the Strong Smith, "we have no stuff that would make a right blade for you. Go down now," said he to two of the boys, "and bring up an old sword that's down in the stable full of rust."

They went and brought up the sword on two hand-spikes between them; it was so heavy that one couldn't carry it. They gave it to Cucúlin, and with one blow on his heel he knocked the dust from it and went out at the door and took a shake out of it; and if he did, he darkened the whole place with the rust from the blade.

"This is my sword, whoever made it," said he.

"It is," said the master; "it's yours and welcome. I know who you are now, and where you are going. Remember that I'm in bondage here." The Strong Smith took Cucúlin then to his house, gave him refreshment and clothes for the journey. When he was ready, the Smith said: "I hope you'll thrive. You have done a deal more than any man that ever walked this way before. There is nothing now to stand in your way till you come to the seven cats outside the turning tower. If they shake their tails and a drop of poison comes on you, it will penetrate to your heart. You must sweep off their tails with your sword. 'Tis equal to you what their bodies will do after that."

Cucúlin soon came to them and there wasn't one of the seven cats he didn't strip of her tail before she knew he was in it. He cared nothing for the bodies so he had the tails. The cats ran away.

Now he faced the tower turning on wheels. The queen of the Wilderness was in it. He had been told by Thin-in-Iron that he must cut the axle. He found the axle, cut it, and the tower stopped that instant. Cucúlin made a spring and went in through the single passage.

The old hag was preparing to sit on the chair as she saw him coming. He sprang forward, pushed the chair away with one hand, and, catching her by the back of the neck with the other, said: "You are to lose your head now, old woman!"

"Spare me, and what you want you'll get," said she. "I have the ring of youth and the rod of enchantment," and she gave them to him. He put the ring on his finger, and saying, "You'll never do mischief again to man!" he turned her face to the entrance, and gave her a kick. Out she flew through the opening and down to the ground, where she broke her neck and died on the spot.

Cucúlin made the Strong Smith king over all the dominions of the queen of the Wilderness, and proclaimed that any person in the country who refused to obey the new king would he put to death.

Cucúlin turned back at once, and travelled till he came to Hung-up-Naked. He took him down and, putting the head on his body, struck him a blow of the rod and made the finest looking man of him that could be found. The man went back to his own home happy and well.

Cucúlin never stopped till he came to the castle of Gil an Og. She was outside with a fine welcome before him; and why not, to be sure, for he had the rod of enchantment and the ring of youth!

When she entered the castle and took the form of a cat, he struck her a blow of the rod and she gained the same form and face she had before the king of Greece struck her. Then he asked,

"Where is your sister?"

"In the lake there outside," answered Gil an Og, in the form of a sea-serpent. She went out with him, and the moment they came to the edge of the lake the sister rose up near them. Then Cucúlin struck her with the rod and she came to land in her own shape and countenance.

Next day they saw a deal of vessels facing the harbor, and what should they be but a fleet of ships, and on the ships were the king of Greece, Lug Longhand, the knight of the island of the Flood, the Dark Grúgach of the Northern Island and Thin-in-Iron: and they came each in his own vessel to know was there any account of Cucúlin. There was good welcome for them all, and when they had feasted and rejoiced together Cucúlin married Gil an Og. The king of Greece took Gil an Og's sister, who was his own wife at first, and went home.

Cucúlin went away himself with his wife Gil an Og, never stopping till he came to Erin and when he came, Fin MacCumhail and his men were at KilConaly, near the river Shannon.

When Cucúlin went from Erin he left a son whose mother was called the Virago of Alba: she was still alive and the son was eighteen years old. When she heard that Cucúlin had brought Gil an Og to Erin, she was enraged with jealousy and madness. She had reared the son, whose name was Conlán, like any king's son, and now giving him his arms of a champion she told him to go to his father.

"I would," said he, "if I knew who my father is."

"His name is Cucúlin, and he is with Fin MacCumhail. I bind you not to yield to any man," said she to her son, " nor tell your name to any man till you fight him out."

Conlán started from Ulster where his mother was, and never stopped till he was facing Fin and his men, who were hunting that day along the cliffs of Kilconaly.

When the young man came up Fin said, "There is a single man facing us."

Conan Maol said, "Let some one go against him, ask who he is and what he wants."

"I never give an account of myself to any man," said Conlán, "till I get an account from him."

"There is no man among us," said Conan, "bound in that way but Cucúlin." They called on Cucúlin; he came up and the two fought. Conlán knew by the description his mother had given that Cucúlin was his father, but Cucúlin did not know his son. Every time Conlán aimed his spear he threw it so as to strike the ground in front of Cucúlin's toe, but Cucúlin aimed straight at him.

They were at one another three days and three nights. The son always sparing the father, the father never sparing the son.

Conan Maol came to them the fourth morning. "Cucúlin," said he, "I didn't expect to see any man standing against you three days, and you such a champion."

When Conlán heard Conan Maol urging the father to kill him, he gave a bitter look at Conan, and forgot his guard. Cucúlin's spear went through his head that minute, and he fell. "I die of that blow from my father," said he.

"Are you my son?" said Cucúlin.

"I am," said Conlán.

Cucúlin took his sword and cut the head off him sooner than leave him in the punishment and pain he was in. Then he faced all the people, and Fin was looking on.

"There's trouble on Cucúlin," said Fin.

"Chew your thumb," said Conan Maol, "to know what's on him."

Fin chewed his thumb, and said, "Cucúlin is after killing his own son, and if I and all my men were to face him before his passion cools, at the end of seven days, he'd destroy every man of us."

"Go now," said Conan, "and bind him to go down to Bale strand and give seven days fighting against the waves of the sea, rather than kill us all."

So Fin bound him to go down. When he went to Bale strand Cucúlin found a great white stone. He grasped his sword in his right hand and cried out: "If I had the head of the woman who sent her soil into peril of death at my hand, I'd split it as I split this stone," and he made four quarters of the stone. Then he strove with the waves seven days and nights till he fell from hunger and weakness, and the waves went over him.

The Lambton Worm

A WILD YOUNG FELLOW was the heir of Lambton, the fine estate and hail by the side of the swift-flowing Wear. Not a Mass would he hear in Brugeford Chapel of a Sunday, but a-fishing he would go. And if he did not haul in anything, his curses could be heard by the folk as they went by to Brugeford.

Well, one Sunday morning he was fishing as usual, and not a salmon had risen to him, his basket was bare of roach or dace. And the worse his luck, the worse grew his language, till the passers-by were horrified at his words as they went to listen to the Mass-priest.

At last young Lambton felt a mighty tug at his line. "At last," quoth he, "a bite worth having!" and he pulled and he pulled, till what should appear above the water but a head like an elf's, with nine holes on each side of its mouth. But still he pulled till he had got the thing to land, when it turned out to be a Worm of hideous shape. If he had cursed before, his curses were enough to raise the hair on your head.

"What ails thee, my son?" said a voice by his side, "and what hast thou caught, that thou shouldst stain the Lord's Day with such foul language?"

Looking round, young Lambton saw a strange old man standing by him.

"Why, truly," he said, "I think I have caught the devil himself. Look you and see if you know him."

But the stranger shook his head, and said, "It bodes no good to thee or thine to bring such a monster to shore. Yet cast him not back into the Wear; thou has caught him, and thou must keep him," and with that away he turned, and was seen no more.

The young heir of Lambton took up the gruesome thing, and taking it off his hook, cast it into a well close by, and ever since that day that well has gone by the name of the Worm Well.

For some time nothing more was seen or heard of the Worm, till one day it had outgrown the size of the well, and came forth full-grown. So it came forth from the well and betook itself to the Wear. And all day long it would lie coiled round a rock in the middle of the stream, while at night it came forth from the river and harried the countryside. It sucked the cows' milk, devoured the lambs, worried the cattle, and frightened all the women and girls in the district, and then it would retire for the rest of the night to the hill, still called the Worm Hill, on the north side of the Wear, about a mile and a half from Lambton Hall.

This terrible visitation brought young Lambton, of Lambton Hall, to his senses. He took upon himself the vows of the Cross, and departed for the Holy Land, in the hope that the scourge he had brought upon his district would disappear. But the grisly Worm took no heed, except that it crossed the river and came right up to Lambton Hall itself where the old lord lived on all alone, his only son having gone to the Holy Land. What to do? The Worm was coming closer and closer to the Hall; women were shrieking, men were gathering weapons, dogs were barking and horses neighing with terror. At last the steward called out to the dairymaids, "Bring all your milk hither," and when they did so, and had brought all the milk that the nine kye of the byre had yielded, he poured it all into the long stone trough in front of the Hall.

The Worm drew nearer and nearer, till at last it came up to the trough. But when it sniffed the milk, it turned aside to the trough and swallowed all the milk up, and then slowly turned round and crossed the River Wear, and coiled its bulk three times round the Worm Hill for the night.

Henceforth the Worm would cross the river every day, and woe betide the Hall if the trough contained the milk of less than nine kye. The Worm would hiss, and would rave, and lash its tail round the trees of the park, and in its fury it would uproot the stoutest oaks and the loftiest firs. So it went on for seven years. Many tried to destroy the Worm, but all had failed, and many a knight had lost his life in fighting with the monster, which slowly crushed the life out of all that came near it.

At last the Childe of Lambton came home to his father's Hall, after seven long years spent in meditation and repentance on holy soil. Sad and desolate he found his folk: the lands untilled, the farms deserted, half the trees of the park uprooted, for none would stay to tend the nine kye that the monster needed for his food each day.

The Childe sought his father, and begged his forgiveness for the curse he had brought on the Hall.

"Thy sin is pardoned," said his father; "but go thou to the Wise Woman of Brugeford, and find if aught can free us from this monster."

To the Wise Woman went the Childe, and asked her advice.

"'Tis thy fault, O Childe, for which we suffer," she said; "be it thine to release us."

"I would give my life," said the Childe.

"Mayhap thou wilt do so," said she. "But hear me, and mark me well. Thou, and thou alone, canst kill the Worm. But, to this end, go thou to the smithy and have thy armour studded with spear-heads. Then go to the Worm's Rock in the Wear, and station thyself there. Then, when the Worm comes to the Rock at dawn of day, try thy prowess on him, and God gi'e thee a good deliverance."

"This I will do," said Childe Lambton.

"But one thing more," said the Wise Woman, going back to her cell. "If thou slay the Worm, swear that thou wilt put to death the first thing that meets thee as thou crossest again the threshold of Lambton Hall. Do this, and all will be well with thee and thine. Fulfil not thy vow, and none of the Lambtons, for generations three times three, shall die in his bed. Swear, and fail not."

The Childe swore as the Wise Woman bid, and went his way to the smithy. There he had his armour studded with spear-heads all over. Then he passed his vigils in Brugeford Chapel, and at dawn of day took his post on the Worm's Rock in the River Wear.

As dawn broke, the Worm uncoiled its snaky twine from around the hill, and came to its rock in the river. When it perceived the Childe waiting for it, it lashed the waters in its fury and wound its coils round the Childe, and then attempted to crush him to death. But the more it pressed, the deeper dug the spear-heads into its sides. Still it pressed and pressed, till all the water around was crimsoned with its blood. Then the Worm unwound itself, and left the Childe free to use his sword. He raised it, brought it down, and cut the Worm in two. One half fell into the river, and was carried swiftly away. Once more the head and the remainder of the body encircled the Childe, but with less force, and the spear-heads did their work. At last the Worm uncoiled itself, snorted its last foam of blood and fire, and rolled dying into the river, and was never seen more.

The Childe of Lambton swam ashore, and raising his bugle to his lips, sounded its note thrice. This was the signal to the Hall, where the servants and the old lord had shut themselves in to pray for the Childe's success. When the third sound of the bugle was heard, they were to release Boris, the Childe's favourite hound. But such was their joy at learning of the Childe's safety and the Worm's defeat, that they forgot orders, and when the Childe reached the threshold of the Hall his old father rushed out to meet him, and would have clasped him to his breast.

"The vow! the vow!" cried out the Childe of Lambton, and blew still another blast upon his horn. This time the servants remembered, and released Boris, who came bounding to his young master. The Childe raised his shining sword, and severed the head of his faithful hound.

But the vow was broken, and for nine generations of men none of the Lambtons died in his bed. The last of the Lambtons died in his carriage as he was crossing Brugeford Bridge, one hundred and thirty years ago.

The Magic Book

THERE IS A SPOT PRETTILY SITUATED near the town of Glossop, known as Mossey Lea. It is notable as having been the home of a great magician, who dwelt there in the olden time, and who was renowned far and wide. He was, perhaps, the most learned and powerful of all magicians who have lived since the days of Merlin, but unfortunately his name has been forgotten. Such is fame.

So renowned was he in his own day, however, that pupils came to him, not only from all parts of England, but even from across the seas. These pupils desired to be inculcated with the mystic lore, and invested with the same degree of skill in the exercise of the magic arts, that their master possessed. Accordingly they left no stone unturned in their efforts after knowledge – that is to say, they were not over-particular as to the means they adopted to secure the end they had in view. They strove to impress upon everyone with whom they came in contact, their vast superiority to ordinary mankind, and generally they proved a big nuisance to the country side.

But there were two of these pupils who were especially curious; they were constantly prying into nooks and corners which were labelled "private;" they were ever meddling with business that did not concern them. By some evil chance, the magician fixed upon these two pupils to act as his agents for the transaction of some business in a town in Staffordshire, and to bring back with them a very remarkable book, which dealt with magic, and which was, moreover, itself endowed with magical powers. Thus the two luckless youths became all unwittingly the heroes of the following Longdendale tradition.

History – as is often the case in these legends of the olden time – has forgotten to record for us the names of the two notable youths, hence we are driven to the necessity of naming them ourselves, in order to distinguish them from each other. So we call one Ralph and the other Walter. It has already been said that they were two curious youths, ever ready to pry into things; and on the night preceding their journey, they indulged in this pastime to the full.

While they were at supper the magician had bidden them to repair to his private chamber ere they retired to rest; and having entered therein, they were treated to the information already recorded – namely, that they would have to make a journey on his behalf, transact some business, and bring back with them a magic book – with the addition of the following piece of advice and warning.

"Look to it that ye heed what I now say," said the magician; "for by the shades, 'tis a matter of mighty import. Ye shall get the book, and ye shall jealously guard it. On no account shall you open it. More I do not vouchsafe to you, but remember my warning. Open not the book at your peril. Now get ye to rest, for to-morrow you must een start with the rising of the sun."

The youths left the room looking very solemn and good, with many promises that they would faithfully remember their master's charges, and what was of more consequence, that they would act upon them. But for all that they did not retire to rest. When they reached the passage leading to their apartment, Ralph said to Walter:

"What thinkest thou of this quest of ours? Is our master treating us fairly in thus keeping secret this matter? We have paid a high fee for tuition in magic, and here he sends us on our first quest, and we are een to know nothing of the mission on which we go."

"Thou art right," said Walter. "'Tis most unfair, and methinks our master has in view the acquisition of some potent power. If we engage in the quest, it is but fair we should share the spoil – the knowledge to be gained."

To which Ralph added, "I am with thee, comrade. And I would know more of this business before I start."

Here he whispered to his companion, and the latter nodded his head in acquiescence. After which the two stole together in silence to the door of the magician's room, and in turn set their eyes to the key-hole, whilst their ears drank in every sound.

The magician was seated before a crucible, muttering certain incantations which are as foreign language to the unlearned. But the two students understood the meaning of the sentences quite well, and the result of their eavesdropping appeared to give them satisfaction. When the magician made signs of coming to the end of his labour, they skipped nimbly away, and sought their beds, chuckling triumphantly as they ran.

It is not to the purpose of the legend to dwell upon the incidents of their next day's journey. Suffice it to say that on that day they were early astir, that they went gaily upon their way, and in due course received the magic book from its owner. Then they set out on their homeward journey, looking very good and innocent until they were well out of sight. But withal both determined to see the inside of that volume before the day was over.

Soon they came to a lonely part of the country, and here they sat down, intending to gratify their curiosity.

"If there is knowledge contained within, then am I determined to drink of the well thereof, and become even one of the wise."

So spoke Ralph, and Walter also said:

"And I am of a like mind, comrade. So bring hither the book, and let us fall to."

They placed the thick volume upon their knees, and quickly undid the handsome clasp which held the sides together, when, lo! a veritable earthquake seemed to have come upon the scene. The ground shook, houses tottered, walls and fences fell down, a tremendous whirlwind arose, which uprooted trees and tossed the forest giants about like little wisps of hay. Even the students were terrified at the result of their curiosity, and as for ordinary mortals, why there is no describing the panic in which they were thrown.

When the luckless students recovered from the first shock of astonishment, they could only bemoan their folly in discarding the warning of so potent a magician as their master, and they were filled with dread as to the punishment they would receive when next they stood before him.

"Of a truth we are undone," said Ralph; "our master will never more trust us."

"We are like to be beaten to death with the tempest," said Walter "Who can stay the power of this evil Spirit, that our mad curiosity has thus let loose?"

Now, luckily, the magician no sooner beheld the tempest than he at once divined the cause of this hubbub of the elements, and with commendable promptitude he proceeded with all speed to the spot where the students lay with the magical volume. Arrived there, he pronounced an incantation, and then by magic means known to himself alone, rapidly stilled the tempest, which the ill-timed curiosity of his pupils had brought forth. In the words of the old chronicle, he "laid the evil spirit, commanding him as a punishment to make a rope of sand to reach the sky."

Which venture no doubt had a salutary effect upon the spirit, for there is no later mention of any similar antics on its part. We may conclude from this circumstance, that the spirit has found the task assigned it as a punishment, greater than it can discharge, and that it is still labouring away at the sand rope, which is not much nearer reaching the sky than it was when the work first begun.

The Bewitched House at Wakefield

IN THE EARLIER HALF of the seventeenth century, and during the Commonwealth, there dwelt in a mud-walled and thatched cottage, in the environs of Wakefield, a "wise woman," as she was styled, named Jennet Benton, with her son, George Benton. He had been a soldier in the Parliamentarian army, but, since its disbandment, had loafed about Wakefield without any ostensible occupation, living, as it appeared, on his mother's earnings in her profession. As a "wise woman," she was resorted to by great numbers of people – by persons who had lost property, to gain a clue to the discovery of the pilferers – by men to learn the most propitious times for harvesting, sheepshearing, etc. – by matrons to obtain charms for winning back their dissipated or unfaithful husbands to domestic life, as it existed the first few months after marriage – and by young men and maidens for consultation with her on matters of love; and, as no advice was given without its equivalent in the coin of the realm, she made a very fair living, and was enabled to maintain her son in idleness, who was wont to spend a great part of his time in pot houses, with other quondam troopers, their chief topics of discourse being disputed points of controversy between the Independents and Presbyterians, and revilings of the Popish whore of Babylon and her progeny, the Church of England. Although not imbued with much of the spirit of piety, Benton, in his campaigning career, had imbibed much of the fanaticism, superstition, and phraseology of the lower class of the Puritans, such of them as assumed the hypocritical garb of Puritanism to curry favour with their superiors, who were, as a rule, men of sincere piety, and, in so doing, somewhat overdid the part by altogether out-Puritaning them in the extravagance of their outbursts of zeal, and in the almost blasphemous use of Scriptural expressions. Such was Benton amongst his companions, and he passed for a fairly godly man. With his mother, however, he cast off all this assumption of religion and the use of Bible phrases, for she was a woman who despised all religions alike, and sneered equally at the "snivelling cant" of the Puritans, the proud arrogance of the Bishops of the Church, and the "absurd drivellings" of the Separatists; but these ideas she was sufficiently wise to keep to herself, or confide them to her son alone. She even went occasionally to church and conventicle, that she might stand well with her customers, who were of all sects. She had, besides, a voluble tongue, and was not deficient in intelligence, so that she was able to converse with all, each one according to his doctrinal bias, so as to leave an impression that she was not opposed but rather inclined to the particular theological dogma then under discussion.

There was, however, a vague idea prevalent in Wakefield that Mother Benton was a witch, had intercourse with the Devil, and was a dangerous person to deal with otherwise than on friendly terms. She was old, wrinkled, and ungainly in features; unmistakable characteristics of the sisterhood. She was possessed of wisdom in occult matters seemingly superhuman, which could only be derived from a compact with Satan. She had a huge black cat, presumably an imp, her familiar, who would bristle up his hair and spit viciously at the old woman's visitors until restrained by her command. On one occasion, however, a handsome young man came from her cottage followed by the cat, which was observed to purr and rub himself affectionately against his legs, who, it was assumed, could be none other than the Father of Evil himself, who had assumed that guise to pay a friendly visit to his servant and disciple. She was also sometimes away from her cottage for a night, and the inquiry arose – for what purpose, excepting to attend a Sabbath of the witches. It is true she had never been seen passing through the air astride of her broom, but it was noticed that whenever she was absent on such occasions her broom, which usually stood outside her cottage door, disappeared also, and was found in its place again on her return.

At this time the belief in witchcraft was universally prevalent, as we find in the narrative of the witches of Fuystone, in the forest of Knaresborough, who played such pranks in the family of Edward Fairfax, the translator of Tasso, about the same time. Indeed it was considered as impious then to doubt their existence as it is now-a-days of their master and instigator, for is there not a Scriptural precept – "Thou shalt not suffer a witch to live?" and was there not a witch of Endor who summoned the spirit of Samuel? Besides, had not many decrepit half-witted old women, when subjected to torture, confessed that they had entered into compact with the Devil, bargaining their souls for length of years and the power of inflicting mischief on their neighbours? It is quite certain that the evidences of Mother Benton being one of the sisterhood of Satan were so palpable that had she not been so useful in Wakefield in her vocation of a "wise woman" she would have been subjected to the usual ordeal, by way of testing whether she were a witch or not. This ordeal consisted of stripping the accused, tying her thumbs to her great toes and throwing her into a pond:

if she floated, it was a proof that she, having rejected the baptismal water of regeneration, the water rejected her, and she was hauled out and burnt at the stake as an undoubted witch, but if she sank and were drowned she was declared innocent; so that, were she guilty or innocent of the foul crime, the result was pretty much the same, excepting in the mode of terminating her existence.

At this time one Richard Jackson held a farm called Bunny Hall, under a Mr. Stringer, of Sharlston, which lay near to Jennet Benton's cottage. Over one of Jackson's fields was a pathway, really for the use of the tenant of the farm, but which was used on sufferance by others, Jennet and her son frequently having occasion to pass along it. Jackson, however, in consequence of the damage done to his crops by passengers, disputed the right of the public, and issued a public notice that after a certain date it would be closed. The people of Wakefield, in reply to the notice, asserted that it was an ancient footpath that had belonged to the public time out of mind, and that they intended to continue the use of it in spite of Jackson's prohibition.

Jennet and her son were the ringleaders of this opposition, and after the closure of the path, passed over the railings placed across the entrance, and were going along as they had been wont to do, when they were met by Daniel Craven, one of Jackson's servants, who told them that they could not be allowed to cross the field as it was private property. An angry altercation ensued, in the course of which George Benton took up a piece of flint and threw it with great force at Craven, "wherewith he cut his overlipp and broake two teeth out of his chaps," and thus having overcome their opponent they went onward and out at the other end. An action for trespass was then laid against George Benton by Farmer Jackson, who appears to have won his cause, as Benton "submitted to it, and indevors were used to end the difference, which was composed and satisfaction given unto the said Craven;" satisfaction of a pecuniary nature, no doubt.

A few days after the judicial termination of the case, 'Jackson v. Benton,' the farmer was riding home from Wakefield market. He had to pass Jennet's cottage on his road, and he thought to accost her in a conciliatory style, as he did not wish to be at variance with his neighbours, especially with one who had the reputation of being "a wise woman," whose services he might require in cases of pilfering, sheep stealing, and the like; in cases of sickness amongst his children, or a murrain amongst his cattle; or in other cases beyond the ken of ordinary mortals; hence he considered it politic to remain on good terms with her, although he had felt it his duty to maintain the action for trespass.

As he approached the cottage, the old woman was seated outside her door, watching a cauldron suspended from cross sticks, in which was simmering a decoction of herbs, to eventuate in a love philtre probably for some love-sick maiden. By her side was seated her black cat, who bridled up and spat viciously at the farmer as he came up.

"Ah, mother Benton," said he, reining up, "busy as usual, I see, preparing something for the benefit of one of your clients."

"It is no business of yours what I am preparing," she replied. "I sent not for you, nor do I want your conversation or interference in my concerns. Go your way, or it may be the worse for you."

"Nay, good dame, be not angry, I came not to interfere with your concerns; I merely stopped on my road home to say 'good even' to you, and to see if I could be of any service to you, for I desire to cultivate the good-will of my neighbours."

"And a pretty way you have of doing so by prosecuting them in law courts for maintaining the rights of themselves and their ancestors for generations past."

"That I was compelled to do, good Jennet, for the maintenance of my own rights. It was a necessity forced upon me, but I bear no ill-will to either you or your son. And see, as a proof thereof, I have brought you a new kirtle from Wakefield," at the same time drawing from his saddlebags a flaming scarlet garment of that kind, which he threw into her lap.

"Farmer Jackson," said she, "come not here with your honied lips and deceitful expressions of friendship. I want none of your gifts," and taking up the kirtle, she rent it into a dozen pieces, and thrust them into the fire under the cauldron.

"Listen to me one moment," commenced Jackson, but the old beldame, rising up into a majestic attitude, interrupted him with, "I will listen no more to your hypocritical palaver. You have done me a grievous wrong in citing my son before your law courts, it is an unpardonable offence, and soon shall you know what it is to incur the wrath of Jennet Benton, the wise woman of Wakefield. Within a twelvemonth and a day, Farmer Jackson, shall you find at what cost you set the myrmidons of the law upon me and my belongings, and from that time to your life's end shall you rue that day's work. It is I, the wise woman of Wakefield, who say it, and see if I am not a true soothsayer, and merit the appellation I bear. That is all I have got to say," and she passed into her cottage, whilst the farmer rode homeward, not without a foreboding of impending evil.

We have many narratives on record of houses that have been the scenes of remarkable disturbances and strange apparitions, of furniture moved from place to place without apparent agency, of domestic utensils thrown about by no perceptible impelling power, and of noises attributable to no human cause, problems that in many cases have never been solved, but which have usually been ascribed to some mischievous goblin, or to the ghost of some unhappy person who has come by death unfairly and by foul means.

Farmer Jackson's house and homestead from this time, for the period of a year and a day, became haunted in this fashion, but here there could be no doubt as to the cause. It was the spell cast over it by the machinations of the witch, Jennet Benton, and it was in fact not a haunted but a bewitched house.

As Jackson rode home he thought of the curse laid upon him by the witch, but being a strong-minded man he did not entertain the current superstition as to the superhuman diabolic power said to be possessed by such persons, and he felt little or no apprehension on that score; yet he inclined so far to the popular belief as to fear that by some means she might cast incantations over his cattle and crops, so as to cause the former to sicken and die, and the latter to wither and come to naught.

On reaching his home he stabled his horse, and going indoors he accosted his wife with some cursory remark, but she made no reply, and he thought to himself, "She is sullen to-night – in one of her tantrums; what's the matter, I wonder."

He then sat down to supper, with his children about him, and a couple of maid-servants employed in some domestic duty, when his wife inquired, "Why are you all so silent; are you all dumb; have you got anything to tell me about the doings at the market, husband, goodman?" "What on earth do you mean?" inquired Jackson; "I spoke to you when I came in, and there has been noise enough among the children since then to waken the Seven Sleepers." Mrs. Jackson still stood staring, with a vacant countenance, and said, after a pause, "Why don't you reply? It seems as if one were in the charnel-house of the church, surrounded by the dead." It then occurred to Jackson that his wife must have suddenly become stone deaf, and by means of signs and such writing as the family had at command, he ascertained that such was the fact; but he dreamt not that it was the beginning of the witch's spell.

A night or two after, one of the children was stricken by an epileptic fit, throwing itself about with great violence and twisting its body with strange contortions, with convulsive writhings, and requiring to be held down by three or four persons to prevent its doing itself an injury.

One morning the swineherd of the farm came into the room where Jackson was sitting at breakfast, and with a scared countenance told him that a herd of swine that had been shut up in a barn the previous night "had broake thorrow two barn dores," and had fled no one knew whither. A search was immediately instituted, but it was not until after two or three days that a portion of the herd was found at a considerable distance from the farm, the remainder being lost altogether.

On another occasion Jackson himself, "although helthfull of body, was suddenly taken without any probable reason to be given or naturall cause appearing, being sometimes in such extremity that he conceived himselfe drawne in pieces at the hart, backe, and shoulders." During the first fit he heard the sound of music and dancing, as if in the room where he lay. He partially recovered the following day, but at twelve o'clock the next night he had another fit, and during its continuance he heard a loud ringing of bells, accompanied by sounds of singing and dancing. He inquired of his wife, who appears by this time to have recovered her sense of hearing, what the bell-ringing and singing meant; but she replied that she heard nothing of it, as also did his man. "He asked them againe and againe if they heard it not. At last he and his wife and servant heard it (what?) give three hevie groones. At that instant doggs did howle and yell at the windows as though they would heve puld them in pieces."

Jackson now became fully convinced that he was enduring all these trials and sufferings from the curse of the witch Jennet, and he expressed this opinion to his friends who came to condole with him. They, with neighbourly feeling, proposed to put the question to the test by submitting the old woman to the usual ordeal of the horse pond; but he would not hear of this, not even yet, with such probable evidence, believing that Satan could be authorised to endow old women with such mischievous powers. By the counsel of his friends, however, he sanctioned the sending a deputation to Jennet to investigate the matter. The deputation went to her cottage and told her their errand, but she only laughed at them. "It is true," said she, "that I called down the wrath of Heaven upon him and his belongings for his cruel persecution of a helpless widow and her orphan son; and if God has listened to my supplication, and sent calamity upon him, it is intended as a warning to him that, for the future, he may be more merciful to the poor and unprotected. If he chooses to blame any one, he must attribute his punishment to a much higher power than a feeble mortal such as I am."

During all this time Jackson's house was rendered almost uninhabitable by noises and apparitions, so that the servants fled from it panic-stricken, and others could not be found to take their places. The commencement of the disturbances was some six months after the utterance of the curse. The family were seated at supper when a tremendous crash was heard in the next room, as if some heavy metal vessel had been flung violently on the floor. Supposing it to be something that had fallen from a shelf or a hook in the ceiling, they went into the room, but found nothing to account for the noise. At other times it would seem as if all the doors of the house were being slammed to, or the windows shaken as by a storm of wind, although there was not the slightest agitation in the atmosphere. Then would occur shrieks as of persons in distress, groans as of sufferers in agonies of pain, and bursts of demoniac laughter, with a flapping of huge bat-like wings. "Apparitions like blacke dogges and catts were also scene," which darted out from under the furniture and usually passed out up the chimney, it being immaterial whether or not a fire was blazing in the grate. Along with all these disturbances in the house and unaccountable illnesses of the various members of the household, the horses and cattle of the farm were subjected to similar inflictions, much to the detriment of Jackson's material prosperity. Week after week news came in of the death of horses, cows, and sheep: and in his deposition at York, Jackson said that "since the time the said Jennet and George Benton threatened him he hath lost eighteen horses and meares, and he conceives he hath had all this loss by the use of some witchcraft or sorcerie by the said Jennet and George Benton."

For a twelvemonth and a day these disturbances, sufferings, and losses continued, rendering Jackson almost bankrupt, and then they all at once ceased.

Being fully convinced that these troubles had been caused by the diabolical incantations of the witch Jennet, he brought a charge against her and her son, at York, of practising witchcraft against him, and they were tried at the assizes on the 7th June, 1656.

The Curse of Echo

IN THE FLOWERY GROVES OF HELICON Echo was once a fair nymph who, hand in hand with her sisters, sported along the green lawns and by the side of the mountain-streams. Among them all her feet were the lightest and her laugh the merriest, and in the telling of tales not one of them could touch her. So if ever any among them were plotting mischief in their hearts, they would say to her,

"Echo, thou weaver of words, go thou and sit beside Hera in her bower, and beguile her with a tale that she come not forth and find us. See thou make it a long one, Echo, and we will give thee a garland to twine in thy hair."

And Echo would laugh a gay laugh, which rang through the grove.

"What will you do when she tires of my tales?" she asked.

"When that time comes we shall see," said they.

So with another laugh she would trip away and cast herself on the grass at Hera's feet. When Hera looked upon Echo her stern brow would relax, and she would smile upon her and stroke her hair.

"What hast thou come for now, thou sprite?" she would ask.

"I had a great longing to talk with thee, great Hera," she would answer, "and I have a tale – a wondrous new tale – to tell thee."

"Thy tales are as many as the risings of the sun, Echo, and each one of them as long as an old man's beard."

"The day is yet young, mother," she would say, "and the tales I have told thee before are as mud which is trampled underfoot by the side of the one I shall tell thee now."

"Go to, then," said Hera, "and if it pleases me I will listen to the end."

So Echo would sit upon the grass at Hera's feet, and with her eyes fixed upon her face she would tell her tale. She had the gift of words, and, moreover, she had seen and heard many strange things which she alone could tell of. These she would weave into romances, adding to them as best pleased her, or taking from them at will; for the best of tale-tellers are those who can lie, but who mingle in with their lies some grains of truth which they have picked from their own experience. And Hera would forget her watchfulness and her jealousies, and listen entranced, while the magic of Echo's words made each scene live before her eyes. Meanwhile the nymphs would sport to their hearts' content and never fear her anger.

But at last came the black day of reckoning when Hera found out the prank which Echo had played upon her so long, and the fire of her wrath flashed forth like lightning.

"The gift whereby thou hast deceived me shall be thine no more," she cried. "Henceforward thou shalt be dumb till someone else has spoken, and then, even if thou wilt, thou shalt not hold thy tongue, but must needs repeat once more the last words that have been spoken."

"Alas! alas!" cried the nymphs in chorus.

"Alas! alas!" cried Echo after them, and could say no more, though she longed to speak and beg Hera to forgive her. So did it come to pass that she lost her voice, and could only say that which others put in her mouth, whether she wished it or no.

Now, it chanced one day that the young Narcissus strayed away from his companions in the hunt, and when he tried to find them he only wandered further, and lost his way upon the lonely heights of Helicon. He was now in the bloom of his youth, nearing manhood, and fair as a flower in spring, and all who saw him straightway loved him and longed for him. But, though his face was smooth and soft as maiden's, his heart was hard as steel; and while many loved him and sighed for him, they could kindle no answering flame in his breast, but he would spurn them, and treat them with scorn, and go on his way, nothing caring. When he was born, the blind seer Teiresias had prophesied concerning him,

"So long as he sees not himself he shall live and be happy."

And his words came true, for Narcissus cared for neither man nor woman, but only for his own pleasure; and because he was so fair that all who saw him loved him for his beauty, he found it easy to get from them what he would. But he himself knew nought of love, and therefore but little of grief; for love at the best brings joy and sorrow hand in hand, and if unreturned, it brings nought but pain.

Now, when the nymphs saw Narcissus wandering alone through the woods, they, too, loved him for his beauty, and they followed him wherever he went. But because he was a mortal they were shy of him, and would not show themselves, but hid behind the trees and rocks so that he should not see them; and amongst the others Echo followed him, too. At last, when he found he had really wandered astray, he began to shout for one of his companions.

"Ho, there! where art thou?" he cried.

"Where art thou?" answered Echo.

When he heard the voice, he stopped and listened, but he could hear nothing more. Then he called again.

"I am here in the wood – Narcissus."

"In the wood – Narcissus," said she.

"Come hither," he cried.

"Come hither," she answered.

Wondering at the strange voice which answered him, he looked all about, but could see no one.

"Art thou close at hand?" he asked.

"Close at hand," answered Echo.

Wondering the more at seeing no one, he went forward in the direction of the voice. Echo, when she found he was coming towards her, fled further, so that when next he called, her voice sounded far away. But wherever she was, he still followed after her, and she saw that he would not let her escape; for wherever she hid, if he called, she had to answer, and so show him her hiding-place. By now they had come to an open space in the trees, where the green lawn sloped down to a clear pool in the hollow. Here by the margin of the water she stood, with her back to the tall, nodding bulrushes, and as Narcissus came out from the trees she wrung her hands, and the salt tears dropped from her eyes; for she loved him, and longed to speak to him, and yet she could not say a word. When he saw her he stopped.

"Art thou she who calls me?" he asked.

"Who calls me?" she answered.

"I have told thee, Narcissus," he said.

"Narcissus," she cried, and held out her arms to him.

"Who art thou?" he asked.

"Who art thou?" said she.

"Have I not told thee," he said impatiently, "Narcissus?"

"Narcissus," she said again, and still held out her hands beseechingly.

"Tell me," he cried, "who art thou and why dost thou call me?"

"Why dost thou call me?" said she.

At this he grew angry.

"Maiden, whoever thou art, thou hast led me a pretty dance through the woods, and now thou dost nought but mock me."

"Thou dost nought but mock me," said she.

At this he grew yet more angry, and began to abuse her, but every word of abuse that he spoke she hurled back at him again. At last, tired out with his wanderings and with anger, he threw himself on the grass by the pool, and would not look at her nor speak to her again. For a time she stood beside him weeping, and longing to speak to him and explain, but never a word could she utter. So at last in her misery she left him, and went and hid herself behind a rock close by. After a while, when his anger had cooled down somewhat, Narcissus remembered he was very thirsty, and noticing for the first time the clear pool beside him, he bent over the edge of the bank to drink. As he held out his hand to take the water, he saw looking up towards him a face which was the fairest face he had ever looked on, and his heart, which never yet had known what love was, at last was set on fire by the face in the pool. With a sigh he held out both his arms towards it, and the figure also held out two arms to him, and Echo from the rock answered back his sigh. When he saw the figure stretching out towards him and heard the sigh, he thought that his love was returned, and he bent down closer to the water and whispered, "I love thee."

"I love thee," answered Echo from the rock.

At these words he bent down further, and tried to clasp the figure in his arms, but as he did so, it vanished away. The surface of the pool was covered with ripples, and he found he was clasping empty water to his breast. So he drew back and waited awhile, thinking he had been overhasty. In time, the ripples died away and the face appeared again as clear as before, looking up at him longingly from the water. Once again he bent towards it, and tried to clasp it, and once again it fled from his embrace. Time after time he tried, and always the same thing happened, and at last he gave up in despair, and sat looking down into the water, with the teardrops falling from his eyes; and the figure in the pool wept, too, and looked up at him with a look of longing and despair. The longer he looked, the more fiercely did the flame of love burn in his breast, till at length he could bear it no more, but determined to reach the desire of his heart or die. So for the last time he leaned forward, and when he found that once again he was clasping the empty water, he threw himself from the bank into the pool, thinking that in the depths, at any rate, he would find his love. But he found naught but death among the weeds and stones of the pool, and knew not that it was his own face he loved reflected in the water below him. Thus were the words of the prophet fulfilled, "So long as he sees not himself he shall live and be happy."

Echo, peeping out from the rock, saw all that had happened, and when Narcissus cast himself into the pool, she rushed forward, all too late, to stop him. When she found she could not save him, she cast herself on the grass by the pool and wept and wept, till her flesh and her bones wasted away with weeping, and naught but her voice remained and the curse that was on her. So to this day she lives, a formless voice haunting rocks and caves and vaulted halls. Herself no man has seen since the day Narcissus saw her wringing her hands for love of him beside the nodding bulrushes, and no man ever shall see again. But her voice we all have heard repeating our words when we thought that no one was by; and though now she will say whatever we bid her, if once the curse were removed, the cry of her soul would be, "Narcissus, Narcissus, my love, come back – come back to me!"

By the side of the clear brown pool, on the grass that Echo had watered with her tears, there sprang up a sweet-scented flower, with a pure white face and a crown of gold. And to this day in many a land men call that flower "Narcissus," after the lad who, for love of his own fair face, was drowned in the waters of Helicon.

HEALERS, SEERS & SOOTHSAYERS

Introduction

WITCHES AND WIZARDS CAN BE A FORCE FOR GOOD. Magic may as easily be used for healing as for harm. It can work in mysterious ways, though: on the one hand here we have, from India, twin Hindu gods of medicine; on the other a Chinese physician who is, quite literally, a dog.

Sometimes the sorcery lies in self-sacrifice. From Kenya comes the story of Wanjiru who, losing her life to save her village in a dreadful drought, comes back to wed her handsome young warrior. Ying Lo, the little boy who, in return for long-forgotten kindnesses to random strangers, finds his life saved, along with his family, fellow-passengers and crew aboard the storm-tossed 'Phantom Vessel' in the Chinese tale.

Witchcraft, wizardry and wisdom can be close kin, we are reminded, but quickness and common sense may be as important as occult learning. Hugh the Conjuror, from Wales, has special powers, but it's old-fashioned smartness that enables him to unmask 'The Two Cat Witches' here. As for the Turkish 'Soothsayer', his methods deliver spectacular results, but owe rather less to lofty mysticism than to low cunning.

Wanjiru, Sacrificed by Her Family

THE SUN BEAT DOWN MERCILESSLY and there was no sign of any rain. This happened one year, and it happened again a second year, and even a third year, so that the crops died and the men, women and children found themselves close to starvation. Finally, the elders of the village called all the people together, and they assembled on the scorched grass at the foot of the hill where they had sung and danced in happier times.

Sick and weary of their miserable plight, they turned to each other and asked helplessly: "Why is it that the rains do not come?"

Not one among them could find an answer, and so they went to the house of the witch-doctor and put to him the same question:

"Tell us why there is no rain," they wept. "Our crops have failed for a third season and we shall soon die of hunger if things do not change."

The witch-doctor took hold of his gourd, shook it hard, and poured its contents on the ground. After he had done this three times, he spoke gravely:

"There is a young maiden called Wanjiru living among you. If you want the rain to fall, she must be bought by the people of the village. In two days' time you should all return to this place, and every one of you, from the eldest to the youngest, must bring with him a goat for the purchase of the maiden."

And so, on the appointed day, the people gathered together again, each one of them leading a goat to the foot of the hill where the witch-doctor waited to receive them. He ordered the crowd to form a circle and called for Wanjiru to come forward and stand in the middle with her relations to one side of her.

One by one, the people began to move towards Wanjiru's family, leading the goats in payment, and as they approached, the feet of the young girl began to sink into the ground. In an instant, she had sunk up to her knees and she screamed in terror as the soil tugged at her limbs, pulling her closer towards the earth.

Her father and mother saw what was happening and they, too, cried out in fear:

"Our daughter is lost! Our daughter is lost! We must do something to save her."

But the villagers continued to close in around them, each of them handing over their goat until Wanjiru sank deeper to her waist.

"I am lost!" the girl called out, "but much rain will come."

She sank to her breast, and as she did so, heavy black clouds began to gather overhead. She sank even lower, up to her neck, and now the rain started to fall from above in huge drops.

Again, Wanjiru's family attempted to move forward to save her, but yet more people came towards them, pressing them to take goats in payment, and so they stood still, watching as the girl wailed:

"My people have forsaken me! I am undone."

Soon she had vanished from sight. The earth closed over her, the rain poured down in a great deluge and the villagers ran to their huts for shelter without pausing to look back.

Now there was a particular young warrior of fearless reputation among the people who had been in love with Wanjiru ever since childhood. Several weeks had passed since her disappearance, but still he could not reconcile himself to her loss and repeated continually to himself:

"Wanjiru is gone from me and her own people have done this thing to her. But I will find her. I will go to the same place and bring her back."

Taking up his shield and his spear, the young warrior departed his home in search of the girl he loved. For almost a year, he roamed the countryside, but still he could find no trace of her. Weary and dejected, he returned home to the village and stood on the spot where Wanjiru had vanished, allowing his tears to flow freely for the first time.

Suddenly, his feet began to sink into the soil and he sank lower and lower until the ground closed over him and he found himself standing in the middle of a long, winding road beneath the earth's surface. He did not hesitate to follow this road, and after a time, he spotted a figure up ahead of him. He ran towards the figure and saw that it was Wanjiru, even though she was scarcely recognizable in her filthy, tattered clothing.

"You were sacrificed to bring the rain," he spoke tenderly to her, "but now that the rain has come, I shall take you back where you belong."

And he lifted Wanjiru carefully onto his back and carried her, as if she were his own beloved child, along the road he had come by, until they rose together to the open air and their feet touched the ground once more.

"You shall not return to the house of your people," the warrior told Wanjiru, "they have treated you shamefully. I will look after you instead."

So they waited until nightfall, and under cover of darkness, the young warrior took Wanjiru to his mother's house, instructing the old woman to tell no one that the girl had returned.

The months passed by, and Wanjiru lived happily with mother and son. Every day a goat was slaughtered and the meat served to her. The old woman made clothes from the skins and hung beads in the girl's hair so that soon she had regained the healthy glow she once had.

Harvest time was now fast approaching, and a great feast was to be held among the people of the village. The young warrior was one of the first to arrive but Wanjiru waited until the rest of the guests had assembled before she came out of the house to join the festivities. At first, she was not recognized by anyone, but after a time, one of her brothers approached her and cried out:

"Surely that is Wanjiru, the sister we lost when the rains came."

The girl hung her head and gave no answer.

"You sold Wanjiru shamefully," the young warrior intervened, "you do not deserve to have her back."

And he beat off her relatives and took Wanjiru back to his mother's house.

But the next day, her family knocked on his door asking to see the young girl. The warrior refused them once more, but still they came, again and again, until, on the fourth day, the young man relented and said to himself:

"Those are real tears her family shed. Surely now they have proven that they care."

So he invited her father and her mother and her brothers into his home and sat down to fix the bride-price for Wanjiru. And when he had paid it, the young warrior married Wanjiru who had returned to him from the land of shadows beneath the earth.

The King and the Ju Ju Tree

UDO UBOK UDOM was a famous king who lived at Itam, which is an inland town, and does not possess a river. The king and his wife therefore used to wash at the spring just behind their house.

King Udo had a daughter, of whom he was very fond, and looked after her most carefully, and she grew up into a beautiful woman.

For some time the king had been absent from his house, and had not been to the spring for two years. When he went to his old place to wash, he found that the Idem Ju Ju tree had grown up all round the place, and it was impossible for him to use the spring as he had done formerly.

He therefore called fifty of his young men to bring their matchets and cut down the tree. They started cutting the tree, but it had no effect, as, directly they made a cut in the tree, it closed up again; so, after working all day, they found they had made no impression on it.

When they returned at night, they told the king that they had been unable to destroy the tree. He was very angry when he heard this, and went to the spring the following morning, taking his own matchet with him.

When the Ju Ju tree saw that the king had come himself and was starting to try to cut his branches, he caused a small splinter of wood to go into the king's eye. This gave the king great pain, so he threw down his matchet and went back to his house. The pain, however, got worse, and he could not eat or sleep for three days.

He therefore sent for his witch men, and told them to cast lots to find out why he was in such pain. When they had cast lots, they decided that the reason was that the Ju Ju tree was angry with the king because he wanted to wash at the spring, and had tried to destroy the tree.

They then told the king that he must take seven baskets of flies, a white goat, a white chicken, and a piece of white cloth, and make a sacrifice of them in order to satisfy the Ju Ju.

The king did this, and the witch men tried their lotions on the king's eye, but it got worse and worse.

He then dismissed these witches and got another lot. When they arrived they told the king that, although they could do nothing themselves to relieve his pain, they knew one man who lived in the spirit land who could cure him; so the king told them to send for him at once, and he arrived the next day.

Then the spirit man said, "Before I do anything to your eye, what will you give me?" So King Udo said, "I will give you half my town with the people in it, also seven cows and some money." But the spirit man refused to accept the king's offer. As the king was in such pain, he said, "Name your own price, and I will pay you." So the spirit man said the only thing he was willing to accept as payment was the king's daughter. At this the king cried very much, and told the man to go away, as he would rather die than let him have his daughter.

That night the pain was worse than ever, and some of his subjects pleaded with the king to send for the spirit man again and give him his daughter, and told him that when he got well he could no doubt have another daughter but that if he died now he would lose everything.

The king then sent for the spirit man again, who came very quickly, and in great grief the king handed his daughter to the spirit.

The spirit man then went out into the bush, and collected some leaves, which he soaked in water and beat up. The juice he poured into the king's eye, and told him that when he washed his face in the morning he would be able to see what was troubling him in the eye.

The king tried to persuade him to stay the night, but the spirit man refused, and departed that same night for the spirit land, taking the king's daughter with him.

Before it was light the king rose up and washed his face, and found that the small splinter from the Ju Ju tree, which had been troubling him so much, dropped out of his eye, the pain disappeared, and he was quite well again.

When he came to his proper senses he realised that he had sacrificed his daughter for one of his eyes, so he made an order that there should be general mourning throughout his kingdom for three years.

For the first two years of the mourning the king's daughter was put in the fatting house by the spirit man, and was given food; but a skull, who was in the house, told her not to eat, as they were fatting her up, not for marriage, but so that they could eat her. She therefore gave all the food which was brought to her to the skull, and lived on chalk herself.

Towards the end of the third year the spirit man brought some of his friends to see the king's daughter, and told them he would kill her the next day, and they would have a good feast off her.

When she woke up in the morning the spirit man brought her food as usual; but the skull, who wanted to preserve her life, and who had heard what the spirit man had said, called her into the room and told her what was going to happen later in the day. She handed the food to the skull, and he said, "When the spirit man goes to the wood with his friends to prepare for the feast, you must run back to your father."

He then gave her some medicine which would make her strong for the journey, and also gave her directions as to the road, telling her that there were two roads but that when she came to the parting of the ways she was to drop some of the medicine on the ground and the two roads would become one.

He then told her to leave by the back door, and go through the wood until she came to the end of the town; she would then find the road. If she met people on the road she was to pass them in silence, as if she saluted them they would know that she was a stranger in the spirit land, and might kill her. She was also not to turn round if anyone called to her, but was to go straight on till she reached her father's house.

Having thanked the skull for his kind advice, the king's daughter started off, and when she reached the end of the town and found the road, she ran for three hours, and at last arrived at the branch roads. There she dropped the medicine, as she had been instructed, and the two roads immediately became one; so she went straight on and never saluted anyone or turned back, although several people called to her.

About this time the spirit man had returned from the wood, and went to the house, only to find the king's daughter was absent. He asked the skull where she was, and he replied that she had gone out by the back door, but he did not know where she had gone to. Being a spirit, however, he very soon guessed that she had gone home; so he followed as quickly as possible, shouting out all the time.

When the girl heard his voice she ran as fast as she could, and at last arrived at her father's house, and told him to take at once a cow, a pig, a sheep, a goat, a dog, a chicken, and seven eggs, and cut them into seven parts as a sacrifice, and leave them on the road, so that when the spirit man saw these things he would stop and not enter the town. This the king did immediately, and made the sacrifice as his daughter had told him.

When the spirit man saw the sacrifice on the road, he sat down and at once began to eat.

When he had satisfied his appetite, he packed up the remainder and returned to the spirit land, not troubling any more about the king's daughter.

When the king saw that the danger was over, he beat his drum, and declared that for the future, when people died and went to the spirit land, they should not come to earth again as spirits to cure sick people.

The Young Thief

ONCE UPON A TIME there was a man and he wished to marry. So he went to the Seers and asked them to foretell his future. The Seers looked at their books and said to him, "If you marry you will certainly have a child, a very beautiful boy, but with one blemish; he will be a thief, the biggest thief that ever was."

So that man said, "Never mind, even if he be a thief; I should like to have a son." So he married, and in due time a child was born, a beautiful boy.

The child was carefully brought up till he was old enough to have a teacher. Then the father engaged a professor to come and teach him every day. He built a house a little distance from the town and put him in it, and that professor came every morning and taught him during the day, and in the evening returned home. Now the father ordered the professor never to let his son see any other soul but himself, and he thought by that means that his son would escape the fate that had been decreed by the Seers; for if he never saw any other person he could have no one to teach him to steal.

One day the professor came, and he told the lad about a horse of the Sultan's, which used to go out to exercise by itself and return by itself, and was of great strength and speed.

Then that youth asked where was the Sultan's palace, and his professor took him up on to the flat roof and pointed out to him the palace and its neighbourhood.

That night, after the professor left, the youth slipped out and came to the Sultan's stables, stole the horse, and returned home with it.

Next day the professor was a little late in coming, so the lad asked him, "Sheikh, why have you delayed today?" The professor said, "I stayed to hear the news. Behold, someone has stolen the Sultan's horse which I told you about yesterday."

Then that lad asked, "What does the Sultan propose to do?"

The old man replied, "He thought of sending out his soldiers, but then he heard of a seer who is able to detect a thief by looking at his books, so he is going to ask him first."

So the youth asked, "Where does that seer live?"

The professor then pointed out the seer's house and its neighbourhood.

That night the youth slipped out and came to the seer's house and found that the seer was out. He saw his wife and said to her – "My mistress, the seer has sent me to fetch his box of books."

So the wife brought out the box containing all his books of magic and gave them to him, and he took them and returned with them to his house.

Next day his professor was late, and when he came he said to him, "Father, why have you delayed?"

The old man said, "I stopped to hear the news. Do you remember the seer of whom I told you yesterday, who was to find out the thief for the Sultan? Well, he has now been robbed of his books of magic."

The youth asked, "What does the Sultan intend to do?"

The old man replied, "He was about to send out his soldiers, and then he heard that there was a magician who is able to detect a thief by casting charms, so he is going to consult him."

Then the youth asked, "Where does the magician live?"

So the old man took him on the roof and pointed out the magician's house and its neighbourhood.

That night, after the professor had gone, the youth went out and came to the house of the magician. He found him out, but saw his wife and said to her, "Mother, I fear to ask you, for was not the seer robbed in like manner yesterday? but the magician has sent me to fetch his bag of charms."

That woman said, "Have no fear; the thief's not you, my child;" and she gave him the bag of charms, and he took them and went to his house.

Next day, when the professor came, he asked for the news, and he said, "Did I not tell you yesterday that the Sultan was going to get a magician to tell him the thief by casting his charms? Well, last night the magician had his bag of charms stolen."

Then the youth asked, "What is the Sultan going to do?"

The old man answered, "He was going to send out his soldiers to catch the thief, but he heard that a certain woman said she knew who the thief was, and so he is going to pay her to tell him."

The youth asked where the woman lived, and the old man pointed out her house to him.

That evening the youth went out, and came to the house of that woman and found her outside, and he said to her, "Mother, I am thirsty; give me a drink of water."

So she went to the well to draw some water, and the youth came behind her and pushed her in. Then he went into the house and took her clothes and jewellery and brought them back to his house.

Next day, when the professor came, he asked the news, and he said, "My son, I told you yesterday that there was a woman who said that she could tell the Sultan the name of the thief. Well, last night the thief came and pushed her into the well and stole her things."

Then that youth asked, "What does the Sultan propose to do?"

The old man replied, "He is sending his soldiers out to look for the thief."

That night, after the professor had gone, the youth dressed up as a soldier, and went out and met the soldiers of the Sultan looking for the thief.

He said to them, "That is not the way to look for a thief. The way to look for a thief is to sit down very quietly in a place, and then perhaps you will see or hear him."

So he brought them all to one place and made them sit down, and one by one they all fell asleep. When they were all asleep he took their weapons and all their clothes he could carry and came with them to his house.

Next day, when the professor came, he asked him the news, and he said, "Last night the Sultan sent his soldiers out to look for the thief and behold, the thief stole their arms and their clothes, so that they returned naked."

Then the youth asked, "And now, what does the Sultan propose to do?"

The old man said, "Tonight the Sultan goes himself to look for the thief."

The youth said, "That is good, for the wisdom of Sultans is great."

That night the youth dressed up as a woman and scented himself and went out. He saw in the distance a lamp, and knew that it was the Sultan looking for the thief, so he passed near. When the Sultan smelt those goodly scents, he turned round to see whence they came, and he saw a very beautiful woman.

He asked, "Who are you?"

The lad replied, "I was just returning home when I saw your light, so I stepped aside to let you pass."

The Sultan said, "You must come and talk with me a little."

That lad said, "No, I must go home."

They were just outside the prison, so at last the youth consented to go in and talk for a little while with the Sultan.

When they got inside the courtyard, the youth took a pair of leg-irons and asked the Sultan, "What are these?"

The Sultan replied, "Those are the leg-irons with which we fasten our prisoners."

Then that youth said, "Oh, fasten them on me, that I may see how they work."

The Sultan said, "No, you are a woman, but I will put them on to show you," and he put them on.

The youth looked up and saw a gang-chain and asked, "What is that?"

The Sultan said, "That is what we put round their necks, and the end is fastened to the wall."

So the youth said, "Oh, put it on my neck, that I may see what it is like."

The Sultan replied, "No, you are a woman, but I will put it on my neck to show you;" so he put it on.

Then the youth took the key of the leg-irons and of the gang-chain, and looked up and saw a whip and said, "What is that?"

"That," said the Sultan, "is a whip with which we whip our prisoners if they are bad."

So the youth picked up the whip and began beating the Sultan. After the first few strokes the Sultan said, "Stop, that is enough fun-making."

But the youth went on and beat him soundly, and then went out, leaving the Sultan in chains and chained to the wall, and he also locked the door of the prison and took the key and went home. Next day the Sultan was found to be in the prison, and they could not get in to let him out or free him.

So a crier was sent round the town to cry, "Anyone who can deliver the Sultan from prison will be given a free pardon for any offence he has committed."

So, when the cries came to that youth's house, he said, "Oho, I want that as a certificate in writing before I will say what I know."

When these words were brought to the Wazir, he had a document drawn up, giving a free pardon to anyone who would deliver the Sultan. Then he brought it round to the prison for the Sultan's signature, and as they could not get it in they pushed it through the window on the end of a long pole. Then the Sultan signed it, and it was given to that youth, who handed over the key of the prison and of the chains and fetters. After the Sultan had been released he called that youth to his palace, and the youth took the horse, and the sage's books of magic, and the magician's bag of charms, and the woman's clothes and jewellery, and the soldiers' arms and clothes, and came to the palace.

When the Sultan heard his story he said that he was indeed a very clever youth, so he made him his Wazir.

This is the story of the man who would have a child, even though he should be a thief.

The Chamber of the Priest-Magician

LET US ATTEMPT TO DESCRIBE the treatment of a case by a priest-physician-magician of Babylonia. The following is a rather obscure one, but by the aid of imagination as well as the assistance of Babylonian representation we may construct a tolerably clear picture.

The chamber of the sage is almost certain to be situated in some nook in one of those vast and imposing fanes which more closely resembled cities than mere temples. We draw the curtain and enter a rather darksome room. The atmosphere is pungent with chemic odours, and ranged on shelves disposed upon the tiled walls are numerous jars, great and small, containing the fearsome compounds which the practitioner applies to the sufferings of Babylonian humanity. The asipu, shaven and austere, asks us what we desire of him, and in the role of Babylonian citizens we acquaint him with the fact that our lives are made miserable for us by a witch who sends upon us misfortune after misfortune, now the blight or some equally intractable and horrible disease, now an evil wind, now unspeakable enchantments which torment us unceasingly. In his capacity of physician the asipu examines our bodies, shrunken and exhausted with fever or rheumatism, and having prescribed for us, compounds the mixture with his own hands and enjoins us to its regular application. He mixes various ingredients in a stone mortar, whispering his spells the while, with many a prayer to Ea the beneficent and Merodach the all-powerful that we may be restored to health. Then he promises to visit us at our dwelling and gravely bids us adieu, after expressing the hope that we will graciously contribute to the upkeep of the house of religion to which he is attached.

Leaving the darkened haunt of the asipu for the brilliant sunshine of a Babylonian summer afternoon, we are at first inclined to forget our fears, and to laugh away the horrible superstitions, the relics of barbarian ancestors, which weigh us down. But as night approaches we grow more fearful, we crouch with the children in the darkest corner of our clay-brick dwelling, and tremble at every sound. The rushing of the wind overhead is for us the noise of the Labartu, the hag-demon, come hither to tear from us our little ones, or perhaps a rat rustling in the straw may seem to us the Alu-demon. The ghosts of the dead gibber at the threshold, and even pale Uru, lord of disease, himself may glance in at the tiny window with ghastly countenance and eager, red eyes. The pains of rheumatism assail us. Ha, the evil witch is at work, thrusting thorns into the waxen images made in our shape that we may suffer the torment brought about by sympathetic magic, to which we would rather refer our aches than to the circumstance that we dwell hard by the river-swamps.

A loud knocking resounds at the door. We tremble anew and the children scream. At last the dread powers of evil have come to summon us to the final ordeal, or perhaps the witch herself, grown bold by reason of her immunity, has come to wreak fresh vengeance. The flimsy door of boards is thrown open, and to our unspeakable relief the stern face of the asipu appears beneath the flickering light of the taper. We shout with joy, and the children cluster around the priest, clinging to his garments and clasping his knees.

The Witch-Finding

The priest smiles at our fear, and motioning us to sit in a circle produces several waxen figures of demons which he places on the floor. It is noticeable that these figures all appear to be bound with miniature ropes. Taking one of these in the shape of a Labartu or hag-demon, the priest places before it twelve small cakes made from a peculiar kind of meal. He then pours out a libation of water, places the image of a small black dog beside that of the witch, lays a piece of the heart of a young pig on the mouth of the figure and some white bread and a box of ointment beside it. He then chants something like the following: "May a guardian spirit be present at my side when I draw near unto the sick man, when I examine his muscles, when I compose his limbs, when I sprinkle the water of Ea upon him. Avoid thee whether thou art an evil spirit or an evil demon, an evil ghost or an evil devil, an evil god or an evil fiend, hag-demon, ghoul, sprite, phantom, or wraith, or any disease, fever, headache, shivering, or any sorcery, spell, or enchantment."

Having recited some such words of power the asipu then directs us to keep the figure at the head of our bed for three nights, then to bury it beneath the earthen floor. But alas! no cure results. The witch still torments us by day and night, and once more we have recourse to the priest-doctor; the ceremony is gone through again, but still the family health does not improve. The little ones suffer from fever, and bad luck consistently dogs us. After a stormy scene between husband and wife, who differ regarding the qualifications of the asipu, another practitioner is called in. He is younger and more enterprising than the last, and he has not yet learned that half the business of the physician is to 'nurse' his patients, in the financial sense of the term. Whereas the elderly asipu had gone quietly home to bed after prescribing for us, this young physician, who has his spurs to win, after being consulted goes home to his clay surgery and hunts up a likely exorcism.

Next day, armed with this wordy weapon, he arrives at our dwelling and, placing a waxen image of the witch upon the floor, vents upon it the full force of his rhetoric. As he is on the point of leaving, screams resound from a neighbouring cabin. Bestowing upon us a look of the deepest meaning our asipu darts to the hut opposite and hales forth an ancient crone, whose appearance of age and illness give her a most sinister look. At once we recognize in her a wretch who dared to menace our children when in innocent play they cast hot ashes upon her thatch and introduced hot swamp water into her cistern. In righteous wrath we lay hands on the abandoned being who for so many months has cast a blight upon our lives. She exclaims that the pains of death have seized upon her, and we laugh in triumph, for we know that the superior magic of our asipu has taken effect. On the way to the river we are joined by neighbours, who rejoice with us that we have caught the witch. Great is the satisfaction of the party when at last the devilish crone is cast headlong into the stream.

But ere many seconds pass we begin to look incredulously upon each other, for the wicked one refuses to sink. This means that she is innocent! Then, awful moment, we find every eye directed upon us, we who were so happy and light-hearted but a moment before.

We tremble, for we know how severe are the laws against the indiscriminate accusation of those suspected of witchcraft. As the ancient crone continues to float, a loud murmuring arises in the crowd, and with quaking limbs and eyes full of terror we snatch up our children and make a dash for freedom.

Luckily the asipu accompanies us so that the crowd dare not pursue, and indeed, so absurdly changeable is human nature, most of them are busied in rescuing the old woman. In a few minutes we have placed all immediate danger of pursuit behind us. The asipu has departed to his temple, richer in the experience by the lesson of a false 'prescription.' After a hurried consultation we quit the town, skirt the arable land which fringes it, and plunge into the desert. She who was opposed to the employment of a young and inexperienced asipu does not make matters any better by reiterating "I told you so." And he who favoured a 'second opinion', on paying a night visit to the city, discovers that the 'witch' has succumbed to her harsh treatment; that his house has been made over to her relatives by way of compensation, and that a legal process has been taken out against him. Returning to his wife he acquaints her with the sad news, and hand in hand with their weeping offspring they turn and face the desert.

The Strange Tale of Doctor Dog

FAR UP IN the mountains of the Province of Hunan in the central part of China, there once lived in a small village a rich gentleman who had only one child. This girl, like the daughter of Kwan-yu in the story of the Great Bell, was the very joy of her father's life.

Now Mr. Min, for that was this gentleman's name, was famous throughout the whole district for his learning, and, as he was also the owner of much property, he spared no effort to teach Honeysuckle the wisdom of the sages, and to give her everything she craved. Of course this was enough to spoil most children, but Honeysuckle was not at all like other children. As sweet as the flower from which she took her name, she listened to her father's slightest command, and obeyed without ever waiting to be told a second time.

Her father often bought kites for her, of every kind and shape. There were fish, birds, butterflies, lizards and huge dragons, one of which had a tail more than thirty feet long. Mr. Min was very skilful in flying these kites for little Honeysuckle, and so naturally did his birds and butterflies circle round and hover about in the air that almost any little western boy would have been deceived and said, "Why, there is a real bird, and not a kite at all!" Then again, he would fasten a queer little instrument to the string, which made a kind of humming noise, as he waved his hand from side to side. "It is the wind singing, Daddy," cried Honeysuckle, clapping her hands with joy; "singing a kite-song to both of us." Sometimes, to teach his little darling a lesson if she had been the least naughty, Mr. Min would fasten queerly twisted scraps of paper, on which were written many Chinese words, to the string of her favourite kite.

"What are you doing, Daddy?" Honeysuckle would ask. "What can those queer-looking papers be?"

"On every piece is written a sin that we have done."

"What is a sin, Daddy?"

"Oh, when Honeysuckle has been naughty; that is a sin!" he answered gently. "Your old nurse is afraid to scold you, and if you are to grow up to be a good woman, Daddy must teach you what is right."

Then Mr. Min would send the kite up high – high over the house-tops, even higher than the tall Pagoda on the hillside. When all his cord was let out, he would pick up two sharp stones, and, handing them to Honeysuckle, would say, "Now, daughter, cut the string, and the wind will carry away the sins that are written down on the scraps of paper."

"But, Daddy, the kite is so pretty. Mayn't we keep our sins a little longer?" she would innocently ask.

"No, child; it is dangerous to hold on to one's sins. Virtue is the foundation of happiness," he would reply sternly, choking back his laughter at her question. "Make haste and cut the cord."

So Honeysuckle, always obedient – at least with her father – would saw the string in two between the sharp stones, and with a childish cry of despair would watch her favourite kite, blown by the wind, sail farther and farther away, until at last, straining her eyes, she could see it sink slowly to the earth in some far-distant meadow.

"Now laugh and be happy," Mr. Min would say, "for your sins are all gone. See that you don't get a new supply of them."

Honeysuckle was also fond of seeing the puppet show, for, you must know, this old-fashioned amusement for children was enjoyed by little folks in China, perhaps three thousand years before your great-grandfather was born. It is even said that the great Emperor, Mu, when he saw these little dancing images for the first time, was greatly enraged at seeing one of them making eyes at his favourite wife. He ordered the showman to be put to death, and it was with difficulty the poor fellow persuaded his Majesty that the dancing puppets were not really alive at all, but only images of cloth and clay.

No wonder then Honeysuckle liked to see the puppets if the Son of Heaven himself had been deceived by their queer antics into thinking them real people of flesh and blood.

But we must hurry on with our story, or some of our readers will be asking, "But where is Dr. Dog? Are you never coming to the hero of this tale?" One day when Honeysuckle was sitting inside a shady pavilion that overlooked a tiny fish-pond, she was suddenly seized with a violent attack of colic. Frantic with pain, she told a servant to summon her father, and then without further ado, she fell over in a faint upon the ground.

When Mr. Min reached his daughter's side, she was still unconscious. After sending for the family physician to come post haste, he got his daughter to bed, but although she recovered from her fainting fit, the extreme pain continued until the poor girl was almost dead from exhaustion.

Now, when the learned doctor arrived and peered at her from under his gigantic spectacles, he could not discover the cause of her trouble. However, like some of our western medical men, he did not confess his ignorance, but proceeded to prescribe a huge dose of boiling water, to be followed a little later by a compound of pulverized deer's horn and dried toadskin.

Poor Honeysuckle lay in agony for three days, all the time growing weaker and weaker from loss of sleep. Every great doctor in the district had been summoned for consultation; two had come from Changsha, the chief city of the province, but all to no avail. It was one of those cases that seem to be beyond the power of even the most learned physicians. In the hope of receiving the great reward offered by the desperate father, these wise men searched from cover to cover in the great Chinese Cyclopedia of Medicine, trying in vain to find a method of treating the unhappy maiden. There was even thought of calling in a certain foreign physician from England, who was in a distant city, and was supposed, on account of some marvellous cures he had brought to pass, to be in direct league with the devil. However, the city magistrate would not allow Mr. Min to call in this outsider, for fear trouble might be stirred up among the people.

Mr. Min sent out a proclamation in every direction, describing his daughter's illness, and offering to bestow on her a handsome dowry and give her in marriage to whoever should be the means of bringing her back to health and happiness. He then sat at her bedside and waited, feeling that he had done all that was in his power. There were many answers to his invitation. Physicians, old and young, came from every part of the Empire to try their skill, and when they had seen poor Honeysuckle and also the huge pile of silver shoes her father offered as a wedding gift, they all fought with might and main for her life; some having been attracted by her great beauty and excellent reputation, others by the tremendous reward.

But, alas for poor Honeysuckle! Not one of all those wise men could cure her! One day, when she was feeling a slight change for the better, she called her father, and, clasping his hand with her tiny one said, "Were it not for your love I would give up this hard fight and pass over into the dark wood; or, as my old grandmother says, fly up into the Western Heavens. For your sake, because I am your only child, and especially because you have no son, I have struggled hard to live, but now I feel that the next attack of that dreadful pain will carry me away. And oh, I do not want to die!"

Here Honeysuckle wept as if her heart would break, and her old father wept too, for the more she suffered the more he loved her.

Just then her face began to turn pale. "It is coming! The pain is coming, father! Very soon I shall be no more. Good-bye, father! Good-bye; good– ." Here her voice broke and a great sob almost broke her father's heart. He turned away from her bedside; he could not bear to see her suffer. He walked outside and sat down on a rustic bench; his head fell upon his bosom, and the great salt tears trickled down his long grey beard.

As Mr. Min sat thus overcome with grief, he was startled at hearing a low whine. Looking up he saw, to his astonishment, a shaggy mountain dog about the size of a Newfoundland. The huge beast looked into the old man's eyes with so intelligent and human an expression, with such a sad and wistful gaze, that the greybeard addressed him, saying, "Why have you come? To cure my daughter?"

The dog replied with three short barks, wagging his tail vigorously and turning toward the half-opened door that led into the room where the girl lay.

By this time, willing to try any chance whatever of reviving his daughter, Mr. Min bade the animal follow him into Honeysuckle's apartment. Placing his forepaws upon the side of her bed, the dog looked long and steadily at the wasted form before him and held his ear intently for a moment over the maiden's heart. Then, with a slight cough he deposited from his mouth into her outstretched hand, a tiny stone. Touching her wrist with his right paw, he motioned to her to swallow the stone.

"Yes, my dear, obey him," counselled her father, as she turned to him inquiringly, "for good Dr. Dog has been sent to your bedside by the mountain fairies, who have heard of your illness and who wish to invite you back to life again."

Without further delay the sick girl, who was by this time almost burned away by the fever, raised her hand to her lips and swallowed the tiny charm. Wonder of wonders! No sooner had it passed her lips than a miracle occurred. The red flush passed away from her face, the pulse resumed its normal beat, the pains departed from her body, and she arose from the bed well and smiling.

Flinging her arms about her father's neck, she cried out in joy, "Oh, I am well again; well and happy; thanks to the medicine of the good physician."

The noble dog barked three times, wild with delight at hearing these tearful words of gratitude, bowed low, and put his nose in Honeysuckle's outstretched hand.

Mr. Min, greatly moved by his daughter's magical recovery, turned to the strange physician, saying, "Noble Sir, were it not for the form you have taken, for some unknown reason, I would willingly give four times the sum in silver that I promised for the cure of the girl, into your possession. As it is, I suppose you have no use for silver, but remember that so long as we live, whatever we have is yours for the asking, and I beg of you to prolong your visit, to make this the home of your old age – in short, remain here for ever as my guest – nay, as a member of my family."

The dog barked thrice, as if in assent. From that day he was treated as an equal by father and daughter. The many servants were commanded to obey his slightest whim, to serve him with the most expensive food on the market, to spare no expense in making him the happiest and best-fed dog in all the world. Day after day he ran at Honeysuckle's side as she gathered flowers in her garden, lay down before her door when she was resting, guarded her Sedan chair when she was carried by servants into the city. In short, they were constant companions; a stranger would have thought they had been friends from childhood.

One day, however, just as they were returning from a journey outside her father's compound, at the very instant when Honeysuckle was alighting from her chair, without a moment's warning, the huge animal dashed past the attendants, seized his beautiful mistress in his mouth, and before anyone could stop him, bore her off to the mountains. By the time the alarm was sounded, darkness had fallen over the valley and as the night was cloudy no trace could be found of the dog and his fair burden.

Once more the frantic father left no stone unturned to save his daughter. Huge rewards were offered, bands of woodmen scoured the mountains high and low, but, alas, no sign of the girl could be found! The unfortunate father gave up the search and began to prepare himself for the grave. There was nothing now left in life that he cared for – nothing but thoughts of his departed daughter. Honeysuckle was gone for ever.

"Alas!" said he, quoting the lines of a famous poet who had fallen into despair:

> *"My whiting hair would make an endless rope,*
> *Yet would not measure all my depth of woe."*

Several long years passed by; years of sorrow for the ageing man, pining for his departed daughter. One beautiful October day he was sitting in the very same pavilion where he had so often sat with his darling. His head was bowed forward on his breast, his forehead was lined with grief. A rustling of leaves attracted his attention. He looked up. Standing directly in front of him was Dr. Dog, and lo, riding on his back, clinging to the animal's shaggy hair, was Honeysuckle, his long-lost daughter; while standing near by were three of the handsomest boys he had ever set eyes upon!

"Ah, my daughter! My darling daughter, where have you been all these years?" cried the delighted father, pressing the girl to his aching breast. "Have you suffered many a cruel pain since you were snatched away so suddenly? Has your life been filled with sorrow?"

"Only at the thought of your grief," she replied, tenderly, stroking his forehead with her slender fingers; "only at the thought of your suffering; only at the thought of how I should like to see you every day and tell you that my husband was kind and good to me. For you must know, dear father, this is no mere animal that stands beside you. This Dr. Dog, who cured me and claimed me as his bride because of your promise, is a great magician. He can change himself at will into a thousand shapes. He chooses to come here in the form of a mountain beast so that no one may penetrate the secret of his distant palace."

"Then he is your husband?" faltered the old man, gazing at the animal with a new expression on his wrinkled face.

"Yes; my kind and noble husband, the father of my three sons, your grandchildren, whom we have brought to pay you a visit."

"And where do you live?"

"In a wonderful cave in the heart of the great mountains; a beautiful cave whose walls and floors are covered with crystals, and encrusted with sparkling gems. The chairs and tables are set with jewels; the rooms are lighted by a thousand glittering diamonds. Oh, it is lovelier than the palace of the Son of Heaven himself! We feed of the flesh of wild deer and mountain goats, and fish from the clearest mountain stream. We drink cold water out of golden goblets, without first boiling it, for it is purity itself. We breathe fragrant air that blows through forests of pine and hemlock. We live only to love each other and our children, and oh, we are so happy! And you, father, you must come back with us to the great mountains and live there with us the rest of your days, which, the gods grant, may be very many."

The old man pressed his daughter once more to his breast and fondled the children, who clambered over him rejoicing at the discovery of a grandfather they had never seen before.

From Dr. Dog and his fair Honeysuckle are sprung, it is said, the well-known race of people called the Yus, who even now inhabit the mountainous regions of the Canton and Hunan provinces. It is not for this reason, however, that we have told the story here, but because we felt sure every reader would like to learn the secret of the dog that cured a sick girl and won her for his bride.

The Phantom Vessel

ONCE A SHIP LOADED with pleasure-seekers was sailing from North China to Shanghai. High winds and stormy weather had delayed her, and she was still one week from port when a great plague broke out on board. This plague was of the worst kind. It attacked passengers and sailors alike until there were so few left to sail the vessel that it seemed as if she would soon be left to the mercy of winds and waves.

On all sides lay the dead, and the groans of the dying were most terrible to hear. Of that great company of travellers only one, a little boy named Ying-lo, had escaped. At last the few sailors, who had been trying hard to save their ship, were obliged to lie down upon the deck, a prey to the dreadful sickness, and soon they too were dead.

Ying-lo now found himself alone on the sea. For some reason – he did not know why – the gods or the sea fairies had spared him, but as he looked about in terror at the friends and loved ones who had died, he almost wished that he might join them.

The sails flapped about like great broken wings, while the giant waves dashed higher above the deck, washing many of the bodies overboard and wetting the little boy to the skin. Shivering with cold, he gave himself up for lost and prayed to the gods, whom his mother had often told him about, to take him from this dreadful ship and let him escape the fatal illness.

As he lay there praying he heard a slight noise in the rigging just above his head. Looking up, he saw a ball of fire running along a yardarm near the top of the mast. The sight was so strange that he forgot his prayer and stared with open-mouthed wonder. To his astonishment, the ball grew brighter and brighter, and then suddenly began slipping down the mast, all the time increasing in size. The poor boy did not know what to do or to think. Were the gods, in answer to his prayer, sending fire to burn the vessel? If so, he would soon escape. Anything would be better than to be alone upon the sea.

Nearer and nearer came the fireball. At last, when it reached the deck, to Ying-lo's surprise, something very, very strange happened. Before he had time to feel alarmed, the light vanished, and a funny little man stood in front of him peering anxiously into the child's frightened face.

"Yes, you are the lad I'm looking for," he said at last, speaking in a piping voice that almost made Ying-lo smile. "You are Ying-lo, and you are the only one left of this wretched company." This he said, pointing towards the bodies lying here and there about the deck.

Although he saw that the old man meant him no harm, the child could say nothing, but waited in silence, wondering what would happen next.

By this time the vessel was tossing and pitching so violently that it seemed every minute as if it would upset and go down beneath the foaming waves, never to rise again. Not many miles distant on the right, some jagged rocks stuck out of the water, lifting their cruel heads as if waiting for the helpless ship.

The newcomer walked slowly towards the mast and tapped on it three times with an iron staff he had been using as a cane. Immediately the sails spread, the vessel righted itself and began to glide over the sea so fast that the gulls were soon left far behind, while the threatening rocks upon which the ship had been so nearly dashed seemed like specks in the distance.

"Do you remember me?" said the stranger, suddenly turning and coming up to Ying-lo, but his voice was lost in the whistling of the wind, and the boy knew only by the moving of his lips that the old man was talking. The greybeard bent over until his mouth was at Ying-lo's ear: "Did you ever see me before?"

With a puzzled look, at first the child shook his head. Then as he gazed more closely there seemed to be something that he recognized about the wrinkled face. "Yes, I think so, but I don't know when."

With a tap of his staff the fairy stopped the blowing of the wind, and then spoke once more to his small companion: "One year ago I passed through your village. I was dressed in rags, and was begging my way along the street, trying to find someone who would feel sorry for me. Alas! no one answered my cry for mercy. Not a crust was thrown into my bowl. All the people were deaf, and fierce dogs drove me from door to door. Finally when I was almost dying of hunger, I began to feel that here was a village without one good person in it. Just then you saw my suffering, ran into the house, and brought me out food.

Your heartless mother saw you doing this and beat you cruelly. Do you remember now, my child?"

"Yes, I remember," he answered sadly, "and that mother is now lying dead. Alas! all, all are dead, my father and my brothers also. Not one is left of my family."

"Little did you know, my boy, to whom you were giving food that day. You took me for a lowly beggar, but, behold, it was not a poor man that you fed, for I am Iron Staff. You must have heard of me when they were telling of the fairies in the Western Heaven, and of their adventures here on earth."

"Yes, yes," answered Ying-lo, trembling half with fear and half with joy, "indeed I have heard of you many, many times, and all the people love you for your kind deeds of mercy."

"Alas! they did not show their love, my little one. Surely you know that if any one wishes to reward the fairies for their mercies, he must begin to do deeds of the same kind himself. No one but you in all your village had pity on me in my rags. If they had known that I was Iron Staff, everything would have been different; they would have given me a feast and begged for my protection.

> *"The only love that loves aright*
> *Is that which loves in every plight.*
> *The beggar in his sad array*
> *Is moulded of the selfsame clay.*
>
> *"Who knows a man by what he wears,*
> *By what he says or by his prayers?*
> *Hidden beneath that wrinkled skin*
> *A fairy may reside within.*
> *"Then treat with kindness and with love*
> *The lowly man, the god above;*
> *A friendly nod, a welcome smile –*
> *For love is ever worth the while."*

Ying-lo listened in wonder to Iron Staff's little poem, and when he had finished, the boy's face was glowing with the love of which the fairy had spoken. "My poor, poor father and mother!" he cried; "they knew nothing of these beautiful things you are telling me. They were brought up in poverty. As they were knocked about in childhood by those around them, so they learned to beat others who begged them for help. Is it strange that they did not have hearts full of pity for you when you looked like a beggar?"

"But what about you, my boy? You were not deaf when I asked you. Have you not been whipped and punished all your life? How then did you learn to look with love at those in tears?"

The child could not answer these questions, but only looked sorrowfully at Iron Staff. "Oh, can you not, good fairy, will you not restore my parents and brothers, and give them another chance to be good and useful people?"

"Listen, Ying-lo; it is impossible – unless you do two things first," he answered, stroking his beard gravely and leaning heavily upon his staff.

"What are they? What must I do to save my family? Anything you ask of me will not be too much to pay for your kindness."

"First you must tell me of some good deed done by these people for whose lives you are asking. Name only one, for that will be enough; but it is against our rules to help those who have done nothing."

Ying-lo was silent, and for a moment his face was clouded. "Yes, I know," he said finally, brightening. "They burned incense once at the temple. That was certainly a deed of virtue."

"But when was it, little one, that they did this?"

"When my big brother was sick, and they were praying for him to get well. The doctors could not save him with boiled turnip juice or with any other of the medicines they used, so my parents begged the gods."

"Selfish, selfish!" muttered Iron Staff. "If their eldest son had not been dying they would have spent no money at the temple. They tried in this way to buy back his health, for they were expecting him to support them in their old age."

Ying-lo's face fell. "You are right," he answered.

"Can you think of nothing else?"

"Yes, oh, yes, last year when the foreigner rode through our village and fell sick in front of our house, they took him in and cared for him."

"How long?" asked the other sharply.

"Until he died the next week."

"And what did they do with the mule he was riding, his bed, and the money in his bag? Did they try to restore them to his people?"

"No, they said they'd keep them to pay for the trouble." Ying-lo's face turned scarlet.

"But try again, dear boy! Is there not one little deed of goodness that was not selfish? Think once more."

For a long time Ying-lo did not reply. At length he spoke in a low voice; "I think of one, but I fear it amounts to nothing."

"No good, my child, is too small to be counted when the gods are weighing a man's heart."

"Last spring the birds were eating in my father's garden. My mother wanted to buy poison from the shop to destroy them, but my father said no, that the little things must live, and he for one was not in favour of killing them."

"At last, Ying-lo, you have named a real deed of mercy, and as he spared the tiny birds from poison, so shall his life and the lives of your mother and brothers be restored from the deadly plague.

"But remember there is one other thing that depends on you."

Ying-lo's eyes glistened gratefully. "Then if it rests with me, and I can do it, you have my promise. No sacrifice should be too great for a son to make for his loved ones even though his life itself is asked in payment."

"Very well, Ying-lo. What I require is that you carry out to the letter my instructions. Now it is time for me to keep my promise to you."

So saying, Iron Staff called on Ying-lo to point out the members of his family, and, approaching them one by one, with the end of his iron stick he touched their foreheads. In an instant each, without a word, arose. Looking round and recognising Ying-lo, they stood back, frightened at seeing him with the fairy. When the last had risen to his feet, Iron Staff beckoned all of them to listen. This they did willingly, too much terrified to speak, for they saw on all sides signs of the plague that had swept over the vessel, and they remembered the frightful agony they had suffered in dying. Each knew that he had been lifted by some magic power from darkness into light.

"My friends," began the fairy, "little did you think when less than a year ago you drove me from your door that soon you yourselves would be in need of mercy. To-day you have had a peep into the awful land of Yama. You have seen the horror of his tortures, have heard the screams of his slaves, and by another night you would have been carried before him to be judged. What power is it that has saved you from his clutches? As you look back through your wicked lives can you think of any reason why you deserved this rescue? No, there is no memory of goodness in your black hearts. Well, I shall tell you: it is this little boy, this Ying-lo, who many times has felt the weight of your wicked hands and has hidden in terror at your coming. To him alone you owe my help."

Father, mother, and brothers all gazed in turn, first at the fairy and then at the timid child whose eyes fell before their looks of gratitude.

"By reason of his goodness this child whom you have scorned is worthy of a place within the Western Heaven. In truth, I came this very day to lead him to that fairyland. For you, however, he wishes to make a sacrifice. With sorrow I am yielding to his wishes. His sacrifice will be that of giving up a place among the fairies and of continuing to live here on this earth with you. He will try to make a change within your household. If at any time you treat him badly and do not heed his wishes – mark you well my words – by the power of this magic staff which I shall place in his hands, he may enter at once into the land of the fairies, leaving you to die in your wickedness. This I command him to do, and he has promised to obey my slightest wish.

"This plague took you off suddenly and ended your wicked lives. Ying-lo has raised you from its grasp and his power can lift you from the bed of sin. No other hand than his can bear the rod which I am leaving. If one of you but touch it, instantly he will fall dead upon the ground.

"And now, my child, the time has come for me to leave you. First, however, I must show you what you are now able to do. Around you lie the corpses of sailors and passengers. Tap three times upon the mast and wish that they shall come to life," So saying he handed Ying-lo the iron staff.

Although the magic rod was heavy, the child lifted it as if it were a fairy's wand. Then, stepping forward to the mast, he rapped three times as he had been commanded. Immediately on all sides arose the bodies, once more full of life and strength.

"Now command the ship to take you back to your home port, for such sinful creatures as these are in no way fit to make a journey among strangers. They must first return and free their homes of sin."

Again rapping on the mast, the child willed the great vessel to take its homeward course. No sooner had he moved the staff than, like a bird wheeling in the heavens, the bark swung round and started on the return journey. Swifter than a flash of lightning flew the boat, for it was now become a fairy vessel. Before the sailors and the travellers could recover from their surprise, land was sighted and they saw that they were indeed entering the harbour.

Just as the ship was darting toward the shore the fairy suddenly, with a parting word to Ying-lo, changed into a flaming ball of fire which rolled along the deck and ascended the spars. Then, as it reached the top of the rigging, it floated off into the blue sky, and all on board, speechless with surprise, watched it until it vanished.

With a cry of thanksgiving, Ying-lo flung his arms about his parents and descended with them to the shore.

The Ashvin Twins

THERE ONCE WERE TWO BROTHERS, divine twins who were the sons of the sky-god Surya. Their names were Dasra and Nasatya and they were the most exquisitely beautiful boys, looks with which they were blessed into adulthood. The Ashvins were bright and friendly, and they attracted only the best attention wherever they flew. They rode in a gilded carriage – gold which appeared tarnished next to the burnished good looks of the Ashvin twins. They flew quickly and travelled widely, for they sought a place among the pantheon of Hindu gods, an honour which had not yet been accorded.

One day, Dasra and Nasatya were stopped in their travels by the sight of the most delicate and elegant woman, who was taking her bath in a stream near her home. This was Sukanya, or 'Fair-Maid', and she was the wife of the aged rishi Chyavana, who had held her hand in marriage for many years and to whom she had pledged her heart and eternal devotion.

The twins were stunned by the sight of her beauty, and they flew to her side, their pearly smiles flashing as they moved forward to greet her.

"You are the most beauteous of all creatures, fair-limbed girl. Who is your father? And how is it that you have been allowed to bathe alone here in these woods?" asked the twins.

"Why I am the wife of Chyavana," said Sukanya, "and I bathe here each day."

The twins shook with laughter. "How could your father bear for you to give your hand to someone so old and near death. You are the very essence of beauty, fair maiden, and yours should have been the choice of every man."

"I love Chyavana," said Sukanya with dignity, preparing to dress.

"Leave your husband," suggested the Ashvins. "Come away with us and have a taste of youth. You'll have a life with us and our beauty will be the perfect complement to one another."

But Sukanya refused their offer and turned to leave her toilet.

But the Ashvins stopped her once again, praying that she should listen to their new request. "We are medicine men," they announced, "and we will make your husband young again, and fair of face. If we do so, fair maiden, will you agree to choose between us a husband for life?"

Sukanya consulted with her husband, who agreed to the plan, and the Ashvins did as they had promised. Within a few moments, Chyavana was at their sides and all three men entered the pool and sank into its depths. There was a pause and then they emerged, all three equal. All three identical.

The three men said in unison, "Choose among us Sukanya."

The fair maiden searched carefully for traces of her husband, and when she found them she chose him to be her lord and husband for the remainder of her life.

Chyavana had suffered no indignities, and from this fateful interlude he had had his youth returned to him. He smiled widely, and in gratitude to the Ashvin twins, he promised to win for them the right to sit with the gods, and share in their offerings.

The twins went on their way again, fleet of foot and then high in their gilded chariot. The happy couple lived together in great joy, gods in their own home.

The Soothsayer's Son

A SOOTHSAYER WHEN ON HIS DEATHBED wrote out the horoscope of his second son, whose name was Gangazara, and bequeathed it to him as his only property, leaving the whole of his estate to his eldest son. The second son thought over the horoscope, and said to himself:

"Alas! am I born to this only in the world? The sayings of my father never failed. I have seen them prove true to the last word while he was living; and how has he fixed my horoscope! 'From my birth poverty!' Nor is that my only fate. 'For ten years, imprisonment' – a fate harder than poverty; and what comes next? 'Death on the sea-shore;' which means that I must die away from home, far from friends and relatives on a sea-coast. Now comes the most curious part of the horoscope, that I am to 'have some happiness afterwards!' What this happiness is, is an enigma to me."

Thus thought he, and after all the funeral obsequies of his father were over, took leave of his elder brother, and started for Benares. He went by the middle of the Deccan, avoiding both the coasts, and went on journeying and journeying for weeks and months, till at last he reached the Vindhya mountains. While passing that desert he had to journey for a couple of days through a sandy plain, with no signs of life or vegetation. The little store of provision with which he was provided for a couple of days, at last was exhausted. The chombu, which he carried always full, filling it with the sweet water from the flowing rivulet or plenteous tank, he had exhausted in the heat of the desert. There was not a morsel in his hand to eat; nor a drop of water to drink. Turn his eyes wherever he might he found a vast desert, out of which he saw no means of escape. Still he thought within himself, "Surely my father's prophecy never proved untrue. I must survive this calamity to find my death on some sea-coast." So thought he, and this thought gave him strength of mind to walk fast and try to find a drop of water somewhere to slake his dry throat.

At last he succeeded; heaven threw in his way a ruined well. He thought he could collect some water if he let down his chombu with the string that he always carried noosed to the neck of it. Accordingly he let it down; it went some way and stopped, and the following words came from the well: "Oh, relieve me! I am the king of tigers, dying here of hunger. For the last three days I have had nothing. Fortune has sent you here. If you assist me now you will find a sure help in me throughout your life. Do not think that I am a beast of prey. When you have become my deliverer I will never touch you. Pray, kindly lift me up." Gangazara thought: "Shall I take him out or not? If I take him out he may make me the first morsel of his hungry mouth. No; that he will not do. For my father's prophecy never came untrue. I must die on a sea coast, and not by a tiger." Thus thinking, he asked the tiger-king to hold tight to the vessel, which he accordingly did, and he lifted him up slowly. The tiger reached the top of the well and felt himself on safe ground. True to his word, he did no harm to Gangazara. On the other hand, he walked round his patron three times, and standing before him, humbly spoke the following words: "My life-giver, my benefactor! I shall never forget this day, when I regained my life through your kind hands. In return for this kind assistance I pledge my oath to stand by you in all calamities. Whenever you are in any difficulty just think of me. I am there with you ready to oblige you by all the means that I can. To tell you briefly how I came in here: Three days ago I was roaming in yonder forest, when I saw a goldsmith passing through it. I chased him. He, finding it impossible to escape my claws, jumped into this well, and is living to this moment in the very bottom of it. I also jumped in, but found myself on the first ledge of the well; he is on the last and fourth ledge. In the second lives a serpent half-famished with hunger. On the third lies a rat, also half-famished, and when you again begin to draw water these may request you first to release them. In the same way the goldsmith also may ask you. I beg you, as your bosom friend, never assist that wretched man, though he is your relation as a human being. Goldsmiths are never to be trusted. You can place more faith in me, a tiger, though I feast sometimes upon men, in a serpent, whose sting makes your blood cold the very next moment, or in a rat, which does a thousand pieces of mischief in your house. But never trust a goldsmith. Do not release him; and if you do, you shall surely repent of it one day or other." Thus advising, the hungry tiger went away without waiting for an answer.

Gangazara thought several times of the eloquent way in which the tiger spoke, and admired his fluency of speech. But still his thirst was not quenched. So he let down his vessel again, which was now caught hold of by the serpent, who addressed him thus: "Oh, my protector! Lift me up. I am the king of serpents, and the son of Adisesha, who is now pining away in agony for my disappearance. Release me now. I shall ever remain your servant, remember your assistance, and help you throughout life in all possible ways. Oblige me: I am dying." Gangazara, calling again to mind the "death on the sea-shore" of the prophecy lifted him up. He, like the tiger-king, walked round him thrice, and prostrating himself before him spoke thus: "Oh, my life-giver, my father, for so I must call you, as you have given me another birth. I was three days ago basking myself in the morning sun, when I saw a rat running before me. I chased him. He fell into this well. I followed him, but instead of falling on the third storey where he is now lying, I fell into the second. I am going away now to see my father. Whenever you are in any difficulty just think of me. I will be there by your side to assist you by all possible means." So saying, the Nagaraja glided away in zigzag movements, and was out of sight in a moment.

The poor son of the Soothsayer, who was now almost dying of thirst, let down his vessel for a third time. The rat caught hold of it, and without discussing he lifted up the poor animal at once. But it would not go away without showing its gratitude: "Oh, life of my life! My benefactor! I am the king of rats. Whenever you are in any calamity just think of me. I will come to you, and assist you. My keen ears overheard all that the tiger-king told you about the goldsmith, who is in the fourth storey. It is nothing but a sad truth that goldsmiths ought never to be trusted. Therefore, never assist him as you have done to us all. And if you do, you will suffer for it. I am hungry; let me go for the present." Thus taking leave of his benefactor, the rat, too, ran away.

Gangazara for a while thought upon the repeated advice given by the three animals about releasing the goldsmith: "What wrong would there be in my assisting him? Why should I not release him also?" So thinking to himself, Gangazara let down the vessel again. The goldsmith caught hold of it, and demanded help. The Soothsayer's son had no time to lose; he was himself dying of thirst. Therefore he lifted the goldsmith up, who now began his story. "Stop for a while," said Gangazara, and after quenching his thirst by letting down his vessel for the fifth time, still fearing that some one might remain in the well and demand his assistance, he listened to the goldsmith, who began as follows: "My dear friend, my protector, what a deal of nonsense these brutes have been talking to you about me; I am glad you have not followed their advice. I am just now dying of hunger. Permit me to go away. My name is Manikkasari. I live in the East main street of Ujjaini, which is twenty kas to the south of this place, and so lies on your way when you return from Benares. Do not forget to come to me and receive my kind remembrances of your assistance, on your way back to your country." So saying, the goldsmith took his leave, and Gangazara also pursued his way north after the above adventures.

He reached Benares, and lived there for more than ten years, and quite forgot the tiger, serpent, rat, and goldsmith. After ten years of religious life, thoughts of home and of his brother rushed into his mind. "I have secured enough merit now by my religious observances. Let me return home." Thus thought Gangazara within himself, and very soon he was on his way back to his country. Remembering the prophecy of his father he returned by the same way by which he went to Benares ten years before. While thus retracing his steps he reached the ruined well where he had released the three brute kings and the goldsmith. At once the old recollections rushed into his mind, and he thought of the tiger to test his fidelity. Only a moment passed, and the tiger-king came running before him carrying a large crown in his mouth, the glitter of the diamonds of which for a time outshone even the bright rays of the sun. He dropped the crown at his life-giver's feet, and, putting aside all his pride, humbled himself like a pet cat to the strokes of his protector, and began in the following words: "My life-giver! How is it that you have forgotten me, your poor servant, for such a long time? I am glad to find that I still occupy a corner in your mind. I can never forget the day when I owed my life to your lotus hands. I have several jewels with me of little value. This crown, being the best of all, I have brought here as a single ornament of great value, which you can carry with you and dispose of in your own country." Gangazara looked at the crown, examined it over and over, counted and recounted the gems, and thought within himself that he would become the richest of men by separating the diamonds and gold, and selling them in his own country. He took leave of the tiger-king, and after his disappearance thought of the kings of serpents and rats, who came in their turn with their presents, and after the usual greetings and exchange of words took their leave. Gangazara was extremely delighted at the faithfulness with which the brute beasts behaved, and went on his way to the south. While going along he spoke to himself thus: "These beasts have been very faithful in their assistance. Much more, therefore, must Manikkasari be faithful. I do not want anything from him now. If I take this crown with me as it is, it occupies much space in my bundle. It may also excite the curiosity of some robbers on the way. I will go now to Ujjaini on my way. Manikkasari requested me to see him without failure on my return journey. I shall do so, and request him to have the crown melted, the diamonds and gold separated. He must do that kindness at least for me. I shall then roll up these diamonds and gold ball in my rags, and wend my way homewards." Thus thinking and thinking, he reached Ujjaini. At once he inquired for the house of his goldsmith friend, and found him without difficulty. Manikkasari was extremely delighted to find on his threshold him who ten years before, notwithstanding the advice repeatedly given him by the sage-looking tiger, serpent, and rat, had relieved him from the pit of death. Gangazara at once showed him the crown that he received from the tiger-king, told him how he got it, and requested his kind assistance to separate the gold and diamonds. Manikkasari agreed to do so, and meanwhile asked his friend to rest himself for a while to have his bath and meals; and Gangazara, who was very observant of his religious ceremonies, went direct to the river to bathe.

How came the crown in the jaws of the tiger? The king of Ujjaini had a week before gone with all his hunters on a hunting expedition. All of a sudden the tiger-king started from the wood, seized the king, and vanished.

When the king's attendants informed the prince about the death of his father he wept and wailed, and gave notice that he would give half of his kingdom to any one who should bring him news about the murderer of his father. The goldsmith knew full well that it was a tiger that killed the king, and not any hunter's hands, since he had heard from Gangazara how he obtained the crown. Still, he resolved to denounce Gangazara as the king's murderer, so, hiding the crown under his garments, he flew to the palace. He went before the prince and informed him that the assassin was caught, and placed the crown before him. The prince took it into his hands, examined it, and at once gave half the kingdom to Manikkasari, and then inquired about the murderer. "He is bathing in the river, and is of such and such appearance," was the reply. At once four armed soldiers flew to the river, and bound the poor Brahman hand and foot, while he, sitting in meditation, was without any knowledge of the fate that hung over him. They brought Gangazara to the presence of the prince, who turned his face away from the supposed murderer, and asked his soldiers to throw him into a dungeon. In a minute, without knowing the cause, the poor Brahman found himself in the dark dungeon.

It was a dark cellar underground, built with strong stone walls, into which any criminal guilty of a capital offence was ushered to breathe his last there without food and drink. Such was the cellar into which Gangazara was thrust. What were his thoughts when he reached that place? "It is of no use to accuse either the goldsmith or the prince now. We are all the children of fate. We must obey her commands. This is but the first day of my father's prophecy. So far his statement is true. But how am I going to pass ten years here? Perhaps without anything to sustain life I may drag on my existence for a day or two. But how pass ten years? That cannot be, and I must die. Before death comes let me think of my faithful brute friends."

So pondered Gangazara in the dark cell underground, and at that moment thought of his three friends. The tiger-king, serpent-king, and rat-king assembled at once with their armies at a garden near the dungeon, and for a while did not know what to do. They held their council, and decided to make an underground passage from the inside of a ruined well to the dungeon. The rat raja issued an order at once to that effect to his army. They, with their teeth, bored the ground a long way to the walls of the prison. After reaching it they found that their teeth could not work on the hard stones. The bandicoots were then specially ordered for the business; they, with their hard teeth, made a small slit in the wall for a rat to pass and repass without difficulty. Thus a passage was effected.

The rat raja entered first to condole with his protector on his misfortune, and undertook to supply his protector with provisions. "Whatever sweetmeats or bread are prepared in any house, one and all of you must try to bring whatever you can to our benefactor. Whatever clothes you find hanging in a house, cut down, dip the pieces in water, and bring the wet bits to our benefactor. He will squeeze them and gather water for drink! and the bread and sweetmeats shall form his food." Having issued these orders, the king of the rats took leave of Gangazara. They, in obedience to their king's order, continued to supply him with provisions and water.

The snake-king said: "I sincerely condole with you in your calamity; the tiger-king also fully sympathises with you, and wants me to tell you so, as he cannot drag his huge body here as we have done with our small ones. The king of the rats has promised to do his best to provide you with food. We would now do what we can for your release. From this day we shall issue orders to our armies to oppress all the subjects of this kingdom. The deaths by snake-bite and tigers shall increase a hundredfold from this day, and day by day it shall continue to increase till your release. Whenever you hear people near you, you had better bawl out so as to be heard by them: 'The wretched prince imprisoned me on the false charge of having killed his father, while it was a tiger that killed him. From that day these calamities have broken out in his dominions. If I were released I would save all by my powers of healing poisonous wounds and by incantations.' Some one may report this to the king, and if he knows it, you will obtain your liberty." Thus comforting his protector in trouble, he advised him to pluck up courage, and took leave of him. From that day tigers and serpents, acting under the orders of their kings, united in killing as many persons and cattle as possible. Every day people were carried away by tigers or bitten by serpents. Thus passed months and years. Gangazara sat in the dark cellar, without the sun's light falling upon him, and feasted upon the breadcrumbs and sweetmeats that the rats so kindly supplied him with. These delicacies had completely changed his body into a red, stout, huge, unwieldy mass of flesh. Thus passed full ten years, as prophesied in the horoscope.

Ten complete years rolled away in close imprisonment. On the last evening of the tenth year one of the serpents got into the bed-chamber of the princess and sucked her life. She breathed her last. She was the only daughter of the king. The king at once sent for all the snake-bite curers. He promised half his kingdom and his daughter's hand to him who would restore her to life. Now a servant of the king who had several times overheard Gangazara's cries, reported the matter to him. The king at once ordered the cell to be examined. There was the man sitting in it. How had he managed to live so long in the cell? Some whispered that he must be a divine being. Thus they discussed, while they brought Gangazara to the king.

The king no sooner saw Gangazara than he fell on the ground. He was struck by the majesty and grandeur of his person. His ten years' imprisonment in the deep cell underground had given a sort of lustre to his body. His hair had first to be cut before his face could be seen. The king begged forgiveness for his former fault, and requested him to revive his daughter.

"Bring me within an hour all the corpses of men and cattle, dying and dead, that remain unburnt or unburied within the range of your dominions; I shall revive them all," were the only words that Gangazara spoke.

Cartloads of corpses of men and cattle began to come in every minute. Even graves, it is said, were broken open, and corpses buried a day or two before were taken out and sent for their revival. As soon as all were ready, Gangazara took a vessel full of water and sprinkled it over them all, thinking only of his snake-king and tiger-king. All rose up as if from deep slumber, and went to their respective homes. The princess, too, was restored to life. The joy of the king knew no bounds. He cursed the day on which he imprisoned him, blamed himself for having believed the word of a goldsmith, and offered him the hand of his daughter and the whole kingdom, instead of half, as he promised. Gangazara would not accept anything, but asked the king to assemble all his subjects in a wood near the town. "I shall there call in all the tigers and serpents, and give them a general order."

When the whole town was assembled, just at the dusk of evening, Gangazara sat dumb for a moment, and thought upon the Tiger King and the Serpent King, who came with all their armies. People began to take to their heels at the sight of tigers. Gangazara assured them of safety, and stopped them.

The grey light of the evening, the pumpkin colour of Gangazara, the holy ashes scattered lavishly over his body, the tigers and snakes humbling themselves at his feet, gave him the true majesty of the god Gangazara. For who else by a single word could thus command vast armies of tigers and serpents, said some among the people. "Care not for it; it may be by magic. That is not a great thing. That he revived cartloads of corpses shows him to be surely Gangazara," said others.

"Why should you, my children, thus trouble these poor subjects of Ujjaini? Reply to me, and henceforth desist from your ravages." Thus said the Soothsayer's son, and the following reply came from the king of the tigers: "Why should this base king imprison your honour, believing the mere word of a goldsmith that your honour killed his father? All the hunters told him that his father was carried away by a tiger. I was the messenger of death sent to deal the blow on his neck. I did it, and gave the crown to your honour. The prince makes no inquiry, and at once imprisons your honour. How can we expect justice from such a stupid king as that? Unless he adopt a better standard of justice we will go on with our destruction."

The king heard, cursed the day on which he believed in the word of a goldsmith, beat his head, tore his hair, wept and wailed for his crime, asked a thousand pardons, and swore to rule in a just way from that day. The serpent-king and tiger-king also promised to observe their oath as long as justice prevailed, and took their leave. The goldsmith fled for his life. He was caught by the soldiers of the king, and was pardoned by the generous Gangazara, whose voice now reigned supreme. All returned to their homes.

The king again pressed Gangazara to accept the hand of his daughter. He agreed to do so, not then, but some time afterwards. He wished to go and see his elder brother first, and then to return and marry the princess. The king agreed; and Gangazara left the city that very day on his way home.

It so happened that unwittingly he took a wrong road, and had to pass near a sea-coast. His elder brother was also on his way up to Benares by that very same route. They met and recognised each other, even at a distance. They flew into each other's arms. Both remained still for a time almost unconscious with joy. The pleasure of Gangazara was so great that he died of joy.

The elder brother was a devout worshipper of Ganesa. That was a Friday, a day very sacred to that god. The elder brother took the corpse to the nearest Ganesa temple and called upon him. The god came, and asked him what he wanted. "My poor brother is dead and gone; and this is his corpse. Kindly keep it in your charge till I finish worshipping you. If I leave it anywhere else the devils may snatch it away when I am absent worshipping you; after finishing the rites I shall burn him." Thus said the elder brother, and, giving the corpse to the god Ganesa, he went to prepare himself for that deity's ceremonials. Ganesa made over the corpse to his Ganas, asking them to watch over it carefully. But instead of that they devoured it.

The elder brother, after finishing the puja, demanded his brother's corpse of the god. The god called his Ganas, who came to the front blinking, and fearing the anger of their master. The god was greatly enraged. The elder brother was very angry. When the corpse was not forthcoming he cuttingly remarked, "Is this, after all, the return for my deep belief in you? You are unable even to return my brother's corpse." Ganesa was much ashamed at the remark. So he, by his divine power, gave him a living Gangazara instead of the dead corpse. Thus was the second son of the Soothsayer restored to life.

The brothers had a long talk about each other's adventures. They both went to Ujjaini, where Gangazara married the princess, and succeeded to the throne of that kingdom. He reigned for a long time, conferring several benefits upon his brother. And so the horoscope was fully fulfilled.

The Soothsayer

THERE WAS ONCE A MAN between forty and fifty, whose grey hairs and beard might have caused him to be mistaken for sixty or seventy. Being skilled in various branches of industry, he managed tolerably to provide for the needs of himself and his wife.

One day on going to the bath his wife saw a great crowd of people. She was informed by the other women, who like herself had come to bathe, that on that day the chief soothsayer's wife was coming to the establishment; that was why there was so much confusion and excitement. While they were speaking the sound of song and music betokened the approach of the wife of the chief soothsayer, and as her husband was a great favourite of the Padishah she had a numerous escort. The bath-woman, in the hope of receiving a valuable present, paid the lady great honour and respect and begged her to choose her place.

Our poor woman, an eye witness of all this favouritism, took her bath and returned home. Chafing at the slight which she, in common with the other women, had experienced, she sought out her husband and said to him: "Either thou must become a soothsayer or I will leave thee!" The man replied: "Woman, it is as much as I can do to procure our daily bread; I have no time to study the soothsayer's art. How could I carry out thy wish?" But the woman repeated her resolve – either he must become a soothsayer or she should leave him.

His wife being of exceptional beauty he did not like the thought of losing her, so he began to consider whether anything could be done. He went to a coffeehouse, and while he was absorbed in thought over the difficulty a friend came up and asked what was the matter. Our man related his trouble. Now the friend was intimate with the bath-woman, and he answered: "Be consoled, brother, I will help thee." With these words he went straight to the bath-woman and put the situation clearly before her. The woman rejoined: "Tomorrow let the man post himself at the gate of the bath, armed with paper, pen, and inkpot, and scribble away like a soothsayer. The rest shall be my affair."

Our man, though he could neither read nor write, went to the stationer's and bought all the necessary materials, after which he took up his stand at the gate of the bath, where every one who passed mistook him for a hodja. The chief soothsayer's wife came as usual to the bath. While the attendants were occupied with her they, on the instructions of the bath-woman, took a costly ring secretly from the lady's finger, and this the bath-woman hid in the mud collected in the gutter, advising the man at the gate of what had taken place.

Soon the chief-soothsayer's wife raised a great clamour over her lost ring. The bathers ran hither and thither in confusion, and while the uproar was at its height the bath-woman said: "A hodja is at the gate who is skilled in revealing the whereabouts of missing articles." Immediately the hodja was fetched in and informed of what was required. Looking very wise and with knitted brows reflecting, he presently said: "The ring will be found buried in the mud in the narrow part of the gutter." The place indicated was searched and behold! there the ring was indeed. The lady, now happy in the recovery of her treasure, gave the hodja much baksheesh, and he went home highly satisfied with his first success as a soothsayer.

A few days later it was reported that the Sultana had lost her ring in the serai. It was believed one of the slaves had stolen it. Every. body and everywhere were searched, but the missing jewel could not be found. When it came to the ears of the Chief soothsayer's wife, she mentioned the hodja as the most likely person to be of use in the matter. He was accordingly sent for, and when he came into the Sultana's presence she said: "Hodja, thou must discover my ring wherever it be. I give thee until tomorrow morning; if by then it is not forthcoming thy head falls." They led him away and locked him up in a room by himself, where he flung himself on the floor crying in the agony of despair: "O Allah, who knowest all things, tomorrow my soul will be in thy hands!"

Now it happened that the slave who had stolen the ring was also suffering indescribable agony at the fear of her crime coming to light. She could not sleep, and at length resolved to risk consequences and make confession to the hodja. In the dead of night she got up and went to the room in which the hodja was confined. Hearing the sound of the key turning in the lock, his fear increased, for he thought it must already be morning. One may imagine his surprise then when the slave fell at his feet and implored: "O best of hodjas, I have the ring; if it becomes known I am a dead woman. O save me! Save me!"

Now thought the happy hodja to himself: "As Allah has delivered me, I must also help this poor creature in her distress." The slave told him everything; then said he to the woman: "Go, my daughter, and without any person seeing thee, let a goose swallow the ring and afterwards break its leg. Do as I command thee and fear not."

When morning broke the hodja was brought before the Padishah, to whom he said: "My Shah, all night I have pondered this thing. Animals are visible in sand. Let all the poultry, cocks, hens, geese, turkeys, and other fowls be gathered together in the garden."

The monarch ordered this to be done without delay, and the hodja followed by the whole court proceeded to the garden. Surveying the assembled fowls and scribbling the while, the hodja espied a goose which limped. Pointing it out he announced triumphantly: "O King, kill this goose and the lost ring will be found inside." The goose was quickly killed, and to the astonishment of every one, there was the ring in its stomach just as the learned hodja had predicted.

He was promoted to be chief soothsayer, besides receiving several konaks as presents. Thus the poor artisan became a very famous hodja.

Cheung Puk-chang, the Seer

THE MASTER, Puk-chang, was a noted Korean. From the time of his birth he was a wonderful mystery. In reading a book, if he but glanced through it, he could recall it word for word. Without any special study he became a master of astronomy, geology, medicine, fortune-telling, music, mathematics and geomancy, and so truly a specialist was he that he knew them all.

He was thoroughly versed also in the three great religions, Confucianism, Buddhism, and Taoism. He talked constantly of what other people could not possibly comprehend. He understood the sounds of the birds, the voices of Nature, and much else. He accompanied his father in his boyhood days when he went as envoy to Peking. At that time, strange barbarian peoples used also to come and pay their tribute. Puk-chang picked up acquaintance with them on the way. Hearing their language but once, he was readily able to communicate with them. His own countrymen who accompanied him were not the only ones astonished, nor the Chinamen themselves, but the barbarians as well. There are numerous interesting stories hinted at in the history of Puk-chang, but few suitable records were made of them, and so many are lost.

There is one, however, that I recall that comes to me through trustworthy witnesses: Puk-chang, on a certain day, went to visit his paternal aunt. She asked him to be seated, and as they talked together, said to him, "I had some harvesting to do in Yong-nam County, and sent a servant to see to it. His return is overdue and yet he does not come. I am afraid he has fallen in with thieves, or chanced on a fire or some other misfortune."

Puk-chang replied, "Shall I tell you how it goes with him, and how far he has come on the way?"

She laughed, saying, "Do you mean to joke about it?"

Puk-chang, from where he was sitting, looked off apparently to the far south, and at last said to his aunt, "He is just now crossing the hill called Bird Pass in Mun-kyong County, Kyong-sang Province. Hallo! he is getting a beating just now from a passing yangban (gentleman), but I see it is his own fault, so you need not trouble about him."

The aunt laughed, and asked, "Why should he be beaten; what's the reason, pray?"

Puk-chang replied, "It seems this official was eating his dinner at the top of the hill when your servant rode by him without dismounting. The gentleman was naturally very angry and had his servants arrest your man, pull him from his horse, and beat him over the face with their rough straw shoes."

The aunt could not believe it true, but treated the matter as a joke; and yet Puk-chang did not seem to be joking.

Interested and curious, she made a note of the day on the wall after Puk-chang had taken his departure, and when the servant returned, she asked him what day he had come over Bird Pass, and it proved to be the day recorded. She added also, "Did you get into trouble with a yangban there when you came by?"

The servant gave a startled look, and asked, "How do you know?" He then told all that had happened to him, and it was just as Puk-chang had given it even to the smallest detail.

The Sun-horse

THERE WAS ONCE UPON A TIME A COUNTRY, sad and gloomy as the grave, on which God's sun never shone. But there was a king there, and this king possessed a horse with a sun on his forehead; and this sun-horse of his the king caused to be led up and down the dark country, from one end to the other, that the people might be able to exist there; and light came from him on all sides wherever he was led, just as in the most beautiful day.

All at once the sun-horse disappeared. A darkness worse than that of night prevailed over the whole country, and nothing could disperse it. Unheard-of terror spread among the subjects; frightful misery began to afflict them, for they could neither manufacture anything nor earn anything, and such confusion arose among them that everything was turned topsy-turvy. The king, therefore, in order to liberate his realm and prevent universal destruction, made ready to seek the sun-horse with his whole army.

Through thick darkness he made his way as best he could to the frontier of his realm. Over dense mountains thousands of ages old God's light began now to break from another country, as if the sun were rising in the morning out of thick fogs. On such a mountain the king came with his army to a poor lonely cottage. He went in to inquire where he was, what it was, and how to get further. At a table sat a peasant, diligently reading in an open book. When the king bowed to him he raised his eyes, thanked him, and stood up. His whole person announced that he was not a man like another man, but a seer.

"I was just reading about you," said he to the king, "how that you are going to seek the sun-horse. Journey no further, for you will not obtain him; but rely on me: I will find him for you." "I promise you, good man, I will recompense you royally," replied the king, "if you bring him here to me." "I require no recompense; return home with your army – you're wanted there; only leave me one servant."

The next day the seer set out with the servant. The way was far and long, for they passed through six countries, and had still further to go, till in the seventh country they stopped at the royal palace. In this seventh country ruled three own brothers, who had to wife three own sisters, whose mother was a witch. When they stopped in front of the palace, the seer said to his servant: "Do you hear? you stay here, and I will go in to ascertain whether the kings are at home; for the horse with the sun is in their possession – the youngest rides upon him." Therewith he transformed himself into a green bird, and, flying on the gable of the eldest queen's roof, flew up and down and pecked at it until she opened the window and let him into her chamber. And when she let him in he perched on her white hand, and the queen was as delighted with him as a little child. "Ah, what a dear creature you are!" said she, as she played with him; "if my husband were at home he would indeed be delighted with you; but he won't come till evening; he has gone to visit the third part of his country."

All at once the old witch came into the room, and, seeing the bird, screamed to her daughter, "Wring the accursed bird's neck, for it's making you bleed!" "Well, what if it should make me bleed? it's such a dear; it's such an innocent dear!" answered the daughter. But the witch said: "Dear innocent mischief! here with him! let me wring his neck!" and dashed at it. But the bird cunningly transformed itself into a man, and, pop! out through the door, and they didn't know whither he had betaken himself.

Afterwards he again transformed himself into a green bird, flew on the gable of the middle sister, and pecked at it till she opened the window for him. And when she let him in he flew on to her white hand, and fluttered from one hand to the other. "Oh, what a dear creature you are!" cried the queen, smiling; "my husband would indeed be delighted with you if he were at home; but he won't come till to-morrow evening; he has gone to visit two thirds of his kingdom."

Thereupon the witch burst into the room. "Wring the accursed bird's neck! wring its neck, for it's making you bleed!" cried she as soon as she espied it. "Well, what if it should make me bleed? it's such a dear, such an innocent dear!" replied the daughter. But the witch said: "Dear innocent mischief! here with it! let me wring its neck!" and was already trying to seize it. But at that moment the green bird changed itself into a man, ran out through the door, and disappeared, as it were, in the clap of a hand, so that they didn't know whither he had gone.

A little while afterwards he changed himself again into a green bird and flew on the gable of the youngest queen's roof, and flew up and down, and pecked at it until she opened the window to him. And when she had let him in he flew straight on to her white hand, and made himself so agreeable to her that she played with him with the delight of a child. "Ah, what a dear creature you are!" said the queen; "if my husband were at home he would certainly be delighted with you, but he won't come till the day after to-morrow at even; he has gone to visit all three parts of his kingdom."

At that moment the old witch came into the room. "Wring, wring the accursed bird's neck!" screamed she in the doorway, "for it is making you bleed." "Well, what if it should make me bleed, mother? it is so beautiful, so innocent," answered the daughter. The witch said, "Beautiful innocent mischief! here with him! let me wring his neck!" But at that moment the bird changed itself into a man, and pop! out through the door, so that none of them saw him more.

Now the seer knew where the kings were, and when they would arrive. He went to his servant and ordered him to follow him out of the town. On they went with rapid step till they came to a bridge, over which the kings were obliged to pass.

Under this bridge they stayed waiting till the evening. When at even the sun was sinking behind the mountains, the clatter of a horse was heard near the bridge. It was the eldest king returning home. Close to the bridge his horse stumbled over a log of wood, which the seer had thrown across the bridge. "Ha! what scoundrel was that who threw this log across the road?" exclaimed the king in anger. Thereat the seer sprang out from under the bridge and rushed upon the king for "daring to call him a scoundrel," and, drawing his sword, attacked him. The king, too, drew his sword to defend himself, but after a short combat fell dead from his horse. The seer bound the dead king on the horse, and gave the horse a lash with the whip to make him carry his dead master home. He then withdrew under the bridge, and they waited there till the next evening.

When day a second time declined towards evening, the middle king came to the bridge, and, seeing the ground sprinkled with blood, cried out, "Somebody's been killed here! Who has dared to perpetrate such a crime in my kingdom?" At these words the seer sprang out from under the bridge and rushed upon the king with drawn sword, exclaiming, "How dare you insult me? Defend yourself as best you can!" The king did defend himself, but after a brief struggle yielded up his life under the sword of the seer. The seer again fastened his corpse upon the horse, and gave the horse a lash with the whip to make him carry his dead master home. They then withdrew under the bridge and waited till the third evening came.

The third evening, at the very setting of the sun, up darted the youngest king on the sun-horse, darted up with speed, for he was somewhat late; but when he saw the red blood in front of the bridge, he stopped, and gazing at it exclaimed, "It is an unheard-of villain who has dared to murder a man in my kingdom!" Scarcely had these words issued from his mouth when the seer placed himself before him with drawn sword, sternly bidding him defend himself, "for he had wounded his honour." "I don't know how," answered the king, "unless it is you that are the villain." But as his adversary attacked him with a sword, he, too, drew his, and defended himself manfully.

It had been mere play to the seer to overcome the first two kings, but it was not so with this one. Long time they fought, and broke their swords, yet victory didn't show itself either on the one side or on the other. "We shall effect nothing with swords," said the seer, "but do you know what? Let us turn ourselves into wheels and start down from the hill; the wheel which breaks shall be the conquered." "Good!" said the king; "I'll be a cart-wheel, and you shall be a lighter wheel." "Not so," cunningly said the seer; "you shall be the lighter wheel, and I will be the cart-wheel;" and the king agreed to it. Then they went up the hill, turned themselves into wheels, and started downwards. The cart-wheel flew to pieces, and bang! right into the lighter wheel, so that it all smashed up. Immediately the seer arose out of the cart-wheel and joyfully exclaimed, "There you are, the victory is mine!" "Not a bit of it, sir brother!" cried the king, placing himself in front of the seer; "you have only broken my fingers. But do you know what? Let us make ourselves into flames, and the flame which burns up the other shall be the victor. I will make myself into a red flame, and do you make yourself into a bluish one." "Not so!" interrupted the seer; "you make yourself into a bluish flame, and I will make myself into a red one." The king agreed to this also. They went into the road to the bridge, and, changing themselves into flames, began to burn each other unmercifully. Long did they burn each other, but nothing came of it. Thereupon, by coincidence, up came an old beggar with a long gray beard, a bald head, a large scrip at his side, leaning upon a thick staff. "Old father!" said the bluish flame, "bring some water and quench this red flame; I'll give you a penny for it." The red flame cunningly exclaimed, "Old father! I'll give you a shilling if you'll pour the water on this bluish flame." The old beggar liked the shilling better than the penny, brought water and quenched the bluish flame. Then it was all over with the king. The red flame turned itself into a man, took the sun-horse by the bridle, mounted on his back, called the servant, thanked the beggar for the service he had rendered, and went off.

In the royal palaces there was deep grief at the murder of the two kings; the entire palaces were draped with black cloth, and the people crowded into them from all quarters to gaze at the cut and slashed bodies of the two elder brothers, whose horses had brought them home. The old witch, exasperated at the death of her sons-in-law, devised a plan of vengeance on their murderer, the seer. She seated herself with speed on an iron rake, took her three daughters under her arms, and pop! off with them into the air.

The seer and his servant had already got through a good part of their journey, and were then crossing desert mountains, a treeless waste. Here a terrible hunger seized the servant, and there wasn't even a wild plum to assuage it. All of a sudden they came to an apple-tree. Apples were hanging on it; the branches were all but breaking under their weight; their scent was beautiful; they were delightfully ruddy, so that they almost offered themselves to be eaten. "Praise be to God!" cried the delighted servant; "I shall eat one of those apples with an excellent appetite." "Don't attempt to gather one of them!" cried the seer to him; "wait, I'll gather some for you myself." But instead of plucking an apple, he drew his sword and thrust it mightily into the apple-tree; red blood spouted out of it. "There," said he, "you would have come to harm if you had eaten any of those apples, for the apple-tree was the eldest queen, whose mother placed her there to put us out of this world."

After a time they came to a spring; water clear as crystal bubbled up in it, all but running over the brim and thus attracting wayfarers. "Ah!" said the servant, "if we can't get anything better, let us at any rate have a drink of this good water." "Don't venture to drink of it!" shouted the seer; "but stay, I'll get you some of it." Yet he didn't get him any water, but thrust his drawn sword into the midst of it; it was immediately discoloured with blood, which began to flow from it in mighty waves. "That is the middle queen, whose mother placed her here to put us out of this world," said the seer, and the servant thanked him for his warning, and went on, would he, nould he, in hunger and thirst, whithersoever the seer led him.

After a time they came to a rose-bush, which was red with delightful roses, and filled the air round about with their scent. "Oh, what beautiful roses!" said the servant; "I never saw such beauties in all my life. I'll go and gather a few of them; I will at any rate comfort myself with them if I can't assuage my hunger and thirst." "Don't venture to gather one of them!" cried the seer; "I will gather them for you." With that he cut into the bush with his sword; red blood spurted out, as if he had cut the vein of a human being. "That is the youngest queen," said the seer to his servant, "whom her mother, the witch, placed here with the intention of taking vengeance upon us for the death of her sons-in-law." They then went on.

When they crossed the frontier of the dark realm, flashes flew in all directions from the horse's forehead, and everything came to life again, beautiful regions rejoiced and blossomed with the flowers of spring. The king didn't know how to thank the seer sufficiently, and offered him the half of his kingdom as a reward, but he declined it. "You are king," said he; "rule over the whole realm, and I will return to my cottage in peace." He took leave and departed.

The Vision of MacConglinney

CATHAL, KING OF MUNSTER, was a good king and a great warrior. But there came to dwell within him a lawless evil beast, that afflicted him with hunger that ceased not, and might not be satisfied, so that he would devour a pig, a cow, and a bull calf and three-score cakes of pure wheat, and a vat of new ale, for his breakfast, whilst as for his great feast, what he ate there passes account or reckoning. He was like this for three half-years, and during that time it was the ruin of Munster he was, and it is likely he would have ruined all Ireland in another half-year.

Now there lived in Armagh a famous young scholar and his name was Anier MacConglinney. He heard of the strange disease of King Cathal, and of the abundance of food and drink, of whitemeats, ale and mead, there were always to be found at the king's court. Thither then was he minded to go to try his own fortune, and to see of what help he could be to the king.

He arose early in the morning and tucked up his shirt and wrapped him in the folds of his white cloak. In his right hand he grasped his even-poised knotty staff, and going right-hand-wise round his home, he bade farewell to his tutors and started off.

He journeyed across all Ireland till he came to the house of Pichan. And there he stayed and told tales, and made all merry. But Pichan said:

"Though great thy mirth, son of learning, it does not make me glad."

"And why?" asked MacConglinney.

"Knowest thou not, scholar, that Cathal is coming here tonight with all his host. And if the great host is troublesome, the king's first meal is more troublesome still; and troublesome though the first be, most troublesome of all is the great feast. Three things are wanted for this last: a bushel of oats, and a bushel of wild apples, and a bushel of flour cakes."

"What reward would you give me if I shield you from the king from this hour to the same hour tomorrow?"

"A white sheep from every fold between Carn and Cork."

"I will take that," said MacConglinney.

Cathal, the king, came with the companies, and a host of horse of the Munster men. But Cathal did not let the thong of his shoe be half loosed before he began supplying his mouth with both hands from the apples round about him. Pichan and all the men of Munster looked on sadly and sorrowfully. Then rose MacConglinney, hastily and impatiently, and seized a stone, against which swords were used to be sharpened; this he thrust into his mouth and began grinding his teeth against the stone.

"What makes thee mad, son of learning?" asked Cathal.

"I grieve to see you eating alone," said the scholar.

Then the king was ashamed and flung him the apples, and it is said that for three half-years he had not performed such an act of humanity.

"Grant me a further boon," said MacConglinney.

"It is granted, on my troth," said the king.

"Fast with me the whole night," said the scholar.

And grievous though it was to the king, he did so, for he had passed his princely troth, and no King of Munster might transgress that.

In the morning MacConglinney called for juicy old bacon, and tender corned beef, honey in the comb, and English salt on a beautiful polished dish of white silver. A fire he lighted of oak wood without smoke, without fumes, without sparks.

And sticking spits into the portion of meat, he set to work to roast them. Then he shouted, "Ropes and cords here."

Ropes and cords were given to him, and the strongest of the warriors.

And they seized the king and bound him securely, and made him fast with knots and hooks and staples. When the king was thus fastened, MacConglinney sat himself down before him, and taking his knife out of his girdle, he carved the portion of meat that was on the spits, and every morsel he dipped in the honey, and, passing it in front of the king's mouth, put it in his own.

When the king saw that he was getting nothing, and he had been fasting for twenty-four hours, he roared and bellowed, and commanded the killing of the scholar. But that was not done for him.

"Listen, King of Munster," said MacConglinney, "a vision appeared to me last night, and I will relate it to you."

He then began his vision, and as he related it he put morsel after morsel past Cathal's mouth into his own.

> "A lake of new milk I beheld
> In the midst of a fair plain,
> Therein a well-appointed house,
> Thatched with butter.
> Puddings fresh boiled,
> Such were its thatch-rods,
> Its two soft door posts of custard,
> Its beds of glorious bacon.
> Cheeses were the palisades,
> Sausages the rafters.
> Truly 'twas a rich filled house,
> In which was great store of good feed.

"Such was the vision I beheld, and a voice sounded into my ears. "Go now, thither, MacConglinney, for you have no power of eating in you." "What must I do," said I, for the sight of that had made me greedy. Then the voice bade me go to the hermitage of the Wizard Doctor, and there I should find appetite for all kinds of savoury tender sweet food, acceptable to the body.

"There in the harbour of the lake before me I saw a juicy little coracle of beef; its thwarts were of curds, its prow of lard; its stern of butter; its oars were flitches of venison. Then I rowed across the wide expanse of the New Milk Lake, through seas of broth, past river mouths of meat, over swelling boisterous waves of butter milk, by perpetual pools of savoury lard, by islands of cheese, by headlands of old curds, until I reached the firm level land between Butter Mount and Milk Lake, in the land of O'Early-eating, in front of the hermitage of the Wizard Doctor.

"Marvellous, indeed, was the hermitage. Around it were seven-score hundred smooth stakes of old bacon, and instead of thorns above the top of every stake was fixed juicy lard. There was a gate of cream, whereon was a bolt of sausage. And there I saw the doorkeeper, Bacon Lad, son of Butterkins, son of Lardipole, with his smooth sandals of old bacon, his legging of pot-meat round his shins, his tunic of corned beef, his girdle of salmon skin round him, his hood of flummery about him, his steed of bacon under him, with its four legs of custard, its four hoofs of oaten bread, its ears of curds, its two eyes of honey in its head; in his hand a whip, the cords whereof were four-and-twenty fair white puddings, and every juicy drop that fell from each of these puddings would have made a meal for an ordinary man.

"On going in I beheld the Wizard Doctor with his two gloves of rump steak on his hands, setting in order the house, which was hung all round with tripe, from roof to floor.

"I went into the kitchen, and there I saw the Wizard Doctor's son, with his fishing hook of lard in his hand, and the line was made of marrow, and he was angling in a lake of whey. Now he would bring up a flitch of ham, and now a fillet of corned beef. And as he was angling, he fell in, and was drowned.

"As I set my foot across the threshold into the house, I saw a pure white bed of butter, on which I sat down, but I sank down into it up to the tips of my hair. Hard work had the eight strongest men in the house to pull me out by the top of the crown of my head.

"Then I was taken in to the Wizard Doctor. 'What aileth thee?' said he.

"My wish would be, that all the many wonderful viands of the world were before me, that I might eat my fill and satisfy my greed. But alas! great is the misfortune to me, who cannot obtain any of these.

"'On my word,' said the Doctor, 'the disease is grievous. But thou shall take home with thee a medicine to cure thy disease, and shalt be for ever healed therefrom.'

"'What is that?' asked I.

"'When thou goest home tonight, warm thyself before a glowing red fire of oak, made up on a dry hearth, so that its embers may warm thee, its blaze may not burn thee, its smoke may not touch thee. And make for thyself thrice nine morsels, and every morsel as big as an heath fowl's egg, and in each morsel eight kinds of grain, wheat and barley, oats and rye, and therewith eight condiments, and to every condiment eight sauces. And when thou hast prepared thy food, take a drop of drink, a tiny drop, only as much as twenty men will drink, and let it be of thick milk, of yellow bubbling milk, of milk that will gurgle as it rushes down thy throat.'

"'And when thou hast done this, whatever disease thou hast, shall be removed. Go now,' said he, 'in the name of cheese, and may the smooth juicy bacon protect thee, may yellow curdy cream protect, may the cauldron full of pottage protect thee.'"

Now, as MacConglinney recited his vision, what with the pleasure of the recital and the recounting of these many pleasant viands, and the sweet savour of the honeyed morsels roasting on the spits, the lawless beast that dwelt within the king, came forth until it was licking its lips outside its head.

Then MacConglinney bent his hand with the two spits of food, and put them to the lips of the king, who longed to swallow them, wood, food, and all. So he took them an arm's length away from the king, and the lawless beast jumped from the throat of Cathal onto the spit. MacConglinney put the spit into the embers, and upset the cauldron of the royal house over the spit. The house was emptied, so that not the value of a cockchafer's leg was left in it, and four huge fires were kindled here and there in it. When the house was a tower of red flame and a huge blaze, the lawless beast sprang to the rooftree of the palace, and from thence he vanished, and was seen no more.

As for the king, a bed was prepared for him on a downy quilt, and musicians and singers entertained him going from noon till twilight. And when he awoke, this is what he bestowed upon the scholar – a cow from every farm, and a sheep from every house in Munster. Moreover, that so long as he lived, he should carve the king's food, and sit at his right hand.

Thus was Cathal, King of Munster, cured of his craving, and MacConglinney honoured.

The Leeching of Kayn's Leg

THERE WERE FIVE HUNDRED blind men, and five hundred deaf men, and five hundred limping men, and five hundred dumb men, and five hundred cripple men. The five hundred deaf men had five hundred wives, and the five hundred limping men had five hundred wives, and the five hundred dumb men had five hundred wives, and the five hundred cripple men had five hundred wives. Each five hundred of these had five hundred children and five hundred dogs. They were in the habit of going about in one band, and were called the Sturdy Strolling Beggarly Brotherhood.

There was a knight in Erin called O'Cronicert, with whom they spent a day and a year; and they ate up all that he had, and made a poor man of him, till he had nothing left but an old tumble-down black house, and an old lame white horse.

There was a king in Erin called Brian Boru; and O'Cronicert went to him for help. He cut a cudgel of grey oak on the outskirts of the wood, mounted the old lame white horse, and set off at speed through wood and over moss and rugged ground, till he reached the king's house. When he arrived he went on his knees to the king; and the king said to him, "What is your news, O'Cronicert?"

"I have but poor news for you, king."

"What poor news have you?" said the king.

"That I have had the Sturdy Strolling Beggarly Brotherhood for a day and a year, and they have eaten all that I had, and made a poor man of me," said he.

"Well!" said the king, "I am sorry for you; what do you want?"

"I want help," said O'Cronicert; "anything that you may be willing to give me."

The king promised him a hundred cows. He went to the queen, and made his complaint to her, and she gave him another hundred. He went to the king's son, Murdoch Mac Brian, and he got another hundred from him. He got food and drink at the king's; and when he was going away he said, "Now I am very much obliged to you. This will set me very well on my feet. After all that I have got there is another thing that I want."

"What is it?" said the king.

"It is the lap-dog that is in and out after the queen that I wish for."

"Ha!" said the king, "it is your mightiness and pride that has caused the loss of your means; but if you become a good man you shall get this along with the rest."

O'Cronicert bade the king goodbye, took the lap-dog, leapt on the back of the old lame white horse, and went off at speed through wood, and over moss and rugged ground. After he had gone some distance through the wood a roebuck leapt up and the lap-dog went after it. In a moment the deer started up as a woman behind O'Cronicert, the handsomest that eye had ever seen from the beginning of the universe till the end of eternity. She said to him, "Call your dog off me."

"I will do so if you promise to marry me," said O'Cronicert.

"If you keep three vows that I shall lay upon you I will marry you," said she.

"What vows are they?" said he.

"The first is that you do not go to ask your worldly king to a feast or a dinner without first letting me know," said she.

"Hoch!" said O'Cronicert, "do you think that I cannot keep that vow? I would never go to invite my worldly king without informing you that I was going to do so. It is easy to keep that vow."

"You are likely to keep it!" said she.

"The second vow is," said she, "that you do not cast up to me in any company or meeting in which we shall be together, that you found me in the form of a deer."

"Hoo!" said O'Cronicert, "you need not to lay that vow upon me. I would keep it at any rate."

"You are likely to keep it!" said she.

"The third vow is," said she, "that you do not leave me in the company of only one man while you go out." It was agreed between them that she should marry him.

They reached the old tumble-down black house. Grass they cut in the clefts and ledges of the rocks; a bed they made and laid down. O'Cronicert's wakening from sleep was the lowing of cattle and the bleating of sheep and the neighing of mares, while he himself was in a bed of gold on wheels of silver, going from end to end of the Tower of Castle Town.

"I am sure that you are surprised," said she.

"I am indeed," said he.

"You are in your own room," said she.

"In my own room," said he. "I never had such a room."

"I know well that you never had," said she; "but you have it now. So long as you keep me you shall keep the room."

He then rose, and put on his clothes, and went out. He took a look at the house when he went out; and it was a palace, the like of which he had never seen, and the king himself did not possess. He then took a walk round the farm; and he never saw so many cattle, sheep, and horses as were on it. He returned to the house, and said to his wife that the farm was being ruined by other people's cattle and sheep. "It is not," said she: "your own cattle and sheep are on it."

"I never had so many cattle and sheep," said he.

"I know that," said she; "but so long as you keep me you shall keep them. There is no good wife whose tocher does not follow her."

He was now in good circumstances, indeed wealthy. He had gold and silver, as well as cattle and sheep. He went about with his gun and dogs hunting every day, and was a great man. It occurred to him one day that he would go to invite the King of Erin to dinner, but he did not tell his wife that he was going. His first vow was now broken. He sped away to the King of Erin, and invited him and his great court to dinner. The King of Erin said to him, "Do you intend to take away the cattle that I promised you?"

"Oh! No, King of Erin," said O'Cronicert; "I could give you as many today."

"Ah!" said the king, "how well you have got on since I saw you last!"

"I have indeed," said O'Cronicert! "I have fallen in with a rich wife who has plenty of gold and silver, and of cattle and sheep."

"I am glad of that," said the King of Erin.

O'Cronicert said, "I shall feel much obliged if you will go with me to dinner, yourself and your great court."

"We will do so willingly," said the king.

They went with him on that same day. It did not occur to O'Cronicert how a dinner could be prepared for the king without his wife knowing that he was coming. When they were going on, and had reached the place where O'Cronicert had met the deer, he remembered that his vow was broken, and he said to the king, "Excuse me; I am going on before to the house to tell that you are coming."

The king said, "We will send off one of the lads."

"You will not," said O'Cronicert; "no lad will serve the purpose so well as myself."

He set off to the house; and when he arrived his wife was diligently preparing dinner. He told her what he had done, and asked her pardon. "I pardon you this time," said she: "I know what you have done as well as you do yourself. The first of your vows is broken."

The king and his great court came to O'Cronicert's house; and the wife had everything ready for them as befitted a king and great people; every kind of drink and food. They spent two or three days and nights at dinner, eating and drinking. They were praising the dinner highly, and O'Cronicert himself was praising it; but his wife was not. O'Cronicert was angry that she was not praising it and he went and struck her in the mouth with his fist and knocked out two of her teeth. "Why are you not praising the dinner like the others, you contemptible deer?" said he.

"I am not," said she: "I have seen my father's big dogs having a better dinner than you are giving tonight to the King of Erin and his court."

O'Cronicert got into such a rage that he went outside of the door. He was not long standing there when a man came riding on a black horse, who in passing caught O'Cronicert by the collar of his coat, and took him up behind him: and they set off. The rider did not say a word to O'Cronicert. The horse was going so swiftly that O'Cronicert thought the wind would drive his head off. They arrived at a big, big palace, and came off the black horse. A stableman came out, and caught the horse, and took it in. It was with wine that he was cleaning the horse's feet. The rider of the black horse said to O'Cronicert, "Taste the wine to see if it is better than the wine that you are giving to Brian Boru and his court tonight."

O'Cronicert tasted the wine, and said, "This is better wine."

The rider of the black horse said, "How unjust was the fist a little ago! The wind from your fist carried the two teeth to me."

He then took him into that big, handsome, and noble house, and into a room that was full of gentlemen eating and drinking, and he seated him at the head of the table, and gave him wine to drink, and said to him, "Taste that wine to see if it is better than the wine that you are giving to the King of Erin and his court tonight."

"This is better wine," said O'Cronicert.

"How unjust was the fist a little ago!" said the rider of the black horse.

When all was over the rider of the black horse said, "Are you willing to return home now?"

"Yes," said O'Cronicert, "very willing."

They then rose, and went to the stable: and the black horse was taken out; and they leaped on its back, and went away. The rider of the black horse said to O'Cronicert, after they had set off, "Do you know who I am?"

"I do not," said O'Cronicert.

"I am a brother-in-law of yours," said the rider of the black horse; "and though my sister is married to you there is not a king or knight in Erin who is a match for her. Two of your vows are now broken; and if you break the other vow you shall lose your wife and all that you possess."

They arrived at O'Cronicert's house; and O'Cronicert said, "I am ashamed to go in, as they do not know where I have been since night came."

"Hoo!" said the rider, "they have not missed you at all. There is so much conviviality among them, that they have not suspected that you have been anywhere. Here are the two teeth that you knocked out of the front of your wife's mouth. Put them in their place, and they will be as strong as ever."

"Come in with me," said O'Cronicert to the rider of the black horse.

"I will not: I disdain to go in," said the rider of the black horse.

The rider of the black horse bade O'Cronicert goodbye, and went away.

O'Cronicert went in; and his wife met him as she was busy waiting on the gentlemen. He asked her pardon, and put the two teeth in the front of her mouth, and they were as strong as ever. She said, "Two of your vows are now broken." No one took notice of him when he went in, or said "Where have you been?" They spent the night in eating and drinking, and the whole of the next day.

In the evening the king said, "I think that it is time for us to be going"; and all said that it was. O'Cronicert said, "You will not go tonight. I am going to get up a dance. You will go tomorrow."

"Let them go," said his wife.

"I will not," said he.

The dance was set a-going that night. They were playing away at dancing and music till they became warm and hot with perspiration. They were going out one after another to cool themselves at the side of the house. They all went out except O'Cronicert and his wife, and a man called Kayn Mac Loy. O'Cronicert himself went out, and left his wife and Kayn Mac Loy in the house, and when she saw that he had broken his third vow she gave a spring through a room, and became a big filly, and gave Kayn Mac Loy a kick with her foot, and broke his thigh in two. She gave another spring, and smashed the door and went away, and was seen no more. She took with her the Tower of Castle Town as an armful on her shoulder and a light burden on her back, and she left Kayn Mac Loy in the old tumble-down black house in a pool of rain-drip on the floor.

At daybreak next day poor O'Cronicert could only see the old house that he had before. Neither cattle nor sheep, nor any of the fine things that he had was to be seen. One awoke in the morning beside a bush, another beside a dyke, and another beside a ditch. The king only had the honour of having O'Cronicert's little hut over his head. As they were leaving, Murdoch Mac Brian remembered that he had left his own foster-brother Kayn Mac Loy behind, and said there should be no separation in life between them and that he would go back for him. He found Kayn in the old tumble-down black house, in the middle of the floor, in a pool of rain-water, with his leg broken; and he said the earth should make a nest in his sole and the sky a nest in his head if he did not find a man to cure Kayn's leg.

They told him that on the Isle of Innisturk was a herb that would heal him.

So Kayn Mac Loy was then borne away, and sent to the island, and he was supplied with as much food as would keep him for a month, and with two crutches on which he would be going out and in as he might desire. At last the food was spent, and he was destitute, and he had not found the herb. He was in the habit of going down to the shore, and gathering shell-fish, and eating it.

As he was one day on the shore, he saw a big, big man landing on the island, and he could see the earth and the sky between his legs. He set off with the crutches to try if he could get into the hut before the big man would come upon him. Despite his efforts, the big man was between him and the door, and said to him, "Unless you deceive me, you are Kayn Mac Loy."

Kayn Mac Loy said, "I have never deceived a man: I am he."

The big man said to him:

"Stretch out your leg, Kayn, till I put a salve of herbs and healing to it. Salve and binding herb and the poultice are cooling; the worm is channering. Pressure and haste hard bind me, for I must hear Mass in the great church at Rome, and be in Norway before I sleep."

Kayn Mac Loy said:

"May it be no foot to Kayn or a foot to any one after one, or I be Kayn son of Loy, if I stretch out my foot for you to put a salve of herbs and healing on it, till you tell me why you have no church of your own in Norway, so as, as now, to be going to the great church of Rome to Rome tomorrow. Unless you deceive me you are Machkan-an-Athar, the son of the King of Lochlann."

The big man said, "I have never deceived any man: I am he. I am now going to tell you why we have not a church in Lochlann. Seven masons came to build a church, and they and my father were bargaining about the building of it. The agreement that the masons wanted was that my mother and sister would go to see the interior of the church when it would be finished. My father was glad to get the church built so cheaply. They agreed accordingly; and the masons went in the morning to the place where the church was to be built. My father pointed out the spot for the foundation. They began to build in the morning, and the church was finished before the evening. When it was finished they requested my mother and sister to go to see its interior. They had no sooner entered than the doors were shut; and the church went away into the skies in the form of a tuft of mist.

"Stretch out your leg, Kayn, till I put a salve of herbs and healing to it. Salve and binding herb and the poultice are cooling; the worm is channering. Pressure and haste hard bind me, for I must hear Mass in the great church at Rome, and be in Norway before I sleep."

Kayn Mac Loy said:

"May it be no foot to Kayn or a foot to anyone after one, or I be Kayn son of Loy, if I stretch out my foot for you to put a salve of herbs and healing on it, till you tell me if you heard what befell your mother and sister."

"Ah!" said the big man, "the mischief is upon you; that tale is long to tell; but I will tell you a short tale about the matter. On the day on which they were working at the church I was away in the hill hunting game; and when I came home in the evening my brother told me what had happened, namely, that my mother and sister had gone away in the form of a tuft of mist. I became so cross and angry that I resolved to destroy the world till I should find out where my mother and sister were. My brother said to me that I was a fool to think of such a thing. 'I'll tell you,' said he, 'what you'll do. You will first go to try to find out where they are. When you find out where they are you will demand them peaceably, and if you do not get them peaceably you will fight for them.'

"I took my brother's advice, and prepared a ship to set off with. I set off alone, and embraced the ocean. I was overtaken by a great mist, and I came upon an island, and there was a large number of ships at anchor near it; I went in amongst them, and went ashore. I saw there a big, big woman reaping rushes; and when she would raise her head she would throw her right breast over her shoulder and when she would bend it would fall down between her legs. I came once behind her, and caught the breast with my mouth, and said to her, 'You are yourself witness, woman, that I am the foster-son of your right breast.' 'I perceive that, great hero,' said the old woman, 'but my advice to you is to leave this island as fast as you can.' 'Why?' said I. 'There is a big giant in the cave up there,' said she, 'and every one of the ships that you see he has taken in from the ocean with his breath, and he has killed and eaten the men. He is asleep at present, and when he wakens he will have you in a similar manner. A large iron door and an oak door are on the cave. When the giant draws in his breath the doors open, and when he emits his breath the doors shut; and they are shut as fast as though seven small bars, and seven large bars, and seven locks were on them. So fast are they that seven crowbars could not force them open.' I said to the old woman, 'Is there any way of destroying him?' 'I'll tell you,' said she, 'how it can be done. He has a weapon above the door that is called the short spear: and if you succeed in taking off his head with the first blow it will be well; but if you do not, the case will be worse than it was at first.'

"I set off, and reached the cave, the two doors of which opened. The giant's breath drew me into the cave; and stools, chairs, and pots were by its action dashing against each other, and like to break my legs. The door shut when I went in, and was shut as fast as though seven small bars, and seven large bars, and seven locks were on it; and seven crowbars could not force it open; and I was a prisoner in the cave. The giant drew in his breath again, and the doors opened. I gave a look upwards, and saw the short spear, and laid hold of it. I drew the short spear, and I warrant you that I dealt him such a blow with it as did not require to be repeated; I swept the head off him. I took the head down to the old woman, who was reaping the rushes, and said to her, 'There is the giant's head for you.' The old woman said, 'Brave man! I knew that you were a hero. This island had need of your coming to it today. Unless you deceive me, you are Mac Connachar son of the King of Lochlann.' 'I have never deceived a man. I am he,' said I. 'I am a soothsayer,' said she, 'and know the object of your journey. You are going in quest of your mother and sister.' 'Well,' said I, 'I am so far on the way if I only knew where to go for them.' 'I'll tell you where they are,' said she; 'they are in the kingdom of the Red Shield, and the King of the Red Shield is resolved to marry your mother, and his son is resolved to marry your sister. I'll tell you how the town is situated. A canal of seven times seven paces breadth surrounds it. On the canal there is a drawbridge, which is guarded during the day by two creatures that no weapon can pierce, as they are covered all over with scales, except two spots below the neck in which their death-wounds lie. Their names are Roar and Rustle. When night comes the bridge is raised, and the monsters sleep. A very high and big wall surrounds the king's palace.'

"Stretch out your leg, Kayn, till I put a salve of herbs and healing to it. Salve and binding herb and the poultice are cooling; the worm is channering. Pressure and haste hard bind me, for I must hear Mass in the great church at Rome, and be in Norway before I sleep."

Kayn Mac Loy said:

"May it be no foot to Kayn or a foot to anyone after one, or I be Kayn son of Loy, if I stretch out my foot for you to put a salve of herbs and healing on it, till you tell me if you went farther in search of your mother and sister, or if you returned home, or what befell you."

"Ah!" said the big man, "the mischief is upon you; that tale is long to tell; but I will tell you another tale. I set off, and reached the big town of the Red Shield; and it was surrounded by a canal, as the old woman told me; and there was a drawbridge on the canal. It was night when I arrived, and the bridge was raised, and the monsters were asleep. I measured two feet before me and a foot behind me of the ground on which I was standing, and I sprang on the end of my spear and on my tiptoes, and reached the place where the monsters were asleep; and I drew the short spear, and I warrant you that I dealt them such a blow below the neck as did not require to be repeated. I took up the heads and hung them on one of the posts of the bridge. I then went on to the wall that surrounded the king's palace. This wall was so high that it was not easy for me to spring over it; and I set to work with the short spear, and dug a hole through it, and got in. I went to the door of the palace and knocked; and the doorkeeper called out, 'Who is there?' 'It is I,' said I. My mother and sister recognised my speech; and my mother called, 'Oh! It is my son; let him in.' I then got in, and they rose to meet me with great joy. I was supplied with food, drink, and a good bed. In the morning breakfast was set before us; and after it I said to my mother and sister that they had better make ready, and go with me. The King of the Red Shield said, 'It shall not be so. I am resolved to marry your mother, and my son is resolved to marry your sister.' 'If you wish to marry my mother, and if your son wishes to marry my sister, let both of you accompany me to my home, and you shall get them there.' The King of the Red Shield said, 'So be it.'

"We then set off, and came to where my ship was, went on board of it, and sailed home. When we were passing a place where a great battle was going on, I asked the King of the Red Shield what battle it was, and the cause of it. 'Don't you know at all?' said the King of the Red Shield. 'I do not,' said I. The King of the Red Shield said, 'That is the battle for the daughter of the King of the Great Universe, the most beautiful woman in the world; and whoever wins her by his heroism shall get her in marriage. Do you see yonder castle?' 'I do,' said I. 'She is on the top of that castle, and sees from it the hero that wins her,' said the King of the Red Shield. I requested to be put on shore, that I might win her by my swiftness and strength. They put me on shore; and I got a sight of her on the top of the castle. Having measured two feet behind me and a foot before me, I sprang on the end of my spear and on my tiptoes, and reached the top of the castle; and I caught the daughter of the King of the Universe in my arms and flung her over the castle. I was with her and intercepted her before she reached the ground, and I took her away on my shoulder, and set off to the shore as fast as I could, and delivered her to the King of the Red Shield to be put on board the ship. 'Am I not the best warrior that ever sought you?' said I. 'You can jump well' said she, 'but I have not seen any of your prowess.' I turned back to meet the warriors, and attacked them with the short spear, and did not leave a head on a neck of any of them. I then returned, and called to the King of the Red Shield to come in to the shore for me. Pretending not to hear me, he set the sails in order to return home with the daughter of the King of the Great Universe, and marry her. I measured two feet behind me and a foot before me, and sprang on the end of my spear and on my tiptoes and got on board the ship. I then said to the King of the Red Shield, 'What were you going to do? Why did you not wait for me?' 'Oh!' said the king, 'I was only making the ship ready and setting the sails to her before going on shore for you. Do you know what I am thinking of?' 'I do not,' said I. 'It is,' said the King, 'that I will return home with the daughter of the King of the Great Universe, and that you shall go home with your mother and sister.' 'That is not to be the way of it,' said I. 'She whom I have won by my prowess neither you nor any other shall get.'

"The king had a red shield, and if he should get it on, no weapon could make an impression on him. He began to put on the red shield, and I struck him with the short spear in the middle of his body, and cut him in two, and threw him overboard. I then struck the son, and swept his head off, and threw him overboard.

"Stretch out your leg, Kayn, till I put a salve of herbs and healing to it. Salve and binding herb and the poultice are cooling; the worm is channering. Pressure and haste hard bind me, for I must hear Mass in the great church at Rome, and be in Norway before I sleep."

Kayn Mac Loy said:

"May it be no foot to Kayn or a foot to anyone after one, or I be Kayn son of Loy, if I stretch out my foot for you to put a salve of herbs and healing on it, till you tell me whether any search was made for the daughter of the King of the Universe."

"Ah! The mischief is upon you," said the big man; "I will tell you another short tale. I came home with my mother and sister, and the daughter of the King of the Universe, and I married the daughter of the King of the Universe. The first son I had I named Machkan-na-skaya-jayrika (son of the red shield). Not long after this a hostile force came to enforce compensation for the King of the Red Shield, and a hostile force came from the King of the Universe to enforce compensation for the daughter of the King of the Universe. I took the daughter of the King of the Universe with me on the one shoulder and Machkan-na-skaya-jayrika on the other, and I went on board the ship and set the sails to her, and I placed the ensign of the King of the Great Universe on the one mast, and that of the King of the Red Shield on the other, and I blew a trumpet, and passed through the midst of them, and I said to them that here was the man, and that if they were going to enforce their claims, this was the time. All the ships that were there chased me; and we set out on the expanse of ocean. My ship would be equalled in speed by but few. One day a thick dark mist came on, and they lost sight of me. It happened that I came to an island called The Wet Mantle. I built a hut there; and another son was born to me, and I called him Son of the Wet Mantle.

"I was a long time in that island; but there was enough of fruit, fish, and birds in it. My two sons had grown to be somewhat big. As I was one day out killing birds, I saw a big, big man coming towards the island, and I ran to try if I could get into the house before him. He met me, and caught me, and put me into a bog up to the armpits, and he went into the house, and took out on his shoulder the daughter of the King of the Universe, and passed close to me in order to irritate me the more. The saddest look that I ever gave or ever shall give was that I gave when I saw the daughter of the King of the Universe on the shoulder of another, and could not take her from him. The boys came out where I was; and I bade them bring me the short spear from the house. They dragged the short spear after them, and brought it to me; and I cut the ground around me with it till I got out.

"I was a long time in the Wet Mantle, even till my two sons grew to be big lads. They asked me one day if I had any thought of going to seek their mother. I told them that I was waiting till they were stronger, and that they should then go with me. They said that they were ready to go with me at any time. I said to them that we had better get the ship ready, and go. They said, 'Let each of us have a ship to himself.' We arranged accordingly; and each went his own way.

"As I happened one day to be passing close to land I saw a great battle going on. Being under vows never to pass a battle without helping the weaker side, I went on shore, and set to work with the weaker side, and I knocked the head off every one with the short spear. Being tired, I lay myself down among the bodies and fell asleep.

"Stretch out your leg, Kayn, till I put a salve of herbs and healing to it. Salve and binding herb and the poultice are cooling; the worm is channering. Pressure and haste hard bind me, for I must hear Mass in the great church at Rome, and be in Norway before I sleep."

Kayn Mac Loy said:

"May it be no foot to Kayn or a foot to anyone after one, or I be Kayn son of Loy, if I stretch out my foot for you to put a salve of herbs and healing on it, till you tell me if you found the daughter of the King of the Universe, or if you went home, or what happened to you."

"The mischief is upon you," said the big man; "that tale is long to tell, but I will tell another short tale. When I awoke out of sleep I saw a ship making for the place where I was lying, and a big giant with only one eye dragging it after him: and the ocean reached no higher than his knees. He had a big fishing-rod with a big strong line hanging from it on which was a very big hook. He was throwing the line ashore, and fixing the hook in a body, and lifting it on board, and he continued this work till the ship was loaded with bodies. He fixed the hook once in my clothes; but I was so heavy that the rod could not carry me on board. He had to go on shore himself, and carry me on board in his arms. I was then in a worse plight than I ever was in. The giant set off with the ship, which he dragged after him, and reached a big, precipitous rock, in the face of which he had a large cave: and a damsel as beautiful as I ever saw came out, and stood in the door of the cave. He was handing the bodies to her, and she was taking hold of them and putting them into the cave. As she took hold of each body she said, 'Are you alive?' At last the giant took hold of me, and handed me in to her, and said, 'Keep him apart; he is a large body, and I will have him to breakfast the first day that I go from home.' My best time was not when I heard the giant's sentence upon me. When he had eaten enough of the bodies, his dinner and supper, he lay down to sleep. When he began to snore the damsel came to speak to me; and she told me that she was a king's daughter the giant had stolen away and that she had no way of getting away from him. 'I am now,' she said, 'seven years except two days with him, and there is a drawn sword between us. He dared not come nearer me than that till the seven years should expire.' I said to her, 'Is there no way of killing him?' 'It is not easy to kill him, but we will devise an expedient for killing him,' said she. 'Look at that pointed bar that he uses for roasting the bodies. At dead of night gather the embers of the fire together, and put the bar in the fire till it be red. Go, then, and thrust it into his eye with all your strength, and take care that he does not get hold of you, for if he does he will mince you as small as midges.' I then went and gathered the embers together, and put the bar in the fire, and made it red, and thrust it into his eye; and from the cry that he gave I thought that the rock had split. The giant sprang to his feet and chased me through the cave in order to catch me; and I picked up a stone that lay on the floor of the cave, and pitched it into the sea; and it made a plumping noise. The bar was sticking in his eye all the time. Thinking it was I that had sprung into the sea, he rushed to the mouth of the cave, and the bar struck against the doorpost of the cave, and knocked off his brain-cap. The giant fell down cold and dead, and the damsel and I were seven years and seven days throwing him into the sea in pieces.

"I wedded the damsel, and a boy was born to us. After seven years I started forth again.

"I gave her a gold ring, with my name on it, for the boy, and when he was old enough he was sent out to seek me.

"I then set off to the place where I fought the battle, and found the short spear where I left it; and I was very pleased that I found it, and that the ship was safe. I sailed a day's distance from that place, and entered a pretty bay that was there, hauled my ship up above the shore, and erected a hut there, in which I slept at night. When I rose next day I saw a ship making straight for the place where I was. When it struck the ground, a big, strong champion came out of it, and hauled it up; and if it did not surpass my ship it was not a whit inferior to it; and I said to him, 'What impertinent fellow are you that has dared to haul up your ship alongside of my ship?' 'I am Machkan-na-skaya-jayrika,' said the champion, 'going to seek the daughter of the King of the Universe for Mac Connachar, son of the King of Lochlann.' I saluted and welcomed him, and said to him, 'I am your father: it is well that you have come.' We passed the night cheerily in the hut.

"When I arose on the following day I saw another ship making straight for the place where I was; and a big, strong hero came out of it, and hauled it up alongside of our ships; and if it did not surpass them it was not a whit inferior to them. 'What impertinent fellow are you that has dared to haul up your ship alongside of our ships?' said I. 'I am,' said he, 'the Son of the Wet Mantle, going to seek the daughter of the King of the Universe for Mac Connachar, son of the King of Lochlann.' 'I am your father, and this is your brother: it is well that you have come,' said I. We passed the night together in the hut, my two sons and I.

"When I rose next day I saw another ship coming, and making straight for the place where I was. A big, strong champion sprang out of it, and hauled it up alongside of our ships; and if it was not higher than they, it was not lower. I went down where he was, and said to him, 'What impertinent fellow are you that has dared to haul up your ship alongside òf our ships?' 'I am the Son of the Wet Mantle,' said he, 'going to seek the daughter of the King of the Universe for Mac Connachar, son of the King of Lochlann. 'Have you any token in proof of that?' said I. 'I have,' said he: 'here is a ring that my mother gave me at my father's request.' I took hold of the ring, and saw my name on it: and the matter was beyond doubt. I said to him, 'I am your father, and here are two half-brothers of yours. We are now stronger for going in quest of the daughter of the King of the Universe. Four piles are stronger than three piles.' We spent that night cheerily and comfortably together in the hut.

"On the morrow we met a soothsayer, and he spoke to us: 'You are going in quest of the daughter of the King of the Universe. I will tell you where she is: she is with the Son of the Blackbird.'

"Machkan-na-skaya-jayrika then went and called for combat with a hundred fully trained heroes, or the sending out to him of the daughter of the King of the Universe. The hundred went out; and he and they began on each other, and he killed every one of them. The Son of the Wet Mantle called for combat with another hundred, or the sending out of the daughter of the King of the Universe. He killed that hundred with the short spear. The Son of Secret called for combat with another hundred, or the daughter of the King of the Universe. He killed every one of these with the short spear. I then went out to the field, and sounded a challenge on the shield, and made the town tremble. The Son of the Blackbird had not a man to send out: he had to come out himself; and he and I began on each other, and I drew the short spear, and swept his head off. I then went into the castle, and took out the daughter of the King of the Universe. It was thus that it fared with me.

"Stretch out your leg, Kayn, till I put a salve of herbs and healing to it. Salve and binding herb and the poultice are cooling; the worm is channering. Pressure and haste hard bind me, for I must hear Mass in the great church at Rome, and be in Norway before I sleep."

Kayn Mac Loy stretched his leg; and the big man applied to it leaves of herbs and healing; and it was healed. The big man took him ashore from the island, and allowed him to go home to the king.

Thus did O'Cronicert win and lose a wife, and thus befell the Leeching of the leg of Kayn, son of Loy.

The Two Cat Witches

IN OLD DAYS, it was believed that the seventh son, in a family of sons, was a conjurer by nature. That is, he could work wonders like the fairies and excel the doctors in curing diseases.

If he were the seventh son of a seventh son, he was himself a wonder of wonders. The story ran that he could even cure the 'shingles,' which is a very troublesome disease. It is called also by a Latin name, which means a snake, because, as it gets worse, it coils itself around the body.

Now the eagle can attack the serpent and conquer and kill this poisonous creature. To secure such power, Hugh, the conjurer, ate the flesh of eagles. When he wished to cure the serpent-disease, he uttered words in the form of a charm which acted as a talisman and cure. After wetting the red rash, which had broken out over the sick person's body, he muttered:

"He-eagle, she-eagle, I send you over nine seas, and over nine mountains, and over nine acres of moor and fen, where no dog shall bark, no cow low, and no eagle shall higher rise."

After that, the patient was sure that he felt better.

There was always great rivalry between these conjurers and those who made money from the Pilgrims at Holy Wells and visitors to the relic shrines, but this fellow, named Hugh, and the monks, kept on mutually good terms. They often ate dinner together, for Hugh was a great traveler over the whole country and always had news to tell to the holy brothers who lived in cells.

One night, as he was eating supper at an inn, four men came in and sat down at the table with him. By his magical power, Hugh knew that they were robbers and meant to kill him that night, in order to get his money.

So, to divert their attention, Hugh made something like a horn to grow up out of the table, and then laid a spell on the robbers, so that they were kept gazing at the curious thing all night long, while he went to bed and slept soundly.

When he rose in the morning, he paid his bill and went away, while the robbers were still gazing at the horn. Only when the officers arrived to take them to prison did they come to themselves.

Now at Bettws-y-Coed-that pretty place which has a name that sounds so funny to us Americans and suggests a girl named Betty the Co-ed at college – there was a hotel, named the 'Inn of Three Kegs.' The shop sign hung out in front. It was a bunch of grapes gilded and set below three small barrels.

This inn was kept by two respectable ladies, who were sisters.

Yet in that very hotel, several travelers, while they were asleep, had been robbed of their money. They could not blame anyone nor tell how the mischief was done. With the key in the keyhole, they had kept their doors locked during the night. They were sure that no one had entered the room. There were no signs of men's boots, or of anyone's footsteps in the garden, while nothing was visible on the lock or door, to show that either had been tampered with. Everything was in order as when they went to bed.

Some people doubted their stories, but when they applied to Hugh the conjurer, he believed them and volunteered to solve the mystery. His motto was "Go anywhere and everywhere, but catch the thief."

When Hugh applied one night for lodging at the inn, nothing could be more agreeable than the welcome, and fine manners of his two hostesses.

At supper time, and during the evening, they all chatted together merrily. Hugh, who was never at a loss for news or stories, told about the various kinds of people and the many countries he had visited, in imagination, just as if he had seen them all, though he had never set foot outside of Wales.

When he was ready to go to bed, he said to the ladies:

"It is my custom to keep a light burning in my room, all night, but I will not ask for candles, for I have enough to last me until sunrise." So saying, he bade them good night.

Entering his room and locking the door, he undressed, but laid his clothes near at hand. He drew his trusty sword out of its sheath and laid it upon the bed beside him, where he could quickly grasp it. Then he pretended to be asleep and even snored.

It was not long before, peeping between his eyelids, only half closed, he saw two cats come stealthily down the chimney.

When in the room, the animals frisked about, and then gamboled and romped in the most lively way. Then they chased each other around the bed, as if they were trying to find out whether Hugh was asleep.

Meanwhile, the supposed sleeper kept perfectly motionless. Soon the two cats came over to his clothes and one of them put her paw into the pocket that contained his purse.

At this, with one sweep of his sword, Hugh struck at the cat's paw. The beast howled frightfully, and both animals ran for the chimney and disappeared. After that, everything was quiet until breakfast time.

At the table, only one of the sisters was present. Hugh politely inquired after the other one. He was told that she was not well, for which Hugh said he was very sorry.

After the meal, Hugh declared he must say good-by to both the sisters, whose company he had so enjoyed the night before. In spite of the other lady's many excuses, he was admitted to the sick lady's room.

After polite greetings and mutual compliments, Hugh offered his hand to say "good-by." The sick lady smiled at once and put out her hand, but it was her left one.

"Oh, no," said Hugh, with a laugh. "I never in all my life have taken any one's left hand, and, beautiful as yours is, I won't break my habit by beginning now and here."

Reluctantly, and as if in pain, the sick lady put out her hand. It was bandaged.

The mystery was now cleared up. The two sisters were cats.

By the help of bad fairies they had changed their forms and were the real robbers.

Hugh seized the hand of the other sister and made a little cut in it, from which a few drops of blood flowed, but the spell was over.

"Henceforth," said Hugh, "you are both harmless, and I trust you will both be honest women."

And they were. From that day they were like other women, and kept one of the best of those inns – clean, tidy, comfortable and at modest prices – for which Wales is, or was, noted.

Neither as cats with paws, nor landladies, with soaring bills, did they ever rob travelers again.

Text Sources & Biographies

The stories in this book derive from a multitude of original sources, often from the nineteenth century and often based on the writer's first-hand accounts of tales narrated to them by natives, while others are their own retellings of traditional tales. Authors, works and contributors to this book include:

Diane Purkiss
Foreword
Diane Purkiss is Professor of English Literature and Fellow in English at Keble College Oxford. She has published widely on witches, fairies, ghosts and the history of the supernatural. She is currently working on a study of witches accused during the period of the trials who believed themselves to be performing magic.

Im Bang, Yi Ryuk and James S. Gale
The work of classical Korean storytellers Im Bang and Yi Ryuk was translated from the Korean by James S. Gale (1863–1937) and published as *Korean Folk Tales: Imps, Ghosts And Fairies* in 1913. Gale was a Canadian missionary, educator and Bible translator who was sent to Korea in 1888. Much of his writing and translation remains unpublished.

George W. Bateman
George W. Bateman (1850–1940) was the British-born author of the famous *Zanzibar Tales: Told by Natives of the East Coast of Africa* (1901), in which he presented stories, 'translated from the Original Swahili', told to him in Zanzibar, by locals 'whose ancestors told them to them, who had received them from *their* ancestors, and so back.' Reportedly many of these tales were the inspiration for several Disney films such as *Bambi*, *The Lion King* and so on.

Abbie Farwell Brown
American author Abbie Farwell Brown (1871–1927) was born in Boston and attended the Girls' Latin School. While attending school she set up a school newspaper and also contributed articles to other magazines. Brown's books were most often retellings of old tales for children such as in *The Book of Saints and Friendly Beasts*. She also published a collection of tales from Norse mythology, *In the Days of Giants*, which became the common text held by many libraries for several generations.

Elsie Finnimore Buckley
Elsie Finnimore Buckley (1882–1959) was an English translator and writer. As a student she excelled at French and went on to translate many historical studies such as *The restoration and the July monarchy* by Jean Lucas-Dubreton (1929) and *The consulate and the empire* by Louis Madelin (1937). But it is for her *Children of the Dawn, Old Tales of Greece* (1909) that she is best known.

E. A. Wallis Budge
Sir Ernest Alfred Thompson Wallis Budge (1857–1934) was an English Egyptologist, Orientalist, philologist and author. Born in 1857 in Bodmin, Cornwall, Budge would leave for London as a

boy, to live with his aunt and grandmother. It was here, including at the British Museum, that he would be able, whilst working at the stationers W.H. Smith, to indulge is growing interest in languages, particularly Biblical Hebrew, Syriac and Assyrian. He studied Semitic languages at Cambridge and then worked at the British Museum in the Department of Egyptian and Assyrian Antiquities, part of which involved helping the museum to build it collection. He is best known today for his many publications on ancient Egyptian religion, history, culture and hieroglyphics, from *The Dwellers On The Nile: Chapters on the Life, Literature, History and Customs of the Ancient Egyptians* (1885) to *The Literature of the Ancient Egyptians* (1914), and countless more.

Margaret Compton

Margaret Compton was born in 1852 and is best known as the author of *Snow Bird and the Water Tiger and other American Indian Tales*, a collection of Native American folk tales written for children and young adults that was based on authentic Native American lore. Originally published in 1895, the book was republished four years after Compton's death in 1903 under the new title *American Indian Fairy Tales*.

Jeremiah Curtin

Jeremiah Curtin (1835–1906) was a Detroit-born ethnographer and folklorist. While much of his work would focus on collecting myths and folktales from around the world, such as *Myths and Folk-tales of the Russians, Western Slavs, and Magyars* (1890) and *Myths and Folk-lore of Ireland* (1890), Curtin would also be renowned for his translations of works by Polish author Henryk Sienkiewicz. Between 1883 and 1891 Curtin's interests would focus closer to home when he worked as a field researcher recording the myths and customs of Native American people, which would later result in the publication of the book *Creation Myths of Primitive America* (1898).

Jonathan Ceredig Davies

Jonathan Ceredig Davies (1859–1932) was a Welsh writer who was interested in different cultures from around the world. He lived for a number of years in both Patagonia and Australia, and visited Spain and France, before settling finally in Wales to devote the rest of his life to studying the history and folklore of his native land, dying at Llanddewi-brefi. His works include *Darlith ar Patagonia* (1891); *Patagonia: a description of the country* (1892); *Adventures in the land of giants: a Patagonian tale* (1892); *Western Australia: its history and progress* (1902); *Australia Orllewinol* (1903) and *Folk-lore of West and Mid-Wales* (1911).

F. Hadland Davis

Frederick Hadland Davis was a writer and a historian – author of *The Land of the Yellow Spring and Other Japanese Stories* (1910) and *The Persian Mystics* (1908 and 1920). His books describe these cultures to the western world and tell stories of ghosts, creation, mystical creatures and more. He is best known for his book *Myths and Legends of Japan* (1912).

Elphinstone Dayrell

Dayrell (1869–1917) collected his tales after hearing many first-hand from the Efik and Ibibio peoples of Southeastern Nigeria when he was District Commissioner of South Nigeria. His collections of folklore include *Folk Stories From southern Nigeria* (1910) and *Ikom Folk*

Stories From southern Nigeria, the latter published by the Royal Anthropological Institute of Great Britain and Ireland in 1913.

George Douglas

George Brisbane Scott Douglas (1856–1935) was a Scottish poet and writer, sometimes writing under the name of Sir George Douglas on account of his rank as baronet. In addition to his *Scottish Fairy and Folk Tales* of 1901, other publications included *Poems* (1880), *The Fireside Tragedy* (1896), *New Border Tales* (1892), *Poems of a Country Gentleman* (1897), *History of the Border Counties: Roxburgh, Selkirk and Peebles* (1899) and *Scottish Poetry: Drummond of Hawthornden to Fergusson* (1911).

Alice Elizabeth Dracott

Alice Elizabeth Dracott was the author of *Simla Village Tales: Or, Folk Tales From the Himalayas* (1906), the source of the story 'The Magician and the Merchant'.

George Grey

Sir George Grey (1812–98) was a British soldier, explorer, colonial administrator and writer, who among various governing positions, was the eleventh prime minister of New Zealand. Among his many achievements, he became a pioneering scholar of Māori culture, publishing *Polynesian Mythology & Ancient Traditional History of the New Zealanders* in 1854.

William Elliot Griffis

Born in Philadelphia, William Elliot Griffis (1843–1928) went on to serve as a corporal during the American Civil War. He studied at Rutgers University after the war and graduated in 1869. He tutored Latin and English to a samurai from Fukui and then travelled around Europe for a year prior to studying at what is now known as the New Brunswick Theological Seminary. In 1870, Griffis went to Japan and became Superintendent of Education in the province of Echizen because of his organisation of schools there. During the 1870s, Griffis and his sister taught at many different institutes and he wrote for many newspapers and magazines. In 1872 he prepared the *New Japan Series of Reading and Spelling Books* and left Japan in 1874, having made many connections and friendships with Japan's future leaders. On returning to the United States he worked in several churches on the east coast but retired in 1903 to write. With the help of his extensive knowledge of Japanese and European culture, he produced a number of books, such as *Japanese Fairy World* (1880), *The Fire-fly's Lovers and Other Fairy Tales of Old Japan* (1908), *Japanese Fairy Tales* (1922), *Korean Fairy Tales* (1922), *Belgian Fairy Tales* (1919) and many more.

Jacob and Wilhelm Grimm

The German academics, folklorists and authors Jacob and Wilhelm Grimm published works individually too, and even began to compile a detailed German dictionary before their deaths, but it is for their collection of fairy tales – including such well-loved stories as 'Hansel and Grethel' and 'Rapunzel' – that they are now principally known. The elder of the two, Jacob, was born in 1785, with Wilhelm born the following year, also in Hanau. Their father died while they were still young, casting the family into poverty and resulting in the two brothers becoming virtually self-reliant. Of all their siblings, they formed the closest relationship, evident in the number of collaborative works they produced. Despite experiencing financial hardship at a number of points in their lives, the brothers were immensely productive academically: they excelled in their studies and developed an interest in philology whilst attending the University of Marburg, and as well as university teaching and librarian posts, they carried out extensive research on the history of the German language and its literature. They began collecting folk tales around their mother's death in 1808, and gradually established a method of recording fairy tales that has become a standard among folklorists. Their first edition of *Children's and Household Tales* was published in two volumes, in 1812 and 1815 respectively, and underwent a number of revisions culminating in the seventh and final editions in 1857.

Francis Hindes Groome
Francis Hinde Groome (1851–1902) was a passionate and precise researcher, commentator and writer on the topic of Romani culture and folklore. He contributed to a variety of publications, encyclopedias and dictionaries as well as publishing his own books, of which *Gypsy Folk Tales* (1899) is his most significant.

H.A. Guerber
Hélène Adeline Guerber (1859–1929) was a British historian who published a large number of works, largely focused on myths and legends. Guerber's most famous publication is *Myths of the Norsemen: From the Eddas and Sagas*, a history of Germanic mythology. Her works continue to be published today and include *The Myths of Greece and Rome, The Story of the Greeks* and *Legends of the Middle Ages*.

Florence Holbrook
Florence Holbrook (1897–1932) was an educator in Chicago schools, and a collector of folk tales from around the world. She reproduced these tales in several children's books and primers, including *The Hiawatha Primer; The Book of Nature Myths; Northland Heroes;* and *Cave, Lake and Mound Dwellers, and other Primitive People.* She was also prominently involved in the early-twentieth-century peace movement.

Douglas Hyde
Douglas Ross Hyde (1860–1949) was the first President of Ireland from June 1938 to June 1945. Besides his political achievements, he was also an academic and scholar of the Irish language who played a prominent part in the Gaelic revival. Related publications that he edited and translated include *Beside the Fire: A Collection of Irish Gaelic Folk Stories* (1910) and *Legends of Saints & Sinners* (1914).

Eleanor Hull
Though born in England, Eleanor Henrietta Hull (1860–1935) was from an Irish family and studied at Alexandra College, Dublin, becoming a scholar of Old Irish. She was co-founder and secretary of the Irish Texts Society and president of the Irish Literary Society. Also a writer and journalist, she published literature, stories, Irish poetry and histories, such as *The Cuchullin Saga in Irish Literature* (1898), *The Poem-Book of the Gael* (1912) and *A History of Ireland and her People* (1931) among other works.

Joseph Jacobs
Joseph Jacobs (1854–1916) was born in Australia and settled in New York. He is most famous for his collections of English folklore and fairytales including 'Jack and the Beanstalk' and 'The Three Little Pigs'. He also published Celtic, Jewish and Indian fairytales during his career. Jacobs was an editor for books and journals centred on folklore and a member of The Folklore Society in England.

W.F. Kirby

William Forsell Kirby (1844–1912) was an English entomologist and folklorist. He was a curator at the Museum of the Royal Dublin Society before going, in 1879, to work at the British Museum in the natural history department, where he remained until his retirement in 1909. He published a large amount of catalogues and scientific work on butterflies, moths and other insects. He also knew many languages and had interests in literature and folklore, with works in these areas including a translation in 1907 of Finland's national epic, the *Kalevala*, footnotes to Sir Richard Burton's translation of the *Arabian Nights* (1886), his own *The new Arabian nights. Select tales, not included by Galland or Lane* (1883), and *The Hero of Esthonia, and Other Studies in the Romantic Literature of That Country* (1895).

Ignác Kúnos

Ignác Kúnos (originally Ignác Lusztig, 1860–1945) was a Hungarian professor, linguist, turkologist and folklorist. After studying the linguistic aspects of the Hungarian and Mordvinic languages, he went on to focus on Turkish language and culture, becoming professor of the Turkish philology at Budapest University. He held various other academic posts including professorships at Ankara and Istanbul Universities, but is perhaps best known for his gathering and translating of folk tales, which resulted in numerous collections published in Hungarian and English, one of which is *Forty-Four Turkish Fairy Tales* (1914).

Andrew Lang

Poet, novelist and anthropologist Andrew Lang (1844–1912) was born in Selkirk, Scotland. He is now best known for his collections of fairy stories and publications on folklore, mythology and religion. Inspired by the traditional folklore tales of his home on the English-Scottish border, Lang complied twelve coloured fairy books which collected 798 stories from French, Danish, Russian and Romanian sources, amongst others. *The Grey Fairy Book* (1900) contains a lone African-inspired story of 'The Jackal and the Spring'. This hugely successful series further encouraged the increasing popularity of fairy tales in children's literature.

Edmund Leamy

Edmund Leamy (1848–1904) was an Irish politician, barrister and journalist who was a member of the Irish Parliamentary Party and MP for various seats throughout his career. But he was also 'one of the brightest and most poetic spirits who have appeared in Ireland' and a writer of fairy tales, which were collected in *Irish Fairy Tales* (1906) and *By the Barrow River, and Other Stories* (1907).

Charles Godfrey Leland

Charles Godfrey Leland (1824–1903) was a qualified lawyer, journalist and civil war veteran whose various interests saw him travel widely and write about many topics. Perhaps most notably, Leland's keen fascination with folklore would lead him to write many books on the subject, covering everything from pagan and Aryan traditions, to studies of Gypsies; his work on Native American tales was published in 1884 as *The Algonquin Legends of New England*.

Thomas Malory

Thomas Malory (*c.* 1415–71) is the known author and compiler of *Le Morte d'Arthur*. Malory originally named the work *The Book of King Arthur and His Noble Knights of the Round Table* but this was changed to the name known today by William Caxton when it was printed in 1485. There are a number of theories surrounding Malory's identity, with the most popular remaining that he was Sir Thomas Malory of Newbold Revel in Warwickshire, a knight and Member of Parliament. He was also accused of a variety of crimes including robbery and attempted murder and was imprisoned a number of times during his life. Recently a different identity has been highlighted, that of Thomas Malory of Yorkshire, due to the works drawing largely from Yorkshire romances and the knowledge of Northern England that Malory shows throughout *Le Morte D'Arthur*. Despite the uncertainties surrounding Malory he remains famous for creating the first full-length English book centered on King Arthur and his knights.

Minnie Martin

Minnie Martin was the wife of a government official, who arrived in South Africa in 1891 and settled in Lesotho (at that time Basutoland). In her preface to *Basutoland: Its Legends and Customs* (1903) she explains that 'We both liked the country from the first, and I soon became interested in the people. To enable myself to understand them better, I began to study the language, which I can now speak fairly well.' And thus she wrote this work, at the suggestion of a friend. Despite the inaccuracies pointed out by E. Sidney Hartland in his review of her book, he deemed the work 'an unpretentious, popular account of a most interesting branch of the Southern Bantus and the country they live in.'

Frederick H. Martens

Frederick Herman Martens (1874–1932) was an author, lyricist and translator, whose work includes a translation of Pietro Yon's 1917 Christmas carol 'Gesu Bambino', a biography of the musician A.E. Uhe (1922), *A Thousand and One Nights of Opera* (1926), *Violin Mastery* (*Talks with Master Violinists and Teachers*) (1919), and fairy-tale translations in *The Chinese Fairy Book* (ed. Dr. R. Wilhelm).

A.B. Mitford, Lord Redesdale

Algernon Bertram Freeman-Mitford, 1st Baron Redesdale (1837–1916), was a writer, collector and British diplomat. He was educated at Eton and at Oxford University, and later went to Japan as second secretary of the British Legation. His stay in Japan and his meeting Ernest Satow inspired the writing of *Tales of Old Japan* (1871). The book allowed several Japanese classics to be exposed to the Western world.

James Mooney

James Mooney (1861–1921) was an American ethnographer who dedicated his life to studying the Native American people. Self-taught in his field of expertise, Mooney lived among the Cherokee people for a number of years, and wrote extensively on various tribes located across the North American continent for the Bureau of American Ethnology in reports and bulletins such as *Siouan Tribes of the East* (1892), *Myths of the Cherokee* (1902) and *Indian Missions North of Mexico* (1907).

Sophia Morrison

Sophia Morrison (1859–1917) was a leading authority on Manx folklore, being a cultural activist, folklore collector and author. Fluent in Manx and French, and proficient in Irish, Scottish Gaelic, Italian and Spanish, she championed the preservation of Manx culture in all forms, from language to folk tales, and her most famous and influential work is *Manx Fairy Tales*, first published in 1911.

M. I. Ogumefu

M. I. Ogumefu, B.A, was the author of *Yoruba Legends* (1929), the source of the story 'The Three Magicians'.

Yei Theodora Ozaki

The translations of Japanese stories and fairy tales by Yei Theodora Ozaki (1871–1932) were, by her own admission, fairly liberal ('I have followed my fancy in adding such touches of local colour or description as they seemed to need or as pleased me'), and yet proved popular. They include *Japanese Fairy Tales* (1908), 'translated from the modern version written by Sadanami Sanjin', and *Warriors of Old Japan, and Other Stories* (1909).

Norman Hinsdale Pitman

Educator and author, Norman Hinsdale Pitman (1876–1925) was born in Lamont, Michigan. His best-known collection of Chinese myths and fairy tales is *A Chinese Wonder Book* (1919). His other works include: *The Lady Elect: A Chinese Romance* (1913), *Chinese Fairy Tales* (1924) and *Dragon Lure: A Romance of Peking* (1925).

W. R. S. Ralston

William Ralston Shedden-Ralston (1828–1889) was a British scholar of Russia and translator of Russian. He graduated from Cambridge with a law degree in 1850, but sought more stable employment when his family's fortunes were squandered in an unsuccessful case arguing a claim to the Ralston estates in Ayrshire, Scotland. He went to work as a junior assistant in the printed-book department of the British Museum where he rose through the ranks by filling a need for someone to catalogue books in Russian. He learnt the language and studied Russian literature. He published translations of Ivan Andreevich Krylov's and Ivan Turgenev's works, as well as *Songs of the Russian People as Illustrative of Slavonic Mythology and Russian Social Life* (1872) and, of relevance to this volume: *Russian Folk Tales* (1873).

A.G. Seklemian

A.G. Seklemian was an Armenian scholar and storyteller who published *The Golden Maiden and Other Folk Tales and Fairy Stories Told in Armenia* in 1898.

Henry Rowe Schoolcraft

Henry Rowe Schoolcraft (1793–1865) devoted a significant portion of his life to interactions with Native American people. In 1822 he served as an Indian agent for the US government covering Michigan, Wisconsin and Minnesota, before later marrying Jane Johnston, who was herself the daughter of an Ojibwa war chief. From his wife Schoolcraft would learn the Ojibwa language and much about their history and way of life. He would go on to write extensively about the Native American people, with works including *The Myth of Hiawatha, and other Oral Legends, Mythologic and Allegoric, of the North American Indians* (1856) and a comprehensive six-volume series titled *Historical and Statistical Information Respecting the History, Condition, and Prospects of the Indian Tribes of the United States* that was published between 1851 and 1857.

Charles M. Skinner

Charles Montgomery Skinner (1852–1907) was an American writer, playwright and journalist, who wrote on a wide range of topics, such as natural history and socialism, but also published collections of myths, legends and folklore, including *Myths And Legends of Our Own Land* (1896).

Lewis Spence

James Lewis Thomas Chalmers Spence (1874–1955) was a scholar of Scottish and Mexican and Central American folklore, as well as that of Brittany, Spain and the Rhine. He was also a poet, journalist, author, editor and nationalist who would found the party that would become the Scottish National Party. He was a Fellow of the Royal Anthropological Institute of Great Britain and Ireland, and Vice-President of the Scottish Anthropological and Folklore Society. He published many books, of which *Myths & Legends of Babylonia & Assyria* (1917) is one of relevance to this volume.

Capt. C.H. Stigand

Chauncey Hugh Stigand (1877–1919) was a British army officer, colonial administrator and big game hunter who served in Burma, British Somaliland and British East Africa. He was in charge of the Kajo Kaji district of what is now South Sudan, and was later made governor of the Upper Nile province and then Mongalla Province before being killed during a 1919 uprising of the Aliab Dinka people. During his time in Africa he managed to write prolifically, from *Central African Game and its Spoor* (1906), through *Black Tales for White Children* (1914), to *A Nuer-English Vocabulary*, published posthumously in 1923.

J.R. Walker

James R. Walker (1849–1926) served as a physician for the Indian Service of the United States government. After gaining his medical qualifications, he first served at Leech Lake Indian Reservation in Minnesota before being transferred to the Colville Reservation in Oregon, then in 1896 to the Indian Industrial School at Carlisle, Pennsylvania. In 1896 he moved to the Pine Ridge Reservation in South Dakota, where he developed his lifelong interest in the Lakota (Oglala Sioux) Indians that was to drive him to become one of the leading scholars of Lakota religion, collecting an invaluable resource of documentary interviews and writings, including the publication in 1917 of *The Sun Dance and Other Ceremonies of the Oglala Division of The Teton Dakota.*

Alice Werner

Alice Werner (1859–1935) was a writer, poet and professor of Swahili and Bantu languages. She travelled widely in her early life but by 1894 had focused her writing on African culture and language, and later joined the School of Oriental Studies, working her way up from lecturer to professor. *Myths and Legends of the Bantu* (1933) was her last main work, but others on African topics include *The Language Families of Africa* (1915), *Introductory Sketch of the Bantu Languages* (1919), *The Swahili Saga of Liongo Fumo* (1926), *A First Swahili Book* (1927), *Swahili Tales* (1929), *Structure and Relationship of African Languages* (1930) and *The Story of Miqdad and Mayasa* (1932).

E.T.C. Werner

Edward Theodore Chalmers Werner (1864–1954) was a sinologist specialising in Chinese superstition, myths and magic. He worked as a British diplomat in China during the final imperial dynasty, working his way up to British Consul-General in 1911. Being posted to all four corners of China encouraged Werner's interest in the mythological culture of the land, and after retirement he was able to concentrate on his sinological studies, of which *Myths & Legends of China* (1922) was one result.

W.D. Westervelt

William Drake Westervelt (1849–1939) was a pastor from Ohio, who moved to Hawaii and became a prominent authority on the island's folklore, publishing numerous articles and works on Hawaiian history and legends, including *Legends of Maui* (1910), *Legends of Old Honolulu* (1915), *Legends of Gods and Ghost-Gods* (1915), *Hawaiian Legends of Volcanoes* (1916) and *Hawaiian Historical Legends* (1923).

Lady Wilde

Jane Francesca Agnes Wilde (1821–96) was a poet, writer, journalist and activist in the Irish nationalist movement, and more famously, the mother of Oscar Wilde. She wrote under the pen name 'Speranza' and her special interest in Irish folklore in particular led to the publication of *Ancient Legends, Mystic Charms, and Superstitions of Ireland* (1888).

Dr R. Wilhelm

Richard Wilhelm (1873–1930) was a German theologian, missionary and sinologist. He is best known for his works of translations of philosophical works from Chinese into German, including his translation of the I Ching and The Secret of the Golden Flower. He also edited The Chinese Fairy Book (1921).

A.H. Wratislaw

Albert Henry Wratislaw (1822–92) was an English scholar, headmaster and clergyman descended from the Czech noble family Wratislaw von Mitrovitz. Before becoming headmaster at Felsted School and later King Edward VI School in Bury St Edmunds, he had visited Bohemia and studied the Czech language, leading to the publication of *Lyra Czecho Slovanska, or Bohemian Poems, Ancient and Modern* (1849). He produced several other texts and books on Slavonic literature and history while in his positions as headmaster, and then rector in Pembrokeshire, before finally publishing *Sixty Folk-Tales from Exclusively Slavonic Sources* in 1889.

W.B. Yeats

William Butler Yeats (1865–1939) was an Irish poet and is considered one of the greatest writers from the twentieth century. He played an important role in the Celtic Twilight, a revival of Irish literature focused on Gaelic heritage and Irish nationalism. Yeats was fascinated by Irish legends, including many Irish heroes in his works and focusing his poetry on Irish folklore. Alongside his poetry he is famous for re-telling and writing short stories (such as in his collections *Fairy and Folk Tales of the Irish Peasantry*, 1888, and *The Secret Rose*, 1897) and plays. Yeats set up the Abbey Theatre in 1899 which held Irish and Celtic performances. In recognition of Yeats' important work he received a Nobel Prize in 1923.

FLAME TREE PUBLISHING
Epic, Dark, Thrilling & Gothic
New & Classic Writing

Flame Tree's Gothic Fantasy books offer a carefully curated series of new titles, each with combinations of original and classic writing:

Chilling Horror • Chilling Ghost • Science Fiction
Murder Mayhem • Crime & Mystery • Swords & Steam
Dystopia Utopia • Supernatural Horror • Lost Worlds
Time Travel • Heroic Fantasy • Pirates & Ghosts • Agents & Spies
Endless Apocalypse • Alien Invasion • Robots & AI • Lost Souls
Haunted House • Cosy Crime • American Gothic • Urban Crime
Epic Fantasy • Detective Mysteries • Detective Thrillers • A Dying Planet
Footsteps in the Dark • Bodies in the Library • Strange Lands
Lovecraft Mythos • Terrifying Ghosts • Black Sci-Fi • Chilling Crime

**Also, new companion titles offer rich collections of
classic fiction, myths and tales in the gothic fantasy tradition:**

Charles Dickens Supernatural • George Orwell Visions of Dystopia
H.G. Wells • Lovecraft • Sherlock Holmes • Edgar Allan Poe • Bram Stoker Horror
Mary Shelley Horror • M.R. James Ghost Stories • The Divine Comedy
Hans Christian Andersen Fairy Tales • Brothers Grimm Fairy Tales
Alice's Adventures in Wonderland • King Arthur & The Knights of the Round Table
The Wonderful Wizard of Oz • The Age of Queen Victoria • Ramayana
One Thousand and One Arabian Nights • Persian Myths & Tales • African Myths & Tales
Celtic Myths & Tales • Greek Myths & Tales • Norse Myths & Tales • Chinese Myths & Tales
Japanese Myths & Tales • Native American Myths & Tales • Irish Fairy Tales
Heroes & Heroines Myths & Tales • Gods & Monsters Myths & Tales
Witches, Wizards, Seers & Healers Myths & Tales

Available from all good bookstores, worldwide, and online at
flametreepublishing.com

See our new fiction imprint
FLAME TREE PRESS | FICTION WITHOUT FRONTIERS
New and original writing in Horror, Crime, SF and Fantasy

And join our monthly newsletter with offers and more stories:
FLAME TREE FICTION NEWSLETTER
flametreepress.com

GOTHIC FANTASY

For our books, calendars, blog
and latest special offers please see:
flametreepublishing.com